THE SHIMMERING ROAD

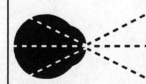

This Large Print Book carries the
Seal of Approval of N.A.V.H.

THE SHIMMERING ROAD

HESTER YOUNG

THORNDIKE PRESS
A part of Gale, a Cengage Company

Farmington Hills, Mich • San Francisco • New York • Waterville, Maine
Meriden, Conn • Mason, Ohio • Chicago

LIBRARY OF CONGRESS CIP DATA ON FILE.
CATALOGUING IN PUBLICATION FOR THIS BOOK
IS AVAILABLE FROM THE LIBRARY OF CONGRESS

ISBN-13: 978-1-4328-5022-7 (hardcover)

Published in 2018 by arrangement with G. P. Putnam's Sons, an imprint of Penguin Publishing Group, a division of Penguin Random House LLC

Printed in the United States of America
1 2 3 4 5 6 7 22 21 20 19 18

For the women who showed me Tucson:
Sylvia, Annette, Laura, Margaret,
Tavie, Carolyn, Isabel, Eva, Diana,
and most of all, Teresa

To say nothing is out here is incorrect; to say the desert is stingy with everything except space and light, stone and earth is closer to the truth.

— WILLIAM LEAST HEAT-MOON

The dream begins with water, always water.

I'm awash in indistinct shapes and hues, anchored only by the feel of it: a warm and steady spray against my back, soothing in its measured patter. Then the colors sharpen, take form, like the lens of a camera adjusting its focus.

Walls of concrete block, painted white, peeling. A metal rod from which a flimsy cloth curtain hangs. Exposed piping. A showerhead.

I'm standing on blue and yellow tile, naked, drenched. The floor dips beneath me toward a drain, but the gathering water can't escape quickly enough. It pools around my ankles, soothing my tired feet.

I close my eyes. Roll my head gently from side to side, release the tension in my shoulders. Thoughts of the outside world buzz at the edge of my mind in an angry swarm, but I push them away. Allow myself to occupy only this moment, to be wholly present in my body, which is no longer mine alone. I run a hand over the swelling curve of my abdomen and smile at the answering kick.

I'm going to be a mother, I think. *Going to put the ugly past behind me and build a future with this child.*

Despite my worn surroundings, I feel clean. My body is full of life and hope and promise. I stretch my arms luxuriously above my head, enjoying the weight of my growing baby, the sensation of running water against my face and heavy breasts.

It never occurs to me that we're not alone.

The sound cuts through everything, the falling water, my sense of calm, my belly. A loud pop, like a firework going off behind me. And I can feel it.

I stumble backward, clutching my stomach, suddenly struggling to breathe. I don't fully grasp what's happening until I see the blood swelling from beneath my hands.

A gunshot.

I've been hit. *She's* been hit.

Two more pops. A pressure in my chest, a burning. Now I'm drowning in the dark, trying to break through, swimming, swimming, until the water becomes blankets and my lungs at last find air.

When I awake, find myself in the safety of my own bedroom once more, there's a wave of relief, intense and fleeting. *That dream again,* I think. Still, I reach down and touch my belly, waiting for some movement, some sign that my baby's okay. Only after I've felt her lazy swish within me do I relax.

She's fine, I reassure myself, *and so are you. The dream hasn't come true.*

But another, darker part of me knows I can't rest easy. *Not yet,* it tells me. *Not yet.*

■ ■ ■ ■

PART I
SIDALIE, TEXAS
JULY 2012

■ ■ ■ ■

ONE

I know, long before Noah parks in the newly paved two-car driveway, that this is not a house I want to own. The upscale brick exterior and sharp white trim, the springy green lawn, the sprawling garage — it's so cookie-cutter cute, so ready for its spot on HGTV. So beautiful, if I were being fair, but I'm not.

As they say in real estate, location, location, location.

After watching me shoot down a dozen other properties that looked exactly like this one, Noah can't have high hopes, but he puts on a good face nevertheless. "This is one of Sidalie's best neighborhoods," he says, and then, noting my wrinkled nose, adds, "Would you at least keep an open mind?"

Our realtor, who has been waiting in her gleaming Grand Cherokee, now rushes over to meet us. "Hey there, honey!" Brandi

15

exclaims, her eyes barely meeting mine before they settle on my pregnant belly. "Look at you! Must be getting close now, Charlotte!"

"She's thirty-two weeks." Noah beams with that can-you-believe-it expression that older women so adore in an expectant father.

Brandi is no exception. "Aw, now, isn't he precious? You've got a proud daddy-to-be right here. I love it!"

Brandi Babcock may possess the name of a porn star, but she has the body of a butternut squash, a solid top that flares out into an epically large backside. In the past few months of house-hunting, I've grown rather fond of her. When not raving about architectural features, she's dishing about the details of her daughter's upcoming wedding, and even though these extravagant nuptials aren't my style, I admire how much she cares. I can only imagine what it would be like to have a mother so invested in my life.

"I just can't *wait* to show you this property," Brandi gushes. "Light, airy, great yard, practically brand-new. And plenty of room to expand the family!" She gives me a little wink, as if multiplying is the secret desire of every woman.

I grin. She must be seriously underestimating my age. At thirty-nine, I have no intention of "expanding the family." In point of fact, Noah and I were blindsided by this pregnancy, and if our nascent relationship has thus far absorbed the shock and left us eager for our daughter's arrival, it's more a function of luck than careful planning.

Brandi's tour goes over about as well as the last twelve. Noah likes the place, and I don't. At thirty-five hundred square feet, the house is absurdly large — "Texas sized!" as Brandi said with a laugh. It also possesses the same characteristics as every other property we've seen, which I can by now recite along with her: crown molding, granite countertops, stainless-steel appliances, master bath with his-and-hers sinks, a pool, a two-car garage. I feel a twinge of homesickness. Flawless, voluminous real estate at ridiculously affordable prices? This is not my world.

"*And* there's an underground sprinkler system," Brandi tells me, as if this is the item that I've been missing, the one that will close the deal.

I move through the house, nodding politely at the right intervals, but when she warns us that the bathroom attached to the garage "needs some work," my body kicks into high alert. Could it be? The shower

17

from my dream with the blue and yellow tile? Surely not in a house this nice.

Noah glances at me, one eyebrow raised. He knows exactly where my mind has gone, and he's right there with me. Since my nightmare began a month ago, we've both kept an eye out for sketchy-looking showers, approached every unfamiliar restroom with caution.

My dreams are not like other people's. They show me things.

"What kind of work does the bathroom need, exactly?" I ask Brandi.

"The sink is stained," she admits. "I think the previous owner washed out some paintbrushes there. It's just a half bath, and I'm sure you'd never use it, but I know how particular you are."

Half bath. That means no shower. Noah gives my hand a reassuring squeeze.

"Well?" Brandi asks me when we've completed the walk-through. "What did you think?"

"It's just so . . . big."

"These New York City girls." Noah shakes his head. "You finally give 'em room to breathe, and they don't know what to do with it."

Brandi laughs. "I can see that!" She puts a hand on my shoulder, preparing to dispense helpful advice. "It seems big now, Charlotte, but you'll want all this space once your baby comes. Children have a way of shrinking a home, you'll see."

Her all-knowing smile gets to me. I can feel my hormones flaring up — it doesn't take much these days. "Thanks for the tip, Brandi, but this isn't my first house. Or my first child."

"Oh no? I thought —"

"I had a son. He died last summer."

I regret mentioning Keegan the moment the words pass my lips. Though pregnancy regularly brings his loss to the forefront of my mind, I recognize that he's a delicate subject as far as others are concerned. People never know what to say about the death of a child. Even the perennially perky Brandi looks thrown off balance.

"I — had no idea," she stammers. "I'm so sorry to hear that."

Noah puts a hand on my waist and nudges me toward the door. He knows this house is a lost cause. "Thank you so much, Brandi, for showin' us the place," he says. "We'll give it some thought."

"Of course," she agrees, ready to get me out of here. "Y'all just call if you'd like another showing."

Back in the car, Noah makes no mention

of the house or Brandi Babcock, but I can feel his disappointment. I stare out the window at all the shiny new houses of Sidalie, knowing how desperate Noah is to own one, wishing I could share in his enthusiasm.

"Maybe we should put this house thing on the back burner for a while," Noah suggests. "The baby's comin' soon. We don't need the extra stress right now."

I grab my water bottle from the center console and take a long drink. "That's probably a good idea. To table the search for a bit."

He doesn't address the thing we both know. That I don't ever want to buy a house in Sidalie. That I'll use every possible excuse to avoid putting down roots here.

Our living situation will remain in a holding pattern for now, the month-by-month lease on our apartment a tenuous compromise that can't last forever. I see his plan, of course, as clearly as he sees mine. He's hoping that, with patience, he can wear me down, that Sidalie will grow on me like a slow fungus, consuming my resistance bit by bit until I capitulate.

It's a battle he may very well win. I know what having a baby does to a person. Odds are good I'll be too tired to fight him once our daughter's here. Sooner or later, I'll stop struggling and submit. Resign myself to living someone else's life, a life I had no hand in choosing.

On our way home, we stop at a Walgreens to pick up more prenatal vitamins. What should be a three-minute errand quickly blows up when Noah is accosted in the parking lot by a plump brunette.

"Noah?!" She has platform sandals and a rock that could probably feed an African village for a year. "Oh my gosh, how *are* you?"

I know the drill by now. She's either one of his landscaping clients, which would be fine, or someone he knows through his ex-wife, which would be awkward.

It's Option B.

"I can't believe I ran into you," the brunette says. "I was just thinking of you guys the other day. I told Tim, we should invite Carmen and her husband over. It's been way too long."

One would think, given the number of times he's been in this exact scenario, that Noah would have developed a more suave approach. That he'd have learned to tell the truth straight off, mention his divorce directly instead of pussyfooting.

Nope.

True to form, he gets that deer-in-the-headlights look and begins rubbing the back of his neck.

"Wow," he says. "Yeah. You and Tim — it's been a while."

"Right? But our son is finally sleeping through the night, so we're, like, trying to have a social life again. Where are you guys living now?" Somehow the brunette remains totally oblivious to the immensely pregnant woman at Noah's side. She probably thinks I'm a relative. They always do. "You moved, right? I drove by your old house a few months ago, and the lawn was a mess. I knew that couldn't be *your* place, ha-ha."

"Yeah, Carmen and I, uh, sold the house," he says, still failing to introduce me. I feel like a giant piece of furniture, a poorly positioned piano or clumsy table that Noah's always trying to get around. "I'm in an apartment right now. Not sure where I'll go next."

She misses his meaning entirely. "Knowing Carmen, you'll probably end up in Houston, living, like, a block from her office. What's the big plan? Partner at the firm by thirty-five?"

Noah scratches his head. "That's her plan," he says. "And you're right, actually. She did get a place in Houston. I think she's . . . doin' okay. From what I hear."

At last, it dawns on the brunette. Her mouth drops open. Her eyes bug. Suddenly she sees me, really sees me, and I know she's jumping to a number of unfavorable conclusions. "Oh my God, I'm *so* embarrassed. Did you and Carmen split up?"

"Yeah." Noah looks apologetic, as if her bad manners and general cluelessness are somehow his fault. "We just reached a point . . . where it made sense."

The woman stares at me, awaiting further explanation. She's already decided that he was cheating, that I was his dirty little secret, that I probably leveraged my pregnancy to break up his marriage. All untrue, but how can one defend oneself against unspoken accusations?

"This is Charlie, by the way." Noah makes no other attempt at introduction, and after some stilted conversation, the brunette drifts away, her smile pinched with tacit disapproval.

I try not to take it personally. The woman was Carmen's friend, after all. Whatever story Noah tells, her loyalties will always lie with his ex-wife. I don't begrudge her that, don't even blame Noah for his ineptitude, although just once, I'd love for him to brag on me instead of freezing up like a kid caught daydreaming in class. *This is my girlfriend, Charlotte Cates,* he could say. *She's a journalist from New York. Did you know she has a book coming out next month?*

But that might read as insensitive. There's no winning here — unless you're Carmen.

Though I've never met the hotshot lawyer who once shared Noah's bed, I feel like I know her, quite intimately, in fact. Because it's not just her ex-husband I've taken on. Somehow, unwittingly, I've inherited her life.

Sidalie isn't a large town, and I can't help but move in her shadow, fall into all of her and Noah's old routines. I shop at her grocery store, dine at her favorite restaurants, receive her mail. *Mrs. Noah Palmer,* the envelopes say, and they're not for me.

Carmen may have left Sidalie, but her family members remain tethered to Noah's landscaping company. Two of her cousins work for Noah, and his lead landscape designer just happens to be Carmen's little sister. Our uncomfortable encounter with the brunette is *nothing* compared to the stink-eye Cristina gives me on the rare occasion I stop by his office.

It's not the life that I imagined when we left Louisiana together just a few months ago, ready to see where our relationship would take us. Things were easy then. I loved our time on the road: stopping to explore tiny towns, sleeping at whatever funky motel we might chance upon, photographing every tacky roadside attraction. When we returned to Noah's native Texas, I hoped that Sidalie would be another pit stop for us, a dot on the map where he tied up the loose ends of his business and then moved on, went somewhere new, built a life from nothing with me and our daughter.

It hasn't worked out that way.

I don't regret my choice to come here, exactly. After my son's death, I needed a change of scene, and our day-to-day existence is, for the most part, a happy one. I only wish we had found a place for *us,* instead of trying to fit me into a place that is so clearly his. So clearly *hers.*

"Sorry about that, hon," Noah mutters as we head into the store. "I don't even remember that woman's name. I think Carmen and I went bowlin' with her once."

I say nothing, just breeze through the aisles to the shelf of vitamins. Inside, though, I'm vindicated. *That,* I think, *is why we're not buying a house here. Ever.*

Living in Sidalie means living with the ghost of Carmen, and even though ghosts are not exactly an unfamiliar presence in

25

my life, this is one phantom I can do without.

Two

That night, as Noah refills my water, I hear a faint metallic clink against my glass.

I look up from my carton of lo mein. Half-eaten containers of Chinese food, crumpled napkins, and a pair of stained chopsticks litter the table. The only thing out of place in this gluttonous scene is the glinting object at the bottom of my water glass.

A ring.

Beside me, Noah awaits my reaction with a goofy, hopeful grin. I love this man deeply, but he should know better. I exhale. Massage my temples.

"Oh, hon. I thought you finally stopped with the marriage stuff."

"Come on, Charlie," he urges me, his twang sweet and coaxing. "Just try it on."

I peer down at the ring. Twirl a strand of lo mein with my chopsticks.

"You really gonna be like that?" He sits back, his thick, sun-browned arms folded across his undershirt.

"I appreciate the gesture, I really do. But you know how I feel about marriage."

"I know, I know." His voice rises as he does his best impression of Charlie Being Unreasonable. *"Real commitment is about more than a piece of paper,"* he mimics. "I get it, already." He sighs. "Would you just wear the ring? We don't have to go through a whole ceremony."

"If it's just for show, then what's the point?"

"It's not for show. It's for our *family.* Our baby girl deserves a daddy who's committed to her mama."

I give him an affectionate pat. "She already has one."

"Not accordin' to the rest of the world." He rises from the table, thumbs hooked in the loops of his jeans. "People look at us, Charlie, they do. They look at you, they see we're not married, and then they look at *me.* And they wonder what kinda asshole I am."

"That's what this is about?" I pick up a dumpling and dip it in soy sauce, not bothering to finish chewing before I speak. "You want to get married so people will stop looking at you? Noah, my wearing a wedding ring is not going to make that woman

in the parking lot judge us any less."

"Yeah." He balls up a dirty napkin and tosses it into an empty container, defeated. "People have a long memory in this town."

I reach into my glass with a chopstick and carefully fish out the ring. It's a simple solitaire diamond on a silvery band, probably platinum. Once upon a time, before my divorce, I would have loved this ring. But Eric cheated, and the divorce happened. My first marriage couldn't even make it to the four-year mark. If I'm going to make mistakes in life, I'd at least like to make new ones.

I set the ring on the table. "I could put it on a chain," I offer, trying to placate him. "Wear it as a necklace."

"Doesn't have quite the same meanin' then, does it?"

"What do you want it to mean? We're together, aren't we? I'm here."

"You're here," he says. "But sometimes I wonder how long."

I give a rueful laugh. "I wonder the same thing about you. *How long is this man in Sidalie? When can we leave?* I wonder that all the time."

He comes up behind my chair and places his hands on my shoulders, his chin resting on top of my head. "I don't have any family left, Charlie, none that counts. Don't even have my dog — he's Carmen's now. A person's gotta have *somethin'* to anchor 'em. For me, it's this town."

How can one be mad at a guy who just wants to belong somewhere? As if sensing that he's gaining ground, Noah sinks his thumbs into the tender muscles of my shoulders, slowly working out knots of tension. The man doesn't play fair.

I wish I could provide him with the clan he feels he lacks, but the fact is I've never had much in the way of family myself. A drug-addicted mother who left when I was too young to remember, an alcoholic father who died when I was fourteen, an aunt and cousins I never see. And while Noah loves my grandmother, the formidable woman who stepped in to raise me, Grandma's eighty-eight years old. She doesn't have a lot of time left.

Just one more way that Carmen outshines me. *She* had a tribe with Sunday dinners, nieces and nephews, an *abuela* who harassed them every weekend about their baby-making plans. I have no one.

I wipe my mouth and push away the rest of the food. "I know you're attached to Sidalie," I tell him. "I get it. Sometimes I miss New York like crazy. At the end of the day, though, there's nothing really keeping us here."

"My company's in Sidalie," he reminds me. "I have forty guys dependin' on me for a salary. After all the years they've given me, you really think I can just walk away?"

"Yes, I do! You have millions of dollars lying around in a bank account you've never touched. You could pay those guys a lifetime of wages and just *go.*"

His face clouds over at the mention of his inheritance. "I don't want that money," he says flatly. "I'd just as soon burn it. It won't bring my father back." These days, we don't talk much about what happened in Louisiana, but in the battle for Most Dysfunctional Family History, I'd have to say he's winning. "If it's the money you're after, woman, you better take off right now."

The accusation of gold digging is a joke, of course. I just sold my house in Connecticut; I'm sitting on plenty of cash. In truth, you couldn't pay me enough to stay in Sidalie. Only the heart would stick this one out.

I follow him down the hall into the bedroom, watch him strip off his jeans and undershirt. He deposits his clothing into the hamper (the man *can* be taught) before flopping onto our bed. His body, taut and

31

tan from all the hours spent at work out-doors, both entices and discourages me. How can I keep up with *that*? He'll never have to worry about stretch marks, baby weight, or C-section scars.

"You comin'?" He holds his arms out as if I might tumble into them. "It's gettin' late."

"I don't want to sleep yet." I linger in the doorway, not quite meeting his eye. Noah lifts his head, and I don't have to say a word. He understands.

"You can't stay awake forever, baby," he says. "I know you're scared you'll have that dream again, but sooner or later, you gotta get your *z*'s."

"Yeah."

"It's just a dream, no matter how many times you have it."

I stare down at my protruding navel and bite my lip. Neither one of us believes that, not completely. I've been seeing myself die in a shower since the end of June, and if experience means anything, that's no ac-cident. "Anytime I see something, it either happened or it's going to happen," I mur-mur. "You know that."

"This is different," Noah insists, settling himself beneath the sheets. "Those were dreams about children. This one's about *you,* about our baby. I read that *What to*

Expect book. They said lots of pregnant women have weird dreams, that it's just hormones."

"Maybe," I say, because beneath his calm exterior, I know he's scared. Losing me, losing his baby daughter — this sudden, unexpected blessing we've both upended our lives to accommodate — is an idea too terrible for him to contemplate.

"I'll go to bed in a minute," I tell him lightly. "Just let me clean up the kitchen a little."

He gives a grunt of assent. Rolls onto his stomach, face squished against the pillow in his signature sleep pose.

Now the only one awake, I'm lonesome. There's a lump in my throat as I clear the table of my remaining Chinese takeout. I repackage the leftover dumplings, slip packets of soy sauce and spicy mustard into a kitchen drawer of items I will never use but can't seem to throw away. The ring remains on the table, a shiny and expensive reminder of our disparate goals for the future.

Suddenly I want to cry. Whether it's the dream, my life in Sidalie, or simply a wave of aftershock from the changes I've experienced in the last year, I don't know. I sit down at the table and crack open a fortune cookie, taking a few bites of the tasteless, hard shell before I read the message inside: *Love takes practice.*

That's it. I burst into nonsensical tears. I am officially a giant, pregnant disaster.

What am I doing here, anyway? Living month to month in this impersonal little apartment, refusing to purchase a more permanent home or solidify our future together in any meaningful way — why did I come to Sidalie at all if I wasn't in it to win it?

Noah's a good guy. He doesn't deserve all my moods and personality flaws, the sudden bursts of grief for my lost son worsened by baby hormones. Noah didn't ask for an accidental pregnancy to rock his life, didn't ask for his fling with some Yankee woman to permanently alter his existence just months after his divorce.

Except, I realize as my eyes fall again on the ring, he *is* asking for it.

I set the ring down in the palm of my right hand. Touch the diamond with my index finger. It's both solid and delicate, beautiful yet hard, a lump of coal shaped by the earth's pressure into something strong and dazzling. I can't wear it, of course, won't let myself get sucked into all that, but I don't want Noah to return the ring, either. I open the drawer of items I can't quite throw away and tuck it in amongst the old phone chargers, hotel soap, and rubber bands.

He's right. I've got to get some sleep.

I head back to our room and climb into bed with him. Begin the elaborate arrangement of pillows that must occur each night before I can sleep with this belly.

From his side of the bed, Noah lets out one sudden, single snore, a noise that sounds remarkably like the low setting of our blender. I feel a rush of tenderness toward him and, almost immediately after, guilt.

"I'm trying to be happy here," I whisper into the dark. "I'm really trying."

I turn on my side. Close my eyes. Stroke my belly and whisper, "Good night, baby girl."

I awaken a little after one a.m., the need to pee as insistent as an alarm. It will be nice, I think, when I no longer have a small person pressing against my bladder 24/7. I roll heavily out of bed and pad down the hallway to the bathroom.

The apartment is quiet except for the low groan of the air conditioner. You'd never know we have a lot of neighbors; Sunview Apartments is inhabited by polite and sensible people who wouldn't dream of making a peep after nine p.m. on a week-night. For a moment I miss New York, the feeling that somewhere there's a diner, a bar, an all-night pharmacy still open and populated by a community of fellow insomniacs. But who am I kidding? I'm not in my twenties. I'm pushing forty, and I'd resigned myself to a quiet suburban existence in Connecticut years before I met Noah. My reservations about Sidalie have nothing to do with the town itself and everything to do with Noah's history here.

Moments later, I stumble out of the bathroom, still half asleep. The moon is high and full as it floods through the skylight, and for a second, I think it's playing tricks on me, casting eerie shadows on the carpet that weren't there when I entered the bathroom two minutes ago.

But they aren't shadows, I realize as I peer down at the trail of dark and blotchy spots. Suddenly I'm awake, far more awake than I want to be. I take a few steps closer, the back of my neck tingling as I realize what I'm looking at.

Footprints. Very *small* footprints, and they're heading for our living room.

I sink down to the floor in an awkward, pregnant squat and gingerly reach out to touch one of the prints. It's thick and wet on my fingers, the smell metallic yet sweet. Blood.

It's not real, I think, but it doesn't matter. I'm already disappearing. Losing myself, giving in to that sweet, dark pull. Around me, the ceiling drops and the walls shift noiselessly, forming a new space. The carpet dissolves beneath my feet, turns to cheap vinyl tile.

The footprints are still there, glistening in the dark. I'm in someone else's apartment, a place that smells of stale smoke and some kind of floral air freshener. A pile of Barbies clutters the floor, bodies contorted into odd shapes, one doll missing a head. I navigate past crayons, an adult-sized pair of flip-flops, an empty water bottle. On the wall, I see a mirror with a shiny metal frame shaped like a sun. I note my own reflection as I walk past, silvery and ghostlike, lips parted, my eyes unnaturally bright.

The footprints continue through a living area to a partially open sliding glass door. I step outside, barely able to make out a small patio. Beyond, the land drops off into an indigo void. All that blue seems to ripple and blur around me, and I think that I'm underwater at first, weedy plant life swaying in the current. Then the air stills. I see the jagged lines of distant mountains, realize it's not ocean flora that I'm looking at but cacti, their plump limbs reaching upward, grasping at the low-hanging sliver of moon.

I hear panting. A whimper. Someone's out there.

I scan the desert landscape until I spot something moving: a shadowy, huddled mass by an immense cactus. The figure seems to sense me, pausing before rising.

A little girl. Chubby, with a mess of tangled black hair, her body quivering like a rabbit. She stares straight at me, half frightened, half hopeful, and I have no idea if she's alive or dead.

Mama? she calls, and when I don't respond, she tries again. *Mama?*

I'm not your mama, I tell her.

The night is hot with no wind, yet I find myself shivering. In the blackness of the night sky, the moon seems to shudder.

I want my mama, the girl says, her voice wavering. *Please. I want my mom.*

I think of my own son, just four years old when he died of a sudden brain aneurysm. Did he utter these same words as I raced to join him at the hospital?

Tell me who you are, I say. *Tell me what you need me to do.*

She tilts her face to the sky and lets out a

low, animal-like keening, to me or God or maybe just the desert moon, I don't know. I feel her cry, an almost physical thing squeezing at my chest, my heart. Then she's silent, just a small slip of a girl against the vast, empty desert.

Above us, the slice of moon swells to fullness. A single crimson flower spreads across its surface in a disturbing, bloody bloom.

I need to go to her. Need to do *something.* I leave the patio, take a few quick strides in her direction, but she's gone now. The desert, too, has vanished.

A mound of blankets, that's all that remains. White blankets with long, dark strands of hair spilling from its folds. She's in there, I know she's in there. I must unwrap her. Must see what I don't want to see.

The moment I extend my hand, I feel a jolt. My body hits a wall.

I stumble back, aware that the desert and the child wrapped in blankets have been replaced by my own moonlit living room and the very solid wall that I've just tried to walk through.

I rub my head. The room is spinning, my head and shoulder shooting pain. I feel a series of sharp, irritated kicks from within as my daughter protests this rude awakening.

The carpet is clean. No sign of bloody footprints.

Am I sleepwalking through my visions now? Wandering through my apartment in some altered state and crashing into walls? *Not an encouraging development, Charlie.*

But at least I'm not dreaming an ugly future for my baby again. She's alive. I'm alive. That has to count for something.

I find my way back to the bedroom, lumber into bed, and begin arranging pillows the best I can, though my hands are unsteady. Sooner or later, that little girl will surface in my waking life, possibly dead. That seems to be how it works.

Noah's still out, absorbed in the kind of deep, untroubled sleep I always envy. For once, I follow his example. Perhaps I've finally grown accustomed to these dreams, or perhaps my physical exhaustion is greater than my anxiety. It doesn't take long to fall asleep again, and when I do, I'm out until the morning.

Noah is already up and showering for work when I awake. Inside the kitchen, I find a pot of decaf coffee waiting for me like a love note. I pour myself a mug, mentally organizing my day. Book promo stuff, mostly, and a magazine article I need to finish.

Over on the counter, my phone begins to vibrate. Not a New York number and not local, either. I answer anyway, bracing myself for a telemarketer.

"Charlie?" The familiar Boston accent doesn't bother with the *r* in my name. "It's your aunt Suzie."

"Suzie! Hi . . ." A phone call from my aunt is a rare occurrence, and generally not a harbinger of anything good. "Is everything okay?"

"Not really." She launches unceremoniously into her reason for contacting me. "I got a call this morning from the Tucson Police Department. Donna's dead."

"Who?"

"Donna," she says. "Your mother."

I grip the handle of my mug, curiously numb. I haven't heard a thing about my mother in decades, haven't known where she was or what she might be doing, and I'm not sure I want to know these things. For all intents and purposes, I've excised her from my family tree. More accurately: she excised herself.

"My mother's dead? In Arizona?" Given what I've heard about her propensity for addiction, I'm amazed the woman survived

41

this long. I've always sort of assumed that she overdosed years ago.

"The cops found her at her daughter's place." From her blasé delivery, you'd think my aunt was discussing an electric bill. "Somebody shot 'em both."

"I didn't even know Donna had a daughter. Besides me, I mean." Without thinking, I take a mouthful of steaming coffee and burn my mouth. "That's so . . . you're saying somebody just came in and *shot* them?"

"The police think it's drug related," Suzie informs me. "No surprise there. A real shame Donna took her own kid down with her, though. I always said you were better off without her."

"The daughter," I begin, "did she —"

"They're both dead. Pretty ugly business from what the officer told me."

"Jesus. That's crazy." I'm not sure what to do with any of this information, how I'm supposed to feel about losing family members I never really had. In truth, I don't feel much of anything, just detached recognition that in the contest for Most Dysfunctional Family History, Noah and I may now be running even. "So . . . are you going to fly out there? To Tucson?"

Suzie snorts. "I haven't had a relationship

with Donna in almost forty years. Too late now."

"Yeah." I'm relieved to hear this is just a courtesy call, not an appeal to explore a portion of my gene pool that I'd rather ignore. "Well . . . thanks for letting me know."

"There's one thing," she says. "I probably shouldn't even bring it up, not with you expecting, but . . ." She sighs. "There's a kid. Donna's granddaughter. She was in the house the night it happened."

I have a sudden flash of the girl in the desert, the bloody footprints, the cries for Mama. And the blankets, dark hair spilling from white folds. My body goes cold.

"What happened to her? The little girl, is she alive?"

"She's all right," Suzie confirms. "Child Protective Services have got her in a foster home for now. But they always go chasing after the family in these situations, looking for someone to take the kid. And I guess there's no dad in the picture, so . . ."

The image of that little girl, her bloody footprints, hangs over me, more awful now that I understand. She must have found her mother dead in that apartment. Found Donna, too. But why appear to me? What good could I possibly do, unless —

"You don't think Child Protective Services

will come to *me,* do you?" I ask.

"Oh yeah," my aunt says. "They're gonna be all over you. Just don't let them guilt you into anything. You and me both know Donna was a piece of shit. You don't owe her jack. But I figured, you know, better warn you what's coming."

"Thanks," I mumble, and find some quick excuse to get off the phone.

I'm not your mama, I told the girl, and it's true. But by some strange accident of blood, I'm her aunt. Does that matter?

Usually, when strange children whisper to me in dreams, I have no qualms about helping. That's how I met Noah, in fact — rushing to the aid of some mystery boy. But this child is different. An echo of a life I never lived. Tangible proof of a woman I'd rather forget.

The urge to walk away is overwhelming.

Still processing it all, I drift down the hall in search of Noah. I find him in the bathroom, toweling off after his shower. His close-cropped dark hair sprays me with a few errant drops as I enter. I can smell the sandalwood soap he uses, a familiar, masculine odor, and suddenly I want to bury my face in his neck and promise him that house in Sidalie.

"What's goin' on?" Noah correctly deduces something's amiss from my knit eyebrows.

"I don't know," I murmur. "I think . . ." I stare at the bathroom floor, trying to mentally work my way around this one, but there's only one conclusion I can draw, no matter how I attack it. "I think we need to go to Tucson."

■ ■ ■ ■

PART II
TUCSON, ARIZONA
AUGUST 2012

■ ■ ■ ■

THREE

For years, I have listened to people describe anything large as "the size of Texas." *I can't wear skinny jeans,* my friend Rae might moan. *Can't you see I've got an ass the size of Texas?* In my mind, this made sense. Texas equals big, a simple equation. But only when Noah and I hit the highway, destination Tucson, do I understand the full extent of such hyperbole. Texas isn't just big — it's endless.

In the Northeast, you can drive eight hours and pass through almost as many states. The coast is littered with rest stops, major cities, tourist destinations. Texas, I quickly learn, is its own world. According to our GPS, the drive from Sidalie to Tucson clocks in at around fifteen hours, and Noah's home state accounts for ten of them. You can drive all day and still find yourself in Texas.

Noah drives the first several hours, looking oddly relaxed as his SUV reaches speeds of ninety-five miles per hour.

"Would you slow down?" I beg, although the speed limit's eighty out here, and we haven't seen any state troopers.

"Mm." He complies for about ten minutes before the pointer on the speedometer begins creeping up again.

I roll down the window a few inches, craving wind, a dash of fresh air, but the sudden blast of heat in my face feels more like cracking open an oven. Noah smirks at this rookie mistake and points to the temperature display in the center console. One hundred and two degrees. From then on, we travel windows up, hermetically sealed in our climate-controlled car.

Early in our journey, we see some encouraging signs of life — exits, towns, industry — but by the time we hit the western portion of the state, there is only highway. Rural desert. Skies you could drown in. Buttes rising up, flat and plodding. *This* is the Texas I always imagined, this hot and dangerous wasteland, not Sidalie, with its manicured, water-wasting lawns, its strip malls and chain stores, and the one enormous building I mistook for an athletic complex until Noah explained that it was a mega-church.

I watch the monotonous desert landscape roll by, fascinated by the people who choose to live in such a place. I have never seen land so empty and unforgiving: cracked dirt dotted with scraggly bits of green, the very occasional attempt at a town delineated only by a sign and a thin scattering of houses in the distance. Living out here, away from the safety net of neighbors and speedy emergency services, you'd have to learn to handle yourself. No wonder Noah keeps a nine-millimeter in the glove compartment. The Wild West is alive and well.

I wonder if Arizona will be more of the same, if Tucson possesses its own breed of culture. Apart from a girls' weekend Rae and I once spent in New Mexico, I haven't seen much of the Southwest.

"You've been to Tucson before, right?" I ask. "What's it like?"

Noah shrugs. "Just another city in a desert. Nothin' special."

"This drive is *long.*"

"Yeah, Arizona's a trek. You get used to it, I guess."

"Used to it? What, were you a trucker in a former life?"

"I drove this route a lot when Carmen was in law school," he says.

The mention of his ex-wife makes me a

bit prickly, but I'm careful not to show it. Noah doesn't usually mention her, and I'm curious. "Where'd she go to law school?"

"Arizona State. She got a scholarship." Though he offers little in the way of detail, I can tell it must have been a source of contention for them, Carmen's going away to school.

"Was that right after you got married?"

"Yep," he says. "It was hard for a few years. My company was takin' off, and I couldn't just up and leave with her. So we did a lotta back-'n'-forth."

"A long-distance marriage," I marvel.

"Yeah," he says. "I don't recommend those."

I want to ask more about her, this woman he spent so much of his life with, but part of me is afraid to know the details, afraid that Carmen's ambition and intelligence will prove me inferior. Ultimately their relationship imploded because she didn't want kids and Noah did. In my rawest, most insecure moments, I wonder if that's the only leg up on Carmen that I have: my womb. My willingness to bear children.

I'd never tell Noah about these fears, of course. I don't want to be a jealous stereo-type.

I shift around in the passenger seat, too

proud to complain about my physical discomfort, but inwardly cursing myself for attempting a car ride of this magnitude when I'm so far along in the pregnancy. We could've flown, of course, but it seemed easier to keep our travel plans flexible, to forgo the hassle of renting a car in Arizona. Unfortunately, I did not factor in my overactive bladder, which I'm currently managing through a combination of mild dehydration and frequent pit stops. I drive for a couple hours to let Noah nap, but driving is even more awkward than being a passenger; my belly bumps up against the steering wheel.

And my discomfort is not just physical. My mind races with questions, worries, and suppositions about the little girl we will soon meet. Michaela Ramos, my niece. According to her caseworker, she goes by Micky. Six years old. Old enough to understand something about death, to understand that neither her mother nor her grandmother is ever coming back. Old enough to understand that someone, or multiple someones, came into her home while she was sleeping and killed the two people she loved best.

And it was Micky who found them dead.

After an intense couple weeks of paperwork, background checks, and polite but persistent phone calls, Noah and I have secured visitation rights with my niece. Tomorrow, we meet with Micky's case-worker, a man with a low, jaded voice named Daniel Quijada. He'll bring us to a supervised visit with the child herself. From there, everything's up in the air. Noah and I will be tasked with some difficult choices, choices with life-altering consequences for the two of us, our daughter, and Micky.

How does one make these decisions? I know nothing about my niece except that her bloodline is unimpressive and her parenting, in all probability, has been wildly inadequate. In my book, mothers and grandmas of quality do not become victims of gruesome drug-related double homicides. Who knows the caliber of screwed-up kid we're about to encounter?

In the passenger seat, Noah awakens from his catnap. He blinks his eyes a few times and peers out the window to see where we are. "Still Texas?" he guesses.

We've been driving since five a.m. and it's after noon now. "Yeah," I say. "Still Texas."

He yawns. "Gonna need lunch soon."

I don't answer, don't shift my gaze from the road.

He studies me, my upturned chin and

hands gripping the wheel at ten and two, in perfect driver's ed formation. "You nervous?"

"Well, sure. I don't know what we're getting ourselves into." It bothers me that he's *not* more freaked out about everything, yet from the beginning, he's approached the topic of Micky with an almost preternatural calm.

That girl needs somebody, he said when I explained the situation to him. *Maybe it's us.* And maybe it is. But how will we know?

Noah touches my arm. "Hey. I know the timin' is bad with the baby and all, but we're doin' the right thing."

"Yeah."

One can't argue with "the right thing." I don't tell him that the prospect of coordinating an additional child's housing, school, doctor visits, and the like leaves me overwhelmed. Don't mention that inviting a traumatized child into our home precisely when our first child is born strikes me as reckless, arrogant even. I want to do the right thing, but unlike Noah, I'm guided by more than untested ideals. I've been a parent before. I know what it entails.

"Can you imagine where you 'n' I would be today if we didn't have grandparents to raise us?" He shakes his head. "I keep thinkin' about that, how we gotta pay it forward. We have a responsibility to this kid."

"Micky," I say, trying her name on like an article of clothing I'm not so sure about.

"Micky," Noah echoes, and then smiles. "Your family's got somethin' against girly-girl names, huh?"

"Her mom's name was Jasmine," I protest. "That's pretty girly." I wince. "Jasmine. Sounds like a Disney princess or a stripper, and I don't know which is worse."

"All right, then." He chuckles. Squints into the searing sunshine. "Guess that's a name we won't be givin' our daughter."

From the highway signs, you'd think El Paso was some kind of mecca. All morning, green road markers have tracked our distance from the city: EL PASO, 479. As if the city were so miraculous, one needs five hundred miles of anticipatory signage. Still, I watch the numbers dwindle, cheering internally when the mileage shrinks from triple to double digits. El Paso is near the state border, just a stone's throw from New Mexico. El Paso means we're getting closer.

With proximity to El Paso comes Mexico, and with Mexico, Border Patrol. We hit a checkpoint in Sierra Blanca, find our vehicle funneled into a lane alongside a green-uniformed agent who asks about our citizenship and destination, his left hand tight on the leash of a vigilant canine. Unlike the cars with brown-skinned occupants or California plates, we move through without much in the way of a real inspection. The unearned free pass makes me feel uncomfortable, a reluctant teacher's pet.

"What does Border Patrol have against California?" I ask Noah, craning my neck to see what's happening to an old Cali-plated station wagon.

"Medical marijuana," he says. "It's legal there, not here. Sierra Blanca's always bustin' folks for weed." He doesn't look back, and I gather that random stops and searches are a Texas quirk he has learned to live with, racial and geographic profiling notwithstanding.

As we speed toward the Franklin Mountains, Mexico looms ever larger in my consciousness. Signs crop up for Ciudad Juárez and the international border, and though I can't see the dividing wall, I imagine it out there, demarcating the line between poverty and possibility. Or not. Maybe I've unfairly bought into stereotypes of an impoverished Mexico — the truth is I've never been to a border town before.

"Hey. Wanna make a pit stop in Juárez?" I

don't know if the suggestion is a noble attempt at consciousness-raising or simple morbid curiosity, but Noah shoots it down regardless.

"Nah. We don't even have our passports."

"Yes, we do," I inform him. "I brought pretty much every form of ID imaginable, just in case. You never know what kind of paperwork Child Protective Services will come up with."

Around us I can see the stirrings of a city: concrete structures, expanding lanes, increased traffic. As if sensing the potential for freedom, my right leg cramps up. Pain shoots up my calf in a series of wild spasms. If I don't get out of this car soon, I'm going to lose it.

"Come on," I urge him. "We need a break. You can get a beer."

"We're not crossin' over," Noah says. "I've spent enough time in Mexican border towns, trust me. They'll hurt your soul."

I imagine dirty barrooms, topless dancers, sketchy alleyways best avoided. Mexico, in my mind, is a bad Antonio Banderas movie. "You think I can't handle a little sin?" I scoff.

"*I* can't handle it. They see you're a gringo, and they're all over you." He shudders. "I've had girls who couldn't be more'n twelve try to sell themselves to me on the street. Nobody should have to live like that."

"Oh." I put a hand reflexively to my belly. "I guess we can skip that. Probably safer, anyway. Never know what kind of creepy bathrooms we might run into."

We settle for El Paso, swooping in for a quick bite at some taco chain I've never heard of and then gassing up in a neighborhood that looks best avoided at night. *Is Juárez really so much worse?* I wonder, noting the run-down motel across the road, its offers of both hourly and weekly rates.

Despite having used the bathroom at the taco joint, I have to pee again. I scan the gas station — too rinky-dink for even a proper food mart — and see a small concrete structure with the word RESTROOM on its dented metal door. Sketchy as all get-out, but it'll do. I scramble out of our SUV, turn sharply around the gas pump, and nearly crash into a young woman passing by.

She bobbles her bottle of Fanta and whirls on me in a flash of jangling bracelets and large hoop earrings.

"Jesus Christ, watch it!" She's a brown-skinned woman with blond-streaked hair and plenty of cleavage, the kind of woman who could address a friend as *homegirl* without sounding ridiculous. She raises a finger as if preparing to cuss me out but stops when she notices I'm pregnant. The dirty look she's been shooting me immediately turns to a big, chummy grin.

"Hey, *mami,* me too!" She gestures to her own belly, which is in that pudgy-but-not-obviously-expecting stage. "You about to drop yours, huh? When're you due? I'm January."

"Congratulations." My armpits are already damp from the heat. "I'm due the end of September." It's an unlikely moment of sisterhood, but haul around new life in your body for a few months, and you feel a certain kinship with others in your situation. "Is this your first?"

She laughs, a low cackle. "Don't I wish." She slaps her gut. "Number five right here. My oldest is sixteen."

I almost say, *You look too young to have a teenager,* but I don't. Because chances are she *was* too young. I think suddenly of my mother, raised in the projects of Boston, just nineteen when she had me. I think of Jasmine, the half sister I never knew, a single mom gunned down in her home. And I think of Micky, facing the kind of hardships I put behind me many, many years ago. I've never dwelled upon my own losses, choosing instead to outrun them, and yet here I am, Micky's present bringing me uncomfortably close.

"Sounds like you have your hands full," I say. "Good luck."

"Yeah, you too." She squints at me, having just worked out my intended destination. "You weren't gonna use that bathroom, were you?"

"Actually, I was . . ."

"Ooh, nah, best not." Her eyes glance over me, quickly assessing my neatly styled dark hair and Anthropologie sundress. "That's not your kinda bathroom, trust me." She jerks her finger at the road behind her. "Go another block down. There's a McDonald's."

I bristle at the implication, however well-intentioned. *You think I'm some stuck-up white lady too good for a gas station bathroom?*

"This bathroom's fine."

She shrugs, and I march over to the little concrete building, determined to show her how Not Like That I am. The door is heavy and sticks, but I tug it open. Release a blast of heat and stench so powerful I almost pass out.

Oh, I think. *Oh.*

The light switch doesn't work, which

might be a blessing or a hazard; in the dim room, I can't fully see all sources of the stink. But as I glance at the contents of the toilet, I can surmise. No air-conditioning and some unmotivated employees mean that unflushed feces and urine have been left to slow-cook for hours, maybe days. And the floor is wet with mystery liquid — a plumbing problem? I don't dare flush yet. I'll just have to go on top of everything else.

I plug my nose, still gagging, and squat-pee as quickly as I can. *May this serve as proof,* I think. *You're not the soft, entitled white woman that lady thought.*

My business done and white guilt temporarily exorcised, I reach for the toilet handle. Flush, and run like hell.

By the time we reach Arizona, the sun kisses the horizon, lighting up the sky in spectacular shades of orange and pink. We're less than two hours from Tucson, but with night approaching and my lower back crying for relief, I'm ready for the first decent hotel we can find. Though disappointed, Noah stops at the first signs of civilization and hunts for lodging.

We hunker down for the night at a battered motel in Willcox. I grab a handful of brochures from the hotel lobby, hoping to get a sense of what the state has to offer. From the flyers, Willcox's big claims to fame are a cowboy museum and a cemetery that boasts the grave of Geronimo's son. As I flip through brochures for the historic copper mines of Bisbee and the infamous OK Corral in Tombstone, I begin to wonder if southern Arizona is like some aging football star yearning for the good old days, or just a shrewd businessman ready to exploit the nation's collective delusions about its past. And future, judging from the casino pamphlets.

Back in our room, I fashion myself a pillow nest and sleepily suggest baby names for our daughter. "Beatrice," I say. "Eleanor. Harriet."

Noah's composing an e-mail to his assistant, Sharlene, only half paying attention. "Those are old-lady names," he tells me.

"No, they're *classic*." I try a new line. "Daisy. Rose. Poppy."

"I'm not a fan of flowers."

"What do you mean you're not a fan of flowers? You're a freaking landscaper, you *love* flowers. Lily? Holly?"

He bangs off one final instruction to Sharlene and then looks up from his tablet. "I love beer, too, but I don't want to name our daughter Guinness."

"Corona, then? Yuengling?" I'm too tired to be anything but silly now. "Or we could class it up with wine. Our daughter, Chardonnay. Or Merlot. Riesling? . . ."

"Riesling is actually kind of pretty," Noah says, and it's the last thing I remember before I fall into a dreamless sleep.

The next morning, as we reach the limits of Tucson proper — which, at its outskirts, still mostly resembles desert — I spot a coyote limping alongside the road. I've never seen one before, and I'm taken aback by his beauty, part wolf, part fox, part dog, pressing forward through the desert's rising sunlight. I pull over into the breakdown lane and slow our car to a stop.

"Whatcha doin'?" Noah asks, looking up from a work e-mail on his phone.

I point back at the coyote, now a short distance behind us on the road. He walks with an awkward little hop-skip, dragging his rear leg along without putting any weight on it.

"He's hurt," I say. "Looks like maybe he got clipped by a car or something. You think he'll be okay?"

"Sure he will," Noah says. "Takes a lot to kill a coyote. They're tough. Wouldn't last a day in the desert if they weren't."

We watch the creature continue along toward us against a backdrop of cacti and green-brown mountains. Even after all the wide, empty spaces of yesterday, the openness of the landscape amazes me. You can see for miles, winding roads, a cell tower, neighborhoods on the edge of the city popping up and rapidly thickening — all the ways that human beings encroach upon what should be uninhabitable land.

The coyote glances over at our SUV, our gawking faces, assessing the danger we might pose. He's unimpressed. Never missing a hop-skip, he limps past us, following the line of highway toward the city, determined and unafraid.

He knows hunger, and he knows thirst. He doesn't worry about needy nieces. He doesn't dream of dying.

FOUR

Daniel Quijada is a burly Latino man with a goatee and hipster glasses. We find his cubicle in the back corner of the Child Protective Services office, an over-air-conditioned building stuffed with desks and fatigued social workers. Daniel's on the phone, sipping a Diet Coke and rubbing his left temple with an expression that begs for death's reprieve.

"No, no, I get it, Sylvia," he says, "I do." He sighs. "He's a tough kid, we knew that going in. I'm just — sorry to hear it's not working out for you. I'll see what I can do about finding him another placement, but quite honestly, I don't have a lot of options right now." He sets down his Diet Coke and selects a red roller-tip pen from his cup. "Of course, and I respect that. But I may need a few days to work something out. Let me get back to you, okay?"

Listening to his end of the call, Noah and

I exchange nervous glances. A foster parent with buyer's remorse? Could this be us someday?

Daniel hangs up the phone and scribbles notes onto a legal pad, nodding wearily in our direction. I can't guess his age. The overweight baby face, thinning black hair, and stocky build could be an old thirty-five or a young fifty, and his desk offers no clues. His workspace is an impersonal testament to obsessive-compulsive disorder, with color-coded binders and alphabetized reference materials. Only a Costco-sized bottle of Tums provides any insight into his inner workings.

"Hi!" I greet him brightly. "I'm Charlotte Cates, and this is Noah." I don't sit down because there are no extra chairs around his cubicle. "We're here about Michaela Ramos."

"Sure, sure. Great to meet you both." Daniel's head bobs up and down, and he grabs a yellow folder from his desk. "We'll just pop into one of the meeting rooms this way." He takes off down the hall and turns into a windowless room with a table, cheap chairs, and glaring lights.

"So. Micky Ramos. You are her . . ." He glances at his file. "Mom's half sister?"

I nod, although the words sound strange.

I've never been someone's sister before.

"And you're considering guardianship?"

"That's why we're here," Noah says. "All the way from Texas. We thought we'd meet with Micky, see how things go, and . . . maybe we can adopt."

I give Noah the side-eye. A child is not some stray dog you play with once at an animal shelter and decide to take home.

"Texas, that's right." Daniel rifles through his pages, probably trying to remember which of his many cases he's supposed to be discussing. "You're looking at an out-of-state placement."

Maybe it's the way my aunt Suzie spoke about Child Protective Services, as if they stand around trying to pawn children off on any halfway-respectable adult who will take them, but I expected a little more excitement from Daniel, a little more enthusiasm at the prospect of unloading Micky on us. Instead, he regards me with what looks like caution.

"You haven't met your niece before," he states.

"No," I admit. "We're here because she's family."

"That's admirable, it really is." Daniel scratches his head. "And visits are a great way to start."

"So how long will this take?" Noah's practically bouncing in his seat, and I know part of him is hoping we'll return to Sidalie in a week or two with a plucky six-year-old in tow.

"Look," Daniel says, lifting his glasses and rubbing his eyes. "I'm going to be straight with you. Transferring guardianship to an out-of-state resident is a long process on both ends. Typically, it takes about six months to move a child from foster care to an out-of-state relative."

"Six *months*?" It's even longer than I would've guessed. "So basically, as soon as she gets settled into her foster home, we'd uproot her?"

"It can be tough," Daniel acknowledges. "Micky will have to change schools, leave her friends, lose any consistency she has in her life right now. I'm not saying you shouldn't seek custody of your niece, not saying that at all. But if you're still in the decision-making phase, I want you to have all the facts."

I brace myself. "And the facts are?"

"This child has been through a severe trauma," Daniel says. "She'll need a lot of support services."

"She still needs a home, though, right?" Noah stubbornly clings to his view of Micky as a sad, vagrant animal. "There's no other relatives tryin' to get custody? Her father didn't suddenly turn up?"

"No, no." Daniel shakes his head. "Her father reportedly lives in Mexico. He's never had any custodial rights, and so far we haven't been able to locate him. That will become another issue down the line, if you choose to adopt. If you find him, he might willingly surrender his parental rights. Otherwise, you'll have to get a court to terminate them."

I close my eyes, imagining all the paperwork and court dates we'll have ahead of us, should we choose to go this route. "You said it could be six months to get guardianship. How long does it take to officially adopt?"

Daniel licks his lips. "On average? For an out-of-state family, we're looking at three, four years."

Noah lets out a low whistle. He thought our trip to Tucson was a simple extraction mission, not a multiyear legal obstacle course. I can see the doubt creeping in as he reevaluates the commitment he was so prepared to make.

"I'm sorry," Daniel says. "I just want to be honest about the process. A lot of caseworkers aren't, and it's the kids who suffer." He tries for optimism. "All this is do-able, really. Six to nine months from now, once you've cleared some hurdles, Micky could be joining you in Texas."

"Do you think that's best for Micky?" I ask.

"That's really up to you two." Daniel folds his hands. Despite his large frame, his fingers are long and slim, his nails neatly clipped. "You've got a baby coming. Before you both sign on for this, you need to make sure you're ready to jump through a lot of hoops." For the first time, I detect a note of compassion in Daniel's voice, not for us, but for Micky. "I'd hate for you both to become a presence in this little girl's life, and then . . . things don't work out. Maybe you change your mind. I've seen that too many times."

"If we don't step in, what happens?" Noah asks. "Who's Micky with now?"

"A great couple with a lot of experience fostering." Daniel's face warms with genuine enthusiasm. "The woman works as an aide at Micky's school. I've dealt with her and her husband before. They're amazing."

"Is there any chance that *they* would want to adopt?"

"Very possibly," Daniel replies, and I know what he's thinking. *Don't mess up a good thing for this kid unless you're all in.*

Noah drums on the table with his thumbs, and I can see the idea of strangers taking my niece doesn't sit well with him. "I think we're gettin' ahead of ourselves, here," he says. "We haven't even met Micky yet, and I'd like to get a look at these folks she's livin' with. Maybe we should get to know her some before we all go makin' up our minds."

"Of course." Daniel stands up. "You have a supervised visit with the therapist in about half an hour. I can give you a lift to Micky's foster home."

"We're going to see where Micky lives?" I thought for sure we'd be in some claustrophobic therapist's office.

"It's not standard procedure," Daniel concedes, "but Micky's had some hard meetings with the police psychologist, and the therapist felt that another office environment . . . well, it might not send the right message."

I hadn't realized that investigators were questioning my niece, although it makes sense. She was present in the house that night. She might've heard something. I wonder what Daniel means by "hard meetings." Did they bombard the poor child with questions? Push Micky to talk about fright-

72

ening things?

"Let's go," I say. "Let's go meet her."

The driving in Tucson is not especially cut-throat by East Coast standards, but Daniel operates his vehicle with the alarming intensity of a New York cabbie. I am simultaneously terrified and impressed by his abrupt lane switches, jerky stops, and who-are-you-kidding-that-light-was-red surges.

"If you weren't so sure about dyin' in a shower, I might be real worried right now," Noah whispers.

We end up in a neighborhood that feels blue-collar and relatively safe. No dingy apartment buildings, liquor stores, pawn-shops, or bus stops with homeless people roasting on the bench as we've seen else-where throughout the city: just homey, somewhat worn-down residences.

Daniel pulls up in front of a single-story brick ranch. The front yard is a dozen shades of brown and gray — a bit dismal to someone not accustomed to desert — but there are neatly placed flagstones leading up to the door and items that indicate children live inside. A boy's bicycle dropped by a shrub. A jump rope. A set of pink plastic gardening tools.

Noah and I exchange a quick glance, and

73

he shrugs, forced to agree: *All right, the house passes muster.* His arms are crossed; he's reserving judgment but still ready to assume the worst about Micky's foster family, perhaps even hoping for some clear-cut incompetence or meanness on their part that might make our decision easy, our role of hallowed rescuers more obvious.

I've heard mixed reviews on foster parents, heard stories ranging from low-class mercenary types who do it for the extra income to saintly couples who transform the lives of at-risk children. When Vonda Lopez answers the door, it's clear that she falls into the latter category.

Micky's foster mother is a tall, thick woman in her fifties, and she answers the door barefoot. I know without asking that she's the kind of woman who gives all-encompassing hugs and uses lots of mayonnaise. For a moment, I imagine what childhood with such a woman would be like — dance classes, hair braiding, idle threats of a butt whooping, Jell-O — and I envy Micky.

That was not my childhood. Not even close.

"Hey-a!" Vonda exchanges a quick hug with Daniel and turns to Noah and me. There's nothing fake about her smile, her crinkly eyes. "So nice to meet you two! And you came all the way from Texas?" At the sight of my pregnant belly, she almost swoons. "Oh my goodness, look at you." She reaches out and cradles my stomach in both her hands, her fingers finding the shape of the baby like a midwife. It's a shockingly intimate gesture made all the more surprising by the fact that I'm okay with it.

"Girl, right?" she says. "You're carrying high."

"Yeah, a girl." I smile shyly. "Do you have kids?"

A boy of about ten appears in swim trunks. Vonda hands him a towel and he dashes out the back door. She laughs, turns back to me. "I've got these guys, and that's enough. Luis and I couldn't have children of our own."

"How'd you choose to foster?" Noah asks.

Vonda bends over and grabs a couple toys off the floor. "We were going to adopt a child from Mexico, actually," she says. "That's where Luis's family came from, and there are plenty of kids across the border who need help. At the end of the day, though, it just costs too much. So here we are. Sometimes you pick your fate, sometimes your fate picks you." She points to the door the boy just ran out of. "Micky's out back with Bryce, if you want to go say hi. The therapist should be by in a few minutes."

"Maybe you could fill us in a little first," Daniel suggests. "Anything we should know? How's she been getting on?"

Vonda considers this. "She's very withdrawn. A lot of trouble sleeping. There have been nightmares, some bed-wetting. She's jumpy, but no aggressive behavior yet."

I don't like her use of "yet," the lifetime of issues that lurks behind that word.

Vonda puts a hand on my shoulder as if sensing my anxiety and gently urges me toward the glass door. "Come on. It'll be better if you just get out there."

The yard is half sun, half shade, with no grass, just pale dirt and colorless gravel. Bryce, the boy in swim trunks, fills up a large water gun in a wading pool. Micky sits several feet away in the shady area, a green Popsicle melting in her hand. Her eyes follow us as we file out onto the patio, but she doesn't engage us. Though the lighting is different and her clothing changed, I recognize the dark hair and small, chubby frame.

My dream. The girl from my dream.

"Micky, honey," Vonda addresses her, "this is your auntie Charlotte I was telling you about. Your mama's sister, remember?"

Micky nods. Stares at me, then Noah.

76

Puts the runny Popsicle to her lips.

"Auntie Charlotte and Mr. Noah are going to stay outside with you a bit until Miss Emily gets here. You remember Miss Emily, right? She played toys with you the other day?"

Micky nods again. Blinks. The Popsicle trickles down her chin in a sticky green trail. Vonda and Daniel huddle by the back door, speaking in hushed tones.

Micky's face remains blank when I go to sit down beside her. "Don't sit on a scorpion," she says, and I leap to my feet, peering around the concrete.

"Are there scorpions?"

"Luis saw one yesterday." She looks up at me through her dark lashes. "He said look before you sit down. And check your shoes."

She relates these recommendations matter-of-factly. I'm not sure she's displaying the appropriate level of alarm. "It doesn't seem very safe to play where there are scorpions. Maybe we should go inside."

"The scorpion Luis saw *was* inside."

Noah chuckles, as if an infestation of deadly animals is somehow amusing. "They don't have scorpions where your aunt Charlie is from," he tells Micky. "You'll have to teach her a few things."

She pokes the ground with her Popsicle

77

stick, stone-faced. I get the message. Schooling ignorant adults is not her thing.

"I'm your mom's sister," I announce, a little too loudly. "Did you know that she had a sister?"

"No," Micky says.

"I didn't know I had a sister either. It was a big surprise."

"She's dead now," Micky tells me. "So you don't have a sister anymore."

I don't know how to answer. Her voice is toneless, but I recognize the self-protection in that flat affect, the refusal to reveal weakness. Should I offer words of comfort? Ask her how she feels? Ignore her weird comment?

Nobody speaks for a minute. Over in the swimming pool, Bryce takes a few experimental squirts with his water gun. "Are you going to have a baby?" he asks.

"I am. My belly's pretty big, huh?"

He shrugs.

"You know, Micky," Noah says, shading his eyes with one hand, "that baby in Charlie's belly is gonna be your cousin. I never had any cousins, but I hear they're pretty fun."

"Why didn't you have any cousins?" Micky asks, almost suspicious.

"Well," Noah begins, "I was raised by my

grandma and grandpa, so I didn't know a whole lotta folks in my family."

"What happened to your mom and dad?" She's watching him intently.

I wince at Noah's screwed-up family, wondering how he'll explain his way around this. Back in Louisiana, we worked so hard to conceal the secrets his grandparents built their life around. I see no need to discuss *that* ugly, violent history.

Evade, Noah, I think. *Make something up.*

"Somebody killed my dad," Noah says.

I cover my face with my hands. It's not the whole truth, of course, but far more than Micky needs. What is he doing, unloading the deaths of family members on her? The girl is only six.

But Micky stares at him, her eyes round with understanding. "My mom got killed," she says. "My grandma, too. Somebody shot them with a gun, and there was blood. Somebody killed them."

"Yeah." Noah glances at me, making sure I'm hearing this. We've been wondering how much Micky knows or understands about what happened. "I heard that. It's pretty scary, huh?"

She won't admit to fear. "Were you there when your dad got killed?"

"Actually," Noah says, "yeah. Sort of. I

was asleep in the car when he got shot."

From his spot by the pool, Bryce catches my eye. He holds up his water gun, takes careful aim, and gets me in the neck. I clutch myself, feigning a dramatic death until it occurs to me this is absolutely the wrong game to be playing at this moment. Thank God Micky isn't paying attention. She's still hanging on to Noah's story, determining how it intersects with her own.

"I was sleeping, too," she tells him, tracing her empty Popsicle stick in the dirt. "Inside my house. Somebody came inside." For a moment, her voice hovers in the burning air, unfinished, and I think she's going to add something. I think she's going to go there, somewhere awful. But she's waiting for Noah, waiting for him to guide her.

"You must really miss your mom," he says, and whatever horrific description might have awaited us is forgotten. She's just a little girl, nodding and squinching her lips together in an effort not to cry. And she doesn't. She holds herself together, miraculously. I should take notes.

All these life-and-death personal disclosures are more than I can stomach. I spring up and dip a hand in the wading pool, where Bryce has busied himself with spraying the neighbor's yappy dog through the fence.

"Mm, that feels nice!" I exclaim, although the water is lukewarm and far from refreshing. "Micky, why don't you come for a swim?"

She casts me a long look. "I don't really like the water."

"Oh. Well." I stop splashing. "Living in the desert must be right up your alley."

Noah shoots me a look he reserves for only my most inane moments. "Let's go inside," he says. "I think Miss Emily just arrived."

Micky watches us rise to our feet and wipe away the gravel dust from our hands and backsides. "Hey," she says as Noah reaches for the sliding door. "When the bad guy killed your dad, did they catch him?"

Noah thinks about how to answer this. "It took a long time," he says, "but the person who did it — well, they're dead now."

"Good," she says.

"How did it go?" Daniel asks us in the car.

Alone in the backseat, I say nothing. Noah and I haven't had time to compare notes yet, but something about Micky terrifies me. Her composure, perhaps, in the face of such terrible events. Where does she get her dark calm, and why don't I possess it? Here I am, an adult woman, still struggling with the occasional crying spell more than a year after my loss. Do I lack the emotional self-command of even a six-year-old?

"Micky's a sweet girl," Noah says, bracing himself against the passenger-side door as Daniel leads us boldly through a massive pothole. "It's hard to imagine everything she's goin' through."

"It looks like she's in good hands, at least," I venture. "Vonda seems very — experienced."

"She's fostered a lot of kids," Daniel agrees.

I can't help but hope that Vonda will let us off the hook, swoop in with all her maternal goodness and nurture this broken child in a way that Noah and I, so broken ourselves, can't. "You said she might adopt?"

"She and Luis have been through a lot of short-term placements lately," Daniel replies, watching me through the rearview mirror. "They're looking for something more permanent. They usually take older kids, but I think they'd be willing to adopt Micky if there were a need."

"No." Noah's voice is sudden, startling in its assurance. "Micky belongs with us."

I lean against the window, pursing my lips. "Hon. I think it's a little early for —"

"We're the right ones, Charlie. Us." Noah twists around in his seat to face me. "She's supposed to be with us. When I was talkin' to her today, I just . . . felt that."

"You two did seem to click." I don't tell him how utterly inadequate that makes me feel. We came to Tucson to bond with my poor orphaned niece, but my motherly instincts have failed me thus far.

"Look," Noah says, focusing on Daniel now. "Suppose we pursue custody. I know it wouldn't be easy, but a lot of that is livin' out of state, right?"

"It complicates things, yes." Daniel veers out of a turning lane and zips through a red light.

"What if we were Arizona residents?"

I snap to attention. Would he really leave Sidalie? He can't be serious.

Daniel runs a hand through his goatee. "Residency would certainly help," he says. He works through the details quickly in his mind. "Charlotte's a blood relative, so we could bypass the home certification and place her with you right away. It would shave a lot of time off the adoption process, too." He raises his eyebrows. "Are you two considering a move?"

83

Noah meets my gaze and smiles, apparently mistaking my stricken expression for one of passionate urgency. "Well," he says, "we are now."

FIVE

I'm all for retaining a degree of independence in one's relationship, but even *my* commitment-phobic ass knows there are certain decisions in life a couple have to make together. Moving to Arizona so that you can adopt a disturbed child? On the list.

I keep up a good game face in front of Micky's caseworker, but by the time Daniel Quijada drops us off at our car, I'm seething. *He didn't ask me,* I think. *Noah, you bastard, this is* my *niece, and you didn't even ask me.* I'm prepared, once we reach the privacy of our own vehicle, to deliver a scathing lecture of epic proportions, to remind him about the true meaning of partnership, to demand that my voice be heard.

Then, I open the car door.

The heat in our vehicle renders all other thought impossible. I let out a sound somewhere between a moan and a gasp. Noah slides into the driver's seat and turns on the car, impervious to the blazing inferno around him.

"Huh," he says, poking the screen of the GPS with his index finger. "It overheated."

I can see why. Empty a bottle of water on our dashboard right now, and I suspect that it would vaporize into a giant steam cloud. You'd have yourself an SUV sauna, the white man's tacky, twenty-first-century answer to a sweat lodge.

"We need to find a hotel," I pant, hoping I can maintain consciousness for the three minutes it will take our air-conditioning to kick in. "Drive. Just drive."

To his credit, Noah has a sixth sense for navigating desert cities. We quickly locate a midrange chain hotel along the highway that, in the oppressive heat of early August, doesn't seem to be commanding a lot of business. After dumping our luggage, we settle ourselves by the pool and guzzle from courtesy water bottles they hand out at check-in.

"Nice view," Noah remarks, and he's not wrong. The electric-blue water crackles with sunlight, and if you ignore all the highway noise, the mountains and expansive sky evoke a sense of freedom never to be found in Manhattan's congested horizon.

"So." I plant myself at the pool's edge and dip a foot in, ready to have it out with him now. "Tell me about this big move you have planned."

He's cleaning a spot on his Oakleys, too preoccupied to catch the edge in my voice. "Don't know yet," he says. "I'm still thinkin' through some details, tryin' to figure how this all can work." He slips his sunglasses back on and sits beside me, the tips of his fingers skimming my shoulder. "You need sunscreen, baby."

"What details are you working out, exactly?"

"The business, mainly. I could probably sell it. Pete Gantos might buy if I wanted to unload it. But he's too green. It would tank if he took over." Noah's sunglasses obscure any view of his eyes, leaving me with only the reflection of my own incredulous face.

"I'm sorry, are you talking about *work*?" My own feelings about Tucson — or Micky, for that matter — do not seem to have factored into his plans whatsoever.

He pauses, like I've laid some cunning female trap for him he can't quite make out. "What do you *want* me to talk about?" he asks carefully.

"Oh, I don't know. The child that you just

unilaterally decided to adopt? Maybe we could talk about that."

His eyebrows draw together in an expression of bewilderment. "I didn't unilaterally —"

"You didn't even ask me!"

"Well, I know, but —"

"You made a major life decision without first consulting —"

"I didn't consult you because you gave me the look!"

"The look?" I blink. Try to reel myself in with a deep breath and entertain the possibility that I'm dealing with a simple case of stupidity here, not total self-absorption. "What look did I give you, Noah?"

"The one where your eyes get all big. Like when you really want something." He wipes his forehead with the back of his hand, flustered. "I thought we were on the same page, babe. You said we made a connection with Micky, and then you gave me that look . . . I thought movin' was what you *wanted.* I mean, you've been tryin' to get me out of Sidalie for months, haven't you? This seemed like the right time, the right reason."

I twist my hair into a knot and wrap it with an elastic from my purse. "So let me get this straight. *Me* wanting to move, us building a better life for our baby . . . not a good reason to leave town. But *Micky,* some weird little girl you just met, *that's* the right reason?"

He's too smart to meet that one head-on. "You think Micky's weird?"

"How could she *not* be?"

"All right," he says. "Well, nothin' wrong with weird. I mean, look at you. And I still love you."

I roll my eyes, insulted. "Me and Micky. Two peas in a weird old pod. Thanks."

"You have more in common with her than I think you realize."

"What, besides our crappy genetics?"

"Did you see how well that kid held it together? She's been takin' care of herself a long time, since long before her mom turned up dead."

"So?"

"So one parent left. The one who stayed didn't do too well by her. The kid's grown up way too fast, and now she's on her own." He gives me a pointed look. "Remind you of anyone?"

"I was never on my own. I had my grand-mother."

"Micky's not on her own either," he says. "She's got us."

I'm about to tell him that is *not* a foregone

conclusion when my phone rings. "Hello?"

A woman with a gruff voice quickly identifies herself. "This is Lieutenant Pamela Soto of the Tucson Police Department. I'm looking for Charlotte Cates." She doesn't sound like she wants to be making this call.

"Speaking." I assume she's part of Donna and Jasmine's murder investigation, although what these people think they'll get from me, I don't know.

"You're Donna DeRossi's daughter, is that right?"

"Biologically, yes." Noah mouths, *Police?* to me, and I nod. "Like I told Detective Vargas the other day, I really didn't know Donna. I'm not sure what you think I can —"

"We need to meet." Lieutenant Soto's tone leaves little room for negotiation. "When would be a convenient time for you?"

It occurs to me that the TPD are getting pretty desperate if they're still pumping me, of all people, for information. But really, what else do I have to do with my time? And maybe Lieutenant Soto can tell me something about Micky, her family and her upbringing. Detective Vargas was a stone wall when he called last week, but Soto's a woman. She might help me.

I glance at my watch. "I could meet you in an hour. What's the station address?"

"An hour?" She sounds surprised. "Are you in town?"

I can see that she and Vargas have not communicated well with each other. "Yeah, I'm in town. Do you want me to come by or not?"

"Yes," she says. "Yes. But don't come by the station. I'll meet you at Dino's on Fourth Ave. It's near the university. A little pizza joint."

Something's not right. Why would a cop — and a lieutenant, a higher-up — want to meet me outside of the station? "Look, I really don't have anything useful for you. Ask Detective Vargas. I can't answer any of your questions."

"I knew your mother," she says quietly. "Maybe I can answer some of yours."

Pamela Soto is about five foot six, with short, dark hair; black eyes; and deeply creased, golden skin of some indeterminate race. Her arms are inked with various tattoos: a wolf, a scorpion, the figure of a man standing atop a circular maze. From her face, I'd put her somewhere in her fifties, but she's remarkably fit. Her black, form-fitting T-shirt reveals broad shoulders and a trim, muscular frame still capable of pursuing a suspect on foot or taking down a bad guy. It doesn't take a genius to surmise she's gay.

"Pam Soto. Thanks for making it out." Though she greets me with a solid handshake, I can tell that my pregnancy has startled her. She avoids looking at my belly the way a man tries not to stare at breasts.

The restaurant, a funky little Italian spot, crawls with university students. I watch a girl with rumpled sex hair and layers of tank tops stretch out in her booth, limbs long and languid in the manner of one who regularly sleeps past noon. Feeling positively geriatric, I join Pam at a corner table, where she has a pizza and pitcher of water waiting.

"So you said you're a lieutenant with the Tucson police?" I can't hide my skepticism; her outfit and physique don't belong on someone with a bureaucratic desk job.

"Was, yeah. I'm retired."

"Oh." So this meeting is 100 percent personal. I'm not sure how to feel about that.

For a moment, she stares at me, eyes taking in the details of my face, searching, not finding what she's seeking. "You must look more like your father," she tells me.

"So I've heard."

"This is . . ." She exhales, and I notice that her hands are shaky. "I'm sorry. I didn't think I'd ever meet you. Donna didn't talk about you much."

My discomfort grows by leaps and bounds each minute. "She left when I was eighteen months old. I doubt she had a lot to say."

Pam offers me a slice of pizza, something with feta and spinach that may easily prove to be the best part of this meeting. I take it.

"So," I ask, though I already have a pretty good idea, "how did you know my mother?"

"We were together the last fourteen years," Pam says. "Love of my life." I remain poker-faced, and she swallows. "I hope that's not a problem for you."

I shrug. "No. But it doesn't change any-thing, either. Donna was an addict who left my dad raising a kid alone. I don't really feel a connection to her."

"What she did to you was inexcusable," Pam says. "But she was just a kid herself back then, Charlotte. It took a lot of years, but she cleaned herself up. Got sober." She watches me inhale my slice of pizza, then thrusts another at me. "Donna had a lot of regrets. I told her ages ago she needed to make her peace with you, but . . . she was ashamed."

"Okay." What am I supposed to say? I

don't need any secondhand apologies on my mother's behalf, don't need Pam's good intentions pressing on old bruises, yet telling her to lay off seems cold. The so-called love of her life was just murdered. I don't like the way she's looking at me, though. Desperate. Probing. Like she wants something.

"The memorial's on Friday," Pam says. "I've already made the arrangements, but if you want to speak or maybe suggest a reading —"

"I didn't even *know* the woman." My words come out more forceful than I intended, and something flickers in Pam's face, a bright light of hope burning out. My guilt is immediate. "I'm sorry. It must be a terrible loss for you. But honestly, I'm just here on the off chance I can help my niece."

"You mean Micky."

"That's right."

"I've been wondering what would happen to her. Poor kid." She shoves more pizza at me and then pours me a glass of water for good measure. A transparent attempt to make me stay longer, but I don't object. "Are you taking Micky, then?"

"I'm not sure that I can. It's complicated."

"Yeah, I get that." She watches me drink, and I can see her planning, considering her angle. This isn't all about healing the past, I realize. Pam's got an agenda.

Sure enough, she leans across the table, a ball of intensity and purpose. Her eyes are so dark they nearly blend with her pupils. "There's something I want you to know about your mom."

"What's that?" I shouldn't have come. Not alone, not without Noah as a buffer.

"The Tucson Homicide Division is handling Donna and Jasmine's death like a drug-related crime."

I try not to roll my eyes, but seriously? Does she think I'll find this information surprising? "Yes, I heard that."

"I was on the force for thirty-five years, Charlotte. I've worked a lot of cases. More important, I knew Donna." She shakes her head. "It wasn't drug related."

"She had a history of substance-abuse issues," I say, wondering if this fact somehow escaped Pam.

"She'd been clean for thirteen years." Pam continues leaning forward in her chair, jaw set, and I can imagine how relentless she'd be in an interrogation. "And even if she'd relapsed, Donna's thing was always junk, not roofies."

"Roofies?"

"Flunitrazepam. Also known as Rohypnol." She gives me a long look. "That's what they found in Jasmine's apartment."

"Rohypnol?" I stop chewing. "You mean the date-rape drug? Why on earth would that —"

"There are people who use it for recreational purposes," Pam explains. "Dumb people. Gets you doing stupid shit you won't remember the next day. Believe me, Donna wouldn't have messed with that crap."

"Okay," I say. "Well, they were at Jasmine's place, weren't they? So the drugs were Jasmine's."

"No. Jasmine partied, but not like that. Her boyfriend was a cop. She was a trashy little thing, don't get me wrong, but she stayed out of trouble."

I raise my eyebrows at this candid description of Micky's mother. Whatever grief Pam feels for her girlfriend's loss, she seems wholly unaffected by Jasmine's death.

"Before I called you today, I spoke with the medical examiner's office. I know a few people over there." Pam peers at me. "You know what the toxicology results were?"

"I'm guessing you'll tell me."

"Neither Jasmine nor Donna had anything unusual in their blood at their time of death. No drugs. Not even alcohol."

"So they were selling. It happens." I rack my brain for a plausible excuse to leave. Somewhere I have to be, something I have to do.

"I've been over Donna's financials with a fine-toothed comb," Pam states. "She didn't have any unexplained sources of income, anything that would indicate extra cash flow. And Jasmine was on goddamned food stamps. She didn't even have a car. Had to take the bus everywhere."

"Then what are you suggesting?" All this misplaced passion exhausts me. "If this wasn't drug-related, what was it? And why was there Rohypnol on the scene?"

"I don't know. But I want to find out."

"I hope you find what you're looking for, I really do. But I've got no horse in this race, Pam."

"I need your help."

I stand up. "Sorry. You can handle this on your —"

"No," she says hotly. "I can't. Don't you get it? You're a relative. I'm *nothing*. Legally, I'm nothing."

She doesn't have to say, *Because I'm gay.* I know what she's getting at.

"You can apply pressure to the team working the case," she urges. "That's the only way things get done. If there's no one there fighting for a victim, they'll expend their resources elsewhere."

I hold up a hand. "This is your battle, not mine. Anyway, you're the one with law-enforcement connections."

"Which is why I'm not the person to push this." Her voice lowers as she realizes that students at a nearby table are staring at us. "Look, I know these guys on the force. They're not bad guys, but they're conservative. Really conservative. We never talked about my personal life, and now suddenly it's part of the investigation, getting thrown in their faces. Please. It'd be better coming from you."

"I'm sorry, but I have to go." I make my way to the door, no longer bothering with good manners.

Pam grabs a couple bills from her wallet, tosses them on the table, and hurries after me. "Think about Micky," she says, blinking away the sudden rush of sunshine. "You leave now, she'll go through her whole life never knowing what happened to her mom."

I fold my arms across my chest. "Never bothered me any."

And with that, I'm gone.

Back in our hotel room, I find Noah looking at Tucson real estate listings on his laptop. He looks up, guilty, and quickly closes out the window.

"I'm not makin' any decisions without you," he says. "I promise."

I've already moved past my earlier hissy fit. "It's fine. It's good for us to have options." I kick off my shoes and peel back the heavy duvet. I want a nap now, not a fight.

He crawls into bed next to me, kisses my ear. Smiles as I luxuriate in the cool sheets. "How'd your meetin' with Lieutenant Soto go?"

"Interesting." I laugh drily. "Very interesting." I fill him in on Pam's relationship with my mom and all her wild conspiracy theories.

Noah listens, chin in hand. "You think she's right?" he asks.

"Right about what?"

"That Donna and Jasmine weren't killed for drugs."

I yawn. "What does it matter? They're dead, aren't they?"

"Okay," he says. "I just . . . I mean, you don't think it affects Micky one way or another?"

"Whether it was a drug lord or just some psycho? I don't see the difference. Either way, Micky woke up and found what she found. And she's gotta live with it."

"Yeah." He shudders. "So did this Pam lady tell you anything about Micky's mom, or what happened to the dad?"

"She said Jasmine was trashy. I didn't ask about Micky's father."

"We gotta find that guy," he mutters. "I want to know who this kid came from, if there's a health history we should know about. I want to make sure he's not going to crop up in the future and try to get access to her." Noah rolls onto his stomach. "Next time you see Pam, you gotta ask."

I stuff a pillow between my knees, trying to ease the weight on my hips. "There won't *be* a next time. Did you hear anything I just said?" I do a quick recap. "The woman is conducting some crazy behind-the-scenes murder investigation and trying to recruit me. She's clearly nuts."

He chuckles. "Yeah, y*ou* involved in an unofficial murder investigation? Where would she get a fool idea like that?"

I ignore his smirk. "I don't want to get caught up in these people and their drama, okay? Not my monkeys, not my circus. Donna DeRossi is dead, and so's her daughter. There's no need to resurrect them."

"Donna's a part of Micky's past, whether we like it or not," Noah says. "And from what you're sayin', so's Pam. Now, I'm not suggestin' you two run around playin' detective." His eyes narrow as if he perceives some actual danger of Pam and I forming a female investigative duo. "But you can't just throw Pam to the wayside 'cause hearin' about your mom makes you uncomfortable. If you can't handle who Micky is and where she came from, then we're not the right home for her."

I press my face to the mattress and say the thing he doesn't want to hear. "Maybe we're *not* the right home for her."

Noah's head jerks sharply in my direction. "You really think you could live with that? Handin' her over to someone else?"

"Someone like Vonda? Yeah. I do."

I can't explain it to him, how badly I want to walk away, to pack up the car and hightail it back to Texas. Even living in Sidalie seems easier than taking on that grave and dark-eyed little creature with her big questions and excess baggage. A child who knew my mother in a way that I never did and never will. A child who, however frozen her emotions may now appear, will one day need to mourn her losses. Will need to feel.

It's the feelings that I fear.

Noah watches me, his face clouded with silent disapproval. "Just get to know the kid before you decide it's a no-go, would you?"

he asks. "Get to know her world. That means talkin' to Vonda and Pam and anyone else we find. Even if you can't be Micky's mom, you can still be her auntie. She needs any family she can get."

"Fine." He's giving me an out. I can meet him halfway. I let out the breath I didn't realize I was holding and reach for my phone. Scroll through the list of recent incoming calls. Hope that I am truly the good person he believes me to be. "If you think it's such a big deal . . . I'll call Pam."

Water. Concrete. Tiles, blue and yellow. I know this place by now.

The water is falling again, gathering around the drain. In my belly, my chest, the agony of lead tunneling through flesh.

Blood. So much blood, flowing, swirling, pooling. And the baby isn't moving.

Gone, I think as I sink slowly to my knees. *She's gone.*

"Charlie?" Someone's calling my name. "Charlie, honey, you okay?"

Hands grasp me by the shoulders, pulling me out of this place. I hear shrieking, so shrill and terrible I cover my ears. But they are *my* screams, I realize. I'm screaming, and I can't stop.

One image replaces another in a single,

rapid blink as Noah shakes me from my vision. I'm in the darkness of our hotel room, hunched over on all fours. Safe, in a pile of rumpled sheets. I close my mouth abruptly and the shrieking ceases. But Noah's brought me back too fast. For a few seconds everything is moving, my waking world as unsteady as my dream.

He switches on the bedside light and studies me with alarm. "Babe?"

I don't speak, just wait for the room to settle. A few slow breaths, and my queasiness subsides. The room becomes familiar again: thick bedding, orange curtains, our open suitcase spilling clothes and toiletries.

Noah leans toward me, wide-eyed, and I see a look of fear so raw, so helpless, that I wonder if he saw what I saw: the gunshot, the drain, the water turning red. But no, I realize. It's me scaring him. Always me.

"You all right?" he asks.

I struggle to sit up. "I think so."

"Were you asleep?"

"Sort of."

"Your eyes were wide open," he tells me. "You screamed and grabbed your belly. I thought —" He falters. "I thought somethin' was wrong with the baby."

"It was the dream," I murmur.

He places a protective hand on my stomach, the panic on his face quickly absorbed by a look of determination. "It's not gonna happen," he says. "We won't let it."

"I can't lose another child," I whisper. "Keegan's hardly been gone a year. I can't do it again."

"It'll be okay." He touches his lips to my forehead, strokes my head. "It's only another six weeks, right? You can just — start takin' baths instead of showers."

I stare down at my round belly. Suddenly the air-conditioning feels so cold. "I don't know. I don't know if I can change the outcome."

"Shhh." He wraps his arms around me, pulling me as snug against his chest as one can pull a woman seven and a half months pregnant.

This is all the comfort he can offer. His touch. His crushing warmth.

I let him hold me. Feel his chest rise and fall, feel his fingers work their way through my hair. He doesn't turn out the light, and I'm grateful. For the remainder of the night, I drift in and out against him. His body is solid, something I can count on, and his skin smells like man, not just any man, but *mine.*

Inside of me, our daughter stretches and

kicks, rolls and dances. *You'll be here soon,* I tell her. And I pray that it's the truth.

Six

Pam's condo lies nestled in a relatively new development in northeast Tucson. The community is sprawling and well-groomed, tidy adobe-style homes set against what a real estate agent might describe as charming mountain views. Beside me, Noah delivers running commentary about the area's potential, still investigating the possibility of our moving.

"Kid friendly," he says when we drive by a swimming pool full of school-age children. "I checked online, and the schools around here are pretty decent."

He's getting ahead of himself again, but I barely notice. As I turn down Paseo de Sed and park in front of Pam's unit, all I can think is, *My mother lived here.*

Pam was gracious, eager even, when I called yesterday. *Come by,* she said, almost begging, and despite my instinctive desire to avoid her — her desperation, her misplaced crusade, her history with a woman I want to forget — I'm here. Noah was right. These are the pieces of Micky's past, and if I can't handle them, I have no business in this child's life.

We follow the brick walkway to a small, neat home pretty much identical to all the others.

"Mediterranean fan palms," Noah observes as he waits for Pam to answer the door. He can't get enough of the trees out here. "Look, I think that's a guajillo. And those are palo verdes, you see that bark?"

Pam appears wearing a white T-shirt and black sweatpants cut off at the knee, her hair looking a little wild. She holds a phone to her ear, frowning as she hashes out details of tomorrow's memorial service. "I just spoke to the funeral home yesterday," she says, beckoning Noah and me into her living room. "No flowers. A donation to Sonora Hope, that's what Donna would've wanted." She pauses for a moment, listening. "No, no. Hell no. Not the whole Catholic shebang. I told the funeral director, let's keep it simple." Pam quickly wraps up her call and then stares at us, a bit disoriented. "So many decisions," she says. "I don't know what I'm doing."

One look at her rumpled clothes and

bloodshot eyes, and I regret my uncharitable behavior at Dino's. I resolve to be more compassionate today, however uncomfortable I find myself.

"You must be Lieutenant Soto," Noah says, realizing no one's going to introduce him. "I'm Noah Palmer. So sorry for your loss, ma'am."

"Call me Pam." She looks a bit dazed, and I wonder if she regrets inviting us over. "Let me — show you the house, I guess."

She leads us through a modest two-bedroom that is clean and comfortable, decorated in warm, eye-catching colors: peach, lime, sunflower. Houseplants hang from the ceiling, occupy end tables, and dominate corners with lush green leaves. I spot brightly painted handicrafts throughout — plates, bowls, ceramic coasters, ornaments, what looks like an altar to the Virgin Mary — all distinctly Mexican in style. Pam must be Mexican American. I wonder how long her family has been in the United States.

"This place is really lovely," I say. "It feels — cheerful."

"Your mom did it," Pam tells me, her lip looking a little wobbly. "She loved decorating." All of her fire and self-possession at lunch yesterday have been replaced with a despondent vagueness, as if the reality of Donna's death has finally hit her. I remember how it was after Keegan died, all the people dropping in, my grandmother and Rae walking me through the practical details of life when I was too paralyzed to attend to them myself. I wonder about Pam's empty home. Where are her friends? Her family?

Maybe it's a good thing we came by.

"I'm glad you called," Pam says. "I came on too strong yesterday, I'm sorry."

I shake my head. "I think I was . . . taking frustrations out on you that I meant for Donna."

"Is that her?" Noah has wandered into the hallway and stands studying a framed eight-by-ten. "Is that Donna?"

Pam glances in his direction. "Yeah, that's her."

Noah motions for me to join him, which I reluctantly do. I've seen hundreds of old photos of my mother, but nothing current. Nothing taken after she left me, in fact. In my mind, Donna has remained a self-absorbed, frizzy-haired girl in bell-bottoms, just twenty years old. To see her on this wall, suddenly in her late fifties, is oddly shocking.

In the photograph, Pam and Donna stand on a beach, arms wrapped around each other, grinning broadly. Hair blows in their eyes. For years I've envisioned Donna De-Rossi toothless on a street corner, but this smiling woman with shoulder-length auburn hair is an altogether different story. Pam's right about one thing: I don't look like my mother. Her round, pink face lacks all my sharp angles and her friendly blue eyes are a far cry from my jaded green. She wears a demure two-piece purple swimsuit with a skirt that hides her upper thighs, and I can see her toenails half buried in the sand, crescents of fluorescent pink. Yes, she could stand some orthodontia, but there's nothing glaringly wrong with her, no glassy, drugged-out gaze or apathetic stare to warn you off. She doesn't look like the kind of woman who would abandon her toddler.

Don't think of her as your mom, I tell myself. *This is Micky's grandmother. That's the only reason she matters.*

"She has such a great smile, doesn't she?" Pam says from behind me, and Noah nods politely.

"How did you guys meet?" he asks.

"A church thing." Pam's face lightens, the pleasure of her memories undercutting, for a moment, the intensity of her grief. "I noticed Donna right away. She was so nervous, like this little animal you might scare away if you talked too loud. We were just friends for a while. She had a boyfriend back then, some asshole. I never thought we'd turn into anything."

I turn away from the photo. "A boyfriend?"

"Yeah. Before me, Donna was always with men."

"Was she bi?" I ask. "Or it just took her a while to figure out who she was?"

Pam smiles as if my attempt to neatly categorize human sexuality is misguided. "She loved who she loved." She takes off for the living room, temporarily reanimated, and grabs a stack of photo albums off the shelf. "Here. I'll show you some more pictures."

What initially sounds like a tedious excuse for Pam to reminisce proves revealing — touching even — in ways I did not anticipate. Because, if the photos are any indication, something happened to Donna De-Rossi once she sobered up, ditched the asshole boyfriend, and fell in love with Pam.

She came alive.

I look at photos of my mother waterskiing on Lake Havasu, pitching a tent amongst the red rocks of Oak Creek Canyon, and standing by a waterfall in the middle of the desert, hands on hips, her smile one of goofy affection.

"Seven Falls," Pam says. "That's just a few miles away. You guys will have to hike it."

I don't remind her that it's over a hundred degrees out and I'm knocked up. In another six months, I might be game. I move to another album, an older one, where the image of a pouty but beautiful girl on the first page captures my attention.

"Is that Jasmine?"

Pam nods. "Yeah. That's Donna's album. You can have it, if you want."

As I flip through the opening pages, it's apparent why Pam doesn't want this book. Every photograph is of Donna's daughter. With her cat eyes, ever-changing hair colors, and less-than-subtle makeup choices, Jasmine doesn't resemble me any more than her mother does. We have similar figures, perhaps — narrow shoulders and a tendency to carry weight in our thighs — but I can't imagine ever dressing mine as she does. I spent years working at *Sophisticate,* a women's fashion and lifestyle magazine, so I'm hardly opposed to showing skin, but Jasmine's outfits are two sizes too small, inappropriate for anyone not trolling the Vegas strip. Some perverse form of sibling rivalry bubbles up within me. *Really, Donna?*

112

I think. *That's the one you stuck around for?*

Beside me, Pam stares down at Jasmine's image with an expression of antipathy that is oddly gratifying. I remember her less-than-flattering description of her stepdaughter yesterday and can't quite argue with the word "trashy."

"I guess you and Jasmine weren't close," I say.

"Jazz was thirteen when Donna and I got together." Pam moves across the living room to the window. "That kid hated me from day one. Said I made her mom gay." She peers out the blinds, watching as a landscaper rakes the gravel. "Her real beef with me was that I wouldn't put up with her shit. The kid never had rules until I came along."

"Donna wasn't big on discipline?" Noah asks, and I know he's mentally filing away whatever he can learn about Micky's early influences.

"Donna was a good person but a lousy mom," Pam says. "She'd spent so many years checked out, wasted, high or whatever, she felt like she owed Jazz. She tried to be her friend, and that's no way to parent." She turns away from the window. "Worst arguments Donna and I ever had were about that girl. Four years we dealt with her crap. When Jasmine moved out, it was the happiest day of my life."

I do some quick math. "She was seventeen when she left? That's pretty young."

Pam shrugs, and I doubt she ever devoted much time to worrying about her step-daughter's well-being. "There was a boy-friend. He was older."

"Was that Micky's dad?" Noah asks.

"No, no. Micky's dad was later. There was a long line of boyfriends, believe me."

"Which one was the father?" Noah seems anxious to establish Micky's paternity, and I wonder if he's planning to Google the man later to make sure he's not a serial killer. I hope so.

"Ruben Ramos." Pam supplies the name without emotion. "Vargas from Homicide has been asking about him, too. I don't know if he's a suspect or if they think he might want custody, but they're trying to hunt him down. Good luck, I told them. Ruben was just some Mexican guy here on a student visa."

"I'd like to talk to him," Noah says. "Before we adopt Micky, I'd like to meet him. You have no idea where he is?"

"His visa expired, and far as I know, he went back home a few months into Jazz's pregnancy. Could be anywhere."

I say nothing, but it occurs to me that

there could be more going on here. If Pam and Jasmine despised each other so passionately, Donna may not have shared all the details of her daughter's love life.

I continue flipping through Donna's photo album. She's not nearly as exhaustive in her documentation as Pam, just scattered snapshots of Jasmine's prom and graduation, a swim party, someone's birthday. Once Micky is born, however, everything changes. Suddenly the pages are filled with this drooling, dark-haired baby. Micky sleeping. Micky staring solemnly. Micky sucking on a pacifier. Micky sucking on a bottle. Micky crying. Micky smiling. Micky examining a toy. Micky bundled up in Donna's arms, asleep, as Donna beams down at her. They go on and on, as loving and as thorough as any doting grandmother's photos.

I feel a strange mixture of gratitude and resentment, happy that Micky had at least one adult in her life who appears to have loved her without reservation, and bitter that this same woman failed her own two daughters so completely.

Noah squeezes my hand. "It looks like Donna and Micky were pretty close," he murmurs, and turns to Pam. "Did you spend a lot of time with Micky, too?"

She closes her eyes for a moment and

touches her forehead. "Jasmine didn't want me anywhere near her daughter. I saw Micky every now and then if Jazz brought her over here. But she usually made Donna come to her place. It was disgusting, the way she used that kid to manipulate her mom."

I don't doubt there's some truth to Pam's depiction of Jasmine as narcissistic and demanding, but I can't imagine Jasmine was the only controlling force in Donna's life. I'm beginning to get a picture of Donna as a pliant peacemaker who catered to the needs of those stronger than she was — a list of people that almost certainly included Pam. Yet somewhere inside her, Donna must have possessed her own hidden reservoir of strength, or else how could she have successfully fought addiction for so many years?

Enough. I put the photo album back on its shelf. I don't want to care about these people.

Noah points to a splashy ceramic plate that's mounted on the wall, trying to shift the conversation to something less fraught. "That's nice. Is it from Mexico?"

Pam nods. "One of the women Donna worked with made that for her."

"Donna worked in Mexico?" Noah raises

his eyebrows.

"Sometimes," Pam confirms. "She worked at a nonprofit that helped women living in Sonoran border towns become financially independent. She spent a lot of time in Nogales."

Inwardly, I groan. A nonprofit to help impoverished women? Is Pam kidding? Why couldn't my long-lost mother be a junkie, a self-involved bitch, some cheap and stupid floozy I'd never miss? Did she really have to Do Good Things? To have been a positive influence in the life of a child? If my mother had value as a human being, if she could demonstrate kindness and compassion in her life, where does that leave me, the daughter she discarded and forgot?

I am thirty-nine years old, and still, the sense of rejection is acute when I realize that for the last thirteen years, Donna De-Rossi ignored my existence not because she was ruled by addiction, not because she was a worthless scumbag, not because she was injured or dead or suffering from memory loss, but because . . . she *chose* to.

I wasn't worth her time.

I swallow back the lump in my throat and tune suddenly back in to Pam and Noah, who have moved on from a discussion of Donna's inspiring international work and are now comparing firearms. I don't love that Noah carries a handgun, but at this point I'm resigned to it. He's had a concealed-weapon permit as long as I've known him, and these days, my bad dreams have left us both feeling vulnerable.

"That can't be standard issue," Noah says as he admires Pam's piece. "What's that, a 1911 subcompact?"

"Yep. Smith and Wesson Pro Series," Pam replies, her head bobbing up and down. "The power of a forty-five, but the smaller barrel leaves you with more options for deep concealment. I can jog five miles wearing this baby, no problem."

Even though Noah is impressed, I'm disturbed that she still has possession of any firearms, period. "Nobody took your gun?" I ask. Her romantic partner just died in a violent shooting. Has the TPD neglected to properly investigate one of its own?

Pam knows what I'm getting at. "I spent the last two weeks answering questions at the station while the team combed this place for evidence," she says evenly, and I realize for the first time that she is dealing with more than just her own grief. "The guys on the unit looked at both guns I own, believe me. If there was any way one of my weapons killed Donna and Jasmine, they would've confiscated it and run ballistics."

"So they have some idea of the type of weapon they're looking for," I muse.

"They must," Pam agrees. "I'm guessing they found casings at the scene. Or it was a shotgun."

Noah watches our exchange with a frown, and I can see he does not want me pursuing this further, especially not with Pam. "Well," he says, "now that you've been cleared, Pam, hopefully Homicide can do their job and find the actual bad guys."

"Cleared?" Pam casts him a half smile. "Oh, I'm still on their radar. Vargas was pretty disappointed when five people confirmed my whereabouts that night. He probably hasn't given up on a murder-for-hire angle, the little fuck." She bites her lip. "It doesn't matter. They'll follow the drugs. They have to. Fifty tablets of Rohypnol need some explaining."

"Good thing you had a solid alibi, huh?" I watch her closely. "Where *were* you that night, anyway?"

"Charlie." Noah covers his face with his hands, embarrassed, but Pam waves him off.

"No, no. That's the way you gotta be. Cautious." She turns to me. "I was at a poker game with some gals. Donna was going to come, but Jazz asked her to babysit, so . . ."

119

She falls silent, and I can only imagine how this final act of Donna's — choosing her daughter over her partner — has added to Pam's feelings toward her stepdaughter.

Noah slides her weapon back across the table to her, signaling the end of our conversation, and secures his own Glock in its holster. "We better get goin'. I guess we'll see you tomorrow at the memorial, though."

Pam turns to me. "I hope . . . you learned a little more about your mom today."

I nod. *More than I wanted to, actually.*

She's still holding her gun as she walks us to the door. Noticing my uneasy expression, she slips the weapon into a nearby drawer. "I take it you don't carry?"

"No."

"Neither did Donna." Her dark eyes glitter. "Be careful. The world's not as safe as you want to think it is."

I consider telling her that firearms are more likely to kill a household member than to be used in self-defense, but I'd be the wrong woman making this argument to the wrong woman. Pam and I are already part of a statistically anomalous group. Just five months ago, I was held at gunpoint in Louisiana. Donna and Jasmine are dead, and my unborn daughter is in danger. If carrying a lethal metal object at their sides offers Pam and Noah some peace of mind, however false and illusory that peace may be — well, maybe they're onto something.

"I know what the world is like," I tell Pam, feeling some small part of my identity crumble as these unnatural words form in my mouth. "You're probably right. I should learn to shoot."

There are several shooting ranges around Tucson, but Pam sends us to the Bullseye Gun Club. "It's where cops go," she explains, and that's all the recommendation Noah needs. He's thrilled at the prospect of arming me, having pushed for this moment ever since the Louisiana incident. To me, it feels like failure, the surrender of my beliefs to a more depressing pragmatism.

No one can blame you for wanting to protect yourself, I think, but I still have a sense that I'm losing something, a purer version of myself, when I enter a place that rents machine guns by the hour and sells human-shaped targets.

From the outside, Bullseye Gun Club looks like a long, rectangular warehouse, innocuous against a mostly empty parking lot. The front of the building has been devoted to a retail and rental store, with weaponry displayed so casually, it feels artificial, like a

Hollywood prop room. On the walls, I spot bumper stickers with slogans like GUN CONTROL IS BEING ABLE TO HIT YOUR TARGET and PUT LOCKS ON CRIMINALS NOT GUNS.

If I'm expecting Hick Central, the man at the counter doesn't quite look ready for a *Deliverance* casting call. In fact, his reddish beard and gold-rimmed glasses call to mind my old friend Dirk, a gay bartender in the West Village. Redbeard has busied himself with a pair of young male customers, clean-cut twentysomethings who also fail to match the Woolly Mountain Man image I somehow have of gun owners. One is a short Latino with an easy smile; his companion is a good-looking white boy with steely blue eyes.

As we wait, Noah and I entertain ourselves by looking over the various paper targets for sale. Beyond your basic dartboard-style target, there are pictures of zombies, were-wolves, and other creatures that gun aficionados apparently enjoy spraying with lead.

"Good to know we can prepare for a gnome attack," I say. "Classy joint."

"Yeah, well. Things might have turned out different for Donna and Jasmine if they'd paid this place a visit," Noah says.

One of the young men at the counter, the guy with the piercing blue eyes, glances sharply back in our direction. I don't know if it's my pregnant belly or flippant remark, but I get the feeling we rub him the wrong way. I stare at the floor and keep my mouth shut.

"All righty." Redbeard slaps a box of bullets down on the counter. "That'll be thirty with the officer discount. You guys are in lane six."

Off-duty cops. Pam was right about this place. I watch as they slip on their protective eye and ear equipment and make their way through a large metal door covered with safety reminders.

"Now, what can I do for you folks?" Redbeard does not seem scandalized by a pregnant woman in a shooting range, but I feel self-conscious nevertheless. "You looking to purchase a weapon today?"

"Actually," Noah says, "I was gonna teach my lady here how to shoot."

"I've got some twenty-twos if you want to start her off easy." The man reaches into the display case and emerges with a dainty little handgun.

Noah's lip curls in disgust. "Aw, come on. Shoot someone with a twenty-two and all you do is make 'em mad. She's gonna use my piece. Nine-millimeter semiauto. Might actually do some damage should it come to that."

Frankly, I'm not sure I want the ability to inflict damage. "Is it safe out there in the shooting area?" I ask, hand pressed to stomach.

Redbeard laughs, and I catch a flash of a shiny gold filling. "Nobody's gonna shoot your baby," he reassures me. "Except maybe you, if you don't follow the rules. Just keep your gun pointed in a safe direction, and don't put your finger on the trigger 'til you're ready to fire. Got that?"

"I got it."

Shooting is easier than I anticipated, but it's also louder. From ten yards, I can set my sights on the target and more or less hit my intended zone, and after fumbling the first few tries, I eventually get a knack for loading a cartridge. The noise, however, I can't adjust to. I recoil every time, flinch whenever a bullet casing is expelled from the chamber, and our daughter seems equally jumpy. I wish I could apologize, explain that I'm doing it for her.

"You're doin' great," Noah says. "Relax."

But I can't relax. Even with ear protection, every bang is a reminder that the object I'm holding could kill someone.

Could kill *me,* kill my baby, if my dream is right.

Adding to my apprehension, the blue-eyed officer a few lanes over keeps staring at us. His friend tries to distract him, nudging him and cracking jokes, but the man's icy demeanor never changes.

"What's his problem?" I hiss to Noah in between rounds of gunfire.

"Probably just some dick with too much testosterone," he says, but he keeps an eye on the guy all the same. We're both relieved when the pair take off and, apart from the range master, we're the only people remaining.

I've all but forgotten the officers when I dash off to use the bathroom fifteen minutes later, but as I pass through the retail store on my way back, I see them. The white guy stands in front of the metal door to the range, arms crossed, blocking my reentrance. His friend leans casually against the counter. They're waiting for me.

I look to Redbeard for some help, but he's on the phone, paying no attention.

"Hey." The white guy meets my eyes with an unblinking blue gaze. "You know Jasmine Cassell?"

I exhale. *So that's what this is about. He must have heard Noah mention Jasmine and*

Donna before. "No," I say. "No, I don't know her. Why? Are you guys working her case?"

His body tenses. "You *do* know her. If you've got any information —"

"Dude." The smaller Latino cop steps in, placing one hand on his friend's shoulder. "Lighten up, huh? You're getting a little scary there." He gives me a winning smile. "I'm Sanchez, and this is McCullough. We didn't mean to eavesdrop, just overheard your boyfriend earlier —"

I put up both hands. "I've never even met Jasmine, okay? Supposedly, she's my sister, but I had no idea she existed until a few days ago."

Sanchez's eyes widen. "Holy shit. You're the sister?" He punches McCullough in the arm to make sure he's getting this. "Charlotte, right? Your name's Charlotte?"

I nod. "Charlotte Cates."

"Vargas *told* me they found a sister." Sanchez bounces on the balls of his feet. "So crazy. Jasmine didn't know about you, either. Friggin' Donna."

McCullough says nothing but stares me down with his chilly eyes.

"I'm sorry," I say. "Have you been assigned to Jasmine and Donna's case?" Sanchez sounds awfully familiar with the victims to be involved in their investigation.

"No, no, we're not Homicide." He shoos McCullough away from the door so that I'm now free to return to Noah. "Me and Mac here work on the Aggravated Assault Unit. Jasmine was Mac's girlfriend."

At the mention of their relationship, McCullough turns away. He rakes a hand through his hair and makes a weird gulping sound.

"My God, I didn't realize." It makes sense; Pam said Jasmine's boyfriend was a cop.

"Mac has been a little on edge after everything that went down," Sanchez explains in a low voice. "He heard you guys talking about Jasmine and he didn't recognize you, so he thought . . . you know. Maybe you knew something."

"Nothing at all," I say ruefully. "Everything I know about Jasmine I got from Pam Soto." I can't resist throwing Pam's name in there to see what kind of reaction I get, but Sanchez only grins.

"You talked to Pam, huh? I bet you got an earful. She and Jazz can't stand each other."

"Yeah, I picked up on that."

"Listen, I don't know what Pam told you, but Jazz was a good person. She had a really rough time growing up because of her mom

— *your* mom." He shakes his head, startled at the idea. "Anyway, don't believe everything Pam says."

"Was Pam really a cop?" I figure it can't hurt to verify her story.

"Oh yeah," Sanchez says. "She headed the Homicide Unit for a while. That woman's got balls of steel. You'd have to, making lieutenant when you're a woman *and* an Indian."

"What the hell are you saying, Sanchez?" McCullough demands.

"Nothing, man." Sanchez remains unruffled. "Not saying TPD is racist or sexist or whatever. Just, you know . . . there's not a lot of Indian women working there."

McCullough rolls his eyes. "Please. Being female, Indian, and a dyke is the only reason Soto made it anywhere. She lights up every little diversity box they gotta check off."

"Dude." Sanchez closes his eyes. "Don't be like that. Seriously."

I have a few choice words of my own for McCullough, but I know better than to tell off a volatile policeman in a gun range. "When you say Indian, do you mean Native American?"

"Yeah, she's Tohono O'odham, I think. Grew up on one of their reservations." Sanchez chuckles. "She won't talk about it, though, unless she's three sheets to the wind."

Our conversation is cut short by the creaking door of the shooting range. Noah emerges, removing his glasses and ear protection with a frown. "I was wonderin' what happened to you. Everything okay?"

I make some quick introductions and then decide it's a good time to head out. "I think we're gonna take off now, but glad to meet you both," I tell the guys. "I'm . . . very sorry for your loss."

As I pass by McCullough, he grabs my arm. "Wait."

I don't like his hand on me, don't like the darkness flickering through his pale eyes. Beside me, I see Noah stiffen, ready to clock McCullough if he doesn't let go of me in a hurry.

"You wouldn't know where I could find Ruben Ramos, would you?"

The question takes me by surprise. What's McCullough want with Micky's dad? "No idea."

He studies me a few seconds, searching for traces of dishonesty, and then releases my arm. There's an awkward silence as Noah, Sanchez, and I all stare at him, and then McCullough disappears back into the shooting range.

Shaken, I turn to Sanchez. "What's his deal?"

Sanchez sighs, apologetic. "Somebody said something about Ruben and Jasmine recently that got Mac a little paranoid, that's all. I keep telling him, Ruben lives in Mexico, chill out, but — I guess he heard some stuff. Listen, you gotta excuse him. He's a little crazed right now. I took him over here to blow off steam."

I smother a smile. *Excellent idea, Sanchez. Give the crazy guy a gun. That always turns out well.*

But, of course, McCullough is a cop. He already had one.

I wait until Noah and I are buckling ourselves into the car before I let loose with my theories. "I don't know about you, but that McCullough guy gives me the creeps. His girlfriend just died, and what's he doing? Trying to track down some guy he thinks she slept with. There's something off about that, don't you —"

Noah cuts me off. "Stop. The police are handlin' this."

"Are they?" I'm so fired up, even the heat can't subdue me. "He's one of them. You really think they're giving him a thorough look?"

"I really think you need to let 'em do their job. Not your monkeys, not your circus, remember?" He pulls out onto the street, his face unreadable beneath his sunglasses. "Anyhow, bein' an asshole doesn't make you a murderer."

"It *could.* Domestic violence is a leading cause of death for —"

"I don't want to hear it. I don't even want you to think it. Honest to God, Charlie, you gotta stay out of this mess."

"But what if he —"

"All the more reason for you not to get involved! He's a goddamn *cop.*" The harshness in his voice is not anger, I realize, but fear. He's scared for me.

"We need to find Micky's dad," I say, figuring we can at least agree on that point. "It sounds like Ruben Ramos might still be in the picture."

"Don't you go sniffin' out trouble now, droppin' us in the middle a some love triangle." Noah knows me too well. "Your only job these next few weeks is to keep you and our baby safe, you understand?"

"You're right," I say. "You're right."

And he *is* right. But that doesn't stop the wheels from turning.

SEVEN

The next morning, the morning of Donna and Jasmine's memorial, we oversleep — a frustrating mistake, given my usual propensity for insomnia. After a frantic scramble to dress and tame my hair and Noah cussing his way through Tucson's numerous traffic lights, we make it to the Remembrance Funeral Home exactly two minutes after the service is slated to begin. They're running late, thank goodness. I am not the jackass who was late to her own mother's funeral.

An usher hands us a program and directs us to the appropriate room. It's a large, sober-looking space with dark wood and an abundance of burgundy. At the front of the room, a pair of framed photographs, lit candles, flowers, and a string of rosary beads honor the deceased. I'm a bit puzzled by the rosary beads. I know my mother was raised Catholic — probably a significant factor in her choosing to have an unwanted child at nineteen — but according to my aunt Suzie, she'd emphatically renounced the Church by the time she left my father and me. Maybe she rekindled her relationship with God in a twelve-step program?

"Lotta people turned out," Noah murmurs, sliding into a bench at the rear of the room.

I nod, glad to see well over a hundred people have shown up. There's nothing more pitiful than the poorly attended funeral of one who died too young, and I know that firsthand. When my father died in a drunk-driving accident — just thirty-seven years old — few people came. I understood why, even at fourteen. He'd been drinking too long, burned too many bridges. To most of the people who'd once cared about him, he was already dead.

I'm happy to see that Jasmine's and Donna's lives still meant something to a great many people. In their own little corner of this sprawling desert city, they mattered.

The service comes to a start as a man with thinning hair, identified in the program as the director of the funeral home, parks himself at the lectern. He welcomes everyone briefly and then reminds us of our purpose. "Today, we remember the lives of Donna DeRossi and her daughter Jasmine

Cassell. As we mourn their untimely departure, so too do we celebrate their passing on to a better world."

I look around the room. No one seems particularly celebratory.

He reminds us of the Kingdom of Heaven, which these women now occupy; leads us in a quick prayer; and then launches into the most generic of Bible readings: *Yea, though I walk through the valley of the shadow of death.* I wonder about Pam's choice to avoid a traditional Catholic mass, whether she was representing the wishes of Donna and Jasmine or simply doing what seemed easiest. This service is hardly irreligious; there's a lot of talk of Jesus Christ, Our Lord, and seeking comfort in God.

They never talk about your anger, these funerals. *Don't feed me the same old line about eternal peace,* I think. *What about the living?*

I want outrage. This is not the funeral of some ninety-year-old grandpa. Donna and Jasmine had responsibilities in this world, a child who depended on them. A child who will spend the rest of her life waiting for people to leave, distrusting anything that looks too stable.

I would know.

When I look down at my own hands, I realize my knuckles are white.

Finally, the funeral director steps aside, making way for the young woman chosen to deliver Jasmine's eulogy. I lean forward in my seat as a hesitant blonde accepts the lectern and begins, haltingly, to speak about Jasmine. They were best friends, she says, ever since their job at the mall. They did everything together. Jasmine was so full of life. The blonde's words are stilted and unoriginal, and her eyes remain glued to her speech throughout, a trembling finger marking her place on the index card as she reads. Once, she loses her place, and the entire room fills with silence, then shuffling, a cough, as we wait for her to get sorted. In the end, the blonde mentions Micky only in passing, noting that Jasmine "tried really hard to be a good mom," and concludes with the observation "Her life was cut way too short, and I know we'll all miss her forever."

This lackluster tribute to the life of a murdered twenty-seven-year-old depresses me. Is that it? All that Jasmine's short life amounts to? I watch the blonde scurry back to her seat, her cheeks flaming, and glance at the program to see who is speaking on Donna's behalf. *Teresa King.* I guess Pam doesn't like public speaking.

I don't know what I'm expecting from this Teresa character, but it's certainly not the poised, sophisticated woman who now appears. She looks a few years older than I am. Large doe eyes, a small nose, and a bow-shaped mouth. Her hair is styled in long, dark waves with the kind of subtle red highlights that require a good salon and a lot of money. The charcoal short-sleeve skirt suit and slim gold crucifix around her neck render her both professional and pious, and when she stands before the congregation and begins to speak, no notes in hand, it's obvious she's an ace.

"For those of you who don't know me," she begins in the clear, unaccented English of a stage actor, "I'm Teresa King, founder of Sonora Hope. For the last eight years, I had the privilege of working with Donna DeRossi, who we remember here today." She pauses, gazes earnestly at her listeners. "All of us here to honor Donna possessed a unique relationship with her. You shared moments of joy and laughter, faced struggles together, or else supported one another in small but significant ways. I can't speak to the side of her that you knew, but I can tell you about the Donna that *I* knew, a compassionate and giving woman who began as an employee but ultimately became a dear friend."

This woman should go into politics, I think. *She's got this down.*

"For those of you unfamiliar with Sonora Hope," Teresa continues, "we're an organization that assists impoverished women living in border towns in the Sonoran region of Mexico. Through the generous contributions of our donors, we can offer these women the skills needed to financially support themselves and their families." She moves quickly past this little plug for her charity. "The most difficult part of our work is finding and gaining the trust of women who are used to receiving the worst that life can give. And it was in that area that Donna excelled." Her voice rises, swelling with emotion.

"Donna had a knack for identifying women in need," Teresa marvels. "Women in abusive relationships. Women forced by economic necessity into the degrading work of prostitution. Women raising their children in the garbage dump of Tirabichi because they could not afford housing. Donna found these women, she befriended them, and she changed their lives."

Though she doesn't belabor Donna's struggles with addiction, Teresa does mention them as obstacles Donna overcame. To hear Teresa tell it, my mother's dark years were the foundation of a deep compassion for those in need and a crucial part of her ability to connect with downtrodden women. The story has all the right ingredients for a Lifetime movie: sin, repentance, and redemption.

By the time Teresa's eulogy has reached its conclusion, there's not a dry eye in the place. I wipe my eyes with the back of my hand, annoyed with myself for having succumbed to such pathos.

"That woman can *talk*," Noah whispers, blinking away a few tears of his own. "Who could top *that* act?"

I feel a twinge of sympathy for Jasmine's bumbling blond friend, her speech seeming even more mediocre in the wake of this rock star. *Poor blondie. You did your best.*

After the service, people linger awkwardly. Some hunt Pam down to offer their condolences; others thank the funeral director, quietly greet friends, or drift wordlessly out. It's an eclectic group of mourners, ranging from those dressed quite formally despite the sweltering heat to one young man who drifts about in shorts and flip-flops. There are a few older children present, but for the most part, people seem to have decided that the funeral of two killed in a bloody double homicide is not a child-friendly occasion. I guess Vonda was right to keep Micky home.

Through the shifting crowds of people, I spot Sanchez in a group of able-bodied young men whose oozing testosterone and collective physique suggest that, regardless of relationship status, their first love is the gym. McCullough, I note, is not among them.

Surely he wouldn't skip Jasmine's funeral?

But then I find him standing against one of the back walls, brooding and handsome in a tie. His murky gaze flickers back and forth between the two exits, observing people as they leave, and I imagine that he's searching for someone who does not belong, someone who might have been involved in his girlfriend's death. Or else keeping an eye out for the mysterious Ruben Ramos. I'm so intent on watching McCullough that I fail to see Pam come up behind me.

"Good-looking guy, if you like that sort of thing."

I whirl quickly around. "Pam. Hi. I was just —"

"Admirin' the view?" Noah says mildly, and I flush, hoping neither of them actually misinterpreted my staring as lustful.

"Glad you two made it out this morning."

Pam appears far more composed today than when we last saw her. I notice the woman at her side, spiky gray hair and a neck tattoo, and wonder if it's her good influence. When battling grief, friends go a long way.

"It was a nice service," I say. "And so many people."

"That was quite a eulogy from Teresa King," Noah adds.

Pam gives him a sour look. "I knew what I'd get when I asked Teresa to speak."

"You don't look real impressed," Noah says, stumped. "I thought she really brought Donna to life. Maybe even got a few people interested in her charity."

"Only thing she's ever after."

"Really?" Noah's disappointed, and I can see that Teresa struck a chord with him. He wants to believe in her and her cause. "She seemed like she really cared about Donna. And all those women, wow."

"You sound like Donna." Pam rolls her eyes. "Everyone has their faults, trust me. Even Teresa King. I'd like to see Vargas banging down *her* door."

Pam's friend pats her on the shoulder, reeling her in. "Pammy here's been listening to Donna fawn over that woman for years," she says by way of explanation. "It gets a little old, that's all."

Pam nods. "You know what the women called her in Nogales? Mother Teresa. Like she's a goddamn saint." She snorts. "Donna always had a little crush on her. All the people working there do. And Teresa, well, she gets off on having groupies."

"It sounds like they do good work, at least," I venture.

"They do," Pam says grudgingly. "Donna loved it there. The stuff she saw, though, it took its toll. Five, six weeks ago some girl killed herself, and Donna about went off the deep end. Because she cared, you know? Those were her women. Teresa — she just spends all her time fund-raising. Doesn't have a clue what's happening on the ground." Her gaze shifts to something behind me. "Speak of the devil," she mutters, and I realize that Teresa is headed our way. The four of us fall quiet, and I wonder if Teresa can tell that we were talking about her.

"Pam. I hope I'm not interrupting." She's a tiny woman up close, scarcely more than five feet in heels, and she smells like something edible, a mixture of vanilla and cinnamon. "I just wanted to thank you. I'm so honored you let me speak today."

"No problem." There is nothing warm or welcoming in Pam's dismissive tone. Whatever the precise source of her jealousy, it must run deep.

"Listen, I don't want to take up too much of your time, but . . ." Teresa looks apologetically at the rest of us. "There's a donor luncheon on Sunday at the Desert Museum of Contemporary Art. We'd originally planned to present Donna with a service award. I thought . . . maybe you could be there to accept it. As a representative of the family."

Pam watches her for a few seconds, waiting just long enough for the silence to become uncomfortable. "I'm not really interested in being part of your show, Teresa," she says at last.

Teresa flushes. "Of course. I understand."

"If you're looking for family representatives, maybe bug Charlotte here." Pam gives me a little nudge in Teresa's direction and, having made what could loosely be termed an introduction, finds pressing business across the room. Pam's friend delivers a brusque good-bye and takes off after her.

"Well!" With a faltering smile, Teresa turns her attention to Noah and me. "Charlotte, was it?" Teresa studies me, and I can see her making a sudden connection with my name. "You're . . . a relative?"

I nod but don't elaborate.

"You've come a long way, then. Assuming you still live on the East Coast?"

I swallow. She knows who I am. How does she know who I am? What did Donna say about me? How many people did she tell?

"We live in Texas now," Noah says. "But we're thinkin' about movin' to Tucson. Sure would make it easier to adopt Micky."

Teresa touches her hand to her heart. "Oh my goodness, you two are taking Micky? You don't know what that would mean to Donna, knowing Micky had a stable, loving home to go to. She's never really had that before."

It's a subtle dig at Jasmine, but probably accurate. I don't tell Teresa that our plans regarding Micky are far from definite. "I hope we can give her what she needs," I say.

"I guess Micky didn't make it to the funeral today?"

"No," I confirm. "Her foster parents felt that all the people might be . . . overwhelming. They're bringing her to the cemetery later to have a more private good-bye."

"Closure is important." Teresa sighs deeply. "Poor Micky. She's been on my mind, ever since I heard. How is she holding up?"

"Time will tell, right? She's lost a lot."

"She has." Teresa touches my hand, her

143

dark eyes welling up. "Listen, I know you didn't really know Donna. But I hope you'll learn more about her someday, about the things she did. Donna and Micky were very close, and . . . I think Micky should know the positive impact her grandma had."

Her words feel both intrusive and true, an echo of Noah's own reminder that having a relationship with my niece entails coming to terms with her family. *My* family.

It would be easier to dismiss Micky's dearly departed as deadbeats with no real value, but the kid deserves more from me. If Donna added something to the world, it's time I know about it. I lift my chin, meet Teresa's teary gaze straight on.

"The donor luncheon on Sunday," I say, "what time does it begin?"

Though Noah's attempts to protect me sometimes come off as old-fashioned rather than chivalrous, I don't object when he offers to bring the car around. Waiting in the funeral home's cool, shadowy vestibule seems vastly preferable to enduring the intolerable temperatures of our vehicle.

"Give me ten minutes," he says, kissing my forehead. "I'll get the A/C goin' for you."

I steal a couple mints from a candy dish and then stand by the window, watching cars do battle in the chaotic parking lot. The funeral attendees trickle steadily out of the building until only a handful remain. One of them, a sniffling brunette with red-rimmed eyes, takes up residence with me at the window. She peers outside, presumably searching for her ride, and then wipes at her eyes, her finger dragging with it a dark trail of mascara. I reach into my purse and hand her a Kleenex.

"Thanks." She dabs carefully at her lower lashes, gathering up the little black flecks. "I hate crying. It's so ugly." She stuffs the dirty tissue in her pocket. "This whole thing . . . I mean, it's un-freaking-believable, right?"

"Yeah," I agree, popping a mint into my mouth in what I hope is a suitably somber fashion. "Hard to wrap your brain around."

"Jazz was, like, my best friend. We live at the same apartment complex and every-thing."

"I'm so sorry." And I am, for a fleeting moment, sorry for her, although my sympathy rapidly diminishes as she continues speaking.

"I totally don't understand why they asked Bree to do the speech. I mean, *Bree*? Just 'cause they bonded over some stupid mall job? What a joke." The thought of this injustice brings forth a fresh round of tears, and it takes a minute for her to get herself together. "You heard it, right?" she sniffs. "Worst speech *ever*? It's like Bree didn't even know her. And then she's up there stuttering like a retard. I mean, wow, those are some top-notch public-speaking skills, am I right?"

I glance around the lobby to see if anyone else is catching this, but I'm on my own. *Does this girl have a personality disorder? Am I supposed to be kind and understanding here?*

"I would have killed that speech," she says. "Well . . . Bree killed it all right." For the first time, she actually looks at me, takes in the identity of the person she's been talking at. "I guess you were here for Donna?"

"Um . . ." I'm too caught off guard to give anything but an honest answer. "More for Micky, actually."

"That's cool." She plays with a strand of her streaky brown hair. "I'm Serena, by the way."

I don't tell her my name or my relationship to Donna and Jasmine, and I don't think she cares. But hey, if she wants to talk, I'll let her. Someone this wildly inappropriate may give me some candid answers about Micky's childhood.

"Serena," I say. "That's a pretty name. It

sounds like you and Jasmine were really close. You must know a lot about her, everything she's been going through lately."

"I dunno." She looks a little defensive. "Probably not since she started dating Doug last year."

"Doug McCullough? What's he like?"

She folds her arms across her chest. "He thinks he's hot shit. And yeah, okay, he's good-looking. But trust me, he's *not* all that."

"So you weren't a fan."

"He told her what to do and who to be friends with." Serena tosses her hair, as if calling attention to her own freedom from male dominance. "Jazz used to be super cool and fun, but when she started seeing Doug, it was always, 'I can't hang out with you, Doug wants to stay in tonight,' or 'No, no, Doug won't let me.' He hated that me and Jazz were friends."

While I can see how McCullough would've been a convenient excuse for Jasmine to avoid this little drama queen, I don't entirely discount Serena's assessment of their relationship. Not that it matters. As far as I'm concerned, there's only one useful metric to judge McCullough by.

"Did Doug get along with Micky?"

She makes a derisive noise. "He didn't

give a crap. They just passed her off to Donna all the time, the two of them." Serena looks about to say something else and then thinks better of it. "Whatever. I'm not gonna talk bad about Jazz today. She was the best mom she could be, I guess."

"Yeah, it must've been hard, raising a kid without a dad." I say this like I've never done it, but of course I have. And it *is* hard. Damn hard. "Did you know Ruben at all?" I ask. "Were he and Jasmine in touch?"

She regards me with sudden suspicion. "Why're you asking me that? You're not in with Doug, are you?"

"No, no. This has nothing to do with Doug." I move away from the window and study a crucifix on the wall. In this particular artistic rendering, Jesus looks more exhausted than pained. Like he's been chasing toddlers, or up at night with a newborn, instead of dying for six hours on a cross. "Here's the thing, Serena. My boyfriend and I, we're thinking about adopting Micky. But Ruben Ramos is her father. He has parental rights until a court terminates them, so I'd really like to speak with him before we go making any big decisions about Micky's future."

"If you find him, at least get some money out of him," Serena advises. "His family's loaded, but I don't think Jasmine ever got a dime."

I think of Jasmine raising a child alone without any financial assistance and can't help but respect the woman. Even my philandering ex-husband managed modest child-support payments, money that allowed Keegan the extras I never had as a kid: a music class, new clothes, a swing set in the backyard. "Sounds like Ruben would surrender his rights without a whole lot of fuss, then."

"Hey, the best way to make a man want something is to tell him he can't have it, right? And Ruben's parents might take Micky. Who knows?" She examines a fingernail, and I can tell that she's growing bored.

I try to reel her back in. "Do you have any idea where I can find him? I heard Jasmine was in contact with him recently. Maybe she mentioned something to you . . ."

She shakes her head, a little bitter. "Not to me. Jazz stopped talking to me about that stuff. But I heard things." She turns her back to the window, throwing her face into abrupt shadow.

"What kind of things?"

"She thought *I* couldn't keep a secret, but Bree? That girl's got no filter. Bree told me some *interesting* stuff, you know what I mean?" Beneath all the smudgy mascara, Serena's eyes glow. "I guess Jazz never got over Ruben. She just couldn't stay away."

I'm losing my patience with all the second-hand gossip and innuendo. "So Jasmine *was* seeing him again." I don't pose it as a question, and she doesn't correct me. "Is Ruben back in the States? Who would know where he is?"

She shrugs. "She didn't tell Bree, so probably no one. I guess Donna might've known. Jazz and her mom were pretty tight. But that's not gonna help you now."

"No," I say, "it isn't." I glance out the window for some sign of Noah, but the lot is still paralyzed by a post-funeral traffic jam. Sighing, I slip another mint into my mouth. "I don't get it. If Jasmine was so into Ruben, why didn't she just break up with McCullough?"

"You serious?" Serena leans back and laughs heartily at my ignorance. "No way. You don't know Doug McCullough. He would've gone apeshit. Jazz was all in love with Ruben. She wasn't gonna sic Doug on him. Do you know what that guy would do to Ruben? And he's a cop. A *white* cop. He could probably get away with it." She's not scandalized, just matter-of-fact, and I can't argue with her. There are a lot of stories

150

McCullough could tell to justify shooting a young Mexican man. This is Arizona, after all, a state still embroiled in legal battles over its controversial show-me-your-papers law. It can't be easy to "look" Mexican here, much less *be* Mexican.

I file all this away to share with Noah later. There's just one more question I have for Serena, one raised by police that surely affects Micky and her upbringing. "Serena," I say, "do you know if Jasmine ever did any drugs?" It is not the most delicate of questions, but I have the feeling she won't mind.

"Just weed," she replies without hesitation. "And we dropped X a few times when we were clubbing. But she stopped all that when she and Doug got together."

I'm cautiously optimistic on Micky's behalf. Having a stoner mom is a lot better than having, say, a cokehead for a mother. "What about roofies?"

Serena looks aggravated. "I already told the cops she never touched that shit. I don't know what they found, but it wasn't hers. And no way it was Donna's," she adds, anticipating my next line of inquiry. "Donna went to meetings like crazy, wouldn't even have a beer."

"So you don't think —"

"You wanna know where any drugs in her

apartment probably came from?" She puts her hands on her hips, looks me square in the eye. "Doug McCullough's on Aggravated Assault. They run into plenty of drugs on the job."

I'm tempted to press her for more details, but she begins waving wildly at two young men across the room. "Rob! Robby!" she exclaims, and I recognize Sanchez and one of his bodybuilder friends. She bounds across the room to them, far more eager to see them than they are her. "Damn, Robby," she says, elbowing Sanchez like some annoying kid sister on a TV sitcom. "I thought you snuck out the back or something. *Estás listo? Ya nos podemos ir.*"

Sanchez responds with a few terse words in Spanish, and I get the sense that he finds this girl as grating as I do. Still, he nods at me as he passes. "Good luck with your baby," he tells me. Serena follows him out, an eager puppy nipping at his heels. She's already forgotten me. I wish I could forget her so easily.

It's obvious that Serena hates McCullough, feels somehow wronged by him, but that doesn't mean she's off the mark. Could McCullough have been collecting drugs from perps? I gaze at the wallpaper, interlocking white flowers on a mustard background, searching for answers. The drugs would have to be about money, I figure, not recreational use. As a cop, he must get drug tested. Or maybe he was using Rohypnol on someone else? Some kinky thing with Jasmine?

I move back to the window, scanning the parking lot for Noah's SUV. Remind myself that police corruption is not my business. If Pam wants to go searching for an institutional cover-up, good luck to her, but I'd prefer to steer clear of whatever melodrama got Jasmine killed. I'm just here to help Micky.

And yet, as Noah finally pulls up outside, I have to admit that Jasmine's tangled love affairs do impact Micky's future. Jasmine didn't cheat on McCullough with just anyone. She chose the one man who had a legal claim to her daughter, the one man I can't ignore.

Whatever secrets Jasmine took with her to the grave — secrets that could be responsible for her death — may lie with Ruben Ramos. If I had my druthers, I wouldn't go within a mile of this mess. But for Micky's sake, I have to find him.

I have to find her father.

EIGHT

After the funeral, Noah and I stop for brunch and head back to the hotel to change out of our Respectful Mourner clothes. We've arranged to visit Micky this afternoon, leaving us a few hours to squander as we please. Though there are decisions to be made, conversations we ought to be having, neither one of us is in a talking mood. We slop on sunscreen and hang around the hotel pool as if on some lame family vacation, willfully avoiding the topic of Donna and Jasmine and, by extension, Micky.

Yet I think of them. My mother. My sister. Their deaths are not nearly as troubling as the knowledge that two weeks ago, they were alive. If Donna didn't want me, that was her decision to make. But I had the right to know my sister, to know my niece. I should've been told.

Huddled in the hot shade of an umbrella,

I watch Noah do laps in the pool, watch him plow through the glowing blue water in an effort to burn off some nervous energy. Part of me wants to join him, but I'm lethargic, preoccupied, and there is no way I'm cramming this lump of baby belly into a swimsuit. Instead, I pull up images of local real estate on my phone. Though Tucson isn't a proper city with an impressive skyline, subway system, and people living on top of one another, it has its own appeal, like an eighties rock ballad you can't resist singing along to at full volume. There's something about the homes here — the simple earthiness of adobe, the brightly tiled floors, the wild and scraggly look of cacti on a patio — that draws me in.

I chug water and exchange a few e-mails with my editor while Noah continues to demonstrate his maddening stamina in the pool. The temperature climbs. My skin, I realize with surprise, is sticky with sweat. I haven't perspired much in the past few days — the desert sun seems to burn away the water within you, kill any trace of moisture long before it can escape your body — but today the air feels thicker, more humid. I notice a mass of clouds beginning to build.

The storm moves in like a creepy guy at a party, a little closer, a little closer, then suddenly, inescapably in your path. The sky darkens and the wind begins to pick up, its hot breath lifting my hair and whipping at the fabric of the sunshade.

"It's gonna rain," Noah says. "Hard. We better get inside."

We're safe in the lobby when the clouds open up. I stare out the panel of windows as a sheet of rain descends upon the pool. The drops fall in thick, diagonal lines, needles piercing the surface of the water in a sort of violent acupuncture. The palm trees rock back and forth, and the gusts rip off a few old fronds, blow them about the pavement and into the pool.

A young man wearing a hotel uniform jogs through the lobby and out into the mess, where, one by one, he closes the umbrellas. He returns, sopping and bedraggled, but cheerful nevertheless.

"Gotta love monsoon season!" he says. "Hopefully it won't hail."

Hail? In August? I turn to Noah with a stricken look, as if to ask, *Did you know about this?* but he's busy watching the storm. A bolt of lightning streaks across the sky, jagged electricity that spreads like nerve endings over the city.

I have to admit, it's breathtaking.

"The plants will love this," Noah says, and

I feel a surge of affection for his one-track mind.

The storm ends — without hail — half an hour later, and we head over to Vonda's. Outside, clouds roll away with astonishing swiftness, and the steely sky yields to an abiding blue. Desert rain, I've learned, is intense yet fleeting, leaving only an oppressive humidity and a few washed-out roads in its wake.

As Noah guides our vehicle through a series of muddy brown puddles, I'm glad we left my little Prius back home. On one road too flooded to pass, I spot a gang of school-age kids kicking and sloshing through rainwater that tops their knees. They squeal and shriek, try to wrestle one another down into the grimy water.

Noah stops the car, trying to reroute the GPS, and I watch the smallest child, a little girl, race into a nearby house and emerge with an inner tube. She sprints into the puddle with everything she's got and then launches herself into the air atop the inner tube, soaking all three boys with her landing.

I grin. "I hope our daughter's like that."

Noah gives a little grunt of agreement, although I don't think he's paying any attention.

I watch the four kids battle for control of the inner tube, marveling at how happy they look, how wholly absorbed they are in their play. Keegan would've loved this crew, would've exulted in these flooded streets. And then I look up at the horizon, see the nearby palm trees and cacti and houses, the mountains beyond them, smoky blue clouds rolling off into the distance, and even, I realize with a pang, a small fragment of rainbow suspended like a promise.

My eyes fill up with tears, and though I know it's probably just the hormones working me over, turning me into some unrecognizably soft and sentimental being, I can't help myself. I want to live here.

Micky waits for us in front of Vonda's house, a yellow plastic bucket in her lap. We're late, quite late, delayed by both the storm and its aftereffects.

I can't tell if Micky is pleased to see us, exactly, but she looks alert, her dark eyes taking in whatever information she can. Behind her, Vonda carefully brushes out Micky's hair, dividing it into pigtails. Vonda smiles when she sees us, probably relieved she doesn't have to explain the sudden disappearance of two more grown-ups to Micky.

"You made it!"

"Barely." Noah wipes his forehead with the back of his hand.

"That was quite a storm." I grin. "I had no idea you got that kind of rain out here."

Vonda laughs, as if pleased by her city and its ability to surprise. "Mid-June through September, that's monsoon season. Gets a little wild now and then, but it's a nice change of pace, in a way." She grabs a hair band off the step next to her and wraps it three times around one of Micky's pigtails. "We liked watching it, didn't we, Micky?"

Micky nods and holds up her bucket, which I now see contains water. "This is how much it rained here," she says. "Two inches."

"A budding meteorologist," I observe. "Cool."

Micky looks at me blankly, then at Vonda.

"A meteorologist studies the weather," Vonda explains.

"Me-tee-or-all-oh-gist," Micky repeats. She mouths the syllables again to herself, filing this word away, and it occurs to me that this child is not stupid. She wants to learn.

"Shall we invite your guests inside, Micky?" Vonda asks. "We can have some lemonade and maybe some of those Rice

Krispie treats we made today?"

Oh, Vonda, I think. *Of course you made Rice Krispie treats. Of course.*

"Can I stay out here a little longer?" Micky asks her.

"Sure, sweetie. Tell you what, I'll run in and get our snack ready. You can talk with your auntie Charlotte and Mr. Noah for a bit. I know you had some questions for them today, didn't you?" Vonda catches our eyes and there's a warning of some kind in her gaze. "You all just let me know if you need anything." She disappears into the house and I wonder what, exactly, we're in for.

Micky doesn't beat around the bush. "Did you go to my mom's funeral?"

"We did." Noah settles himself on the step beside her.

I lean against the door behind them, fairly sure that if I sit down here, I will not be able to rise again under my own power.

"Were there a lot of people there?" Micky asks.

"*So* many." I understand all too well why this matters. "Your mom and your grandma must have had a lot of people who loved them."

She twists around to get a good look at me. "Did they get buried?"

160

I hesitate. We're treading on dangerous ground now, walking a fine line between the honesty I think children are due and the fear that too much information can feed. "I'm not sure," I say, which is the truth. I don't know what Pam's burial plans were for Jasmine and Donna. But Micky doesn't let me off that easy.

"When you die, they bury you in the ground, right?" she persists.

"Sometimes."

"My mom and my grandma . . . are they in the ground now?"

For all I know, Jasmine and Donna were cremated, but I don't think the concept of burning people up and then hauling around their ashes will ease Micky's mind any. "I think so," I say, wishing I were anywhere but here. "I think they've been . . . laid to rest now."

I look to Noah for some guidance, some sign that I'm doing okay, but he's quiet, mulling over her questions. Maybe he thinks that, as the veteran parent, I know what I'm doing, but in four and a half years, Keegan never required any explanations of this kind.

"Vonda says their bodies are in the ground but their spirits are flying in heaven." Micky looks skeptical, as though she suspects Vonda might have been trying to sell her something.

I take a deep breath. I am the last person in the world who should be explaining the afterlife to young, impressionable children. My own experiences have left me more unsure, not less. "Nobody really knows for sure what happens when you die," I tell Micky. "Some people believe in heaven, and some people think . . . that dying is like going to sleep. Only you don't wake up."

Her grip on the yellow bucket tightens. "Who's right?"

"I don't know." I'm aware that answer is even less satisfying to a child than it is to an adult. "What do *you* think?"

She gnaws on her lip. "I think it's really dark under the ground. It must be scary."

Instantly I regret being so candid with a six-year-old. She can't understand death, not really. All she wants is a little certainty, someone controlling the reins. "I'm sure they're in heaven, honey," I say. "Vonda's right."

"Is heaven far away? Like, could I go there?"

That's it. I nudge Noah with my knee. Let him field this one.

"You want to go to heaven?" Noah asks softly, and Micky nods. "I bet you want to see your mom and your grandma again,

162

huh," he murmurs, and she nods again, gazing into her bucket with a heaviness that it pains me to see in a six-year-old.

"People can't go to heaven while they're still alive," Noah says. "But that doesn't mean your grandma and your mom are gone. My Daddy Jack died more'n a year ago, but I still feel him with me sometimes."

Micky lifts her head. "Does your Daddy Jack talk to you?"

Noah smiles. "Yeah," he says, "sometimes he does."

I raise my eyebrows. This is news to me.

"Every now and then I hear his voice in my head," Noah explains. "Like if I'm confused, or feelin' scared. He reminds me how to be a good man."

Micky looks at him with large, intense eyes. "I saw Grandma in my dreams. Is it real?"

"Does it feel real?" Noah asks.

"I don't know. She didn't talk to me. She just watched."

"I'd say that means your grandma's got her eye on you," he says, ruffling her hair. "She's keepin' you safe."

He's so ready to be a father. To be *her* father. But Micky has a father, and we need to settle things with him before we go making decisions about who this child belongs to. No sense letting Noah get attached to someone he might lose.

"Hey, Micky?" I ask. "Do you know if your mom had a friend named Ruben?"

At the mere mention of his name, her face shutters up. One finger finds its way to her mouth. "I don't know."

"Did your mom talk about him?" I press. "Maybe she went to visit him sometimes?"

Micky shrugs and continues sucking on her finger, giving up nothing. The poor kid has obviously been instructed to keep her mouth shut. *Excellent parenting, Jasmine, relying on your kindergartner to cover up your cheating.*

"I don't know about him," she mumbles. "You shouldn't ask me."

"Honey." Noah leans forward. "Your mom can't get in trouble anymore. You can tell us about him. We're your family, you got that? You don't need secrets."

She hesitates. Searches his face for signs of deceit or trickery, and eventually relents. "Ruben by the beach," she says softly.

"Ruben lives by the beach?" I cast Noah a triumphant look.

"My mom went to the beach with him on the weekend sometimes," Micky says. "If Doug had to work. But two times, I got to go, too."

"You went to the beach?"

"Yeah. We all went swimming in the ocean, but the waves were too big and they knocked me over. That's why I don't like the water."

I'm puzzled how Jasmine could afford beach vacations. "Did you take an airplane?"

"No," she says. "We borrowed Grandma's car. It was a long drive. I took Grandma's iPad and I watched *Tangled* two times. And then we were there."

My friend Rae's daughter was briefly obsessed with *Tangled*. Two *Tangled* viewings must be a three- or four-hour drive. Is there really oceanfront just four hours away from the Tucson desert?

"So, you went to the beach with your mom and Ruben," Noah reviews. "What else did you do?"

Micky screws up her face, trying to recall details. "Well, he was working at the blue hotel. We had to wait for him while he made all the drinks. He gave me some little umbrellas."

Noah and I exchange quick glances. *A bartender?*

"So Ruben was — nice?" I prod.

"Yeah," Micky says. "He got me a shark jaw with all the teeth in it. From a real shark, but he bought it at a store. And he

165

made good sand castles."

I can scarcely believe what we're hearing. Micky met her father. Spent time with him, probably recently. "Do you remember the name of the hotel Ruben works at?"

She blinks. "It was just . . . the blue hotel."

Micky may be running out of useful information, but I sense that we're on the verge of a breakthrough. I motion for Noah to take over and I duck into the house, where Vonda is mixing up a pitcher of powdered lemonade.

"Vonda, how far are we from the ocean?"

"The ocean?" She taps the last bits of fluorescent yellow powder from the pouch, unbothered by the abrupt entrance and odd question. "Hmm, let's see. Rocky Point is, oh, two hundred miles away."

"Rocky Point?"

"That's what Americans call Puerto Peñasco," she explains, stirring the lemonade with a large wooden spoon. "It's a beach town in Mexico. The university kids go there to party because the drinking age is eighteen, and I think they get a bunch of retired folk, too. The RV crowd."

"So you can drive there?"

"Sure. You'd need a passport, but sure."

"Does Micky have a passport?"

"I wouldn't know," Vonda says. "We can't

take Micky out of state without special permission, much less out of the country." She pours a glass of lemonade over ice and offers it to me. "If you need to know, you should ask the police. You're next of kin. I'm sure they'd let you into Jasmine's apartment, and you'll probably want to sort through Micky's stuff there anyway. Or try the apartment manager, they could help."

She's right, of course, and I feel a bit dense for not having considered that avenue myself. Although if there was clear evidence of Ruben's whereabouts in Jasmine's apartment, wouldn't investigators have found and seized it by now? Wouldn't McCullough, as jealous as he is?

It doesn't matter, I decide. Whatever we might find or fail to find in that apartment, Noah and I already have enough information about Ruben Ramos to pull this off. Bartender, blue hotel, Rocky Point. We can find Micky's dad.

I thought that convincing Noah to make the trek to Rocky Point would be a slam dunk, but it's soon clear that I've misjudged him. We're sharing a colossal ice-cream sundae inside a chilly shop when I tell him my plan.

"No," he says, almost spitting out a gob of

whipped cream. "No freakin' way." From the look on his face, there's no room for negotiation.

I scoop out a spoonful of peanut butter topping, mystified by his resistance. "I thought you'd be all over this. You've been saying all along how much you want to meet Micky's dad. Get a family health history and all that."

"But just marchin' off to Mexico hopin' we find him? That's plain crazy."

"Why?" I stare at him, trying to understand. "Ruben Ramos is out there. No one can adopt that kid if he still has parental rights. Not us, not Vonda, not anyone. What happened to getting to know Micky's world? This man is part of it, Noah. We have to try."

"No, baby, *we* do not. Somebody else can handle it."

He's scared, I realize suddenly. *Scared of my dream.*

"Who do you think is going to handle this?" I ask quietly. "The police? McCullough? I mean, Jesus, if McCullough gets ahold of the guy, Micky could have two dead parents on her hands."

Noah slaps his plastic spoon down, jiggling our slightly lopsided table. "Ruben coulda been the one who killed Jasmine and

168

Donna, you ever think of that?"

The possibility has of course occurred to me, but I find it unlikely. "Ruben can't even get into the country. He's a Mexican citizen, remember?"

"Not bein' a citizen hasn't stopped plenty of folks," Noah points out. "And don't you think it's suspicious, him and Jasmine havin' some kinda relationship, and then she dies, he disappears, and —"

"He didn't necessarily disappear, Noah."

"Yeah? Then how come no one can find him?"

"Jasmine was cheating on her boyfriend with this guy. Her volatile, possessive, gun-owning boyfriend. You think she'd just hand out Ruben's phone number and address to everyone she knows?" I munch thoughtfully on a frozen chunk of brownie. "She was keeping the whole thing under pretty tight wraps. Ruben might not even know she's dead."

I'm thinking aloud, but as soon as I say it, the idea makes sense. If Ruben's living in Rocky Point, how would he know what happened to Jasmine? Who would have told him? Nobody but Jasmine — and possibly Donna — even knew where he was, and it's not like he'd be following Tucson news.

Given law enforcement's difficulty locating the guy, Jasmine must have done a decent job covering her tracks with Ruben, which means she probably wasn't using her cell phone to communicate with him. A smart move. It would've been too easy for McCullough to stumble across a missed call or an unknown number, too easy for him to answer the wrong phone call while she was driving or in the bathroom. And the international fees wouldn't be cheap. The more I think about it, the more I'm convinced: Ruben doesn't know.

"Someone has to tell him." I frown, sliding a restless foot across the tiled floor. "Someone has to let Ruben know what happened."

Noah's eyes blaze. "Okay, let's say you're right. We find this blue hotel, we find Ruben. What if he wants Micky? What then? He gets to whisk her off to Mexico?"

"That would be for the court to decide." I dig out one final bite of ice cream, let the sweetness melt slowly on my tongue. "That girl at the funeral thought Ruben's parents might want Micky. It's worth looking into, at least."

"It sounds like you're trying to get rid of her. Make her someone else's problem."

"I'm trying to give her a family!" I retort. "Ruben is Micky's father. And not just biologically, Noah. He *knows* her. They hung out together. They made sand castles."

"He met her twice." Noah scowls. "Big deal. She doesn't even know he's her father."

"Maybe he doesn't want a relationship with her," I agree. "But what if he does? It wouldn't have to be custodial. You said yourself, she needs all the family she can get." I go for the jugular. "You grew up without a dad. What would *you* have given to know your father?"

My words have the intended effect. Noah has always felt his father's absence acutely, and learning details of the man's murder this past winter has only intensified his feelings of loss. "Shit," he says, and I know that I'm winning, though from the stubborn set of his jaw, I haven't won yet.

I reach across our wobbly table and take his face in my hands. "I know what you're scared of, and it won't come true. You said yourself the dream won't come true."

For a moment, he lets me hold him, meets my gaze with an expression both fierce and tender. Then he breaks away. "I'm not willin' to bet your life on that."

I want to tell him that if my nightmare is really a premonition of my future, there may be no escaping it. Doesn't trying to change your future always cement it? I think of Oedipus and Macbeth, both trying to dodge ugly prophecies and, in doing so, inadvertently running headlong into the very futures they feared. But now is not the time to have a philosophical discussion about fate or free will.

"It would just be one night," I tell him. "If we can't find Ruben, fine. We gave it a shot."

"It's too dangerous. I don't want you in Mexico."

I can understand where he's coming from. That old shower with the blue and yellow tile would be right at home in the seedier part of a Mexican beach town, and Noah can't bring his gun across the border. We'd be vulnerable. But the truth is, we're vulnerable here, too. Tucson is a relatively high-crime city with an abundance of firearms in circulation, and that sketchy little shower could be in any of its run-down buildings.

"My dream could've been anywhere, Noah," I remind him. "Mexico, Arizona, Texas, I don't know. Could be Canada, for all I can tell."

"What's your point?" he demands. "I should be scared all the damn time? I *am,* Charlie. I already am."

"My point is that we can't run away from it. Any place we run to — that could be it."

"You're askin' me to just sit around and wait for somethin' to happen. You're sayin' there's nothin' I can do." The desperation in his voice — the absolute impotence — leaves me aching. Noah likes to tackle his problems straight on. He's not used to worrying about what lurks in the shadows, and yet that's exactly what I've given him: a monster he can't see, can't fight, can't possibly conquer. I've made him helpless.

"I can avoid showers," I say. "That's something. And if I see anything from my dream, we'll hightail it out of there."

He's torn, caught between his natural optimism and an almost primal fear. I take his hand and my fingers curve around his.

"I'm going to be all right, I promise. What matters right now is Micky."

He closes his eyes, inhales, and chooses, against all odds, to believe the best. Maybe because it's better than believing in death.

"Okay," he says. "Okay."

NINE

I spend the evening on my laptop trying to pinpoint Ruben's whereabouts. The search term "Rocky Point blue hotel" yields no obvious hits, but Google lists only about fifty hotels across the city. I sort quickly through each entry, and yet, on web page after web page, I don't spot any blue buildings at all.

There are pools, of course, their chemical-treated water appearing as hypnotic blobs in the aerial photos, and the beachfront resort sites never fail to flaunt the cerulean waters of the Gulf of California. Ultimately, though, the buildings are all the kind of whitish neutrals that only a card of lyrically named paint samples could distinguish between. I find something pink and another hotel in an eye-burning shade of mustard, but that's as colorful as Rocky Point gets.

"How's it goin'?" Noah's stretched out on the hotel bed behind me, looking peevish after a long phone conversation with his assistant, Sharlene. Some irrigation company in Sidalie screwed up one of the town's sprinkler systems, and Noah's crew must now salvage a dozen waterlogged flower beds. I don't want to add to his bad mood with the news that we're heading blind into Rocky Point tomorrow, don't want to provide him with ammunition to back out, so I duck the question.

"Looks like there are some nice resorts," I say. "Where should we stay?"

He shrugs. "Wherever's safest. A good area with good security."

"I'll see what I can find." All the major hotels look safe to me, but I figure Noah will feel better if I pretend that, after exhaustive research, I've found us the Fort Knox of Mexican hospitality.

Another forty-five minutes online produces no new leads on Ruben's blue hotel. I'm starting to have doubts. Could there have been some other beach town Micky and Jasmine visited? Was Micky mistaken when she said that Ruben worked at a hotel? Unlike most seaside resort towns, Rocky Point skews heavily toward condos and timeshares. If Ruben works from one of those, we'll be sorting through another two or three hundred properties across the city, easy. There's no way Noah and I could cover that kind of ground in one day.

I grab a sheet of paper and make a list of properties with a restaurant or bar on the premises. Next, I wade through a series of articles about Rocky Point, trying to narrow down the most likely areas: Playa Mirador, Choya Bay, Sandy Beach. The more I read, the more immense this city of less than sixty thousand starts to seem. And the names are driving me crazy. Some are English, others Spanish, some a mishmash of the two, and some referred to in English *or* Spanish, depending on what source I'm looking at. As someone who speaks about twenty words of Spanish total, it takes me a while to realize that Choya Bay and Bahía la Cholla are one and the same.

Frustrated, I accomplish other tasks. Purchase Mexican auto insurance online. Map out tomorrow's route to Rocky Point. I'm changing into my pajamas, about to admit defeat, when it finally occurs to me that my failure to locate this mythical blue hotel may lie not in poor research skills but in my decision to take high school French.

"Noah."

He's fallen asleep on top of the covers, one arm dangling off the side of the bed, his cheek mashed against the comforter. I nudge his shoulder and he snorts.

"Hnh?"

"What's the word for 'blue' in Spanish?"

" '*Azul,*' " he tells me without ever opening his eyes or fully waking up.

"*Azul,*" I repeat. The word is familiar. "Is that A-Z-U-L?"

"Mm-hm." He nestles his face deeper in the folds of the comforter, and I have to admire his ability to conduct conversations while unconscious.

I pick up my list of hotels with restaurants or bars inside and groan. There it is, the third item on my paper. Vista Azul Resort. I could've ended this search hours ago. Micky wasn't telling us the color of the building her father worked in, but the name.

It isn't the satisfying *Gotcha, Ruben* that I was hoping for, but I'll take it.

Not wanting to spend a couple of decades in a Mexican prison, we leave Noah's gun with Pam.

I'd prefer not to tell her the true purpose of our visit to Rocky Point — she'll inform the TPD, and potentially ruin our chances of having the first crack at Ruben — but Noah dismisses my pleadings as insane and irresponsible. "Someone has to know where we are," he says.

Upon arriving at Pam's, however, he spills his guts so immediately and so thoroughly, I realize he's got another agenda altogether: he thinks she can talk me out of going.

"Ruben, huh? In Rocky Point?" Pam finishes watering a plant in her living room and regards me impassively. "You weren't going to mention this to the investigative team?"

"Mention what?" I cross my arms, defiant. "That a six-year-old made an offhand remark about going to the beach with Ruben a couple of times? I'm just playing a hunch, Pam. I could be wrong about this. If we find him, of course I'll let the police know."

She cracks a half smile that says she doesn't entirely believe me. "Why do you want to get to him so badly, anyway? You could chat with Ruben after he's been cleared as a suspect. What's your rush?"

"He could run," I say. Does she think I'm stupid? "Your guys obviously don't have enough to extradite, and all it takes is one visit from McCullough to spook him. As soon as Ruben knows that guy is on his tail, he could disappear."

"What if he's dangerous?" Noah demands. "Shouldn't we be worried about this guy?"

I brush off the suggestion. "I don't think

he killed anyone. But even if he did, what happened to Jasmine wasn't random, it was personal. He has no grudge against *us*."

"If he killed her, then he killed Donna, too," Noah points out. "Not because it was personal, but because she was there. So maybe rethink how dangerous he could be."

It's a fair point. "Pam," I say reluctantly, "you know more about this than we do. What's the theory right now?"

Pam lifts her watering can to another hanging plant and wets her lips with her tongue. "I've talked to a few folks," she says. "My theory is that Jasmine was the target. Donna was just . . . wrong place, wrong time. Hardly anyone knew she'd be babysitting that night. And I sure don't buy all this bullshit about drugs." She plucks a dead leaf from the plant and rolls it between her fingers, agitated.

"You're assuming Jasmine was the target because it happened in her apartment?" I ask.

She nods. "And because of the crime scene."

"Dare I ask?" Part of me doesn't want to know, but curiosity — an ugly, morbid curiosity — rears its head before I can stop myself.

Pam looks me over as if assessing whether

or not I can handle the details. Maybe she has no one else to confide in, or maybe she sees more in me than just a pale, pregnant women clad in cheerful florals. For whatever reason, she gives me a try.

"They were sitting at the dining room table," she says. "Donna was still in her chair when they found her. Two shots to the head from a distance of four to six feet. Didn't look like she was running, so they're guessing she was killed first. She probably didn't suffer." Pam recites these facts in a quiet, affectless voice, but beneath it, I can still feel her loss, a black hole exerting its own gravitational pull. I wonder if her time leading Homicide has made this easier for her or if having seen these cases up close only sends her imagination into overdrive.

"Jasmine was discovered on the floor next to the dining table," Pam continues. "She was shot four times, once in the shoulder, three times in the chest. They also recovered a bullet in the wall behind her, probably a miss."

Noah whistles. "Somebody was pissed off at Jasmine."

"Yeah." Pam sounds like she knows the feeling.

"Was she trying to get away?" I ask.

"She didn't get far," Pam observes drily,

"but that's what it looks like. We don't know exactly how much time elapsed between the two deaths. Could've been seconds, or this guy could've held her at gunpoint for several minutes."

"It must've been fast," I say. "Micky was in that apartment. She would've heard the first shot, wouldn't she?" I don't want to believe that Jasmine spent her final moments pleading with some psychopath for her life.

"The shooter didn't necessarily know Micky was there," Pam says. "And there was a party going on outside that night. It was loud."

Noah clears his throat. "Whoever it was . . . he didn't mess with them, did he?"

I'm not even sure what he's getting at until Pam replies, "No sign of sexual assault. If that's what the Rohypnol was for, it didn't go down according to plan."

Noah breathes a sigh of relief.

"So." Pam sets down her watering can and folds her arms. "You still want to make this trip to Rocky Point?"

"Not if you think we shouldn't," says Noah. "I don't especially like the sound of Ruben."

Instead of weighing in, Pam dispenses a few facts. "Here's what I know about

Ramos," she says. "According to US Customs and Immigration, his student visa expired in December of 2006, and he hasn't returned since. If he's in Rocky Point right now, he couldn't have killed these two women unless he made it in and out of the US undetected. Now, I'm not saying our border security is infallible, but that sounds awfully premeditated for a domestic dispute with his girlfriend."

Noah bites his lip. "Okay. I trust your judgment, Lieutenant."

"So you won't get the police involved yet?" I ask. "We just need a day, that's all."

"You're really sticking your neck out for this kid." Pam studies me, bemused. "Why? A week ago, you didn't even know her."

I rest my hands on my belly, feel my daughter stirring inside of me like the answer to her question, though not one I can articulate. "I don't know. It's what needs to be done," I say, and there's something in Pam's reaction to those words — a haunted look, her breath drawn in sharply with startled recognition — that tells me she's heard this logic before.

Donna, I intuit with some discomfort. *I'm sounding like my mother.*

"You've got twenty-four hours," Pam says. I want to hug her. "Thanks."

"Twenty-four hours," she repeats gruffly. "And then I'm gonna have a chat with Vargas. In the meantime, if you do find Ruben, you don't go anywhere alone with him, okay? You stay in public places, you don't hang out with his buddies, and you never, ever mention that he's a suspect in these murders. If you get a bad feeling, if anything sets your spidey senses tingling, you get outta there and you give me a call pronto. Got it?"

I smile. "Got it."

Though much shorter, the drive to Rocky Point feels at least as desolate as our journey through Texas. This is straight-up desert, a single-lane highway with few cars. I spend the first fifteen minutes playing with my adjustable chair, trying to achieve maximum comfort in the passenger seat before I accept that it's a lost cause.

We're not far out of Tucson when a sign informs us that we are entering Tohono O'odham Indian Reservation lands. I remember Sanchez saying that Pam grew up on a Tohono O'odham reservation and wonder if it was this one. Living in Connecticut, the only reservation lands I knew of were home to Mohegan Sun and Foxwoods, a pair of opulent casinos that don't exactly call to mind the dire economic straits of many native people. As we drive through Sells, Arizona, the capital of the Tohono O'odham nation, I realize I've never seen what actual reservation living looks like.

Sells is a barren little town with a population in the two thousands, and maybe it's the New Yorker in me, but imagining this place as the capital of anything saddens me. The homes are small and blocky, with laundry flapping on a line outside, a statue of the Virgin Mary perhaps, or else a few horses pent up in a modest-size yard. A community college on the outskirts of the "downtown" area resembles a juvenile detention center more than a place of higher learning. Half-melted traffic cones divert traffic around a crumbling section of highway.

Maybe to the Tohono O'odham people, it's a sanctuary, a refuge — but to me, Sells looks like a prison. The kind of place you put people you want to forget.

"Is this crappy piece of land really the best the government has to offer?" I ask.

Noah casts me a sidelong glance. "Honey, they're desert people. They've been livin' in the desert for ages. They *choose* to live here. Nobody's makin' 'em."

But I wonder how much choice a child born here has, what kind of tools they might be given to prosper in the outside world. Suddenly Pam's success in the Tucson Police Department seems all the more miraculous, and I can understand what my mother must have seen in her, the fierce determination and courage Pam must have employed as she clawed her way up.

"I'm just saying, this doesn't exactly look like a land of opportunity."

Noah shrugs, ever the pragmatist. "What would you rather do?" he asks. "Round all the kids up and send 'em to one of those Indian boarding schools, like they used to? I'll tell you one thing. I don't know when sittin' around feelin' sorry for someone ever helped 'em any."

Is this his polite way of calling me a bleeding-heart liberal?

I don't ask. We have another hundred-odd miles to drive together.

For a road so barren, Highway 86 appears to have a disturbing number of traffic accidents. We pass several memorial sites on the side of the road: white crosses staked in the dirt and draped in flower wreaths, Jesus and Mary figurines, a message on a telephone pole in pink spray paint. ♡ *U 4EVR,* someone has written, *RIP JOEY.*

As we pass through yet another hilly region populated with tall, treelike cacti, Noah lets out a long sigh of contentment. "I hope you're enjoyin' this," he says.

I yawn, trying to calculate how much longer I can hold in my pee. "Enjoying what? The cacti?"

"It's a saguaro forest. Saguaros only live in the Sonoran Desert. This is special."

I peer out at all the looming saguaros: thick green central columns with rounded tips, their branches jutting upward on the sides like arms. Though it's hard to gauge their precise height through the car window, most are much taller than a human being. They look like every cartoon cactus you've ever seen, and if one slapped on a mustache and a sombrero and came to life, I would only be sort of surprised.

"Biggest cactus in the US," Noah tells me, "but you get a drought, and it can take 'em ten years just to grow a couple inches." He scans the horizon, and I can just imagine him big-eyed under those sunglasses, taking it in with the shiny wonder of a kid. "Their flowers don't bloom until night, you know."

"Night-blooming flowers?" It sounds like some romantic fairy tale, not a fact of desert survival. "Why? Too hot?"

"Nocturnal pollinators, probably."

"You're better than a Snapple cap." I run a hand across the top of his head. His hair tickles my palm; the buzz cut is starting to grow out.

"This right here . . ." He lifts one hand from the steering wheel and gestures all around us. "This is the Southwest done right. I mean, can you imagine this place at sunset?"

For an instant, I can — the dark, spiny silhouettes of the saguaros against a fluorescent orange sky — but the winding, unlit roads and all those highway memorials prove a more powerful image.

"What happened to Mr. Protective?" I ask. "Are you suggesting we drive to Mexico in the dark?"

"No, of course not," he says, chastened. "I bet it's quite a sight, that's all."

I smile. Until we came to Arizona, I didn't fully realize how deep Noah's love of horticulture extended. Before, I'd looked upon his knowledge of trees and shrubbery as a professional necessity. Only now, as he spouts facts about a desert terrain he's never had to landscape, do I understand his work is not just a job but a vocation. The guy loves plants. Loves watching them, learning about them, tending patiently to them. It's

187

a promising skill set, I think.

He'll be so good with our daughter. He's already so good with Micky.

I don't know how I found him, if it was dumb luck or a gift from the cosmos, but somehow, as we travel along this winding desert road together, I feel a sense of immense contentment. I'm achy, sluggish, and thirsty, but this is where I want to be. Even when he breaks out the Dixie Chicks CD and, God help us all, tries to sing along.

I don't remember falling asleep, but the next thing I know, Noah's tapping my thigh. "Charlie," he murmurs. "Wake up, baby."

My eyes flicker open. "Unh?"

Outside, I see the border crossing, customs agents moving leisurely about, pausing to speak with drivers. A traffic light indicates whether vehicles should proceed or stop for inspection. SONOYTA, the sign says.

"We're here," Noah tells me. "This is Mexico."

■■■■

PART III
PUERTO PEÑASCO,
SONORA, MEXICO

■■■■

TEN

The Vista Azul proves to be a fairly nice establishment, clean and bright, the walls of its lobby a piercing turquoise color that almost justifies the hotel's misleading moniker. When Noah has determined that it meets his safety requirements, we proceed to the check-in counter. One thing is quickly apparent to me: at two hundred dollars a night, there's no way Jasmine could afford this place. Either Pam is wrong about the drug angle, or Ruben was the one financing these stolen visits. I try to imagine Jasmine standing in this lobby, anticipating a weekend with her lover. Did she worry about McCullough's finding out, I wonder, or was secrecy half the fun?

After receiving the key to our room, Noah asks the girl at the desk about the hotel bar. She directs us to a corridor on our right in surprisingly good English. "The Cantina del Mar is open until three," she informs us, as if I, in my current state, might possibly be boozing until three a.m.

"Do you know if Ruben Ramos is working there today?" I ask. There's no reason the hotel staff would have any knowledge of the bartenders' schedules, but she's young and pretty with big pouty lips, and I've seen enough of Jasmine's taste in men to guess that Ruben is probably no slouch himself. Attractive people have a way of noticing each other.

Sure enough, the girl's eyes widen at his name, and she laughs, almost involuntarily. "Ruben? He could be here today. He works many Saturdays."

I reach for Noah's hand and give it an excited squeeze. This wasn't all in my head. I did it. I found Micky's dad. We don't even bother stopping by our hotel room; without any discussion, we head for the restaurant.

The Cantina del Mar looks like every Tex-Mex chain restaurant I have ever seen. Somehow I expected something other than sombreros and clusters of chili peppers hanging from the walls. This can't be authentically Mexican, can it? But as I observe the dozens of red-faced tourists, mainly American, I understand the business decision to give the people what they want. Which is, from the looks of things, hamburgers and colorful alcoholic beverages. I remember Micky saying that Ruben gave her little umbrellas, and indeed, they're everywhere, their toothpick handles laden with orange slices and maraschino cherries, topping off every cocktail.

An old man with a shock of white hair comes to seat us, but I politely decline, explaining that I've come to speak with Ruben Ramos about an urgent matter.

The old man leans over and touches my belly. "Ah, you have something belong to Ruben, I think," he says in heavily accented English, and when I turn to him, thoroughly horrified by the insinuation, he cackles with delight. "I joking you! Only joking!" He points at the bar. "There is your man, okay?" He gives me a friendly pat on the shoulder and then takes off, still chuckling over his little jest.

I scan the bar, my gaze skipping past a bald man and a world-weary woman and settling on their young male coworker. My eyebrows rise. *Ruben Ramos. Well, then.*

He has dark, shaggy hair to his chin, just enough scruff to be sexy, and dimples that he's not afraid to use. In a white collared shirt with the sleeves rolled up, he comes off as both casual and effortlessly handsome, and if his forehead is dotted with perspiration from working all day in the heat, well . . . let's just say it's not a bad look for him. I have to give Jasmine props. Though far from my type, the man is beautiful. He looks like a surfer or a frat boy, all fun and games and debauched merriment, the antithesis of McCullough's blue-eyed intensity.

I watch Ruben hand a drink to a dyed-blond woman in her fifties, watch his flirty smile, the way he laughs at something she says — something not nearly as amusing as he's making it out to be, I'd warrant — and responds with a cheeky remark of his own. Unsurprisingly, she tips him very, very well.

"Looks like he's got his own fan club," Noah says, and only then do I see the row of young women on the left side of the bar. A group of sloppy-drunk twentysomethings, the women giggle uproariously at one another and vie for Ruben's attention in ways they probably wouldn't want shared on YouTube.

"Ruuu-ben!" a brunette slurs. "I need a straaaw. Can you get me another straaaw?"

"I need ice!" her friend calls. "I'm, like, *so hot*. Can you bring me ice? Oh my God, I just want to melt ice *all over my body.*"

"Ooh, yes!" a third woman agrees. "Come melt ice all over our bodies, Ruben! That is totally how I want to spend my afternoon."

The three laugh outrageously as he presents them with a straw, a cup of ice, and a smile far more good-natured than their behavior merits. "Ladies," he says, managing to look as though their antics are charming and amusing, not an embarrassment to women everywhere. The moment he turns his back to them, though, his expression becomes one of fatigue. He must get this a lot.

"What do you think?" I ask Noah, fidgeting. "Should we just — go talk to him? Maybe we should wait. He looks busy." The thought of trying to hold a conversation with this man is making me light-headed. Those dimples are lethal, and I don't do well with hotties.

"I'll handle it," Noah says, approaching the bar. I follow behind him, trying not to look like an awkward teenage girl hiding behind her father.

Ruben spots us immediately, only too happy to get away from his intoxicated groupies. "What can I get you, sir?" he asks Noah in a voice that seems to caress the English language. The man belongs on a soap opera or the cover of a romance novel, not here, living, breathing, smoldering away in the flesh. Poor Jasmine. Of *course* Ruben was her weakness, the one she could never quite move beyond. They were young when they met. He was the father of her child. And just look at him.

"Ruben Ramos, right?" Noah says, and Ruben looks a bit thrown when he hears his name. "Listen, what time are you off work? We need a word with you."

"A word . . . ?"

"It's about Jasmine," Noah tells him.

I assess Ruben's reaction to the name. Though his eyes register recognition, he seems more worried about Noah than the woman he's purportedly been involved with for months.

"You are . . . Jasmine's friend?" He studies Noah, hesitant, and I realize he's afraid he's about to get his ass kicked. A legit fear, I guess, for someone in the business of screwing girls with boyfriends.

"I'm Charlie." I step forward. "I'm Jasmine's sister, and that's my boyfriend, Noah. When can we talk to you? It's very important."

"Sister," Ruben says, relieved. "Okay. She never tells me she has a sister." He calls to the female bartender. *"Rosario! Voy a tomar un descanso."* Without warning, he leaps up over the bar and joins us, suddenly so close that I can smell him, an unsettling mixture of cologne and mansweat. "Sit down, mama," he tells me. "We can talk right now."

Though I'm not exactly looking forward to the conversation with Ruben, my nerves turn into indignation when Noah dismisses me from the scene. "Go call Pam," he whispers in my ear. "Let her know who we found."

"What?" I stare at him. *Now?* I'm tempted to object, to insist that Noah be the one to call her, but I don't particularly want to be left alone with Ruben, either. Sulking, I plod off to make the phone call, which, being international, proves a pain in the butt. It takes a good fifteen minutes to inform my cellular service provider that I am in Mexico, enable international calls, and work out the correct sequence of digits necessary to dial the United States.

Back at Cantina del Mar, I find the men hunched together at a table in the corner, each nursing a bottle of beer. From the outside, they look like buddies, just a couple of dudes drinking stoically together while their girlfriends are off shopping or getting pedicures. For a strange, flickering instant, I yearn for a different reality, a world in which I know Jasmine, spend time with her, a world in which our children celebrate birthdays and holidays together, Keegan and Micky growing up the tightest of cousins.

"There you are," Noah says when I plop down in the empty seat beside him. "I was startin' to wonder."

Ruben stares at the beer in his hand, scarcely moving. Not upset, not angry, not displaying any emotion other than frozen bewilderment. I know then, without asking, that Noah has told him about Jasmine. What I initially mistook for calm and companionable drinking is actually shock.

"I'm sorry." I stare at the splintered edge of the wooden tabletop. "We were hoping you already knew."

"No." Ruben takes a long drink from his bottle — Tecate, some cheap Mexican brand — and continues to stare at the table. "She didn't call me awhile. I was thinking . . . she is busy. Or her boyfriend is around. I never thought that she is *dead.*"

"Was it unusual for her not to call?"

"No. We only meet together . . . sometimes. And I can't call her because, *pues,* the boyfriend."

"Right," I say, nodding. "He's a pretty jealous guy, huh?"

"Yes. He looks in her phone to see the numbers that call. She uses the phone of her mother and we do Skype." Ruben's English is faltering as he struggles to comprehend what's happened. "This is . . . very crazy. Jasmine is always a girl . . . very alive."

I glance at Noah, trying to get a sense of what they've already talked about, if he's brought up Micky yet. I highly doubt it. Asking probing questions and bringing up thorny issues isn't really Noah's bag, and in this case, his instincts are probably right. We should let Ruben talk a bit longer about Jasmine before springing Micky on him. No need to appear disrespectful.

"So, Ruben," I begin, looking for a safe warm-up question, "how did you and Jasmine meet? I never heard the whole story."

"I was on a summer program at the University of Arizona," he says, fingers playing with a piece of his floppy hair. "A business course. This was seven years ago." He rubs the back of his neck with one hand, and I get the sense that this memory isn't a particularly happy one for him. "We go on some dates, and then . . . *pues.* She gets pregnant." He glances at me, and I can see him wanting to make a good impression on Jasmine's sister. "I wanted to stay with her, but my visa expired. And my parents, they wanted me home. They don't want me to marry an American."

I get the feeling Ruben comes from a pretty well-off family if he dabbled in university courses in the US and his parents were advising against a legitimate path to American citizenship. "So you guys just lost touch after that?" I ask.

"I saw her sometimes," he says quickly. "In Nogales or here, in Rocky Point. I met the baby." He seems to think he should get points for bothering to meet his own offspring, and I have to bite the inside of my cheeks to keep from giving him a piece of my mind. "Please understand. I was a student at Tecnológico de Monterrey. The distance was big. Jasmine and I, we both meet other people."

"Looks like your paths crossed again, though, huh," Noah says.

Ruben gives a long sigh and takes another drink of beer. "Two years ago, I have a big fight with my parents. I'm upset how they try to control me with their money, you know? So I come here, to Puerto Peñasco. It's a good place to find work when you speak English. And I like the life here. The beach, the parties."

The girls, I add mentally.

"So did you contact Jasmine?" I ask, although I'm certain he didn't. Some men like a few obstacles in their relationships, can handle challenges like geographical distance and a kid. Ruben is not that man. If Jasmine resurfaced in his life, I'm pretty sure it's because she fought her way back in.

"I was not thinking about Jasmine when I came back," Ruben admits. "We don't talk for so long. But then she visited Puerto Peñasco with her friends in November and we . . ."

"Bumped into each other?" Noah supplies, which strikes me as quite the euphemism.

"Yes. A happy accident."

"She did tell you about the boyfriend, right?" Though his tone is mild, Noah can't quite mask his feelings about infidelity. I cringe inwardly. We need to be empathetic, not to come across as Judgey McJudgerson, Chief Inspector of Moral Virtues.

Ruben doesn't appear particularly fazed by the subject of Jasmine's boyfriend, however. "I think the boyfriend is not a big problem," he says. "A man who can't make his woman happy, he will not keep her. I make her more happy than her boyfriend, then okay, it is her choice, right?"

For a second, his golden-brown eyes search mine, daring me to imagine just how happy he is capable of making women. I drop my gaze, disgusted and yet blushing fiercely. *Her choice indeed.* Ruben's version of feminism, I take it. Every woman deserves the freedom to choose . . . to sleep with him.

"We have fun, me and Jazz." Ruben turns to Noah now, seeking manly understanding. "This was all we are looking for together. Just fun."

For "fun" I substitute the word "sex" and have a pretty good idea of what this relationship meant to Ruben.

"Jazz always was a party girl," I say, and shoot him a knowing smile, as if I knew her, as if she confided in me about all their antics. "She would try anything once."

He laughs, a little nervous about what I might be referring to.

"You guys used Rohypnol together, right?"

Noah kicks me gently under the table, and his message is unmistakable. *Shut the hell up. Don't ruin this for us.* I realize that I'm not playing by the safety rules that Pam laid down for us, and I'm probably putting Ruben on the defensive, but the presence of those pills in Jasmine's apartment has been bothering me.

"Rohypnol?" Ruben's eyes dart from my face to Noah's. "I don't know what that is."

"Doesn't matter," Noah says, swiftly steering us back on course. "We mostly wanted

202

to talk with you about Micky. We heard you saw her a few times."

"Oh." Ruben looks uncomfortable at the mention of his daughter. "Yes. That was maybe not a good idea, but Jasmine wanted us to meet."

She was hoping you'd fall in love with your daughter, I think. *Hoping Micky could reel you in, even though Jasmine never could.* I want to both hug and slap Jasmine for her folly. Ten minutes with Ruben has shown me what wishful thinking this was. The guy would never sacrifice his own pleasure for someone else's benefit, and that's half of parenting in a nutshell.

"Expecting you to be a father to Micky after all these years is a little silly," I say, trying to get on his good side. "It doesn't sound like Jasmine really thought that through."

Ruben jumps on this, grateful for an out. "No, she doesn't think. It can confuse a child, you know? I said I will meet her, but Jazz has to promise not to tell Micky I'm her father. I always know Jasmine and I, this is not forever, and Micky is only a *pequeñita,* a little girl. Bad for her to have a father who comes and disappears again."

"Good call," I say, and I'm not being facetious. Micky will have enough daddy issues as she grows up without throwing blatant rejection at age six into the mix. "So . . . did Noah tell you why we're here?"

"He tells me Jasmine is dead." Ruben swallows. "That someone shoot her."

"Right. She's dead, and so is her mother. We're trying to figure out who will become Micky's legal guardian." I place my hands upon the table, forcing myself to look at him.

His eyes widen. "Me? Hey, no, no. Micky is a good kid, but my life is not for a child. Too crazy, these hours, and . . . sometimes I'm not home. I can't give her . . . *estabilidad.*"

"No, of course not," I agree, and the rush of relief is enormous. The more distance we can put between this guy and Micky, the better. "We'll find a home in Arizona for her. We just wanted to make sure you were okay with that. Since you're her father."

"Do it," he says quickly. "You can take her. You two are . . . good people. I can see."

"You'll need to give up your parental rights," Noah says, tired of my beating around the bush.

"We'll be contacting a lawyer to figure out the exact process," I say, "but we wanted to make sure that, conceptually at least, you're okay with that. With giving her up."

"Sure." Ruben nods vigorously. "I'm okay. This is . . . the best thing for Micky." He grabs a pen from his pocket and scribbles a series of numbers on a napkin. "You get these papers and you fax me at Vista Azul, okay? I know a girl at the desk. Anything you need, I can do."

I don't know whether to rejoice or cry at how willing he is to sign away his daughter. Noah reaches for my hand, sensing my surge of emotion, but his attempt to offer comfort is undercut by an ugly flash of honesty from Ruben.

"Listen," he says, "maybe you can answer this question." He plays with the label on his beer, peeling at the edges with his thumb. "Did Jasmine try to get some money from me?"

For a second, I think that he is, in his sexy, broken English, accusing her of stealing. "Money?" I echo. "What do you mean? Did she take money from you?"

"Cómo se dice . . ." He frowns, trying to find the words. "Money for a child. When the law says a father has to pay the money."

"You mean child support?" When I finally realize what he's getting at, the urge to take a swing at him is strong. I can feel Noah, too, tensing up beside me. "As far as I know, Jasmine never sought any child support, no.

205

She knew you were out of the country. The courts couldn't really do anything."

"Okay," Ruben says, unable to disguise his satisfaction. "Good. Someday maybe I want to go back to the States. And I don't want the police to arrest me because of the child support." He tries to laugh, as if this last part were a joke.

I manage a weak smile in return, but all I can think is, *Hello, motive.* "You think Jasmine would've done that to you? Sue you for child support?"

"That girl?" He shakes his head, and in that moment I see traces of the spark between them, an admiration for Jasmine flashing in his golden eyes. "With that girl, a man can never know."

As I stand outside our hotel room fumbling with the key, Noah finally loses it. "Bastard," he mutters. "What a waste of oxygen."

"You mean Ruben?" I jerk the door open. "We don't have to like him."

"Good, 'cause I don't." Noah tosses our overnight bag onto the bed with a frown. "He's bad news."

"I'm just glad we found him. It's good to know there aren't rare genetic disorders in his family, just a little childhood asthma, right?" I glance around our hotel room, determining what exactly two hundred dollars has bought us for the evening. The walls and furniture are beachy in that airy pastel oh-look-a-painting-of-a-shell way, and the tan carpeting has obviously been selected for its ability to conceal sand. Not quite an advertisement in *Coastal Living,* but serviceable. I duck into the bathroom, making it a point to inspect the shower before I get too comfortable here.

"Look familiar?" Noah says from behind me.

The shower is a gleaming white with a turquoise curtain; it smells of bleach. I smile at the distorted image of my face in the chrome showerhead. "Never seen it before in my life," I tell him.

"You're still not showerin' here," Noah says, and as hot and sticky as I feel, I don't argue. "So what did Pam say when you called? Was she surprised?"

"I don't know. She said she was going to call Vargas. Told me to be careful."

"McCullough's gonna hear about this," Noah says with some satisfaction. "Ruben better watch his back."

"You don't look too worried on his behalf," I observe.

"Whatever's comin' to that guy, he deserves it."

"You're really advocating vigilante justice here?" His hatred for Ruben surprises me. Apart from getting a little too worked up about sports games, Noah isn't normally a violent or aggressive person. "What is it about this guy that eats you? The cheating? Because you know that's all McCullough cares about."

Noah stares at me as if insulted by the question. "The man's got no respect for women, that's what eats me! Did he really look that broken up about Jasmine to you? Hell no. Disposable as a paper towel, that's what she was to him. And Micky, he couldn't unload *her* fast enough." He sits on the edge of the bed and yanks a boot off. "McCullough might not be doin' it for the right reasons, but I think he'll get the outcome right."

I sit down next to him. "Look," I say, "Ruben's a self-absorbed asshole, sure, but so was Jasmine by all accounts. She made some bad choices, too."

"Yeah, well, she didn't deserve to die for them."

"You really think Ruben killed her? Her and Donna both?" I don't want to believe it, don't want to add another terrible thing to Micky's bloodline.

"Maybe," he says, less sure of himself now.

He removes his other boot and tosses it onto the carpet.

"But why? To avoid child support? Even if she was threatening him with it, I don't think he wanted back into the United States *that* badly."

"Drugs, then. She was in and out of the country seein' him, wasn't she? He coulda had her runnin' drugs."

"What, you think Ruben's a part of some big, scary cartel? That he used Jasmine as some kind of mule?"

"Could be."

I can't help but laugh. "I'm sorry. The floppy-haired dude who flirts with old-lady tourists? You *really* think that guy can stop thinking about his pecs long enough to participate in the international drug trade?"

"Those people come in all shapes and sizes, Charlie." Noah's jaw tightens. "Carmen used to tell me stories."

I bristle at the mention of his ex-wife.

"Carmen's law firm deals with all kinds of border stuff," Noah continues, as if I might find this "insider knowledge" impressive. "She's defended a lot of Americans who got caught smugglin' crap over the border, guys with some pretty shady Mexican contacts, and the thing Carmen always said —"

"I get it, I get it. Appearances can be

deceiving. One should not unfairly profile drug runners." The last thing I need right now is Noah's imparting nuggets of wisdom from his brilliant lawyer ex. I liked Carmen better before I knew the woman had brains, when I could picture her as some superficial housewife with no real interests beyond spending money.

Noah's too hung up on his wild Ruben theories to notice my momentary flicker of jealousy. "You have to admit," he muses aloud, "a bartender in a rich tourist town isn't a bad cover."

"I think you overestimate Ruben's intelligence."

"Yeah? Well, I think you *under*estimate it." He gives me a long look that seems to imply I was too flustered by Ruben's good looks to assess the situation properly. "He lied about Rohypnol, I can tell you that much. There's no way that guy doesn't know what Rohypnol is. He works at a *bar,* Charlie. That's where people use that stuff. I mean, what self-respectin' bartender doesn't keep an eye out for dudes slippin' Rohypnol and GHB in drinks? Unless he's the one druggin' girls himself."

"Maybe Rohypnol has a different name in Mexico. Anyway, I doubt he has to drug girls to get action."

"There are some scary-ass creeps out there, babe. You don't know what he's into."

I sigh. "Okay. Let's say you're right and he's this evil bartender rapist. Why would Jasmine end up with his pills? I mean, fifty tabs of Rohypnol? That's weird."

Noah considers this. "Maybe she found 'em, or was sellin' for him —"

"So he's a rapist *and* a drug lord?"

"— or she coulda bought 'em herself in Rocky Point. You can buy stuff in Mexican *farmacias* that will get you twenty years in prison in the States. She's white. They probably didn't search her car too hard when she crossed the border."

I smile as I heave myself to my feet. "Can I just point out that, beyond the fact that you have no coherent theory here, you're starting to sound as wildly speculative as — well, me?"

He groans. "Oh God, I *am*. You . . . you're a bad influence."

He watches me peel off my shirt and bra and root around our bag for articles of clothing not damp with sweat. The sight of my breasts, swollen from pregnancy, proves more than enough to clear his mind of Ruben. "Look at you," he says, grinning, "I swear those girls are gettin' bigger every day."

I cast him a suggestive smirk, suddenly ready to take advantage of our impromptu seaside vacation. "Get 'em while the getting's good. Our child-free days are numbered."

Noah slides slowly and purposefully off the bed. "Woman," he says, his voice low and husky as his lips brush my neck, "I'm gonna be all over you like wet on water."

The next morning, as we drive home from Rocky Point, I'm flying high. We found Ruben, we secured his promise to terminate parental rights, and I'm safe. The baby, too, is safe — enjoying a sugar rush, in fact, from the bottle of apple juice I just drank.

I've taken the wheel today, giving Noah a break from all the driving, and the combination of speed, sunshine, and endless open skies is intoxicating. I'm in control. For the first time, I allow myself to consider the possibility that my nightmare is just that: a nightmare, and not a premonition. My worst fear given form and shape in the darkness of my subconscious, but ultimately insubstantial, a shadow that disappears in light.

Ahead of us, the road shimmers in the heat, solid concrete made suddenly fluid. I want to believe in this desert magic, believe that my dreams are just another kind of mirage, nothing to be trusted.

There are virtually no other cars on the road, and I haven't been paying much attention to speed limits, so when I spot two cars pulled over on the shoulder far ahead, my first reaction is to slow down. Parked behind a silver, older-model Corolla is a white SUV with a green stripe and official lettering on its side. Definitely governmental, possibly a cop. I reduce my speed even further.

"Border Patrol," Noah says, just as I'm close enough to read the words on the vehicle for myself.

Wearing a hunter-green uniform, sunglasses, and heavy black boots, a Border Patrol officer stands by his SUV, speaking into what looks like a walkie-talkie. Only as we drive past do I see the man behind him, his brown arms pressed to the side of the vehicle, preparing to be searched. In the backseat of the Corolla, I swear I can make out a child's face. Staring. Frightened.

"What did that guy do?" I ask, disturbed by this scene. "Is he illegal?"

Noah shrugs. "Who the hell knows," he says. "They stop everyone." For a few seconds, the statement hangs in the air, uncomfortable and demonstrably false.

"Well," he says, shifting in his seat, "not *everyone.*"

I stare at my arm on the steering wheel, pale with just a few summer freckles and never more than fifteen minutes from a sunburn. I know who Border Patrol stops. I know it's not me.

PART IV
TUCSON, ARIZONA

ELEVEN

Noah is noticeably calmer after he's re-trieved his gun from Pam's place. I'm a bit surprised Pam doesn't question us about our encounter with Ruben, but she's on her way out when we catch her.

"Off to meet a friend," she says, which sounds emotionally healthy and not entirely true. I suspect the "friend" is connected to whatever private investigation she's con-ducting, but for once, I shut my mouth. The voice of my third-grade teacher, Ms. Man-cini, echoes in my head: *Keep your eyes on your own paper.*

I heed Ms. Mancini's advice. Today we're attending the Sonora Hope luncheon at some art museum, accepting the service award Donna's no longer here to claim, and that is nerve-racking enough. Why borrow trouble?

With half an hour to kill before the dreaded luncheon, Noah and I stop at a park near Pam's place and try to map out the coming week beneath a shady mesquite tree. He hasn't been to the gym in a few days, and all that restless energy is starting to seep out; he begins doing pull-ups from an overhanging branch.

"I say we head home after this Sonora Hope thing." He drops to the ground and runs a hand through the tree's hanging pods. "We can come back next weekend to visit Micky."

"I'm not going back to Sidalie yet." I loll against the trunk, sleepy in the heat. "Book a flight tomorrow if you want, deal with your business stuff. But I should stay. There's so much left to do."

He sighs. "I'm not gonna leave you alone here. What's so important it can't wait a few days?"

I pick up a fallen mesquite pod and crack it open, studying the seeds. "One, we need a lawyer, an Arizona lawyer, to draw up whatever documents Ruben has to sign. Two, I'd like to get into Jasmine's apartment and collect Micky's stuff. And three . . ." I toss the broken pod back on the ground. "Before we make any decisions about Micky, I want to look at some houses. Get a feel for what it might be like living here."

"Yeah?" After all his bold talk of relocation and adoption, Noah sounds unsure about taking such concrete steps. "You really think we can make a go of it in Tucson?"

"Maybe." I meet his eyes, finally ready to force a topic that we've been hitherto avoiding. "While we're figuring out the future, it might be time to sort out your financial plans. You've got a lot of money sitting around, Noah."

He kicks the dirt with the toe of his boot. "We've got plenty to do without worryin' over that."

"If you want to donate all of your inheritance, that's fine, I get it. But we need to budget accordingly."

"Budget?" He repeats the word like it's foreign to him, which I suppose it is. For years, he's had an accountant handling his company books, and Carmen must have dealt with their personal finances.

"What's your next move, career-wise?" I ask. "If we move to Tucson, are you going to work for someone else? Retire? Start a new company? Your inheritance is a factor in those decisions, that's all I'm saying."

"I haven't thought it through yet," he admits, scratching the back of his neck.

"You need a financial adviser."

"You mean *we* need one." He frowns. "We make this decision together. It's *our* money, you got that?"

"It was gifted to you," I protest. "It's yours."

"If we were married, it would belong to both of us."

I smile and close my eyes. Though not about to have the marriage talk with him, I can appreciate that it comes from a good place. "Have you thought about organizations you'd like to donate to? Any special causes you care about? Or should we just write Sonora Hope a big fat check and be done with it?"

Noah scoops up a plastic wrapper from the ground and throws it into a nearby trash can. "We're talkin' a whole lot of money here, Charlie," he says. "This would have to be a damn good lunch."

Tucked along the southeast corner of Saguaro National Park, the Desert Museum of Contemporary Art stands as a sophisticated architectural experiment, a collection of sharp corners and angles that appear starkly beautiful against the vast expanse of sky. Though its clean lines call to mind some fantastical, futuristic city, the building is situated on an empty patch of desert land well beyond the Tucson sprawl. I'm surprised that someone would choose to put a museum way out here, and yet, as we pull into the parking lot, I find the place reasonably busy.

"Do you *see* these cars?" Noah gapes. "Man."

He's right. The surrounding vehicles read like a checklist of luxury brands: BMW, Audi, Lexus, Land Rover. This is a side of southern Arizona we've not yet seen.

We follow a winding walkway past a series of square and rectangular water pools leading to the entrance. The front wall of the building consists mainly of tinted glass, and by the time we make it through the doors, I'm itching to know who operates this museum and where they get their funding.

The lobby contains a number of pieces mounted from the ceiling and displayed on platforms of varying heights, but its centerpiece is a massive loop of clay, pounded flat and rolled into a lopsided tube, with metal coils wrapped around it. On one side of the tube, a pile of feathers encircles a single upright bone. I glance at the accompanying placard, which identifies the artist as Jenni Rook and the title as *Consumption.* Noah stares at Rook's creation with an expression of both concern and bewilderment, and I grin, making a mental note never to take him to MoMA.

Sonora Hope is holding its presentation in the museum's event room, which consists of a small stage, several round dining tables with place cards, and an open space in the back for mingling. Presently, the room is half full with about forty men and women engaged in polite conversation.

"Didn't know this was black-tie," Noah grumbles, although none of the men in the room are actually wearing ties. Collared shirts, yes, and linen pants or polo shorts or seersucker bottoms of any length . . . but not ties. In his loose, many-pocketed shorts and rumpled button-down, Noah sticks out like a turkey in a den of peacocks.

Maybe people will think he's one of the museum's exhibiting artists. That could get him a pass.

Lunch itself is a tame affair, filled with remarks on the weather and discussions of summer homes in Montana and Colorado. We're seated with a pair of husband-and-wife cardiologists and some kind of entrepreneur with a much younger girlfriend. I know the drill. I ask our companions a dozen questions, look fascinated by their answers, good-naturedly tease one of the cardiologists about his golf game. We make it through our meal without any mention of Donna and my relationship to her.

I'm glad when Teresa King finally appears to kick off the donor lovefest. I want to get this over with. Teresa looks much as she did at Donna and Jasmine's funeral, except that her clothing choice today is a more upbeat shade of blue and her makeup can't quite conceal the circles beneath her eyes. She quickly introduces herself — though it's apparent from the abundant applause that everyone present is already familiar with her — and welcomes us all.

"As many of you know," Teresa begins, "my involvement with Sonora Hope is, first and foremost, a personal one. I'm Mexican by birth, American by luck. I spent my early years begging on the streets of Nogales, trying to help a young, single mother make ends meet."

Heads nod, and I gather Teresa's history is widely known and likely part of her persona, although it's news to me.

"My mother died before her twenty-fifth birthday, and I was sent to an orphanage at the age of eight," Teresa tells the sympathetic crowd. "For most Mexican children in this situation, opportunity ends here, as few families are willing to adopt an older child. But I was fortunate. I won the lottery, you might say, for I was adopted by a family, and not just any family — an *American* family." She pauses, gazing out at her audience. "Not a day passes that I don't marvel at my many blessings. Not a day passes that I don't wonder if I deserve them."

The room waits. For one tense second, Teresa appears lost, as if she's forgotten who she is and what she's doing, but she recovers quickly.

"I founded Sonora Hope in 2002 in memory of my mother, Jimena Ríos, who fought hard to raise and protect her children. Today, as we approach our organization's ten-year anniversary, I'm proud to report that we have helped hundreds of women — women just like my mother — to become more educated, more enterprising, more financially self-sufficient." She stops speaking as a round of enthusiastic applause breaks out, and gives us all a tired, hollow smile until it dies down. "The fantastic thing about this organization is the positive way that it affects everyone involved, both recipients *and* donors. Today we celebrate the people who have made Sonora Hope a success and remember that giving is never a one-way street."

As she introduces the first speaker, a Nogales woman named Marilena, I overhear the male half of the cardiologists whispering. "A little off her game today, don't you think?"

"It's Donna," his wife responds in a low voice. "The woman who got murdered, remember? Teresa's a wreck about it. They were pretty close."

I can't help but wonder what "pretty close" might mean. Was Donna's admiration for this woman more than just the silly crush Pam described? Is there some part of that story that Pam left out, one that justifies her hostility toward Teresa? I glance at Noah, but he's immersed in the words of this Marilena character, showing no signs of having heard the people behind us.

Short and squat, with a lean and angular face, Marilena is a plain woman with one outstanding feature: a drooping left eye that never blinks. From the story she tells, she must be about my age, but her hair is streaked with gray, her skin deeply creased around the eyes and forehead. It comes as no surprise that life has prematurely aged her. In slow, choppy sentences, Marilena details a life of abuse with a husband who once beat her so badly that she subsequently lost all vision in her left eye. She describes fleeing with her four children, finding themselves homeless, and eventually taking refuge in the garbage dump of Tirabichi, joining a community of scavengers that earned their living by selling recyclable trash.

Ordinarily, listening to some foreigner fight her way through English would grate on my nerves, yet somehow Marilena's determined struggle to conquer the language becomes heroic, a metaphor for her life in this hardscrabble border town. By the time she reaches the Magical Intervention by a Sonora Hope Employee part of her saga, my lip is quivering and my arms are wrapped around my own belly, hugging my unborn daughter. Marilena smiles proudly as she tells the roomful of potential benefactors about the small hotel that she now runs, four rooms to rent plus a room for her and her children.

"I am so grateful to the people like you," she says, pressing her hands together as if in prayer. "Finally, we have this roof on our head."

Noah and I exchange agonized glances, and I know that he would, in this moment, gladly give every last penny of his inheritance to needy Mexican women. Always a skeptic, I find myself torn. I can feel my defenses going up; I want to dismiss Marilena's story as fake, something concocted to tug on the heartstrings of donors. It's too awful to accept as someone else's reality — and I haven't exactly led a life of sunshine and rainbows myself. Yet while my father struggled for years with alcoholism and its resulting money problems, he certainly didn't beat me. And when I gave my cheating husband the boot, I still had a home, a career to support my son and myself. I did not have to live, quite literally, amongst the trash.

This woman has to be lying, I think. And yet there is something in Marilena's thin face, the kind of fierceness and fortitude that only comes with desperate circumstances. She's a survivor. It's a relief when she finally leaves the stage and Teresa introduces the next speaker, an employee of Sonora Hope named Albert Mangusson.

Already perilously close to bawling, I don't actually pay much attention to Albert's speech. Instead, I distract myself by discreetly surveying my fellow audience members and trying to guess what lucrative industries they work in. Doctor, lawyer, sales and marketing, something tech-based — it's far easier to assign imaginary professions than listen to more horror stories of inequity, and Albert makes my quest to ignore him immeasurably easier with his low, lilting tone. He's a lanky, balding redhead, inoffensive and utterly forgettable, and I have effectively blocked him from my thoughts until, for reasons I don't hear, he speaks my mother's name.

I look up, but he seems to be talking about something else now, the void his work at Sonora Hope filled after a difficult divorce, the support he drew from his phenomenal coworkers. Albert's experiences are supposed to be inspiring, and they probably are, but I just want to get out of here, to end the emotional onslaught.

I already know how bad this world is, I want to tell them. *I lost my son to it.*

I pull on Noah's sleeve. "What was that he said before about Donna?"

"Just that they were friends," Noah whispers, irritated by my interruption.

When I finally accept the service award on my mother's behalf, it's anticlimactic, Teresa's praise a rehash of what I heard at the funeral. Standing in front of the crowd and being identified in public as Donna's daughter is not the revelation I was expecting. It feels dishonest, like I'm lying to them all.

Shiny plaque in hand, I return to the table no different, no closer to understanding who my mother was and why she made the choices she did.

After the ceremony has ended and everyone is hobnobbing, glasses of champagne in hand, I scan the crowd for Albert Mangusson. Noah, unabashed by his wrinkled attire, has joined the ring of Teresa devotees, and I'm glad. I want to ask Albert about my mother, want to learn about this other side of her that came out in her work, and for reasons I can't explain, I don't want Noah to be part of this conversation.

Albert is not, as it happens, hard to locate. He stands alone in a corner, nibbling on a pastry as clumps of stylish people ignore him. He doesn't look self-conscious or in any way lonely, and I have the sense that he's used to being invisible, drifting amongst people without ever really being seen. When he's finished with his dessert, he moves toward the door, casting a final glance back at the circle around Teresa before divining that his presence is unnecessary. I scramble into the lobby after him.

"Mr. Mangusson!" My voice echoes slightly in the space.

He stops walking and turns around, spots me bounding across the room toward him with all the grace and elegance of a loping panda. Despite the short distance, I'm a

229

little winded when I reach him.

"I was wondering if you had a minute."

"I have several minutes," he says. "Sit down, please." He touches my elbow and urges me toward a bench. We sit on opposite ends, and I find myself suddenly shy. This is the first time I've discussed my mother without using Micky as my shield.

"I just . . . wanted to talk to you about Donna, if that's okay. Since you two were friends."

"Of course, of course." Albert's head bobs up and down a little too vigorously. "Wow. So you're Charlotte." For a few seconds we sit staring stupidly at each other, and then he leans forward and gives me an awkward hug. "I'm so glad to meet you."

Somehow the fact that he knows my name — and so did Pam, so did Teresa — is more than I can bear. I find myself crying, a rush of salty, silent tears that slide down my cheeks and into my shaky fingers. Albert hurries over to the museum's ticketing desk and retrieves a tissue for me. For a moment, his kindness only makes me cry harder.

"I'm sorry," I mumble, wiping at my face. "I don't mean to dump on you."

"No, no, no," he protests. "You must be . . . going through a lot right now." He puts a reassuring hand on my shoulder, and

I can see that he must be good at his job, able to respond with compassion when the situation calls for it, gentle enough to win the trust of even the most hardened woman. "Please," Albert says, "ask me anything you want about Donna. She would've been so happy to have you here."

Through my tears, I give a short, dry laugh. "Somehow I doubt that."

"Why's that?" He looks genuinely puzzled.

"It's pretty clear she didn't want me around. She could've reached out to me at any time, and she didn't."

Albert doesn't immediately reply, but the look on his face says that he is weighing his words carefully. "I'm not sure how much you know about your mother's past," he says at last. "But it was an ugly one. From what she's told me, there were a lot of years she wasn't fit to speak to you. Maybe it's a gift she didn't."

I pick at my cuticle. "I'm not saying I wanted her around. I'm just saying, you know, she *wasn't*. So, pardon me for saying so, but I don't think she'd care that I'm here now."

Albert nods with the empathetic-yet-detached expression of a therapist. "I under-stand why you'd feel that way. My sense of things — and this is just from conversations with Donna, I don't pretend to know her mind — but my sense was that she was waiting for you to make the first move."

"Well, that's just . . . *cowardly.*" I spit out the word with more anger than I intended.

"I guess it is." He smiles at me, a little sad. "Donna never had much in the way of self-esteem. I didn't know her when she was using, so it always seemed strange, this kind, capable woman with all that self-doubt. I don't think she ever forgave herself for all the years she lost."

"Years she *wasted.*"

"Yes," he agrees, "years she wasted. Donna knew her good intentions weren't enough to fix things. She tried, you know, but . . . I think she took it pretty hard when you went to live with your grandmother."

I stare at Albert's watery blue eyes, uncomprehending.

"After your dad passed," he says, uncertain, as if he might've mixed up the details. "When she tried to get custody of you."

I'm about to tell him that he's wrong, that Donna wasn't in touch with anyone in our family, that she didn't even know about my dad's death, but I stop. Because how would Albert know about my father's death and my going to live with Grandma . . . unless Donna told him? The full significance of what he's just said hits me, alters everything I thought I knew about Donna DeRossi, that phantom of my childhood.

"She *knew* about that?" I whisper. "Donna knew my dad died?"

Albert hesitates, as if this question somehow puts him in an indelicate position. "Listen, Charlotte," he says slowly, "I don't know exactly what your family told you, and it's certainly not my place to —"

"Please," I say. "I'm sorry to put you in the middle of this, but whatever you know about my mother, I need to hear it."

Albert dabs at his forehead with his sleeve, trying to remove the sudden beads of perspiration that have appeared. Gone is that calm, reassuring exterior. Now he looks about as comfortable as a polar bear in a Florida zoo. "I only know what Donna told me," he cautions me, "but her story was that after your dad passed away . . . Jim? Was that your dad's name?"

I nod.

"Right. So after Jim died, Donna decided that she would take you. She was having a sober period and thought she could manage you. Jasmine was two, maybe three back then? And your mom thought it would be nice for her to have a big sister. Thought you all could be a family."

"I don't understand," I say. "No one ever told me about this. No one even mentioned her."

"I guess when Donna discussed the idea with her sister, it didn't go over too well."

I think of my aunt Suzie, her casually informing me of my mother's death. *You and me both know Donna was a piece of shit,* she told me. *You don't owe her jack.* It's not hard to imagine that Suzie would have objected, probably strenuously, to my mother's attempting to get custody of me. And who could blame her?

"So, Suzie told her to buzz off, and that was it?" I ask.

Albert seems wrongly concerned that I'll be furious with Suzie over this. "Your aunt had a lot of valid points," he says quickly. "She was worried about Donna's sobriety, how long it would last. And, you know, she was right. Donna started using again within the year. It took her a long time to really, finally get clean."

"Oh, I know I wasn't missing out," I assure him. "Suzie was looking out for me. I owe her one."

"Right," he says, relieved. "Anyway, I think that's why your mom didn't contact you. Her sister convinced her that you were better off if she stayed away."

"I can't believe she told you all this," I say. My gaze wanders upward and settles somewhere in the rafters above us.

"We were good friends," Albert says softly. "She was really there for me after my divorce. And I think the nature of our work made it easy to . . . share things. We saw problems so much worse than our own." He swallows, permitting himself a moment of his own grief. "I'll miss her every day, I really will. And it's not just a personal loss. The whole organization is feeling this. Earlier this summer, one of our girls in Nogales killed herself, and now we lose Donna. It's just . . . getting hard to fight the good fight. Even Teresa's struggling."

I feel like a jerk now, blubbering about my relationship with some woman I never even knew when the man across from me has just lost a very real and valued friend. "I'm sorry," I tell him. "I hope . . . Sonora Hope has resources for you. You must absorb so much stress on the job."

"I wouldn't trade it." He stands up from the bench, signaling that our conversation has come to an end. "Listen, it was great to meet you. I hope I didn't say anything today to cause problems."

"No." I spread my legs in an unladylike squat and rise to my feet. "I appreciate your honesty. You . . . clarified some things for me."

He gives me a business card and then leans in for a one-armed hug. "Take care, Charlotte. And if you have any questions, don't hesitate to call."

I'm not asleep, not even close to dreaming, but as he wraps his arm around me, I feel something crackle through me. Heat. My skin blazing. It hurts to swallow. There's a fire in my throat, a hot coal searing me from the inside. My voice burns away. I look up at Albert, stricken, but his face is distracted, his mind elsewhere. When he moves away from me, the pain subsides.

It's a message, I think, but not from Albert.

I grab his sleeve before he can get away. "Albert? Do you have any kids?"

"A ten-year-old," he says. "I was just going to call him, actually."

I remember that Albert is divorced. "I guess he's with his mom right now?"

"Yeah. He was supposed to come hear me speak today, but . . . he's not feeling well. A cold or something. At least that's what his mother told me." He shrugs, but I can see his sadness at the idea his son may have blown him off. "Maybe he just wanted out."

"Oh, no." My skin has cooled now, the

fire in my throat subsided. "I think he's really sick."

Albert smiles. "Maybe." He takes his phone from his pocket and prepares to dial his son. "His mom has never been a fan of doctors."

"You should take him," I say, "just to be on the safe side. I hear strep throat's been going around."

Back in the event room, I find Noah still hanging with the Teresa crowd. Although people have arranged themselves around her, Teresa herself says little, allowing her admirers to do all the talking. She smiles and manages to laugh when appropriate, but I can see what Albert was saying about her struggling. There's a vagueness in the way she listens, and her hands flutter about her face and hair, indecisive, searching for a place to land.

When she spots me, she abandons her chattering pack of fans and grasps me by the arm. "How's Micky?" she asks. I imagine Teresa at eight, a scrawny, dark-eyed orphan grappling with her mother's death, and I understand why her thoughts are now with this little girl.

"Holding up," I say. "Micky's holding up."

Behind her, the well-dressed cluster of

philanthropists watches us, trying to figure out why Teresa has broken ranks to speak with me. At their rear, Noah lifts his hand in greeting, the wart on an otherwise designer crew.

"I've been thinking we could start a memorial fund," Teresa says in a rush. "Something in Donna's name, but the proceeds would go to Micky. Would that be all right with you?" She glances at my stomach. "Raising a child is so expensive, and Donna was one of our own. I'd like to help."

If I were in a different sort of mood, I might laugh at the absurdity of one offering financial assistance to a couple with a considerable fortune languishing in a Swiss bank account.

"Money's not a problem," I tell her, "but I certainly do appreciate the thought."

I wave Noah over and nudge him firmly toward the door, too drained by my conversation with Albert to engage in social niceties any longer. My eyes are probably still pink and puffy from my unexpected sob session, and I can feel a headache moving in, dark and menacing, like the clouds of an oncoming monsoon.

Who were you, Donna? I want to ask. *Were you good or were you bad? A saint or sinner?*

These are the wrong questions, I know, too reductive, too binary to encapsulate a human being. I should stick to facts, ask only that which has a clear answer.

Who killed you?

TWELVE

On Monday morning, I set out to accomplish the task I most dread: clearing out Jasmine's apartment.

It needs to be done, of course. Investigators have finished their work inside, and now someone must take charge, gather Micky's toys and clothes and dispose of Jasmine's belongings. These are the duties that normally fall to family members, I reason, and technically that's what I am. I can't imagine one of Jasmine's friends — histrionic Serena or inarticulate Bree — doing the job. Pam certainly can't be bothered.

And yet, as I stand outside the Desert Village Apartments, I feel a kind of panic rising up in my throat at the prospect of seeing the place where my sister lived and died. Perhaps I shouldn't have come alone, shouldn't have left Noah back at the hotel discussing a rather dubious workman's comp claim with Sharlene. When I grabbed the car keys and told him I was leaving, I expected opposition. Instead, he gave me a distracted thumbs-up. Either he's starting to doubt the validity of my dream, or work has him too frazzled to think straight.

I wander along the winding paths between buildings, frowning at this first glimpse into Micky's upbringing. Desert Village consists of about a dozen buildings, each a dismal shade of yellow-brown. Situated across from a money-wiring service and a checks-for-cash establishment, Jasmine's home was chosen, safe to say, for its low rent and proximity to a bus stop.

The grounds, from what I can make out, are bare-bones. Scraggly trees protrude from red gravel; soda cans and an empty bag of potato chips litter the walkways. At the center of the complex, a tall black fence encircles the pool. The bars of the fence and the lock on its gate give the whole swimming area a dishearteningly jail-like appearance. The pool itself is empty except for a young mother with a child in floaties.

On one of the buildings I spot a sign marked LEASING OFFICE, so I follow the trail of cigarette butts to its door. I've been a little worried that the staff here will turn me away without proof of my relationship to Jasmine, but I needn't have worried. The thickset, heavily lipsticked woman manning the office is only too thrilled to grant me access to Jasmine's place.

"Thank God you came." She produces the key so fast I suspect it's been there on her desk awhile, waiting for any takers. "We didn't know who to call. Only emergency contact Miss Cassell had on her application was her mom, and of course, she's dead, too." She blinks, as if it is belatedly occurring to her that this is not the most sensitive of comments. "It's terrible," she adds. "I'm real sorry for your loss."

"I didn't really know Jasmine," I confess, not wishing to be the recipient of any unearned sympathy. "But she's a half sister, so I guess I should take care of this."

"Somebody has to. Half sister's good enough for me." Realizing I'm not some heartbroken relative, the woman assumes a conspiratorial tone. "This place has been crazy since it all went down. It's not good for business, you know, all those cops."

"I bet." This is not a population that would find a strong police presence comforting. "Are they asking a lot of questions?"

"Oh, yes. They knocked on all the doors, went around leaving little cards. Here at the office, they've been asking about some of the residents, trying to get personal information." She presses her brightly colored lips together in disapproval. "Two people dead, and I don't think they have a clue."

"Somebody must have heard something," I say.

"You'd think, right? But Miss Cassell's building has three vacant units. Andrew Dakin, he's in eight oh six, and he wasn't even home that Saturday. He spends weekends with his girlfriend in building two. Probably about time for them to get married, but you know how men are." She rolls her eyes. "The other couple in building eight, the Delgados, they go to bed early. Mrs. Delgado told me she heard gunshots and screaming at maybe half past eleven — her husband slept right through it, of course — but she thought it was just a video game."

"Really?" I can't conceal my skepticism. "Mrs. Delgado couldn't tell the difference between real screaming and a video game?"

"You can't blame her," Office Lady tells me. "The kids were having a big party over at the pool that night. They scream their damn heads off, those fools. And they play their music so loud, my God, it's a wonder any one of 'em still has their hearing."

"You don't get complaints?"

"The sign clearly says the pool is closed after ten," the woman says, not actually answering my question. "But you know teenagers. They jump the fence. What are you gonna do?" She throws up her hands as if to indicate her complete helplessness in the matter. "They set off firecrackers, too, sometimes."

"Well . . ." I retreat a few steps. "I guess all that explains how nobody heard anything. Thanks again for the key."

"Oh, it's no problem. I'm just so glad you're here. When the cops left the other day and nobody showed up to claim anything, I was afraid *we* were gonna get stuck with that mess."

"Is it dirty?" I ask, and she gives a short, disbelieving laugh.

"You serious? The police don't clean up for you when somebody dies, ma'am. That's on the families. On *you.*" She looks me over, assessing my readiness for this job. "Honestly," she tells me, not unkindly, "you're better off hiring a cleaner before you ever set foot in there."

My fist tightens around the key. I wrote freelance articles for a crime magazine back in my twenties, and yet it never occurred to me that after the CSI teams leave, the grim residue of death remains someone else's problem.

"Have you been inside?" I ask.

"No," she replies, "but I heard a couple detectives talking one day on my break. They said it was a bad, bad scene. I just praise God that Miss Cassell's little girl didn't get harmed. Poor baby."

At this mention of Micky, I feel my resolve crystallizing. I've come all the way out here. I can't leave without at least grabbing some of her clothes, some items from her previous life that she can hang on to when everything else is changing.

"What number is the apartment?"

"It's eight oh two," the woman informs me as I back out the door. "Ground floor, over by the pool. Miss Cassell's paid up through the end of the month, which means you've got until the thirty-first to clear out. Otherwise, *someone's* gotta pay for September."

I make some noise of acknowledgment and weave around to the pool area. The sky has darkened a shade since I entered the office. Perhaps we're in for another storm.

Apartment 802 has no distinguishing features, nothing on the exterior that hints at the dark events that occurred inside. I place my key inside the lock, feel it resist my push at first, then reluctantly click open.

The moment I step inside, I'm met with a nauseating mixture of heat and stink. The stench startles me, since Jasmine's and Donna's bodies were discovered relatively quickly, but of course there must have been blood. A lot of blood. That wouldn't age well. To exacerbate matters, whoever exited the apartment last turned off the air-conditioning, a cost- or energy-saving measure that left any lingering body fluids to vaporize in the high temperatures.

I cover my nose and mouth and gingerly observe my surroundings.

Although it's dim inside, I can make out a few familiar details, images from my dream of Micky that give me goose bumps. Barbies and crayons scattered about. A mirror with a shiny, sun-shaped metal frame. And on the cheap vinyl flooring, small bloody tracks.

I fumble for the light switch, afraid to see what this room holds but more afraid of things I can't see. The bulb overhead hums and flickers once before illuminating the scene.

Blood. Mostly just a lot of blood, dried into a rusty brown crust that seems to be flaking in places. With the exception of Micky's little footprints, the ghastly details are confined to the dining area. A sense of the unreal settles over me. If it weren't for the ungodly odor, I could disengage completely, forget that two living, breathing women died in this space.

I glance down at Micky's tracks, following them with my eyes as I try to retrace her movements. The trail seems to originate from a large pool of blood, long congealed, to the left of the dining table. A series of smeary marks leads to another sizable blob on the wall nearby. I note four long streaks clawing at the floor.

Fingers, I think. *Jasmine's fingers.*

Pam told me that Jasmine got shot in the chest several times. She must have leaned against the wall and left that big stain before dragging herself — or collapsing, from loss of blood — to the ground where Micky found her. It may not have taken Jasmine long to lose consciousness, but for at least a couple minutes, she had to have known that she was dying. Had to have seen who killed her.

I return to my study of Micky's footprints, trying to hold back a rising feeling of despair. Her bloody tracks don't travel in a single, obvious trail the way they did in my dream; they're chaotic, moving in circles, smeared in one place as if Micky's foot slipped. This child was frantic. She found her mother and didn't know where to go, what to do.

And Donna?

My eyes venture to the other side of the table, settling on a high-backed chair in the corner that Micky's prints appear to avoid. Spatter. Tiny white chips. Pink flecks.

No wonder Micky didn't approach her grandmother. I, too, keep my distance.

Suddenly desperate for fresh air, I hurry out of the apartment, leaving the door ajar behind me. I no longer feel the heat, am only vaguely aware of laughter coming from a neighboring building's stairwell. I just want air, clean air. Want to fill my lungs with molecules not tainted by death.

I should feel something, anything, about the gruesome scene I've just come from, but my mind skips right over Donna and Jasmine, just keeps going back to Micky. Imagining what she saw that night. Wondering how I can possibly take on a child with so many problems.

Donna and Jasmine couldn't have been dead for long when Micky found them, not if she was tracking footprints everywhere. I don't know exactly how fast blood coagulates on vinyl, but I'm guessing Micky discovered them within the hour, and probably sooner. Perhaps she heard the gunshots her neighbors didn't. Perhaps she heard her mother screaming, arguing with her killer.

Perhaps she lay huddled in bed, waiting for it all to pass.

The more I think about it, the more frightened I am by what Micky may have overheard. I know that she's been questioned by police psychologists and she's seeing some sort of therapist, so I've assumed that she knows nothing of real value. But would she tell the police if she did? Jasmine taught her to lie and omit details of Ruben. What other secrets might the child choose to keep?

"Hey!"

A pale blond boy of eleven or twelve peers down from the second floor of building seven. His friend joins him and both stare at me.

"You going in there?" the blond boy calls. "That's where those ladies died!"

His friend hits him in the chest. "Dude. She's probably, like, *related* to them. Or she's a detective or something."

"She's not a detective," the blond boy scoffs. "Look, the yellow tape is down. That means all the detectives finally left. Besides, she's preggers."

"She could still be a detective," his friend retorts. "Some of them wear regular clothes to try and fool you."

The blond kid has already lost interest in

me. "We should go in," he says, nudging his buddy. "Look, the door's open. I dare you. I dare you to go in."

"No way."

"Wuss. I'll give you five dollars."

"Yeah, right. *You* do it."

"For five dollars? Fine."

As the two negotiate the terms of the dare, I duck back inside, taking care to lock the door behind me. It's not the most comforting sensation, being locked in with all this gore, but I don't want some stupid kid to wander in and be traumatized for life.

Find Micky's room, I tell myself, *then get the hell out.*

As it happens, the task is not so simple. The apartment has only one bedroom, one dresser that Jasmine and Micky apparently shared. Either the investigative team pulled all the clothing out and then stuffed it back in or Jasmine was the laziest laundress imaginable, because her items are mixed indiscriminately with her daughter's. My fingers sift through Jasmine's frilly bras, silk panties, and tiny camis to locate a couple pairs of Micky's shorts, her Disney princess nightgown, and an orange tank top.

I toss these items into a hamper and move on to the next drawer, trying not to gag. Though I'm breathing through my mouth to avoid the putrid smell, I swear I can still *taste* it, old blood souring the air.

When I've grabbed enough little-girl clothing to fill the basket, I search for keepsakes that Micky might like to have. A box of polished stones that she's apparently been collecting, a dog-eared copy of *The Three Little Javelinas,* a gold bracelet engraved with the word "Michaela." And then I dive into the photographs. Jasmine isn't much for frames, but her bedside table is cluttered with glossy prints, like someone who hasn't yet joined the digital age. I sift through them — her and McCullough, mainly, and a bunch of friends, but I eventually find a couple shots of her and Micky. I tuck them into an old envelope for safekeeping and stuff them into my pocket. I should go. Drop off Micky's clothes with Vonda and call a cleaning service, something that specializes in biohazards, to deal with this place.

Yet I don't leave. In my vision, I followed Micky's footprints to the patio, found her hiding outside. What's out there?

I glance back at Jasmine's living area, past the chair and couch to the sliding doors. Find myself unlatching the glass door and tugging on the handle. The panel glides noisily back, and I step onto the patio.

I'm expecting desert, the indigo void I saw when I dreamed of Micky. Jagged lines of distant mountains, weedy plant life swaying as if in an aquarium. Instead, I find a tiny concrete area enclosed by an adobe wall about four feet high. The wall serves no purpose I can see other than to block out an ugly view: storage sheds that Desert Village must rent out, and a highway underpass.

Jasmine has at least made some effort with this patio. Wind chimes hang from the wall, adding an occasional jingle to the highway clamor, and a potted money tree occupies one corner, though it's starting to look a bit droopy. A blue-and-white-striped lawn chair faces the wall. I sit down, letting the noise of the road wash over me. I imagine that Jasmine liked it out here.

Her life couldn't have been an easy one. Low-level jobs, government assistance, a string of relationships that flamed out, no transportation beyond friends with cars and unreliable city buses, an accidental child with a man she loved but could never have. At twenty-seven, Jasmine didn't even have her own bedroom. She must have wanted more, so much more, but this was what she got, all she'll ever get.

This apartment should've been her safe

place, not her death site.

And now a memory tickles my brain, something left undone. The bathroom. I need to check the bathroom here, to make sure it isn't the one. I start to heave myself off the chair and then pause midway up.

Through the open door behind me, I hear something.

A thumping, followed by a male voice much too deep to belong to one of the boys on the stairwell. "Goddamn it!" he shouts, and I'm fairly sure someone has just tripped over the laundry basket I left by the front door.

Someone in the apartment. Someone with a key.

There must be a hundred legitimate reasons for a person to be rummaging through Jasmine's apartment, and yet I can't think of a single one. The investigators had a week to pry this place apart. Why would they be back? And from the way the woman in the leasing office was talking, the management wouldn't set foot in this place, not if they didn't have to.

I slump deep into the chair, afraid to move, afraid to draw attention to myself. Any minute the man in the apartment will notice the door to the patio cracked open, and then what?

My first thought is McCullough. Jasmine might've given him a key. But why would he be prowling around her apartment? What could he possibly have left here that's so valuable it justifies his returning to his girlfriend's grisly death site? And whatever it is, wouldn't the cops have already found it?

The stranger is definitely looking for *something.* I hear the sounds of drawers and cabinets being slammed, pots and pans banging around. What might Jasmine have hidden in her kitchen? Could this guy be searching for the Rohypnol that the TPD confiscated? I have zero desire to encounter some sketchy drug contact of Jasmine's, especially not the kind who specializes in rape drugs.

I stagger to my feet. Make a split-second calculation about personal safety and then hurl my pregnant self over the four-foot patio wall. Not the most graceful maneuver, and I land with a painful thud that pleases neither me nor the baby. Still, it beats confronting a man who may or may not have murdered my mother and sister.

I drag myself around to the side of the building and stand, back pressed to the wall, contemplating my next move. I want to know who the hell is in that apartment.

I circle around front and park myself near the pool, where I have a good view of the door to apartment 802 and enough witnesses to assure my safety. After about twenty minutes of waiting around, my nerves give way to hunger and I succumb to the allure of a nearby vending machine. Beneath the envelope of Micky and Jasmine photos, I discover a crumpled dollar bill in my pocket. I'm trying to smooth it out on the corner of the machine, periodically glancing over at Jasmine's door, when someone appears beside me. I recoil, arm flying out across my chest in a defensive posture.

Sanchez.

I almost don't recognize him in his T-shirt and running shorts. He looks decidedly uncoplike, so sweaty and casual, I think for a moment that he might live here. But the TPD can't pay *that* badly.

"Sorry to surprise you," he says with his easy smile. "Just thought I'd say hello. What are you doing in these parts?"

I try to relax, to return his friendly smile, but all I can think is, *Why is he here? Is he the one? How did he sneak up on me like that?*

"I'm here to pick up clothes for Micky," I

say. The wrinkled dollar bill flutters in my hand.

"Ahh." He breaks out his wallet and hands me a crisp dollar for the vending machine. "That was *you* with the laundry basket. You left the back door cracked, too."

"Right." So it was him. "I left for a little bit. I was going to come back." I have no idea how to convincingly explain why I left or what I've been doing the past twenty minutes. Thankfully, Sanchez doesn't ask. I purchase some chips, watch the bag drop down.

"Word of advice," Sanchez says, bending down to retrieve my snack, "don't leave that place unlocked. Not for any amount of time. You got a lot of curious people in the surrounding apartments, people who would love to see what's inside. Out of respect to your sister, and Donna, too . . . you won't let them in, right?"

"I'll be more careful." I wait, wondering if he'll offer an explanation for his presence, tell me what he was looking for in Jasmine's place, but he provides nothing more than a sympathetic face.

"I'm real sorry you had to go in there." He lays a hand on my shoulder. "It's not for the faint of heart."

His touch makes my skin crawl. "Oh, I

wouldn't say I'm faint of heart."

"Obviously not. You didn't even turn on the air-conditioning."

I stuff my tattered dollar back in my pocket, adjusting the envelope to make sure the pictures don't get crushed. Sanchez glances at the envelope, and though his smile doesn't change, I can feel his curiosity boring into me like a drill.

"You find something?"

"Just a few pictures. They're not for me."

Though his eyes widen, Sanchez doesn't get to question me further. From across the grounds, a girl calls out his name in a high-pitched squeal. "Robby!"

He swears under his breath as Jasmine's frenemy from the funeral, Serena, comes scampering toward us. I forgot that she lives here, too.

"Hey, *cabrón.*" She links elbows with Sanchez, gives him a cheeky smile. In a bikini top and very short cut-off jeans, she's cute, but not gorgeous. Certainly no Jasmine. "Is Mac with you? That dude keeps turning up on my doorstep wanting to talk. He's, like, stalking me or something." Judging by her self-satisfied smirk, McCullough's attention isn't exactly unwelcome.

Sanchez edges away from her. "He's not here."

"No? Then where's he at?"

"I don't know. We're partners, not Siamese twins."

Serena giggles. "You might as well be attached." There is something ugly in her smile, the kind of glee one sees in a child burning ants or pulling the legs from a spider. "You boys do a lot together, after all."

Sanchez turns red. "Watch it," he says, and I gather that there's more to her little jab than meets the eye.

"I better go grab Micky's clothes," I murmur to no one in particular. "Catch you later."

THIRTEEN

Noah greets me in the lobby of our hotel like a grateful princess being rescued from a tower. He's a bit of a stress case. As he fills me in on the workman's comp claim that has monopolized his morning, I can't help remembering the relaxed, easygoing guy I fell in love with back in Louisiana. What happened to that man? Was he just some transitional, post-divorce version of Noah I'll never see again?

"Are you *really* going to be able to move to Tucson?" I ask, handing him the sandwich I bought while out. "You're so wrapped up in this company, hon. Can you honestly walk away?"

The question makes him squirm. "We can make it work," he insists. "I could do two weeks here, two weeks there. Maybe if I kept an apartment in Sidalie —"

"Whoa, *what*?" This is a far cry from the drop-everything-and-move plan that he started with. "I know we both want to help Micky, but let's not bite off more than we can chew. I'm not looking for a half-time dad, Noah."

His cheek twitches, and I know that I've hit a nerve. "You're right." He peels back the wrapper from his sandwich, checking the contents. "We'll . . . figure it out." It's hardly a solution, but if he wants to sweep the matter under the rug for now, I'll let him. I don't have the energy for conflict.

We sit down in the lounge, and while Noah devours his sandwich, I tell him about Jasmine's apartment, using many colorful adjectives and similes to describe the smell. "Just what I wanna hear while eatin'," he says, suitably grossed out. He's less impressed by what I consider to be the climax of the tale: my run-in with Sanchez.

"There are a lotta reasons he could've been there," Noah points out. "He's friends with McCullough. Maybe he was helpin' the guy out, pickin' up his stuff so McCullough didn't have to go in."

"Sanchez was searching the kitchen," I say. "What would McCullough have left in the kitchen that he wanted back so badly?"

Noah shrugs. "Alcohol, an iPod? Who knows? But it could be perfectly legit."

"You just don't think Sanchez is sketchy."

"No, I don't. He seemed like a nice guy." He pauses. "Did you get a look at Jasmine's bathroom?"

"It's not the one in my dream."

"Good," he says. "And how was the rest of your day?"

I check items off on my fingers. "Dropped Micky's clothes off with Vonda, called a cleaning team to deal with Jasmine's apartment, and I've got an agent showing us houses tomorrow morning."

"How about the adoption lawyer?"

"Haven't looked into it yet." And I'm not sure it's worth my time if Noah's suddenly having doubts about moving.

"You know who could help with adoption stuff? Teresa King."

"Teresa?" I scoff. "Come on. I know you think she's some kind of all-powerful goddess, but —"

"Her husband is the CEO of an international adoption agency," Noah says.

"Oh."

"I'm guessin' they have a few lawyers on staff." He wipes his hands on his jeans. "She could probably recommend somebody."

"Oh," I say again. "I'll call her, then."

"I have a better idea," Noah tells me. "We'll drive over. You can see where your mom was workin' all these years."

I'm about to tell him that she was my *mother,* not my *mom,* and I don't really care about the details of her life, personal or professional, but something stops me. I remember what Albert told me yesterday, that Donna tried to get custody of me all those years ago. Tried in her totally insufficient way, but tried nevertheless. I can't be mad at Donna forever. Not when I'm about to have a daughter of my own.

"Okay," I say. "Let's go."

Sonora Hope has a modest suite in an office park that also houses a podiatrist, a hypnotherapist, and an optician. No sooner have I parked the car than Noah's phone begins to ring. He glances at the screen and sighs.

"It's Cristina. I better take this."

I make a face. Though Carmen's sister is a very competent landscape designer as far as I can tell, she's high maintenance and unfailingly rude to me.

"You don't *have* to answer," I say.

Noah closes his eyes. "If I don't, she'll suck Sharlene into all her drama, and you know what happens once the two of them get goin'."

I bite the inside of my cheek. "Fine. I'll leave you to it. Come find me when you're off the phone."

I'm not holding my breath on his turning up anytime soon. Cristina's calls tend to be long rants that require inspirational athletic-coach-type speeches from Noah. It's a semi-dysfunctional dynamic that, according to Noah, annoyed Carmen even more than it does me.

I follow signs to suite E, where the Sonora Hope offices are located. I never do make it inside, though, because on the side of the building, I spot Teresa leaning against a Dumpster with a cigarette in hand. She doesn't notice me at first, just stands, morose, in her own little world. This is the first time that I've seen her in something other than a public-speaking capacity, and without an audience and a podium, she seems smaller. Fragile. Her hair is pulled back into a long ponytail with flyaway tendrils that frame her face, and she wears white capris, a flowery yellow tunic. In the bright sunshine, makeup can't conceal her wrinkles, her age, and the smell of the Dumpster isn't adding to her glamour either.

"Teresa." I feel bad about interrupting what may be a rare private moment for her.

She looks up, startled. The cigarette continues to burn in her hand, little more than a stub now. A chunk of ash falls from the tip to the concrete. "Hi," she says. "Were you . . . looking for me?"

"Was just in the area and I had a question to run by you." Explained thus, my presence sounds decidedly stupid. "I probably should've called."

"No, it's fine." She blinks once. Suddenly seems to register my belly and then scrambles to stamp out her cigarette. "We'll go inside. You shouldn't be around smoke."

"No, no," I protest, not wanting to be a killjoy. "This is your break. One cigarette is not going to kill this baby. I smoked a couple myself before I knew I was pregnant."

Teresa glances at me to see if I mean it and determines that I do. She pulls out a pack of Virginia Slims, her fingers jittery. "Some people go a little crazy when they see these," she says, lifting one from the box. "My husband hates them."

"We all need our little vices, right?"

She gives an exhausted laugh and roots around for her lighter. "We do indeed. So. Charlotte. What can I do for you?"

"It's an issue with Micky, actually. Noah thought you might be able to help."

"Me? Sure. How?" She looks genuinely eager to be of service, and I wonder if she has some kind of compulsive helping disorder, if she ever slows down enough to think about her own needs.

"I'm trying to track down a good adoption lawyer for Micky." I don't tell her that Noah and I may not be the ones doing the adopting. I want to preserve her good opinion of us. "The situation is a little complicated because Micky's dad is Mexican, but I heard your husband heads an adoption agency."

"Mexikids International." She pauses to light her cigarette. "They have a *great* attorney working for them, Andrea Rincón. Give me your number, I'll have her call you." She whips out her cell phone and lets me program my number in. "Anything else you need?"

"That's it," I say. "Thank you so much." I turn, about to leave, and then stop. "How are *you,* Teresa? How are *you* doing?"

"Me?" She takes a deep drag off her cigarette and exhales slowly. "Well. I would say I'm feeling . . . pretty fucked up, actually."

Somehow I was not expecting this lovely, petite woman to drop an F-bomb. "Of course you are. Sorry. That was a stupid question."

"No, *I'm* sorry," she says. "I'm not usually

like this, I've just . . . hit my breaking point, I guess. The whole organization is going through some . . . difficult losses. Donna was the worst by far, but . . . not the only."

"You mean the girl who killed herself?" I ask.

"Oh, God. You heard about her?" She doesn't look happy to know the story is making the rounds.

"Albert mentioned it in passing."

"Leticia." She pronounces the name as only a native Spanish speaker could, smoothing the syllables softly: *Leh-tee-see-ah.* "They called her Lety. I didn't know her personally — these days I'm so busy fundraising, I don't really get out in the field anymore. Maybe I've drifted too far from the actual work." She stares at her cigarette. Brings it to her lips as if disgusted with herself. "You blame yourself, of course. Wonder if you could have prevented it . . ." She glances down, and I notice her toenail polish is chipped. "Some of our staff members were very fond of that girl."

"Like Albert?"

"Like your mother. Lety was one of her favorites." For a few seconds, I think Teresa might burst into tears, but she's too cool for that. She swallows it down, powers through. "Bad things happen to our women sometimes, that's just an unfortunate fact. But it's especially hard when they're young. Lety was only fifteen."

"Jesus." I want to ask why a fifteen-year-old would take her own life, but it seems callous, prying. "You're certainly juggling a lot," I say. "I wish there was something I could do."

"You *are* doing something." Teresa turns her head away to avoid blowing smoke in my face. "You're taking Micky. Believe me, there is no better gift you could give your mother. She had no illusions about Jasmine, and if Micky ends up in a better situation with you and Noah . . . Well, that's *something* at least. One good thing from all this." She stops. "God, that sounds awful."

"I understand. You don't want to feel like their deaths were pointless."

"Yeah." Her hand brushes my belly. "Is this your first baby?" I think she's searching for a happier topic of conversation, but that's not what she has walked into.

"Second baby, actually. My son passed away last summer."

"Oh, no," she breathes. "I didn't realize."

It's a conversation killer, my lost child, and I don't dwell on the subject. "Do you have children?" I ask, wondering what the hell Cristina could possibly be blabbing to

Noah about all this time.

"No. Jonathan, my husband, never wanted any. He's always been very career-driven."

"And you? Did you want children?"

"Oh . . ." She doesn't actually answer my question. "I guess it's worked out. I couldn't have managed Sonora Hope if I had a family to worry about."

"You guys must be quite the dynamic duo." I smile.

"It's a good partnership," Teresa says dully. "We both work with needy families in Mexico. It's nice to have . . . a common cause." Her voice is devoid of warmth or affection, and I have the feeling that this marriage is dead. Has been dead for a while. No wonder she works so tirelessly for her charity. Perhaps Teresa's passion has had nowhere else to go.

I draw back from the subject of her husband. "So what does Mexikids do, exactly? Just helps childless American families get babies, or —"

"No, they don't typically deal with babies," she says. "In Mexico, children have to be at least five to be eligible for adoption."

"Oh." I'm surprised. "So it's all older kids?"

"Unless the Mexican Central Authority makes an exception."

"Why would they do that?"

"If a child has health issues, a disability. Special needs that won't be provided for if they remain in Mexico, basically." She glances at me. "Are you considering an international adoption?" Although her tone remains polite, she looks a bit concerned that Noah and I might have plans to drag some third child into our makeshift family.

"No," I say. "God, no. Hats off to people who can do it, but I've got my hands full." I try to imagine the kind of parents who adopt older children, sick children, handicapped children from other countries, how huge their hearts — and bank accounts — must be. My old coworker Bianca adopted a little girl from China, and it cost her and her husband forty grand. *Better than surrogacy,* she told me when I expressed dismay at the price. *That'll set you back six figures.* Until Bianca shared the details of their six-year baby ordeal, I'd never before considered the random good luck of my own fertility. It makes me sad to think of kind and capable parents like Vonda and Luis, unable to adopt from Mexico because of the cost.

"Well," I say, now rethinking my decision to stand in a nicotine cloud, "I should probably go."

Teresa turns abruptly toward me, her eyes glassy. "I loved your mother, you know. Maybe not the way she wanted to be loved. But I did love her."

I'm not sure what exactly she's confessing to here. "Were you and Donna involved?"

I expect her to take offense or commence evasive maneuvers, but to my surprise, she smiles wistfully. "No. I'm a nice little Catholic girl. Some things you just can't change." She fingers the cross around her neck. "Pam's the only one who ever worried about *that*."

So my mother did not die as the result of some sordid lesbian love triangle.

"But you do think Donna had — feelings for you?" I ask.

Teresa tilts her head to the side. "They weren't for me. Not really. In my line of work, you get to be larger than life pretty quickly, and sometimes the people around you . . . well, they can't distinguish between the person and the image."

"Occupational hazard, I guess."

"With fund-raising, it's a gift, you know. People *want* to give us money. They make it easy. But personally?" She tosses her cigarette onto the pavement and crushes it carefully beneath the toe of her sandal. "I'll never be the woman Donna thought I was.

The woman everyone thinks I am. It's hard to know that about yourself. I'm just this . . . fraud who can never measure up."

She studies my reaction, appearing both exhilarated and frightened at having said this out loud.

"Imposter syndrome," I murmur.

"What?"

"It happens to a lot of successful women." I don't tell her that when I was managing editor at *Sophisticate* we ran a whole series on the topic. "They think all their achievements are a result of luck. That they've conned people into believing they're smarter or more talented than they really are."

"But I *have*," Teresa says. "They don't want *me*, not one of them. They want the woman with the microphone."

"That's still you," I point out.

"No. That's 'Teresa King, founder of Sonora Hope.' " She recites the name and title with a sarcastic flourish. "I'm Teresa Ríos. I was born in Nogales. Take away my American citizenship, and do you know what the difference is between me and the women I help?"

I shrug.

"Me neither," she says. "Me neither."

FOURTEEN

On Tuesday morning, our new realtor greets us outside the first property he's showing. He wears a golf shirt, khaki shorts, and large aviator sunglasses, and his hair is slick with gel. Though he's probably close to Noah's age, he smells like a frat boy — Axe body spray, or something like that. His skin emits waves so intense that I wonder briefly if my gestating child will suffer grave birth defects with prolonged exposure.

"Charlotte! How are you? You weren't lying about that baby you've got coming, huh? Great to see you! Oscar Perez." He speaks in one high-pitched, grinning breath and punctuates his own name with a hand that slashes through the air like a guillotine, so abrupt it takes me a second to realize I'm supposed to shake it.

"Charlie," I say. "Call me Charlie."

I can already see that this first house is nothing special, a spacious ranch in a nice neighborhood of nearly identical single-family residences, but Oscar grabs Noah's hand and pumps it with no absence of zeal as he embarks upon a Mickey Mouse–on–speed soliloquy. "You must be Noah. So glad to meet you. Can't wait to show you two this property, I really think you're going to like it, hits all the items on your list and then some. Now, I know we're working under deadline here, so let's get started, and I'm hoping you can hang on to that baby just a little longer there, Charlie — you look ready to pop! — but at least wait until you get a look at this gorgeous kitchen, 'kay?"

He drapes an arm around my shoulders and urges me toward the house. He's so over-the-top, his whole demeanor such an impossible caricature, that I find myself strangely entertained.

Inside the house, I scan the large foyer, note the skylights. Compared to all the flawless homes we've seen in Sidalie, it's underwhelming, but there's a lot of natural light and plenty of square footage. We could make it work, if we wanted to. We could make anything work.

Convinced of my chronic pickiness, Noah seems to be bracing himself for the worst. He's listened to me find complaint with items I can now admit were ridiculous: the color of a granite countertop, the shape of a Jacuzzi, the placement of a light switch. When I respond cheerfully to Oscar's unwarranted praise of the high-ish ceilings and so-so appliances, Noah's eyebrows just about hit his hairline.

"Is it the fumes?" he whispers, and I gather I'm not the only one who has noticed our agent's profusion of body spray. "Are they makin' you woozy?"

"I don't think so." I laugh. "I'm just ready to do this now." I don't tell him how good it feels to picture a future together outside of Sidalie, away from his old life with Carmen. It would seem like gloating.

"Baby." His eyes widen. "I think you're nestin'."

Oscar takes us to three more suburban ranches, all nondescript but suitable. I find positive, noncommittal things to say about each, drawing more furrowed brows from Noah and manic enthusiasm from Oscar, who seems to believe that volume and exaggerated facial expressions are the way to close a sale.

Still, as I envision a life in Arizona, I find myself torn. I like Tucson, its positive, relaxed vibe, its promise of a new beginning. But am I really ready to take on all the challenges my niece entails? To juggle whatever profound psychological issues Micky has with the demands of an infant? And I can't quite shake the feeling of unease that touring all these bathrooms produces. Those seconds before I first enter always send me into high alert, my eyes scanning the room for something familiar, something dangerous: concrete walls, exposed piping, blue and yellow tile. Yet these half-remembered dream elements bear no resemblance to the serviceable bathrooms Oscar shows us. These houses seem safe, my fears unfounded.

"We've seen four places now," Oscar says, trying not to betray his impatience, "and I'd like to know where your head's at. What you like, what you're missing. Which one's your favorite?"

"They're all fine," I tell him. "I mean, it's just a house. Whatever keeps the rain out, right?"

Noah blinks. "Who *are* you?"

"Let me show you both one last property," Oscar says, correctly calculating that my indifference is not moving us any closer to an actual purchase. "Ten Mawith Drive. M-A-W-I-T-H, program that into your GPS. Just came on the market three days ago. It was designed by a couple of artists, and it's a beaut, environmentally friendly, very custom. Has a lot of character."

For once, Oscar's not overselling. Located in a suburban-verging-on-rural area, the house is far from the ranches that we've spent our morning wandering through. It's smaller but funkier, and the exterior is in a blocky pueblo style that feels geographically distinctive. Really, though, it's the landscaping that catches my eye. Instead of the meticulous paving and stonework we've been seeing, 10 Mawith Drive is nestled in what appears to be actual desert. The pathway to the house is flanked by a variety of cacti, trees, shrubs, and even a few boulders that imbue the land with a natural, slightly unkempt look.

Noah touches my arm and points silently to a nearby flowering bush where a tiny, shimmering little creature vibrates against a blossom. I gasp. A hummingbird.

"There's a patio in the back," Oscar says quickly, "so don't worry about space for the kids to play. Come on inside, and I'll show you what we've got going on."

Noah and I grin at each other, and for a moment, all the other details cease to matter. We're just some shining, expectant couple looking to buy our first home together. He puts a hand on the small of my back, gently guiding me in the front door, and for once, I don't feel that flash of annoyance, the urge to snap, *Jesus, Noah, I'm not crippled.*

No way around it, the interior of the house screams *Artist!* The floors are nearly all Saltillo tile, the ceilings have exposed beams, and both the kitchen and bathroom walls are decorated with colorful Mexican ceramic tiles. Painted in electric shades of orange, purple, and green, the bedroom walls suggest fruity sherbets and contain hand-painted images of birds, a tree, a fanciful village, a sun and moon.

"I don't know about that," Noah says. His tastes have always run toward the traditional, and with his old-school upbringing, I'm sure that painting on the walls seems like sacrilege.

"Kind of tacky, kind of cute," I say.

"Of course you'll want to repaint," Oscar tells us, "but that's a minor thing. If you look past the quirky murals, I think you'll see the bones are there."

From the doorway of a small, pistachio-colored bedroom, I mentally arrange baby furniture. Changing table, dresser, rocking chair, a crib over by the tree mural — it would all fit, though just. There's a large window on the rear wall, and I peer outside, taking in the view of the back patio. A hammock wedged between trees. Silent mountains on the horizon, greenish brown and craggy. Room for the kids to run around, as Oscar said, but also a hot tub. I imagine soaking beneath the stars on a cool desert night. Not bad.

I move away from the window, my vision blurring. The sunshine is getting to me, making my head buzz. I touch my temple, about to ask for Tylenol, and then I feel it. That telltale crackle passing through, showing me.

The room goes dark, daylight flipping off like a switch. Window full of moonlight, and the tree mural still there, its branches spreading across the walls like outstretched hands. In the space that I'd imagined placing my daughter's crib, I now see a bed, and in it, a girl, or the shadow of one.

She's propped up on one elbow, her face tilted upward to a larger, adult shadow. I take a few steps closer. Who am I seeing? The previous occupants of this house? Did something bad happen to them?

But as I move closer to the girl, I realize that she's no stranger from the past. Though the hair is longer, the face thinned out, I know this child. It's Micky. An older Micky.

The adult shadow bends over her, fusses

with her blankets. When it turns a few degrees, I recognize Noah's familiar silhouette. He stoops to kiss Micky good night, his hand lingering on the top of her head, and the easy affection between them is a palpable presence in the room. As the buzzing in my head fades and the picture flickers out, all I can think is, *I guess this isn't supposed to be the baby room, after all.*

"Well?" Noah asks, and only then do I realize that he's beside me, Real Noah, not Future Noah in the Dark. "Not really your style, right, this house?"

I shield my face from the streaming sunlight, still a little dazed. "It has . . . possibilities."

"The outdoor area is pretty amazin'," Noah ventures. "You saw the hot tub?"

"Yeah."

"Nice view, enough space. Artsy, but . . . I mean, we could change what you don't like."

"Definitely artsy," I agree.

He interprets my reticence as a lack of enthusiasm. "Hey," he says, trying to swallow back his disappointment. "You don't have to settle. We'll keep lookin'. This was just a scoutin' mission, right?"

But I can't let him pull back, not now. Not after what I've seen.

This is a house for children. A house for a family. A house where Noah can tuck Micky into bed and kiss her good night, his hand lingering on the top of her head.

This house is already ours. And Micky, however conflicted I may feel about her, is evidently ours as well.

"This is it," I tell Noah. "This is where we should live."

He pauses. Checks to make sure he's heard me correctly. "What?"

"I think we should make an offer."

"On this place? You're serious?"

A few yards away, I can see Oscar perking up, the quiet *ka-ching* of dollar signs in his eyes as he works out his potential commission. I lean into Noah, trying to quash all lingering doubts — his and mine both — with a show of certitude.

"We should do it. We should do everything."

Noah looks around us. Breaks into a grin. "Wow," he says. "Just like that, huh? Leave Sidalie? Get another kid? Wow. Okay. Let's make an offer."

We wander through the house again, brimming with ideas, too swept up in the moment to recognize the cliff we might be walking off. The baby will get the orange sun-and-moon room; the downstairs alcove will be my office. As we plan, I can feel the struggles of the past few months fading from view, a feeling of release as I grasp that my purgatory in Sidalie will soon end. Now our new life rushes toward us with exhilarating speed.

It's only the next day, after we've drawn up the papers at Oscar's office, after our offer has been accepted and we sit toasting our bright future together over mocktails, that I realize. I saw a future for Noah and for Micky in that house.

But I didn't see me. I didn't see our daughter.

I call Pam Wednesday evening, ostensibly to tell her about the house but mainly to check on her emotional well-being. "How are things going?" I ask. I'm stretched out on a recliner in our hotel room while Noah throws on some workout clothes.

"I'm hanging in," Pam says. "I guess." Her voice is hard to read over the phone. "It's a little weird living here without Donna."

"I bet."

"I never realized she had so much *stuff*. Everywhere I look, there's something. I don't know what to do with it all."

I know what she means. After Keegan died, the *stuff* began to seem so important.

Each object became an extension of him somehow, a story from his short life I couldn't bear to look at or to part with. It wasn't until April, a full nine months after his death, that I finally emptied my house in Stamford, let him go — most of him, anyway. I still have three large boxes of my son's possessions in Sidalie, carefully whittled down to the items I most cherish: a handful of children's books, a framed Maurice Sendak print from Keegan's nursery, a baby blanket that my grandmother knit for him. Losing a lover is not the same as losing a child, but I can sympathize with Pam. I know what absence feels like. It is a low, melancholy tune that never stops playing, and the happiest moments of our lives only serve to raise its volume, to remind us, *You are not with me.*

"You don't have to deal with Donna's stuff yet," I tell her. "Give yourself time."

"Feels like I have too much of that," she says. "I don't know what to do with myself. Hell of a time to be retired."

From the doorway of our room, Noah gestures that he's leaving. *Gym,* he mouths, and holds up his cell to let me know it's on him. I give him a thumbs-up, watch him go.

"Listen," I tell Pam, "my guy just ditched me for some quality time with a bench press. If you're looking for a distraction, I could come by with Chinese in half an hour."

"Make that sushi and you've got yourself a deal," Pam says.

I wait a couple minutes to let Noah get settled into his workout and then head down to the lobby, car keys in hand. If I tell him where I'm going now, he'll want to come with me, to keep an eye on me, but we've had more than enough Together Time lately. From the car, I send him a quick text. *Kinda bored. Going to visit Pam for a bit. Sounds like she could use company.*

I don't expect him to like it, but what's he going do? Come after me?

Not when I've got the car.

Pam's home is different at night. Less cheerful. With just a few weak lamps on, the colors are muted, the wall ornaments shiny and dark. Donna's hanging plants spill downward in shadowy tangles. Pam leads me to the kitchen table, where a catalog of what appears to be surveillance equipment lies open. I glance at a few of the products on the page: tiny cameras, hidden recording devices, night goggles.

"Is that a cop thing?" I ask. "Or are you just especially paranoid?"

"It's not paranoia when two people end up dead," she says, unruffled. "You want a drink?"

"I don't drink."

She gives me a strange look. "I didn't mean alcohol. I know you're pregnant."

I laugh. "Of course you do. Sorry. I never drink, and I'm just so used to —"

"Explaining yourself? Yeah. I don't drink alcohol, either." She removes a pitcher of ice water from the fridge and pours us each a glass. "Socially awkward sometimes, turning down a beer."

"Yeah, well." I take the water that she offers. "My family tree has a lot of addicts. If it keeps me off that particular branch, I'm okay with a little social awkwardness." I begin unpacking our sushi order, unable to conceal my enthusiasm. "So we've got *unagi,* dragon roll, Alaskan roll, *futomaki,* and spicy tuna." Looking at the feast before me, my previous avoidance of sushi during pregnancy now seems moronic and vaguely insulting to generations of Japanese mothers.

"Looks good. Thanks." Pam settles down at the table with me. She's wearing a black T-shirt and athletic shorts this evening, and I realize that I've never seen her wear anything not black or white. I wonder if this is a reflection of an intense all-or-nothing personality or just the sign of someone who can't be bothered to match colors. "So where exactly is this house you and Noah found?"

"About fifteen minutes from here." Her mention of Noah reminds me to check my phone for texts. Just one, I discover. *Have fun w/ Pam,* Noah tells me. *PLS be careful.* I look up, smiling. "Mawith Drive," I say. "Our new house is on Mawith Drive."

"Mawith," she repeats. "Huh. That's O'odham. It means 'mountain lion.' "

"Really? I hope the name isn't descriptive."

"Just some developer getting cute, I'm sure."

"I didn't realize you spoke O'odham." I glance at her. Shove a disc of *futomaki* in my mouth.

"I haven't in ages. Probably forgot most of it."

I remember the way my high school French came back a decade later in Paris, long-forgotten words suddenly bubbling up from my throat, the phlegmy pomposity of the French *r* like riding a bicycle. And I was never even fluent in French. "I bet you'd remember O'odham if you went reaching for it," I say. "At least the basics. Like . . .

how do you say 'sun' and 'moon'?"

"What do *you* care?" Her voice is unexpectedly sharp.

I don't know how to reply. I asked about the words "sun" and "moon" because I love how they sound in French, *soleil* and *lune,* the way they ease off the tongue like poetry. Because I wondered what the sun and moon sound like to the Tohono O'odham people. From the way Pam's looking at me, though, daring me to exoticize her culture or romanticize her history, I realize that's the wrong answer.

Pam's hand tightens around her glass of water. "I left the res at sixteen," she says. "Far as I'm concerned, it can stay right where I left it."

"Okay." I wonder what made her turn her back on where she came from so completely. Was she running away from something? Looking for something better? "Do you still have family there?"

"It's been forty years. Who the hell knows?"

"You weren't close to them, then." Something she and Donna had in common, I gather.

Pam looks annoyed that I'm pursuing the topic. "I was close to my grandfather. Hung around until he died, and after that, nothing in the world could've kept me there." She stabs at a spicy tuna roll with one chopstick. "You think your family tree's got problems, you should get a look at mine. Diabetics and drunks, the whole damn thing."

"Even your grandfather?"

"No. Not my grandfather." She softens at the mention of him but doesn't offer anything further. I set aside my curiosity, sensing that any discussion of loved ones long gone is dangerous ground. Pam's recent losses are quite enough for her to contend with; no need to expose old wounds. I have wounds of my own to contend with. I get it.

"Sorry. I didn't mean to pry."

She picks at something in her teeth. "If you want to dredge up secrets, let's talk about someone too dead to care. You want to hear what turned up in your sister's apartment?"

I lean forward in my chair. "You know I do."

"Nudie pics."

I sigh. "That sounds about right. Although . . ." I consider this for a moment. "Why would Jasmine keep pictures of herself in her own apartment? I thought the whole idea of nude pictures was to give them to some deadbeat boyfriend so he can

287

post them all over the Internet when you break up."

Pam cracks a sardonic grin. "The pictures weren't of Jasmine."

I raise an eyebrow. "Who?"

She shakes her head, still smiling. "A woman, mostly. All those years Jazz went on about how 'disgusting' it was to see her mother and I together, how 'unnatural' we were . . . and she's got a memory card full of coochie shots. You gotta love it, right?"

I can see why this brings her a certain dark satisfaction. I gulp down my glass of water. "Who's the woman?"

"Can't tell. There's no face shots, just a lot of blurry body parts."

"Then how do they know it's not Jasmine?"

"The tits were wrong." She rolls her eyes. "Jasmine had pierced nipples."

"Of course she did." I don't want to be judgmental about female sexuality, but everything I learn about Jasmine — Micky's *mother,* damn it — tests the limits of my acceptance. "So they think Jasmine took the pictures? Of some other woman?"

Pam drenches a piece of sushi with soy sauce and wasabi. "Can't prove it, but the memory card was in her house. Taped up into the top of a drawer like it meant something to her. And the pictures were definitely taken in her apartment."

"Do they think Jasmine had a girlfriend? I mean, what's the theory?"

"Threesome," Pam announces. "There's a guy in some of the pictures, too. A few action shots with him and the girl. No view of *his* face, either."

I'm not even surprised. Jasmine is starting to seem downright predictable. "Did they identify the guy? Because if it's Ruben, and those photos were taken in her apartment — well, that would prove he'd been in the US recently, right?"

"It's a white guy in the pics, that's all they know." Pam shrugs. "But these photos predate McCullough and her latest fling with Ruben, as far as I know. They were time-stamped over a year ago."

"Are they being treated as part of the murder investigation?"

"You bet your ass they are," Pam says. "We don't know why Jasmine had those pics. Could've been blackmail. Could've been motive. Vargas is pulling out all the stops to ID the guy and girl."

"Does McCullough know about this?" I ask. I don't know how he'd react, but I'm guessing not well.

"If he didn't before, he sure does now.

Sexy photos — well, it's hard to keep 'em under wraps in an organization full of guys."

Suddenly I remember Sanchez going through Jasmine's apartment yesterday, opening drawers in the kitchen. Could he have been searching for these pictures, unaware that they were already in Homicide's possession? "Pam," I murmur, "you said they found the memory card in a drawer, right?"

She nods.

"What room was the drawer in?"

"I don't know. Why?"

I hesitate. I want to trust Pam, but Rob Sanchez is a cop. Retired though she may be, Pam obviously still has connections to the Tucson police, and her loyalties to them likely extend far beyond whatever bond she and I have forged in the last nine days. "No reason. Just curious."

Pam doesn't buy it. She studies me with the carefully neutral face of a poker player, as if reading her opponent, trying to get a sense of my hand. Still, she says nothing.

"So are they getting close?" I try to redirect the conversation. "You think the pictures will lead to some kind of break-through?"

"Hope so." Pam stares down at her sushi, and I see that she's not about to share whatever private theories she may harbor. "Jasmine was bad news, that's all I know," she says brusquely. "She invited all kinds of chaos into her life, and it got her killed. Got Donna killed, too." She notices my empty water glass and stands up. "You want some coffee or something?"

"Tea, if you have it. Something herbal?"

"Herbal tea, I shoulda known." She plucks a tea bag from a drawer and, without warning, turns sentimental. "Chamomile. Just like your mom."

I want to tell her I'm a coffee drinker by nature, that I'm avoiding caffeine purely because of the baby, and tea drinking is not some familial similarity between Donna and me, but even I know that it's silly to protest something so trivial. I can give Pam this one. I watch as she sets the kettle on the stove and fires up the gas.

"Tash," she says. *"Tash* and *mashath."*

"What?" It sounds like gibberish.

"Sun and moon," she explains. *"Tash* and *mashath."*

I smile when I understand this gift she's giving me. O'odham words. A piece of her past. *"Tash,"* I say, trying to pronounce the word as she does, yet failing. "That's 'sun'?"

She nods. "You make the *sh* sound a little farther back in your mouth."

Before I can offer another poor attempt at O'odham, someone knocks at the door. Three knocks, quick and deliberate. Pam looks up, seeming to calculate the chances of an interesting visitor versus an annoyance. She moves to answer it. I wait a few seconds and then follow her.

It's McCullough. His eyes are bloodshot and his T-shirt clings to his body, damp with sweat, but when he sees Pam, he nods curtly. "Evening," he says. "Hope you'll pardon the interruption."

"Hey, Mac." Pam's face betrays no surprise, but her dark eyes miss nothing. "What's going on?"

"Just wanted to be the one to tell you." He's breathless but triumphant. "They've arrested Ruben Ramos."

Her eyes narrow. "Oh yeah? Who got him?"

"The Mexican authorities. Down in Rocky Point."

"Ah. So that's where he's been at." Pam feels me tensing up behind her and raises a finger, almost imperceptibly, behind her back. The gesture is slight but unmistakable. *Let me handle this.* "So what do they have on him?" she asks. "Something to connect Ruben to the murders?"

"He wasn't arrested for murder," McCullough says. "He was arrested for sexual assault."

FIFTEEN

Eager to get on with his night, McCullough dispenses the facts as quickly as he can. "You know Homicide can't share details of the investigation," he says, glancing at me. "But I do know Vargas and some of the guys went down to Rocky Point yesterday to speak with the local police. They had a lead Ramos was down there."

"Hard for him to hurt Jasmine if he's living in Mexico without a US visa," Pam says. "Did Vargas question him?"

"I think so. But they didn't have enough to take him into custody."

"So when did these sexual assault charges —"

"Early this morning. The story is Ramos met some woman at a bar, they went back to her place, and he assaulted her."

"A tourist?" Pam asks.

"A local woman. Who happened to be a cop."

"Huh," Pam says.

"He's a fucking rapist," McCullough spits. "He's gonna rot in prison. And not some cushy US facility, either."

Pam registers neither excitement nor anger at this news. "Well," she says, "I know you've been keen to find him. I hope this makes it easier for you."

He doesn't like that: sympathy. "I thought you'd want to know. Since you cared about Donna."

She heaves a long, slow sigh, and I realize that in a side-by-side comparison of toughness, McCullough offers Pam no contest at all, despite being six inches taller. Beside her, he looks like a kid, a confused rookie. "Come on, Mac," she says. "You really think Ruben killed Donna? Or Jasmine, for that matter?"

"I don't know what he did," he says, "but I'd say a Mexican prison is a pretty damn good place for him."

"I get that, buddy." Pam clamps a hand on his shoulder. "I do. He screwed you over big-time."

His blue eyes smolder. "You don't even care, do you? You don't care what happens to him."

"Not the way you do," she says. "Ruben took something from you. I don't think he

295

took something from me."

McCullough's body goes rigid. He pulls away from her.

"I'm glad you came by," Pam says. "And listen. I know it's all shit now, but you'll get through this. You just stay outta trouble, okay?"

He storms back to his car like some misunderstood teenager offended by the advice of a well-meaning parent. Pam watches him screech off in his car before she shuts the front door. She heads back to the kitchen and loads up her plate with dragon roll. "Poor kid," she says, and it takes a second for me to realize that she's talking about McCullough.

"Really? That's what you think of him?"

"He's a decent guy. A little intense, and his taste in women sure hasn't done him any favors, but he's okay."

I sink back into my chair. Has Pam been working amongst testosterone so long she's started thinking like one of them? "Frankly, I'm surprised Detective Vargas isn't more interested in McCullough as a suspect," I say. "He's a bit of a hothead, isn't he?"

"He had plans with Jasmine the night she died," Pam says evenly. "Got called in last-minute to cover a shift and canceled on her. I'm sure he feels responsible."

"Maybe he *is* responsible."

"He was on duty. With his partner."

"You mean Rob?"

She gives me an odd look, and it occurs to me that maybe normal people don't call him Rob. I've only heard Serena, Jasmine's crazy friend at the funeral, address Sanchez by the nickname.

"You know the guy?" Pam asks.

"We chatted a few times."

"Then I'm sure he told you about the rigorous questioning he and McCullough both went through."

I've made a misstep, casting doubt upon the integrity of her fellow officers. "I wasn't accusing anyone," I say, trying to backpedal. "Just thought they always go after the boyfriend first."

"How about you trust law enforcement to do its job?" Pam says, which gets my hackles up again.

"Why? It doesn't sound like *you* trust them. Weren't you the one conducting your own little side investigation because you thought Vargas was barking up the wrong tree?"

She casts me a thin-lipped smile. "Blinded by grief, I guess."

"Bullshit. You're really trying to pretend that you're going to leave this alone? How stupid do you think I am?" Inside me, my daughter begins to kick, as if picking up on my indignation and offering some of her own. "I saw where your head was at last week. Finding bad guys is your thing. Right now your choices are figure out who killed Donna or sit around dealing with the fact that she's dead. I know what *I'd* choose."

"Pretty feisty, for a woman who's about five minutes from popping out a baby."

"Tell me I'm wrong."

"You're not wrong."

We're on the same side again, I can feel it. She likes my getting fired up, challenging her. I try to capitalize on her goodwill. "Pam," I say, swallowing, "I need your honest opinion. This thing with Ruben. I mean, he's Micky's *father.* Do you really think he assaulted someone?"

"Who just happened to be a cop?" She laughs. "Not a chance. This is Mexico we're dealing with."

"Meaning what?"

"Meaning if United States law enforcement started whispering in their ear about Ruben and some unsolved double murder . . . well, they have their own way of handling things. Ten to one, the cop that Ruben assaulted was someone that they planted."

I've heard stories, read things, of course, but it's hard to reconcile all that with the highly Americanized resort Noah and I saw in Rocky Point. "Are the cops really *that* corrupt?"

"It's the whole government, not just the police force." Pam pulls a strip of avocado off her dragon roll and chews it thoughtfully. "You can get away with anything in Mexico, as long as you give the right people a cut. And on the flip side, even if you follow the law to the letter, you piss off the wrong person and . . ."

"You think Ruben pissed the wrong person off?" I frown. "McCullough sure had it in for him."

"I doubt McCullough has that kind of reach." Pam prods at her sushi with her chopsticks, not actually eating. "This smacks of politics. Rocky Point depends on its American tourists. Sexual assault charges are a convenient way to hustle Ruben off, maybe let Vargas and them get another crack at him later, keep everyone happy."

"Maybe he really *did* assault someone," I suggest. "Went back with some drunk woman to her place and . . . you know. That could've happened."

"It could've."

"You don't look like you believe it."

"Ruben's family has money, right?"

"Yeah," I say.

"It's not uncommon for Mexican police to arrest someone on bogus charges and then ask wealthy family members for 'bail.' Of course, once they get their money, they don't necessarily release the guy."

I see what she's getting at. "If these charges are manufactured, then it's my fault he's in jail, Pam. I was the one who found him. He wouldn't have been on anyone's radar if I hadn't told you where he was." I feel a little sick when I realize what I've done. I don't have a high opinion of Micky's father, but I wasn't looking to stir up trouble for him, certainly not trouble of this magnitude.

"They would've tracked Ruben down eventually," Pam says. "Give them a little credit. This isn't all on you."

"Maybe, maybe not." I take the final sip of my tea and stare down at the empty mug. I know nothing about the Mexican judicial system, what kind of access an American might get to an inmate. Can Ruben sign away his parental rights while in prison? Will his arrest prolong the adoption process for Micky? "It's late," I tell Pam. "I'd better get back."

She doesn't argue. "Noah's waiting for

300

you, huh."

"Yeah."

"I'll walk you out." She doesn't look at me as she speaks. "I appreciate it, you know. You coming over here. Checking up on me and all that."

"Not a big deal. I wish there was more I could do for you."

"It *is* a big deal," Pam says gruffly. "You don't owe me anything, I know that. You're here because . . . you have a good heart."

"Thanks."

"I just wish Donna could've met you. She would've —"

"Don't." In my haste to retreat, I stumble backward off her front step, catching myself on the rails before I fall. "This is about you and me, not Donna, okay?"

"Okay," she says, but even I know that I'm wrong. Like it or not, my relationship with Pam will always be about Donna. It's inescapable.

"I'll be in touch," I tell her. "And if you hear anything else about Ruben . . ."

"I'll let you know."

Back in the car, I buckle myself in, flip on the A/C. Before I've pulled away from the curb, my phone lights up with a text from Noah. *It's past your bedtime. You alive?*

I'm annoyed. While it's true that I've been

going to bed early recently, that doesn't mean I can't stay awake like a grown-up every now and then. *Dead as a doornail,* I type back, then catch myself before I hit Send. No need for snark. With everything that's happened, I can't blame Noah for being a little nervous.

I'm alive, I reply. *Back soon.*

That night, I'm awakened from a decent stretch of sleep by acid reflux. I sit up in bed, fumbling around in the dark for my water bottle, something to calm the burn. That's when I hear the music.

Low at first. A distant pounding that moves closer, like the subwoofer of some sporty car pulling up beside you at a stoplight. Soon it's so loud I swear the room itself is pulsing. Are the people next door having a middle-of-the-night dance party? What the hell? Noah, of course, doesn't stir, which means I'll have to call the front desk myself. Irritated, I slide a bare foot onto the carpet, feel it vibrating beneath me.

It happens so fast this time. The change is liquid and immediate, the hotel gone, my body upright and unburdened by the weight of pregnancy. The music is everywhere.

The lights are blurring lines of neon pink and purple, the air thick with smoke and sweat and throbbing music. A flashing silver disco ball casts fragments of light across the dark walls, pale flecks that swirl around the room in dizzying circles like a school of ghostly fish. The pounding club beat travels up through my calves and thighs, urging my hips to action, yet I resist.

I don't want to dance. Not here.

It's a sticky, creaking establishment that trembles with the music. Some attempt has been made at a nautical theme: fishing nets draped from the ceiling, shells affixed to the walls, a small glow-in-the-dark trident suggestively aimed at the crotch of a giant blow-up mermaid. She's blond, of course, and possesses both a vacant smile and huge plastic breasts adorned with obscene red nipples. But that's what they're here for. That's what they want.

They're everywhere, all around me in the dim room. I can smell them. Men. The stink of their bodies, their alcohol-drenched breath. I see their shadows moving around the floor, their eyes bright and glowing in the dark, like rats. Their gazes range from hungry or leering to impassive, disgusted even, and they consume me. Claim me. First with eyes, then with hands, a mess of hot, relentless fingers that start at my ankles and work their way up my legs. I don't fight them, don't protest. There is something routine about this groping, something pathetic and necessary, however unpleasant.

I leave my body behind, let myself swim in the spinning light of the disco ball, around and around and around until I'm giddy. Exultant.

Now the room is underwater. The men brush against me, but they're only fish, slippery bodies who can do me no harm. I am a mermaid come to life, ensnaring them with my sultry song of flesh, drowning them, drowning us all in the pink and purple lights, the crushing waves of music.

When I come up for air, the building is empty, the space dark. I'm alone but for one figure, a watchful shadow, her eyes fixed on me from across the room. A young woman.

She leans against a counter, chin in hand, dissecting me with her fierce gaze. Her features are approximate, smudgy even, a half-drawn pencil sketch. Long, dark hair. A pert nose, defiant lips. And radiating from her in thick, black waves that make the air shimmer: anger.

Who are you? I ask.

She crosses her arms. *Lety,* she says. *I'm Lety.*

I recognize the name. She's the girl who

killed herself, the fifteen-year-old in Nogales whose death broke Donna's heart. But what am I supposed to do for one dead by her own hand? She already made her choice.

What do you want? I ask.

She steps away from the counter, and I realize she's wearing only the skimpiest of clothes. Towering heels, fishnet thigh-highs, a shiny black bra and thong. I recoil. Was that her at the club, getting groped by all those men? Teresa didn't tell me the poor girl was a stripper.

Lety approaches me with a *click, click, click* sound, surprisingly steady on her precarious heels. She stands in front of me, hands clamped into two tight fists.

Mi hermanita, she tells me. *My little sister, Yulissa. You have to help her.*

Up close, I can see she's short, even with the extra three or four inches of shoe. And her youth — I see that, too. Beneath the makeup and the sexy costume, she's just a kid, a small and sullen teenager rolled in layers of attitude. Hardly a match for all those men, all those hands reaching for her beneath the lights. No wonder she wanted out.

I can't, Lety, I say. *I can't go to Nogales. I'm sorry.* I have the crazy urge to explain to her that I'm a little overbooked right now. That whatever crisis her sister is going through, it's just not a good time for me.

Why? Por qué no? She leans in, and her breath is cold, so cold, when she whispers in my ear. *Are you afraid of that shower?*

I stare at her. Who is this girl, and how does she know what I've been seeing?

Is it real? I whisper. *That scene in the shower, is it real?*

Lety runs a hand through her long dark hair. *What you see is always real.*

Then what do I do? The scene I keep seeing — how do I stop it?

You come to Nogales, she says, stepping back into the darkness. *You help Yulissa.* Her face has gone smoky, her body dispersed like steam, but I still catch her final words. *It's what your mother would've wanted.*

Sixteen

When I come to, I'm standing between two elevator doors. At some point in my waking vision, I must've wandered into the hotel corridor. Now I find myself half inside the elevator, half planted in the hallway. The automatic sensors don't permit the doors to shut on me, and so they're caught in an endless loop: attempting to close, detecting me, dinging, opening again. I glance at the placard to make sure I'm on the right floor and step back into the hall.

All things considered, Noah reacts fairly well to my banging on the hotel door at three a.m. After I provide him with a pseudo-logical explanation about wanting ice and forgetting my room key, he puts his gun back in its holster and promptly falls asleep.

I don't tell him about Lety. I'm still turning it over in my mind, trying to understand. Is she offering me a way out, an outcome other than that blue and yellow tiled bathroom? If I go to Nogales, can I really change the ugly future that has haunted me for weeks?

I crawl back into bed. Huddle up against Noah, seeking comfort in his slow, unchanging breaths. In the end, I have no choice, and that, I suppose, makes it easier.

If helping Lety's sister means a chance to save my daughter, I'll do it. Of course I'll do it.

I walk through the day a distractible mess, trying to figure out where to begin my search for Yulissa and how to convince Noah to get on board. I sit zombielike through a meeting with Micky's caseworker, absorbing only snippets as Daniel and Noah discuss our plans to become Arizona residents.

At some point, Andrea Rincón calls. It takes me an embarrassingly long time to realize that she's the adoption lawyer Teresa promised to put me in touch with. We make an appointment for next week, which I forget to write down.

When it's time to get Micky after school for our scheduled visit, Noah's rethinking the wisdom of dragging me out. "Are you sure you're up for this today?"

I tell him I am. I tell him I can't wait to see my niece. I don't tell him I'm collapsing under the weight of all these girls who need me, my daughter, Micky, and now this Yulissa character who could presumably follow in her sister's suicidal footsteps if I don't somehow fix things. That, I keep to myself.

Noah has chosen mini-golf for our first unsupervised visit with Micky, and so Vonda lends us a booster seat and the three of us drive to a nearby course. Though we slather ourselves with sunscreen and buy large bottles of water to stay hydrated, I quickly conclude this was not the brightest idea. After three holes in 107-degree weather, the undersides of my breasts and belly have transformed into busy waterways of sweat, and I'm about ready to pass out from heat exhaustion. Micky, too, is flushed and perspiring, yet when I offer her a break, she declines, chin up, shoulders back.

She's never played mini-golf before, but she takes in everything that Noah does, imitates his stance, tries to duplicate the way he grips his club. When she hits the ball too lightly or too hard, her bottom lip pokes out as if the error pains her. A perfectionist, I determine, although where she got that from remains a mystery. Neither Ruben nor

309

Jasmine appeared overly concerned with excellence.

Eventually, feeling anxious and faint from the sun, I seek relief in the shade of a windmill and refuse to budge while Noah and Micky play out the remainder of their game. From a safe distance, I watch them attack the fourth hole, watch Micky's look of concentration as she squares herself up for a shot and Noah's patient, encouraging nod. Her ball sails unscathed between two mounds and nearly reaches the cup. Noah offers her a high five, which Micky returns after some hesitation. She sticks her fingers in her mouth, and for the first time, I think I see the hint of a smile tugging at the corners of her mouth.

I'm glad I sat this one out. *These two are fine without me,* I think, but then the image of his putting her to bed in the new house comes flooding back, cryptic, unsettling. Maybe Micky is not meant to be mine. Maybe she's Noah's, the one thing he'll have left when the baby and I are gone. Maybe today is a prelude of things to come, a preview of my absence.

I can't let that happen.

I dig around in my wallet for the card Albert gave me at the Sonora Hope luncheon. He knew Lety. Perhaps he knows Yulissa, too. I dial his number.

"Charlotte!" Albert sounds oddly excited to hear from me. "I was going to call you."

"Really?"

"I wanted to tell you," he says. "I took my son to the pediatrician. He had strep throat, just like you said. We're lucky we caught it."

The news doesn't surprise me the way it once would've, but it's good to know I'm getting better at interpreting my impressions. "Well," I say, "at least strep is easy to treat, right?"

"You'd think," says Albert, an edge to his voice. "But my ex-wife took Josh to a homeopath, who said it was a simple fever. They'd been giving him these *herbs* instead of antibiotics. I'm glad you mentioned strep. I honestly don't know if I would've taken him in otherwise."

I know better than to trash his ex, even if she's made a questionable parenting decision. "It sounds like your son is in good hands now. I hope he feels better soon."

"Enough about me," Albert says, sensing my change in mood. "What's on your mind?"

Noah and Micky have finished another hole now and stepped out of view. I kick off my sandals, give my swollen feet some breathing room. "I was hoping you could

311

help with something. Did you or Donna ever work with a girl named Yulissa?"

"Yulissa," he repeats. "The name is familiar."

"I think Yulissa's sister received services from Sonora Hope. Lety? The girl who committed suicide."

"Oh." Albert's voice falls a little at Lety's name. "To be honest with you, I really didn't know Lety's family situation. She was your mother's case."

The thought of Donna hovers there for a second between us, ghost mother and missing friend. I hold the phone away and drizzle my water bottle over my head, my cheeks, my eyelids.

"Do you know where Lety lived?" I ask. "Where she was from?"

"She lived downtown, I think. Worked as a dancer before she came to us."

The dancer part I already know. I saw the skimpy outfit and all those hungry men. "How did a fifteen-year-old get *that* job?"

"I'm sure she lied about her age. Underage girls aren't exactly a rarity on that scene. Can I ask what this is about?" Albert has been a good sport; I owe him some kind of explanation.

"It's . . . for an article I'm writing."

He's skeptical. "You're writing about Lety

and her sister?"

"No, no." I cringe. Squinch up my toes, bracing myself for the lie. "There's this magazine I used to work for, *Sophisticate.*" That part is true. That part makes the fiction easier. "I thought . . . maybe I could write a little feature piece about Sonora Hope. The kind of work you're doing."

"That would be great for donations," Albert says. "*Sophisticate* is really popular with our target donors." He means rich women. "Why Lety, though? Sonora Hope has done a lot of good work. Why focus on the one we couldn't help?"

I have to spin the Lety angle somehow. "I think it would help to contrast a tragic story like Lety's with the success story of someone like . . ." I grasp for the name of the one-eyed woman at the presentation. "Marilena." I clear my throat. "I want readers to understand that there are real life-or-death consequences for these women, you know? To show how high the stakes are."

Albert doesn't reply for a few seconds, and I can tell that selling out a dead teenager to drum up some dollars doesn't sit well with him.

"You could talk to Marilena," he says at last. "She's always happy to speak about the program, and she knew Lety quite well." I

313

wait for him to say more, but that's apparently all I'm getting. "Let me get back to you about this, Charlotte. I'll chat with Teresa, and we can get you some leads. As you can probably imagine, we're very strict about confidentiality, but I think if we approached a few specific women, got their permission . . ."

I make some noise to indicate my assent, but the truth is I barely hear him. I wander the mini-golf course in a daze, past hills and winding chutes, past a pirate ship and a gaping gorilla mouth. I have to find the club that Lety worked at. I have to talk to Marilena. *Someone* has to know about this girl.

Follow Lety's trail, I reason, and sooner or later, I'll find her sister.

Getting Noah to venture into Mexico again will not be easy, but I know his weak spots, will do my best to exploit them.

"So Albert called me," I say after we've dropped Micky off at Vonda's. "Remember him? That guy from the Sonora Hope presentation?"

"Sure." Noah frowns as a couple of kids in University of Arizona shirts dash foolishly in front of our car. "What'd he want?"

I play it casual. Try not to sound like I

care. "We were talking about me maybe writing an article. Just a little piece to get Sonora Hope some exposure."

Noah, God bless his predictable heart, lights up. "That's a great idea! For *Sophisticate*?"

I nod.

"Baby, that's *perfect.* Good publicity, that's worth its weight in gold." He pulls out into a line of cars. We're in the Tucson version of rush hour now. "I assume there's no hurry on this, right? Just whenever you got some time?"

"It would probably be right away. But if it's just a couple thousand words, I could knock that off pretty quick. I don't know." I feign reluctance. This will work best if he thinks he's convincing me, getting his own way.

"You don't sound too excited."

"Well, we're so busy right now," I say. "And I'd need a day or two in Nogales for research."

"Oh." That's all it takes. One mention of Nogales, and he abandons the knee-jerk optimism. "Maybe in a few months, then. After the baby."

"I don't think that's an option. I think it's — time sensitive."

He falls quiet. Our car creeps along, waiting to make a left turn. When Noah finally speaks, I realize that for all my strategizing, he sees through this act of mine, at least partially. "You wanna go," he says, "don't you."

"I'm guessing you won't want me to."

"I think it could be dangerous. That bathroom . . ."

"I know." I don't say anything for a minute. Let him sit with it. Try not to press my case, the fastest way to get him digging in his heels. Finally, I can't stand the silence. "What if we didn't spend the night? Just crossed in and out of Mexico on foot during the day? Americans cross the border all the time. It wouldn't have to be a big deal."

He heaves a deep sigh. "I still don't like it."

"I could help a lot of people by writing this article."

The light goes green, and traffic funnels forward. We just make our turn. "If this was all about helpin' Sonora Hope, we could give them money ourselves," Noah says. "It's the story you want, isn't it? You see a story you can't resist, and you have to go chasin' it. Is this how it's always gonna be with you? You need dumb risks to feel alive?"

He's angry. Angry at me for trying to manipulate him, angry at me for wanting to

316

put myself and our baby in harm's way. I've played this all wrong. Should've just told him the truth straight off.

"It's not just the story, okay?" I slump forward, head in hands. "There's a girl."

He glances at me and knows. Knows immediately. "Oh, Jesus. You *saw* somethin'?"

"You know that girl Donna worked with who killed herself? Lety?"

"You saw *her*?"

"She wants me to find her sister. Help her somehow."

He frowns. "The sister's in Nogales?"

"I think so."

"You *think*? You think but you're not sure? You want to run off to some place that could get you killed, just like in your dream, because you *think* you need to find some girl?" He grips the steering wheel so tight I worry for a moment he's going to tear it off the dashboard. "That's bullshit. That's *bullshit,* Charlie! That's not fair to ask of me and you know it."

I search for a good retort, a logical reason to make this trip, but come up empty.

"Why does it have to be you?" Noah's close to tears. "Why now, when we've got everything to lose?"

I don't know the answer to his question until Lety's words have already left my lips.

317

"It's what my mother would've wanted."

It is the rawest and most honest thing that I could say, one that acknowledges so many parts of myself I'd rather keep hidden. That, despite everything I've ever said, my mother matters. That, in my own pathetic way, I'm searching for a connection to her.

The admission makes me want to crawl under a rock, but for Noah, it's a silver bullet. His shoulders sag.

"Tomorrow, then," he says in a voice that's all but broken. "We can go tomorrow. We'll find the sister."

I don't know how to respond to my own victory. It doesn't feel like I've won.

"We'll go durin' the day, like you said." His eyes are on the mountains, the sky, the road, anywhere but me. "In and out, that's it. And I'm not leavin' your side for a minute. Every time you gotta pee, I'm right there with you, no arguments."

"No arguments," I promise. "I wouldn't dare." I study his face, now hard and remote. Wish that I could kiss him, hold him, bring him back to me somehow. I already regret the whole plan.

What does Lety know about my future, and what power can she possibly have to change it? She's just some fifteen-year-old girl who succumbed to her darkest urges.

Killed herself and then realized she had unfinished business.

"We don't have to go." I touch Noah's shoulder tentatively. "I could just . . . ignore everything Lety told me."

His body stiffens at my touch. "I know you don't believe in God, Charlie. But I do." He still won't look at me. "I don't know what you're bein' called to do. But I'll help you do it."

■ ■ ■ ■

Part V
Nogales, Arizona,
and Nogales,
Sonora, Mexico

■ ■ ■ ■

SEVENTEEN

About an hour south of Tucson, the twin cities of Nogales rise up out of the desert, separated by more than just a wall. From the moment we pass through the metal, full-height turnstile, it's clear we've entered another country, another world. Unlike Rocky Point, there are no cushy resorts, no high-rise hotels or pristine blue swimming pools. The Nogales of Mexico is a flurry of activity, street merchants hawking their wares, cars surging across intersections, men on doorsteps yelling suggestive comments at passing women. Noah's presence and my pregnancy ensure that no leering remarks come my way, but they offer little protection from aggressive vendors and sketchy cabbies who urge us toward their taxis in broken English.

And everywhere I look: *farmacias.* They spring up like dandelions, assaulting us at every corner with advertisements for all the prescription drugs they think Americans will like. WELLBUTRIN, LIPITOR, ZYRTEC, RITALIN, HGH, but mainly VIAGRA VIAGRA VIAGRA.

"Need some Viagra?" I ask Noah.

He puts a hand to his chest, shaking his head. "Knife to a man's heart you'd even ask."

I'm glad he's finally feeling good enough to joke around. The drive south was not exactly filled with levity; he sat in the passenger seat, brooding and agitated, responding to any attempts at conversation with one-word answers as he fiddled with his phone.

Maybe that was the worst of it, I think. *The waiting. The anticipation.*

Now we're here, wandering the dingy streets, enveloped in a haze of exhaust fumes and fried food. My sense of dread has lifted, and purpose has taken over. If my mother could spend years trying to improve life for local women, surely I can handle one. Yulissa must be somewhere in this city.

"Marilena's hotel is about a mile from here," Noah says, consulting the directions he scribbled down earlier. "We can start there and see if Marilena knows anything about Lety's family."

I glance down at the list of strip clubs I've compiled. "And if she doesn't? Should we just go through this list systematically? I think I would recognize the club she worked at if I saw it."

Noah makes a face. "Let's hope Marilena comes through for us. I'd just as soon skip those joints if we can."

On that point, we are in total agreement. What I know about strip clubs in Nogales I have gleaned mainly from skin-crawling posts online, bulletin boards that American men use to "rate" sex workers around the world. Per their reports, Nogales has a handful of strip clubs near the border and a red-light district with brothels a few miles in. The women are "not as good as Bangkok, but on par with Tijuana" says one poster, and "kinda robotic, don't look into it" according to another, who went on to chronicle his encounters in terms so explicit I became physically ill and had to shut down my computer. The "dancers" in these clubs, I've learned, are also invariably prostitutes.

The toll that must have taken on fifteen-year-old Lety only intensifies my desire to find Yulissa. I don't want this girl to end up like her sister, convinced that death is better than the life she's living.

Noah has already taken off down the

street, anxious to complete our task and be out of this city. Ignoring the cries of persistent vendors — "beautiful clothes for a beautiful mama!" — I jog after him.

"Are we walking the whole way?"

"Or we could get a taxi." He points at one of the grinning cabbies, a man with a beard and sweat-soaked shirt who waves wildly at me and yells, "I drive you! I drive you! Where you want to go, *señora*?" the instant I make eye contact.

Suddenly our whiteness, our American citizenship, seems ostentatious, embarrassing. We can walk among the people of Nogales, but they all know what we are. There is no hiding our privilege, no pretending that we don't have more than the locals that we pass.

I lower my eyes. "I can walk."

Donna wasn't the kind of woman who took a cab to travel one measly mile. I won't be that woman, either.

When Marilena shared her Sonora Hope success story, I did not imagine that her happy ending involved a place like the Hotel del Viajero. I pictured — foolishly, I see now — a quaint bed-and-breakfast, a Spanish-style courtyard with bougainvillea and perhaps a fountain. The Hotel del Viajero is a narrow three-story building wedged between a shoddy department store and a restaurant. I have the uneasy feeling that its clientele consists mainly of American males looking for a place to pass out drunk or cavort with local prostitutes. I hope I'm wrong.

Inside, a young boy of about eleven or twelve stands behind a faux-wood counter flipping through a comic book. Behind him, a doorway half obscured by a curtain divides the proprietor's living area from the small lobby. Though there's an air-conditioning unit mounted in the wall, it doesn't appear to be working; any movement of air in this inferno comes from a single oscillating fan that does little more than rustle the pages of the boy's reading material as it swivels by.

The boy looks bored, half asleep when we enter, but he snaps to attention at our arrival and adopts a welcoming smile. "Hello. You want a room?" He's sunny and polite. Well trained.

"Hey," Noah says. "Are you Marilena's son? We're tryin' to track somebody down, a young lady."

The child stares at him, uncomprehending, and so Noah slips into Spanish, tries again. Although I can't make out what he's saying, I hear the names "Marilena," "Yulissa," and "Lety." From the boy's perplexed face and vigorous head shaking, I gather that Marilena is not available and he doesn't know any Yulissas. On the subject of Lety, however, he is quite chatty. He and Noah launch into a spirited discussion that leaves Noah looking dumbfounded and asking, *"Aquí? De véras? Aquí?"* several times while the boy nods solemnly. *"Aquí, señor. Aquí,"* he says.

I wait for Noah to translate, but when he finally does turn to me, it's with a question. "The club you saw," he says, "where Lety worked. Do you know what it looked like?"

"There was a mermaid," I say. "It had an ocean theme."

Noah turns to the boy, his Spanish stumbling now, but evidently still good enough to convey the basics. Light dawns on the child's face.

"Ah!" he says. "Treasure Island!"

I try not to wonder why a kid that age can distinguish one strip club from another.

The boy, meanwhile, gestures outside, giving directions that Noah asks him to repeat twice. At last, reasonably sure he's got a handle on it, or just too well mannered to ask a third time, Noah thanks him and propels me quickly out the door.

"Well?" I whirl on him, impatient for an update. It didn't occur to me before, but my mother must've spoken pretty decent Spanish. I have no idea where or when she learned. "What did the kid tell you?"

"He thinks Lety worked at a club called Treasure Island. It's a few blocks away."

"That's it?" I wait for him to provide further details, but he's gazing down the street, trying to orient himself. "You guys talked awhile. That's really all you got?" I can't shake off the nagging feeling that he's keeping something from me.

Noah glares in my direction and flips down his sunglasses. "I'm gettin' you to this club, aren't I? How 'bout a thank-you? You wanted to find it, and I did."

I refrain from grouching back at him. These temperatures could make anyone irritable, and he's not exactly thrilled to be here. "Maybe we should wait at the hotel until Marilena gets back," I suggest. "She might know where Yulissa is."

"I'm not hangin' around here," Noah says flatly. "That place gives me the willies."

I glance back at the Hotel del Viajero, watch a broad-shouldered man in a loud pineapple-print Hawaiian shirt approach the premises. He glances over at us for a moment, and his large sunglasses are like mirrors, reflecting back everything around him yet betraying nothing of the man beneath. He looks far too well-off to frequent Marilena's hotel, and I shudder to think what activities Pineapple Guy has planned there. I remember, on our drive from Texas, Noah telling me how much he hates border towns. *They'll hurt your soul,* he said, and I know what he means now.

I'm not sure what Marilena's son told him today, but I don't press for details. One thing I learned from the Internet last night: there are things in life I'd rather not know.

Treasure Island is not a discreet establishment. Even from a distance, you know exactly what you're getting. A neon sign, currently unlit, announces the merchandise in plain terms: GIRLS. The building's red concrete exterior features the painted silhouettes of curvaceous women and, across one of the women's crotches, the image of a treasure chest. TREASURE INSIDE, the wall boasts. From the bilingual signage, I gather that the establishment gets its share of Americans. Located on a dubious, graffiti-filled side street, Treasure Island would be substantially seedier in its peak night hours. Now, when it's still early on a weekday, few folks seem to be craving nude entertainment. I cling to this as evidence of human decency, however flimsy.

Noah and I amble slowly down the street, neither one of us excited to reach our destination. We pass a liquor store, an ATM, a couple of sleepy-looking bars just starting to show signs of life, and a pair of little boys sharing a Coke under an awning. In the shade of a doorway, a scrawny dog naps, his tongue lolling. He gazes over at us with one eye, determines that we have neither food nor water, and resumes his rest.

Outside Treasure Island, a jittery young man in shorts and a collared shirt moves up and down the sidewalk, having been tasked with coaxing passersby inside. I'm trailing several feet behind Noah, the only male on the street, so it doesn't surprise me when the hawker zeroes in on him. "*Señor!* Come see the most beautiful girls in Nogales! Private dance for a good price! Lunch special today! Two girls for the cost of one!"

Noah looks like he might throw up. He hangs back a minute, allowing me to catch up, and takes my hand. For once, the gesture is not protective but defensive. I'm his shield.

When the hawker sees me, flushed and swollen and baby-heavy, he steps out of our path and nods deferentially. The moment we approach the entrance of Treasure Island, however, he breaks into a grin. Scurries ahead and opens the door for us. "You tell them Bernardo sent you, yes?" I feel his gaze slide over my belly as he wonders what kind of kinky pair we are, and I want to ask him why he works here, to pointedly inquire if he has a daughter.

It's a stupid urge, I realize. Having a daughter — or any children — would be reason enough to do his job. They have to eat, after all.

Inside, Treasure Island is dark and cool. There are no windows, just black walls and black fabric sealing out all natural light. In the seconds before my eyes adjust, I feel the panic of sudden blindness. Then I become aware of shapes. A bar lined with stools, glass bottles gleaming. Tables, mostly empty. A few men seated, alone or with friends, heads all tilted toward the dancer. Moving on a raised platform to some thumping Spanish pop song, she's hard to see — boots and hot pants, hair that whips around her face, brief flashes of flesh bathed in dim, purply-blue light. I can't tell if she's old or young, pretty or plain, and I suppose that's the idea of all this darkness. To conceal. To let fantasy rule.

I head for the bar, mainly because it's the

farthest point from the stage and I don't want to sit amongst all the gawking men. The whole room possesses a trippy, underwater quality that makes me feel off balance, a little dizzy even, but as I scan the room, I begin to discern certain distinctive features: the disco ball, the blow-up mermaid, the shells and netting dangling from the ceiling and walls.

We're in the right place. Lety's place.

On the rear wall, I notice a detail not in my dream: a row of small booths with curtains drawn. In the gap between curtain and floor, I see a pair of tennis shoes and the high heels of a woman on her knees. All the reviews I read online come flooding back, the "services" performed for very little money by women expected to fake enthusiasm for their work. How did my mother remain hopeful she could make a difference? She must have seen and heard such depressing things.

I take a seat at the bar and let Noah order us bottled water. He tips the bartender absurdly well — no need to piss anyone off with our presence — and we wait.

A pair of women in halter tops and skimpy bottoms approach us almost immediately. The older one is thin, with sharp features that she tries to soften with big, fluffed-out hair. When she smiles, I see she's invested a lot in good dentistry. Her companion is shorter and plumper, a curvy body and girlish face. She sidles up to Noah, and her breasts graze his arm.

"You buy your man private dance," the sharp-faced woman tells me with a smirk, "then you the woman of his dreams."

I remove a few twenties from my pocket. "No dance. We just want to talk." In that moment I wish, rather absurdly, that Noah and I were wearing wedding rings.

The sharp-faced woman takes my bills. "Talk?" she says, one eyebrow lifting.

"There was a girl who worked here." Noah discreetly removes his arm from the vicinity of Curvy Girl's breasts. "Leticia. Lety. Did you know her?"

The women glance at each other. The sharp-faced dancer, clearly possessed of superior English skills, answers. "Lety no work here no more," she says.

"I know," I say. "She's dead."

This is no surprise to either woman. The sharp-faced dancer puts her hands on her hips, suspicious. "What you want with Lety?"

"I'm looking for her sister, Yulissa," I say. "Do you know her? Did Lety ever mention her?"

The woman turns to her young coworker, says something in Spanish. They converse quickly. "We don't know Yulissa," she announces, but I can't tell if she's telling the truth.

"But you knew Lety," Noah persists. "Do you know where she was from? Where her family might live?"

"She *work* here, she don't talk of her family." The woman shrugs. "She leave in April, and we don't talk."

The thumping Spanish pop song ends. On the stage behind us, the dancer receives a lukewarm response from her sparse audience.

"Why did Lety leave?" I ask the sharp-faced woman.

"Lety . . . *cómo se dice* . . ." She searches for the words in English and can't find them. *"Fue despedida."*

"She was fired." Noah translates for me with a frown.

The younger, curvier woman picks up the thread of our conversation and gestures to her stomach in explanation. "Too big."

It's unexpected, given that this girl isn't exactly a waifish gazelle herself. "They fired her because she got too fat?"

"No," the girl tells me. *"Estaba embarazada.* Like you. Baby." She points to her

335

stomach again.

The news sits in my throat, making it hard to breathe. Fifteen-year-old Lety was pregnant. Pregnant enough to be showing in April, to be fired. Four months along, I'd guess, maybe five if she carried it well. And she died just a couple months later. Why didn't someone tell me?

I know the answer will not be good, but I ask anyway. "What happened to the baby?"

The curvy girl folds her arms. "Is dead. The baby and Lety is dead."

"Are you saying she killed her own baby? She killed her baby and herself?" That would explain why Albert and Teresa neglected to mention Lety's pregnancy. You don't tell a very pregnant woman about another very pregnant woman doing away with herself and her unborn child. No wonder Albert was reluctant to have me write that article.

Neither of the two dancers will confirm Lety's role in her baby's death, however. They exchange a glance, and the curvy girl eyes us suspiciously.

Finally, the sharp-faced woman moves in closer to us. "You are a friend of Lety?" she asks.

"Kind of," I say.

"I tell you what is true." She's so close

now I can see where her over-plucked eyebrows are starting to grow in. "Nobody care for us. Nobody care for Lety and her baby. We are like the garbage to them."

I don't know who she means by "them." Her clients? The club owners?

"Lety die, and nobody care. They say, eh, she is *una puta.* She must do the drugs, she must love a bad man."

"I don't think I understand . . ."

The curvy girl puts a hand on her friend's shoulder, trying to silence her, but the sharp-faced woman has had enough. Gone is the sexy prowl. Her face is cold and hard.

"I hear what happen to Lety. The whole *barrio* know. One shot here" — she forms a gun with her thumb and index finger and points it to her gut — "and two shots here." She touches her chest. "They can tell me Lety is dead, okay? They can tell me she was no good. But they cannot tell me she kill herself."

My hands go cold. An unpleasant shiver moves down my spine. The dancer's re-enactment of Lety's death has struck a chord in me, jogged loose a memory, and I can't breathe.

Gun. Stomach. Chest.

"But who?" Noah's saying. "Who would want her dead?"

The woman shakes her head, unable to answer, or else unable to understand. But I understand. I understand perfectly. I remember what Pam told me at the funeral, the very first time I heard about Lety. *Five, six weeks ago some girl killed herself, and Donna about went off the deep end.*

That means Lety died in late June. Right around the time that I began having my nightmare.

Gun. Stomach. Chest.

My hand closes around Noah's wrist, tugs him toward the club's exit.

"What are you doing? We still haven't found out about Yulissa. Don't you think we should —"

"No." I nudge him toward the door, now desperate to get out of there.

"You feelin' okay, darlin'? Or . . ." He trails off when the sunlight hits us, dazzling, burning hot. Yet even outside, awash in heat, I find myself shivering.

Is it real? I asked her in my dream. *That scene in the shower, is it real?*

Your dreams are always real, Lety told me, and she was right. They're always real, but never mine.

"Charlie?" Noah asks. "What's goin' on?"

I stare at my half-frozen hands, helpless. "That dream I've been having," I whisper.

"About the shower." My heart aches for Lety. For the baby that never was. "She's been showing me, Noah, over and over again."

"Are you sayin' — ?"

"It wasn't about me. It was never about me." My voice cracks as I say the words. "Lety wants me to know who killed her."

Eighteen

It should feel better than it does, knowing that my daughter and I are not in imminent danger, knowing that the violence I've dreamed of again and again is not my fate. And yet, it doesn't. Doesn't feel better at all. When the dream was mine, at least there was hope, hope that I was wrong, hope that the future was not fixed, that my own free will might somehow change the outcome. Now there is nothing I can do for Lety or her baby. Their deaths are written in stone, irrevocable and unspeakably cruel.

"Maybe you're wrong," Noah says. He wants to believe me, wants to cast aside this shadow that's been hanging over us, but he's cautious, too. Doesn't want to let down his defenses prematurely.

"I'm not wrong," I murmur. "That girl said Lety was shot in the stomach and the chest. That's what I've been *seeing*. That's what I've been dreaming. All this time, she's been showing me, and I didn't get it. I thought it was me."

"Still . . ." Noah takes my hand, gallantly helping me leap over a puddle of sludge on the sidewalk. "You can't take that one dancer's opinion as proof. Sometimes people kill themselves in violent ways. We don't *know.*"

"How does somebody shoot herself more than once in the chest? And what are the chances that Lety would even have a gun?" I can't rid myself of the tearful lump in my throat. "Of all the ways to die, why would a fifteen-year-old girl go to the trouble of getting a firearm?"

"Maybe she already had one," he says. "For protection."

"If she really wanted to end her life, there's a *farmacia* on every corner. She had better options, Noah. It didn't have to be bloody. Didn't have to be painful. And you said yourself, she had people who wanted to help her. She had Sonora Hope. If she was going to kill herself, it would've been in April when she lost her job. But in June? She had things to live for."

"You'd think." He bites his lip, and I can see the emotions warring within him: relief that we no longer have this grim vision hanging over us, fear of what we could be getting ourselves into. "What about Yulissa?" he says at last. "If Lety wants you to find out who gunned her down, why'd she send you after her sister?"

"I don't know. Maybe Yulissa knows who did it. Maybe she's in danger, too."

"Don't pregnant women usually get killed by their baby daddies?" Noah asks.

"Statistically, yes. But if Lety was prostituting herself, she may not have known who the father was. We should find out if there was a boyfriend. Or a pimp."

Noah looks about to say something and then catches himself. Takes a deep breath. "Right now, the best thing we can do is go home."

I stop walking. A nearby vendor takes this as a sign of encouragement and begins waving sunglasses in my direction, assuring me of his excellent deals.

"That's it? You want to go home and pretend this never happened?"

"We'll go back to Tucson first. Wrap things up over there. Get the ball rollin' with Micky."

This is in no way a satisfying answer. "What the hell, Noah? Yesterday you said God was calling on me. Now you're all, *Aw, let it go to voice mail.* I thought you wanted to help."

"I *did* help. We found out what happened to Lety, didn't we? Maybe that's enough." He searches for a compromise, something to pacify me. "We can . . . go to the police. Let them figure out who did what."

But I won't settle for that, not after what Pam told me about Mexican law enforcement. Not after what happened to Ruben. "The Nogales police were happy to write Lety off as a suicide," I point out. "And I have nothing but my dreams and an angry stripper to say otherwise. You think the police are going to lift a finger on my say-so?"

"Probably not," he concedes. "But I still think we should leave. We can't change it, so let's . . . focus on what's ahead."

I'm caught between fury and bewilderment. "Are you saying it's ethically permissible to bow out? That we should let some psycho who shot a fifteen-year-old girl and her unborn child — a *viable* child — just walk away? Leave the sister to fend for herself because, hey, it's not our problem?"

"It's *not* our problem," Noah says.

Tears spring to my eyes. "I don't think you'd be saying that if Lety were a white girl from some middle-class American family."

The accusation hits Noah hard. He seems

to weigh my words, asking himself if I'm right. Finally, he takes me by the elbow and removes me from the line of foot traffic. "We don't have the resources to fix this now, Charlie. Our responsibility to our own livin' baby is bigger than our responsibility to one who's dead."

I know he wants me to absolve him, but I won't do it.

"Yulissa is *alive,*" I say. "That's why Lety came to me."

I look around us, at these dirty streets. Behind us, a little girl peddling gum attacks another pair of white tourists, her face twisting into a look of practiced destitution. I know that she is playing them, preying upon their guilt and pity, and yet I also know she needs that money. I know that someone, probably her mother, sent that child out to sell *chicle* because they could not provide for her. My child will have everything. But this child? What will she have?

For a moment, I understand Teresa and the burden she must carry, having risen from this kind of poverty. It's survivor's guilt, pure and simple. She flourished, and others did not.

"I love your big heart," Noah says, stroking my belly as if to remind me of my little passenger. "But someone's gotta care for *our* baby. Right now, that's you."

I stare down at the broken sidewalk. I'm alone in this, I realize. It's between me and Lety now.

Noah misinterprets my silence as agreement. "Come on." He kisses my head, and though the gesture is almost certainly meant to be tender, it strikes me as patronizing. "We'll get some food and then head back to Tucson. You can do all the investigatin' you want once we're on the right side a the border."

We speak very little at lunch. The restaurant is nicer than one would expect from the exterior, clean, colorful, and air-conditioned. I nibble on an avocado salad and take a few halfhearted bites of a bean and cheese burrito. Noah inhales his food with his usual efficiency and kicks back with a beer.

A mariachi band drifts from table to table, taking requests. I wonder if they like their work or if parading around in giant hats and traditional black suits loses its charm when you have to play "La Bamba" for the five hundredth time. This must be a popular spot for tourists; I recognize the man in the Hawaiian pineapple shirt I saw at Marilena's hotel, dining alone.

My mind, of course, is with Lety. I can't shake all that she's shown me of her life. Because it wasn't just images, some silent film of another person's existence that I viewed passively from the sidelines. I know how it felt to *be* Lety. I know the club, the men, the way she lost herself in the music, left her body behind when they reached for her. And I remember her final minutes. That feeling of hope as she stood in the shower, smiling at the kicks of her baby, looking forward to a future that seemed so close, so possible, just seconds before it was torn from her.

How can I separate myself from Lety, ignore her brutal death, having seen what I have seen? I thought it was me. I thought it was *my* baby. I can't simply set aside her pain, decide that as long as it's not mine, it doesn't matter.

Take away my American citizenship, and do you know what the difference is between me and the women I help? Teresa asked.

I didn't know. I still don't. But I can't help feeling that my purpose in coming to Arizona is tied to Yulissa. And tied, through Lety, to my mother.

It's what your mother would've wanted, Lety said of my visit to Nogales. Now I wonder what, exactly, she meant by it. A fifteen-

346

year-old expectant mother shot in late June. Donna and her daughter shot just one month later. Can these murders really be a coincidence?

"Would you like me to box your food, *señora*?"

I look up, see our genial server awaiting my response. I don't particularly feel like lugging around a doggie bag the rest of the day, but letting food go to waste in this city seems like an unforgivable display of wealth. "Sure," I mumble. "Please."

With the skill of a consummate professional, the waiter slides all our plates into the crook of his arm, loads up with glasses and silverware, and heads for the kitchen. I watch him move, admiring his dexterity in some vague way, though my thoughts are elsewhere.

"We gotta schedule our home inspection for Ten Mawith Drive," Noah says, trying to bring me back. "You excited?"

"Excited?"

It bothers me that he has already moved on, pushed the violence from his mind. If anything, he's *happy*. Giddy with relief that the bloody death we've so dreaded belongs to someone else. It feels like the worst kind of schadenfreude, but I swallow my opinions. Starting in on Noah won't solve anything right now, and we'll have plenty to argue over soon enough. Because after I talk to Albert, to Teresa, to anybody else at Sonora Hope who might know something of Lety and her sister — after that, I will have to return to Nogales.

Noah pays for our lunch in US dollars and leaves the waiter a fat tip. He grabs my plastic bag of leftovers as if half a burrito in a styrofoam container might be more than I can manage to carry. "Got your passport?" he asks.

I finger through my purse a few seconds before producing the slim, navy rectangle. "Got it."

My ticket out. Worth more than I'll ever know.

The lines to reenter the United States on foot aren't overly long, and they move quickly. We wait outside a grubby building where a couple of lanes lead up to uniformed Customs and Border Protection agents. Once we're inside, the ceilings and floors are an institutional tile, and with the waist-high turnstiles, it's not unlike a metro stop, though the lighting here is better.

Noah, in good spirits, has given up engaging me in conversation and now focuses his efforts on the retired couple behind us.

They're considerably more receptive to his chatty remarks than I am, and in no time, the woman is opening her bags and narrating for him the details of their shopping exploits in Nogales, explaining which child or grandchild will receive each purchase and why.

I glance over at the other line of folks waiting to gain entry, a quiet crew with papers or passports ready and, in most cases, little in the way of luggage. Amidst the line of tired, patient faces, I notice one that is familiar to me: the man in the Hawaiian shirt I saw at the Hotel del Viajero and later at our restaurant. I study the splashy print of his shirt. Pineapples. Brown pineapples with streaky green crowns. An Arizona resident, I figure. A shirt that tacky strikes me as a distinctly American tourist feature, like Germans wearing socks with sandals.

The CBP agent, a young woman with a lot of eyeliner, seems to know the Pineapple Guy. They greet each other warmly, friendly smiles and a joke about the weather. His voice, I note, has a slight accent, and when he produces his passport, I see that he's a Mexican citizen, after all.

Before passing through, he leans toward the female officer and speaks confidentially into her ear. She nods, smile vanishing. Her eyes scan the other lines, and then she looks directly at me. Pauses. Looks back at Noah. Pineapple Guy offers her a cheerful salute and continues merrily on his way.

Something about this whole exchange makes me uneasy.

"Ma'am?"

I look up, startled, and find the customs agent in my own line — bald, with milky-blue eyes — watching me with a look of profound boredom.

"Citizenship?"

I hold out my passport. "American."

He glances at my photo, an unflattering shot taken for a trip to Hong Kong my ex-husband and I made years ago. Back then, I wore my hair short and bobbed, and it must have been humid out that day because my flustered half smile is framed by a halo of frizz.

"Did you do any shopping today?" the bald agent asks.

"No, just visiting," I tell him. "I'm a journalist."

My answer does not interest him in the slightest. "Have a nice day."

Behind me, Noah finally stops gabbing with the retired couple and steps up to the desk. I see the young female agent gesture to her bald coworker, an abrupt cutting motion with her hand. He snaps to attention, suddenly awake.

"What's in the bag?" he asks Noah, pointing at my leftover lunch.

"Food," Noah says.

"Can you open that, please?"

Noah removes the Styrofoam container and obediently unhooks the fasteners. When he lifts the lid, his mouth falls open. My breath catches. There are no avocado slices, no remnants of my burrito inside. Just leaves, dried and green.

Even from several feet away, it looks like marijuana.

"That's not mine," Noah says helplessly. "There must have been a mix-up at the restaurant."

"Please place your hands against the wall," the bald agent announces, and the female officer waves in another agent for backup.

This is not good.

"But that's not *mine*!" Noah repeats, and suddenly everyone is looking at him, all the bored faces lighting up with curiosity. Behind him, the woman Noah's been blabbing with shares a look with her husband. *He seemed so nice,* it says.

"Hands against the wall, sir." Although the bald officer remains polite, there's a warning in his voice now. "I need to give

351

you a pat-down."

Grudgingly, Noah submits to this little bit of humiliation. I wait, hoping this will somehow get cleared up, that they'll discover it's just someone's bag of oregano, but before I know what's happened, they have him in handcuffs.

"This way, sir." Baldy directs him away from the line of pedestrian traffic and points Noah toward a room with an imposing metal door. "I'm going to have to place you under arrest."

As they're leading him off, Noah shoots me a final glance. He's afraid, I see, but not for himself. It's me he's worrying over, me hanging around this dusty border town, alone.

I watch him mouth one single, urgent word.

Go.

NINETEEN

We never should have come to Nogales. The thought cycles through my head over and over again, an endless loop of self-recrimination. Noah said it was too dangerous. He warned me. And now here we are.

I don't know who the man in the pineapple shirt is or how we ended up on his bad side, but he clearly knew what Customs and Border Protection would find in that container. He was at the restaurant. He must've had a hand in putting it there. But why? What was he doing at the Hotel del Viajero? What did we unknowingly stumble on?

I should be scared. Scared for Noah, scared for me, scared for our daughter. That would be the normal reaction. Instead, I'm furious. If that asshole thinks setting up Noah is going to make me mind my own business like a good little girl, he's got another think coming.

First things first: I need to get Noah out

of there.

I head straight for the CBP administrative building. After waiting in line for ages and getting passed around a handful of office workers, I finally find a woman who takes pity on me. She listens to my story, and though it's clear she thinks I'm one of those totally-in-denial stand-by-your-man chicks, she at least explains the process. They'll collect Noah's personal effects, she says, and field-test the leaves. If it's really marijuana, he'll be placed in a holding cell for US citizens until an agent from Homeland Security Investigations comes to handle his case. That agent will determine whether or not they have enough evidence to charge him.

"Will they let him call me?" I ask.

"Sure," she says. "Usually takes a few hours, but you'll hear from him. And if it's all a big mistake like you say, they'll release him right away."

Fingers crossed for a quick release, I settle into a twenty-four-hour McDonald's on the American side of the border and wait. For three and a half hours, I stare at my tray of fries, check that my phone is operational, and chase my own circuitous thoughts with the panting stupidity of a dog going after its own tail.

Is Pineapple Guy a drug smuggler? Why was he following us? What's his business with Marilena's hotel? Did he know that we were asking about Lety?

When Noah finally does call, he has no interest in discussing my theories. "I want you to get outta there," he tells me. "Catch a flight to New York. Go visit your grandmother or Rae. I want you to be safe. Somebody was messin' with us, and I don't want them goin' after you."

I ignore his instructions. "Have they charged you with something? Do you have a court date?"

"Right now it's simple possession. But it's Friday. I probably can't get before a judge until Monday."

"They can't put you in jail all weekend!" I protest. "Can't you post bail or something?"

"Not until a judge sets it." He sounds tired. "I'll get this taken care of, okay? I'll find a good lawyer. But you need to leave Arizona. Promise? I want you safe."

"I'll keep the baby and me safe, I promise." I make no commitment to leave Arizona. Now that we know my visions of fatal showers aren't a personal threat, I'm not worried about my own well-being. "You're sure you're all right?"

"Yeah. But if I ever catch the guy who did

this . . . I'll give these folks a legit reason to lock me up, I swear."

He doesn't sound nearly frightened enough. Carrying marijuana across a US border is a big deal. This could mean jail time for him, a permanent criminal record. I try to imagine my life without Noah. I know how hard it was to raise Keegan on my own, and I certainly don't want to take on two children under those circumstances. Then it occurs to me. If Noah's convicted, there won't *be* two children for me to raise. Ever. Child Protective Services would never place Micky with someone who has a history of drug possession.

We need a lawyer, and we need one fast. Someone smart, capable, and experienced at handling drug charges at a United States border.

The air-conditioning vent above my head lets out a sudden blast of cold air, and I cross my arms, shivering. There's only one person for me to turn to, and though she's the last person I want to invite into our lives, we're out of options.

"Noah," I tell him, "I'm calling Carmen."

Noah doesn't exactly jump for joy at the idea of my contacting his ex-wife. One might even say he strenuously objects: *Don't you call her, damn it, don't you dare!* But the facts speak for themselves. Carmen has defended drug smugglers before. She's obviously intelligent, having earned herself a free ride through law school. And on the rare occasion that they speak, she and Noah are civil to each other. At the very least, she can recommend somebody, remove some of the legwork for us. Who else do we have to go to?

That is how, for the first time ever, I find myself on the phone with Noah's ex-wife.

"Carmen Palmer," she says after the receptionist connects me. My heart sinks a little when I hear that she still uses Noah's last name.

"Hi." I haven't planned the encounter and suddenly find myself scrambling for words. "This is Charlie Cates. Noah's, um . . ." I have no good word to identify myself. "Girlfriend" sounds so trivial, and "baby mama" is hardly the relationship I want to communicate to Noah's ex. I skip past my nonexistent title. "I'm calling because Noah has run into some trouble and I thought . . . you could help, maybe. That you might know someone. A lawyer. Someone in Arizona."

"I'm sorry, are you talking about Noah *Palmer*?"

"Yes."

"My ex-husband?"

"Yes." The vent continues to pump out its frigid air. My arms break out in goose bumps.

Carmen is silent for a second. "Who *is* this?"

"Charlie Cates."

"Charlie," she says, and then something clicks. "*Oh,* got it. I was just . . . thrown off by the nickname." She doesn't dwell on it, doesn't betray any feelings of anger, jealousy, or resentment. Instead, she remains cool and professional. "Okay, Charlie. Explain to me what kind of trouble Noah's in."

"He's been arrested at the United States border." I pick up my tray of fries and slide into another booth, one not directly beneath a vent. "He was returning from Mexico, and . . . somebody planted weed in the bag. They arrested him and charged him with possession."

"Well, shit." Carmen gives an incredulous laugh. "How many ounces was he carrying?"

"Ounces? I don't know. It was in a baggie."

"Are we talking, like, a handful of pot?" Carmen asks. "Or more like a sack?"

"God, I don't know." I close my eyes. "Small, I guess. Not a lot."

"Okay." She exhales loudly. "What point of entry?"

"Nogales. The pedestrian crossing."

"Seriously? He's in Arizona?" Carmen doesn't wait for an answer. "Of all the states for him to need rescuing from, this is pretty fucking funny. I went to law school there, you know. And let me tell you, he was *not* wild about my going." I can practically hear her rolling her eyes. "I just hope he appreciates the irony, because it's certainly no thanks to him that I'm qualified to help right now."

I wonder if she's doing this on purpose, flaunting the depth of their history to me, putting me in my place. "So . . . you're going to help him?" Despite Noah's high praise for her abilities as an attorney, I was kind of hoping she'd hand me over to a colleague.

"I'll fly out tonight. Can you have someone get me at the airport?"

Her willingness to drop everything to help Noah both relieves and unsettles me. "I can get you."

"Great." She sighs and murmurs, almost to herself, "Smuggling pot. *That's* unexpected."

My temper flares. "He didn't, though! I mean, you don't actually believe he was carrying drugs, do you? Because I'm telling you, somebody planted that stuff, and I have a pretty good idea —"

Carmen silences me with a dry chuckle. "Whoa, there, tiger. It's sweet that you're so loyal and all, but from now on, you let me do the defending."

Truth be told, I'm a bit nervous about laying eyes on Noah's ex-wife. Somehow, in the almost eight months he and I have been together, I've never seen a picture of Carmen. I know a handful of facts about her — that she sold their house and moved to Houston back in April, that she retained possession of Gonzo, their Labrador retriever — but Noah and I have never discussed her at length. I've always assumed his reticence on the topic is simply another sign of his being a gentleman, that he doesn't want to speak ill of a woman he spent so much of his life with. Now, though, I begin to wonder. He *told* me they divorced because Carmen didn't want children, but what if his version of events isn't the whole story? Perhaps his reluctance to mention her is evidence of pain and not discretion, the mark of a wound that hasn't healed.

I arrive early at Tucson's trifling airport, having vastly overestimated the time I'd need to park and meet Carmen's flight. With just twenty gates and only a handful of airlines to its name, Tucson International is no Phoenix. I pace around the nearly empty concourse, concocting wild theories about Lety and the man in the pineapple shirt until at last Carmen's flight lands.

Not knowing what she looks like, I scrawl the word PALMER across a napkin to hold up to exiting passengers. This embarrassing display proves unnecessary. The flight from Houston is small, and when Carmen does make her way out, I have no doubts about her identity. Not because she looks like her sister — she's not nearly so girly and made up as Cristina — and not because she's the only young, professionally dressed Latina who steps off the plane. There's something else I see in her, something beyond the long, dark hair and shrewd black eyes. A style, a sharpness. A quickness to her step, even in heels, that says, *Don't screw with me.*

In short, I see a younger version of myself.

Looking down at my own maternity garb, a billowing white-and-tomato-colored sundress with all the shape and elegance of a potato sack, I feel about a hundred years old. Even worse, I feel suburban. Domesticated. Carmen Palmer looks like the kind who would have a loft in the city and a posse of raucous girlfriends to go out drinking with.

"Excuse me." I step out in front of her, trying to flag her down. "Are you Carmen?"

Whatever she was imagining, I obviously don't fit the bill. "Oh," she says. "Yes, hi. You must be Charlie." Her gaze flickers over my belly, noting it, dismissing it almost as quickly. "Thanks for picking me up. I hate dealing with rentals."

"No problem. I'm just . . . so glad you could make it."

"Well." She smiles grimly as she adjusts the strap on her laptop bag. "Noah and I have certainly had our ups and downs, but he doesn't quite deserve prison, in my book."

"I'm glad you feel that way." I can't bring myself to look her in the eye. The knowledge that this woman was physically intimate with him — many, many times — makes me feel a little sick to my stomach. "I don't think I'd be quite so generous with my ex, honestly."

Carmen's already ahead of me, following the signs for parking. "He gave me the dog," she says with a backward glance. "That goes a long way."

■ ■ ■ ■

Even though I'm anticipating a long and awkward drive back to Nogales, Carmen proves bizarrely friendly. "I remember buying this car," she says, hopping into the SUV and rifling through Noah's CD collection with a knowing smile. "His singing voice is criminal, isn't it? But he just won't stop." Though she says nothing about my pregnancy or my relationship with Noah, she asks where I'm from, what I did before coming to Texas, and gets a little gushy when she learns about my work for *Sophisticate*.

"You're kidding me!" she exclaims. "I *love* that magazine. What have you written for them? Anything that I would know?"

"Probably not." I try not to notice the way the fading light plays upon her unreasonably great hair. "I was an editor the last several years."

"Did you ever meet any celebrities?"

"Sure. I did some interviews, met some high-profile people at industry events. You get a lot of freebies with that job, people angling for magazine coverage."

"That's amazing." She laughs. "I don't know what I was thinking, going to law school. Clearly, there were better options.

And now you're living in *Sidalie*? Why?"

All the small talk strikes me as absurd, a ridiculous diversion from the panic I'm feeling, but when I try to discuss Noah's case, she raises her hand, waving me off. "No, no. You are not going to stress out about this, you poor thing," she says. "I can't believe you got saddled with this craziness. But it's not your problem anymore. It's mine, okay? I'll make it right, I promise."

She sounds so sure of herself, so confident that she can get Noah back, that I almost burst into grateful tears. Her kindness is so surprising, so bighearted, and it makes absolutely no sense to me at all until she asks, "So how do you like working for Noah?"

At first, I think I've misheard her. "What?"

"He's so disorganized, isn't he?" she prods. "I told him for years to get an assistant. He was always, 'No, no, I can handle it.' I'm sure you've made his life much easier."

I inhale sharply as I realize her error. *Oh my God. She thinks I'm Sharlene.* An understandable mistake, when I consider it. Carmen's sister has undoubtedly kvetched about Sharlene for the past few months; the hotheaded Cristina and cool, efficient Sharlene have been at odds with each other

364

ever since Sharlene began working for Noah. And "Charlie" is not an unthinkable nickname for "Sharlene," nor is it a stretch to believe that Noah's personal assistant might've been the one tasked with finding him a lawyer.

Do I tell her?

For a moment I'm tempted to brush it all under the rug, to play the role of Sharlene and ensure her civility and cooperation a while longer. Sooner or later, though, she'll learn the truth, and then what? How much worse would things be if I knowingly deceived her?

I put on my big-girl panties and come out with it. "I think there may be some confusion. I'm not Noah's assistant."

"Oh, I'm sorry. What's your title?"

"I don't work for him."

She turns slowly to me, suddenly aware this is going somewhere unpleasant. "You said your name was Charlie. I thought . . . aren't you Sharlene?"

"No," I murmur. "I'm Charlotte." From the blank look on her face, my name means nothing to her. Cristina must have spared her sister the details of Noah's new life, seeing no need to hurt her. On the one hand, I'm impressed the little blabbermouth kept it to herself. But on the other . . . the job now falls to me.

"This baby," I say, because it's the simplest way I know to explain things, "it's Noah's."

Carmen blinks. "Really," she says. "Then maybe you'd like to explain what the hell I'm doing in this car with you."

"You asked if someone could meet you at the airport. I thought . . ."

"You thought *what*? That I wanted to meet my successor? Spend *time* with you?" She practically spits out the words. "My God, you could've *told* me who you were!"

"I thought you knew."

"Of *course* I didn't know! I didn't even know you existed! And what the — you're *pregnant*?" She pulls her arms in against her chest as if protecting her own uterus from this horror. "Believe me, if I'd known that I'd be stuck dealing with Noah's preggo girlfriend, I would *not* have come."

"Oh really?" I don't like this answer. "So you came because you thought you'd get some alone time with him?"

"I came because you said he needed help and I am a decent human being," she snaps. "But I think I'm entitled to have feelings."

I grip the steering wheel a little tighter. "Exactly what kind of *feelings* do you have, Carmen?"

"Um, not wanting to be around my ex-husband's new woman? You know we got divorced in *December*? That's nine months ago, and look at you!" She gestures in disgust at my baby bump. "I mean, wow, he must've been really broken up, huh?"

"He said you'd been separated for months."

"*Four* months. It wasn't that long." She sits tensely beside me, legs crossed, spine straight, and I don't know what to say, how to defend myself.

"Nothing about our relationship was planned."

She casts my belly a long, contemptuous look. "Are you sure about that?"

"Are you implying I intentionally got pregnant?"

"Are you implying that you didn't? Because there's this thing called birth control, you know. Works great. Any moron can keep from getting knocked up these days."

I grit my teeth and let her have that one. In her position, I'd be angry, too.

"Just tell me one thing," Carmen says softly. "One thing, and I don't want to know the rest of it —"

I don't let her finish. "He didn't cheat on you, if that's what you're after."

She searches my face for any signs of

deceit. "Do you swear to me?"

"You guys were married for ten years. You really think he's the kind of man who doesn't respect his marriage vows? You really think he'd be unfaithful?"

"That's not an answer," she says coolly.

"He wouldn't and he didn't," I say. "I swear." I try not to go off on her, but it's hard. I'm wound so tight, and she's *here,* a convenient target of my ire simply by virtue of her proximity. *But you've been cheated on,* I remind myself. *You know that it matters.* I take a careful breath, steady myself. "I met him in Louisiana. January, when your divorce was already final. One night, and we both got more than we bargained for."

Something in her deflates, and I wonder if I've actually done her a disservice. Maybe it would've been easier for her to hate us, to have words like "adultery" and "infidelity" on her side. It certainly made it easier for me to move past my ex.

We're close to the American Nogales now, a few minutes from city limits. In the dark, I can just make out the rolling hills dotted with buildings, the sudden burst of industry that springs up on both sides of the border. I already regret calling Carmen. She's just another layer of stress and guilt to add to everything else right now.

"Look," I say, "I understand if you don't want to help Noah, I do. But if that's the case, tell me now. Because I'm going to need to find someone else, fast. A lawyer who can fix this."

She doesn't answer for a moment, just opens my glove box and rifles through it until she locates a broken-tipped pencil. I watch her gather up her mane of long black hair, wind it expertly into a knot, and then jam the pencil in. She looks over in my direction, all business now, every hair in place. I can no longer read the hurt or anger in her face, although I'm sure it's there, simmering beneath the surface, preparing to boil over.

"He'll have his arraignment on Monday," she tells me. "I'll stay until then. But if they won't plea down to probation, then Noah's really up shit's creek. He'll need someone else, someone who's in it for the long haul. That's obviously not me." She turns to stare out the passenger-side window, so that I see nothing but her neatly knotted hair. "Not anymore."

TWENTY

The fanciest hotel in Nogales, Arizona, is probably not, by Carmen's standards, very fancy. It's a chain hotel that comes in at less than a hundred dollars per room, and I can just see Carmen wrinkling her nose at the salmon color scheme as I check us in at the front desk.

High maintenance, I observe with a certain amount of satisfaction. *I could've guessed as much.* She's a *Sophisticate* fan, after all. Who knows what she'll bill us for her time.

Once settled into my hotel room, I take a long shower, grateful that at least I no longer have to fear my own demise while doing so. The baby responds to the sound of falling water with curiosity, poking her hands and feet in a series of sudden and bizarre bulges across my abdomen. I poke her back.

"It's just water," I tell her. "It won't hurt you. We're okay now, little girl. No more worries."

She's not even born yet, and I'm already telling her lies. We're far from okay. Noah's absence chafes, wears away at me until my mind is raw and red and sore. And the person responsible is still out there. How do I find him?

I try to conjure up a mental image of the man in the pineapple shirt but find I'm fuzzy on details. He had broad shoulders, dark hair, and a receding hairline, yet I remember little about his face, neither handsome nor ugly. All I can picture is that damn shirt, so loud and eye-catching it distracted from all the rest of him.

I work shampoo through my hair, catch a whiff of coconut and something citrus. Review the key facts with growing unease. Clearly, Pineapple Guy can move freely back and forth across the border. He has something against Noah and/or me. And I might not recognize him when he inevitably changes his shirt. I need to watch my back.

Pineapple Guy, it turns out, is not the only thing I've got to worry about.

As I'm rinsing out my hair, the heaviness comes, a soporific chill that settles over me like a layer of snow. I look down, see blood spiraling toward the drain. Those blue and yellow tiles hover behind my eyelids, creeping closer with each blink.

Lety's reminding me of my promise.

"I can't help you now," I say, but the words are slurred, dragging against my tongue. Somewhere there's a rancid smell, an unpleasant rotting odor that worms its way into my nostrils, urging me firmly to the other side.

I turn off the shower. Grab a towel and stagger over to the hotel bed, leaving patches of damp carpet in my wake. I just want to sleep, to nestle up with these plump pillows and give myself over. I plunge into the downy comforter, press my cheek to the freshly laundered cotton.

But something's wrong. Instead of softness, sharp corners. Rough edges tearing at my skin. Mounds of metal and tire and plastic and old cardboard. Cans and wrappers, discarded containers, soggy newspaper, a broken doll — they're rising up around me, enclosing me in a fortress of refuse.

I know she's summoned me here, but I don't know why.

Lety?

The second that I call her name, she's beside me, huddled amongst all the junk. Something about her face is fuller, softer than when last I saw her. And her dress —

she's ditched the sexy stripper gear in favor of a shapeless white-and-tomato-colored maternity ensemble. *My* dress, I think, because now I'm wearing it, too, standing beside her like some taller, paler twin, our big boobs and watermelon bellies a perfect match.

The sight terrifies me.

I'm not like you, I tell her, but she only mouths the words back at me, her hands moving with my hands, her expressions mirroring mine. She's not Lety at all, but my own reflection. My reflection with Lety's face.

Around us, the wall of trash re-forms into a single peak. I struggle to my feet and shade my eyes from a blinding sun. Beside me, Lety does the same. We labor uphill, across bumpy, rolling ground that seems to shift beneath us. Lety's gasping breaths echo my own; she matches me stride for stride. We have to get to the top of this hill, although I'm not sure why.

At last, with a final surge, I reach the summit, survey swelling piles of garbage, wipe the sweat from my hairline. What am I doing here? Why am I seeing this?

A movement underneath my left foot gets my attention. I jump back, sensing that I'm standing on something living — a rat perhaps, or some other scavenger. When I look down, however, I see a person. Brown-eyed, golden-skinned, with poorly cut bangs. A girl, watching me.

I drop to my knees, offer her a hand, try to help her up, but she's caught in the mess of garbage, her body wedged in tight. I try to brush away the other scraps of trash to unbury her, but as I do, it becomes clear that I'm not dealing with garbage at all.

I'm standing on a tower of people. A mass of human bodies. Stacks of brown limbs in brightly colored clothing, black hair spilling from the crevices. And eyes. Quiet, blinking eyes that fill me with panic. These people are alive.

I let out a startled noise, not a scream, but a strangled exclamation. Feel a hand on my arm, calming me. Lety's there, small yet strong, no longer my reflection but a flesh-and-blood creature of her own. She stoops down to the little girl that I've been trying to dig out. Dips her hands into the sea of bodies, trying to lift her up.

The hill begins to shudder beneath us. From the pile of bodies: hands. So many hands. Palms up, fingers curled. Asking for assistance. Waiting to receive.

Yulissa, Lety says, still tugging on the child. *You see? You have to help.*

I can't! I gesture wildly around me. *Don't you get it? There's too many, Lety! I can't help them all.*

Lety presses her cheek to the child's matted hair and shakes her head. English is not enough, not enough to reach me, and so she speaks to me with her eyes, wordless and eloquent.

Not all of them, her eyes say. *Just this one. You can help this one.*

I awake to the sound of a text message going off somewhere near my head. The blinking blue numbers on the bedside clock flash twelve o'clock, which can't be right. I grope around for my phone and determine that it's Saturday, ten a.m. How did I sleep so late?

The text, I see, comes from Pam: *where r u?*

Nogales, I reply. *Where are YOU?* I sit up in bed and try to remember what I did with my prenatals. Life may be going to hell in a handbasket, but my daughter still needs her vitamins.

My phone chimes loudly, heralding the arrival of another text. *on a date,* Pam writes, and I have to read it twice to make sure I understand her. Pam? On a breakfast date? Is she about to embark upon the most ill-advised rebound relationship ever? And why is she telling *me* this?

Congrats? I type as I fill the hotel's plug-in coffeepot with water. *Seems a little soon.*

def too soon, Pam responds, and then posts a digital photograph to our exchange. I squint down at what looks like a random picture of a man and woman in a Starbucks, their heads bent together in intimate conversation or perhaps just nuzzling. An unremarkable photo and inelegantly shot, but I can see what she's getting at. Although only the back of the woman's head is visible, the man is without a doubt McCullough. Pam's on a date, all right — someone else's.

This raises a number of questions, not least being when Pam went from thinking McCullough was "a decent guy" to worthy of tailing. I don't for a moment imagine she just bumped into these two.

Think he was cheating? I ask.

probably. Pam doesn't dwell on her discovery, significant as it may be. *what r u doin in nogales?*

I tear open a packet of coffee and load up the coffeemaker. *Sonora Hope stuff,* I answer, intentionally vague. I prefer not to explain Noah's arrest, not to a cop, not if Carmen can make it all go away.

Pam's next message gives me serious

pause, however. *u know any reason sanchez would b following u?*

"Sanchez?" The suggestion is so strange I find myself saying his name aloud. Where does Pam come up with this stuff? Before I can inquire further, though, someone knocks on the hotel door. I set down my phone. It has to be Carmen — she's the only one who knows I'm here. Still, I look through the peephole for confirmation. Can't be too careful.

Sure enough, Carmen's standing in the hall yakking on the phone. I throw open the door.

"Any news?"

She holds up a finger, the ultimate in cheap power moves. Make me wait, just to show that her time is more valuable than mine.

Whatever, Carmen, I think. *Get Noah out of jail, and I'll play all your little games.*

I finish fixing my cup of badly brewed coffee, all the while covertly assessing how attractive she is. Minus the baby gut, I'm taller and thinner, but she has better hair, a more curvaceous figure. While my face is comprised of angles and cheekbones, hers is round and youthful, her makeup strategically applied to make her look older. I guess "young" is not a look that works in your favor when you're a defense lawyer.

She continues to yap away on the phone, even giving me a faux apologetic look at one point. A work colleague, from the friendly banter and legal jargon. I get the feeling that she works with a lot of men. There's a toughness she adopts, a coarse keeping-up-with-the-boys sense of humor that says she's learned to navigate a male world.

"So," she announces when she's finally ended her call, "I just met with Noah."

I take a sip of terrible coffee and try not to imagine them together in the close confines of a jail cell, Carmen heroically arriving to free him. "Well? Can you get him out of this?"

"They've got everything they need to bust his balls," she says. "This isn't going to be easy, but I think I can swing it. Unless, of course, there's something you aren't telling me."

"Me?" I bristle. "Like what?"

"Oh, I don't know." She studies a fingernail, feigning indifference. "It's a little weird, the sudden appearance of weed in your personal belongings. Any idea how it got there?"

"That sounds like an accusation."

She gazes at me appraisingly for a few

seconds. Without waiting for an invitation, she brushes past me into my hotel room and settles herself in the mango-colored armchair. I shut the door behind us, wondering what I'm in for now, what wild allegations she's going to throw at me. Yet Carmen doesn't lose her cool. She props herself up on one elbow, slouchy and casual.

"Look," she tells me, "I'm a defense lawyer. I don't usually like to know too much about my clients. But this is personal. I don't want anything bad to happen to Noah. So please, I have to ask . . . what were you guys doing in Mexico?"

"Shopping," I say tonelessly.

"That would be a great answer, except that neither one of you bought a damn thing."

I leave my nasty coffee on the counter and sit on the edge of the bed, stone-faced. "What did Noah tell you?"

"See now, that's the thing." She works her fingers through a long strand of her hair. Tilts her head to one side. "He sounded a little crazy, to be honest. He said you were trying to find some girl. Some girl you *dreamed* about."

"Huh." I can feel my jaw tighten. *Really, Noah? You told your ex-wife about this?* "That sounds pretty crazy, all right."

"Maybe it's not. He said you see things. Dead children." Carmen's watching me with the easy, open face of a therapist, but I don't trust her. Not for a second. "Is that true? Do you think you have, like, special powers?"

"Why? What does it matter?" I want to punch her. She's making me sound like some total head case.

She puts her hands in her lap and bends toward me, still in therapist mode. "We both want what's best for Noah, right?" she asks. "If the pot is yours, maybe you should own up. You don't want secrets like that between you. And they'd go easy on a first-time offender. I'm sure we could find medical uses to justify —"

"Screw you, Carmen. *It wasn't mine.*"

"Okay." She extends a nyloned leg and lets her designer pump dangle from her toes. "It's just that the whole story is . . . kind of fishy. You can see how it might look to a judge."

I can see how it would look to a judge, all right.

"Listen," Carmen tells me, "I can get Noah a good deal, no problem. He'd be out of there faster than a sneeze through a screen door. It would go on his record, but he's got his own company, so it's not like he'll be scaring off employers."

"All right. Then what do you need me for?"

She exhales, a slow hiss through her teeth. "He told me today he won't accept any plea deals. You know why?"

"Micky," I murmur. "They'd never let us adopt Micky."

"Exactly." Carmen flops back in the chair. "He's being totally irrational about this. You need to talk to him. Get him straightened out before his court appearance on Monday."

"Straighten him out how? Tell him to accept blame for something he didn't do?" I knead my forehead with the tips of my fingers, trying to stave off the headache that's coming. "Somebody slipped us that bag, Carmen. Either they were using us to run drugs, which seems unlikely, or they were deliberately trying to get us in trouble."

"That also seems unlikely."

"But it *happened*. And I'm pretty sure I saw the guy who did it. He pointed us out to the CBP agent. He knew what we were carrying."

She studies me. Frowns as if I'm describing some paranoid hallucination. "You saw this?"

"Yes! He had a Mexican passport and he

was wearing a Hawaiian shirt with pineapples. The agent he talked to seemed to recognize him. For all I know, he's got some racket going with CBP."

"You're sure he picked Noah out of the line?"

I nod. Know that my certainty doesn't mean jack to her.

"Well," she says, not exactly brimming with confidence, "I guess I could ask for the footage. Look for people who crossed the border yesterday around the same time you did."

My heart jumps at the thought. "Please. Please do that. I want to know his name."

If we can find out who Pineapple Guy is, figure out why he's gunning for us, we just might discover a connection to Lety, to Yulissa. Maybe even to my mother.

Carmen stands up and takes a few steps toward the door. "I'll see what I can do. No promises." She pauses in the middle of the room, hands on her hips, squinting at a point somewhere behind me. "This Micky kid. You guys are really going to take her?"

"We might."

"But you're already . . ." She chews on her lip. "I mean . . . isn't one kid enough?"

"She's my niece," I say. "Her mother was murdered. I'm her only family."

Carmen doesn't speak for a moment, and I'm both curious and scared of her thoughts. "So what makes you think Noah will be a decent father?" she asks at last. It's a fair question.

"I don't know. The fact he wants to be one."

"I just don't get it." She folds her arms, hugs them to her chest. "He was always *so* against having kids. We both were, you know. Him with a dad who ran off, and me, one of four. We always said just the two of us, that was enough. And then suddenly . . . it wasn't."

I don't know what she wants me to do. Express sympathy? Apologize? Explain the change of heart that ended their marriage?

Carmen hugs herself a little tighter. "I always figured if he could change his mind so quickly, he'd eventually change it back again," she says. "But now, with two in the works . . . well, there's no going back, is there? Once you've got 'em, they're yours. Whether you want 'em or not." She blinks, suddenly self-conscious. "I'm sorry, I'm not trying to be a jerk. And I don't want him back or anything like that. It's just . . . weird. After so many years, you think you know someone."

She seems genuinely flustered, not malicious, and that makes her comments all the more worrisome. What if she's right? What if he *does* change his mind about children? There's no Undo button. Our baby is coming, however he feels about it.

I'm not about to share my doubts with Carmen. "Where do we go from here? Legally, I mean."

She shrugs. "If Noah gets his head out of his ass, I'll get him a sweet deal. I'm pretty good at what I do." She smiles faintly. " 'Slicker than pig snot on a radiator,' that's what Daddy Jack used to say."

I'm acutely aware that I'll never get to meet Noah's grandfather, never get to reminisce about his cute Southernisms.

"The way I see it, Noah has two options," Carmen says. "Suck it up and plea, or keep spouting this little conspiracy theory of yours and hang his hat on a jury trial."

I look up. "You think he'd have a shot with a jury?"

"Nope," she says. "Not a prayer. So if you've got some sway with Mr. Stubborn, now would be the time to exercise it."

And then she's off, leaving me with only the discomfiting memory of her high heels, glowing skin, and trim, baby-less figure.

Oh, Charlie, I think. *What have you unleashed?*

■ ■ ■ ■

Despite Lety's colorful attempts at communication, I've pretty much forgotten about her when Albert calls. My head is full of Noah as I squeeze into a maternity tank top and grab my phone.

"Hi," Albert says. "Just thought I'd check in about your article."

"Oh. Yeah." The article, of course, is barely on my radar at this juncture. I consider spilling the beans to Albert about our troubles at the border but decide against it. Drug arrests aren't something you advertise. The fewer people who know, the better.

"I don't know if you're still interested in Lety's story," Albert begins, "but I grabbed her file yesterday."

"You did?"

"I got curious after we talked," he admits. "Donna didn't always keep up with her field notes, but there was some information in there you could probably use."

"Lay it on me. You never know what could be helpful."

"Looks like Leticia Medina came to Sonora Hope in April as a referral from Marilena. Lety was about five months pregnant." The unborn baby hangs for a second in the air before Albert continues. "Donna immediately arranged for medical care. Lety had several doctor's visits, some prenatal tests. Everything looked good."

"Then why would she kill herself, Albert? If she was being so well cared for, why would Lety end her life? And her baby's, for that matter." Does he know it was murder? Does he suspect?

"I have no idea," he says. "She must've had . . . outside pressures. That's the whole point of your article, right? The everyday realities these women face. Sometimes Sonora Hope can help, but sometimes . . . well, there's only so much one organization can do."

"Was there anything in Lety's file about her family?"

"It didn't say where she was from originally," Albert replies, "but according to Donna's notes, Lety lived in Tirabichi for a few years before she got the dancing gig."

"Where's Tirabichi?"

"Up in the hills. Tirabichi is a Nogales garbage dump. There's a settlement there, about thirty families who make their living sifting through trash and collecting recyclables."

Garbage. Of course. I collapse sideways

onto the bed, phone still pressed tightly to my ear.

Lety tried to show me. She wanted me to know where she came from.

"It's hard to imagine literally living in a dump," I tell Albert, and my voice sounds remarkably normal for someone feeling so shaky. "This could be . . . a powerful angle for the article."

"I thought you might say that," Albert says wryly. "That's why I'm calling. I'm going up there with a few volunteers this afternoon to distribute protective gloves. Would you like to come along?"

"Sorry, did you say you're handing out *gloves*?"

"The recyclers often cut themselves when picking through the trash," Albert explains, "and then of course they're open to all kinds of infection without the money to treat it. So we go out there a couple times a year just to make sure folks have something to protect their hands. The kids, too."

"Right," I breathe. "That's — a great idea." I pause for a minute, daring myself to make this decision. Tirabichi, a community of garbage people. Lety wants me there, obviously. But do I go back into Mexico? What if Pineapple Guy is waiting for me, ready to make trouble at the border again?

How do I know it's safe?

"You could get some photographs," Albert suggests, sensing that I'm on the fence. "I think your readers would be blown away to see how these people live. And honestly, I'm really proud of the work we do there. We'll be delivering clean drinking water, too. If you come along, I can get you interviews."

I think of Lety and her baby, shot dead in the shower, their murder somehow disguised as a suicide. And I think of Donna, of Jasmine, shot dead in that putrid-smelling apartment. It's a violent world, and these events could be unrelated. But I'm starting to doubt that.

"Albert? Did my mother ever do work at Tirabichi?"

He seems surprised by the question. "Of course. That's where she found Marilena."

"The woman with the hotel," I say.

"We really helped her get started," Albert murmurs. "Marilena is the kind of success story that keeps me in this. And Donna was the one who first connected with her. Donna connected with everyone out there, really. I haven't been to Tirabichi since she died, but . . . I'd imagine the families are all taking it pretty hard."

I know then that I'm going. That I can't

stay away, can't ignore Lety's message. That it's probably a good thing Noah's in custody right now because if he knew what I was planning, he might try to bodily restrain me.

"All right, Albert," I say. "This afternoon. I'm in."

Lety was right. This is what my mother would've wanted. This is the only path I can see to the truth — not just about Lety and her sister, but about Donna, too. To say I have no misgivings about venturing back into Nogales would be a lie, but my concerns aren't limited to just one side of the border. Not when I glance out the window a few minutes later and spot a familiar figure peering into the window of my SUV.

He's gone by the time I make it out to the parking lot, but it's clear now that Pam's question earlier was not so far afield. Do I know any reason Sanchez would be following me? Sure I do, and it's the same reason Pineapple Guy is causing trouble.

I'm getting close to something. Very, very close.

Twenty-One

From the back of a rattling Sonora Hope van, I take in the sun-drenched hills of Nogales. Here, on the steep dirt roads that our vehicle strains to climb, poverty is no longer city-flavored, not composed of shiny merchandise for tourists or tall, crumbling buildings. Instead, the houses are squares of plywood, roofs of corrugated tin, cut-out windows sometimes lacking frames or glass. They look like playhouses, their exteriors still under construction or else painted startling colors — pink, lavender — and edged with stacks of tires to prevent erosion in the perilous sloping land.

Albert sits in the passenger seat, well accustomed to our surroundings, squinting as he cleans the lenses of his sunglasses. Carlos, a retiree-turned-volunteer, drives. The van's radio is broken, but Carlos sings Spanish songs to us in a cheerful baritone. He has the A/C on, of course, but it barely reaches the back, where I sit cross-legged amongst the boxes of gloves and cases of water that we have come to deliver. I take a long drink from my own water bottle. Peel the thin fabric of my shirt from my sticky skin and try to invite in some air.

Having seen Tirabichi in my dream, I have some idea of what to expect, but it still surprises me when the van pulls up the rocky path and I see it all in three vivid dimensions: the mountains of trash, the human dwellings constructed from waste, the trees adorned with whatever plastic bags caught a breeze, and the strangely pastoral green hills rolling in the valley below. This is the stuff of postapocalyptic action movies, the kind of bleak and gritty setting Hollywood directors spend millions trying to achieve, only with more sunlight, more color.

It's two p.m., and we're approaching the worst of the day's heat. I spot a couple people working their way through one of the trash piles. "They're up at dawn," Albert says, waving to someone through the window. "Seven days a week, whenever the trucks come, there they are. It's not a life for the lazy."

Carlos guides the van down a trail well worn by municipal vehicles and parks. He comes around to open the back and helps me jump down. The smell is everything you'd expect from a landfill in August. I breathe through my mouth. Take stock of the people I see scattered about, foraging for the dump's hidden treasures. No one looks particularly happy or despondent, I decide. Just focused, like anyone with a job to do.

A few of the residents have already spotted the van and come to say their hellos. A white-haired woman ducks out of a little house made from sheets of metal and blankets, her thin lips rising up in a smile when she sees Albert.

"*Buenos días, guapo!*" she calls, and Albert grins.

"*Doña Imelda! Cómo le va?*"

They aren't as dirty as I anticipated. I was picturing tattered clothing, faces blackened like coal miners, and while their hands are stained, the T-shirts and shorts and loose dresses on Tirabichi's inhabitants are no more ragged than what you'd find in any Goodwill or Salvation Army store. I wonder if they receive their clothes from another nonprofit or if they scavenge these, too.

About half the folks we encounter know Albert. They greet him with smiles, waves, warm exclamations in Spanish. Heat and a lack of running water mean that no one here smells too good, but Albert doesn't seem to notice. He asks how everyone is doing, listens to their answers with concern or pleasure, and I detect no condescension, no superiority or ego in his interactions. His eyes tell the people of Tirabichi that they are important, that they are his equals, and his respect for them is so natural, so unaffected, I want to cry.

Hang on to this, I tell myself. *Good people really do exist in the world.*

Maybe, I think, my mother was one of them. Maybe, after all those years of living in the darkness, she became a candle, doing her best to light the way. I wish that I had known her, this woman she became.

Albert introduces me to people as we go, switching effortlessly in and out of Spanish. I'm particularly fascinated by the children I meet. Victor, Graciela, Pablo — no longer nameless kids inhabiting a dump, but bright-eyed, wisecracking young people who speak readily with me while Albert translates. A teenager, Victor has lived in Tirabichi for nearly a decade. It's what he knows, he says, his home, and he never wants to leave. Graciela, a girl about Micky's age, proudly shows me her collection of dolls, each one salvaged from the depths of the dump. Pablo, a student at the local school, describes a surprisingly normal life of schoolwork, friends, and squabbles with his siblings.

I didn't know it would be like this. Not sad-sack charity cases, just *people* living here.

"So where'd you learn Spanish?" I ask Albert when we finally get a minute to ourselves. For a pasty redhead, he boasts some impressive language skills.

"I lived in Honduras a couple years after college," he tells me. "Peace Corps."

If I weren't nearly eight months pregnant and in love with another man, I would likely be crushing over Albert. He's not much to look at, but he's so *kind.* I wonder why Pam chose Teresa as the target of her jealousy. If you look past Donna and Albert's age difference, surely Albert was the one to watch: divorced and lonely, a close friend who shared a mutual passion for her work.

"What do you think?" Albert asks, pushing his sunglasses back onto the bridge of his nose. "Are you getting enough material for your article?"

"Definitely." I watch a man in a Diamondbacks cap haul several scraps of metal over to a pile. The article I never meant to write takes shape in my mind so swiftly and clearly I can almost forget the real reason that I'm here.

"Albert!" The man deposits his final load of metal and approaches us. "You come to visit?" He wears jeans and a pair of beat-up cowboy boots, and his leathery, sun-darkened skin speaks to a life spent laboring outdoors. He's the first person here to speak English, I note. "How you doing?"

"Doing fine, Duardo," Albert replies. "This is Charlotte Cates. She's a journalist. *Una periodista,*" he adds when the man squints at the word "journalist." "She's writing a story about Sonora Hope."

"Nice to meet you, ma'am." Duardo smiles, but he stares at the ground as if he doesn't quite dare to look me in the face. I wonder if he dislikes the idea of American journalists sniffing around or if he's simply uncomfortable around pregnant women. "You see Marilena lately?" he asks Albert.

"I was going to stop by Marilena's place when we finished up here, actually."

Duardo tilts the visor of his baseball cap down toward his eyes, a vain attempt to block the sun. "She have the baby last month?"

"No," Albert says, heaving a sigh. "I don't think she did."

My ears perk up. Marilena didn't look like

someone who'd just had a baby when I saw her at the presentation last weekend.

"Three babies now, eh?" Duardo shakes his head. "Bad news. She visit a doctor?"

"I don't know."

"Living here do it, man. I bet they throw the chemicals here, you know, the *maquiladoras*. Maybe they kill her babies, those chemicals."

Albert raises his hands palm up as if to indicate his complete lack of knowledge on the subject. "She hasn't even lived here the last couple of years," he says. "I don't know what it is."

"Regina's baby, too," Duardo murmurs. "And now Ysabel. She tell you? She say she going to move away from here. And Doña Imelda with the cancer." He removes his cap and wipes his hairline. Settles his hat back on his head. "Maybe something in the water."

"Yeah, I don't trust the water around here," Albert agrees. "That tank you guys use — it doesn't look that clean." He gestures to the contents of the van behind us. "Make sure you grab a couple cases before we go, okay? And gloves."

"Thank you." Duardo nods at me, too polite to ignore me outright, but not quite making real eye contact. *"Señora."*

Albert has drifted off to confer with Carlos about something, and Duardo moves as if to join him. I pounce before he can make his escape. "Maybe you could help me, Duardo." This is my first and probably only chance to speak to someone without requiring a translator. "You live here, right?"

"A little while." He nudges a flattened soda can with his shoe, unenthused about speaking to me. "I hope I leave soon."

"Your English is great," I tell him. "Where'd you learn?"

"I live in Phoenix eight years and take classes at a church. I come here in February."

Why on earth did you come back? I want to ask, but the question seems rude. "Did you . . . miss your family?"

"My family is in Phoenix," he says. "They are waiting for me." He gazes at a nearby pile of garbage, his eyes cloudy. "I have no papers. Immigration find me, and they send me back."

"Oh." I should've seen that one coming. "I'm sorry. That's rough."

"Yeah," he acknowledges. "I try to cross the border in May, but . . . I run into some trouble in the desert. So. I have to save money and use a *coyote* next time." He lifts his eyes to mine, suddenly defiant. "You can write that in your newspaper. Write how I have a little boy in Phoenix and his mama need my paycheck."

"I'll write all that," I tell him, and I mean it. "Can I ask . . . why'd you pick Tirabichi?" With English skills this good, surely he has better options.

"Everything here is free." Duardo shifts awkwardly, and I see something in him that I didn't see in any of the other residents: shame. "When they deport you, they leave you in Nogales with nothing. You have a few nights at San Juan Bosco, maybe some meals. But you are alone in the city. No money, no job. I have no family there. Tirabichi is . . . a place to go."

My face must betray my feelings.

"Here is not so bad." He shrugs off my pity quickly. "I make money recycling, more than at the *maquiladoras.*"

I heard him tossing around this word earlier with Albert. "You mean the factories?"

"The American factories pay five dollars a day. But I have days here I make six or seven dollars. So this is better."

I don't ask how much he earned in Phoenix. It would be cruel, like asking him to measure how far he's fallen.

"I hope you can be with your son," I say.

398

"Me too." Duardo wipes the back of his neck. "He have his birthday next month. Five years. I want to be home." His lips come together in a thin line, and he adjusts his visor low over his eyes so that I can't see his face. *"Buenas tardes, señora."*

Albert returns from his powwow with Carlos, and together we watch Duardo shuffle through the dump, his skinny shoulders slumping. For a moment, I think he's the saddest man I've ever seen. He doesn't just live in garbage. He feels like garbage.

"Nice guy," I say, swallowing back the lump in my throat. "You think he'll make it back into the States?"

"Possibly," Albert says. "But not legally."

The subject is too depressing to pursue, so I move on to another bummer. "I didn't realize Marilena was pregnant."

"She isn't. Not anymore."

I glance at him. "Has she really lost three babies? Because that's a *lot,* Albert. And it sounds like she's not the only one."

"Yeah." Albert rubs his face, and I know it's bothering him, too. "There have been some problems," he says. "Stillbirths. I don't know exactly. These aren't families that can easily afford another child, so at first I thought maybe the women were having, you know . . . abortions." He lowers his voice when he pronounces the word. "But these seem to be problems very late in pregnancy. Or complications in birth."

I imagine carrying my baby to term only to lose her in labor. Suddenly I want out of here. Don't want to inhale the foul air. Don't want to imagine the harm that it could be causing my daughter. "So these issues might be environmental?"

"Maybe. Marilena lived here for several years before we helped her purchase the hotel. It's possible that prolonged exposure could cause some kind of long-term damage. Hard to be sure, since people here aren't getting much in the way of health care services, but look around us." He gestures with one hand. "There's no way of knowing exactly what these trucks are dumping."

We watch silently as a pair of boys wrestle a tireless bike frame out from one of the trash piles. It looks like a disfigured hunk of paint-chipped metal to me, but they see potential in it. Possibility. Together, they carry it over to one of the makeshift dwellings and begin discussing their plans in excited tones.

Albert smiles a little and trudges back toward the van. He pulls out a case of bottled water. "Doña Imelda?" he calls.

"*Tengo el agua.* You just show me where you want it."

It doesn't take long to figure out that I am not as strong and selfless as Albert and Carlos. Skipping lunch was definitely a mistake. An hour of heat, dizzying stink, and low blood sugar leaves me light-headed. Stubborn as I am, I'd push myself until I drop, but Carlos sees me wobbling on my feet and intervenes.

"Your skin is clammy," he says, touching my forehead. "You're going to faint if you keep on." He digs the keys to the van from his pocket. "I've got crackers in the glove compartment. Go sit in the van for a few minutes, okay? Eat something. You'll feel better." He sees me about to protest and holds up his hand. "You won't get material for this article if you're passed out." Carlos slips into the driver's seat of the van and starts the air conditioner for me.

Embarrassed, I settle into the passenger seat and put my head between my knees, let the rushing blood bring clarity. The blowing air has finally started to cool somewhat when I feel good enough to sit fully upright again. I fetch a half-opened package of stale saltines from the glove box and force myself to consume a few. This is probably no worse

401

than what the residents of Tirabichi eat every day, after all.

Through the windshield of the van, I watch Albert and Carlos hand out gloves to a cluster of kids outside one of the shacks. The children range from three or four to around twelve, and their use of the gloves does not entirely align with Sonora Hope's lofty health and safety goals. They dangle gloves in one another's faces, slap at each other, or, in the case of one child, fill them with bottle caps. I'm starting to question the efficacy of this whole program when I hear someone shouting, a word both unexpected and familiar.

"Yulissa!"

At first I think it's Lety's voice, that in my semi-delirious state, I'm having another vision. But when my head snaps left toward the source, I find that it's Doña Imelda herself, standing in the doorway of her ramshackle home, hands on hips.

"Yulissa!" she yells again.

Over in the ring of boisterous children, a wiry girl with uneven bangs looks up from her glove-slapping assault on a friend. She rolls her eyes in annoyance, shouts over her shoulder in Spanish. *"Momentito!"*

It's her. I've found her.

I crane forward in my seat, trying to get a

better look. Memorizing her choppy, short haircut, her knobby legs and scabby knees. Her clothes are too big for her. The yellow cotton shorts fall halfway down her calves, and her sleeveless shirt covers her bottom, drapes loosely at her not-quite-budding breasts. I turn the key in the ignition to stop all the unnecessary gas consumption and clamber quickly from the van.

Yulissa has grudgingly responded to Doña Imelda's summons and stands sorting boxes of recyclables when I get there, plastic bottles in one box, aluminum in another, scrap metal in a third. She looks none too pleased to be there, and when I see what the other kids are up to — outfitting the old bike frame they salvaged earlier with over-sized tires — I can understand why. She's missing all the fun.

"Hi," I say. "Yulissa, right? Are you Lety's sister?"

I have no reason to believe she speaks English, but the girl knows her own name at least. Nods at me, uncertain, like she might be in trouble.

"Yes," she says in heavily accented English. "Lety my sister." She points at me. "American?"

"Yes, I'm American."

She gazes at me hopefully, as if waiting

for some kind of invitation. Does she think I'm one of the Sonora Hope workers with something to hand out? I wish I knew what she's after. What Lety was after, for that matter. All this time I've focused on finding Yulissa, and yet now that I've succeeded, I have no idea what to do for her.

Albert has ducked into the caretaker's house, so I can't rely on him for translation, but I do spot Duardo stretched out under a sunscreen fashioned from cardboard.

"Duardo?" I head over to his would-be awning and squat down beside him. "I need to speak to that girl over there. Can you help?"

He props himself up on one elbow, blinking away the sun. I've rousted him from a nap. "Yulissa?" he asks sleepily. "Why? She is only a kid."

"I want to talk with her about her sister. Lety."

Duardo sits up, at full attention now. "No," he says. "Not Lety."

"Why? Did you know Lety?"

"We all know Lety. She bring money for her sister every week. She pay Imelda to keep Yulissa safe."

"Is Doña Imelda still taking care of Yulissa?" I ask. "Now that no one pays for it?"

"She try." Duardo sighs, and I gather that

the old lady's efforts are not entirely successful. "Imelda has a cancer. She have some bad days." His eyes flicker over to Yulissa, who has filled one of her boxes and now struggles to carry it inside Doña Imelda's hut. "Why you want to talk about Lety? You make that girl sad."

"Lety wanted me to help her sister," I say. "I'm just trying to figure out how."

Whatever stupidity Lety got herself involved in, whatever got her killed, I must confess grudging admiration for her devotion. At fifteen, I had no one to worry about but myself. Lety had both a little sister and an unborn child depending on her. This girl was tough.

"It sounds like Doña Imelda is Yulissa's guardian," I say, trying to work out Lety's grand plan for me. "If Imelda gets too sick to take care of her, what happens?"

"I don't know." Duardo eyes me suspiciously. "You want to put her in a home for orphans? That is your idea?"

"Would that really be so awful?" It's a serious question. Is a Mexican orphanage worse than living in a garbage dump?

Duardo gives me a look so black I wonder if he speaks from personal experience. "Bad things can happen to the children there. Is better Yulissa stay here."

"You already told me you can't wait to get out of here, Duardo. If this place isn't good enough for *you,* don't tell me it's good enough for Yulissa."

"Not good. *Better.* "

"What would Lety have done?"

Duardo's face turns distant and morose. "She have plans," he says. "She is just a kid, but she have plans. She want a good life for her sister and her baby."

"What kind of life?"

He stares at his hands, the stained lines and grooves of his palm. "I tell them about Phoenix," he says. "About my son. How he was born American. Lety want that, too."

"You're saying Lety wanted to have her baby in the United States?"

Duardo's eyes fill up with tears. "I say I will take them," he says. "When I go home, I will bring them with me. I make this promise to Lety."

Call me cynical, but his concern for a young prostitute strikes me as suspect. "Were you two —"

"No! She have a baby growing in her." His face wrinkles up in horror at the thought, and I think that I've insulted his honor as a gentleman until he adds, "That *jaina* have a dirty body, all the places she go."

Fair enough, I think.

"I want to help those kids, Lety and Yulissa," Duardo tells me. "To be a good man." He crosses himself. *"Dios es mi testigo, lo juro."* If he's lying about the nature of their relationship, it's pretty convincing.

"I heard Lety killed herself. And the baby. Do you know anything about that?"

Duardo doesn't answer immediately. He picks at the worn knee of his jeans, a series of horizontal strings stretched across a two-inch hole, and although I can see he doesn't buy the official story, he says nothing to dispute this version of events. "Lety promise she take Yulissa away," he says. "Then she die. Yulissa cry so much. You don't talk to Yuli about this, please. It make her too sad."

I watch Yulissa, still sorting recyclables with a sour expression. She's not like Victor, I realize, the boy who wants to live in Tirabichi forever. Like Duardo, she will never be happy here. She has dared to imagine more.

"Duardo," I ask, "where was Lety living when she died?"

He shakes his head. "Ask Marilena. She come here a lot. She know all the women."

I remember Albert saying that he intended to visit Marilena after Tirabichi, and I resolve to grill the woman for info. There's

407

just one last piece of information I want from Duardo, something that might point to the identity of Lety's killer. "The baby," I say, "do you know who the father of Lety's baby was?"

Duardo's mouth lifts slightly in a sad smile. "How can I know?" he asks. "*Lety* don't know."

I sigh. It was a stupid question. "I guess . . . there were a lot of men."

Duardo lies down beneath his cardboard sunshade, satisfied I'm not going to harass poor Yulissa and now ready to resume his nap. I wander back to the van, eyes stinging from a potent combination of garbage and failure.

I know what Lety wants from me now, and it's not justice for her or her unborn daughter. It's a life for the one still living, an American dream for the sister who must carry on without her. Yulissa's position at Tirabichi is a precarious one, given Doña Imelda's poor health. Lety wants her cared for.

But Lety has misjudged me. I already have a child — or two — on the way, and whatever happens with Noah, I can't raise another needy kid. I don't even speak Yulissa's language. Short of adopting her, what can I really do? Smuggle the girl into the

United States? I don't need another run-in with CBP.

Sometimes, I realize with a certain amount of self-loathing, it is easier to lament the dead than save the living.

TWENTY-TWO

The van skids down the winding, hilly road on its way to the Hotel del Viajero. "Just a quick check-in with Marilena," Albert says. "To see how she's handling things." An oblique reference, I assume, to her lost baby.

From the way Albert and Duardo have spoken of her, I gather that Marilena is Sonora Hope's unofficial den mother, a mentor to women in the program and an occasional recruiter. I remember her presentation at the Desert Museum of Contemporary Art, remember the history of domestic abuse that left her blind in one eye. As a hotel owner who rose from nothing, Marilena has the kind of compelling story that any journalist would slaver over, but my interest in her is more personal.

She knew my mother. She knew Lety. And, for whatever reason, the man in the pineapple shirt came to visit her hotel yesterday.

From the passenger seat, Albert tries to be a good host, pointing out items of local interest as we pass. A sprawling public mural made by graffiti artists. A street that has been known to flood and sweep cars away during a monsoon. A metal statue of a gigantic naked man shoving a spear into something.

"That's El Mono Bichi," Albert tells me with a grin. "He's slaying the beast of ignorance." It all looks rather homoerotic to me, but I nod. Do my best to appear interested, despite the grand conspiracy scenarios I'm silently entertaining.

The death of all these Tirabichi babies can't be a coincidence, and Duardo's hypothesis about environmental hazards doesn't sound so far-fetched. Perhaps the *maquiladoras* really are dumping toxic waste at Tirabichi, something causing a rash of stillbirths amongst that population, maybe even Doña Imelda's cancer.

What if the man in the pineapple shirt is employed by one of the *maquiladoras*? If he works for an American company, that could explain his ease in crossing the border. Maybe Lety stumbled upon proof of his company's wrongdoing. How a fifteen-year-old stripper/prostitute would secure such evidence, I don't know. But if Pineapple

411

Guy killed Lety to silence her, it might explain why he saw Noah and me as a threat when we went asking around about her.

And Donna? Couldn't this provide a motive for my mother's death as well? Pam, Teresa, and Albert all mentioned how devastated Donna was by Lety's death, but perhaps her response denoted more than simple grief. Whatever Lety knew, she could've shared with Donna.

When we reach the Hotel del Viajero, Carlos double-parks out front. "I'll stay with the car," he says. "Just in case."

"Do they ticket a lot around here?" I ask, and Carlos chuckles.

"No," he says, "but they break into a lot of cars."

Albert and I hop out of the van and make our way into the hotel. Today, Marilena mans the front desk, and the air conditioner, now repaired, hums as it pumps cool air into the lobby. In the familiar territory of her own business, Marilena looks far more relaxed than she did at the Sonora Hope presentation. She wears a light blue Mexican muumuu embroidered at the neckline with flowers and a pair of birds, and her hair is pulled back into a long, graying braid. Somehow her drooping left eye manages to convey wisdom and experience rather than a tragic past.

"Albert!" Marilena intercepts him and applies kisses to both his cheeks. The gesture comes across as warm and motherly, despite the fact that Albert is probably the older of the two. Hearing his name, two of Marilena's children burst through the curtains that lead to the family's living quarters. The younger child, a girl I'd guess to be in early elementary school, squeals and begins checking his pockets. Sure enough, she finds a bag of Tootsie Rolls.

"Thank you, thank you!" She tears the wrapper off one and offers another to her sister.

Beaming, Albert presents me to the three of them. "This is my friend Charlotte. She's writing an article that will hopefully attract some big donors." He doesn't mention my connection to Donna; I suppose he knows it's a sensitive subject.

Marilena shakes my hand with unmitigated enthusiasm while her daughters cast me sidelong glances, their mouths full of Tootsie Rolls.

"So," Albert asks, leaning against the counter, "how *is* everything?"

"Lo mismo." Marilena smiles. "Hot. You went to Tirabichi today?"

He nods. "I heard Ysabel lost the baby."

"A few weeks ago, yes."

He sighs heavily. "How is she taking it?"

"You don't worry about Ysabel. Hard now, better later. This is a new start for her. She is going to leave Tirabichi. I talked to Teresa. The program can help her."

"Good," says Albert. "She deserves it. Ysabel is so smart. She could do well for herself."

"Very well," Marilena concurs.

"How about you?" Albert's face grows very sober. "I know Ysabel isn't the only one who —"

"Shhh." Marilena presses her fingers firmly to her lips. "I have enough blessings. God makes no mistakes." She bustles away from him, busies herself with a tacky arrangement of plastic flowers by the front window. The window is covered with white metal bars, which says plenty about the neighborhood we're in, but Marilena's face brightens when she peers outside.

"Ah! Look here! My friend Quico is coming. Albert, you met him once." She turns to me. "He is a friend to our work. You can talk to him for your article."

"Great," I say.

But when I look out the window and get a glimpse of Quico, I know that he's the last person in the world I want to talk to.

414

Because, even though his pineapple shirt has been replaced with a garish red hibiscus print, I'm pretty sure I recognize the figure on the other side of the street, waiting for the traffic to part.

My heart begins to pound wildly. I need to get out of here. Can't let him see me, which means the front door is a no-go.

"Where's the bathroom?" I ask, half in a panic. Marilena starts to draw back the curtain to her own quarters, but her older daughter shakes her head.

"Rey is still in the bathroom, *mami,*" she reports.

"Upstairs, then," Marilena says, handing me a key. "Room two." She opens a door to the left, revealing a musty little stairwell.

"Thank you!" I gallop up the stairs as fast as my pregnant legs will carry me, not daring to look back when I hear the bells of the front door jingling.

I don't think he saw me. But I can't be sure.

On the second floor, I stand outside room 2, trying to catch my breath. The stairwell is hot and smells like spoiled vegetables — not such a bad odor after Tirabichi. From downstairs, the voices of Albert, Marilena, and this Quico character rise and fall in Spanish. Polite greetings and pleasant conversation, from the sound of it.

Maybe Quico won't know who I am. Maybe I can wait him out.

It's perfectly possible, of course, that I'm being ridiculous, that I've misidentified this fellow or only imagined his role in Noah's arrest. But I'm not taking my chances. I pat my pocket, ensuring that my passport is still on my person. At this point, climbing out a fire escape and making a dash for the border may be the most prudent course of action.

Unfortunately, the building has no obvious exit on this floor, just the hall, doors to the two guest rooms, and the stairwell leading both up and down. The solitary window is barred, just like the one downstairs — a safety precaution that makes me feel caged, not protected. *Do they really need barred windows on the second floor?* I wonder. *Is there some sort of evil Mexican Spider-Man who scales walls at night?* I may have seriously underestimated the criminals of Nogales.

I consider using the key Marilena gave me to enter room 2, but something about that door gives me a bad feeling, makes me feel claustrophobic. I'd rather find the roof.

Up to the third floor, then, where the air is even hotter, even dryer.

I'm instantly disappointed. No roof access. No fire escape. Just another barred window and a pair of locked guest rooms.

Is Mexico undeveloped to the point of entirely lacking fire codes? My frustration mounts. How do I get out of here?

The sound of a door opening echoes in the stairwell below. I hear footsteps, slow and heavy as they move from the first to the second floor. I flatten myself against the wall as best I can, barely breathing, but there is nowhere for me to hide. If someone ventures up another floor, they'll find me.

I keep my ear trained to the sound of footsteps. A pause. A knocking. Silence.

I wait. Wince as my daughter's fist or foot pops me just south of my belly button. She can taste my adrenaline. She knows we're in danger.

Beneath me, footsteps again, retreating to the first floor. The door to the stairwell slams shut, and then I hear nothing.

Was that Quico out there? Was he looking for me? Marilena referred to Quico as her friend, and he seems to make fairly regular stops at her hotel. Is she a part of something bad? Is Albert?

I head back down to the second floor. As far as I can see, I've got two options. I can face Quico with a smile, like I've never seen him before in my life, and then find some excuse to get out of there as soon as possible — assuming he lets me. Or I can see what's in room 2, on the off chance there's a window with a fire escape. Sneaking out would give me some lead time, an obvious advantage.

It's a no-brainer, and yet something in me resists the idea of room 2. Something in me knows what I will find.

Marilena's key fits neatly into the lock. With a quick turn to the right, the knob releases, and I find myself inside the shadowy quarters.

First impression: no exit. The sole window is occupied by an air-conditioning unit. Someone took considerable time to secure the unwieldy device, screwing side panels into the cinder-block wall that will make its removal all but impossible.

The room itself has an L shape, a sharp corner leading to an alcove with a slanted overhang. It's tidy but shabby, fit for a nun or monk or some other ascetic — an odd look when I perceive the Hotel del Viajero to be more of a rent-by-the-hour establishment than a home for the holy. There's not even a phone, and the mattress is just big enough to cram two people on.

I rummage quickly around, searching for something I might use as a weapon just in case. An old television, a cheap plastic ashtray, a small ceramic cross with no real heft — nothing helpful. The key I'm holding is probably my best bet. I slip it between my index and middle fingers, the jagged metal end pointed outward like they teach you in women's self-defense classes.

I hope I'm being paranoid. Oh God, I hope I'm being paranoid.

But there it is, like a low, insistent buzzing in my spine. Something behind me. Lety? I whirl around, but there's no one there, just the alcove. And, I realize, a door I didn't see before. A white vinyl accordion door that leads to the bathroom.

I understand, even before I grip the cheap handle and slide it open, what's waiting for me. A room I know too well.

Walls of concrete block, painted white and peeling. A metal rod from which a white cloth curtain hangs. Exposed piping, a showerhead. Blue and yellow tile. I've died in this room so many times.

I stand in the doorway, spine still crackling, pulsing with an almost electric current, and yet the rest of me remains curiously numb. No surprises here. Everything is as I've dreamed it, strangely mundane now that I'm really seeing it before me.

But for one thing. One wrong detail.

My eyes fall again on the shower curtain. It's not just conceptually white, that mold-tinged gray that quickly triumphs in damp environments. No, this is a gleaming white, the white of toothpaste-commercial smiles and beachy linens in a summer catalog. Too new. No traces of wear. Someone must've replaced this curtain not so long ago.

I push aside the folds of fabric and study the tiled floor. The grout is gray with age but clean. No unexplained stains. No one could fault Marilena's housekeeping. And still.

I ease toward the doorway, suddenly ready to take my chances downstairs with Quico.

The moment I turn my back, I hear a noise. The shuddering of old pipes. A rattling, as the water pressure builds and spray bursts forth. A few tiny droplets graze my neck, warm and wet, setting all my hairs on end.

I don't want to look, don't want to see what's waiting there behind me in that shower, but I force myself.

Nothing but water pooling in the drain. *You know what happened here,* Lety seems to say. *Do I really have to show you?*

I reach out and grip the faucet, jerking the handle. The showerhead sputters twice and shuts abruptly off. I need to leave room 2. Now.

I'm just inches from the door when I hear a scraping at the lock, someone standing in the hallway outside, about to come in. My fingers tighten reflexively around the room key. Its jagged edge still points outward, ready for trouble.

Lety may have died here, naked and vulnerable, too surprised by her assailant to put up a fight. That doesn't mean I will.

TWENTY-THREE

Marilena's one good eye is black and un-readable as she peers at me from the crack of the door, like a lizard or a bird scanning its environment for prey. For an instant, I feel relief — she's not Quico — but something in her iron stare strikes me as off. The warmth she displayed with Albert has evaporated; now her lips form a tense line, a rather frozen approximation of a smile.

"*Señora?* You are okay?"

"Fine, thanks." I should leave the room, of course. It makes no sense to stand here in this unbearable heat, sweat gathering in my armpits and between my breasts, and yet I can't bring myself to approach her. "I was just — looking around. You have a nice little place."

"Thank you," she says. "I am a lucky woman." She stands in the doorway, left hand behind her back, not budging. Waiting to see what I'll do next.

"Is Albert ready to go?" I ask.

"He went to do a small job for me." She doesn't tell me when he'll be back, doesn't move from the doorway. She has me cornered here, in this little room.

"And your friend Quico?" I ask brightly. "Is he still here?"

"Señor Ortega went with Albert." She doesn't say, *It's just you and me now.* She doesn't have to.

I file away the name Quico Ortega, wondering what he told her. That I've been asking around about Lety, I suppose. Or maybe Albert mentioned it. I haven't been terribly discreet in my inquiries.

"I look forward to meeting Señor Ortega." I lean casually against the wall, trying to appear unsuspicious and at ease, as if her presence isn't scaring the crap out of me. "You said he works with Sonora Hope?"

"He works for the government of Sonora," Marilena says. "But he admires our work."

A government job might explain Quico's ability to cross the border easily. "Sounds like a good person to have in your corner," I say.

"Oh, yes. I value his friendship." Marilena cocks her head to the side and observes me with her single intelligent eye. "You are tired?" she asks.

I hope that my fear is manifesting as exhaustion. "Yeah, I haven't been sleeping well."

"Your baby is coming soon, yes? It is hard to sleep when the body grows so big." She doesn't mention her three stillbirths, but I can feel them hanging in the air, unspoken. Did losing three pregnancies drive her to the brink? Are they part of her grudge against Lety? My racing thoughts no longer make sense. I just wish that I could see her left hand, see what she's holding.

"Maybe you want *una siesta*?" Marilena suggests. "I can turn on the cool air. This bed is very comfortable."

"No, no. No need to run up your electric bill." I produce a rather constipated smile. "We should . . . go downstairs. I'm so sweaty and gross, I'd just ruin the sheets anyway."

"A shower, then? To feel fresh?" Her voice is mild, but it slides across my neck and shoulders like ice water. Perhaps this room is not an accident. Perhaps she wanted me here.

Is she the one who did it? Is she the one who pulled the trigger?

"You're so kind," I say faintly. "But I think I'll just wait with Carlos in the van. He's probably getting lonely."

This is it. Either she lets me pass or she kills me. One thing I know, and I hope she does, too: the concrete floor of this guest room is a lot harder to clean than that shower.

Marilena doesn't speak for a moment, and I imagine that she's assessing the threat that I might pose living versus dead. She doesn't know how much I know (not much, if we're being honest) and how much of a potential irritant I might be in the future (very irritating indeed). On the other hand, disposing of a Charlie is not the same as disposing of a Lety. I'm not an orphaned prostitute. I'm a pregnant American journalist. People would come asking.

Marilena pushes the door open a few inches wider. "All right, then." Her lips press thin again. "You tell Carlos hello from me. Albert will be with you soon."

I don't wait around for Albert. I'm no longer sure I can trust him. I don't know if I can trust Carlos, either, but he seems like my best bet. With a look of terror not at all difficult to manufacture, I bang on the passenger side of the waiting van, clutching my lower abdomen as if in pain.

"I'm having contractions," I tell him. "You

need to get me back into the States *right now.*"

It's an Oscar-worthy performance, and Carlos swears as he tears down the busy streets, trying not to take out any pedestrians. The line for vehicle entry back to the States isn't too terrible, but Carlos wants to jump the queue.

"We'll tell them you're in labor," he says. "They'll let us through. They'll have to."

Given how things turned out for Noah, I'm not looking for any drama with Customs and Border Protection. "I can make it. We'll get through." I give Carlos a weak smile, the picture of valiant maternal determination, and then, for good measure, try to look like my insides are seizing up.

As the line of cars crawls forward, Carlos glances periodically over at me to make sure I haven't yet delivered a child in his van. Once across the border, he deposits me in front of a Nogales hospital that looks more like a strip mall or collection of office suites. To his credit, he offers to escort me inside, but I tell him no, he'd better go retrieve poor stranded Albert. Carlos is only too happy to take off. Laboring women are somehow vastly more alarming to him than impoverished families living amongst garbage.

The return to American soil fills me with intense relief. *From here on out,* I promise myself, *you're staying the hell out of Mexico.* But I'm not about to roll over and play dead. I will dig up whatever dirt I can on this Quico Ortega.

Since I'm already at the hospital — having made a big show for Carlos of hustling inside — I plant myself in the air-conditioned waiting area and sort through my messages. Work e-mail, a couple missed calls, and a text from Carmen updating me on her progress with Noah.

Still being an idiot, she reports. *TELL HIM TO ACCEPT A DEAL.*

Whatever fight I had left gushes out at her words. I try to picture Noah in jail and discover I don't want to. He could be locked up with international smugglers, addicts, rapists. We've had far too many close calls lately. Carmen is right. If accepting probation as part of a plea deal is the only way out, then so be it. Maybe we weren't meant to adopt Micky. Maybe my vision of Micky in the house on Mawith Drive was wrong.

I scroll through my missed calls and determine that Carmen isn't the only one who has been trying to get in touch with me. Pam has called twice this morning, a fact that brings me a modicum of comfort.

Like it or not, she's the best friend I have in Arizona, and I need her connections like I never have before.

Pam doesn't waste any time with pleasantries when she answers her phone. "Are you still in Nogales?" she asks.

"Yeah." I have a feeling she already knows this, that she's just testing my answers against her existing knowledge to see if I'm trustworthy. "How'd you know Sanchez was following me?"

"Oh, I know a few things," she says. "Not enough, not yet. But a few things."

"Care to share?"

She lays her first card on the table. "Pretty sure I got an ID on the girl in those naked pictures Jasmine had."

This isn't the kind of information I was looking for, but I run with it. "Who is she?"

"Serena Alexander. An old friend of Jasmine's."

"Serena," I echo, the name familiar. "I know her. She was at the funeral. I talked to her a bit."

"Yeah? What'd you think of her?" Pam has already made up her mind about Serena, I can tell, just wants confirmation of her own bad opinion.

"Total narcissist," I say. "Serena was pissed she wasn't asked to deliver Jasmine's eulogy. And she had a chip on her shoulder about McCullough."

"She say why?"

I try to remember the girl's words. "She said Jazz used to be fun until he came along. And then they stopped hanging out."

Pam sniggers. "Those pics give me a pretty good idea what kind of 'fun' those girls were having together. You think Serena is the jealous type?"

"She did seem a little . . . imbalanced," I concede. "But wasn't there a guy in some of those photos?"

"Yeah, I've got my suspicions about that. Gotta see how it all plays out, though." She makes a low hissing sound with her breath. "Crazy, isn't it? All those years I tried to keep Donna from getting sucked into Jasmine's drama, and now here I am. Guess I always knew where that girl was headed."

Now I understand why cops aren't supposed to work cases they have personal ties to. Pam is so determined to make these murders Jasmine's fault that she's failed to explore Donna's life in any depth. If I'm going to secure her help, I'll need to tread carefully here.

"So." She emerges from her Jasmine-hating bubble and finally gives a thought to someone else. "What are you guys doing in

Nogales, anyway?" She says the word like it's a food she has a bad reaction to.

"You remember that girl Lety that Donna worked with?" I keep my voice down and one eye on the hospital patrons.

"The girl who killed herself, sure."

"I think she was murdered, Pam. Somebody killed her and then covered it up."

Pam reacts without interest. "It's possible. The kid came from a rough background."

"I think her murder could be linked to Donna's."

That gets her attention. "How?"

I gnaw on a fingernail. Of course Pam wants facts, solid proof. What did I expect? "I don't know yet," I admit. "I'm thinking Lety knew something that got her killed. Whatever it was, she could've told Donna."

"You're saying Donna knew something so explosive that someone from Nogales tracked her down to Jasmine's house and killed them both?"

When stated this way, my theory sounds inane. "Maybe."

Pam keeps her opinions to herself, though I can hear the skepticism in her questions. "What exactly do you think Donna knew?"

"Some of the women she worked with have been suffering from stillbirths and cancer." I peer around the hospital, suddenly wishing I hadn't chosen such a public venue to discuss this. "There could be an environmental cause. American factories dumping toxic waste. That kind of thing."

"I'm sure there's plenty of American factories dumping toxic waste in Nogales," Pam says. "But you're wrong if you think anyone cares. The Mexican government likes American dollars, the people of Nogales need jobs, and nobody on this side of the border gives a crap about how their stuff gets made as long as it's cheap. The whole idea of some international cover-up . . . why bother?"

She has a point, a cynical yet valid point. "Maybe it's drugs, then. A smuggling ring. That would explain the Rohypnol in Jasmine's place."

"You're reaching," Pam tells me.

"Come on. You don't think it's weird that both Lety and Donna got shot within a month of each other?"

"If Donna knew about some big illegal operation going on, she would've told me," Pam states.

Not if she was somehow involved, I think. *Maybe you didn't know my mother as well as you think you did.* Insulting Donna's memory won't get me anywhere, though, so I try another approach.

"I guess it doesn't matter, anyway." I sigh. "Your old police connections — it's not like they extend to Mexico. If someone from Nogales *did* kill Donna, we couldn't touch them, right? They'd just get away with it."

I can hear Pam bristling, rising to the challenge. "I don't care if the person who hurt Donna is from friggin' Jupiter," she growls. "One way or another, I'll find the bastard. They're going down, I will make sure of that."

I feign doubt. "I don't know, Pam. It's a whole different country. You said yourself the police are totally corrupt. We should probably stay out of it."

Pam doesn't speak for a moment. She knows what I'm doing, can see my not-so-subtle efforts to manipulate her. "What is it you want me to do?" she asks at last.

"Not much. I give you a couple names, you do some digging. That's it. Can you do that? Even if they're Mexican citizens?"

"Probably," she says cautiously. "But I think we're dealing with something a lot closer to home. You said yourself this Serena girl's a loose cannon. If she and Jasmine had a thing going —"

"See what you can find, and then I'll let it go. First, I need to know about a woman named Marilena. Donna met her a few years ago at Tirabichi."

"Marilena Gallardo," Pam supplies. "I know who you mean. Messed-up eye, husband used to beat her up. You think she's mixed up in something?"

"Pretty damn sure." I shiver at the memory of that old shower. "I'm also looking at a guy named Quico Ortega. Supposedly he works for the Sonoran government. Sound familiar?"

"Never heard about him," Pam replies. "But Quico's a nickname. You're probably looking for an Enrique or Francisco. If he's got a government job, he shouldn't be too hard to find."

"Thanks, Pam."

She knows that I haven't told her the whole story. "Hey," she says, her instincts reflecting her years as a cop, "you and Noah doing all right? Did you run into some kind of trouble with these guys?"

"Well . . ." I laugh darkly. "Since I'm already calling in favors . . . I don't suppose you have any pull with federal judges?"

I have dinner with Carmen that night at a local steakhouse. It's a faded restaurant with a stale odor and worn leather furniture from the fifties. In Brooklyn, this place would be a fun, retro hangout for hipsters to ironically enjoy a bygone era; in Nogales, this seems to pass for present-day glamour. Under different circumstances, I would've delighted in watching the clichéd dating rituals unfold around me, men playing fast and loose with their cash, women fiddling with their hair and giggling at unfunny jokes. Tonight I'm in no mood to be amused. Noah's spending his night in the county jail; tomorrow he'll be transported north to a federal facility.

"I don't understand," Carmen mutters, already on her second glass of pinot noir. "He's being so pigheaded. And for what? One little kid you hardly know — that's not worth jail time."

She's right, of course, but I'm not about to take her side.

"Did you get a record of pedestrians who crossed the border yesterday?" I ask.

"I requested the video footage," she says. "But it's a weekend. Maybe Monday they'll cough it up."

"We're looking for a man named Enrique or Francisco Ortega," I tell her. "Big man, thinning hair, goes by the nickname Quico. I think he works for the Sonoran government."

Carmen frowns. She wants to dismiss me as a crackpot, I know, but my specificity has her reevaluating. "Who is he?" she asks. "What would he have against you and Noah?"

I don't bother trying to explain the intricacies of Lety's death, of Donna's and Jasmine's murders. "I'm a journalist," I say. "And the pot was in *my* bag. Maybe he didn't like the story I was working on."

She raises her eyebrows. "You were doing some kind of investigative piece?"

"Yeah," I say. "On Tirabichi. Trying to figure out why the women there keep suffering stillbirths. One of my sources alleges that companies may have been illegally dumping hazardous waste. I'm still trying to substantiate that." It's hot air, mostly, but it sounds better than the investigating-a-dead-prostitute-I-dreamed-about truth.

"Why didn't you say something before?" Carmen breathes. "I can work with this." She puts down her wineglass a little too firmly, and some sloshes over the side. "People won't care about the environmental stuff, but corrupt Mexican government officials trying to silence a member of the press — that could fly. That's something I can spin."

"Not yet." I slice off a hunk of steak and load it onto my fork. "I don't want this out yet. My information's too shaky."

"Charlie. Noah is in jail. He could get up to a year for this. We have to get him out, preferably before his arraignment on Monday." Carmen examines her mostly empty salad plate, the pile of croutons she shoved to the side. She pops one into her mouth, evidently deciding to risk the carbs. "After Monday, you guys are on your own."

"You're really going to leave?" I have mixed feelings about this.

"I told you before. I'll stick around this weekend, and then I'm out." She picks up another crouton and traces little figure eights in her vinaigrette. "I can send you another lawyer from my firm, someone good. He won't be cheap, but —"

"Is it because of me? Am I the reason you won't stay?"

Carmen finishes chewing and wipes her upper lip with her napkin. When at last her eyes meet mine, there's a look of vulnerability I haven't seen before. "It's because of *me*," she says. "I have to take care of myself, that's all."

I can only imagine what Carmen's been going through the last twenty-four hours, having to divide all her time between her ex-husband and his pregnant girlfriend. If the prospect of her bowing out on us makes me feel strangely abandoned, I can understand where she's coming from.

"Okay," I say. "If you could line someone else up . . . I'd appreciate it."

For the rest of the meal, Carmen and I avoid speaking. She orders another glass of wine and then spends her time "dealing with a work thing" on her phone, which may or may not be a total fabrication. Eventually, the waiter arrives and gives Carmen the check. It feels like a minor insult, as though he's evaluated us both and decided she's the financially responsible adult.

"I'll take that." As I reach out to grab the bill, my fingers brush hers.

A crackling sensation. An impression washing over me in a sudden wave.

My body pressed flat against a wall. Numbness.

In my right hand, a white plastic stick.

If I don't look, maybe it will vanish. If I close my eyes, maybe that pink plus sign will fade.

The end of everything. This is the end of everything.

I withdraw my hand sharply from Carmen's, unsure exactly what I've seen. A pregnancy test, of course. But why? All the possible implications swirl through my mind.

"Sorry," I mumble when I see she's staring at me. Somehow I pry my credit card from my wallet. Try not to look too thrown as I slap it down.

Is Carmen *pregnant*? But she couldn't be. She was drinking all that wine. And the crap she gave me before about unintentional pregnancies — there's no way.

Still, I can't shake the feeling of unease. I don't see things by accident. There's always a reason.

Carmen says she has a few errands to run, so I give her my car keys and let her drop me off at the hotel. A few paces short of the room, my phone begins to vibrate. I get a bad feeling when I see the caller ID.

"Charlotte? This is Vonda Lopez, Micky's foster mom?"

"Hi!" My voice is absurdly bright; the last thing I want is for her and Child Protective Services to find out Micky's potential dad is facing drug charges. "How are you guys doing?"

"I don't know." She sounds flustered. "Listen, I'm probably silly for even asking, but I just wanted to check. Did you send someone by to see Micky this evening?"

"What?" The phone suddenly feels very heavy in my hand. "No. Why?"

"Oh, gosh," she says. "Are you sure?"

"Yes, I'm sure. Vonda, what happened?

Who came by?"

She gives an unhappy sigh. "Micky was playing in the front yard after dinner. I was finishing up with the dishes. And when I came out . . . she was talking to someone. A man." She pauses, and I can feel her turning it over in her head, working through all the nasty possibilities. "I got upset, of course, some stranger in my yard speaking to this little girl, but he said he knew you and Noah. That you'd asked him to check up on her. It felt . . . off. I mean, why would you give someone my address?"

"I didn't." I fight back a feeling of nausea. To know that I'm responsible for Noah's incarceration is horrible enough. But to have jeopardized Micky through my own foolish actions — how can I forgive myself? "What did he look like?" I ask.

"Um . . ." Vonda searches for details. "About my age, I'd guess. Fifty-ish? Big guy. He had a red shirt. With flowers."

"And you spoke to him?"

"Yes. He had a slight accent. He told me his name was —"

"Quico," I murmur.

"Oh," she says, and gives a relieved laugh. "You *do* know him."

■ ■ ■ ■

PART VI
TUCSON, ARIZONA

■ ■ ■ ■

TWENTY-FOUR

I don't want to alarm Vonda, but I don't want her greeting Quico Ortega with open arms if he shows up at her place again, either. "That guy you saw tonight is not my friend," I tell her. "If he ever comes back, you bring Micky inside and you call the police, okay?"

I expect Vonda to freak out and demand answers, but she only lets out another long sigh. "I was afraid of this. Is he a relative?"

"No. But I think he knew Micky's grandmother. They may have had some . . . issues."

"I'll keep an eye open," Vonda promises. "If he comes around again, we might want to talk to Daniel about getting Micky a different placement. For safety reasons." She sounds surprisingly matter-of-fact about the whole thing, and it occurs to me that this woman must have encountered her share of sticky situations.

"Thanks for calling," I say. "I know you'll be extra careful. Tell Micky that I'll visit soon." My throat tightens as I realize that, without thinking, I have just excluded Noah. Part of me doesn't expect him to get out. Part of me is preparing to be alone again.

"You have a good night," Vonda says, and then mumbles to herself as she hangs up, "I *knew* something about him wasn't right."

Of course you knew, I think, staring at the hotel wall. *He wanted you to know.*

Quico could've given a different name, changed his clothes, anything to throw us off. Instead, he went out of his way to mention me. Claimed to be my friend. Clearly, he wanted Vonda to call me, to let me know that he'd stopped by. I sit on the edge of the bed, hands gripping fistfuls of sheet, trying to control my breathing.

Quico Ortega knows who I am. Knows about my relationship with Micky and, by extension, Donna.

This is my fault. I thought that, having made it across the border, I was safe. I never imagined someone dragging my niece into it. If Quico had wanted to hurt her, he could have. I know she's just a pawn, a way to get to me, to remind me of my vulnerabilities. But that doesn't mean she's not in danger.

What the hell does this man think I know?

Marilena must've told Quico I was there at the hotel today. It didn't take him long to find out where Micky was living — and foster placements are supposed to be confidential. Whatever connections he has in the United States are certainly well-placed. That, or he's been watching Noah and me much longer than I thought. No doubt about it: Quico's presence tonight was a warning. One I'd do well to heed.

Stay out of this, he's telling me. *I know who you love.*

By Sunday morning, I'm a puffy-eyed wreck operating on just a couple hours of sleep. Last night, Carmen promised to tell me the details of Noah's transfer as soon as she received them, but she isn't answering her phone or hotel door. I roam through the parking lot and discover the car she borrowed is still missing. Did she even make it home last night?

Worst-case scenarios flutter through my brain. Quico Ortega abducting Carmen to teach me a lesson. Carmen sneaking off for a steamy jail visit with Noah. I know things are bad, but what if they're worse than I realize?

I call the jail, hoping to schedule a visit or

a phone call with Noah before they move him. A pleasant administrator informs me that Noah Palmer is "currently unavailable."

"What does that mean?" I ask. "Was he already transferred?"

His response is both polite and vague. "I don't have that information. You might want to contact the inmate's legal representative."

Inmate. Noah's an inmate now.

"I've been trying to reach the inmate's lawyer all morning," I say. "He has to appear in court tomorrow. Somebody must know something."

"It's Sunday," the administrator announces, as if I've been on a drunken bender and lost track of the days. "Try contacting the attorney tomorrow during business hours."

That leaves me with no news, no car, no Carmen. Am I supposed to sit idly by trusting that Noah's ex-wife has my best interest at heart? That she'll keep me apprised of the situation? We haven't even discussed her fee. My decision to involve her in our legal issues now seems incredibly shortsighted. What if she's been providing us with terrible counsel all along, pushing Noah to plead guilty in a twisted attempt at revenge?

If she's not back by noon, I'll report the car stolen.

With a trial lawyer's sense of timing and flair for drama, Carmen sends me a text at 11:52. *Pack ur bags & meet in parking lot 30 mins.* Though aggravated by the cryptic message, I tear through my hotel room, tossing toiletries and sweaty garments into my suitcase. They must have transferred Noah this morning, which means we're headed north.

I make it outside fifteen minutes before the appointed time, giving my imagination ample opportunity to run wild. What if Carmen didn't write that text? What if someone else shows up in our car? Quico Ortega, perhaps. It could be a setup. I must be a forlorn sight indeed, a massively pregnant woman perched on her suitcase, awaiting her doom in the shade of a hotel awning.

At a quarter to one — late! painfully late! — Noah's car pulls into the parking lot. I don't get a look at the driver, but when the car stops in front of me, passenger-side out, I know it's not Carmen. She's riding shotgun, her shoulders hunched up strangely, guarded. Our eyes meet, and there's a flash of dread, pure dread, when she sees me.

A warning? Who the hell is driving that car?

"Can I help you with your bag, ma'am?"

It takes a moment for me to realize that

it's him, that it's Noah offering me his services with a lopsided grin.

He looks exhausted, his eyes pink and glazed from lack of sleep. And he's scruffy, too, his face scratchy against me as he buries his head in my hair. My body goes limp at his touch, all the tension spilling out in an embarrassing display of tears. Has it really only been two days?

"Aw, honey." Noah brushes his thumb across my cheek. "We got through it. Don't cry."

The parking lot is a sea of concrete and glaring sunlight reflecting off vehicles. Across the street, IHOP seems to be doing a brisk business. Not the most romantic setting for a reunion, but I'll take it.

Still, I don't want to get my hopes up.

"Are you out? Are you *really* out, or just on bail?"

"I'm really out. They dropped all charges."

I exhale. "Hallelujah. I thought I was going to have to be a single parent again."

"No, no, no. You really think I'd miss the birth of my baby girl?" He says it like he had some choice in the matter, like he's personally responsible for his own release. As he moves in for a kiss, I'm suddenly aware of Carmen still sitting in the car, inspecting her fingernails, trying not to watch us. I feel a twinge of guilt, an odd current of anger on her behalf. He doesn't have to rub it in.

I duck the kiss and hand him my suitcase.

Carmen steps from the car, offering up her seat to me the way one might for a pregnant woman on the subway. "I'll sit in back," she says, and with that one act — allowing me the front seat in a car that was half hers just a year ago — I know how wrong I've been to fear her. Whatever Carmen's feelings for Noah may be, she knows it's over. And she's much too proud to ever lick her wounds in public.

I don't know what to say as we climb into the vehicle, but I need to recognize this woman somehow. "Carmen . . . I wish I knew how you pulled this off."

"No idea." She smooths out the bottom of her dress. "Unless Customs and Border Protection thought it would be impolitic to drag Mexican government officials into Noah's little mess."

My eyes widen. "You told them about Quico?"

"I made a few calls." She's underplaying it; a stunt like this took a lot more than a few calls. No wonder she never made it home last night.

"What did you *say*?"

"Just that if CBP reviewed their video footage of Friday afternoon, they'd have clear evidence that a Mexican official was aware of the drugs Noah had on him."

Oh God, I think. *Quico's not going to like this.*

"I also mentioned an exposé you're writing on government corruption in Nogales," she continues, "and suggested that it might be simpler to maintain good border relations if they released your companion. With a promise that your story wouldn't go public, of course." She raises a delicate eyebrow. "I assume you can agree to that?"

"Yes. Of course."

Noah frowns. "What's this about corrupt Mexican officials? If there's shady business goin' on in Nogales, maybe Charlie *should* be writin' about it."

I tap him gently on the thigh to shut him up. "Later. I'll explain later. Right now, the only thing you need to know is that we owe Carmen. Big-time." I give him a severe look. "I'd say a thank-you is in order."

Noah scratches his neck, suddenly embarrassed by his debt. "Thanks, Car."

In the back of the SUV, Carmen shrugs.

"We should celebrate," I say. "Can we take you somewhere, Carmen? We're heading back to Tucson, right? There must be something fun on the way."

Her fingers fly across the screen of her iPhone, already booking a ticket. "Just the airport, thanks."

Back in Tucson, we drop Carmen off six hours early for an evening flight. She has work to catch up on, she says, and the airport will have good Wi-Fi. Though I'm not at all certain that tiny airport will have decent connectivity, I let it slide. If she wants to get away from us that badly, I won't stop her.

All Noah wants is a decent shower and a bed, so we get a room at a chain hotel near the airport that he's amassed frequent-sleeper points with. I let Noah rid himself of all the institutional grime before I attempt to broach any serious topics with him. My motives are not purely altruistic; he acquired an odor in captivity that I'm eager for him to lose, a pungent blend of sweaty strangers living in unnaturally close quarters and without access to deodorant. Only when he has scrubbed away the last of these way-too-manly fumes and stands in front of the mirror, shaving, do I finally tell him my news.

"I found the bathroom. I found the shower."

He glances over his shoulder at the hotel shower, failing to catch my drift.

"Not this one," I clarify. "The one in my dream."

He stops shaving and peers at my reflection in the mirror, his eyebrows knit. "Are you sayin' —"

"I saw the place where Lety died."

Noah doesn't move. His chin is still covered in shaving cream, the razor in his frozen hand pointed upward. "You went back into Nogales?" he says. "Without me?"

"I had to. Lety kept visiting me, she wasn't going to let it rest —"

"You could've *died.*" He turns on me slowly, and I watch it hit, the wave of fear and anger at the outrageous chance I took in his absence. "Damn it, Charlie, what is *wrong* with you? How am I supposed to trust you when you pull shit like this? They could've killed you and the baby both! You couldn't stay away from that hotel for forty-eight frickin' hours?"

"Wait, wait, wait." My eyes narrow as the full meaning of his words registers. "You *knew* that bathroom was in Marilena's hotel? How the hell did you know that?"

His anger flickers for a second, not yielding, but erecting defenses against my imminent attack. "Marilena's kid told me.

When I asked him about Lety. He said she stayed at the hotel for a while. That she died there. Room two."

I remember his long exchange with the boy at the hotel and feel all the color draining from me. "You knew and didn't tell me? You *knew*?" That whole terrifying scene with Marilena could've been avoided.

"I was gonna tell you once we made it back to Tucson, except . . . we never made it back to Tucson."

"Noah, you asshole! I went in that place *alone*! Why didn't you *say* something?"

"Because I know you!" he retorts. "Because as soon as you found out she died there, you'd want to go. And it was obviously a dangerous place to be."

"So dangerous you didn't even warn me!" I grab a hand towel off the sink and throw it furiously on the floor, where it lands with an unintimidating *foop*. The gesture is much less satisfying than I'd anticipated. "What about that whole visit to Treasure Island? Did you seriously let me wander around some skeevy strip joint trying to question these poor exploited women about something you already knew the answer to? Oh my God, I *hate* you!"

Noah has resumed shaving in brisk, semi-violent strokes down his jawline. "We were tryin' to find out *who* killed Lety, not where they did it. And we still don't know that, do we? Or why."

He's right, of course. Though I suspect Quico was involved in Lety's death, I don't believe he actually pulled the trigger. My money's on Marilena. The way she looked at me with that one dead eye and offered me a shower — it was her. It had to have been her. But I don't know why, don't know if Lety's death was somehow linked to Donna's, to Jasmine's.

"Next time you find out where someone was tragically gunned down, maybe give me a heads-up," I say crossly. "Is there anything else I should know about? Anything else the kid told you?"

"I don't think so." Noah turns on the faucet and rinses the whiskers from his razor. "Is there anything else *I* should know?"

"Oh, a few things maybe." I lean against the bathroom doorway. "Like, I found Lety's sister."

"You found Yulissa?"

"She's about ten years old," I tell him. "Lives in a garbage dump, of all places. I think Lety's been bugging me because she wants me to get Yulissa into the US. Honestly, though, I don't see how we can pull that off. Even if we could battle through the whole adoption process, I'm at my limit with two kids."

"Glad we agree," Noah says with a frown.

"Also, the marijuana CBP found? I don't know how, but I think some Mexican official named Quico Ortega planted it. He happens to be friends with Marilena, the woman who owns the Hotel del Viajero. Where Lety died."

"Well, look at you, Nancy Drew."

"Nancy Drew?" I sigh. "No way. Is this the body of a sixteen-year-old girl detective? More like that pregnant cop in *Fargo* . . ."

Cracking a smile, Noah wipes the last bit of shaving cream residue from his face with some water and grabs a bottle of aftershave. "So that's where we're at? We think some random guy in the Mexican government has it in for us?"

"He's not random. I just told you, he's connected to Marilena. And I think she's the one who killed Lety. My guess is that Marilena's kid mentioned you were asking about Lety, and she and Quico didn't like it."

"Sounds . . . pretty messed up." Noah rubs his eyes, and I wonder how much of this he's even absorbing, tired as he is. "We can fix this if we just stay outta Mexico, right?"

"Maybe," I say. "I don't know." When I tell him about Quico's visit to Micky, his face hardens.

"I don't like this," he says. "How the hell does this guy even know about Micky? Has he been followin' us in Tucson?"

"I don't know, but you see what all this points to," I say.

Noah gives me a blank look, officially too sleepy to connect the dots.

"Jasmine and Donna getting shot — it must be related."

"Why?"

I roll my eyes. "Donna knew Marilena through Sonora Hope. Marilena killed Lety. And then Donna turns up dead, too."

He makes his way to the bed, only half hearing me. "So?"

"So . . . maybe Donna had a little side business going with Marilena and Quico. Running recreational drugs. That would explain the marijuana *and* the Rohypnol found in Jasmine's apartment. And it fits with Donna's history of drug use."

"I don't know, Charlie." Noah yawns. "A little Mary Jane isn't quite the same as a date-rape drug. And Pam said Donna never had any extra money comin' in."

I sit on the edge of the bed, eager to hash out the details even if he's not fully with me. "Maybe Donna was getting paid in prescription drugs," I suggest.

"Sounds like you *want* your mother to be the bad guy." His tone is mild, but I can see the obnoxious hint of amateur psychologist in his eyes, and I don't want to go there.

"I think it's more than a coincidence that Donna and Jasmine and Lety were all shot within five, six weeks of each other," I tell him. "Pam and Vargas, they've been assuming Jasmine was the main target, but it could've been Donna."

"Could've been," Noah says with another yawn. "Although I wouldn't sell your sister short. From everything we've seen, she had a way of pissin' folks off."

Late that afternoon, a monsoon hits. The sky darkens, and the steady stream of airplanes booming overhead stops, soon replaced with the rumbles of distant thunder. When the clouds finally open up, it's positively biblical. Rain crashes to the earth in sharp lances, flooding the courtyard in less than ten minutes, its sound reverberating off every surface it touches: concrete, metal, glass. I watch from the window of our hotel room as the palm trees bow and shiver in the wind and a bench blows onto its side. Something tells me Carmen won't make it out of Tucson tonight.

Spread-eagled across the bed on his stomach, Noah sleeps through the roar of rain and thunder.

As I listen to the drops pattering against the roof, I think he's got it right. I steal one of his pillows and begin building up my nest. Nap time.

I don't know how long I doze — it's a light, half-conscious sleep, with hazy thoughts that dissolve like cotton candy on a tongue. My awareness of the storm, of Noah's heat beside me, fades in and out. At some point, I notice the rain has stopped, and it's there, in the sudden, sleepy quiet, that I feel a beckoning.

Goddamn it, Lety, I think. *Not again.* I'm pretty sure that in the past two weeks, I've dealt with more of these visions than in the entire preceding year. I hope this is temporary, a bizarre side effect of late pregnancy and not my new normal.

For a moment, I resist the pull. Grab a pillow, trying to anchor myself in the hotel room. Dig my fingernails into the palm of my hand, hoping pain will keep me present. It's no good. I can remain conscious, but I can't dismiss that tugging need. It's like having to pee; you can delay but never defeat the urge.

I sigh. *Let's get this over with already.*

And then I'm under. Really under. Swimming, in fact.

Night. My arms, long and strong, carve through dark waters. The gently bobbing waves part as I plow through. Above me, the sky is a black sphere without starlight. Only a thin slice of moon cuts through the gloom, a slash of light against a canvas of nothing.

For a moment, I don't know why I'm swimming, what I'm swimming to, but then I see a shape. Bouncing on the sea's shiny surface, a baby. *My* baby?

I dive toward her, terrified that she will sink, that I'll lose her to the softly slapping waves. When I reach the child, however, I know it's not my daughter. Not Lety's unborn girl, either. This is a boy, a black-haired infant boy with strange, unblinking eyes.

I reach to gather him in my arms, to protect him from drowning, but my hands find nothing solid to grasp. He's water, I realize. No form, no flesh, just rivulets running from my fingertips, insubstantial as a reflection. And yet the baby continues to stare, his eyes both alert and indifferent. I don't like it. Something in me knows this dream is not like the others.

What are you? I whisper.

The reply comes to me not as sound but as thought, a whisper from within. *A possibility, once.*

I don't understand, I say. *Did you die?*

I was never born.

The infant vanishes, wiped away like sand-scribbled words in an oncoming tide. On the horizon, I spy a faint blush. The inky night sky turns to blue. All around me, the ocean drains away, swiftly absorbed into the earth, leaving me on an open plain of warm sludge. I kneel in the muck. Wipe my soiled hands against my thighs.

The dark-haired child is back, sitting cross-legged across from me in the mud. He's bigger now, older — about Keegan's age, I'd guess — but I know it's him from those empty eyes. He sits perfectly upright, no tension in his body, just a peculiar stiffness, as if he were carved from wood. I lean forward, getting a closer look at him in the rising light. Though his features seem to shift upon inspection, I detect a common element, a face they seem to borrow from.

I draw in a sharp breath when I realize. This is Carmen staring back at me. Her nose, mouth, cheekbones, chin, and forehead arrange and rearrange themselves, mutating in endless combinations.

What do you want? I ask, now on my guard.

Again he speaks to me without words. *I want nothing.*

Then why are you here? I demand.

She can't forgive herself.

I know he's talking about Carmen. I know this boy is hers. *That has nothing to do with me,* I tell the boy. *Whatever it is you think she needs — I'm not the right person to do it. I don't even* like *her.*

As I'm lining up my arguments, preparing to explain the precarious nature of my relationship with Carmen, the boy melts. Turns to mud. A totally unfair and yet effective way to end a debate.

I stand up, knees coated in filth. The sun rises rapidly in the sky as if in time lapse, and the ground loses its moisture, hardening and cracking in the heat. I spin in a circle, searching for something on the horizon, a destination. I see nothing but a small and withered tree in the distance, its twisted limbs in silhouette against the bright sunlight. I jog toward it.

When I'm just a few yards away, I spot the boy again. His body unfolds from the shadow of the tree trunk. He's even older now, taller, his hair cropped short. A child, but not so very far from adolescence. And he still has those unsettling eyes that refuse to blink.

I fold my arms across my chest. *Let me guess. This time you turn to dust, right?*

His expression remains neutral.

You could just leave me alone, I suggest. *It would be easy. You don't even exist.*

I exist in her mind. That's enough.

It's maddeningly intimate, these words inside my head. I draw closer to the figure by the tree, peer at the oddly morphing face. In one instant, a nose like Carmen's. Then a shift, and it's her round cheeks I find in his unstable face. I squint at him, and all his features ripple at once, a watery surface struck by a stone. When they've solidified again, I see an echo of someone else. My stomach begins to hurt.

Noah. This boy would've been Noah's.

Why are you showing me this? I kick at the tree's thick roots. *They aren't even together anymore. Why can't you go away?*

The young boy stares directly at me, his gaze blank. No feeling, no humanity at all. He doesn't care about Carmen or Noah or me because he isn't real. He never was.

She won't let go of me, he says. *She won't*

let go.

It's evening when I wake up, nearly eight o'clock. Noah remains blissfully unconscious, and I can only imagine the sleepless nights in a holding cell that have produced such exhaustion. I'm drowsy myself, but my stomach demands food. I wriggle into one of my shapeless sundresses and head downstairs to the hotel bar and grill.

The place is nearly deserted when I arrive, but I recognize one of its patrons immediately. She's sitting at the bar hunched over a beer and a plate of potato skins, shoveling cheese-and-sour-cream-laden chunks into her mouth with self-hating abandon. I'm not surprised to see her here. Somehow I expect it.

"Carmen."

Although she flinches at the sound of my voice, she doesn't look especially astonished to see me, either. "*Please* take these away." She pushes her plate at me. "I'm a danger to myself."

"I take it your flight got canceled?"

"There was flooding from the storm. I leave first thing in the morning." She hesitates and then taps the stool beside her at the bar. "You can join me if you like."

I can't tell if she actually wants me to stay.

Don't know if I actually want to. Fragments of my dream play in the back of my mind, uncomfortable and insistent. The son she and Noah might've had but didn't.

I'm supposed to talk to her, of course, yet something in me resists. I don't know what our conversation might set in motion, don't want to serve as some inexplicable instrument of fate if the ultimate purpose is one I can't live with. What if she and Noah still love each other? What if mentioning this child somehow brings them back together?

"Sit," Carmen tells me, annoyed by my indecision. "I won't bite."

I sit. "Did Noah tell you we were at this hotel?"

"No," she says. "But I should've guessed. Frequent-sleeper points, right?" She rolls her eyes as if to communicate his tiresome predictability. I manage the ghost of a smile, but frequent-sleeper points are just another reminder of their long history together. There are so many things she knows about him that I don't.

The bartender approaches and I order a Shirley Temple. It'll be my first in a long while — my time in Louisiana turned me off to that particular drink — but tonight I'm feeling brave. Could use the sugar rush.

I clear my throat. "Thank you again for

making the trip out here. I don't know what we would've done without your help."

"Yeah, well." She doesn't know what to do with the compliment. "I'm not sure what y'all stumbled across, but I'd watch your back. You used up your Get Out of Jail Free card this time around. Next time could get ugly."

I nod, thinking of Lety. I know how ugly it could get.

The bartender arrives with my drink, a glass of ruby-colored liquid topped with an orange slice and a pair of maraschino cherries. I take a cautious sip, trying to figure out a good entry point to the conversation I want to have. In the end, though, she's the one who finally speaks.

"Can I ask you something?" She tilts her head to the side. "I don't mean to be rude, but . . ."

I steel myself. "Go ahead."

"Are you excited? About the baby? I know it wasn't really planned."

I wonder if she and Noah discussed this while he was in jail. Wonder what he said. "Of course I'm excited. Nervous, obviously, too, because everything's going to change. But mostly excited." The words sound false and defensive even to me. I bite into the orange slice, strip away the flesh from the peel with my teeth. Allow myself a shade more honesty. "Like, sixty percent excited and forty percent scared out of my mind."

She gives me a quizzical smile. "That's pretty scared."

"I know what I'm getting into this time. I don't have that new-parent arrogance in my corner anymore."

"Noah told me about your son. I'm sorry."

It's a well-intentioned apology, like so many others, that I don't know how to answer. "Me too."

"You must think there's something wrong with me, not wanting kids."

The comment irritates me. "I don't know what kind of person you think I am, Carmen, but being a mother has never been the sum total of my identity. And I certainly don't expect everyone else to make the same life choices I do."

"Oh, that's right. You're one of those godless Manhattanites, aren't you?" She gives me a wry smile. "You guys have it pretty good. But I'm Catholic. My mother has been pushing for grandkids since I was eighteen. And with my *abuela* . . . reproduction is like a responsibility. In her eyes, my sister and I are failing in our most basic civic duties."

I don't respond. My mind is on the pregnancy test I saw her holding at the restaurant last night, on the boy who looked like Noah. *A possibility, once,* the boy said. And I know. This is my opening. She has brought up the subject of her own accord; now is my chance.

"You were pregnant once, weren't you?" I keep my eyes focused on my ice cubes.

"What?"

"A long time ago, you were pregnant." I picture the older version of the boy in my dream and try to guess his age. "Thirteen years, is that about right?"

Her eyes widen. She runs her thumb along the rim of her beer, circling it over and over, debating whether or not to answer. "Twelve," she says at last. "Twelve years." She's still for a moment. When she speaks again, her voice is unsteady. "How would you know that?"

"I'm crazy, remember? I see things."

"That doesn't . . . I never told anyone. Not Noah, not *anyone.* I know you're a journalist, but even you . . . how could you possibly get access . . ."

"I couldn't."

She folds her arms, deeply unsettled, no longer sure of herself. "I don't understand. That wasn't just a lucky guess."

"I shouldn't have said anything. It was a

long time ago. I'm sure you've put it behind you."

We're both quiet for a moment. I know, of course, that she hasn't put it behind her, but if she doesn't want to talk about her pregnancy with me, I can certainly understand. We are hardly friends. I'm probably the last person in the world she wants to discuss this with, and I'm not convinced I want to have this conversation myself.

And yet, for some reason, she doesn't shut me down. "I guess . . . I've been thinking about it lately," she says.

"Was it . . . a miscarriage?"

Carmen's quiet for a second, privately weighing her reply before she turns to me, half defiant and half terrified. "It was an abortion," she says. "I had an abortion."

She looks far more startled than I am at hearing these words spoken aloud, and I have to remind myself that she grew up in Texas. She's Catholic. Not a cafeteria Catholic like my aunt Suzie, but a first-generation-born-to-Mexican-immigrants Catholic. Having moved in largely liberal circles, I've known women who spoke matter-of-factly about their abortions, without guilt, without sadness. *I was sixteen and he was an asshole,* an acquaintance once told me, and that was all the justifica-

468

tion she needed. But that is not the culture Carmen grew up in.

"I'm sorry. I wasn't trying to pry." I rest an elbow on the bar. "Usually when I see things, I'm supposed to . . . act on them in some way. I guess in this case I don't know what to do."

"I thought it was crazy," she says, "what Noah said about you. It *is* crazy. I don't get it." Her attention snaps back to me. "Are you going to tell him?" she demands.

"Tell Noah? No way. This isn't mine to tell." Frankly, I can see no upside whatsoever in sharing this with him.

We sit there for a moment, not speaking, this strange thing looming between us. It occurs to me that awkward silence is not the reaction I would want from someone after revealing a long-held secret. "Carmen," I say tentatively. "Do you want to talk about it?"

She shrugs as though it doesn't matter one way or another, and yet she begins to talk, the words spilling from her. "I was in my final year of college," she says. "Noah's landscaping business was kind of exploding, and we'd just gotten married. Neither one of us wanted kids, we were both clear about that, and then . . . I found out."

"Why didn't you tell him? Did you

think . . . he wouldn't have supported your decision?"

Carmen bites her lip. "We'd been fighting a lot. About me going to law school in Arizona."

I remember what Noah said about long-distance marriages, how he didn't recommend them. "That must have been hard."

"They were offering me a full ride, a complete scholarship, and he wanted me to walk away. How could I do that? I was the first person in my family to go to college, and here the school was ready to pay for my degree. A *law* degree." She shakes her head. "When the pregnancy happened, I didn't know what he would want. But it didn't matter. I knew what *I* wanted." Her upturned chin relaxes somewhat when I don't appear overtly shocked or appalled by this statement. "I guess I was scared," she admits. "Scared that he'd use my pregnancy as an excuse to keep me in Texas. And then . . . I'd miss my chance."

I try to imagine Noah using a child to control someone, squashing his partner's professional ambitions to pursue his own. It doesn't square with the man that I know, and yet I don't discount Carmen's version of events. The Noah that I know now may be quite unlike the twenty-one-year-old he was then. A person can change a lot in the course of a dozen years.

"You must have felt very alone," I say. "Did you ever have regrets?"

"No," she says. "Not really. I've never wanted to be a mother. I love my nieces and nephews, but that's not the same. And my job is great. I'm good at it."

I wait, sensing there's more.

"I always wondered," she acknowledges. "How life would be different if we'd had a kid. I mean, how could you not? Especially after Noah and I split up. It was just like, would we still be married? Would a kid have kept us together? Or maybe we'd have split up even sooner, I don't know."

"The road not taken."

She stares at me for a second as if suddenly remembering who I am. "I shouldn't be talking about this with you." Still, her own curiosity gets the better of her. "What did you mean when you said you 'saw' it? What did you see about me, exactly?"

I can't tell her about the boy. That would be cruel, giving a gender, a face, to a possibility she walked away from so many years ago. Instead, I remember the boy's words. *She can't forgive herself. She won't let go.* There was nothing accusatory in those words. No anger, just a statement of fact. I

471

look at Carmen, watch as she nervously fingers her bracelet, and I can't imagine the weight that she has been carrying all these years.

"I think what I saw was a message for you."

She squints at me, skeptical but listening.

"The kid that you've been imagining all these years . . . you don't have to punish yourself anymore. You can forgive yourself."

"That's it? Instant absolution?" She gives a low, shaky laugh. "Come on, how many Hail Marys should I say? I took a life. That's a cardinal sin."

"If Hail Marys are your thing, knock yourself out. But . . . you have your life, Carmen. You worked hard for it. And you can't really live it if you're always second-guessing one decision."

She nods, thinking it over. "You really want your baby, don't you?"

"Yes. I do."

"And you lost a child."

My hands ball up into fists. "This baby is not a replacement for Keegan," I say. "It doesn't work like that. Nothing will ever replace him, okay? There will never be a day I don't miss him."

"I didn't mean that. I just meant . . . it's hard to hate you. I mean, I do, kind of. But

I don't wish bad things on you. You've had enough."

I wish that I could explain it to her. That my daughter is not a second chance but another chapter. "I didn't even want another child," I tell her. "I didn't think I could handle it. I still don't know if I can. But then here she is, and . . ." I rest my hands on my belly. "This is my baby. No matter how scared I am, I can't help but love her. Maybe that's hard for you to hear, but —"

"No," she says. "Actually, that makes it easier."

"Easier?"

Carmen's voice is low and husky. "If I'd chosen to have a child with Noah, a child I didn't really want . . . you wouldn't be here right now. Waiting for a child you *do* want." She looks up, and the lights of the bar reflect in her dark eyes. "It makes sense, doesn't it? Somehow, it all makes sense."

TWENTY-FIVE

I wake up the next morning to find Noah bent over his laptop, examining an accounting spreadsheet. "Been up since four," he tells me, rubbing his screen-glazed eyes. "My sleep's all off."

I check the time, discover that Carmen's already departed on an early flight. I don't mention our encounter to Noah. Whatever we discussed last night was between her and me.

"So what's the plan?" I yawn. "Are we heading back to Sidalie today?"

"Tomorrow," he says, scrolling down an expense column. "We should have one more visit with Micky before we go. That Quico guy knows where she lives, and I don't like it. We need to have a Stranger Danger talk with that kid."

I don't tell him that Vonda's already been through all that with Micky. I want to encourage his fatherly instincts. Maybe they can make up for my own stiffness with my niece.

"I'll call Vonda," I suggest. "Micky's got school today, but we could take her out for dinner."

Noah doesn't answer. An e-mail has just come in, something heavy-duty from the crease in his forehead.

"What is it?"

He doesn't speak at first, just stares at his computer, frozen.

"Noah. You look shell-shocked. What happened?"

Finally, he gets up. Paces around our small hotel room. Takes a deep breath.

"An offer," he says. "Pete Gantos made me an offer. He wants to buy the company."

I don't understand his slack-jawed reaction. "That's great news, isn't it?"

He doesn't seem to hear me.

"Babe. Is he lowballing you? Were you hoping for more?"

"No," he says, slowly emerging from his haze. "It's a good offer. I just . . ." He sets his computer down on the bed and massages his temples. "I've spent my whole workin' life buildin' up the business, you know? And Pete . . . he's got a lot to learn. I hand him the reins, he'll run the place into the ground in a year."

I don't like the turn this is taking, the silent deliberation going on in his head. "So you're not sure you want to sell?"

"I don't know."

"Hon." *Rescue this, Charlie, before it gets bad,* I think. *Talk him down.* "You don't really think you can effectively manage the business from Tucson, do you? Look how hard it's been the last week or two. The company needs a hands-on owner."

"Yeah. I can't do that from Tucson."

I wait, but he says nothing more. Panic flares up inside my chest as I realize what this could mean. Still, I keep my voice steady, try to extract an honest answer from him. "Are you having second thoughts about moving?"

He tugs on his fingers, cracking his knuckles. "We're not locked into anything," he says. "We haven't done the home inspection yet. We could still cancel the contract for the house."

"That's what you want? To cancel the contract and head back to Sidalie?" I know, as soon as the words leave my mouth, that I can't do it. I can't go back. "What about Micky? You were so gung-ho about adoption."

"We could still adopt her. It would just take longer."

476

I don't respond. What is there left to say? We're on the verge of several major life changes, and he's getting cold feet.

"Fine," he says, reading the disapproval in my silence. "I'll sell the company if that's what you want. You left behind some things to be with me, you want me to lose somethin', too. Fair's fair, I guess."

I am not about to let him saddle me with that kind of lifelong resentment, the years of *big bad Charlie made me give away my company* sulks. "This isn't a contest for who can be the biggest martyr, Noah. At some point, if neither of us is getting what we really want, maybe we aren't meant to be together."

He lets out a long sigh. "That's not what I was sayin'. It's just that I've been in Sidalie mosta my life. I like it there. It works for me, you know?"

"It hasn't been working for me," I say quietly.

"Because you haven't given it a chance."

"I've been giving it a chance for *months.*" His failure to recognize my efforts is the biggest insult of all. "I've been trying to fit into your life, Noah, I really have. But at the end of the day, it's still *your* life, not mine. It's the life you had with Carmen."

"There's nothin' wrong with that life!"

477

"It's wrong for *me*!" Tears prick my eyes. "Why are you doing this? We had a plan. We were going to move here for Micky, to keep her life consistent. What's changed?"

Noah draws in a breath, internally debating whether or not to say something before going for broke. "Did you ever think that maybe you're usin' Micky as an excuse to get outta Sidalie?"

"Wait . . . what?" If he's trying to derail our argument, this accusation is certainly effective.

"You've been tellin' me all along you weren't sure about us takin' her," Noah says. "And I kept pushin'. But maybe you're right. Maybe we're not the ones."

"What are you talking about? Micky loves you."

"I'm only half the equation, Charlie." He can't look at me as he speaks. "Every time we're with Micky, you get this wall around you. This spaced-out look like you wish you were somewhere else. That kid needs someone to show up for her, to show up big. And I don't know if it's you."

I don't know either. I've never known. I've relied on Noah's confidence, Noah's faith in me, to propel us forward, and now even Noah has his doubts. What does that say about me? If I can't rise to the challenge of raising Micky, what kind of person am I? What kind of shriveled, damaged heart will I bestow upon my baby daughter? Has Keegan's death left me too bereft to fully give myself to another? There are no words. I slip into the bathroom and lock the door behind me. Turn on the shower. Slump to the bathroom floor and wonder what will happen when our daughter's born.

I remember the vision I had of Noah and Micky in the new house, his putting her to bed, and begin to cry. Hot, ugly, wreck-your-face tears that just won't stop.

I thought I knew where we were going. I thought we were going there together. But maybe the future is fluid, not fixed. Throw one pebble, and maybe you've transformed the surface, altered everything.

Maybe my path is one I'm meant to walk alone.

Curled up in a ball by the hotel pool, I almost ignore Pam's call. Trying to sound normal on the phone with Vonda was hard enough. I'm not sure I can handle Pam's probing questions and nose for trouble. But the prospect of wallowing in my own heartache proves worse. I pick up on the eighth ring, right before she gets kicked to voice mail.

"How's it going?" Pam asks, immediately jumping to the one topic I'd rather avoid. "Any news with Noah?"

"He's out," I say. "They released him yesterday."

"That's great news. Glad you got things sorted." Pam doesn't guilt me for not telling her sooner. "I wish I could've pulled some strings, but I don't have an in with Homeland Security. Those HSI guys, they do their own thing."

"How about you?" I ask, shielding my face from the sun. In my scramble to leave the hotel room, I forgot to grab my sunglasses. Now, squinting myself into a headache, I regret my haste. "Did you do some digging on Marilena or Quico?"

"Did my best. You want to hear it?"

"Shoot."

"So I've got a Francisco Ortega, fifty years old, losing a little hair on top. Works for the Sonoran Office of Family Rights. Sound like your man?"

"That's him," I confirm. "But what's the Office of Family Rights? I thought he'd be a lawmaker or something."

"Nope. Basically, his office deals with some pretty messed-up families and tries to figure out where to put the kids."

"You mean like Child Protective Services?" I'm thinking of Yulissa, wondering what will happen to Lety's sister if I don't get involved.

"Yeah, it's pretty much the same crap we've got here," Pam assures me. "Reunification, placement with a relative or in a children's home. They pass along some of the really hard-luck cases to American families. Your Quico guy, for example, works with a lot of disabled kids."

I remember what Teresa said, that Americans can legally adopt young children from Mexico only if the kids are disabled or ill and unable to receive care in their own country. Finding homes for unwanted children does not seem like the sort of work that a murderer of pregnant teenage girls would gravitate toward. Could this man really be tied to Lety's death?

"That's it? That's all you found?"

"He does a lot of philanthropic work on the side, raising money for single mothers in poverty. That's his association with Sonora Hope."

"That doesn't sound terribly threatening," I admit.

"On paper, Francisco Ortega is an upstanding guy," Pam says. "And he definitely didn't kill Donna."

"How do you know?"

481

"He was at a fund-raiser that night in Hermosillo."

The doors to the pool area open, and I glance over, hopeful that Noah has come after me. Instead, a man with an earring hustles his two boys out to the other side of the pool.

"What about Marilena?" I ask, closing my eyes. "Did you get anything on her?"

"Harder to track," Pam says. "She's thirty-seven years old, been operating that hotel for about four years now. The building's in her name. No sign of her for several years before that, but there wouldn't be, not if she was living in Tirabichi. As far as I could find, she's Sonora Hope's poster child."

"Could she have been in Tucson the night Donna and Jasmine were killed?"

"There's nothing to suggest she was."

I can't conceal my frustration. "She and Quico can't *both* be squeaky clean. Didn't Donna ever say anything about her? Something off, something she didn't like?"

"Are you kidding?" Pam snorts. "Donna loved that woman. Marilena was her ground soldier in Nogales. She brought a lot of women into the program."

A splash. Something wet hits me in the face. My eyes flicker open, and I realize belatedly that I'm the victim of synchronized cannonballs. The boys peer up at me from the pool's turquoise waters, grinning at their handiwork. Embarrassed, their father barks out a scolding.

I don't know what to think. Could I have invented this whole thing in my head? Misinterpreted Quico's exchange with the CBP officer and my conversation with Marilena in room 2? Neither one of them has shown any demonstrable signs of violence or ill intent. I'm still troubled by Quico's visit to Micky, but if he knew Donna, perhaps he was just checking on her grandchild. My conspiracy theories hinge solely on a dream.

"Do you think I'm way off base here, Pam?"

Her voice is measured and smooth, an answer unto itself. "I have no doubt you guys ran into trouble at the border, that some dick running a little weed set you up. Whether Francisco Ortega was involved . . . well, we don't have any evidence of that."

I'm quiet, watching the boys attempt handstands in the shallow end.

"I might have something to make you feel better," Pam says. "Something big."

"What's that?"

I can hear the grin in her voice, her teeth flashing like a Cheshire cat's. "I'll pick you up at three," she says, "and you'll see."

My exchange with Noah is a frosty one.

"I'm going out with Pam this afternoon," I tell him.

"Fine." He doesn't look up from his computer. "I'll stay here and work."

"I figured. I know how important your work is to you."

He ignores the snipe.

"Vonda said we can take Micky to dinner at five thirty," I say. "If I'm not showing up big enough for you two, then please, send me home early."

I wait for him to tell me he was wrong, that everything he said earlier about my lack of warmth toward Micky was a mistake, or at least join the fight I'm picking. All I get is, "Five thirty, got it." He continues messing with his computer, shutting me out, shutting me down, until I finally drift away in a cloud of my own dissatisfaction.

At precisely three o'clock, Pam shows up in her beat-up white Wrangler. I don't recognize her at first. She's wearing a baseball cap, the visor pushed low over her sunglasses, and a plain white tank top that shows off her tats and gym arms.

"That's quite the getup," I observe. "You working undercover today?"

It's a joke, but Pam remains straight-faced. "Pretty much."

Uh-oh, I think.

She drives us to a swanky-for-Tucson restaurant with a French name that she mispronounces, and I know even before we enter the establishment that she's under-dressed. Fashion cluelessness, it would appear, is something my mother's partner has in common with my own. No wonder Donna admired Teresa — poise and grooming were in short supply at home.

Eager to shuffle us out of view, the restaurant's crisp hostess seats us in the rear, where we are less visible to incoming customers. Only then does Pam remove her hat and glasses. Only then do I wonder if her casual dress was an act, a strategic move to keep us out of view. But who are we hiding from?

An annoyingly pretty waiter who is almost certainly planning his move to LA fills our glasses with cucumber-and-mint-infused water. Pam peers down at a floating green sprig. "Moments like these, I'd about kill for a beer," she says.

This strikes me as a bad sign. "What's up? You said you had something big."

She nods. "I've been keeping an eye on some of Jasmine's friends these last few days. Their behavior's been pretty interesting."

"What do you mean 'keeping an eye on'?"

She holds out her iPhone to me, a video clip cued up on the screen. I press Play and find some jerky footage of a door. Desert Village Apartments, I realize. The outside of Jasmine's place. It's night, and the scene is yellow and grainy from the building's exterior lights. After several seconds without any action, the camera sweeps suddenly across the grounds, past the empty pool area, and zeroes in on two moving shadows. The recording follows these shapes to Jasmine's apartment, and then the picture quality deteriorates even further with an attempt to zoom in. Still, the building light is just bright enough to make out a blurry face.

"Is that McCullough?"

"Doug McCullough, stopping by the scene of the crime," Pam confirms. "Always thought he was a good kid, but maybe not." Her mouth forms a tight little line. "Jasmine had a way of getting to people, bringing out the worst in them."

I ignore that comment and focus on the video, where the figure beside McCullough stands unlocking the door to 802. Both disappear into Jasmine's apartment. I shudder, remembering the inside. Not the kind of scene you'd think a grief-stricken boyfriend would want to spend time in.

"When was this video taken?" I ask.

"I shot it last night."

I frown. "Why? What were you doing hanging around Jasmine's place?"

"Wanted to see what Mac was up to." Pam shrugs. "One a.m. those two show up. A little weird, going through a dead girl's apartment at that hour, don't you think?"

The idea of Pam staking out Jasmine's apartment in the wee hours of the morning — or worse, following people around like some creepy stalker — is almost as concerning as McCullough's unexplained appearance, but I don't tell her that.

"The other guy's got a key," I note. I rewind the video and study the figure of the second man, but he's obscured by McCullough. "Is that Sanchez?"

"Bingo."

"What are they after?"

"I don't know. They were in there over an hour. Didn't look too happy when they came out, so I don't think they found what they were looking for. I'll show you the video —"

"No, that's okay." I don't need further evidence of Pam's bizarre pursuit. "The CSI team went through every inch of that place, didn't they?"

She nods. "These boys must think they missed something."

"Sanchez has been out there before, you know," I tell her. "I ran into him last Monday when I stopped by Jasmine's place."

"Oh? You didn't mention." Pam takes a slug of her cucumber-mint water like she's downing a shot.

"That memory card with the pictures — Sanchez and McCullough must know about those, right?"

"Sure," says Pam. "They aren't a well-kept secret."

"McCullough's a jealous guy. Maybe he's trying to figure out who was in those photos."

"Those pics were taken before Jasmine and McCullough were even an item."

I give her a look. "Jasmine has photos of a sexual encounter that happened at her place, which she was probably involved in, and you think McCullough cares *when* it happened? Come on, Pam."

"Point," Pam says with a chuckle. "I'm sure Mac's been getting flak about it from the guys at work. Slutty girlfriend and all that."

"I still don't understand what stake Sanchez has in this," I muse. "You said the guy in the photos was white, right? Not Hispanic?"

"Yeah, there's no way it was Sanchez. Not with that pasty white ass. But I've got a theory." She smirks, and I can tell there's something she hasn't told me. "Only one way to test it."

"What's that?"

She jerks her head toward the restaurant's waiting area several feet behind me. "Be casual."

I glance over my shoulder, past a couple empty tables. My eyes bug when I see McCullough pacing around by the hostess, eyes on the door, clearly waiting for someone. "How long has he been here?"

"A couple of minutes."

"Is he here to see us? Did you call him?"

"Nope."

"Then how did you know he was coming?"

She's enjoying this entirely too much. "I told you, I've been keeping an eye on things. And an ear, from time to time."

"Who's he meeting?"

She picks up the menu, ignoring my question. "Keep your voice down and don't stare."

"What if he *sees* us?"

"I've been tailing this guy for four days. Long as I keep my distance, he doesn't see shit." Pam gives a dry laugh. "If he was one of my boys, I'd bench him for cluelessness. Anyway, looks like he's got something else to focus on right now."

I try to peer over my shoulder, to see what she's zoned in on, but Pam shakes her head.

"Don't turn around." Both her voice and face remain completely natural. "They'll walk right by us." She puts a hand to her forehead and raises the menu, casually shielding her face from view. Now I understand the hat and glasses she wore before.

Seconds later, a young brunette passes by us in heels and a minidress. Doug McCullough tags behind her with a sour expression.

"That's Jasmine's friend," I whisper. "Serena. The one in the pictures."

"Uh-huh." I'm not telling Pam anything she doesn't already know.

We watch them sit down at a table on the other side of the restaurant. Though I can't make out any of the words that pass between them, their body language is remarkably incongruent. Serena looks happy, giggly even, as she pores over the menu. McCullough says little and responds mainly with scowls.

"I don't get it," I say. "He doesn't look like he wants to be here."

"No," Pam agrees, draining the remainder of her water. "It was like that in the coffee shop the other day, too. She's got something on him. Be nice to find out what, wouldn't it?"

"Oh no." I recognize the danger much too late. "You've got a plan." There's no big lead, no super-secret clue, just some hare-brained scheme.

"A minute or two, that's all I need from you," Pam says. "You see where they're sitting? We hit the jackpot."

It doesn't take a surveillance expert to see what she means. McCullough and Serena's table borders a four-foot partition. With all the hanging plants, someone could easily stand on the opposite side of the partition and listen in.

"The restrooms are behind that divider," Pam says. "Over by the kitchen. Easiest thing in the world for you to pull off."

"Me?" I hold my head in my hands. "No. Just no. I am not hiding behind some freaking plant."

"Not asking you to." Pam grins and hands me a tiny circular piece of black metal. "You're going to the bathroom and then, on your way back, you reach up, like you're admiring the leaves, and drop that in the planter."

I *could* probably use a trip to the restroom if we're being honest, but depositing spy equipment to conduct an unauthorized investigation of a cop? Not my field, thanks. How did I miss the fact that Pam is totally off-her-rocker crazy?

"Bugging their conversation is illegal, Pam, and you know it."

"It's a transmitter, not a recording device," she argues. "Takes some legwork out of overhearing a public conversation, that's all. And I'm not gathering evidence, just hoping to get something that can point me in the right direction."

"Then *you* do it."

"All right." My refusal doesn't faze her any. "I just thought, if he spotted you, it would be no thing. If McCullough sees *me* here, the game's up."

I glance at Serena and McCullough, hesitating. There's *something* going on with them. Could McCullough have been the guy in those photos? What implication would a Serena-Jasmine-McCullough threesome have for Jasmine's death? Did Jazz become an unwanted third wheel?

For someone who had nothing good to say about McCullough at the funeral, Serena certainly seems to delight in his company now. She tosses her hair, confident, a bit flirtatious. McCullough, on the other hand, looks queasy.

Pam's right. This girl has something on him. Something that must have come into play after her bitter comments about him after the memorial service.

Could McCullough have killed Jasmine? He and Sanchez were supposed to have been on duty that night, but if McCullough wanted to stop by his girlfriend's place, Sanchez might've covered for him. Could still be covering for him.

Serena lived at the same apartment complex as Jasmine. She could've seen something, heard something. Maybe they were in on it together. Either way, Serena seems to like having a cop in her pocket.

I give Pam a scathing look, annoyed at both her and myself that she's exploited my curiosity so successfully.

"I'm going to the bathroom, but I am *not* bugging anyone, do you understand?"

"Fine," she says. "Of course, if you happen to hear anything . . ."

I shoot her another dirty look. She's getting what she wants. She doesn't need to rub it in.

Twenty-Six

Standing against the partition, I wait my turn for the bathroom while trying to avoid waitstaff traffic in and out of the nearby kitchen. There are just two single-occupant restrooms. I let a woman with both a toddler and an infant leapfrog me in line for the ladies' room, buying me extra time. Any actual need to pee I had recedes with nerves.

I get out my phone, partly to look occupied, but also to see if Noah has called or texted an apology for our fight earlier. He hasn't. A waitress passes by, her arms full of drinks, and I step out of her path, edge just a little closer to McCullough and Serena's table. The hanging plants have large gaps between them, so I angle myself carefully.

Three quick steps backward, and I'm behind the hanging plant nearest their table, its spidery leaves scratchy against the back of my head. Now, if I sort through the bar chatter, I can just make out their conversation on the other side of the divider.

"They'll figure it out," McCullough's saying. "It's only a matter of time. This is a *murder* investigation. They're throwing a lot of resources at it."

"Would you chill out already? You're overthinking this." Serena's chewing as she speaks. "The situation is under control, trust me."

"Trust you? Why would I trust you?" he demands. "You're the whole reason I'm in this. You told us you got rid of that card, and here we are, all the photos you said you deleted getting passed around the Homicide unit. What the *fuck*?"

"I *did* delete them," she says calmly. "Just not the copies I gave Jazz."

"And here's where I run into problems with you, Serena. Because what kind of jealous, insane little bitch gives her friend pictures like that?"

So Jasmine *didn't* take those photos. She wasn't even there.

"Oh, Mac. They were so good, I just had to share." Serena laughs, a high-pitched, nasal sound that must grate on McCullough even worse than it does me. "Seriously, though, you can relax. Rob never took pictures of your *face*. I mean, what are they gonna do, identify you from a dick lineup?

Even Jazz wasn't totally sure it was you."

Two servers stop to gossip beside me, and I lose the next minute to their complaints about table 16. Just my luck. Sidelined by rants about a vegan right when things are getting interesting. It takes almost Herculean strength to keep myself from peeking around the plant to see what Serena and McCullough are up to. When the waiter bitch session finally breaks up and I tune back in, McCullough is still obsessing over the photos.

"What about the ones of Sanchez?" he asks. "What did you do with all those?"

"I only gave Jazz the you-and-me pics Rob took. Don't worry, I deleted all the gay shit."

"There was nothing gay," McCullough protests, as if deeply offended by the idea. "I didn't even touch him."

Serena snorts. "You *watched* each other. That's pretty gay."

My mind races, trying to arrange all the pieces, to figure out what's going on. Clearly McCullough and Sanchez had some kind of ill-advised sexual encounter with Serena a while back, but what's he so scared of?

"You couldn't let her have one good thing without pissing on it, could you?" McCullough asks. "You just *had* to let her know you had me first. Had to give her photographic evidence."

"I *did* have you first," Serena tells him sweetly. "Anyway, she was my best friend, and it was *her* apartment. She had a right to know what went on."

"Don't pretend you were her friend. You waited, what, a year to give her those photos? She was barely speaking to you. Just admit it. You were jealous."

She sighs. "Why would I be jealous of her inheriting my sloppy seconds?"

"Because I *loved* her. Really loved her. But you . . . you were just a piece of ass on a night me and Sanchez were too drunk to think straight."

Serena has no snappy comeback for this one. I suspect his insult has hit the mark. "Well," she says at last, "if that's how you feel, I don't want to waste your precious time here. I should probably go stop by Homicide. Who's the lead detective? Max Vargas? I'm sure he'll understand about the gay stuff."

I can't help myself. Her threat is just too brazen. I peer around the hanging plant's long green tendrils and finally get a look at them. Her hands are on her hips, her breasts thrust forward, triumphant. She has him by the balls, and he knows it. Both are far too absorbed in their weird little power game to

497

notice my gawking just a few feet away.

He's going to blow, I think. *Back off, girl, if you know what's good for you.* But Serena doesn't know or doesn't care.

"They're probably wasting a lot of manpower on these pictures," she continues, just in case McCullough needs further incensing. "I should really spare them the trouble, don't you think? Save some tax dollars?"

McCullough grabs her roughly by the wrist and yanks her toward him. I flinch at the violence of his gesture, look wildly around for Pam. Serena, however, looks thrilled.

"Ooh, Dougie. Getting a little rough with me, huh?" He releases his grip on her, and she slides back into her chair with a smirk. "Wouldn't be the first time."

"I could kill you," McCullough murmurs. "With my own two hands."

"Hey, I'm not the one who cheated on you."

"Of course she cheated on me! She saw those pictures, what was she supposed to think? I bet you didn't even tell her they were old."

Serena rolls her eyes. "News flash! She was cheating on you long before she saw those pictures."

"I don't believe you."

"Believe whatever you want. But I don't blame her for going back to Ruben. That guy is *hot.* She always said he was like some kind of animal in bed. You know what he liked to do to her?"

McCullough leans across the table and puts a hand on her throat. "Shut. Up."

So much for staying in hiding. I need to act before the situation escalates to something dangerous — if it hasn't already.

Pam, thank goodness, is one step ahead of me. She chooses this tense moment to wander over to their table, gnawing casually on a slice of artisanal bread. "Mac," she says, her expression benign. "What are you doing here, buddy?"

He removes his hand from Serena. "Nothing," he says. "Just grabbing lunch with my friend. But she's leaving now."

Serena looks about to disagree, but Pam's cool and appraising gaze convinces her otherwise. "Later, Dougie," she mumbles, and flounces off.

"So. You checking up on me?" McCullough stares down at the table.

Pam spreads her hands as if to assert her innocence. "I'm just like you, man. Grabbing lunch with a friend." She scans the restaurant — as if she hasn't known where I was this whole time — and waves to me.

"Charlotte! Come join us."

Although less than thrilled about his two new dining companions, McCullough plays the game, gives me a little nod of acknowledgment when I sit down. "Hi," he says stiffly.

"Well, now." Pam grabs a knife from McCullough's table and begins to butter another slice of bread. "Did I hear you're in some shit over those photos that turned up in Jasmine's apartment?"

"You heard that?" McCullough slumps back in his seat. "Goddamn it." He stares up at the ceiling for a minute.

Pam gives him a long look. "Sneaking around doesn't look good, Mac. You should come clean with Vargas before they put it together for themselves."

He nods miserably. "It's just . . . it was a year ago. One night. We were drunk, you know?"

"You and Sanchez," she says.

"There was nothing gay." He glances at me as if I might contradict him. "I don't care if that's *your* thing, Pam. Whatever, it takes all kinds. But *I* like women. And Serena, she was just . . . there."

"And Sanchez was just there. With a camera," Pam observes.

"It was Serena's phone." McCullough's

leg jigs furiously as he speaks. "I don't know what she did with all the photos, but she gave Jasmine that memory card way after the fact. Just to be a bitch. She said Jasmine had prints, too, but we can't find them." He turns to me, unable to meet my eyes. "Did you take them? From Jasmine's apartment?"

"Me?" The suggestion surprises me.

"Sanchez said you found some pictures in there. That you were going to give them to someone."

Now it all makes sense, Sanchez's concern when he saw me at Jasmine's apartment with the envelope of photos. *They're not for me,* I told him, which must have set his worried mind into overdrive.

"I took a few photos from Jasmine's room," I concede, stifling a laugh, "but they were for Micky. Pictures of her family, not amateur porn." These guys went to such comical lengths to avoid any appearance of man-love, I almost want to see the incriminating snapshots for myself.

"Explains why Sanchez was following you," Pam tells me, her thoughts running parallel to my own.

McCullough, meanwhile, has been reduced to begging. "Please don't let this get out. The guys at work — you don't even know."

"Is Serena blackmailing you?" Pam asks. "We could slap her with extortion charges, get her off your back."

"It's never anything direct." McCullough twists his napkin. "She just . . . she's been asking for stuff, you know? Like, she wanted me to take her to lunch today. *This* place." He makes a sweeping gesture with his hand as if to indicate the extravagance of her request. "I've been scared to say no to her. Scared of what she'll do."

I no longer care about McCullough and Sanchez and the uncomfortable aftereffects of their sexcapades. "You don't think Serena killed Jasmine, do you?" I ask.

"No," he grants. "She's crazy, but not homicidal. And she's scared of guns."

We're wasting time here. Jasmine and her dubious friendships have been a red herring all along. Donna is the key to these murders. We should be uncovering all the details of her life, not her daughter's. Yet even knowing this, I can't refrain from satisfying my perverse curiosity. "Why were the three of you getting busy in Jasmine's apartment, anyway? Where was *she*?"

"She had a lot at the bar that night." McCullough stares at the table, rakes a hand across the back of his head. "She passed out in her room. It's stupid. The only reason I was there was 'cause I liked her, and then . . . this other stuff happened."

Pam licks a bread crumb from her index finger. "Alcohol will make a person do stupid things. We've all been there, buddy."

I should've come in my own vehicle. Now I'm stuck here waiting on Pam, who looks only too ready for a three-course meal. As I'm devising a polite way to get her out of the restaurant, my phone blurps with a text alert. I tear through my purse to get a look.

Not Noah, but Vonda, and I don't have time to feel disappointed when I see her message. *Micky had rough nite yesterday,* she writes. *Seemed to be remembering stuff from when her mom/gramma died? Just want to warn you before your visit.*

My eyes widen, and I curse under my breath. What the hell does *remembering stuff* mean? This is not the kind of thing you just send someone in a text.

"What?" Pam demands. "What is it?"

"Micky's foster mother. It's nothing."

Before I can stop her, she's snatched the phone from me. Her face darkens as she scans the message. Pam slides the phone back across the table.

"Call her," she says.

"Call who?"

"Micky," Pam says. "See what she knows."

"I'm going to see her in an hour," I object. "It can wait."

"No," Pam insists. "It can't. Call this Vonda person. I want to know what Micky told her. If the kid saw or heard something that night, I want to know about it *now.*"

McCullough goes rigid when he realizes what we're discussing. He leans forward, a little too ready to start kicking asses and taking names.

"Shouldn't we just let Detective Vargas handle this?" If only I had my car, some way to make a quick exit. "No offense, guys, but this isn't your case."

"If this was a police issue, the foster mom would've contacted them already, right?" Pam sounds perfectly reasonable, but I remain uneasy. "Micky found her mother dead — she must have a lot of nightmares about that. It's probably nothing. But we need to be sure."

"Right now?"

McCullough lays both hands flat on the table, and his thumbs begin to twitch. "Right now. We follow every lead."

I inhale. "All right." I dial Vonda's number and hit the speaker button. We all listen to her phone ringing. Part of me hopes that Vonda won't even answer, that we can sidestep this weirdness, but no.

"Hello?"

"Vonda, hi. It's Charlie. I just . . . wanted to hear a little more about what's going on with Micky."

"Yeah, I'm glad you called." Vonda briefs me quickly. "Micky had a bad night. Screaming, crying, calling for her grandma. She's had nightmares before, but that was the worst I've seen. I'm going to talk to her doctor about sleep meds."

"How's she been today?" I ask.

"A little off," Vonda reports. "This afternoon she was talking about the night her family died. It was hard to understand. She kept asking what happened to Grandma's friend, but I couldn't tell if she was talking about her dream or something real."

"Grandma's friend?" I glance at Pam. Her jaw tightens, but otherwise her expression remains inscrutable.

"I guess, you know . . ." Vonda seems uncomfortable broaching the subject. "Didn't her grandmother live with a woman? A . . . friend? Anyway, Micky said she heard them in the apartment that night, Grandma and the — the friend. She heard them talking. I don't know. Maybe it was part of the dream? And she said something about blood. All the blood in the dining room."

McCullough and I exchange a surreptitious glance. In her awkward attempts to gloss over Donna's lesbian relationship, Vonda has nevertheless divulged what could be a game changer.

Could Pam really have been there at Jasmine's apartment? Did Micky hear her? But what about Pam's poker game that night, her unbreakable alibi? For the first time it occurs to me that everything I know about this case has come from Pam.

"Anyway . . ." Vonda is eager to leave this conversation behind. "I'm going to check in with the investigator tomorrow to see if any of this matters. I just wanted to give you a heads-up in case Micky said something or seemed strange."

"Thanks, Vonda," I say, clearing my throat. "I'll keep that in mind."

We say quick good-byes and then McCullough, Pam, and I sit around staring at the table. I wait for Pam to offer an explanation, to confirm or deny her presence that evening, but she says nothing. The nothing says plenty.

Maybe there was no poker game. Maybe there was no alibi. Maybe Pam has been the prime suspect all along, and I believed every lie she fed me.

"Well," she says, standing suddenly. "I

guess we all heard enough." Pam studies us both for a few long seconds. Something strange passes over her face, an emotion I can't quite identify. *"Adiós, muchachos,"* she says with a wave. "I'll see you on the other side."

"The other side of what?" I ask with a nervous laugh, but she's already gone. I look to McCullough for answers. "What was *that* about?"

McCullough has removed his phone and holds it in his hand before him as if it weighs a hundred pounds. "I have to call Vargas."

I swallow. "You really think —"

"If Pam was there . . . that changes everything. They've gotta question the kid again."

"Maybe it was just a dream."

McCullough's leg has begun to jiggle again. "No," he murmurs. "No, I think Micky heard her. She knew Pam. She would've recognized her voice. Vargas has been saying all along Pam was involved. I just thought . . . I mean, Vargas is such a tool . . ."

I don't want to believe this about Pam, a woman I've spent time with, a woman I've come to grudgingly respect. "That doesn't make sense. Why would she hurt Donna?

Pam *loved* Donna."

"Who the hell knows what goes on inside other people's relationships?" The whole table quivers now with the strength of his jittery leg. "You've seen Pam. She's sober now, but it wouldn't take much to send her over the edge."

I think of my father. "Donna couldn't stay away from addicts. It's like she had a sixth sense for them."

"Well." McCullough shrugs. "That's how she and Pam met. Alcoholics Anonymous."

"Pam told me they met at a church event."

"Probably did. A lot of churches host AA meetings." He picks up his phone and tosses some twenty-dollar bills on the table. "I have to make this call. Homicide's gotta get on this pronto. And you . . ." His blue eyes move quickly over me. "You stay the hell away from Pam."

TWENTY-SEVEN

There's no time to internally debate Pam's guilt or innocence; she's left me without a ride. Before I can go begging Noah, however, I receive a call from someone who will not be joining my fan club anytime soon.

"This is Andrea Rincón of Mexikids. I'm looking for Charlotte?" Her tone makes me wonder what exactly she has planned for Charlotte, should she find her.

"Speaking." I scramble to recall Andrea Rincón, to determine what she wants from me.

"I'm the adoption attorney," she reminds me with ill-concealed annoyance. "Teresa King put us in touch. We were supposed to meet half an hour ago at the Sonora Hope office. To discuss Michaela Ramos?"

"Oh! Andrea! I'm so sorry!" I have some recollection of scheduling this appointment, although I didn't write it down. Why didn't I write it down? "I must have . . . lost track of time. Are you at the office? Can I still come by?"

"I guess so." She sounds understandably grumpy.

"Listen, while I have you on the line . . . can I ask you a weird legal question?" It's been bothering me since I received the text from Vonda. "If Micky witnessed something the night her mother died — like, heard someone she knew in the apartment — would she have to testify in court?"

Andrea lets out a low whistle. "This is Donna DeRossi's granddaughter you're talking about?"

"Yeah."

"Wow. I wish I could help, but that's really not my area of legal expertise." Her only advice is not the least bit lawyerly. "Get the kid some therapy. A whole lot of therapy."

As soon as we're off the phone, I call Noah. He sighs when I explain my scheduling screwup, which now conflicts with our Micky outing.

"You want me to call Vonda and cancel?" he asks.

"No, no. You go ahead and get Micky, and I'll take a cab over to Sonora Hope," I advise. "That lawyer lady was pissed. If I bow out now, we won't get another meeting with her."

We both know that Micky would rather see Noah than me, and I wasn't looking forward to the visit anyway. Not with his studying the interaction, looking for signs that I'm an insufficient parent. *Just jump this next hurdle,* I tell myself. Tonight, there will be time for Noah and me to address our fight, to talk about the things that matter. Like whether we can raise our *own* child together, much less someone else's.

I wait for the taxi, my heart full of questions.

Andrea Rincón is civil but brisk when I arrive. "You just missed Teresa," she announces, and it feels like a reprimand for my lateness. "She sends her regards."

A husky woman in her forties, Andrea possesses a sharp nose and an equally sharp attitude to match. She herds me through the lobby, past Teresa's office with its shiny gold nameplate, past a few empty cubicles and Albert, who greets me with a startled expression.

"No baby?" he asks, and I realize that the last he heard of me, I was making a beeline for the border, claiming to be in labor.

I give him my best *Oops* face. "False alarm."

Albert sees Andrea tapping her foot impatiently and waves me on with a smile. "It happens."

Andrea and I land in a small conference room where, without ceremony, she launches into the legal minutiae of adopting Micky. For twenty minutes, she outlines the legal barriers I'll encounter should I pursue custody of Micky and estimates how ridiculously long each step might take. She echoes Daniel Quijada's advice that securing custody will be a far easier, faster process if Ruben Ramos terminates his parental rights.

The thought of Micky's father wasting away in a Mexican prison only intensifies my feeling that our trip to Arizona has done more harm than good. Who are we kidding, Noah and I, trying to pretend we're stable enough to take on another kid? Still, I nod and listen and try to ask Andrea good questions. Try to look like the calm and competent parent I wish I were instead of hyperventilating at the number of documents we'll need to file.

No wonder there are so many children in foster care. Adoption really does require the stamina of a marathon runner.

When she's finished her piece, Andrea scribbles down some names of Tucson-area child psychologists who specialize in post-traumatic stress disorder. "I have a meeting with a client I need to get to now," she says, handing me the slip of paper. "Good luck with all this." She gathers up her briefcase and we head out of the conference room. As we pass Albert, Andrea pauses. "I almost forgot. Teresa wanted me to tell you. There's a box of stuff from your mother's desk on that table behind you if you want to go through it. Otherwise, it'll all get thrown out."

I peer over my shoulder and spot a large cardboard box labeled DONNA in red marker. My heart beats a little faster. "Shouldn't that go to Pam?"

"Pam and Teresa aren't on the best of terms," Andrea says drily. "And I'm sure there's nothing valuable." She slips from the office, leaving me with these remnants of the stranger who happens to be my mother.

I look around, worried Albert might be observing my reaction from his desk, but he's lost in his computer screen. The box sits, a mundane testament to Donna's employment here that inexplicably frightens me.

It's been hard enough to visit my mother's home, but her presence there was at least muted by Pam's. Something about sorting Donna's possessions — items that belonged to her and her alone — terrifies me. It's what a daughter does when her mother dies. If I take this box, however trivial the contents, I am acknowledging what I have lost. There will be no reconciliation, no chance for her to apologize or explain or tell me that she's proud of who I've become in her absence. That door has closed.

I remove the first item from the box, ears burning. A file folder with photocopies of receipts, request-for-reimbursement forms. I flip through: gas, mostly, from Donna's frequent drives down to Nogales. Looks like she was there two or three times a week. I work my way through the rest of the box. A canister of tea. A stuffed rabbit. A paperback romance novel with a hunky hero on the cover that seems to suggest Donna never lost all interest in men. No office supplies — someone must've taken those. And then, not halfway through, a slim white box that stops my heart.

The label is clear and unapologetic: *Rohypnol, 2 mg. 30 comprimidos.*

I open the box, noting the Spanish on the label, and find three sheets of untouched pills inside. *What the hell were you up to, Donna?* I glance over at Albert, but he's sitting at his desk, brows knit, his mind elsewhere.

Didn't the police come here? Surely they must have searched Donna's desk, her personal belongings. How did they miss this?

I take a deep breath. Remind myself I have no idea what Tucson Homicide knows or doesn't know. *You're going to have to tell them.* I drop the pills back into the box and sink down into a chair. I wanted to believe in my mother's sobriety. I wanted to believe that people can change, that they can overcome their personal demons, yet after finding these pills, I'm forced to reevaluate.

I cover my face with my hands, not sure why my disappointment is so acute, why the actions of a woman I never knew should matter.

Whatever Donna was doing with Mexican date-rape drugs in her possession, it can't have been good. She was involved in something, something that got her killed. Maybe Pam was involved, too, was present that night and knows more than she's telling.

I remember what my aunt Suzie said when she broke the news of Donna's death: *The police think it's drug related. No surprise there.* Nearly forty years without speaking to Donna, and Suzie still had her pegged. Because people don't change. My selfish, shitty mother remained selfish and shitty.

And she brought her daughter down with her.

The unfairness of Jasmine's death hits me hardest. Everyone has assumed that she was somehow to blame, and yet this wasn't her fault. She was supposed to be out with McCullough, not home getting slaughtered over some stupid drug deal. Jasmine may not have been much of a mother to Micky, but she didn't have to die, didn't deserve to die.

My phone rings, startling me from my thoughts. It's Noah.

"Hey," I say, trying to swallow the hopelessness I feel. "What's up? Did you get Micky?"

"No," he says, and his voice is from another planet, breaking with each word. "She's gone, Charlie. Micky's gone."

TWENTY-EIGHT

"Gone?" It's a strange word, one with so many shades of meaning, and I can feel some part of myself detaching, hardening against bad news. "What do you mean Micky's gone?"

There are numerous ways, I've learned, to be gone. You can be gone like my son, alive one minute and dead in the next. Or gone like my mother all those years, cutting yourself from the lives of those who need you with the swiftness and precision of a scalpel. Or gone like my father, physically present, but lost in his own relationship with alcohol. *Which kind of gone is Micky?* I wonder distantly. What new loss will I have to accommodate?

"She's missin'," Noah says. "Someone took her."

It takes a couple minutes, but I eventually extract the story from him.

When Noah arrived at Vonda's house, no

one answered the doorbell. He found the door unlocked and discovered Vonda lying on the kitchen floor, unconscious but breathing, the back of her head bloody. He called 911 and immediately began searching for Micky.

Thinking she might've gone to seek help for Vonda, he asked a pair of neighborhood boys if they'd seen her. One reported that Micky had left not too long ago with an unfamiliar adult female. The boy was unable to describe Micky's companion except to say that she wore sunglasses and a hooded sweatshirt. Her car, he said, was "big and white." Micky seemed to know her.

"It was a *woman,*" Noah says, as if this subtlety might somehow have escaped me. "Someone she knew with a white car."

"Pam," I whisper. "It was Pam. I never should've let her walk out of that restaurant."

"What would Pam want with Micky?" Noah scoffs.

I duck into the conference room, making sure I'm out of Albert's earshot. "Micky heard something," I say in a low voice. "The night that Donna and Jasmine were murdered, she heard something. Something Pam doesn't want anyone knowing about."

"Even if that were true . . . how would

Pam even know where Micky was?"

"Pam's been tailing everyone," I murmur, remembering the weird video she took in the middle of the night. "She could've followed us there at some point, easy. The woman's unhinged, Noah. She tried to get me to bug McCullough today. We've got to find her before she hurts Micky."

"None of this makes any sense," he protests. "Pam wouldn't hurt that kid, not knowin' how much she meant to Donna."

"You don't understand." I don't waste precious time laying out every dirty little detail. "I talked to Vonda earlier. Micky heard Pam at Jasmine's apartment that night, okay? Micky placed her at the scene. *Micky is the only witness.* And Pam knows that."

Noah doesn't speak for a few seconds, trying to absorb this. "You think Pam . . . you think she killed them?"

"I don't know." I hear sirens in the background. "Are the police there?"

"Yeah," he says.

"Tell them what I told you. Tell them they need to find Pam. Now."

"I'll tell them. But they don't have a warrant. They can't just bust into her place." He still doesn't sound entirely convinced that I'm right. "Pam knows me. Maybe I

519

should go over. I could talk to her."

"That's not a good idea."

Nausea gathers in my stomach as I imagine Noah showing up on Pam's doorstep, demanding to see Micky. Would Pam hurt him? The woman certainly knows her way around a firearm.

I hear voices in the background, and then Noah exhales. "I gotta go," he says. "Sit tight. I'll call you when I know more."

Sit tight? Easy for him to say.

I wander back over to the carton of my mother's items. The box of Rohypnol lies perched on top like an ugly accusation. I stuff it in my purse; the police may need it later.

What *was* Pam doing at Jasmine's apartment that night? What were she and Donna mixed up in? After all her crazy investigations, all her outward displays of grief, could Pam really be the one who killed my mother?

"You can take that whole box with you," Albert says from behind me. He's spun around in his chair, watching me. "You don't have to sort it all out here."

It takes a moment for his words to register, to realize he's trying to get rid of me. "It's just junk," I say, backing away from the table. "You guys can throw it away."

I should leave. But I don't know where to go, what to do. Sit tight, Noah advised. Translation: wait around for his call. It's not a very attractive option.

I take a few steps toward Teresa's office and absently run a finger over the gold nameplate outside. The door is half open, the lights off. *Teresa's not sitting idly around her office,* I think. *She's busy saving the world. And here you are, unable to save the one person who really needs you.*

I stare at my feet. *Where are you, Micky?*

"Sounds like you're having a hard day." Albert has turned off his computer and has his bag in hand, not-so-subtly hinting that it's closing time.

"How much did you hear?" I ask.

"Nothing really," he says. "But you look pretty blown out. Listen, I'd let you hang around, but I've got to pick up my son."

I nod, but my mind is on Pam, trying to figure where she might be. Has anyone called her? Maybe *I* should call her. Maybe this is all a misunderstanding and she's trying to protect Micky, not hurt her. I reach into my purse, feel around for my phone. Just as my fingers close around it, something inside Teresa's office catches my eye. A movement from behind her desk.

I approach the doorway, the back of my

neck tingling. "Albert, is someone else here?"

Albert shakes his head. "It's past six. That's late for this crew."

It's relatively dark in Teresa's office, but now I see it again. A shadow that stands behind the desk and then moves quickly out of view.

"There's somebody in there," I say.

"I don't think so . . ."

I enter the office, my whole body on high alert. I can't see anyone inside, just the outline of a desk and chair, a window with the blinds drawn, a filing cabinet. I flip on the lights.

The walls of the room are covered with framed articles about Sonora Hope, photographs of Teresa smiling with influential donors, a few awards. My eyes sweep the room for any signs of someone, but it's a small office. There's only one place someone could be hiding: under the desk.

I circle around, forgetting, for a few seconds, to breathe. Peer underneath. Nothing.

"We really shouldn't disturb Teresa's things," Albert says from the doorway.

"No, of course." Now I'm embarrassed. "I'm sorry. I just . . . thought I saw someone." I reach to turn off the light on my way out and stop. My fingers freeze in midair at the image I see before me, about six inches to the right of the light switch.

A glossy page from *Arizona Living,* half text and half photograph, in a varnished wooden frame. On either side of Teresa, two men grin for the camera, both sporting tuxedos. Teresa, wearing a lavender formal gown and a demure smile, holds up a plaque for some exceptional-nonprofit award she's received. What stops me in my tracks is not the award but the man standing to her left.

It's Quico.

I quickly scan the caption. *Sonora Hope founder Teresa King celebrates the success of her nonprofit with husband and CEO of Mexikids International Jonathan King and Sonoran director of Family Rights Francisco Ortega.*

"Charlotte?" Albert is drumming his fingers on the wall, the polite façade rapidly fading. "I need to lock up."

I point at the photo. "Do they work together? Those three?"

He sighs. Steps into the office to get a look at what I'm ogling. "Ortega is one of our partners in Mexico. Kind of smarmy, but comes with the territory, I guess. And the other guy is Teresa's husband."

"Does her husband work with Sonora Hope?"

"No, his organization does for-profit adoptions. They have nothing to do with us."

Except they do, I think as I follow him blindly back to the lobby. The three of them laid out in a row — it's plain to me now. They have everything to do with one another. There's a bitter taste in the back of my throat as the realization hits.

Teresa King works with women, vulnerable women. Women with no men, or else bad men, in their lives. Women struggling to support themselves and, in many cases, their children.

Jonathan King facilitates adoptions in a country with strict rules about who may be adopted. No child under five, Teresa told me — unless that child is disabled or sick, requiring care he or she could not receive in Mexico.

And Quico? According to Pam, Francisco Ortega's responsibilities include overseeing American adoptions of Mexican children.

What a neat, efficient little machine they've made.

I put my hand to my belly. Blink. Stare at the fluorescent ceiling lights until they've burned themselves into my vision, floating white circles that travel the length of the office with my gaze.

No wonder Marilena, the most successful recipient of Sonora Hope's assistance, has lost three children. No wonder Ysabel, who also lost a child, will find herself well cared for by the organization afterward. There were a lot of pregnant women in that program. And now I know why.

Albert was wrong. Duardo was wrong. These mothers didn't lose their babies because they were exposed to toxic waste. They didn't lose their babies at all.

They sold them.

TWENTY-NINE

Albert locks the door behind us and surges toward the parking lot. "Sorry to rush you out," he says, "but I have to pick my son up from practice."

I study him for some sign that my questions about Quico and Teresa have made him nervous but find none. He's impatient but nothing more. I've delayed him from performing a fatherly duty.

The man has no idea who it is he's working for.

One thing I know: a person with a secret can be dangerous. Quico, Marilena, and Teresa share a secret, and I'm willing to bet the farm that secret was responsible for Lety's death. Perhaps others knew, too. Donna. Teresa's husband.

So many people with something to lose.

Poor Lety. Young and pregnant, out of options. She must've gone to Marilena for help. She must've promised them her baby.

Maybe Lety was playing them all along, bleeding the program of whatever resources it could offer while she planned her escape to the United States. Or maybe, in the beginning, Lety truly meant to give her daughter up. Maybe, as her pregnancy progressed, she fell in love.

Either way, I know how it felt to be Lety that moment in the shower before she died. She believed in her own future as a mother. She had no intention of giving her child away to some Americans.

Someone made her pay for that, but who? Is Lety's death connected to Donna and Jasmine's? To Micky's abduction?

I need to know just how dangerous Teresa King is.

I jog through the parking lot after Albert. "What color car does Teresa drive?"

He peers over his shoulder at me. "A white Range Rover, I think. But I told you, she already left for the day."

A big white car. Uh-oh.

"When did she leave?"

"I don't know." Albert unlocks the door of his own little red hybrid. "She was chatting with Andrea, and then . . . she left. Something came up, I guess. Right before you got here."

Right before you got here, that's the part I

don't like. It corresponds a little too neatly with Micky's disappearance.

I told Andrea Rincón over the phone that Micky might have overheard someone in Jasmine's apartment that night.

Andrea talked to Teresa.

Teresa left just before I arrived.

Micky disappeared shortly after.

The sequence of events forms a clear if circumstantial line. I drift away from Albert, racking my brain for some idea of where Teresa might have taken Micky.

My odd behavior has begun to concern poor Albert. "Charlie," he calls, "what is this about? Is everything okay? Did something happen?"

"Something's going to happen." I keep walking, eyes on the pavement. "If I don't stop it."

Grandma's friend. As I wander through the parking lot searching for the trappings of a plan, it all seems rather obvious.

Micky told Vonda that she'd heard "Grandma's friend" in her apartment the night Donna was murdered. She didn't mean Pam, safely accounted for at her poker game. She meant Teresa. Teresa who deals in black-market babies. Teresa who probably ordered Lety's death. Teresa who would do anything to save her own hide, even if it meant executing a friend.

Maybe Donna finally learned the truth about all those pregnant women in the program. Or maybe she had always known, but killing Lety was a step too far. One way or another, Donna became a threat, one Teresa felt she had to deal with.

I pass another set of office suites as I weave my way back toward the entrance of the development. I'll call a cab . . . just as soon as I can figure out where to go.

No wonder Pam ran off when she overheard Vonda's phone call. *Grandma's friend.* She must have known exactly who Micky was talking about. Noah and I may have been taken in by Teresa's sad history, her inspiring road to success, but Pam wasn't. Pam has never trusted the woman.

Which explains why Teresa chose Jasmine's place to commit her bloody murders. She didn't dare attack Donna in her condo. Not with Pam around. Not with all those guns.

Teresa knew about Donna's troubled relationship with Jasmine, must have known that Donna was often left to babysit her granddaughter. Maybe Teresa was watching her, waiting for an opportunity. Maybe Donna herself revealed her plans. *Jasmine's*

out again tonight, looks like I'm babysitting.
And so Teresa came late, when she knew
that Micky would be asleep.

She hadn't anticipated Jasmine's being
home. Jasmine was supposed to be out having fun with McCullough, not stuck home
with her mother.

When they saw Teresa on their doorstep,
they must have let her in. Perhaps the three
made small talk, and Micky, only half
awake, heard them speaking. Who knows
how long Teresa sat with them before the
situation turned ugly? Maybe she hadn't
gone with bad intentions. Maybe they
argued and things got out of hand.

But the Rohypnol. Why the Rohypnol?

I dial Noah's number, hoping I can inter-
cept him before he dashes off to Pam's place
and makes an idiot of himself. He doesn't
pick up. I send off a quick text: *CALL ME.*

I have to work out my next move. Have to
anticipate Teresa's. As I hurry through the
parking lot, only dimly aware of my surroundings, a white Wrangler screeches to a
stop just inches from hitting me. The near-
collision breaks me from my haze.

"Jesus Christ, Charlie, what are *you* doing
here?" Pam leans out the window, staring
me down with a disbelieving squint.

An ally with a set of wheels — exactly

what I need right now, if only I can trust her. What choice do I have?

I dash over to Pam's open window. "I need to find Teresa."

"You're a little late. She left about an hour ago."

"Have you been watching her?" Maybe Pam knows where she is. Maybe we have a chance.

"I wasn't *watching* her exactly. Let's just say I keep tabs on her movements."

Whatever sketchiness Pam has been engaged in, I'm grateful. Without waiting for an invitation, I run around to the passenger side of her vehicle and climb in. "Teresa's got Micky," I say. "We've got to find her."

"Micky? But why —"

"She thinks Micky can ID her. That Micky heard her at the apartment that night."

A look of sudden comprehension falls over Pam. "Micky's foster home — is it over on Arollo?"

"Yeah," I say. "Was Teresa over there?"

"Shit," says Pam. "Shit, shit, shit. I *knew* something was up with her. She's been driving by this house on Arollo a few times a week. And last week she drove by Jasmine's place a couple times. It didn't sit right, that she knew the address. But I thought . . . I mean, those pictures. And Serena seemed

531

so unstable . . ."

I don't blame Pam, not really. Twenty minutes ago I was ready to pin this all on *her.*

"I should've told you back at the restaurant," Pam says. "When Vonda said that thing about 'Grandma's friend.' I should've told you to watch out for Teresa. But I had to be sure."

"*Are* you sure?"

"I went to see an old friend from Homicide this afternoon. About Teresa's alibi."

"Does she have one?"

"Home with her husband, watched television, very hazy with the details. Husband corroborated her story, but I think he's covering for her. *His* story was more solid. He remembered several TV shows that night and was on the phone with his sister 'til late."

"He may not have pulled the trigger, but the husband's in on it," I tell her. "His company, Mexikids — I think it's the middleman for a bunch of illegal adoptions. Americans getting babies from Mexico. Sonora Hope is basically paying these women to breed."

"Babies," Pam mutters. "So *that's* Teresa's deal. I should've known. There were always a couple of them with a bun in the oven. I used to tell Donna, you really want these gals to move up in the world, maybe start handing out birth control." She frowns. "The paperwork, though. Adoption is a bureaucratic nightmare. How are they getting past all that?"

"Francisco Ortega," I say. "This Quico guy I was telling you about. He works for the Office of Family Rights, remember? He must be signing off on it, forging records. Maybe there's a doctor or two getting a cut. Saying the kids have health issues, developmental disabilities, to get an exception."

"That's sketchy as hell," Pam says. "Wouldn't the adoptive parents figure this out? If the paperwork says the baby has problems and then the kid is normal — they must know something's off."

I think of Bianca, waiting six years and shelling out forty grand to adopt her Chinese daughter.

"I don't think you understand how desperate some people are to be parents, Pam. If they're getting a healthy baby, they might be happy to cut a few corners." My thoughts return to Micky and I feel sick. "What do we do? Can you send out an APB or something? We have to find Teresa. What if she's taking Micky to Mexico?"

"Last I checked, Teresa was headed west,

not south."

"Then what are you doing here?" I glance at her sideways. "I thought you came looking for her."

"Figured it might be good to stop by the office while she was out. See what turned up."

I don't ask her to elaborate; whatever she had planned, I'm better off maintaining my ignorance. "I can show you what *I* found in there." I fish the package of Rohypnol out of my purse. Toss it into her lap. "That was in a box of Donna's things."

Pam studies the package a few seconds, turning it around in her hands with her usual indecipherable expression. "We'd better find Micky," she says. "If Teresa's really got her, that kid's on her way to dead." She reaches over to open the glove box. Inside, I see a stack of square devices that look like GPS systems, each with a different colored sticker on the back.

"Grab the one with the red dot," Pam tells me. "That's Teresa."

"Are you serious?" I can't help but laugh, a thin, shaky sound, as I remove the device and plug its cord into the cigarette lighter. "You've been tracking Teresa?"

"Not just Teresa." Pam mounts the square on her dashboard. "I told you, I've been keeping an eye on things."

I wonder who the other colored dots belong to, which additional persons of interest Pam's been watching, but I don't ask. Her obsession with illegal surveillance equipment may be the only chance we have.

Pam punches a couple buttons and the screen lights up. "We'll find Teresa. As long as she hasn't switched vehicles, we've got her."

"You're crazy," I say with admiration.

"Completely crazy," she agrees. "Maybe crazy enough to find Micky. Let's just hope she's alive."

THIRTY

According to the locator, Teresa's vehicle is traveling on the outskirts of the city on a long and winding road through the mountains called Gates Pass.

"We're lucky the satellites caught that," Pam says, cutting boldly into traffic. "You can't count on the reception out there. Which direction is she headed? In or out of the city?"

"Um . . ." I study the dot on the map, trying to trace its movement. "Out, I think?"

"Not too many folks out that way," Pam remarks. "Looks like she wants some privacy." Her eyes are bright and incredibly alert, and I can't help wondering if she's had anything to drink today. "I'd say Mother Teresa's out there looking for a dump site. That's good."

I feel like throwing up. "How exactly is that *good*?"

"She's had the kid for, what? An hour? If

she's leaving town, then she hasn't disposed of the body yet, and that's a piece of luck." Pam accelerates rapidly and just catches the last of a yellow light before she turns. "Maybe she's having second thoughts. Or running into logistical issues. Either way, Micky's probably still alive."

"You think there's a chance Micky might already be dead?"

"Not if Teresa has any brains. You don't want to drive around with a dead kid in the back of your car. If something goes wrong and you get caught, you're better off with an abduction charge than first-degree murder. She's a smooth one, Teresa. She could probably talk her way out of abduction."

Pam's focus and preternatural calm leave me wondering about her. A child's life hangs in the balance, and yet she remains levelheaded, logical. Is this just years of police work kicking in, allowing her to detach? Or is part of her *enjoying* this? God only knows how many times she must have envisioned a confrontation with Donna's killer in the past few weeks. Maybe this is what she's wanted all along. A hunt.

"How far are we from Gates Pass?"

Pam considers. "I'd say she's got a fifteen-, twenty-minute jump on us."

"That's not so much."

"It's enough if she's got her spot all picked out. She's heading into the desert. It wouldn't take long."

"I don't think she's planned this." I won't let myself believe in the worst. "Teresa heard about Micky remembering things completely by accident. She's flying by the seat of her pants here."

"Hope so," Pam says. "That's when they screw up."

Suddenly the map goes blank. The little dot that represented Teresa's car vanishes. A message flashes across the screen. *Searching for signal.*

I draw in a sharp breath. "What happened?"

"Bad reception. That, or she found the transmitter."

But the light blinks back on a minute later. Still Gates Pass, just farther down the road. "There she is!" We're still in business.

I pick up my phone and try to call Noah again. He's still not answering. Maybe he's caught up in police questioning. Or else he's extricated himself somehow, stands banging on Pam's door, convinced that she's got Micky. I send him a quick text: *Don't waste time looking for Pam. Teresa has Micky & I think she killed D&J. Trying to find her. Please call.* I don't tell him that I'm with Pam this very moment. It would sound a bit schizophrenic, considering that I just convinced him Pam was Micky's abductor. I don't know how seriously Noah will take anything I say at this point.

In the meantime, Pam flies through traffic, clipping through side streets until she hits Speedway Boulevard. Auto shops, Mexican drive-through restaurants, dive bars, a billboard for a male strip club, heating and air-conditioning repair — all the signs of the city soon begin to thin. We're headed for the mountains.

As the road ventures into less populated territory, the desert springs up around us, saguaros and trees and shrubs and cacti of various shapes and sizes all reclaiming their territory. The road climbs gently upward to a higher altitude. We pass a few small streets leading off to developments, expensive homes nestled just outside the city with what have to be incredible views. But I can't think about real estate right now.

"She's on Kinney Road," I announce.

"Headed north or south?"

"North. She's going north."

"Parkland," Pam says with satisfaction. "Saguaro National Park. You leave a body out there, the rangers will notice the buzzards pretty quick. She's got no idea what she's doing."

I give a little cry of dismay when I see the map blink out. "We lost her again! The whole thing is down."

"It's us," Pam says. "We're in the mountains."

And it's true. All around us now, standing taller and taller against the horizon, craggy rock looms. The sun hangs low in the sky, imbuing the stone formations with a shadowy orange, and on the sloped, rugged hills, a saguaro forest flourishes, the kind that Noah would be sighing over. We race past a pair of scenic viewing areas, where a few cars have stopped to catch the sunset. I keep an eye out for Teresa's white Range Rover but spot nothing.

"Hang on," Pam says as we round a bend in the road. "This is going to get interesting."

Before us, the mountain road barrels suddenly and steeply downward. There are no guardrails, nothing to stop our vehicle from plummeting off the side of the cliff except for Pam's driving skills, which, given her choice to accelerate, now strike me as less than sterling.

"What the hell are you doing?!" I grab the door to brace myself.

"Trying to catch up!" Pam answers, and

then we're going down, so fast that the world around me slows, and what should be a blur of rock and road and falling sunlight appears with astonishing clarity, sharp as a series of photographs in my mind's eye.

The car hooks right at a curve in the road, and I see, in one split second, the valley stretched out below us, the arms of the distant saguaros reaching up as if preparing to field our flaming, mangled wreck. I tilt my body toward the center of the car, convinced that any misplaced weight will send us hurtling off the edge. Then the sun hits us, shattering my vision with its final burst of light, searing my retinas with its explosive gold.

At least I won't see us die, I think, and we descend into the glowing valley. The car hits a series of hills, but Pam doesn't let up. My stomach lurches as we catch air, fly weightless, land with a jolt, and speed on toward the next dip, the next curve.

It ends as abruptly as it began. "Kinney Road," Pam says, coming to a half stop before she turns north. "Any reception yet?"

In our frantic flight down the mountain, I forgot about the locator. The map is back, I see, Teresa's car hovering in place a few miles ahead of us.

"She's stopped," I say. "She must have

pulled over. Oh my God, Pam, *hurry.*"

Pam hits the gas. I press my hands to the dashboard, peering into the horizon, searching for some sign of Teresa's vehicle. The road twists and dips through desert land, allowing me limited visibility. We're close. Nearly there, if only Micky can hang on a little longer.

The dot on the screen begins to move again.

"You think you can run from me, Terry-girl?" Pam croons. "Oh, no. Pammy's gonna find you."

I try to tune out Pam's creepy use of third person. She's all that I have, and I don't want to absorb the full extent of her crazy right now. "Would you slow down? She could've left Micky on the side of the road somewhere, and I won't see her if you're zooming by."

"If she left Micky somewhere, it's already too late," Pam says. "We're going after Teresa. You're in or you're out."

I wonder if I've made a mistake. Pam has her own agenda here, one that may have nothing to do with Micky. I hesitate. Do I get out of the car? Wander along the road, looking for suspicious tire tracks, hoping against hope that something leads me to Micky before the dark extinguishes any hope of finding her? Or do I stick this out a while longer with a woman whose mental condition is becoming increasingly questionable? A quick glance back at the locator, and I have my answer.

"She's veering off the road! Some side loop a few miles ahead."

Now Pam slows down, her body tense and awaiting instruction like a hunting dog. "Tell me where. Tell me when I'm getting close."

The sun has dipped below the horizon, and the bourbon-toned shadows deepen. Soon, Teresa will slip through our fingers, take refuge in the night. I direct Pam down the unpaved loop Teresa has turned onto, my eyes analyzing every shape and color in the surrounding land, training on any motion. Pam flips on her headlights, trying to fight back the dusk.

If it were any later, any darker, I would miss it entirely: a pale strip peeking out from a cluster of distant saguaros.

"There, on our left! Stop!"

Pam can't possibly see what I'm talking about, but she operates on blind faith. Her brakes squeal, and she swerves wildly off the road, crashing through some desert shrubs before she comes to a halt. Together, we survey the terrain.

Teresa's vehicle sits parked about fifty yards away, a pale, metallic phantom amongst the sparse and spiky desert.

I jump out the passenger side, ready to run and search for Micky, but Pam stops me. "Wait until I say. We don't know how ugly this will get." She draws her gun and approaches the Range Rover with a grim, purposeful stride.

I stand by Pam's car, watch as Teresa steps out of her vehicle. Though her brow is furrowed with concern, she certainly doesn't look like someone whose plans to do away with a six-year-old have just been interrupted. "Pam?" Her gaze drops to the weapon in the other woman's hand. "What's going on? What are you doing here?"

"Where's Micky?" Pam demands. "Is she with you?"

Teresa doesn't seem to have heard the question. "My God, would you put that down? I really don't think you need to point that at me."

"I really think I do," Pam says pleasantly. "Charlie!" She motions to me with her index finger, satisfied that Teresa's not putting up a fight. "Check the backseat of her car."

I jog over to the Range Rover. The doors are locked, but I shine the flashlight on my phone into the tinted rear windows. I can just make out some file folders, a laptop bag, a sweatshirt, old food wrappers — Teresa is not as neat and tidy as she presents herself — but there's no sign of Micky.

"She's not in the backseat."

Teresa appears mystified by my search. "Have the two of you lost your minds? Why on earth would I have Micky?"

"Check the trunk," Pam says.

"It's locked," I remind her.

Pam glares at Teresa. "How about you open that for us?"

Teresa fishes her keychain out of her pocket, fingers trembling as she searches for the right button. Finally, her car beeps. "Have a look around, and then please leave me alone," she says. "I don't know what you two are doing here, but waving a gun at someone is not the way to make friends."

I rummage through the trunk, working through layers of reusable shopping bags, gym clothes, a stack of books and DVDs.

I turn to Pam. "Micky's not back here. What do we do?"

"Where is she?" Pam takes a few steps closer to Teresa. "Where the hell is Micky?"

"How on earth would I know?" Teresa asks. "I hardly know her! You think I'd go skipping off to the desert with her in the middle of the night? Really, Pam! Do you hear yourself? You're not making any sense!"

"Is she dead?"

"Who?"

Pam slaps her across the face, hard. *"Is Micky dead?"*

Teresa falls to her knees, cradling her cheek with her hand. "You're scaring me," she whispers.

Pam is scaring me, too. What if we're wrong? What if Teresa's not responsible for Micky's disappearance, and we're wasting precious time, serving up nothing more than a lawsuit and possible assault charges?

Pam removes something from her pocket, tosses it to the ground where Teresa kneels. "Tell me what this is." She watches as Teresa fumbles with the box, removes a sheet of tablets.

"Pills?" Teresa looks up at me helplessly. "Are these pills? It's too dark. I can't read the label."

"Charlotte found this in your office."

"With Donna's things," I add quickly. "That box you left me."

"Oh." Teresa hesitates. "*Those* pills. I found them in Donna's desk when I was cleaning out her things."

"Why didn't you bring them to the police?" I ask.

"I have an organization to protect," Teresa says. "Those pills would hardly make for good publicity. Take them, if you think they're important. I don't know why Donna had them."

"Those weren't her pills, and you know it." Pam spits out her words. "You think you can throw them in a box and pass them off as hers? Use Charlotte to hand them in to the police and make Donna look bad? *Those weren't Donna's.* I know Donna. I *know* her."

"Charlotte!" Teresa appeals to me now. "This woman is threatening me with a gun. Would you please call for help? And maybe check the trunk of *her* car while you're at it."

Her words send a nasty little shiver down my spine. I couldn't have been that wrong about Pam. Could I?

Pam seems to sense my doubt. "Teresa's right," she says, suddenly calm. "We need to get someone out here before I lose my cool. Let me talk to Vargas." She holds out her hand. "Give me your phone, Cates. We'll get this sorted."

I know, the second her callused hand closes around my cell phone, that she's not making that call. Instead, Pam gives me a scornful glance and chucks my phone under her car. "Teresa's getting to you," she tells me reproachfully. "Snap out of it. We're not playing by the rules here, got that? We're doing things my way. Donna was your mother. This is for you, too."

She turns back to Teresa, her voice as hard as Tucson rock. "You tried to dose Donna, didn't you? That's what the Rohypnol was for. You're a little woman, you're not up for a fight. Slip her a few roofies, that would've made your job easier, wouldn't it?"

"This isn't going to make things right, Pam." Teresa's begging now. "Please let me go. Please. I don't know where Micky is. I don't know."

Pam punches the side of her SUV, leaving a dent. "Don't stand there lying to me, you little bitch. There was Rohypnol in that apartment, and you're the one who left it there. Maybe it was meant for Donna, and she wouldn't take it. Maybe you were trying to get Jasmine out of the way. I don't know why, but I know those pills are yours."

"Pam . . ." I don't know how to stop this. Don't know how we've gone so far off the rails.

"I'm willing to bet you gave Micky something, too," Pam says, circling her. "Got her from Vonda's house and slipped her something, is that what happened? That would keep her from causing you any trouble, wouldn't it?"

Teresa is too intent on bargaining to respond. "You're distraught," she says, "and that's perfectly understandable. It's hard to lose someone. But you know I wouldn't hurt a child, you know —"

Before I know what she's doing, Pam has pointed her gun directly at Teresa's head. "The next lie that leaves your mouth will have you eating bullets," she says.

No one's going to find us, I realize. We're on our own, just like Pam wanted. This is her victory. This is her revenge. But I'm not sure she has the right person, not sure her own twisted mind hasn't bent the truth into something it can handle.

Can I stand by and watch her kill an innocent person? Or a guilty one, for that matter?

"Put the gun away, Pam," I plead, now properly terrified. "We came here to find Micky, and you're not helping."

"Are you really falling for her bullshit?" Pam whirls on me in disgust. "Come on, Charlotte. What do you think she's *doing* out here in the desert?"

"I just wanted to get out of the city!" Teresa's on the verge of tears. "I just wanted to be alone. To see the sunset. Watch the stars come out."

Pam shakes her head. "If Micky isn't in that car, then you killed her. And if that little girl is dead, Teresa — if that little girl who was the center of Donna's world is really dead, then so help me God, you will experience the kind of pain you never thought possible. I will rip you into goddamned pieces and feed them back to you. Now I will ask you one more time. *Where the hell is Micky?*"

Teresa waves her hand around vaguely and begins to weep.

"Is she in the car?" Pam asks.

"In the car," Teresa repeats, and I imagine a torture victim parroting back whatever they're supposed to say.

"Pam," I implore. "This is not justice. This is not going to bring Donna back."

"I'm not looking for Donna," she says coldly. "I'm looking for Micky. Go check the passenger seat."

"No," I say. "I can't let you do this. I know you want to believe Teresa is the bad guy here, but maybe it's time to look at facts. Maybe Donna isn't who you thought she was."

"Go check the front seat," Pam says, ignoring me.

"You don't know what Donna was involved in," I persist. "You can't know. Maybe she knew about the babies. Maybe she was part of this whole adoption scam. Maybe . . . maybe *she* killed Lety."

"If you won't do it, then get out of the way." Pam breezes past me and stops at the front passenger-side door of the Range Rover. She grasps the door handle with her left hand, still pointing her gun toward Teresa with her right.

The door of the SUV starts to swing open, and as it does, I hear shots.

I whip my head back to Teresa, sure that she's been hit, that Pam has lost her temper and her mind once and for all, but Teresa remains on her knees, arms extended before her as if praying to some higher power. She's not injured.

For a split second, I think that Pam must've missed, that everything's okay, that there's still a chance of talking her down.

Then I realize Teresa has not been praying. She's been aiming.

Her hands grasp the kind of small handgun that Noah once derisively referred to as a "pocket pistol." *Shoot someone with a twenty-two and all you do is make 'em mad,* he said at the gun range, but when I look at Pam, see the dark flower spreading across her side in one single, deadly bloom, I know

551

that Noah was wrong.

Pam turns around looking more aggravated than frightened by the bullets she's just taken until she sees her own right hand. Whether through luck or skill, Teresa has hit her trigger hand. Her fingers slick with blood and no longer able to grip the weapon, Pam drops to her knees and tries to take cover behind the Ranger Rover's open door. She's fast, but not fast enough.

Teresa shoots her again. I can't see where the bullet lands, but Pam's body flinches at the impact. She topples sideways. Drags herself toward the rear of the car and tries to handle her gun left-handed, cradling the bloody fingers of her right hand between her legs.

"Charlie!" Pam's voice is strained. "Micky's in the car."

I run to the Range Rover while Teresa moves to deal with Pam. On the car floor, at the base of the passenger seat, I discover a large pile of white blankets. And from the folds of the blanket, black against the pale cotton, hair. Long, dark strands of hair.

"Oh God," I whisper. "Oh God. What did you do, Teresa?" I gather the blanketed mass into my arms, try in vain to peel away fabric from Micky's face, but Teresa's voice hits me like another bullet from behind.

"You aren't going anywhere. Don't move."

I look over my shoulder, still holding the child in my arms. Teresa has me in her sights, though she doesn't look particularly happy about it.

A few feet away, Pam writhes on the ground, half babbling, half weeping. "I'm gonna kill you, Teresa. I'm gonna take you down, I swear."

I can't see where her gun has fallen. Teresa must've picked it up or else kicked it away. Pam lies there impotent and wounded, probably bleeding out.

Do I run? Try to get help?

I unwrap a piece of blanket, find Micky's small hand clenched in a fist. "Is she dead?" I whisper. "Is Micky dead?"

"I gave her a pill." Teresa sounds strangely apologetic. "To make her comfortable. I didn't want her to be frightened."

So Pam was right about the Rohypnol. Pam was right about everything. If I had just stayed out of Pam's way, if I had trusted her instincts instead of falling prey to Teresa's pleas for help — we could've gotten out of this. We could've won.

Teresa takes a few steps closer to Pam. Even in the dimming light, I can see that she's uncharacteristically rumpled, her suit jacket disheveled on one side, her arm partly out of the sleeve. On her right side, a strap hugs tight against her body.

A shoulder holster. The bitch had a shoulder holster.

"You were never good for Donna," Teresa says, bending over Pam, "but this brings me no pleasure. None at all."

I wonder how long Pam can live without medical help, if there's something I can do to stanch the bleeding. Teresa sees me looking and frowns.

"Leave her there," she orders. "You hold Micky."

I remove the blanket from Micky's body, drawing her in tight. Run a hand through her straight, thick hair. I would've brushed it for her at night. Slow strokes, careful not to pull, the way I imagine mothers do it.

My eyes well up with tears. Thank God she's unconscious.

Over in the dirt, Pam barely moves. Shock must be setting in. Her mouth forms a small O, begins to open and close like a fish's. She's flat on her back now, chest heaving, her gaze fixed on some distant point in the sky. The first stars have appeared, and I wonder if Pam sees them, if she's swimming in her mind's eye, gulping down stars, inhaling their ancient light.

All that blood, I think. *She has to be losing*

so much blood.

How did this situation turn so quickly? The three of us — Pam, Micky, and I — we were all so alive this morning.

It didn't have to go like this. I could've prevented it. If I hadn't told Andrea Rincón about Micky's memories. If I hadn't interfered with Pam's plan. If I hadn't come to Arizona at all. Without my poor choices, all three of us would be safe. I touch my belly. All four of us. I can imagine my aunt Suzie's unemotional assessment of events. *A real shame Charlotte took her own kid down with her. Just like her mother.*

"I don't understand." I'm rocking Micky back and forth, more for me than her. "You could've helped people, Teresa."

"I *do* help people," she retorts. "Women, children, families. I help them."

"You sell babies. That isn't helping, it's exploiting."

She brushes off her dirty knees. Disregards the groaning sounds that Pam is making. "I never did it for the money, don't you understand? I did it for the women. Women who were pregnant but couldn't raise a child. Women who needed a chance. I *saved* those babies from the kind of childhood that I had."

"You broke the law."

It's too dark to see much of Teresa's face now, but I can hear her indignation, her fury. "Those mothers were looking for abortions!" she exclaims. "In case you didn't know, *that's* illegal, too, in almost every province of Mexico. Our women could've ended up dead from some dangerous procedure. They could've been arrested. Instead, their babies were born and given to families that wanted them. They received excellent maternal care. Donna and I, we did the right thing, and don't you ever try to tell me otherwise!"

Pam's quiet moans are getting to me. If only there were something I could do, something to stop her hurting. "Marilena gave you three different babies, and she made a pretty penny doing it," I tell Teresa. "Are you really trying to pretend every one of these pregnancies was an accident?"

"Things . . . have changed," she acknowledges reluctantly. "In the beginning, Charlotte, they really needed us. We were the only option. But later . . . they just wanted the money, those mothers."

"Then why did you continue? You weren't helping children, Teresa. Those babies were brought into the world to turn a profit."

"It still helped the women," Teresa insists, and her need to justify herself speaks volumes, I think, about her own guilt. "Two thousand dollars is not much in the United States, but it'll buy you a house in Nogales. There was still so much good to do. And the families, these adoptive parents, they'd waited so long. It was a win-win."

"Not for Lety," I say.

"No." Her voice turns quiet. "Not for Lety."

My chest and arms are damp with sweat from holding Micky to me. I realize that I can't hear Pam anymore; she must've passed out.

"What happened to Lety wasn't my fault," Teresa says. "I wasn't a part of that decision."

"How did Lety even get involved in all this?"

"She lived in Tirabichi once. She knew Marilena. She left to work at one of those nasty clubs for a while, and of course, she got pregnant. She came to Marilena, wanting to give up the child."

"And?" I keep an eye on Teresa's .22, hoping she'll get distracted by her story and leave me with an opening.

"We said okay. My husband found a couple who had been fighting infertility for nearly a decade. They were so excited, so ready. They had the money. But then Lety backed out. Seven months pregnant, and she backed out."

"Why?"

"How would I know? She was Donna's little pet. I never even *met* her. From what Donna said . . . I guess Lety had some crazy idea about coming to the United States. 'Why should I give my baby to Americans? I want to *be* an American.' That sort of thing. She had some whole scheme cooked up, thought she could find a way across the border."

"So you killed her?"

"I told you, I never laid eyes on her," Teresa says testily. "That was your mother's domain, not mine. Lety is dead because she got . . . pushy. She wanted to keep her baby *and* she wanted the money. So she started threatening Donna. Saying that she'd go to the government, expose us, all that. After everything we'd done for her during the pregnancy. Food, shelter, medical care — she turned on us."

Poor Lety, I think. *You were too young, too stupid to know what a dangerous game you were playing.*

She was just a kid. Fifteen years old with big dreams for herself and for her child. And for the sister she never stopped looking out for. I know what Lety saw in that shower, the moment all her hopes for the future ended, and something terrible occurs to me now.

"Was my mother . . . was Donna the one who shot her?"

Teresa laughs at the idea. "God, no. Your mother wanted to pay Lety and be done with it. To make it go away. Marilena and I, we tried to tell her. You let one girl railroad you, then they'll all do it. It was obvious Donna had no backbone, so I told Marilena to handle it." She pauses. "I didn't know . . . I didn't know that Marilena would take such drastic measures."

"Were you upset?"

"At Marilena? Yes, of course. But she was only protecting her family. Her livelihood. She knew we had a good thing, didn't want some silly teenage girl ruining it. I didn't agree with her *methods,* Charlotte. I wish she'd never done it. But she wasn't acting out of evil, just . . . survival."

It's probably how Teresa sees herself: acting out of survival, not evil.

"What did Donna think of all this?" I ask.

Teresa sighs. "When she found out what had happened, Donna just about lost her mind. She blamed herself. Wanted to run off to the police and tell them everything. As if that would've done any good." She sounds tired. "We had a lot of fights about it." It's not an admission she wants to dwell on. "Listen. Donna was my best friend. I knew her better than anyone. Better than Pam did, obviously, and a whole lot better than Jasmine. Donna and I . . . up until the end, we had no secrets. We were true friends."

"True friends?" I can't contain myself here, can't play into this level of self-delusion. "She's *dead* because of you, Teresa."

"She was going to throw it all away! Not just her own life but mine. My husband's. All the women in Nogales who needed us, the families waiting for their babies. She was going to hurt every one of us just to ease her own little conscience. I couldn't let her do that, Charlotte! It wasn't her choice to make, don't you understand?"

"I understand." And somehow I do. I don't believe she's right, but I understand.

"I wanted to be gentle," Teresa says. "Painless, so she'd never know. Rohypnol would've made it easy . . . she could've walked out with me, gone to sleep . . . never felt a thing."

"Except Jasmine was there."

She nods. "Jasmine was there. But I couldn't back out. Donna was planning to contact Nogales law enforcement. I had to do it." I wonder if it's the so-called good girl in her that feels compelled to confess all now. I wonder if, in her strange way, Teresa seeks forgiveness. "I tried to slip her some pills, but Donna wouldn't take anything, wouldn't eat or drink. She was still on her crusade about Lety, 'doing the right thing.' She was so naïve. We had . . . a disagreement. And then Jasmine threatened to call her boyfriend. I had to act."

"You killed Donna first. Why?"

"Because I loved her! I didn't want her to have to see her child hurt. Whatever you might think of me, I'm not a cruel person."

Teresa's sense of compassion in the face of cold-blooded murder baffles me.

"I should've taken care of Micky that night, I know that now. I knew there was a possibility that she'd heard something, and I should've done it then. Instead of putting her through all this. That poor baby." She reaches out toward the bundle in my arms, runs an awkward hand across the back of Micky's head. Even unconscious, Micky flinches slightly at her touch.

Teresa's winding down, the need to explain herself to me now satisfied. I have to do something, do it now. Delay her plans. If I ran now maybe I could escape. Maybe.

But I'd be leaving Micky, drugged and defenseless, to this woman. I can't do that. Micky is my responsibility, just as much as the baby girl I'm carrying inside me.

"I think you're overreacting, Teresa," I find myself saying in a strangely steady voice. "This isn't life or death here. Micky had a few bad dreams, that's all. There's nothing that can tie you to Donna and Jasmine. You can let the kid go."

Teresa laughs, a soft, regretful laugh. "Oh, Charlotte. You have such a fighting spirit. Your mother would've admired that."

"Pam pulled a gun on you," I press. "I saw it myself. She was ready to put a bullet in your head. Shooting her was self-defense, and that's what I'll tell the cops."

Teresa doesn't seem to hear me. "Donna always wanted to meet you, you know," she says. "But she said you'd be ashamed of her. You with your glamorous life in New York, working at your fancy magazine." Her hair grazes my arm, giving me chills. "It's strange, isn't it? You were just a name on a masthead to her, a face on the Internet. But I *know* you now. Better than your own mother."

Teresa's getting to me, finding my tender spots. Is she lying, just to rile me? Did Donna really keep tabs on me? Follow my career? I have a hundred questions, but before I can voice them, a pair of headlights comes around a bend in the road.

Hope surges up in me. Maybe it's a park ranger. Pam said they keep an eye on the land out here. Or maybe it's Noah, although how he'd have tracked us down, I can't imagine. But why would someone come down here if they weren't looking for us? The loop doesn't go anywhere.

I lift Micky's body, trying to get a sense of its weight, trying to guess how fast and how far I might be able to run while carrying her. She's a sturdy kid, and I'm not exactly built for speed these days. We'd have two chances — fat and slim.

The headlights continue in our direction, bumping down the unpaved road at a leisurely pace.

"Get down," Teresa hisses at me, tapping the gun in my direction. "Down behind the car."

I comply, mind racing as I work out what to do. Teresa is small. If I launch myself at her, I might be able to wrestle her gun away, but not before she takes a few shots. How can I fight her and still protect my baby? Still protect Micky?

I run a hand over Micky's clenched fist, smooth her fingers with my thumb. It's then, her hand against my palm, the head-lights sweeping toward us, that Micky uncurls her fist, reveals the secret she's been keeping all this while. A white circular pill.

The Rohypnol. She didn't take the Ro-hypnol Teresa gave her.

I study Micky's face and, to my shock, one dark eye peeps warily open. We stare at each other for just a second before her eye blinks shut. *Holy hell. The kid's awake.* More than awake. She's been playing possum this entire time.

How could a six-year-old be so much smarter than I am? She didn't trust Teresa. Not for a minute.

The headlights, meanwhile, have moved past us, following the loop back to the main road. The driver must have been lost. Once again, we're out of luck.

I give Micky's hand a quick squeeze, not sure if her consciousness is a good thing or a dangerous one.

"It's dark now." Teresa stands up. "I think we should go for a walk." She's lost all inter-est in conversation. There's a briskness to her voice now, an efficiency as she steels herself for the unpleasant task before her, and I wonder if this is what she's been wait-ing for all along: the cover of darkness.

"Are you just going to leave Pam lying

here?" I ask, stalling for time. "We're not that far off the road. Someone will see her, see her car. As soon as the sun comes up, someone will find her. The police can probably tie her to you, Teresa. You'll need an explanation."

"Enough." Teresa waves a hand at me as if warding off a pesky bee or fly. "I'll figure this out. I just . . . first things first. We'll go for a walk, and we'll decide. We'll decide what to do."

I know this is not a walk Micky and I will ever return from, know that she intends to get us deeper in the desert, away from the scrutiny of any more passing cars, and do her dirty work. Still, I pretend to believe her. "Okay," I tell her. "I'll help you. We'll figure it out together."

"You carry Micky," she instructs me. "I need to walk. I need to see the stars. Come on."

I heave Micky up in my arms, her head against my shoulder. With her chest pressed to mine, I can feel her heartbeat now, pounding like a kettle drum in her rib cage. Her limbs are tense, not floppy. Ready for flight. How did I ever think she was unconscious?

"You lead the way, Teresa."

"No," she says. "You go. I'm right behind you."

That bitch is going to shoot us in the back. But I proceed like it's no big deal, fall into step ahead of her. We're still too close to the road. She wants us farther out.

I walk toward the blackening expanse of desert, taking in the shape of the land, the silhouettes of the saguaros against the vast, sleepy sky. Get a feel for Teresa's movements a few yards behind me, as she location-scouts for our burial ground. The air is dry and still but alive with the buzzing of insects, the rustling of small creatures in the brush.

Now.

I duck into the shadow of a saguaro and loosen my grip on Micky. Plant her firmly on her feet and press my lips to her ear.

"Run," I tell her. *"Run."*

THIRTY-ONE

Adrenaline flows through me, the purest kind of high. As I take off through the desert, there's no room for fear. Only Micky. Only my baby.

I hear gunshots, Teresa screaming my name. Several clicks, followed by a string of swears. She must've run out of bullets. I don't know how long it will take her to reload, but we're not sticking around to find out.

"Go!" I shout at Micky, blocking her body from behind with my own. "Go, go, go!"

It's hard, though, in the dark. There are so many shadows to navigate, rocks that turn beneath my flimsy sandals, low-lying prickly plants that I don't see until I've got a mess of stickers in my calf. The pain doesn't even register.

My plan is to follow the unpaved loop back to the main road and flag down a car as soon as we see headlights, but Micky takes off in her own direction and we've soon lost sight of the loop altogether. I don't care. I follow at Micky's heels. Let her run. Let her put all the distance she can between us and the woman who already claimed two members of her family.

"Keep running," Teresa calls to us, and I hear the loud click of a newly loaded cartridge sliding into place. "Go ahead. You think I can't find you?"

I can't tell from her voice how far away she is, but it's clearly not far enough. When I glance back to get a look, I can see her silhouette, a small black shape against the starry horizon. She begins to move toward us.

Micky stumbles on a plant nub, and I catch her before she plummets face-first into something large and spiny. *We can't keep running aimlessly,* I think. *Sooner or later one of us will twist an ankle or impale herself on a cactus.*

I peer over my shoulder again. Although she's still too far for a clean shot, Teresa's gaining on us. She can see the movement of our shadows, and she's faster. Micky may have had the better strategy all along — staying still.

I grab Micky by the shoulder and yank her down to the ground with me. We scuttle across the dirt, better shielded from view now by the plant life, and park ourselves in a spray of flowering shrubs that seem to lack the standard desert armor. Now the night is our friend, the darkness a screen.

Not so far off, a light blinks on and begins to scan the ground. Teresa's footsteps crunch through the dirt. Light sweeps across the desert floor in haphazard circles, passing over us once, then twice, but never pausing long enough to indicate she's seen us.

One small motion, one ill-timed cough, could give us away.

I don't know how long we wait, crouched on all fours, the sound of our own breathing impossibly loud. We listen to Teresa as she wanders around, calling to us with words alternately reassuring and threatening. Micky, to her credit, does not move a muscle. I've never seen a child hold so still. Finally, after my right foot has fallen asleep, Teresa appears to give up, if only temporarily.

"All right, then!" Her tone is one of forced cheer, like a parent talking up vegetables or family fun time, not some nut job who has just killed a woman. "Enjoy your night, girls! I'll see you at first light. Unless, of course, the rattlesnakes get you."

It's a ridiculous parting shot, but effective. Because . . . *rattlesnakes*? At night? Only now do I fully consider the number of creatures that could be roaming around this desert, unseen.

Teresa trudges off, and in time I hear the sounds of a car engine. In the distance, a pair of headlights blinks on, jerking along the desert floor before coming to a stop. She must've made it to the loop, and there she remains, high beams still on, guarding the road. Making sure we don't try to flag down help. As if there were anyone to flag down.

The car door slams. I can't see Teresa, can barely make out her vehicle. Her footsteps are faint, far off, but in the immense night, it's hard to determine the direction. Then her noises stop all together. She's somewhere in the dark, waiting for us to reveal ourselves.

I wonder if Pam's keys are still in her car or on her person. If we could somehow double back to her SUV, we might have a chance. Or, if I could get myself oriented, we could try to hike back to the main road. But I can't risk it yet. Not until I know where Teresa's hiding.

I cup Micky's face in my hands, fingertips searching for any dirt or scratches. "Are you okay?" I whisper, finally daring to speak. If I can't trace Teresa from her sounds, then she hopefully can't trace us, either.

"Yeah," Micky says. "But Vonda. I came into the kitchen and she was bleeding."

I remember what Noah said, that he'd found Vonda laid out with a head injury. "She's going to be fine," I promise Micky. "Really. Don't worry about Vonda."

"Charlie?" Her voice is racked with guilt. "I'm sorry."

"For what?"

"I got in Teresa's car. But you're not supposed to get in the car with strangers."

"Oh, Micky." I give her an awkward hug, not quite sure exactly which part of her I'm grasping in the dark, but hoping it's comforting nevertheless.

"I thought she was Grandma's friend," Micky murmurs. "And Vonda was bleeding. Teresa said we had to get help, so I got in her car. But she's the one who hurt Vonda, isn't she?"

"It's not your fault, what Teresa did. She's a very, very bad woman."

"She tried to make me take a pill with juice. She said it was a vitamin to make me strong."

I find her wrist, follow it to her fingers. Hook my index finger around hers. "You didn't take it, though, did you? You knew she was lying."

"I pretended."

"That was really smart. But how did you know to pretend you were asleep?"

"We were driving around and she said the pill might make me sleepy," Micky explains. "She said it was okay to nap. I didn't want her to know I didn't swallow it. So I pretended I was sleeping. And then she put a blanket on me."

"That must've been really scary."

"She has a gun," Micky says quietly. She stirs the dirt with her finger. "Is Pam going to die?"

I don't tell her that Pam is probably already dead. That lying around mortally wounded while all the desert animals search for dinner would likely be worse than death. "Right now I'm just worried about you and me, honey. Let's just think about you and me."

"Okay," she says, and then, after a moment, asks, "Does this mean you and Noah won't keep me?"

"Keep you? What do you mean?"

She rearranges herself on the dirt. "That's why you guys come visit me, isn't it? To see if you want me."

"Who told you that? Vonda? Mr. Quijada?"

"I just know," she says. "Noah likes me, I think. But you aren't sure."

Have our intentions really been so transparent, my own reservations so obvious? We thought we were getting to know her, making our decision in private. I didn't realize Micky knew she was being interviewed, knew exactly which member of the hiring committee was behind her and which wasn't. No wonder she's never been at ease with me. Noah's criticism wasn't so far off base.

"Oh, Micky," I breathe. "I'm so sorry. I didn't mean for it to be like that. It's not that I don't want you, I just . . . well, it's complicated."

"I'm not mad." There's a long pause, and then Micky's voice emerges from the night in a soft confession. "My mom didn't want me either."

She waits to see if I'll disagree, but I've already determined that her bullshit detector is too sophisticated for me to bother with polite protestations. "Why do you think that?" I ask.

"I heard her tell Bree. How things were good until she had me. And how she never gets to do what she wants anymore."

Part of me hates Jasmine in this moment. Hates that she was given this sweet little girl she didn't ask for, didn't deserve. "Your mom wasn't ready to be a mother," I say. "*Anybody's* mother. That was *her* problem, Micky. You didn't do anything wrong."

"She said I made Ruben leave."

"Ruben?"

She nods. "He's my dad. I'm not supposed to know. But I do. He left my mom because he didn't want her to have a baby."

A memory flutters back of my own father, drunk and melancholy one night, waxing philosophical about my mother. She was a topic he rarely broached, and I absorbed every detail, greedy for information about the woman who had left us. *Donna used to laugh until she cried,* he told me. *Giggles, that's what I called her. Everything was always funny to her. Everything except you.* He peered at me suddenly with sad, bleary eyes. *Getting pregnant, there was nothing funny about that.*

He hadn't meant to hurt me, but the words lodged in my brain, turned my legs to lead. *I ruined my mother,* I thought. *I made her stop laughing. I made her go away.*

It isn't until I hear Micky, so ashamed she made her father leave, that I realize I still believe all these things. I ruined Donna's life. I made her stop laughing. I made her go away. I drove her to addiction.

Remind you of anyone? Noah asked when I cataloged Micky's issues, and I realize now how right he was. This girl and I are more alike than I ever wanted to admit, her wounds very like my own.

All the hesitation, the reluctance to open my heart to her — it hasn't been about timing or circumstance, hasn't been about losing Keegan or even being pregnant with another child. It's about fear, the rawest and most private kind of fear. Because I can't help Micky face her losses without facing my own.

I reach for Micky's hand, not the least bit sure we'll make it through this night, not the least bit sure I can ever be enough for her if we do.

"I want you, Micky," I say softly. "I want you."

I turn on my side to get a better look at her, to reassure her of her value in this world, and it is then, in the wake of this profound emotional epiphany, that something bites me on the leg.

"Motherfucker!"

I don't do well with pain. I've never broken a bone, never recovered from major surgery, and the contractions of early labor had me begging for an epidural. I've always avoided the whole lift-weights, run-on-a-treadmill, or wiggle-around-like-a-backup-dancer-in-a-Rihanna-video thing because let's be honest: exercise hurts. Given a choice, I will always choose the option that doesn't hurt.

This time, I have no choice. This time, it hurts like hell.

The pain in my leg, like a woman in the throes of grief, goes through several stages. At first, it feels like a cigarette branding my skin with its embers. I leap to my feet, pulling Micky up with me, and peer at the ground. It's too dark to see anything.

"Something. Bit. Me." My jaw is clamped so tight I can barely get the words out.

"A rattlesnake?" Micky backs away from the area where we were sitting.

"I don't think so . . ." We would've noticed a rattlesnake, heard its telltale rattle, wouldn't we? This had to be something small.

That's when the pain transforms, begins to spread outward, wriggling beneath the skin like a series of burning worms. I bite down on my hand to keep from screaming. I can't speak, can produce only a strangled *unh*.

Micky's six-year-old knowledge of venomous desert creatures proves just extensive enough to frighten without helping.

"Maybe it was a spider," she says. "Mr. Gittle, the gym teacher at my school, he got bitten by a brown spider a long time ago and now he can't feel anything in his toes. Or it could be fire ants." She pauses. "Are you sure it was a bite? Maybe you got stung. By a bee or a wasp, those can kill you. Or a scorpion."

I want to ask her how serious each of these scenarios would be, if an encounter with a desert spider or scorpion could prove fatal, but I'm the adult. I can't let this situation get any scarier for Micky than it already is. And frankly, I'm too busy smothering the involuntary cries of agony that well up in my throat to really hold much of a conversation.

I limp a few yards with Micky, anxious to put some distance between us and whatever creature got me, but the pain in my leg is too overwhelming to continue. So much for outrunning Teresa. I slump down, leg extended in the dirt before me, as the burning sensations continue to ripple across my thigh. There's a numb patch now just above the knee, and I imagine the poison doing battle with my tissue, turning my nerve receptors into mush. What will happen if the venom reaches my baby? Did my daughter and I escape Teresa only to fall victim to some tiny, unidentified insect assassin?

I take deep breaths, try to slow the beating of my heart, the movement of tainted blood through my veins. This has to be worse than a bullet.

Micky rests on her knees beside me, and I'm glad she can't see my face. "Charlie? Are you going to die?"

The edges of my vision begin to blur, then focus, and blur again. "Not tonight," I say through gritted teeth, and it's as much a promise to myself as to Micky. "Not tonight."

The hours roll by, long and sluggish. Before, I thought of the desert as a wasteland, too barren, too harsh to sustain real life, but the night proves me wrong. Dark shapes sail and swoop against the sky — bats, I realize, chasing insects. More than once, we hear the brush around us moving, the crunch of footsteps nearby, and though my heart races every time and I'm sure that Teresa has found us, it's always some animal. I shudder and try not to think of Pam, lying out there for the lizards and coyotes and whatever else to explore. I hope her death was quick, that she never saw them coming.

At some point, we hear strange grunting sounds several yards off, chewing, and then a high-pitched squeal. My heart's in my throat, but Micky leans forward, listening intently.

"Javelinas," she tells me.

"What?" I can scarcely think straight. The pain in my leg hasn't subsided, has in fact spread, and is accompanied by numbness, tingling, and random bouts of violent twitching that make me wonder if my limb is possessed.

"Piggies," Micky says reverently. "Javelinas are desert piggies. I *love* them. I saw them at the zoo with Grandma."

The sweetness — the unbearable sweetness — of this memory nearly undoes me. Here I am, hunted by a crazy woman, taken down by a potentially lethal creepy-crawler, and Micky is finding a reason to be happy. Happy on the worst night of our lives.

Except it's not the worst night, I remind myself, not for either one of us. Not yet. My worst night was losing Keegan, the night I entered an empty house and knew there would be no first day of kindergarten, no high school graduation, no echo of the boy I loved in the face of a man. Micky's worst night was losing Donna, losing Jasmine. On those nights, we were alone, more alone than we had ever been. But not tonight. Tonight is not the worst.

With each breath I take, I repeat this like a mantra. *Tonight is not the worst.*

The waiting, I find, is almost as excruciating as the pain. I don't sleep. Can't sleep. Not with the fire burning in my leg, the questions burning in my head.

I think of Noah, how frantic he must be. He must've read the text I sent him, must know that I was in pursuit of Teresa. I should've told him where we were going. One text, one stinking text, could have been enough. But now? Who — besides Pam with her legally and morally ambiguous spy gear — would ever think to search this particular stretch of desert land for us?

Maybe I won't make it home. Maybe Noah will be left to pick up the pieces alone.

I imagine him back in Sidalie, forced to sort through my belongings, one day finding the engagement ring he gave me in the junk drawer. Why did I put it in the junk drawer? It doesn't belong there, his offering of love and commitment. It isn't junk.

Something tickles my wrist. I recoil sharply, flick a small ant from my arm. Wonder what time it is. Wonder if the venom will eventually render me unconscious.

It's so tempting, despite my leg, to head

back to Pam's car. Her keys have to be around somewhere, and my phone should still be under the Wrangler where Pam threw it. It might still have a charge. Even if I couldn't find the keys or phone, I might be able to arm myself. It didn't look like Teresa took Pam's gun.

But what would I do with Micky? Leave her here alone? Bring her with me into harm's way?

Teresa might be there, waiting.

At some point, Micky drops off to sleep on me, her head wedged in the portion of my lap not eclipsed by baby belly. I put a hand on her cheek. She's cool, so cool next to the heat of my toxic skin.

God, I'm thirsty. I haven't peed in several hours, must be severely dehydrated. And I haven't felt my baby move in a long, long time. I won't think about what that means.

I listen for sounds of Teresa, try to focus my distorted gaze. At some point, the distant headlights of her car blink out. Perhaps she's switched them off herself. Perhaps her battery has died.

I'll see you at first light, she said, and she's right. Once the sun comes up, Micky and I have no way to hide.

The rising light is nearly imperceptible at

581

first, a deep blue that edges onto the horizon, slowly flushing out the black. No one is coming to help us, that much is obvious. Not Noah, not the police, not some random passing car. Whatever I'm going to do, I'd better do it now while I still have the shadows on my side. Another thirty, forty minutes, and Teresa will have a clear view for miles.

My leg is agonizing, a blazing inferno with dead spots, and my vision comes in drippy waves. The right side of my face feels like a pincushion, needles piercing the skin — the venom has spread that far upward. I can't make it all the way back to the main road, which leaves me with just one option.

I rouse Micky gently from her sleep. "We have to go," I whisper. "You're going to follow me back to Pam's car, okay? When we get close, I'll go ahead and you wait until I tell you it's safe, understand?"

Micky understands all too well. "What if you don't come back?" she asks, fingers hovering around her mouth.

"If something happens to me and it looks like you're in trouble, you run," I tell her. "You run for the road and you follow it until you see a car."

"Okay," she says, but her tone is dubious. I don't blame her. If Teresa shows up, we're pretty much sitting ducks, end of story.

Still, she rises to her feet. We begin our limping journey through the dwindling dark.

It's unnaturally quiet as we walk, just the occasional songbird and the soft padding of our shoes. At this hour, beneath an endless indigo sky, the desert looks like an ocean floor, murky outlines of rocks and silt and weedy plant life. The saguaros ripple and flex in my distorted vision, anemones in the current. *Like my dream,* I realize. *My very first dream of Micky.*

This was the world waiting for me when I stepped outside Jasmine's apartment and saw my niece crying for her mother beneath the desert moon. *Mama?* she asked, and I thought that Micky was calling for the mother she'd lost. But what if I was wrong? What if she was calling for the mother she needed? Calling for *me.*

Suddenly I'm sure of something: this familiar patch of desert land, this place I dreamed of — it's no accident. Every choice I've made since I came to Arizona has been leading me here.

When Pam's car comes into view, I believe we just might make it. The early morning feels so calm, so extraordinarily peaceful, it's hard to believe that something bad happened here last night. I leave Micky crouch-

583

ing by a thorny bush. We don't exchange a word, but I kiss her on the forehead. Give her hair a quick ruffle.

Then I'm jogging, or as near as I can come to it on my gimpy leg, bracing myself for the sight of Pam's body. I want her keys. I want her gun. I know she went down near Teresa's Range Rover, but Teresa moved her vehicle last night, so there's nothing to mark the location.

I see no trace of Pam at all, not even the blood-soaked earth she surely left in her wake.

Teresa must have been cleaning up after herself. She could've loaded Pam into the Range Rover last night, I realize. But how would she have been strong enough to lift the woman? Pam's got at least fifty pounds on her.

It occurs to me that Teresa might not be alone. She might've called for reinforcements — her husband, maybe, or Quico.

I have no idea how many people are out here.

Increasingly dizzy, I give up on finding Pam's body and stumble instead toward her Wrangler. The creeping daylight only highlights how bad my vision has gotten, imbuing the landscape with that psychedelic, watery sheen. And my leg is starting to feel like it's been shot full of Novocain.

I try the driver's-side door first, peering over my shoulder the entire time so no one can startle me from behind. Give the rear door a half-hearted tug. Both locked. My phone is my last hope. If it's not under there where Pam tossed it, I'm out of luck.

I peer under the carriage, but it's too dark to see anything. I lie down on the dusty ground. Grope around with one arm, praying that my hand finds an iPhone and not another angry desert creature.

Rocks. Something with teeny prickers that embed themselves in my fingers. No phone. I wedge my head and shoulder beneath the car, still fishing.

Suddenly I feel the weight of the entire vehicle shift above me, down and then up. Someone moving inside. The click of doors unlocking.

I roll out as fast as I can, but I'm too late. Teresa's standing over me, gun pointed directly at my face. She must've spent the night in the Wrangler. And here I am, flat on my back, served up nice and easy so she won't even break a nail.

"Looking for this?" With one hand, she tosses my cell phone onto the dirt beside my head. "I knew you'd be back. A woman always wants her phone."

She's still wearing her work clothes from yesterday, still in heels as she leans forward to deliver a parting shot to my head. It's the heels that get me: three-inch spikes with a cute little bow. No way. No freaking way.

With every ounce of force I have left, I kick her in the ankles.

I have the vague urge to yell, "Timber!" as she crashes sideways into the car. The gun goes off in her hand. I scramble across the ground, trying to crawl out of her path, to protect my belly. In the side of the car, a tiny bullet hole announces her miss.

Teresa regains her footing. Kicks off her broken heel, furious.

I don't see what happens next. Somewhere behind my eyelids, light explodes in pale starbursts, lifting me out of pain and fear. Is it the poison? Has Teresa shot me? Perhaps I am dead. Perhaps this is how life ends, not in darkness, but in a sudden, dazzling light.

I blink. Realize that someone is peering down at me. A woman.

She has shoulder-length auburn hair and blue eyes that crinkle at the corners, but it's something else in her I recognize. Beyond this older woman's face, I feel the girl she once was.

She bends down, presses her fingertips to

my cheek, and I feel the memories washing over me like water. Her cheap perfume. Her fingers snapping open a can of Tab. Her blowing raspberries on my tummy, trying to make me laugh. The way she applied mascara, eyes open wide, as if surprised by what she saw in the mirror. Impossible memories — I was much too young — and yet they're there.

Hi, bunny, she says, and that, too, is familiar, an old nickname I haven't heard in decades.

"Mama?"

But she's already retreating. She can't stay. I know she can't stay. She brings her hand to her lips, then lets her fingers fall back toward me. A kiss. She's blowing me a kiss good-bye. *I should've had a lifetime with you,* she murmurs, and her words are an apology, a regret, and a wish all rolled into one. I feel my vision blurring, though whether from light or tears or animal venom, I can't say. I wipe my eyes. Find myself huddled in the dirt again, kneeling in the shadow of the Wrangler. I'm alive, categorically alive, though maybe not for long. Teresa limps toward me, seething, one foot bare, her gun trained on my head.

She flounces toward me like a woman about to slap her lover, her fury almost comical. The remaining high-heeled shoe throws her whole gait off, but the .22 in her hand assures me that she means business.

I should be afraid, but I'm not. Not when I catch sight of the woman behind her.

Standing against the jagged mountains, Pam is the most solid thing I've ever seen, no insubstantial dream but a force of nature. Her shirt is torn and soaked in red, the finger of her right hand tied tightly in stained cloth. With the first strands of a not-yet-risen sun lighting her from behind, she looks like a wounded angel.

She's battered, bloody, limping. Unsteady on her feet, but not unsteady in her aim. *That* is dead-on accurate.

Three bangs reverberate throughout the valley. Silence, and then Teresa pitches forward onto me, crushingly heavy.

"Well," says Pam as I roll Teresa's body off me a little too aggressively, "my work's done."

Before I can thank her, for my life and for my daughter's, she collapses.

THIRTY-TWO

When I open my eyes, the first thing I see is Noah. Noah and the sterile white surfaces of a hospital room. The hospital setting is neither unexpected nor unwelcome, but Noah's eyes, red from crying, alarm me.

"Where's Micky?" I ask, and he startles at the sound of my voice.

"You're awake." The corners of his mouth lift into something resembling a smile. "Nice to see you."

"Where's Micky?" I repeat.

"Downstairs in the cafeteria with Vonda."

"She's okay?"

He nods. "She's a trouper, that one. Gave a statement to the police, cool as you please. She's been askin' for you."

"What about the baby?" I reach down and touch my belly through the flimsy hospital gown.

"Her blood pressure was pretty high for a while. They thought they might need to do a C-section at first, but looks like she's calmed down. They wanna keep an eye on you both a bit longer, make sure. How you feelin'?"

I lift my leg experimentally, try bending it at the knee. "Numb. But most of the burning's gone. What *was* that, anyway?"

"They think you got stung by a bark scorpion," Noah tells me. "You had a pretty bad reaction. They gave you antihistamines and a lot of Tylenol, remember?"

Now that he says it, I do have a vague recollection of some nurse handing me pills, although I don't think I knew what they were. I'm a little disappointed all that suffering required nothing more than some over-the-counter medicine, but it's comforting to know my organs haven't been irreparably damaged by one pissy scorpion.

I take a deep breath and prepare for the news I don't want to hear.

"And Pam? What happened to Pam?"

Noah takes my hand, folds my fingers against his palm. I wait for him to tell me, to pronounce the words "she's dead." Instead, his voice is laced with disbelief. "Do you believe in miracles?"

Miracles, I think, are beside the point. "Are you saying she's alive?"

"Took three bullets, but she's alive. I'm

tellin' you, that cat's got nine lives."

I laugh, a crazy, brittle laugh filled with a relief I can't adequately express. "Her shirt — it was all bloody. I thought she'd bleed out for sure."

"The bullet barely penetrated her skin," Noah says, pointing to his own side to illustrate. "Just missed her rib. That one was the least of her worries. She lost a finger, and she'll need some rehab on her ankle."

"Guess you were right about twenty-twos. All they do is make a person mad."

"Pam's in the ICU," Noah informs me, lest I think she walked away unscathed. "But she's conscious. I just spoke to her myself."

"Was she upset with me?"

"At *you*? Why would she be upset?"

"I should've trusted her. She knew Teresa was full of shit, but I . . . I wasn't sure."

Noah wilts at the mention of Teresa. "You weren't the only one who got Teresa's number wrong," he says, and I can tell he's been beating himself up about it. "Anyway, Pam wasn't upset. She was . . . peaceful."

"Peaceful" is the last word I'd ever use to describe Pam. "Don't tell me she had some near-death experience."

"Something like that."

"White light, bright tunnel? Heavenly

591

voices speaking to her from above?" I say it like it's a joke, but in truth, the memories of my mother still burn bright in my mind.

"I don't think it was like that." Noah glances at me, considering how to tell it. "Pam said she saw Donna. That Donna came to her in the night, told her to watch out for you and Micky."

"Huh."

"You don't believe her."

I shrug. "The human brain does some interesting things in a trauma situation. I saw some weird stuff myself." I don't tell him that I, too, saw Donna, that she blew me a kiss. My mother is a topic I will need to spend some time alone with. "Can you bring Micky in?" I change the subject before he can question me. "I'd really like to see her."

"Sure. I'll head over to the cafeteria. She can come up when she's done with dinner."

He starts to stand, but I grab at his sleeve. There's one more thing we need to settle. "Noah?"

"What, sugar?"

"Before I see Micky, I need to know. I need to know if we're going to take her. If we're going to move out here and make a go of it, or . . ."

He sighs. "Five minutes awake, and you

wanna do this?"

"I'm sorry. But she asked me last night if she was going to come and live with us. Things changed out there, Noah. I think I understand her now."

I don't tell him that I've already made up my mind. That Micky is my child, that for her sake, my life needs to be here, in Arizona. If Noah is going to leave Sidalie, he needs to make the choice freely. I won't bully him into it.

He leans back in his chair and stares at the ceiling. I can see this won't be a simple yes-or-no answer.

"When you and Micky went missin', I got to thinkin'," he says. "About our life and what I wanted it to be. All the stuff we've been fightin' over."

"And?"

"And I realized you were right about a lotta stuff. The whole marriage thing — you were right." His head dips in defeat.

"You mean, you don't want to get married?" The air has mysteriously vanished from my lungs. Being right, in this instance, carries no satisfaction.

"I guess I had this idea it was gonna fix things," he admits. "I've been so busy worryin' about what's right for the baby and what other folks'll think. But it's not about them, it's about us."

I sit up in my bed, body suddenly rigid. "You don't think we should be together?"

"No," he says. "I'm not sayin' *that.* Just that we don't need to go runnin' into anything. What you've been tellin' me all along." He leans forward, urging me to understand. "Bein' around Carmen kinda cleared my head, you see? I couldn't help but remember. How I felt back then, marryin' this girl I thought I had forever with." He shakes his head. "We were so over-the-moon happy, Charlie. And that wasn't enough."

I turn my head away from him on the pillow. Curl up. I don't need to hear how happy he and his ex-wife once were.

"You were right," he tells me. "People can't get married 'cause of all the things goin' on around 'em. It's gotta be 'cause of what's goin' on *inside* 'em. You and me, we've got time to grow that. We don't have to be all in a hurry."

"We haven't had a lot of time to focus on just us."

He smiles. Strokes my cheek, coaxing me out of my protective ball. "Things happened so fast, I've pretty much never known you as anyone but pregnant, hormonal Charlie. I dunno who you'll be. Got no idea what to expect after the baby arrives. But I'm in. I'm in this."

"Where?" I ask. "Where, exactly, are you in this?"

"I did a lot of thinkin' on that, too."

"What did you come up with?"

"Well," he says. "I started thinkin' about Boone, this dog we had when I was a kid. Boone got cancer, right? And Nanny and Daddy Jack, they said it was time to put him down."

I grab my head as if in physical pain. "Oh my God, Noah. Are you seriously answering a question about our future with a dead-dog parable?"

He waves me off and continues with his story in earnest. "I loved that dog, okay? I was goin' nuts. 'No, no, you can't put down the dog!' I was all worked up."

I bite my tongue and wait for the punch line.

"Anyway, Daddy Jack said somethin' that stuck with me. He said, 'Let the dog remember a life that was good. Don't make him stick around until it's bad.' "

I grip the rail of my bed. "Are you the dog here, Noah? You don't want to stick around until it gets bad?"

"No, no." He looks vexed, as if his meaning should've been perfectly clear. "I'm talkin' about Sidalie. Saying that I had a good life there. But maybe, just maybe, I've stuck around too long. That it's time to let that dog die."

I could laugh or cry; instead, I choose some awkward hybrid of the two. Tears coupled with a fit of giggles that rapidly disintegrates into a string of unladylike snorts. "Oh, hon . . ." My eyes are welling up even as I gasp for air. "Oh, hon, I love you so much." When I finally compose myself, I realize there's one last question. "What about your company?"

"I've got an idea about that." He takes a deep breath. "I split ownership with Pete Gantos. That means it's still half mine. He'll handle the day-to-day, and I'll advise, maybe start up a little branch out here. I'm gonna have to go back to Sidalie now and again," he warns, "but I'll be livin' in Tucson. With you and the kids. Fair?"

"Fair."

"So. You still want that house on Mawith Drive?"

"Yeah." I grin. "I want it."

"All right, then. Here we are, and here we stay. I'm not gonna lie, this whole thing scares me shitless. But I'm gonna try. Gonna do my damnedest."

"All anyone could ask," I say. "Now go

get Micky. We've got to tell her."

It won't be easy, I know. Newborns are hard. Micky, with everything she's been through, will be even harder. But at least we have a chance. A chance to be reasonably-happy-with-the-occasional-road-bump ever after. That's worth fighting for.

I watch him go, hope taking root in my chest and spreading upward. This is not the life that I imagined for us when we first left Louisiana. But I think it's the one we're meant to have.

Noah has been gone scarcely five minutes when I hear a polite knock, although the door to my room is open. A doctor?

I glance over and spot a man standing in the doorway. Though there's something familiar about the broad shoulders and receding hairline, it's the pink collared shirt with its splashy hula-girl print that gives him away. I draw in a sharp breath.

Quico.

"Ms. Cates. I am so glad to see you are recovering." His genial tone does not sound like it belongs to a man who covers up the murder of pregnant women or frames innocent Americans for drug possession. He looks like he should be barbecuing ribs in a backyard somewhere or scratching a large, good-natured dog behind the ears.

I glance around my hospital bed, trying to locate a button that might call in the nurse, but Quico holds up a hand.

"Please, no need to be alarmed. I want no trouble with you. I thought we might talk." His speech is so careful, his accent so precise — not at all what I would've expected from this man with a penchant for tacky Hawaiian shirts.

"We have nothing to talk about."

"No?" He arches an eyebrow. "How surprising. I imagined that you would have . . . questions for me."

"I don't even know who you are." It's a lie, and we both know it.

"How rude of me." With a knowing smile, he offers me his hand. "Francisco Ortega. I'm the director of the Sonoran Office of Family Rights."

"The Office of Family Rights, huh?" I don't take his hand. "Nice shirt."

He glances down at the hula girls and laughs. "I'll tell my daughter you said so."

"Your daughter?"

"I'm color-blind. She picks all my clothes."

The fact that he has children momentarily throws me, though it shouldn't. "Why are you here?"

"To apologize for my associates," he says.

"They've behaved badly."

"You mean Teresa and Marilena?"

He nods. "Their actions don't reflect well on me, I know. I want to assure you that I'm handling this problem."

"Handling it how?" I sit up a little straighter, try to maintain my dignity despite the too-short hospital gown. "Is Marilena going to turn up dead next?"

He gives me a look of mild offense. "That is not how I deal with my problems, *señora.* What I'm going to do is much simpler. I will end this service that we provided and find some other way to help the families of the Sonoran state."

"You mean no more selling babies."

"It will disappoint a great many people, I'm afraid, but it seems prudent, in light of . . . these unfortunate incidents."

"Why are you here? What does this have to do with me?"

"It has nothing to do with you. And yet, you've been quite curious about these matters, haven't you?"

"Curious?" I manage a thin laugh. "Sure, I'll admit I had a few questions. But I think I've got the general gist of things now, thanks."

"In my country, we do not value curiosity as you Americans do."

599

"I gathered that. When you planted drugs on my boyfriend, that really drove the point home."

He only shrugs. "Your friend Albert told Teresa you intended to write an article about Lety's death. And then — you showed up at Marilena's hotel. One shouldn't approach the hive and then complain of a sting. I had to act, Ms. Cates."

I still can't discern his intentions. "You put an awful lot of energy into intimidating me. Are you afraid of me, Quico?"

He settles into the chair beside the bed, the one that Noah just vacated, and regards me gravely. "I think you misunderstand. I'm afraid *for* you. You're a bright woman, soon to have two young and vulnerable children. Your lover, he is free from jail. You have nothing to gain and everything to lose."

"What are you saying? You want me to turn a blind eye to everything that's happened?" Anger eclipses my fear. I can't forget the shower in room 2, the blood swelling beneath my hands as I realized my baby had been shot. "Lety is dead," I tell him. "Her child never took a breath."

He remains solemn. "Justice comes from a divine hand, *señora*. You and I, we're only human. Leave it to our maker to punish the bad."

600

"But Marilena —"

"Marilena made a reckless decision, and not one I endorsed."

"You knew. You knew what she did, and you did nothing. You knew about Teresa, too, didn't you? That she killed Donna and Jasmine."

"I've always let Teresa handle her own affairs," he says calmly. "It's a good policy. Nonintervention. I suggest you practice it."

I'm quiet for a moment, working through my options. I could shout my story from the rooftops, write a fiery exposé, and maybe someone would listen. Maybe there would even be an investigation, a scandal, a little international brouhaha. Maybe dozens of children born in Mexico and illegally adopted by Americans would be torn from the families who raised them and returned to their country of origin, all the opportunities that came with their American citizenship abruptly rescinded.

If I speak out, who will I help? More important, who will I hurt?

"Teresa is dead," Quico reminds me. "Your mother and your sister — they have been avenged. What can you hope to win now?"

It's a good question, and one I find that I can answer.

"Two things," I say slowly, still working through the details as I speak. "My silence isn't free."

"And here I thought you were a woman of such high principles." He clucks his tongue. "I don't advise blackmail. Blackmail caused Lety all her trouble."

"I don't want money. Just a couple favors. Nothing a man like you can't handle."

He gives a low, benevolent chuckle. "What is it you want?"

"Ruben Ramos," I begin. "Micky's father. I want him released from prison."

"Ruben Ramos," he repeats. "I don't know this name."

"He was arrested in Puerto Peñasco on some bogus sexual assault charges. There was some suspicion that he might be involved in Jasmine's murder. Obviously, he wasn't. I trust you have the judicial connections to clear his name?"

"Sexual assault?" Quico gives me an amicable smile. "I think I can manage that. And your second request?"

I take a deep breath and tell him what I want. He listens carefully and accepts my terms. Extends his hand as if to seal our deal.

I stare down at his hand, the fine dark hairs on his knuckles, the thick gold wedding ring. Can I really make this dirty bargain? Is there any better choice?

Quico cocks his head to one side, sensing my hesitation. "I'm a nice man, *señora*. A family man, not so different from yourself. Today, I can give you something that you want. Take this now, this offer. Better to get something you want than something you don't."

I'm a fighter by nature, not the kind to sit idly by after witnessing such a flagrant abuse of power. But in this case, who would I be fighting for? I can't get Lety back. Can't resurrect my mother or my sister. Quico inhabits a world I'll never understand, a world built upon corruption. He plays by different rules. Two small victories and the safety of my family — it's more, I suspect, than some walk away from this man with.

I swallow back the bitter taste in my throat and put my hand in his. We shake.

■ ■ ■ ■

Part VII
Tucson, Arizona
December 2012

■ ■ ■ ■

THIRTY-THREE

The house is ready. The floor has been cleared of stuffed animals and burp rags, board books and baby gear. Any unpacked boxes have been stashed in closets or under beds, out of sight if not mind.

And I *may* have overdone it with all the decorations.

Balloons congregate on the living room ceiling, trailing their ribbons, and twisty orange and yellow streamers form trippy spiderwebs around the room. The fruity walls we haven't yet repainted add yet another layer of color to this madness. A large sign that Noah and I penned hangs across the mantel: WELCOME, MICKY!

Today is the day. Today Micky leaves Vonda's loving care, and our family is complete.

We've planned a modest little gathering to mark the occasion, invited the folks who have made our move to Arizona bearable. I'm no hero. With the exception of some deviled eggs that Noah proudly slopped together, all the food has been purchased. I'm too tired, too strung out on life with an infant to pass myself off as some domestic goddess. Since my book was released back in September, I've been swamped with publicity work, and then my daughter came, landing in our lives with all the subtlety of a grenade.

It's been a lot to juggle, though in some respects, not as difficult as I'd feared. Though the media has been happy to consume my biography of Louisiana's wealthy Deveau family, my own family drama has generated very little interest at all.

There were a few news stories in the beginning, local coverage that focused mainly on Teresa's desert showdown with a TPD veteran. Several journalists wrote profiles of Teresa's life, mostly pieces of the tragic-fall-from-grace variety that suggested her challenging childhood had forever damaged her. Other articles examined the tenuous future of the Sonora Hope organization as a whole now that the reputation of its charismatic founder was forever tarnished. In the end, the two women Teresa killed warranted only a brief mention.

Police never did nail down a motive for Donna and Jasmine's murders, which made the story less attractive to national outlets. *Believed to be a work-related dispute,* some sources said. Others attributed the murders to drugs, mentioned Donna's lifelong problems with addiction, theorized Teresa had been under the influence.

Jasmine was nothing but a footnote in the whole affair. She wasn't rich, didn't have a bright future laid out before her or that shiny blond goodness that people like to see in victims. She was just another anonymous woman dead too soon.

In some strange way, I came to value my sister's life only when I saw how little anyone else did. Here was a young woman with few advantages, raised by a neglectful mother, pregnant herself at twenty and then abandoned by the baby's father, and yet she'd kept on. She worked her crappy mall jobs, dutifully filled out the paperwork for public assistance, ensured that Micky had housing and clothes. There is something strangely heroic about carrying on when the world thinks that you are disposable. Jasmine wasn't a good mother, by any stretch of the imagination, but whatever mistakes she made, she raised a great kid. I can forgive the rest.

As I look around our tacky, decked-out living room, I wonder what Jasmine would've thought of all of this. Was she the type to get sentimental about holidays and special occasions, or would she have rolled her eyes at our handmade sign? I'll never know.

"She's fallin' asleep," Noah says from behind me. "What do I do?"

I turn to find him jiggling our daughter in his arms, his forehead creased with worry.

"If she's tired, let her snooze," I tell him. "It's not a big deal."

"But everyone's gonna want to see her," he frets. "And all the noise — it'll wake her up."

"They've all seen a crying baby before. Just put her down in the bouncy seat. It'll be fine."

The care he takes when he straps her in makes me smile — that look of concentration and concern, always afraid he'll screw something up. *You will,* I want to tell him. *We all do, over and over.*

For weeks, I couldn't believe that we had survived that long, dark desert night at all. I'd awaken at dawn and watch the moon fade from the sky, moved to tears by the sight of another sunrise. *Tash and mashath,* Pam told me. The sun and moon. And then, if you're lucky, the sun again.

That was how I chose my daughter's name.

"Tasha," I told Noah. "What about Tasha?"

"Sweet and simple," he said, before I could even explain the significance. "I like it."

She came in late September, two days before her due date, weighing a respectable seven pounds, seven ounces. Enduring the sting of a bark scorpion did absolutely nothing for my pain tolerance, as it turned out: I still hollered for that epidural.

Tasha Palmer-Cates is now fully alert in her bouncy chair, despite her father's prediction of sleep. She doesn't resemble Keegan as a baby. She's neither blond nor bright-eyed, but instead a small replica of her father: dark hair, dark eyes, and a face more square than round, which is accentuated by her rather flat head. I watch her small fingers grasp at the air before balling into a fist. Noah needn't have worried about her napping. Tasha seems to know that guests are coming and wants to be part of the action.

When Vonda arrives, our daughter breaks out an enormous gummy smile. What a ham.

It's a small crew that we've assembled,

but a good one: Vonda and Luis, Daniel Quijada, Albert Mangusson, and Pam. Albert's son has come along, and though he was initially unenthused to be dragged to some boring adult function, he has since paired up with Bryce, Vonda and Luis's foster child, and the two boys are running around the backyard, whooping it up. It feels good, the sound of children playing in this house.

Micky, our guest of honor, sits quietly on the sidelines, observing all the activity with a solemn expression. I don't try to draw her into the group. Like a frightened wild animal, she'll come when ready. And who could blame her for being nervous? On this day she is acquiring a new home, two new parents — foster parents on paper, but with more permanent designs on her — and an infant sister to boot.

Part of me wonders if we've made a mistake in making a big deal of this, but then Micky comes up beside me, one finger in her mouth, and offers a shy smile. "Did you get me a cake?" she asks.

"Chocolate," I say, and her smile broadens.

I can't help but wish, in some impossible, aching way, that Keegan were here to share in this day. He and Micky would've made quite the pair, his exuberance and her gravity the perfect yin and yang. Instead, he will always be the missing piece, a child neither Noah nor my girls will ever know, though he forever shaped me as a mother.

I make my rounds, catching up with guests, plying them with food, answering questions about Micky's schooling and Tasha's sleep cycles. Pam isn't usually one for babies, but she's feeling sentimental today. She lays Tasha down on her chest, the index finger on her right hand conspicuously missing as she cradles Tasha's head. Tasha, Micky, and me — we are the pieces of Donna that remain. We are the family that she bequeathed to Pam.

I'll always have questions about Donna DeRossi, but after helping Pam clean out her condo last week, I have something more. In a drawer of old letters and important documents, I found three issues from my tenure at *Sophisticate:* February 2002, October 2005, March 2009. I knew their significance immediately — each masthead reflected a new promotion for me at the magazine. Associate editor. Features editor. Managing editor.

It is bittersweet to know that, from her distant city in the desert, my mother was watching me make my way in the world, silently rooting for my success.

Across the room, Tasha's eyes have begun to droop. Pam strokes her head and speaks to her quietly, lulling my daughter to sleep with her words. "What a special day." Vonda appears at my side and surveys the room with me. "We'll miss Micky, but I'm so happy for her. For all of you."

"And *your* family?" I touch her wrist, eager for an update. "How's Yulissa?"

"Good!" Vonda breaks into a megawatt grin. "She's good! We went to visit her again last week. Luis and I, we're very optimistic. The papers are coming along at lightning speed, at least as far as this stuff goes. Mr. Ortega has really been a godsend."

Not exactly a godsend, I think, but I'm glad to hear that Quico is holding up his end of our deal. "And Yulissa still wants to leave Nogales?"

"She's been praying for it," Vonda says. "Literally, praying. For years. Her sister, the one who died, was always talking about coming to the States. So when Luis and I showed up, she thought it was a sign, a gift from . . ." She trails off, too choked up to finish the thought. "She's scared, of course. But she said her sister would be so proud."

I only hope Yulissa's story has a happier ending than Lety's. "It's a big adjustment for a kid."

"Sure," Vonda agrees. "I've seen plenty of kids over the years from all kinds of crazy home situations, and you really never know. But she's a bright kid, Charlie. A *nice* kid. Nice goes farther in this world than a lot of people think." She's so hopeful, something in her shining when she speaks about this girl, and I think that maybe the bargain I made with Quico was a good one if it brings these two together.

But I'll always have my doubts. Never be sure that I made the right call.

It's almost time for Micky's cake, but first I have to hunt down Albert's son and Bryce, hustle everyone inside to participate. I dash onto the patio, calling their names.

The boys burst out from behind a rock, and I shoo them toward the door with promises of dessert. I'm about to follow them in when I hear a noise coming from the hot tub, the sound of jets. I glance over and nearly have a conniption when I notice that the cover has been pulled back.

Were the boys goofing around in here without permission? What were they thinking? Someone could've drowned!

I reach over to switch off the jets, both frightened and furious, and abruptly stop. Because there, rising up from the frothy water like a trick of sunlight, is a girl. Too bright to observe directly, but unmistakable in my peripheral vision, her head bent back and armpits hooked over the rim of the tub.

"Lety?"

She's not the Lety that I've known in dreams, all world-weary attitude and toughness. There's a lightness to her now, something playful, childlike.

La vida buena, eh? she says with a grand gesture of her hands. *The good life.*

I glance back at my house, try to imagine what my home must look like to a girl who spent her formative years in a garbage dump. Resist the urge to burst into tears remembering what I have. What Lety didn't.

"Yeah," I manage. "It's good. It's pretty damn good."

Yulissa . . . she have this?

I don't look at her, but I can sense her there in the space where light meets water. "I don't think Vonda and Luis have a hot tub. But your sister will have a good life when she gets here." I squint upward into the cloudless blue. "As good as she can make it."

My wish, Lety says, wistful. *Always my wish. La vida buena.*

"You got it. What you always wanted." I rest my elbows on the side of the tub. "Not

616

for you, I know. Not for your baby. But you made it happen for Yulissa."

She doesn't answer, doesn't state the obvious. That it's not enough.

"It's all that you could do, Lety. All *I* could do. I'm sorry."

Suddenly the water jets shut off. The noise dies, and the water stills. A dramatic exit? But there's nothing supernatural going on here, I soon realize. I've accidentally hit the switch with my forearm.

Whatever I thought I saw in the hot tub — hallucination, apparition, desert mirage — is gone.

I turn back to the house. Through the sliding glass door, I see my people: my fussy daughter, my stoic niece, the man I hope I'll one day marry. And I see my friends, the odd assortment of folks who are a part of my life now because of Donna, a woman I came to know only after she was gone.

Lety is right. It's a good life. And not just because of the hot tub.

As I reach for the handle, she leaves me with one parting word. Breath against my ear, so gentle it just might be a breeze; the whisper of a girl's voice so faint, it just might be the mesquite trees.

Gracias, she says.

"You're welcome," I say, and then I go inside.

AUTHOR'S NOTE

Though the people and events of this novel are fictional, the community of recyclers at the Tirabichi garbage dump was, for decades, very real. Once a neighborhood consisting of some thirty families, the Tirabichi community was devastated by a suspicious fire in March of 2015, which claimed fifteen homes and the life of a recycler. In April, the Nogales municipal council ordered the closure of Tirabichi. The following month, another unexplained fire burned down six more homes, effectively driving out most of the residents who remained.

When I visited Tirabichi, the community was a ghost of its former self. Still, the longtime caretaker invited me into his home. His ingenious dwelling repurposed many items that others might have dismissed as trash, including a hollowed-out mattress that served as a porch overhang. A pair of residents who had not yet moved on showed me all the bottles they had been collecting for the recycling center. At the edge of the dump, overlooking the rich green valley below, a wooden cross marked the recent death of a resident.

Today, no one knows exactly where all the displaced members of the Tirabichi community have ended up. Resources in Nogales can be scarce and opportunities — legal ones, at least — hard to come by. I hope that, against the odds, these former recyclers and their children are healthy and safe.

ACKNOWLEDGMENTS

Throughout my work on *The Shimmering Road,* I was fortunate to have the assistance of several knowledgeable individuals. Their advice improved the quality of my manuscript considerably; any factual errors or inaccuracies in the novel are entirely my own.

Thank you to the US Customs and Border Protection agency, which gave me clearance for a behind-the-scenes tour of its DeConcini port of entry into Nogales. Public Affairs Officer Marcia Armendariz was both personable and patient as she answered my procedural questions.

Attorney Thea Gilbert, who serves on the National Association of Counsel for Children and practices in Tucson, kindly answered legal questions that I had about the intricacies of adoption, and Sue Schmelz, from the Arizona Department of Child Safety, also provided valuable advice.

I am grateful to — and deeply impressed by — Scott Nicholson, an American charity worker living in Nogales, who led me through one of the city's poorest neighborhoods and introduced me to the remaining residents of Tirabichi. Scott has an unimaginably huge heart, and I am truly in awe of the work he does for HEPAC, the Home of Hope and Peace, an organization that seeks "to create a healthy community in Nogales, Mexico, where citizens do not feel that their only choice for survival is to risk their lives in the desert in an attempt to immigrate to the United States." To learn more about HEPAC, visit www.hepacnogales.org.

My fabulous team at Putnam has been such a pleasure to work with. Katie McKee, Stephanie Hargadon, Carrie Swetonic, Alexis Welby, Ashley McClay, Christine Ball, Sally Kim, and Ivan Held are all so very good at what they do. I am particularly lucky to have the feisty and tenacious Kerri Kolen as my editor. She does the work of seven, and she is, in large part, the reason I am living this multibook dream.

Interning at the Zachary Shuster Harmsworth agency at age nineteen and then becoming a client fifteen years later is one of the greatest plot twists of my life. I'm so glad to have Esmond Harmsworth representing my work.

To parent two young children while producing four-hundred-page novels under deadline is no easy task, and I could not accomplish it without the help and support of people like Deb Hoff, C. M. Brown, Jeff and Liz Wise, Rosaleigh Young, and Ellen Madigan.

Finally, love and gratitude to my husband, Spencer Wise, who gamely agreed to explore Tucson and Nogales in August, though he hates the heat; who listens as I talk through plot problems and provides tech support when I'm stumped; who tries to soft-sell my book to everyone he meets. Thank you for making it all possible, Spence.

ABOUT THE AUTHOR

Hester Young holds a master's degree in English with a creative writing concentration from the University of Hawai'i at Mānoa, and her work has been published in literary magazines such as *The Hawai'i Review*. Before turning to writing full-time, she worked as a teacher in Arizona and New Hampshire. Young lives with her husband and two children in New Jersey.

The employees of Thorndike Press hope you have enjoyed this Large Print book. All our Thorndike, Wheeler, and Kennebec Large Print titles are designed for easy reading, and all our books are made to last. Other Thorndike Press Large Print books are available at your library, through selected bookstores, or directly from us.

For information about titles, please call:
(800) 223-1244

or visit our website at:
gale.com/thorndike

To share your comments, please write:
Publisher
Thorndike Press
10 Water St., Suite 310
Waterville, ME 04901

THE VOTER DECIDES

The four geographical areas sampled

THE VOTER DECIDES

ANGUS CAMPBELL

GERALD GURIN

WARREN E. MILLER

Survey Research Center, University of Michigan

With the assistance of
SYLVIA EBERHART and ROBERT O. McWILLIAMS

GREENWOOD PRESS, PUBLISHERS
WESTPORT, CONNECTICUT

Originally published in 1954
by Row, Peterson and Company, Evanston, Illinois

Reprinted with the permission
of Harper and Row, Publishers

First Greenwood Reprinting 1971

Library of Congress Catalogue Card Number 73-138211

ISBN 0-8371-5566-5.

Printed in the United States of America

Preface

In the fall of 1948, the Survey Research Center of the University of Michigan carried out a small-scale study of the presidential election of that year. Although restricted in scope, this project was reported in some detail in the hope that it might serve as a "pilot study to the definitive investigation" of voting behavior in subsequent elections.

In March, 1952, the Carnegie Corporation of New York made available to the Survey Research Center, through the Committee on Political Behavior of the Social Science Research Council, a research grant to make possible a nation-wide study of voting behavior in the 1952 presidential election. The present report is the first major publication of the results of this study.

Our list of acknowledgments of assistance given during the course of this study is a long one. Our most obvious obligation is to the Carnegie Corporation whose support made the study possible. We express herewith our appreciation of their willingness to invest a substantial grant in our research proposal. The Corporation is not, of course, in any way responsible for this publication, and is not to be understood as approving by virtue of its grant any of the statements made therein.

This project is the outgrowth of a series of meetings of the Social Science Research Council's Committee on Political Behavior. While this committee has not taken direct responsibility for any specific research project, it has given considerable attention to the present study, both in its planning phase and during the preparation of this report. The committee cannot of course be held accountable for what appears in these pages, but the authors wish to acknowledge its very valuable support and counsel. The members of the Committee on Political Behavior are David B. Truman (chairman), Conrad M. Arensberg, Alfred de Grazia, Oliver Garceau, V. O. Key, Avery Leiserson, and M. Brewster Smith. Professor Key was chairman of the committee during the development of this study.

Special reference should be made to Dr. Pendleton Herring, President of the Social Science Research Council. As an ex officio member of the Committee on Political Behavior and as a political scientist, Dr. Herring participated in a number of discussions of this project and has followed its development with continuing interest.

We have also had the assistance of a group of our colleagues at the University of Michigan who have served as an Advisory Committee to the project. This local committee has met at frequent intervals to discuss various problems which arose during the conduct of the study, and we are grateful for its interest and advice. The members of this group are Professors Arthur W. Bromage, Amos H. Hawley, Daniel Katz, Theodore M. Newcomb, and James K. Pollock.

A number of our other associates at the University of Michigan have also taken an interest in the study and have contributed in one way or another to it. For various kinds of assistance we wish to thank George M. Belknap, James C. Davies, Samuel J. Eldersveld, Ronald Freedman, Morris Janowitz, and Dwaine Marvick.

It will be apparent to the reader that the present study has drawn on the previous thinking and research of numerous other students of voting behavior. We are particularly indebted to Professor Paul F. Lazarsfeld, whose pioneering work in this field has served as a model for much of what has followed.

Our most immediate debt, of course, is to our colleagues in the Survey Research Center. Rensis Likert played an important role both in the early planning of the study and in its later development. Stephen B. Withey also contributed advice and assistance. Charles F. Cannell, as head of the Center's Field Staff, was responsible for all field operations. Leslie Kish, head of the Sampling Staff of the Center, supervised the design and selection of the sample. Jane Benjamin directed the coding of the interviews. Joan Abramson and David F. Miller served as research assistants at different stages of the study. Unnamed, but greatly appreciated, are the hundred or more Center interviewers who gathered the data on which this report is based.

The breadth and complexity of the data which were assembled in this project pose serious problems of presentation. It will become apparent to the reader that the full range of analysis which could be undertaken with the data at hand is very broad indeed and vastly beyond the limits of any single volume. Considerations of time and space have imposed limitations on the scope and detail of the data which could be discussed in this report. In some cases tables have been included with only brief comment, primarily for the purpose of indicating the possibilities of subsequent analysis. As a consequence, the reader will encounter many intriguing aspects of the data which appear to have been disregarded in the discussion and will think of numerous cross-tabulations which might have been presented, but are not. It is hoped that additional analyses carried forward independently of this publication will answer some of the questions which are not adequately treated here.

Ann Arbor, Michigan   ANGUS CAMPBELL
February 21, 1954   GERALD GURIN
                                                  WARREN E. MILLER

Contents

Foreword

The survey that this book reports will be regarded by students of politics as a highly significant step in the development of the art and substance of their trade. Yet since it depends on methods of observation not ordinarily at the command of political analysts, be they academic or journalistic, a few words may be in order by way of introduction from a political scientist habituated to the older modes of study.

In this volume we have the most impressive analysis yet made of a national election by the survey method. It should arouse great interest among students of politics, since it demonstrates strikingly how the survey technique supplements our older methods of observation. It brings new problems within reach, and it permits more assured handling of some of the old problems. The traditional means by which we have sought to understand politics have built a respectable body of lore about the nature of the political process. Yet those methods do not always produce satisfactory results. Ivory-tower excogitation, a practice by no means limited to academic precincts, yields persuasive insights, as well as comprehensive descriptions pleasing in their grand architecture but often suspect. Individual field inquiry, in which a good deal of shoe leather is worn out in quest of communicative participants in the political process, permits description with a tone of verisimilitude. Some types of political phenomena, of course, stand out like a red barn when the sun shines on the winter snow and can be identified by the most cursory observation. Even so, only the most doubtful judgments may be made about such dimensions as the frequency, the extent, the magnitude of what one sees. Furthermore, some sorts of political phenomena, especially some features of mass behavior, are simply not perceptible by the older ways of observation.

The invention of the sample survey created a powerful new instrument for the observation of the political process. The most obvious applications are in the study of electoral behavior, but in the long run extensions will doubtless be made to many other matters such as those the political philosophers speculate about when they consider "the nature of the state." A great advance of the sampling method consists in the capacity it gives to make inferences about total populations from the characteristics of relatively few cases. Questions of frequency of occurrence, of magnitude, of incidence, become much more manageable.

Other features of the sample survey also fix its qualities as a tool of analysis. By its nature the survey permits the ready pooling of observations made by many men. The analytical techniques adaptable to the data make possible the identification of phenomena and the isolation of relationships otherwise perceptible chiefly by surmise, if indeed at all. The form of survey data facilitates internal checks on the correctness of interpretations as well as corroboration, refutation, or supplementation by other investigators.

The use of the sample survey in the analysis of voting behavior is, of course, no longer new. Yet this application of the method by the Survey Research Center of the University of Michigan to the 1952 campaign must be ranked as especially notable both for its finished technique and for its contribution to our substantive knowledge of electoral behavior. The highly developed techniques—of sampling, of data collection, of analysis—underlying this volume represent a cumulation of the tricks contrived by many investigators. They owe something to the polling organizations which both popularized opinion sampling and made us wary of it. They build also on techniques developed by other scholars who have used the survey method. Most of all, they rest on the long experience of the authors and their associates of the Survey Research Center in the conduct of national sample surveys on a wide variety of topics. In consequence, from the standpoint of technique, the study here reported bears to Mr. Gallup's 1936 election poll somewhat as the new Cadillac does to the first Model T.

On the substantive side, a differentiating feature of this survey is that its planning involved an effort to harness the skills and curiosities of several disciplines. By an accident of the academic division of labor, social psychologists early acquired an understanding of the mysteries of sampling. They quickly applied the technique to political studies. These forays produced results of genuine significance; yet social psychologists at times, or so it seemed to political scientists, were as aliens moving on strange terrain and failed to examine questions that students of politics would have given priority. By a variety of means —consultation, staffing, and immersion in the literature of politics— the Survey Research Center staff has sought to feed into the survey apparatus the kinds of problems, that concern political scientists as well as those that preoccupy social psychologists. In consequence, the inquiry has its roots quite as much in political science as in social psychology.

What does the survey machinery produce when it is set to work in the observation of a presidential campaign and election? An adequate appreciation of the breadth and variety of the findings can be had only from a reading of the entire report, yet the major elements may be quickly indicated. The materials of Part One, in the main, describe the behaviors and attitudes of the voters in the election of 1952. What was the process by which people made up their minds in 1952? What was the extent and nature of public interest and participation in the campaign? How did groups of people—occupational categories, income levels, unionists, metropolitan dwellers, and so forth—vote? How did people perceive parties and candidates? On all such matters Part One presents the facts. An incidental, but significant, overtone is the emphasis on the peculiarities of the behavior of voters in 1952 and on the theme that elections are likely to differ vastly from time to time—a proposition whose neglect has, on occasion, brought political prognosticators to grief.

Students of politics at least will probably regard Part Two as the major contribution of the study. While that part deals, as does the first, with the election of 1952, it develops a new framework for the analysis of electoral decision. That system of analysis aids in explaining the election of 1952 but it also contributes toward a better understanding of electoral behavior in general. In brief, a scheme or theory is devised for ordering the data on motivation of voters in terms of party identification, candidate orientation, and issue orientation. The authors establish the independence of each of these variables and indicate some of their interrelations in the 1952 polling. By the identification and measurement of these variables, a means has been found to explain to a considerable degree variations in participation and variations in the direction of the vote. The analytical scheme takes into account the baffling complexity of voting behavior, yet its concepts and categories may turn out to be of a sufficiently high level of generality to fit a wide range of voting situations. If so, this scheme will differ markedly from simpler voting behavior theories which so often seem to hold good for only one election.

While the report and the appended special studies touch an astonishing number of aspects of the election of 1952, some readers will doubtless find no mention of points of particular interest to them. Some of these omissions will be cured by subsequent publications based on the survey data. Others resulted from the choice of topics on which to center attention, a process of selection somewhat affected by the nature of the survey method. The survey apparatus, unlike a camera, does not record an image of the entire scene toward which it is aimed, but only of those parts that have been singled out in advance. These choices of centers of attention have to be made a good while before the unfolding of the campaign. Such a schedule creates an opportunity for second-guessing about matters that should have been inquired into, questions that might as well have been omitted. Further, some questions are beyond reach by a national survey. No findings are reported, for example, on the Irish of Boston, the farmers of Iowa, or the Democrats of Birmingham. Segments of the population so small escape detection in a national sample. On some questions of interest to the political scientist, no material will be found simply because such matters cannot be analyzed by a sample survey. Useful though it may be, this method leaves many questions to be dealt with by older modes of political analysis.

The experienced research worker will be impressed by the high degree of technical virtuosity evident throughout, both in the collection of data and in its analysis. While people are astonishingly responsive to the importunities of interviewers, the conduct of a study of this sort amounts to considerably more than asking people questions about what they feel, believe, know, or do, and recording the answers. One aspect of the art consists, paradoxically enough, in the putting of questions that will yield information about people of which they may not be fully aware themselves. What people tell about themselves does not automatically exude from the stacks of completed interview schedules. Another phase of the art consists in the extraction of the more or less hidden meaning from the data. Examination of the interview schedule (Appendix E) in relation to the text of the report will make apparent the order of ingenuity requisite for the transformation of the raw data into meaningful interpretation. While much of the analysis rests on conventional methods, some of the techniques will be appraised as most elegant by the connoisseurs of these matters.

Some readers may still view skeptically inferences about the nation's electorate based on interviews with a couple of thousand persons. While skepticism is never unseemly, the more appropriate posture may be one of awe that inferences with so narrow a margin of error may be derived from so small a sample. The statistically sophisticated will take the analysis in stride. For the benefit of others, it ought to be said that an ineradicable chance for error inheres in even the most perfect sampling procedure. Yet the probability that particular characteristics of the sample mirror characteristics of the total electorate may be calculated by relatively simple statistical methods. These probabilities for the various estimates of this study are set out in Appendix F.

One quality of the analysis that will evoke praise in some circles and perhaps impatience in others is the pervading restraint of statement. At point after point the scholar of speculative bent will observe that the authors have stonily ignored opportunities to soar out through the boundless blue in imaginative explication of the possible immediate or future significance of particular bits of data. On the whole, there prevails in the exposition a dead-pan insistence on the limitation of inferences strictly to the data. In explanation of this manner of the authors, it can only be said that habituation to explicit methods of analysis tends to dampen intellectual boisterousness. When they rely on the sorts of procedures used here, investigators are subjected to the disciplining etiquette of the scientific tradition, sanctioned by the painful but humbling knowledge that no matter how reasonable one may seem he can turn out to be magnificently wrong—and be found out.

While these remarks have been addressed primarily to the professional student of political behavior, they should not becloud the fact that this book has something for everyone with a concern about American politics. What sorts of Southerners voted for Eisenhower? Were the egg-head college graduates largely in the Stevenson camp? Did the women really turn the trick for the Republicans? Did the election mark a widespread popular acceptance of Republican conservatism in domestic policy? What happened to the farmers between 1948 and 1952? On these and many other questions the general reader, so beloved of publishers and booksellers, will find treatments of great interest. At points the presentation requires, as befits a difficult and complex subject, the closest attention. Yet the technical terminology has been kept to the minimum consistent with the necessity for precision of statement.

Professional politicians, or their brain trusters, will find it worth while, and perhaps disturbing, to ponder many of the findings. What did the Republicans have in 1952 other than General Eisenhower? Under what conditions will the Democrats who voted Republican in 1952 return to their party? Are current national policies well calculated to make permanent the 1952 accretions to Republican strength? Can the Southern swing to the Republican party be made lasting? On what terms? What appeals are most likely to move the voter in 1954? In 1956? The answers to such questions are not neatly set out in the pages that follow, but suggestive materials are there for those whose vocations compel them to fret about such matters.

V. O. KEY, Jr.

Cambridge, Massachusetts
January 11, 1954

I

Introduction

The American presidential election is a massive and complex social phenomenon. Every four years the campaigns to elect a president draw millions of Americans into action in support of their candidates and tens of millions into the voting booths on Election Day.

Certainly no single research project can encompass the entire range of political events that make up a presidential election. There must be selection of the area of data to be investigated and of the method of analysis to be applied to it. Many different kinds of studies have been carried out, all having the general objective of providing a better understanding of what goes on during the elections. There have been studies of the registrations, the primaries, the nominating conventions, the campaigns, the media, the pressure groups, the party workers, the candidates, and, of course, the voters. They have drawn their information from historical and legal documents, public records, election statistics, special informants, and cross-section samples. They have provided a very substantial literature regarding the presidential elections.

In the present study we shall be concerned not with legislators, politicians, wardheelers, office-seekers nor any of the other special kinds of people that have particular political importance, but with the general public. That is to say, we are interested in the citizenry, the nearly one hundred million people of legal age who by reason of their citizenship are entitled to vote. Our broad interest is in the political life of these people, their participation as individuals in the total political process. Our specific interest, in the project to be reported here, is in their political behavior during the 1952 presidential campaign and election.

Most analyses of public participation in elections have depended on the election statistics which become available after the votes are counted. These are usually reported on a precinct or county basis, and they have made possible a variety of useful studies of factors related to the vote. Aggregate data, such as election statistics, do not permit analysis on an individual basis, however, and this means that many problems of great interest cannot be explored through this source of data.

The methodology of the sample survey makes it possible to reach and obtain information from great masses of people on an individual basis. Thus we are able to learn about perceptions, attitudes, interests, and behaviors, because our data come from personal interviews with individual citizens. We are able to describe the characteristics of the total population, because these individual respondents are carefully selected to represent the total, of which they are a very small sample.

The present report is based entirely on data gathered through the sample survey method. This procedure was employed because it is the only research method which could provide the kinds of data required by the objectives of the study.

The Objectives

Our study was designed with six major objectives in view. They were as follows:

1. To identify the voters and nonvoters, Republicans and Democrats, within four major geographical areas, in regard to:
   a) socio-economic characteristics,
   b) attitudes and opinions on political issues,
   c) perceptions of the parties and the candidates;
2. To compare these groups with the corresponding groups in the 1948 presidential election;
3. To trace the resolution of the vote with particular attention to the undecided and changing voters;
4. To study the impact of the activities of the major parties on the population;
5. To analyze the nature and correlates of political party identification;
6. To analyze the nature and correlates of political participation.

It was clear from the beginning that it would not be possible to pursue all these objectives with equal emphasis. The objective of greatest theoretical interest to the group of political scientists, social psychologists, and others who planned the study was that dealing with participation. This was given high priority. On the other hand, it was evident that the study could not undertake a full investigation of the activities of the political parties during the election period. This objective was least adequately dealt with. Although certain minor objectives were added during the course of planning, the six major objectives set the basic pattern for the study. They determined the design of the sample, the content of the questionnaires, and the ultimate analysis of the data. The reader will find all these objectives represented in the present report.

The Methods

The procedures used in the study reported here followed the design employed by the Survey Research Center in its study of the 1948 election.[1] A nationwide sample, selected by methods of probability sampling to represent all citizens of voting age living in private residences, was interviewed by representatives of the Center during the seven weeks preceding the election of November, 1952. These same people were interviewed again during the six weeks following the election. These two interviews, the first approximately an hour in length, and the second about a half-hour, were collated for each respondent and they provide the data for the study. A detailed description of the sampling procedures and reproductions of the interview questionnaires are given in the Appendix.

The Two Samples

Since all the data of this study derive from either the pre-election or the postelection sample, it is advisable to state the characteristics of these samples in explicit detail at the outset. The pre-election sample consisted of 2,021 people. This total is subdivided in some phases of the analysis into four geographical areas: the Northeast, the Midwest, the South, and the Far West (see Frontispiece). These areas were sampled at an equal sampling rate (somewhat less than one in 50,000) except in the Far West, where the sampling rate was doubled in order to build up the sample of that relatively thinly populated area. The number of cases by areas was: Northeast, 448; Midwest, 618; South, 509; and Far West, 446. In all presentations in this study in which the West is treated separately from the rest of the country, the full Western sample (446 cases) is used. In all presentations in which the West is combined with other areas of the country to show national totals, half of the Western sample is omitted so that this area will be represented in its proper proportion.

The postelection sample consisted of 1,714 people. Of these, 1,614 had been interviewed in the pre-election survey. The discrepancy between the 2,021 interviewed before the election and the 1,614 who were reinterviewed after the election resulted from two facts: (*a*) The

[1] Memoranda describing the methods of study design, interviewing, coding, sampling, and analysis employed by the Survey Research Center are available on request. For a general statement of survey research methods, the reader is referred to the relevant chapters in Leon Festinger and Daniel Katz (Eds.), *Research Methods in the Behavioral Sciences* (New York: Dryden Press, 1953). The Survey Research Center study of the 1948 election, referred to in this and subsequent chapters, is reported in Angus Campbell and R. L. Kahn, *The People Elect a President* (Ann Arbor: Institute for Social Research, 1952).

extra loading of the Western sample in the pre-election survey (222 cases) was dropped in the postelection survey. (*b*) It proved impossible for reasons of change of address, illness, or refusal, to reinterview 185 people from the pre-election sample who ideally should have been included in the postelection sample. However, 100 people who for one reason or another were missed in the pre-election sample were interviewed in the postelection survey. These, when combined with the 1,614 reinterviewed people, made up the total postelection sample of 1,714 cases. In order to avoid confusion, most of the tables which will be presented are based on the sample of 1,614 people who were interviewed both before and after the election.[2]

Throughout this report, the number of cases on which percentages are based is given. This permits the reader to estimate the reliability of the information which is presented. Reference to the Appendix statement regarding sampling errors should prove helpful in this connection.

Turnout and Party Choice

The major dependent variable in the present study was, of course, the vote itself. Since so much of the analysis which will be presented here will be devoted to the explanation of why people did or did not vote, and why they voted as they did if they did vote, it is appropriate in these introductory paragraphs to examine the record of the survey in its measurement of the two basic voting variables, turnout and party preference.

Of the 1,614 people interviewed in October and again in the postelection survey, 74 per cent said they had voted. According to the election statistics, 61.6 million people are reported to have voted for president. It is very difficult to estimate how much discrepancy exists between these two figures. If turnout is computed by dividing the total number of people officially counted as voting by the total number of people of voting age (approximately 98.5 million), the result would be near 63 per cent, and the discrepancy would appear sizable. However, it must be noted that the survey was not designed to represent the entire adult population. It excluded the following categories of people: (*a*) non-citizens; (*b*) the institutional population, living in prisons, hospitals, homes for the aged, etc.; (*c*) the "floating" population, people with no fixed addresses, traveling salesmen, people in transit to new addresses, hoboes, etc.; (*d*) military personnel living in

---

[2] The characteristics of the 185 respondents who were lost from the October sample and the 100 who were gained in the November sample were very similar to those of the 1,614 respondents who were interviewed in both surveys. Consequently, their inclusion or exclusion from the total sample does not have any significant effect on the data presented.

military installations or outside the country; and (e) mental incompetents living in private homes.

It is not known how many people of voting age fell into these five categories at the time of the survey. The total was certainly not less than five million and might well have run as high as ten million. It is apparent that a very small proportion of these people vote, either because of legal disfranchisement, physical or mental incapacity, or failure to meet residence requirements. It is also evident that the universe the survey represents contains virtually all of the voting population, and that within this universe the turnout must have been substantially higher than 63 per cent.

It would not be unreasonable, of course, to expect in a survey of voting that occasional individuals would say they had voted although in fact they had not. Several researchers who have checked the precinct records of their respondents have found this type of over-reporting.[3] It is safe to assume that some respondents in the present study gave themselves credit for a vote they did not actually cast. It seems clear, however, that this was a very small proportion of the total sample.

In the postelection survey, each respondent who said he had voted was asked how he had voted for president and congressman and, if there were contests in his state, for senator and governor. Their reports are compared in Table 1.1 to the proportions of the total vote recorded in the election statistics as going to the two parties.

TABLE 1.1

DIVISION OF THE 1952 TWO-PARTY VOTE AS RECORDED IN
ELECTION STATISTICS AND IN THE POSTELECTION SURVEY

OFFICE	ELECTION STATISTICS		POSTELECTION SURVEY	
	Republican	Democratic	Republican	Democratic
President	55.5%	44.5	58%	42
Congressman	49.8%	50.2	51%	49
Senator	54.3%	45.7	55%	45
Governor	46.8%	53.2	47%	53

None of the survey results shown in Table 1.1 digresses from the election statistics by a margin larger than that which might be attributed to sampling error alone. However, the largest discrepancy is found in the case of the presidential vote, and it seems likely that this

[3] A check of this kind would have been highly desirable in the present study. Because of the anonymity of the respondents, however, it was not possible.

two or three percentage-point over-report of the Eisenhower vote is not the result of sampling deviation, but of errors of report. If this is indeed an expression of a "band-wagon" effect following the Eisenhower victory, it is perhaps most noteworthy that the effect is so small.

One additional reference to election statistics should be brought to the reader's attention at this point. In the text which follows, a number of comparisons are made between the 1952 presidential vote and the vote for Truman and Dewey in 1948. In some cases—in Chapter V, for example—the record of the 1948 vote is taken from the Survey Research Center's study of that election carried out in November, 1948. In other cases, use is made of the 1952 respondents' report of their 1948 vote, as they remembered it when interviewed in the present study.

When we examine the distribution of the 1948 vote as reported by our respondents in 1952, we find a larger Truman vote than was actually cast. According to the election statistics of that year, Truman received 50 per cent of the votes cast for president, Dewey received 45 per cent, and 5 per cent went to the minor candidates, mainly Wallace and Thurmond. However, in reporting their 1948 votes, our 1952 respondents gave Truman 57 per cent, Dewey 41 per cent, and 2 per cent to the minor candidates. An inspection of Table 1.2 will disclose two factors which seem to be mainly responsible for this distortion: (a) It is apparent that the minor party vote was under-

TABLE 1.2

1948 PRESIDENTIAL VOTE BY REGIONS AS REPORTED IN
ELECTION STATISTICS AND IN THE 1952 PRE-ELECTION SURVEY

"IN 1948, YOU RE-MEMBER THAT TRU-MAN RAN AGAINST DEWEY. [IF VOTED] WHICH ONE DID YOU VOTE FOR?"	NORTHEAST		MIDWEST		SOUTH		FAR WEST	
	Election Statistics	1952 Survey	Election Statistics	1952 Survey	Election Statistics	1952 Survey	Election Statistics	1952 Survey
Truman	47%	52%	50%	54%	53%	77%	50%	52%
Dewey	48	46	48	46	32	19	46	46
Other	5	2	2	*	15	4	4	2
Total	100%	100%	100%	100%	100%	100%	100%	100%

* In all the tables in this report, the asterisk is used to denote an entry of less than one-half of one per cent. The dash is used to denote an entry of zero per cent.

reported in all four areas by our 1952 respondents, and the Truman vote was correspondingly over-reported. This probably resulted in large part from the wording of the question (see Table 1.2), which concentrated their answers on Truman and Dewey. If we assume that the missing minor party voters reported themselves as having voted for Truman (a very likely probability), we shall find that the data for the three regions outside the South conform closely to expectation. (b) In the South an additional factor was apparently present, an unwillingness to admit having voted for Dewey. This is the only region of the four in which the Dewey vote was not reported with reasonable accuracy, and the understatement there no doubt reflects the special political character of that region.

These discrepancies between the survey data and the criterion data drawn from election statistics must be regarded as defects of the survey. In the case of the 1952 data, these defects would appear to be minor. It is highly improbable that they could exert any significant influence on the analysis which is presented in this report. The error in the recall of the 1948 vote is more serious, but the reader should keep in mind that the error is largely a confusion of Democratic and third party votes rather than a confusion of Democratic and Republican votes. This fact makes these data more useful than they might otherwise have been.[4]

The Organization of the Report

The presentation of data in this report is organized in two major parts, followed by a short concluding chapter. Part One, entitled "The Character of the 1952 Election," is composed of four chapters devoted to a description of the voters : their previous voting record and the development of their 1952 decision to vote, their interest and participation in the campaign, their perception of the parties and candidates, and finally their demographic characteristics. Whenever possible, comparable data from our 1948 survey are also presented so that contrasts and similarities between the two elections may be seen.

Part One is intended to accomplish two objectives. In the first place, it is our expectation that the kind of "social accounting" it presents will have interest in itself for students and practitioners of politics. The project was conducted on a national basis in order to give the data national significance, and it was patterned after our 1948 study in order to make a comparison of the two elections possible.

The second purpose of the presentation in Part One is to provide a background for the analysis carried out in Part Two. The argument of the latter is based on a conception of the individual citizen acted upon by forces having relevance for him in the realm of political behavior. We are concerned with individual motivation. We approach this problem not at the level of external factors such as campaign appeals,

[4] It may be noted that all of the data presented in this report are reproduced exactly as they came from the two surveys. No attempt has been made to "improve" the data by introducing adjustments or other "corrections."

personal conversations, or other isolated aspects of the total stimulating situation leading up to Election Day, but rather at the level of the intervening variables of attitudes, perceptions, and group loyalties which mediate between the external environmental facts and the individual response. We have attempted to identify the major components that make up the total matrix of forces influencing the individual vote. It is hypothesized that these factors interact dynamically to determine the individual's behavior in the area of politics, stimulating his participation when they reinforce each other, inhibiting it when they are in conflict.

The reader will observe that while Part One deals specifically with the 1952 election and its relation to the election of 1948, Part Two uses the data of the 1952 election to demonstrate relationships which we believe to have more general significance. It is assumed that the three motivational factors which are considered in Part Two have relevance to all presidential elections, and that the type of analysis undertaken in Part Two might equally well be applied to the circumstances of any such election.

Part One

THE CHARACTER OF THE 1952 ELECTION

II

Conflict and Resolution in 1948 and 1952

The year 1952 was one of reversal of trends in American politics. Most dramatic was the overthrow of a Democratic regime which had held power in Washington for 20 years. Almost as impressive was the great increase in turnout of voters, with over 61.5 million people going to the polls, as compared with about 48.5 in 1948. The losing candidate for the presidency polled more votes—almost two and a quarter million more—than had the winner in 1948.

What gave rise to this great increase in the vote, and why did the vote go so heavily to the Republicans? These are the two questions with which this book is mainly concerned. In this opening chapter we propose to examine some of the characteristics of the vote as we observed it in our 1948 survey and again in 1952. We shall need this descriptive comparison of the two elections to provide a setting for our later analysis of factors which influenced the 1952 vote.

The Course of the Decision

It will be recalled that the pre-election polls of 1948 indicated a Republican victory, and that with few exceptions political forecasters seconded the predictions of the poll-takers. The Democratic victory in 1948 was an "upset," an upset resulting from crucial developments in the minds of the voters during the final weeks of the campaign.[1] It was the memory of that bitter experience that gave the pollsters pause in 1952, even though their data showed Eisenhower leading by a clear margin. Ironically, had they simply projected their pre-election percentages to a prediction of the election, as they had done disastrously in 1948, they would have come very close to the actual vote. For 1952, in contrast to 1948, was a year in which intentions reached in October were carried firmly into action in November.

What was the course of development of these voting decisions? In order to provide the fullest possible answer to this question, we would have had to design our study so as to interview our respondents

[1] For a full discussion of the factors affecting the 1948 predictions, see *The Pre-Election Polls of 1948* (New York: Social Science Research Council, 1949).

repeatedly over the period covered by the conventions and the campaign. We could thus have recorded each individual decision, or shift in decision, that took place during this period. Although our study was not based on this extended "panel" design, we did interview our respondents twice, once just before the election and once just after. These two sets of interviews make it possible for us to compare October intentions with November actions.

Comparing October, 1952, to October, 1948, we find a marked difference in the amount of uncertainty still remaining in the last month of the two campaigns. In 1948, the number of voters who were still undecided in October—19 per cent of the adult population, according to our survey at that time—was so great as to make prediction hazardous. The conventional assumption that these people would

TABLE 2.1

RELATION OF OCTOBER VOTING INTENTIONS TO VOTING BEHAVIOR
IN 1948 AND 1952 PRESIDENTIAL ELECTIONS

VOTE FOR PRESIDENTIAL CANDIDATE	INTENTIONS IN OCTOBER REGARDING VOTE FOR PRESIDENT							
	Will Vote Republican		Will Vote Democratic		Don't Know		Won't Vote	
	1948	1952	1948	1952	1948	1952	1948	1952
Voted Republican	71%	89%	5%	7%	19%	47%	5%	7%
Voted Democratic	14	4	66	79	40	38	10	4
Voted for minor party or vote not ascertained	2	*	4	1	10	2	1	1
Did not vote	13	7	25	13	31	13	84	88
Total	100%	100%	100%	100%	100%	100%	100%	100%
Number of cases	170	648	163	517	102	103	119	330

split their votes in the same proportions as the rest of the voters was one of the factors that led the poll-takers into error. By contrast, as of October, 1952, only 6 per cent of our national sample said they had not yet decided whom to vote for. In 1948 those undecideds who voted—and a majority of them did so—supported Truman two to one (Table 2.1); in 1952 the undecideds did split their votes like the rest of the voters, but their number was so small that, even if they had not, they would not have overturned the election.

The greater decisiveness in the late stages of the 1952 campaign, suggested by the low ratio of undecided voters in the pre-election survey, is also expressed in findings from the postelection study. In

1948 large numbers of people who in October apparently intended to vote did not vote at all (Table 2.1). In 1952 the percentages of such instances were reduced by half. Similarly, late shifts from one candidate to another, so damaging to the rejected candidate, played a significant role in the 1948 vote, when an appreciable number of people who planned in October to vote for Dewey changed candidates by Election Day. In 1952, late shifts from one candidate to the other were far fewer and balanced out to the advantage of neither candidate.

The effects of these differences between 1948 and 1952 are summarized in Table 2.2. There we see that although 32 per cent of the

TABLE 2.2

VOTING INTENTIONS (OCTOBER) AND VOTING BEHAVIOR, 1948 AND 1952 PRESIDENTIAL ELECTIONS (IN PERCENTAGE OF TOTAL SAMPLE)

VOTING BEHAVIOR COMPARED TO INTENTION	1948			
	TRUMAN		DEWEY	
	Intended to Vote for Him 28%	Voted for Him 32%	Intended to Vote for Him 29%	Voted for Him 27%
Voted as intended	19%	19%	21%	21%
Lost to candidate because:				
Did not vote	7		4	
Voted for opponent	1		4	
Voted other	1		—	
Gained by candidate because:				
Had intended to vote for opponent		4		1
Had been undecided†		9		5

	1952			
	EISENHOWER		STEVENSON	
	Intended to Vote for Him 40%	Voted for Him 43%	Intended to Vote for Him 32%	Voted for Him 31%
Voted as intended	35%	35%	26%	26%
Lost to candidate because:				
Did not vote	3		4	
Voted for opponent	2		2	
Gained by candidate because:				
Had intended to vote for opponent		2		2
Had been undecided†		5		3
Not ascertained	*	1	*	*

† Including a few who had not expected to vote.

sample reported voting for the winner in 1948, only 19 per cent said in October that they were going to vote for him and then did so.   The large remaining share of his vote came partly from people who had intended to vote for his opponent and partly from people who had been undecided.   In 1952, on the other hand, 43 per cent of the sample reported voting for the winner, of whom fully 35 per cent had told us in October that they intended to vote for him.   If we base our figures on only those who voted, we may say that in 1948 only two-thirds of the voters acted in accordance with intentions stated a few weeks before the election, whereas in 1952 four-fifths did so.   This does not necessarily mean that these relatively firm October intentions in 1952 were reached without conflict and uncertainty in the minds of the voters.   On the contrary, we shall see later in this chapter that there was a great deal of indecision during the 1952 campaign, just as there had been in 1948.

What was the course of events that lay behind this crystallization of voting intentions in October?   Was there a growing wave of Eisenhower support which reached its crest on Election Day?   Did the two parties begin the campaign on an equal footing, or were the Democrats fighting a losing battle from the very start?

The October-November change is not the only information our study offers regarding the course of the decision.   In the postelection survey, each respondent who reported that he had voted in the election just past was asked "How long before the election did you decide that you were going to vote the way you did?"   Of course we would not expect people to be able to answer such a question with complete accuracy; but the answers do enable us to divide those who felt they had known from the beginning how they would vote from those who by reason of conflict or procrastination had not come to a decision until later. Since we should not expect that errors in recall would differ systematically for those who voted one way and those who voted the other, a comparison of the responses of the two party groups should tell us whether they differed on this rough measure of the time at which their decisions crystallized.

By the use of this recall question, we are able to estimate how the division of sentiment regarding the two candidates stood at successive points during the pre- and postconvention period.   If we consider only the people who eventually voted for one or the other of the two major candidates, and look at their choices at the time they made their decisions, we find that General Eisenhower led Governor Stevenson from the very beginning.   Of those voters who said they had their minds made up—

1. Before the conventions, 52 per cent voted for Eisenhower.
2. At the time of the conventions, 60 per cent voted for Eisenhower.

3. During the campaign, 58 per cent voted for Eisenhower.
4. By the last two weeks of the campaign, 58 per cent voted for Eisenhower.

These percentages are cumulative and give an approximation of what a survey would have shown at each of these points during the election period. It is of interest that there was a slight Republican majority among those who had decided how they were going to vote even before the nominations were held. This majority increased when the nominees were known and held very stable through to Election Day.

An interesting contrast appears when we look at the same data from the 1948 election. Precisely the same question was asked voters in our postelection survey of that year. Of the 1948 voters for the two major candidates who said they had their minds made up—

1. Before the conventions, 49 per cent voted for Dewey.
2. At the time of the conventions, 52 per cent voted for Dewey.
3. During the campaign, 51 per cent voted for Dewey.
4. By the last two weeks of the campaign, 47 per cent voted for Dewey.

Although the fact that the 1948 data are based on a relatively small sample suggests caution in their interpretation, it appears that at the time of the nominations Dewey held a slight lead over Truman which he maintained through most of the campaign; but the decisions made during the final period of the campaign erased this advantage and elected Mr. Truman.

Thus we see that the 1948 and 1952 presidential elections afford a number of contrasts of interest to students of political behavior: first, the much greater public involvement in the 1952 election as expressed in the difference in turnout; second, the early and persistent division of voting intentions in 1952 in favor of the eventual winner; and third, the greater late-campaign stability of the individual voters' convictions regarding their chosen candidates. Related to these contrasts, of course, is the fact that after electing the Democratic party's candidate in five consecutive elections, in 1952 the voters decisively elected the candidate of the Republican party.

The Components of the Vote

Where did the flood of Eisenhower voters come from? Did the great increase in the Republican vote come from the ranks of young voters participating in a presidential election for the first time? Did the activated voters, those who had sat out the 1948 election, come into the electorate as a pro-Eisenhower bloc? Did the 1948 Republicans and Democrats stand by their 1952 candidates, or were there serious defections?

Table 2.3 shows us the basic components of the 1952 vote. There we see that both parties drew to the polls people who had not voted in 1948. The support of these voters was divided between the two

TABLE 2.3

RELATION OF 1948 TO 1952 VOTING BEHAVIOR IN
PRESIDENTIAL ELECTIONS

1952 VOTING BEHAVIOR	1948 VOTING BEHAVIOR				
	Voted for Dewey	Voted for Truman	Neglected to Vote	Not of Voting Age	Total Sample†
Voted for Eisenhower	90%	28%	20%	33%	43%
Voted for Stevenson	4	61	17	25	31
Voted otherwise, or vote not ascertained	*	1	1	—	*
Did not vote	6	10	62	42	26
Total	100%	100%	100%	100%	100%
Number of cases	429	592	467	96	1,614

† Included here but not represented in the preceding four columns are people who reported voting for Thurmond or Wallace in 1948 and some whose 1948 voting behavior was not ascertained.

candidates in about the same proportions as that of voters as a whole. The same holds true for the first-time voters—those who reached voting age after 1948. Both these groups that accounted for the increase in turnout gave Eisenhower a majority, but no larger a majority than the rest of the voters gave him. In other words, while they contributed to the Eisenhower victory, they did not contribute disproportionately. Much more striking is the record of the people who had supported the Democratic candidate in 1948. Roughly one-quarter of Truman's 1948 supporters voted for Eisenhower. Although this figure is probably slightly inflated because of the over-report of the Truman vote (see page 6), there can be no doubt that there were serious defections in the Democratic ranks. Shifts in the opposite direction—from Dewey to Stevenson—were negligible in percentage.

The relative influence of all these groups on the final vote may be seen more clearly if we present them as fractions of the total vote of each candidate, as is done on the opposite page in Figure 2.1. We must be sure to keep in mind in examining these data that every vote for a candidate counts equally, whether it comes from a new voter, a defector, or a party regular. It is clear that both candidates in 1952 received the largest portion of their support from their loyal partisans who had followed the party banner in 1948. This is the solid core which both parties depend on when they go into an election. In 1952 this core was a much larger proportion of the Democratic total vote than it was of

Of those who voted for Eisenhower:	Of those who voted for Stevenson:	
56%	3%	had voted for Dewey
24	74	had voted for Truman
1	1	had voted for minor candidates, or vote was not ascertained
13	16	had neglected to vote in 1948
5	5	were too young to vote in 1948
1	1	were people whose 1948 vote was not ascertained

FIG. 2.1

the Republican, although in actual numbers of voters the two party followings did not differ greatly in this respect. Each party added to its core vote a sizable number of newly activated voters and a somewhat smaller number of young voters. Each drew a small number of people who had voted for minor parties in 1948. The coup de grace was administered to the hopes of the Democratic party, however, by the addition to the Republican total of a substantial number of erstwhile Democrats. Had these 1948 Democrats stayed with Stevenson in 1952, General Eisenhower would not have gone to the White House.

Indecision and Conflict

The evidence seems to be clear that the campaign of 1948 was a much closer contest than was that of 1952. While in 1948 the issue was in doubt until the very end, the Eisenhower victory was strongly foreshadowed from the very beginning. This does not mean, of course, that the 1952 decision was clear-cut and easy for every individual voter. Procrastination and conflict were reported by many 1952 voters just as they had been in 1948, and in both years this indecision was most common among Democrats who were trying to decide whether or not to bolt their party.

One indication of indecisiveness on the part of the voter is delay in reaching his final choice of candidates. Although earlier studies[2] have attributed late decisions largely to indifference, there is considerable

[2] Lazarsfeld, P., Berelson, B., and Gaudet, H., *The People's Choice* (New York: Columbia University Press, 1948).

evidence in the present study that delay in voting decision is for many people a much more dynamic process than simple lack of interest would imply. We find data regarding time of voting decision in Table 2.4. Two kinds of comparison are possible in this table, time of decision in 1948 and 1952, and time of decision of Republican and Democratic voters.

TABLE 2.4

RELATION OF VOTE FOR PRESIDENT TO TIME OF
VOTING DECISION, 1948 AND 1952

"HOW LONG BEFORE THE ELECTION DID YOU DECIDE YOU WERE GOING TO VOTE THE WAY YOU DID?"	1948			1952		
	Dewey Voters	Truman Voters	All Voters	Eisen-hower Voters	Steven-son Voters	All Voters
Before the conventions	42%	36%	37%	27%	35%	31%
At the time of con-ventions	34	22	28	40	27	34
During the campaign	13	14	14	18	24	20
Within two weeks of election	3	14	9	10	7	9
On Election Day	2	3	3	1	4	2
Do not remember	2	1	1	1	—	1
Not ascertained	4	10	8	3	3	3
Total	100%	100%	100%	100%	100%	100%
Number of cases	178	212	421	687	494	1,195

It will at once be remarked, if we begin by considering the two elections, that there was no great difference between 1948 and 1952 in the proportions of voters who located their point of decision at various stages of the campaign. In both years, two-thirds of the voters said they had decided how to vote by or before the end of the conventions, and the proportion who said they had waited until the last two weeks is also the same for the two elections. This similarity must be viewed with some caution. In 1948, of those people who were still undecided in October one-third did not vote (Table 2.1); of the much smaller percentage who were undecided in October, 1952, only one-eighth did not vote. Thus, the findings based on the recall question, which was asked only of people who had voted, understate the total extent of indecision in 1948 through eliminating the relatively large group who evidently did not resolve their indecision in time and ended by not voting at all. Had this group finally voted, they would have increased the proportion of late deciders in the 1948 electorate appreciably.

Considering only voters, however, there is no difference in the two years in their reported time of decision.

When we divide the voters into their two parties in each year, as in the remaining columns of Table 2.4, we see a marked difference between 1948 and 1952. In 1948 early deciders constituted only 58 per cent of Truman's vote, but 76 per cent of Dewey's; in 1952, by contrast, both candidates received two-thirds of their respective votes from early deciders. Again, in 1948 the proportion of Truman voters who felt they had not made up their minds until two weeks or less before Election Day was three times as great as that of Dewey voters; in 1952 there was no such difference between the supporters of the two candidates. As we have seen earlier, the 1952 election was one in which decisions reached during the campaign months maintained rather than changed the choice that was crystallizing before the campaign began.

Do our data give us any explanation for the difference between the two years in the time of decision of the Republican and Democratic voters? An analysis of the previous voting records of these people provides a key. We know from our 1948 study that the waverers who made up their minds late in that campaign were largely former Roosevelt supporters who for one reason or another were flirting with the idea of voting for Dewey. Their conflict over factors associated with the two candidates apparently delayed their final decision until the latter phases of the campaign. In 1952 the situation was somewhat more complex, but the influence of conflict, especially among former Democrats, was again demonstrated in the time of decision.

To carry out this analysis we shall divide the voters into five groups: those who voted for Truman in '48 and Stevenson in '52; those who voted for Dewey and for Eisenhower; those who voted for Truman and for Eisenhower; those who did not vote in '48—whether because they were too young or for other reasons—and voted for Stevenson in '52; and the 1948 nonvoters who voted for Eisenhower in '52. (We shall omit the group who switched from Dewey to Stevenson, a group which was so small that too few cases appeared in the sample to be studied.) To facilitate discussion, we shall call these groups regular Democrats, regular Republicans, switchers, new Democrats, and new Republicans, respectively, although these names are based solely on votes for president and are therefore not applicable to the general political behavior of some of the people so classified.

In Table 2.5 we see the time of voting decision as recalled after the election by the people within each of the five groups. There we see that the regulars were earliest in deciding how they would vote. Whether Democratic or Republican, nearly four in ten of the regulars knew even before the conventions that they would vote for the candidate of the party they had supported four years before. Among the switchers, only one in seven had decided before the conventions to vote Republican. The new Democratic voters were between the switchers and the regulars in proportion of preconvention deciders; but new Republicans were no more likely to have chosen their man before the nominations than were the switchers.

TABLE 2.5

RELATION OF 1948–1952 PRESIDENTIAL VOTING PATTERN TO TIME
OF VOTING DECISION IN 1952

| TIME OF DECISION | 1948 AND 1952 VOTE FOR PRESIDENT† | | | | |
	Dewey, Eisenhower	No Vote, Eisenhower‡	Truman, Eisenhower	No Vote, Stevenson‡	Truman, Stevenson
Before the conventions	37%	16%	14%	29%	37%
At the time of conventions	44	41	32	29	27
During campaign	12	23	29	25	23
Within two weeks of election	4	13	20	7	6
On Election Day	*	1	2	7	3
Do not remember	*	1	1	—	—
Not ascertained	3	5	2	3	4
Total	100%	100%	100%	100%	100%
Number of cases	385	125	165	104	362

† Voters who switched from Dewey to Stevenson were uncommon; therefore too few appeared in the sample to be treated here.
‡ Voters who came of age after 1948, as well as others who did not vote in 1948, are included.

By the time of the conventions, when the candidates were known but before the campaigns were under way, 81 per cent of the regular Republicans, 64 per cent of the regular Democrats, but only 46 per cent of the switchers, had their minds made up. The new voters were between the regulars and the switchers. Very late deciders—those who decided within two weeks of the election—were more frequent among the switchers than in any other group.

The crucial fact here is that wavering Democrats were responsible for most of the late decisions in both 1948 and 1952. In 1948 former Roosevelt voters who had been considering Dewey either returned to Truman in the late stages of the campaign or did not vote at all. Relatively few of them finally decided for Dewey and cast their vote for him.   In 1952 many former Democrats were again tempted to cross party lines, and this time the temptation was apparently stronger: a large number of them made their decision for Eisenhower, late in the campaign in many cases, and supported him on Election Day.   In both years, people who had voted Republican in the previous presidential election were notably infrequent among the late deciders.

It will also be noted that on the average the regular Democrats tended to arrive at their decision later than the regular Republicans. This fact suggests that the forces that drew so many former Democratic voters to Eisenhower in 1952 also affected some who stayed with the Democrats in 1952, creating a certain amount of indecision and conflict, although not ultimately capturing their votes.   Conversely, the absence of forces that might have turned usual Republican voters toward the Democrats in 1952 is evidenced not only by the fact that such switches were few, but by the very early crystallization of the regular Republican vote.   The tendency of regular Republicans to reach their decision earlier on the average than regular Democrats offset the amount of vacillation among the Truman-Eisenhower switchers, with the result that, as we have seen, the average time of decision of Eisenhower voters as a whole was very similar to that of the Stevenson voters.

One other comparison in Table 2.5 is of interest.   Although new Democrats were a little later in reaching their decision than regular Democrats, they were much closer to the regular Democrats than new Republicans were to regular Republicans.   Although by itself this particular datum will not bear much interpretation, it will become significant in connection with comparisons to be made later of the two groups of new voters.

When we look at the October intentions of our five groups, as shown in Table 2.6, we get much the same impressions as those resulting from the recall question.   Again we see that the final decision had been reached at that time by a greater proportion of the regular Democrats and Republicans than any of the other groups, and that the switchers included the largest proportion of people whose vote was not yet stabilized.

A second question which was intended to reveal the relative decisiveness with which the voting decision was made was, "Did you ever think during the campaign that you might vote for [opposite candidate]?"   The answers to this question show us differences of the expected kind among the voting groups (Table 2.7).   Such a question may have different meanings for different people, and probably not all who answered affirmatively had considered the possibility with equal earnestness.   Nevertheless, we can accept the finding that those who voted for Stevenson were more likely to have thought about voting for

TABLE 2.6

RELATION OF 1948–1952 PRESIDENTIAL VOTING PATTERN
TO VOTING INTENTION IN OCTOBER, 1952

VOTING INTENTION IN OCTOBER, 1952	1948 AND 1952 VOTE FOR PRESIDENT				
	Dewey, Eisenhower	No Vote, Eisenhower	Truman, Eisenhower	No Vote, Stevenson	Truman, Stevenson
Will vote for Eisenhower	95%	75%	67%	9%	3%
Will vote for Stevenson	1	6	12	79	86
Do not know; undecided	3	6	16	8	7
Will not vote	1	11	3	2	3
Not ascertained	—	2	2	2	1
Total	100%	100%	100%	100%	100%
Number of cases	385	125	165	104	362

Eisenhower than vice versa, and that among the Eisenhower voters the switchers were the most likely to have considered voting for Stevenson.

Table 2.7 also presents a comparison of the 1948 and 1952 survey data on consideration of the opposing candidate. The findings are similar to the 1948–1952 comparison on time of decision observed in Table 2.4. They are affected by the same large drop-out of uncertain people in 1948 that was noted in connection with Table 2.4. Had these people voted they would doubtless have increased the proportion of the 1948 electorate who oscillated between the two candidates. As it was, however, the proportions of voters who considered the opposing candidate were very similar in the two years.

One further evidence of conflict expressed in the 1952 vote, the splitting of ballots, needs to be reviewed in this chapter. The freedom to vote for different parties in executive and legislative offices is one of the peculiarities of the American political system, and it is a freedom which is widely exercised. The total phenomenon of ballot-splitting deserves more detailed examination than we can give it here; our interest at this point is in its significance as an indication of divided motivations in the mind of the voter.

One-third of the voters cast split ballots in 1952 (compared with a little over one-quarter in 1948). Outside the South, Eisenhower supporters were a little more likely than Stevenson supporters to split their ballots—the proportion was about one-third in both cases

TABLE 2.7

RELATION OF 1948–1952 PRESIDENTIAL VOTING PATTERN TO CONSIDERATION GIVEN TO VOTING FOR THE OPPOSING CANDIDATE IN 1952

"DID YOU EVER THINK DURING THE [1952] CAMPAIGN THAT YOU MIGHT VOTE FOR [THE OTHER CANDIDATE]?"	1948 AND 1952 VOTE FOR PRESIDENT					ALL VOTERS	
	Dewey, Eisenhower	No Vote, Eisenhower	Truman, Eisenhower	No Vote, Stevenson	Truman, Stevenson	1948	1952
Yes	12%	22%	31%	36%	21%	19%	22%
No	88	78	67	64	78	73	78
Other	—	—	1	—	1	3	*
Not ascertained	—	—	1	—	*	5	*
Total	100%	100%	100%	100%	100%	100%	100%
Number of cases	385	125	165	104	362	421	1,195

(Table 2.8). Ticket-splitters outside the South usually voted the entire national ticket of one party, shifting only when they came to state or local candidates. In the South, most voters chose one of two voting patterns: either they voted a straight Democratic ticket, or they voted for Eisenhower while splitting their tickets. A quarter of

TABLE 2.8

RELATION OF VOTE FOR PRESIDENT TO SPLITTING OF BALLOT, 1952 ELECTION; IN THE SOUTH, ELSEWHERE, AND IN THE COUNTRY AS A WHOLE

ALLOCATION OF VOTES FOR ALL CANDIDATES IN 1952†	THE SOUTH		ALL OTHER REGIONS		ENTIRE COUNTRY		
	Eisenhower Voters	Stevenson Voters	Eisenhower Voters	Stevenson Voters	Eisenhower Voters	Stevenson Voters	TOTAL
Voted straight ticket	26%	93%	65%	69%	59%	75%	66%
Split away from their presidential votes:							
At national level only	8	3	2	4	3	4	3
At state or local level only	13	3	24	19	23	15	19
At both levels	53	1	9	8	15	6	12
Total	100%	100%	100%	100%	100%	100%	100%
Number of cases	104	111	583	383	687	494	1,181

† The questions were: "Whom did you vote for for president?" "How about the election for United States senator? Did you vote for a candidate for senator? Whom did you vote for?" "How about the vote for congressman? Did you vote for a candidate for Congress? Whom did you vote for?" "How about the vote for governor here in [your state]? Did you vote for one of the candidates for governor? Whom did you vote for?" "How about the elections for other state and local offices? Did you vote a straight ticket or did you vote for candidates from different parties? [If voted a straight ticket] Which party did you vote for?"
    Those who voted a straight ticket except in the case of senator or congressman are categorized as splitting "at the national level only." Those who voted for the presidential and congressional candidates of one party, but for some or all of the state and local candidates of the other party, are shown as splitting "at state or local level only." Those who voted for the presidential candidate of one party, but for one or more candidates of the other party at both the national and local levels, are shown as "splitting at both levels."

the Southern Eisenhower supporters voted a straight ticket; over 90 per cent of the Southern Stevenson supporters voted a straight ticket.

Table 2.9 summarizes the performances of the groups we have classified according to their 1948 and 1952 votes for president. Regular Democrats were the least likely of all voters to split their tickets, but new Democrats and regular Republicans were only a little more likely to do so. The commonest voting pattern of ballot-splitters in these three groups was to vote for the presidential and congressional candidates of one party, shifting to the other party only for state or local candidates.

Consistent with their other indications of vacillation and conflict, the Truman-Eisenhower switchers were most likely to have split their ballots.   Only one-third of this ambivalent group embraced the entire

TABLE 2.9

RELATION OF 1948–1952 PRESIDENTIAL VOTING PATTERN TO
SPLITTING OF BALLOT, 1952 ELECTION

ALLOCATION OF VOTES FOR ALL CANDIDATES IN 1952†	1948 AND 1952 VOTE FOR PRESIDENT				
	Dewey, Eisenhower	No Vote, Eisenhower	Truman, Eisenhower	No Vote, Stevenson	Truman, Stevenson
Voted straight ticket	70%	59%	36%	70%	77%
Split away from their presidential votes:					
At national level only	3	2	4	4	4
At state or local level only	20	22	28	17	14
At both levels	7	17	32	9	5
Total	100%	100%	100%	100%	100%
Number of cases	385	125	165	104	362

† For the questions used and an explanation of the categories, see Table 2.8.

Republican ticket when they crossed party lines to vote for Eisenhower. An equal number supported Democrats at both the national and local levels.

The behavior of the new Republicans also attracts our attention in Table 2.9.   Four in ten split their tickets (compared with three in ten new Democrats), and like the switchers many voted for Democratic candidates for Congress as well as for local office.   This fact, together with the finding (Table 2.5) that relatively few new Republicans reached their presidential voting decision until Eisenhower's candidacy was expected or known, suggests that on the average the new Republicans may be less firmly attached to the Republican party, even on the national level, than new Democrats are to the Democratic party, and that psychologically many of them were more like switchers in 1952—"Democrats for Eisenhower"—than like Republicans.

Finally, the reader will note that Table 2.9 documents very clearly the manner in which General Eisenhower ran ahead of the Republican ticket. All of the three groups of Eisenhower voters gave a significant fraction of their vote to Democratic candidates for the House and Senate. This was least true of the Republican regulars, but since they were the largest of the three groups their defections from the party ticket were not insignificant. There were also Stevenson voters who supported Republicans at the congressional level, but their proportions were not large, and they were obviously outnumbered by Eisenhower voters supporting Democrats.

Summary

We have now reviewed an array of data regarding the development of the 1952 presidential vote. We have compared the election of 1952 with that of 1948 and have found a complicated pattern of contrasts and similarities.

On the one hand, it is clear that the 1952 campaign was from the beginning a more one-sided contest than was true in 1948. It seems also true that there was less uncertainty in the minds of the 1952 voters as the election approached, less last-minute switching from one candidate to the other, and less failure to carry through on voting intentions. In these respects, the 1952 voters appear to have been more highly motivated, more decisive, and more unequivocal in their voting decisions than were their 1948 counterparts.

However, when we examine the character of these individual decisions we find at least as many people who showed evidence of conflict in reaching their decision to vote in 1952 as we found in 1948. There were just as many who reported putting off their decision until late in the campaign, there were an equal number who gave serious consideration to the candidate they finally voted against, and there were even more who split their ballots between the two parties.

To resolve this apparent contradiction, we must anticipate our later argument regarding the motivation of the voter. The burden of that argument (to be developed in Chapter XII) holds that the total motivation to vote was higher in 1952 than it had been in 1948. Moreover, it maintains that the increase in forces on the voters in 1952 was largely favorable to the Republican candidate and was sufficient to tip the total balance of forces in his direction.

In contrast to 1952, 1948 was a year in which voters generally were not highly motivated, and in which the balance of partisan forces on the voters was much more even. Consequently, many people were uncertain both as to whether they would vote and how they would vote. Among those who did vote, indecision and conflict were found largely among Democrats attracted for one reason or another to the Republican candidate. A sizable number of Democrats considered voting Republican at some time during the 1948 campaign, only to change their minds at the last minute and return to the Democratic fold. In 1948 the factors favoring the Republican candidate were strong enough to create much indecision among many Democrats but not strong enough to hold their votes.

The 1952 election also created considerable conflict in the minds of the voters, and this conflict was again concentrated largely among Democrats attracted to the Republican candidate. In 1952, however, the increase and greater inbalance of motivating forces resulted in a situation in which, in spite of conflict, more people made a definite decision to vote, more people stayed with the decision once made, and more people carried the decision into an actual vote. For one reason or another, Democrats were attracted to the Republican camp in both 1948 and 1952, but in 1952 this attraction was strong enough to prevent a repetition of the last minute uncertainty and change which took place in the previous election.

III

Public Interest and Participation in the Campaign

The effectiveness of political motivation may be measured by the degree to which it brings about political action. The most crucial demonstration of the strength of the forces motivating the public comes on Election Day, and in 1952 the high turnout of voters provided a convincing record of the level of public concern with that election.

Of course, voting is not the only way that the public can participate in a presidential election. The campaigns offer countless opportunities for the interested citizen to express his impulse to support his candidate or party. In 1952 there were organized "Volunteers" and "Independents" and "Citizens" for Eisenhower and Stevenson all over the country. Crowds turned out to greet the presidential candidates' campaign trains. Candidates for state and local office spoke at countless luncheons and dinners and rallies. Television and radio brought the sights and sounds of campaign activities into millions of homes time and again. One had the impression of tremendous activity. How many citizens took part in it?

A number of questions in both the pre- and postelection surveys in 1952 were designed to obtain some estimate of the extent of participation in the campaign. These covered several kinds of participation, ranging from actual canvassing in behalf of a party or candidate, through informal attempts to influence the votes of friends and neighbors, and on down to the passive participation of the stay-at-home radio-listener, television-viewer, and newspaper- or magazine-reader. An attempt was made also to measure the extent of psychological involvement in the outcome of the presidential election—to discover how many citizens felt they "cared" who won.

Participation

Three questions dealt with direct participation in organized campaign efforts: (a) "Did you give any money, or buy tickets, or anything, to help the campaign for one of the parties or candidates?" (b) "Did you go to any political meetings, rallies, dinners, or things like that?"

(c) "Did you do any other work for one of the parties or candidates?"[1]

The answers are tabulated in Table 3.1. Of the total sample, 4 per cent reported that they had contributed financially in some way to a party or candidate, 7 per cent attended campaign meetings of some kind, and 3 per cent did some sort of party work. As we would expect, people who participated in one of these ways were often the ones who participated in the other ways. Altogether, a little over 11 per cent of all adults—one person in nine—took part in these organized party efforts. To political enthusiasts these figures may appear discouragingly small, for their size can be evaluated only against the yardstick of one's expectations. But it must be remembered that each of the figures, even the smallest, represents several million people scattered over thousands of communities.

In percentage of active partisans, Stevenson and Eisenhower supporters did not differ appreciably but, as there were more Eisenhower supporters, the active Eisenhower partisans exceeded Stevenson workers greatly in actual number. The questions were not restricted to activity on behalf of the presidential candidates only, but it is safe to assume that most people who engaged in some activity did so in support of the party of their presidential choice.

Many more people were informally involved in the campaigning than took part in organized party work. About a quarter of the sample, including even people who did not themselves vote, reported that in talking to others they had attempted to gain converts for their side. Here Eisenhower voters appear to have exceeded Stevenson people, not only in actual number, but even in percentage.

From the information on voting behavior and the responses to these four questions—the three about organized party work and the one about informal, individual "campaigning"—we may construct a crude but serviceable scale of political activity by means of which people may be sorted into three categories: (a) those who voted and also participated in the campaign; (b) those who voted but took no other active part; (c) those who did not vote. Some nonvoters were more involved politically than others and did talk politics in a partisan manner, or even in a few cases contributed money and effort to party work; but as the act of voting is, except in uncommon circumstances, the *sine qua non* of political participation for the ordinary citizen, these people are grouped in our scale with other nonvoters. The results of this classification, hereafter referred to as the *index of political participation*, appear in Table 3.2. This index is frequently used in succeeding chapter,

[1] A fourth question, "Do you belong to any political club or organizations," produced too few affirmative responses to support statistical analysis—approximately 2 per cent of the total sample.

particularly in Part Two, as a device for measuring the relation between political attitudes, or other characteristics, and involvement in politics.

Vicarious participation in campaign activities is available to practically every American through the mass media of communication. The

TABLE 3.1

RELATION OF VOTING BEHAVIOR AND CHOICE OF PRESIDENTIAL
CANDIDATE TO PARTICIPATION IN CAMPAIGN

NATURE OF PARTICIPATION	VOTED FOR:		DID NOT VOTE, BUT PREFERRED: †		TOTAL SAMPLE‡
	Eisenhower	Stevenson	Eisenhower	Stevenson	
Organized party activities "Did you give any money or buy tickets or anything to help the campaign for one of the parties or candidates?" Yes	6%	4%	1%	2%	4%
"Did you go to any political meetings, rallies, dinners, or things like that?" Yes	9%	8%	1%	2%	7%
"Did you do any other work for one of the parties or candidates?" Yes	5%	3%	2%	*	3%
Answered yes to one or more of the above	15%	11%	3%	4%	11%
Informal participation "Did you talk to any people to try to show them why they should vote for one of the parties or candidates?" Yes	36%	28%	15%	12%	27%
Number of cases	687	494	175	202	1,614

† Those who reported not voting were asked, "Who would you have voted for if you had voted?"
‡ Included here is a small number of cases of people who voted or would have voted for minor-party candidates or whose votes or preferences were not ascertained.

TABLE 3.2

The Index of Participation†

DEGREE OF PARTICIPATION	VOTED FOR OR PREFERRED:‡		TOTAL SAMPLE
	Eisenhower	Stevenson	
High (voted, and engaged in other political activity)	32%	23%	27%
Medium (voted, but did not engage in other activity)	48	48	47
Low (did not vote)§	20	29	26
Total	100%	100%	100%
Number of cases	862	696	1,614

† For the kinds of participation on which the index is based see Table 3.1.
‡ Included here are nonvoters who specified the candidate they "would have voted for" if they had voted.
§ About 4 per cent did not vote but participated in other ways, chiefly by "talking to people." They are included in the "low" category.

people in the survey were asked whether they had read about the campaign in newspapers, listened to any campaign speeches on the radio, watched any campaign programs on television, or read about the campaign in magazines. Almost 95 per cent said the campaign had reached them through at least one of these media (Table 3.3), 81 per cent said it had reached them through at least two, and one out of every six adults had been reached by all four media. Asked whether they "read [listened, watched] quite a lot or not very much," 65 per cent replied that they had followed the campaign "quite a lot" in at least one of the four media.

There was no great difference between Eisenhower and Stevenson voters in the percentages who followed the campaign (Table 3.4), but there was some tendency for Eisenhower voters to utilize a greater variety of news sources. Almost one-fourth of Eisenhower's voters reported getting information from all four sources, whereas only about one-sixth of Stevenson's did so. The Eisenhower voters also reported much more magazine reading and somewhat more newspaper reading.[2] These differences may be less an evidence of the political influence of the media than of the socio-economic differences—in level of education and of income—of Republicans and Democrats.

The mass media are, of course, the chief avenues by which the parties

[2] The survey data on mass media in the campaign are much more extensively treated by the present authors in "Television and the Election," *Scientific American*, May, 1953, **188**, No. 5.

TABLE 3.3

RELATION OF NUMBER OF MASS MEDIA IN WHICH CAMPAIGN
WAS FOLLOWED TO VOTING BEHAVIOR

VOTING BEHAVIOR	NUMBER OF MEDIA USED†					TOTAL SAMPLE
	None	One	Two	Three	Four	
Voted for Eisenhower	13%	27%	39%	50%	58%	43%
Voted for Stevenson	17	24	32	34	30	31
Did not vote	70	49	29	16	12	26
Total	100%	100%	100%	100%	100%	100%
Number of cases	92	218	481	551	272	1,614
Proportion of total sample	6%	13%	30%	34%	17%	100%

† The four media represented are newspapers, radio, television, and magazines. The following questions were asked: "We're mainly interested in this interview in finding out whether people paid much attention to the election campaign this year. Take newspapers, for instance. Did you read about the campaign in any newspaper?" "How about radio? Did you listen to any speeches or discussions about the campaign on the radio?" "Did you watch any programs about the campaign on television?" "How about magazines? Did you read about the campaign in any magazines?" After each of these questions respondents who answered affirmatively were asked, "Would you say you read [listened, watched] quite a lot or not very much?" but the percentages here include all who made any use of the media, whether "quite a lot" or "not very much."

TABLE 3.4

RELATION OF VOTING BEHAVIOR TO NUMBER OF MASS MEDIA
IN WHICH CAMPAIGN WAS FOLLOWED

NUMBER OF MEDIA†	VOTED FOR:		DID NOT VOTE	TOTAL SAMPLE
	Eisenhower	Stevenson		
None	2%	3%	15%	6%
One	8	11	25	13
Two	27	32	32	30
Three	40	38	21	34
Four	23	16	7	17
Total	100%	100%	100%	100%
Number of cases	687	494	419	1,614

† The four media represented are newspapers, radio, television, and magazines. For the questions on which the data are based, see the footnote to Table 3.3.

seek to reach the electorate, but personal canvassing is still employed by both parties. In response to the question, "Did anybody from either one of the parties call you up or come around and talk to you during the campaign," 12 per cent reported that they had been thus solicited. Inasmuch as our inquiry into these postcampaign recollections of such calls was very limited, the data obtained were not very substantial. In general, they pointed to a tendency among workers of both parties to neglect previous nonvoters, and also to concentrate a large part of their efforts on the particular kinds of voters who would be expected to support the party they represented.

Sense of Involvement in the Outcome

Interest and psychological involvement in politics may exist without producing any of the particular outward manifestations examined above. It is possible to be much concerned about the outcome of an election without interjecting one's political beliefs into social conversation and without going to rallies. Conversely, although one must assume that, as a rule, voting is an evidence of interest and nonvoting an evidence of lack of interest, in individual cases the rule may not apply. As a part of the study, three direct questions were asked in the pre-election interviews concerning three somewhat different aspects of interest in the 1952 election.

Responses to the first of these, ". . . would you say that you have been very much interested, somewhat interested, or not much interested in following the political campaigns so far this year," are summarized in Tables 3.5 and 3.6. Over one-third said they were very much interested, one-third said they were somewhat interested, and a little more than one-quarter were not interested. Eisenhower voters tended to be more interested than Stevenson voters, but this difference did not appear among the nonvoting supporters of the two candidates. We would expect degree of interest to be associated with inclination to vote, and we see in Table 3.6 that there is such a relationship: interested people were much more likely to vote than uninterested people. But it may be noted, as the first indication of a phenomenon we shall observe repeatedly, that interested Democrats were somewhat less likely to vote than interested Republicans. (It may be noted, too, that one out of five voters, for either candidate, said in October that they were not even "somewhat" interested in following the campaign.)

The statement that one was interested in following the campaign undoubtedly could have different meanings to different people. It might, for example, refer to what is sometimes called spectator interest. In that case, the election would be on a par with other competitive spectacles, and interest would not necessarily be accompanied by a

TABLE 3.5

Relation of Voting Behavior and Presidential Preference to Interest in Following the Campaign

"Would you say that you have been very much interested, somewhat interested, or not much interested in following the political campaign so far this year?"†	Preferred Eisenhower			Preferred Stevenson			Total Sample
	Voters	Nonvoters	Total	Voters	Nonvoters	Total	
Very much interested	49%	19%	44%	39%	18%	33%	37%
Somewhat interested	32	31	32	37	36	37	34
Not much interested	18	48	23	23	43	29	28
Not ascertained	1	2	1	1	3	1	1
Total	100%	100%	100%	100%	100%	100%	100%
Number of cases	687	175	862	494	202	696	1,614

† This question was asked in the pre-election interview in October. The classification by vote or—in the case of nonvoters—preference is based, as in the preceding tables, on data obtained in the postelection survey.

TABLE 3.6

RELATION OF PRESIDENTIAL PREFERENCE AND INTEREST IN THE CAMPAIGN
TO VOTING BEHAVIOR

VOTING BEHAVIOR	PREFERRED EISENHOWER			PREFERRED STEVENSON		
	Interested in Following Campaign :†					
	Very Much	Some-what	Not Much	Very Much	Some-what	Not Much
Voted	91%	80%	59%	84%	72%	57%
Did not vote	9	20	41	16	28	43
Total	100%	100%	100%	100%	100%	100%
Number of cases	367	277	205	228	257	202

† The question on which these groupings are based is shown in Table 3.5.

sense of concern about the outcome. Hence another question, ". . . would you say that you personally care a good deal which party wins the presidential election this fall, or that you don't care very much which party wins?" About one-tenth said they cared not at all, and another fifth cared little (Table 3.7). Eisenhower voters were the most likely to care very much, while supporters of Eisenhower who did not vote were most likely to care very little. Here again we observe that the degree of interest is much more closely related to voting among Republicans than among Democrats. Over one-quarter of the Stevenson followers who cared a good deal did not vote (Table 3.8).

The third question directed at measuring concern was, "Do you think it will make a good deal of difference to the country whether the Democrats or the Republicans win the elections this November, or that it won't make much difference which side wins?" About one in every three adults felt it would make no difference at all (Table 3.9). Two out of five thought it would make "some" difference. Only one in five said it would make a "good deal" of difference. Those who voted for one presidential candidate did not differ in this respect from those who voted for the other. Nonvoting Eisenhower supporters were again very low in their expression of concern over the election. Among Eisenhower followers, those who thought the outcome of the election would make a good deal of difference to the country were more likely to vote than those who thought it would not (Table 3.10). Among Stevenson followers, this was not true. Almost one-third of the Stevenson people who thought the outcome was important did not vote.

Failure to vote may spring from any of several causes. The technical cause, inability to meet residence requirements for eligibility to vote,

TABLE 3.7

RELATION OF VOTING BEHAVIOR AND PRESIDENTIAL PREFERENCE TO DEGREE OF CONCERN ABOUT OUTCOME OF ELECTION

"WOULD YOU SAY YOU PERSONALLY CARE A GOOD DEAL WHICH PARTY WINS THE PRESIDENTIAL ELECTION THIS FALL, OR THAT YOU DON'T CARE VERY MUCH WHICH PARTY WINS?"	PREFERRED EISENHOWER			PREFERRED STEVENSON			TOTAL SAMPLE
	Voters	Nonvoters	Total	Voters	Nonvoters	Total	
Care very much	36%	17%	32%	26%	24%	25%	28%
Care somewhat	38	28	36	44	40	43	38
It depends	*	1	1	1	1	1	1
Don't care very much	18	33	21	19	18	19	20
Don't care at all	6	19	8	8	13	9	10
Don't know or not ascertained	2	2	2	2	4	3	3
Total	100%	100%	100%	100%	100%	100%	100%
Number of cases	687	175	862	494	202	696	1,614

TABLE 3.8

RELATION OF PRESIDENTIAL PREFERENCE AND CONCERN ABOUT OUTCOME
OF PRESIDENTIAL ELECTION TO VOTING BEHAVIOR

VOTING BEHAVIOR	PREFERRED EISENHOWER				PREFERRED STEVENSON			
	Concerned about Outcome of Election:†							
	Very Much	Some- what	Not Much	Not at All	Very Much	Some- what	Not Much	Not at All
Voted	90%	84%	68%	53%	72%	73%	72%	61%
Did not vote	10	16	32	47	28	27	28	39
Total	100%	100%	100%	100%	100%	100%	100%	100%
Number of cases	274	311	183	72	176	298	131	67

† The question on which these groupings are based is shown in Table 3.7.

was evidently not much of a factor in 1952. Only 12 per cent of the people who reported that they had not voted said they were disfranchised because of inability to meet such requirements; in terms of the total population, this means 3 out of every 100 adults living in private households (whereas 26 out of every 100 were nonvoters). In any case, we would not expect this factor to involve Democrats appreciably more than Republicans. In some places Negroes, who were very strongly pro-Democratic even in 1952, are debarred from voting by local customs and institutions, a fact that influences the Democratic showing somewhat, although their proportion in the total population is small.

Aside from the effect of residence requirements, there are obviously a variety of other obstacles that may prevent even a highly interested person from voting. Sickness, absence from home, conflicting obligations, and other personal considerations undoubtedly take their toll of the potential electorate. Earlier research has indicated, however, that the major reason for failure to vote is apathy—lack of motivation.[3]

[3] See, for example, Harold F. Gosnell, *Non-Voting: Causes and Methods of Control* (Chicago: University of Chicago Press, 1924); James K. Pollock, *Voting Behavior: A Case Study* (Ann Arbor: University of Michigan Press, 1939); and G. M. Connelly and H. H. Field, "The Non-Voter—Who He Is, What He Thinks," *Public Opinion Quarterly*, Summer, 1944, **8**, 175–87. For theoretical discussions of political indifference or apathy, see David Riesman and Nathan Glazer, "Criteria for Political Apathy," in A. W. Gouldner (ed.), *Studies in Leadership* (New York: Harper & Brothers, 1950), 505–59; and Morris Rosenberg, "The Meaning of Politics in Mass Society," *Public Opinion Quarterly*, Spring, 1951, **15**, 5–15.

TABLE 3.9

RELATION OF VOTING BEHAVIOR AND PRESIDENTIAL PREFERENCE TO PERCEPTION OF IMPORTANCE OF ELECTION TO THE COUNTRY

"Do you think it would make a good deal of difference to the country whether the Democrats or Republicans win the elections . . . or that it won't make much difference which side wins?"	Preferred Eisenhower			Preferred Stevenson			Total Sample
	Voters	Nonvoters	Total	Voters	Nonvoters	Total	
A good deal of difference	22%	11%	20%	22%	24%	23%	21%
Some difference, minor differences	43	33	41	42	35	40	40
It depends	1	1	1	1	—	1	1
No difference	30	44	33	30	29	30	32
Don't know or not ascertained	4	11	5	5	12	6	6
Total	100%	100%	100%	100%	100%	100%	100%
Number of cases	687	175	862	494	202	696	1,614

TABLE 3.10

RELATION OF PRESIDENTIAL PREFERENCE AND PERCEPTION OF IMPORTANCE
OF ELECTION TO THE COUNTRY TO VOTING BEHAVIOR

VOTING BEHAVIOR	PREFERRED EISENHOWER			PREFERRED STEVENSON		
	Importance of Outcome to the Country :†					
	Much	Some	None	Much	Some	None
Voted	89%	83%	75%	69%	75%	73%
Did not vote	11	17	25	31	25	27
Total	100%	100%	100%	100%	100%	100%
Number of cases	170	325	322	157	257	236

† The question on which these groupings are based is shown in Table 3.9.

The tables we have presented in this chapter have demonstrated that a sizable minority of the public had virtually no interest or concern with the 1952 election, and that, at least among the potential Eisenhower supporters, fewer of these apathetic people did vote than did those who were involved in the election. The fact that a good many of the apparently disinterested people actually voted, however, implies that they were activated by other factors than personal concern with the outcome of the election.

Summary

The assumption of a responsive and participating electorate is one of the basic propositions underlying the democratic concept of government. We have seen in this chapter the extent to which the public actually took part in the 1952 election.

If we regard passive attention to radio or television speeches or newspaper articles as participation in the campaign, then it can be said that virtually the entire public took part in the 1952 election. If we think of voting as the *sine qua non* of participation, the figure was still quite high—three out of four of the people our sample represented, although many of these voters seemed to have very little interest in how the election came out. If we consider only the more individual, less institutionalized, forms of activity, we find that the proportion of political "actives" dropped off to a very small minority of the total population.

Despite the appearance of feverish public interest which characterized the 1952 campaign, it seems evident that the bulk of the political activity that went on during that period was concentrated in a fraction of perhaps one-tenth of the public. They were the meeting-goers, money-givers, party-workers. Most people took the campaign much more casually, and approximately one person in three did not seem interested enough to care which party won.

If we think of these differences in extent of participation as reflecting differences in strength of motivation, we would conclude that the population divides into contrasting groups of strongly and weakly motivated people, with the bulk of the public falling between these extremes. We shall examine the characteristics of political motivation more fully in Part Two of this report.

IV

The Popular Image of the Parties and the Candidates

A prominent subject of debate in the 1952 election postmortems was the question of who won the election—the victorious party, or its candidate? This question was not peculiar to 1952, but it seemed particularly relevant to that election because of the dramatic change of control of the national government and the fact that the winning candidate was not a political figure but a popular military hero never before associated with a political party. Such a question is an obvious oversimplification, and our research does not undertake to answer it in this form. Voting behavior is a complex involving many factors, some of them doubtless varying in relative weight from time to time, but all to be taken into account in any serious attempt to understand why people vote as they do.

Voting behavior does not take place in a vacuum. At any given time at which we choose to observe it, we are confronted first with the particular features of the political environment that happen to be most prominent at that time. In 1952 these were such as to focus our attention strongly on the people's reactions to the candidates as well as the parties. Hence, in this chapter we shall attempt to delineate the people's perceptions of Eisenhower and Stevenson as revealed in response to direct questions and also in spontaneous comments throughout the interviews. We shall deal in the same way with perceptions of the two parties. We shall present data bearing on several aspects of the popular perceptions of the parties and candidates: their relative popularity, the specific positive and negative characteristics most prominent in the public mind, and the differences between these perceptions and comparable perceptions in 1948.

It should be stressed that this chapter does not attempt a motivational analysis of the 1952 vote. The images people had of the parties and candidates undoubtedly bore some relation to their motives for voting as they did, but the reader is cautioned not to interpret this relationship too directly.

Perceptions of the Parties

Most of the data on the respondents' perceptions of the parties were gathered in four questions asked in the pre-election interview. Each respondent, regardless of his own political inclinations, was asked the following questions:

> I'd like to ask you what you think are the good and bad points about the two parties. Is there anything in particular that you like about the Democratic party? (What is that?)
>
> Is there anything in particular that you don't like about the Democratic party? (What is that?)
>
> Is there anything in particular that you like about the Republican party? (What is that?)
>
> Is there anything in particular that you don't like about the Republican party? (What is that?)

In addition to the responses to these specific questions, favorable and unfavorable references to the parties in response to other questions in the pre-election interview were also recorded. Many respondents made such comments in answering the question about whether they thought it would make a difference to the country who won the election, in giving the main reasons for their vote intentions, and so on. From a tabulation of all these responses, it is possible to construct descriptions of the two parties as they existed in the minds of the people at the time of the pre-election interviews.

Let us first compare the two parties with respect to the number of people who made any kind of favorable comments about them (Table 4.1). In order to distinguish between attitudes toward the parties themselves and attitudes toward their candidates as personalities, we exclude from this tally people whose only favorable remark about a party was that they liked its presidential candidate. Those who made any other kind of approving reference are counted. As shown in Table 4.1, a larger proportion of the total sample, voters and nonvoters, made such references to the Democratic party (65 per cent) than to the Republican party (48 per cent). This difference seems to be more in accord with the usual party identification of the population (which we shall see in Chapter VII is more often Democratic than Republican) than it is with the 1952 vote. Considering voters alone, we see that most (78 per cent) of the people who voted for Eisenhower had something good to say about the Republican party, but even more (91 per cent) of Stevenson's voters said something favorable about the Democratic party. More striking than this difference, however, is the difference that occurred in the positive perceptions of the parties one

TABLE 4.1

FREQUENCY OF FAVORABLE REFERENCES TO THE PARTIES†

	REFERENCES TO REPUBLICAN PARTY			REFERENCES TO DEMOCRATIC PARTY		
	Eisenhower Voters	Stevenson Voters	Total Sample	Eisenhower Voters	Stevenson Voters	Total Sample
Made one or more favorable references	78%	21%	48%	50%	91%	65%
Made no favorable reference	22	79	52	50	9	35
Total	100%	100%	100%	100%	100%	100%
Number of cases	687	494	1,614	687	494	1,614

† The direct questions and other sources on which these data are based are shown in the text. Not counted here as making favorable comments are people whose only favorable reference to a party was that they liked its presidential candidate.

voted against. Whereas only one-fifth of the Stevenson voters commented favorably on the Republican party, one-half of Eisenhower's voters commented favorably on the Democratic party. While some such finding might have been expected on the grounds that many Eisenhower supporters had previously voted Democratic, the party defectors did not contribute all the difference in these proportions.

The greater popularity of the Democratic party apparent in these positive reactions is partly offset by the fact that unfavorable remarks about the Democratic party were also more common (Table 4.2),

TABLE 4.2

FREQUENCY OF UNFAVORABLE REFERENCES TO THE PARTIES†

	REFERENCES TO REPUBLICAN PARTY			REFERENCES TO DEMOCRATIC PARTY		
	Eisenhower Voters	Stevenson Voters	Total Sample	Eisenhower Voters	Stevenson Voters	Total Sample
Made one or more unfavorable references	36%	77%	51%	83%	43%	58%
Made no unfavorable reference	64	23	49	17	57	42
Total	100%	100%	100%	100%	100%	100%
Number of cases	687	494	1,614	687	494	1,614

† The direct questions and other sources on which these data are based are shown in the text. Not counted here as making unfavorable comments are people whose only unfavorable reference to a party was that they disliked its presidential candidate.

although not much more. In other words, the Democratic party elicited more feeling, both of approval and of disapproval, than the Republican party, but with a net of greater apparent popularity.

From this rough estimate of the relative popularity of the two parties, we can proceed to a consideration of the nature of their appeal and lack of appeal, and thence to a reconstruction of the popular images of the parties.

The specific statements made by the respondents regarding the parties were coded out of the interviews in much greater detail than can be presented here. However, the individual items have been combined into a series of broad categories (as in Table 4.3 and succeeding tables) designed to conform to the objectives of the basic study design. A few brief quotations from the interviews will illustrate the content of these categories:

PARTY LEADERS: "I like some of their men that have held office." "President Roosevelt helped us." "I just like the man who is running." "General Eisenhower—that's enough right there."

PARTY IDENTIFICATION: "It's just that I was raised up to be a Democrat." "It's just that I'm fully Democratic." "Just the habit of being a Republican." "I like everything about the Republican party." "The Democrats as a whole stand together better than the Republicans regardless of the issues. We stand by our party."

DOMESTIC POLICIES AND ISSUES: "The Democrats propose some pretty good reforms. Their stand on things like aid to education is good, for example." "They helped me by getting this social security through." "Seems like we have more prosperity when the Democrats are in office." "I think they will straighten out our corrupt government." "They favor the principle of most production creates most profit." "They'll try to keep taxes and prices more on a lower level." "They're more conservative."

FOREIGN POLICY: "I like the way they deal with other countries." "They were good to Europe with the Marshall Plan." "They don't want to foot all the bills for foreign countries." "I think they will get us out of this cold war." "I don't like to bring Korea into this, but the Republicans are the only ones who said that that situation could be brought to an end."

ASSOCIATION WITH CERTAIN GROUPS: "They stand for the working class people." "They pay us farmers more for the stuff we raise." "They are for the people in place of business." "They favor the small businessman more than the Democrats."

"TIME FOR A CHANGE": "One thing is that they're the party out of office. A new broom sweeps clean. When a person's on a job too long, he gets stagnant and decadent." "Time for a change. One party in power too long tends toward corruption. Gets too securely lodged."

Using these six rubrics, Table 4.3 presents a summary of the favorable comments made regarding the two parties. A number of interesting differences may be seen. First of all, comments favorable to both parties dealt more with domestic affairs than with any of the other

TABLE 4.3

FAVORABLE PERCEPTIONS OF REPUBLICAN AND DEMOCRATIC PARTIES

FAVORABLE REFERENCES	MENTIONED IN CONNECTION WITH:	
	Republican Party	Democratic Party
Party leaders	13%	7%
Party identification; traditional party allegiance	8	11
Domestic policies and issues	33	43
Foreign policy; ability to handle Korean War	13	3
Association with certain groups (working people, farmers, etc.)	2	32
"Time for a change"	13	—
Made no favorable reference	49	35
Total	**	**
Number of cases	1,614	1,614

** Columns total more than 100 per cent because some people gave more than one reason for liking the Democratic or Republican Party.

categories. This emphasis is especially marked in references to the Democratic party, particularly if one considers the "association with groups" category as a response referring to domestic policy. The most striking difference in the images of the two parties lies in this group-association category. One out of three people spoke favorably of the Democratic party as the party of the "common people," the party that had helped the working man, the farmer, etc. Only a handful of people spoke favorably of the Republicans in these terms.

The other remarks on domestic policies, though numerous for both Democratic and Republican parties, also show differing perceptions of the two parties. The three main domestic issues mentioned in favor of the Republican party were those involving "corruption," economy, and taxation. Of the sample, 8 per cent remarked that the Republicans might provide a "more honest" government than that of the Democrats, might "clean up the corruption" in Washington; 9 per cent said that the Republicans were more "economy-minded," that they would "spend less money" and "balance the budget"; 8 per cent mentioned that the Republicans might "lower taxes."

The favorable perceptions of the Democratic party in the domestic sphere, on the other hand, were dominated by one major issue. Although some spoke favorably of Democratic social welfare policies, particularly the social security program, the one domestic issue in favor of the Democrats that stood out most clearly was that of economic prosperity. Fully 26 per cent of the sample population spoke favorably of the Democrats as the party that has meant "prosperity" and "good times," "higher wages" and "more jobs." In contrast to this, only 6 per cent spoke favorably of the Republican party in terms of broad economic conditions, most of these hoping that the Republicans might be able to do something about "inflation" and the "high cost of living."[1]

Looking again at Table 4.3, the difference between the party perceptions in terms of foreign affairs provides an interesting contrast to the domestic area. Whereas domestic issues were more prominently mentioned in favor of the Democratic party, foreign affairs were almost exclusively an area favorable to the Republicans. Only a minority of the population mentioned foreign affairs as reasons for favoring the parties, but most of those who did favored the Republicans.

These perceptions of foreign and domestic policies, taken together with the sizable mention of the "time for a change" argument, reflect very well the major arguments and "issues" defined by the two parties during the campaign. Corruption, economy, taxation, Korea, and "time for a change" were all points that Republican speakers stressed during the months preceding the election. The Democrats, on the other hand, strove to build up the image of their party as the party of "the people" and the party that had brought prosperity and good times, the two points which, as we have noted, were most heavily accented by our respondents in talking about the favorable points of the Democratic party.

Differences between the reactions to the parties in terms of party identification and party leaders, though less striking than the differences in terms of issues, are also of some interest. Most of the positive references to Republican party figures were to their presidential candidate; 8 per cent of the total sample mentioned Eisenhower

---

[1] Further evidence of this tendency to identify the Democratic party with economic well-being was obtained in response to a question designed specifically to measure the respondents' perception of the election in terms of their economic interest. The following question was asked in the pre-election interviews: "Do you think it will make any difference in how you and your family get along financially whether the Democrats or Republicans win? (How is that?)" About half of the respondents said that the election outcome *would* make a difference in their economic situation, and of these twice as many felt they would be better off if the Democrats won than felt their condition would improve under the Republicans.

as a reason for liking the Republican party. In connection with the Democrats, on the other hand, only 1 per cent of the sample mentioned Stevenson as a reason for liking the Democratic party. The majority of the favorable references to Democratic party figures were to Roosevelt.

Responses to the parties in the category labeled "party identification" consist mainly of spontaneous references to the respondents' own traditional party allegiance. At one point in the pre-election interview, people were asked directly with what party they identified themselves (Chapter VII); their answers to that question are not included here. Not many people mentioned their personal party identification in their spontaneous comments regarding the parties, but those who did were a little more likely to mention it in connection with the Democratic party than with the Republican.

Turning now to a consideration of the unfavorable perceptions of the parties, the findings, in general, complement those observed in connection with the positive party responses. Factors mentioned in favor of one party tended also to be mentioned in criticism of the other party. Thus, as shown in Table 4.4, the favorable perception of the Democrats as the party of "the people" is paralleled by some tendency to criticize

TABLE 4.4

UNFAVORABLE PERCEPTIONS OF REPUBLICAN AND DEMOCRATIC PARTIES

UNFAVORABLE REFERENCES	MENTIONED IN CONNECTION WITH:	
	Republican Party	Democratic Party
Party leaders	7%	11%
Party identification†	8	7
Domestic policies and issues	31	43
Foreign policy; Korean War	4	15
Association with special interest groups (mostly "upper classes," "rich people")	11	1
One party in power too long; "time for a change"	—	9
Made no unfavorable reference	48	42
Total	**	**
Number of cases	1,614	1,614

** Columns total more than 100 per cent because some people gave more than one reason for disliking the Democratic or Republican party.

† Unfavorable references in this category consist of responses which involved rejection of the party as a whole or certain factions of the party, rather than the rejection of specific policies or people. (For example: "I just seem to have a natural dislike for Republicans." "I'm just a Republican and I don't see no good in the Democratic party." "I don't like anything about them—they're crooks and not honest.")

the Republicans as the party of the rich and privileged. Foreign policy and the handling of the Korean War, which appeared as predominantly pro-Republican arguments, also emerge as predominantly anti-Democratic arguments. "Time for a change" is an argument mentioned prominently both in support of the Republican party and in criticism of the Democrats.

This parallelism breaks down to some extent when the domestic issue category is considered. The tendency for more people to favor the Democrats because of their domestic policies is not paralleled by a tendency for more people to criticize the Republicans in this area. On the contrary, somewhat more people criticized the Democrats on the basis of domestic policies and actions, as Table 4.4 demonstrates. However, in the specific content within this broad category, the findings on the unfavorable party perceptions are completely consistent with the favorable ones. Regarding domestic affairs, the three major anti-Democratic comments, like the pro-Republican ones, had to do with "corruption," economy, and taxes: 15 per cent of the sample criticized the Democratic party on the "corruption" issue; 12 per cent criticized it for "too much government spending," the "high national debt," etc.; 12 per cent voiced disapproval of the Democrats by criticizing "high taxes." The big anti-Republican domestic argument, like the main pro-Democratic support in this area, dealt with economic depression: 21 per cent of the sample identified the Republicans in some way with depressed economic conditions, sometimes referring to their past experience in the depression of the early thirties, sometimes expressing a fear about what a Republican victory might mean for their future economic well-being.

The specific content of the unfavorable perceptions of the party leaders also is of interest. Only a small proportion of these comments referred to either Stevenson or Eisenhower. This fact is consistent with the results we shall note in our later consideration of the popular images of the candidates, which indicate very little public rejection of either presidential candidate. The largest number of disapproving comments directed at any political figure were about President Truman, who was referred to critically by 7 per cent of the population.

As we have already seen (Tables 4.1 and 4.2), favorable and unfavorable perceptions of the parties are highly related to the respondents' voting behavior, with Stevenson voters tending to accent the positive aspects of the Democratic party and the negative aspects of the Republican party, and Eisenhower voters tending to stress the positive aspects of the Republican party and the negative aspects of the Democrats. There is not much relative difference between the Eisenhower and Stevenson voters, however, in the particular aspects of the parties that they responded to. That is, there is no particular tendency for Stevenson and Eisenhower voters to stress different characteristics when talking about their own or the opposite party. Thus Eisenhower voters, in comparison with Stevenson voters, are much more favorable to the Republican party and much more critical of the Democratic party in all major categories of response (Tables 4.5 and 4.8). Stevenson voters, in turn, are more favorable to the Democratic party and more critical of the Republicans in all the major areas coded (Tables 4.6 and 4.7).

TABLE 4.5

RELATION OF VOTING BEHAVIOR TO FAVORABLE PERCEPTIONS OF REPUBLICAN PARTY

Favorable References to Republican Party	Eisenhower Voters	Stevenson Voters
Party leaders (mostly Eisenhower)	20%	8%
Party identification; traditional party allegiance	14	2
Domestic policies and issues	57	11
Foreign policy; ability to handle Korean War	23	4
Association with certain groups (working people, farmers, etc.)	3	*
"Time for a change"	25	4
Made no favorable reference	19	76
Total	**	**
Number of cases	687	494

** Columns total more than 100 per cent because some people gave more than one reason for liking the Republican party.

TABLE 4.6

RELATION OF VOTING BEHAVIOR TO FAVORABLE PERCEPTIONS OF DEMOCRATIC PARTY

Favorable References to Democratic Party	Eisenhower Voters	Stevenson Voters
Party leaders (mostly Roosevelt)	6%	11%
Party identification; traditional party allegiance	5	18
Domestic policies and issues	31	63
Foreign policy; ability to handle Korean War	2	6
Association with certain groups (working people, farmers, etc.)	19	55
Made no favorable reference	50	9
Total	**	**

** Columns total more than 100 per cent because some people gave more than one reason for liking the Democratic party.

TABLE 4.7

RELATION OF VOTING BEHAVIOR TO UNFAVORABLE PERCEPTIONS OF REPUBLICAN PARTY

Unfavorable References to Republican Party	Eisenhower Voters	Stevenson Voters
Party leaders	7%	9%
Party identification	5	14
Domestic policies and issues	15	52
Foreign policy; Korean War	3	8
Association with special interest groups (mostly "upper classes," "rich people")	4	23
Made no unfavorable reference	63	21
Total	**	***

** Column does not total 100 per cent because a number of the responses were not appropriate for any major category and therefore are not included in the table.
*** Column totals more than 100 per cent because some people gave more than one reason for disliking the Republican party.

TABLE 4.8

RELATION OF VOTING BEHAVIOR TO UNFAVORABLE PERCEPTIONS OF DEMOCRATIC PARTY

Unfavorable References to Democratic Party	Eisenhower Voters	Stevenson Voters
Party leaders (mostly Truman)	18%	5%
Party identification	11	3
Domestic policies and issues	65	29
Foreign policy; Korean War	26	12
Association with special interest groups (mostly "upper classes," "rich people")	1	*
One party in power too long; "time for a change"	17	3
Made no unfavorable reference	17	57
Total	**	**

** Columns total more than 100 per cent because some people gave more than one reason for disliking the Democratic party.

Although the general relationships between voting behavior and party perceptions shown in Tables 4.5 to 4.8 do not add much to the previous discussion, some of the specific figures may be noted. As has already been observed, a large proportion of people who voted for Eisenhower had some favorable perception of the Democratic party. It is evident in Table 4.6 that this favorable perception is heavily concentrated in the area of domestic affairs. Almost one-third of the Eisenhower voters had something approving to say about Democratic domestic policy and activity, and one-fifth talked favorably of the Democrats as a party that helped the working people, farmers, or other subgroupings of the population. We have also observed that many Stevenson voters criticized the Democratic party, criticisms which are also heavily concentrated in the domestic area (Table 4.8). Also, the observation that foreign issues constituted an area almost exclusively favorable to the Republican party is underscored by the fact that even the Stevenson voters more often criticized the Democrats in this area than approved them : 12 per cent of the Stevenson voters criticized the Democratic handling of foreign affairs (particularly the Korean War), as opposed to only 6 per cent who had something good to say about the Democrats in this area (Tables 4.6 and 4.8).

Although not presented in the tables, it may also be of interest to note how often the main specific domestic issues were mentioned by the party protagonists. Democratic "corruption," "government spending," and "high taxes" were specifically mentioned in criticism of the Democratic party by 24, 21, and 18 per cent, respectively, of the Eisenhower voters. Almost as large proportions of Eisenhower voters mentioned these issues when commenting favorably on the changes they felt the Republicans might make if elected. The importance of the "prosperity" theme for the Democrats, on the other hand, is indicated by the fact that 41 per cent of the Stevenson voters praised the Democrats and 36 per cent criticized the Republicans on this issue.

These strong relationships between party perceptions and voting choice should be interpreted with caution, particularly with reference to imputations of causality. We cannot assume from the fact that a person stressed a particular item in talking about the parties that this factor had any necessary influence on his vote. The fact that many Republican voters mentioned "corruption" does not mean that these people voted for Eisenhower "because of" the corruption issue. We have already noted that the main points mentioned by people in describing the parties were all arguments that had been heavily stressed in newspapers, radio, and television in the months before the election. These arguments were thus among the slogans that were readily available to people as rationalizations for their voting choices. A conservative evaluation of the importance of these various issues should be based on the *relative* extent to which different issues stressed by the two parties were accepted by the electorate, rather than on the absolute number that accepted any one of them. Although it may be impossible to interpret the importance of the fact that many people mentioned an argument that party orators and editorial supporters were stressing day after day, the fact that such an item was mentioned by relatively few people may be taken more safely as a sign of the relative unimportance of an issue.

The importance of the presumably big campaign issues that received considerable mention from the electorate should be evaluated, then, by a consideration of and comparison with the presumably big campaign issues that received very little response in the interviews. The most interesting fact, in this connection, is that only 3 per cent of the population mentioned the argument that the Democratic administration had been "soft to communism" and was "infiltrated with Communists," in spite of the fact that this argument was very prominent among the campaign stimuli to which the voters were subjected. It would appear from this that the "communism-in-government" issue was a relatively unimportant one, less meaningful to the electorate than the issues of "corruption," "government spending," etc. Similarly, the almost complete lack of criticism of the Republicans in terms of foreign affairs, in spite of the fact that Republican "isolationism" was one of the Democratic campaign arguments, suggests that this was not particularly important in influencing a vote for Stevenson, certainly much less important than the identification of the Republican party with depressed economic conditions.

Perceptions of the Candidates

One of the most striking aspects of the 1952 election was the apparently great personal attraction of the winning candidate. The crowds that thronged to see him, the buttons and the chants proclaiming "I like Ike," seemed to evidence a dramatic appeal rarely encountered in American presidential candidates. What was the image of Eisenhower to which the American people were responding? Did they see him as a strong leader, a warm and kindly father figure, the person capable of ending the international crisis?

Although the 1952 election will probably be remembered as the "Eisenhower Election," the Democrats also presented an unusual candidate. His refusal to campaign for nomination, his intellectualism, his willingness to take positions unpopular with his audiences, do not conform to the usual stereotype of the American politician. What impact did Stevenson have on the American public? Did he help or hurt the Democratic cause?

Because of the unusual qualities of both major candidates, the 1952 election affords a particularly favorable opportunity to study attraction to a candidate as a force influencing voting behavior. Chapter IX of this volume will deal with the general concept of "candidate orientation" and will attempt to develop this aspect of total political orientation as one of the factors important to the analysis of motivations underlying voting. In the present section of this chapter we shall be concerned with the public's perceptions of the candidates, of their policy positions, their party representativeness or nonrepresentativeness, their experience, and "personalities." From these data should emerge the images of the candidates as they were seen by the public during the campaign.

The data on the respondents' perceptions of the candidates were gathered in a manner similar to that used for perceptions of the parties. Each respondent was asked specifically what he liked and what he disliked about Eisenhower and Stevenson. Responses to these questions, together with favorable and unfavorable references to the candidates that appeared in response to other questions in the pre-election interview, were assembled and categorized.

TABLE 4.9

FREQUENCY OF FAVORABLE REFERENCES TO THE CANDIDATES†

	REFERENCES TO EISENHOWER			REFERENCES TO STEVENSON		
	Eisenhower Voters	Stevenson Voters	Total Sample	Eisenhower Voters	Stevenson Voters	Total Sample
Made one or more favorable references	89%	53%	68%	38%	70%	47%
Made no favorable reference	11	47	32	62	30	53
Total	100%	100%	100%	100%	100%	100%
Number of cases	687	494	1,614	687	494	1,614

† Not counted here as making favorable comments are people whose only favorable reference to a candidate was that he was a Democrat or Republican.

Following the same procedure used in the preceding section, a rough measure of the relative popularity of the two candidates may be obtained by comparing the numbers of people who made any kind of approving references to them during the course of the pre-election interview. As seen in Table 4.9, a much larger proportion of the sample made such references to Eisenhower than to Stevenson (68 against 47 per cent). (These include approving references to any aspect of the candidate—his experience, position on issues, campaign, personal qualities, etc.—except the statement that he was liked because he was a Democrat or Republican.) That this difference is not just a function of the larger number of Republican voters is indicated by the fact that it remains when the vote is controlled. Of the Eisenhower voters, 89 per cent made favorable references to Eisenhower, whereas only 70 per cent of the Stevenson voters mentioned their candidate favorably. Of the Stevenson voters, 53 per cent mentioned something favorable about Eisenhower, whereas Stevenson was thus spoken of by only 38 per cent of the Eisenhower voters (Table 4.9).

As in the case of the party perceptions, this apparent evidence of Eisenhower's greater popularity is offset somewhat by the fact that unfavorable references to Eisenhower were also more common (Table 4.10). However, this difference in the negative references to the two candidates is not as great as the difference in favor of Eisenhower in the proportions of people who made favorable comments.

TABLE 4.10

FREQUENCY OF UNFAVORABLE REFERENCES TO THE CANDIDATES†

	REFERENCES TO EISENHOWER			REFERENCES TO STEVENSON		
	Eisenhower Voters	Stevenson Voters	Total Sample	Eisenhower Voters	Stevenson Voters	Total Sample
Made one or more unfavorable references	33%	67%	45%	57%	19%	35%
Made no unfavorable reference	67	33	55	43	81	65
Total	100%	100%	100%	100%	100%	100%
Number of cases	687	494	1,614	687	494	1,614

† Not counted here as making unfavorable comments are people whose only unfavorable reference to a candidate was that he was a Democrat or Republican.

Evidence of Eisenhower's greater popularity may also be inferred from the responses to another question in the pre-election interview. An attempt was made to have the respondents evaluate the candidates without consideration of their party connections. Although it is no doubt difficult for most people to make such a psychological separation, still it is significant that Stevenson voters were more likely to express the opinion that, of the two, Eisenhower would make a better president than were Eisenhower voters to give this opinion regarding Stevenson (Table 4.11).

A further measure of the relative appeal of the two candidates may be derived from an examination of the respondents' evaluations of the two parties. As we noted in the discussion of the perceptions of the parties, special tabulation was made of those people who mentioned the presidential candidates as reasons for liking the parties. These responses give some indication of the salience of the attitudes toward the candidates. According to this measure, Eisenhower was a more positive figure for Republican voters than Stevenson was for the Democratic voters. Of the Eisenhower voters, 13 per cent said that they liked the Republican party because of its presidential candidate, whereas only 3 per cent of the Democratic voters said that they liked the Democratic party because of Stevenson.

These various findings, then, support the general impressions one gained during the course of the campaign about the relative appeal of the two candidates. It should be noted, however, that the data do not indicate an overwhelming preference for Eisenhower, nor do they necessarily imply that there was any striking rejection of Stevenson by

TABLE 4.11

RELATION OF VOTING BEHAVIOR TO CANDIDATE PREFERENCE

"Now adding up the good points and the bad points about the two candidates, and forgetting for a minute the parties they belong to, which one do you think would make the best president?"	Eisenhower Voters	Stevenson Voters
Eisenhower	82%	16%
Stevenson	9	72
No preference	8	11
Not ascertained	1	1
Total	100%	100%
Number of cases	687	494

the American electorate. As we observed above, more people made unfavorable comments about Eisenhower than about Stevenson. It seems rather to have been the lack of knowledge about Stevenson that worked to his disadvantage, with Eisenhower's greater popularity being partly a function of being better known.

Granting that Eisenhower was a more widely popular candidate than Stevenson, what was the nature of his greater appeal? And what was the popular image that finally evolved of the less well-known Stevenson?

Just as in the case of the parties, a great variety of comments were made by the respondents regarding the candidates. It was necessary to combine these items into a manageable number of categories. In devising this outline of major categories, three main objectives were kept in view: (a) An attempt was made to distinguish references to the personal characteristics and abilities of the two men, references to their support of certain policies and group interests, and references to their party representativeness. (b) In order to test hypotheses about factors related to different types of orientations to leadership figures, certain distinctions were made within the broader category of "personal" responses. Separate note was made of responses to the candidates in functional terms (that is, having to do with their experience and competencies, their ability to do the job), responses to the candidates as strong, decisive leadership figures, and comments which suggested a personal attraction to the candidates (for example, comments on the candidates' "likeableness" or "warmth," which are referred to as "personal attractiveness" in the tables that follow).[2] (c) Within all of these main categories, an attempt was made to tally separately the specific content categories that had particular relevance to one or the other man—for example, Eisenhower's military background or Stevenson's intellectualism.

When the positive perceptions of Stevenson and Eisenhower are compared (Table 4.12), some interesting differences emerge. One notes first of all, as has already been discussed, that many more people made comments about Eisenhower than about Stevenson. Therefore, to choose the items that were especially favorable to Eisenhower one must look for a very heavy preponderance of pro-Eisenhower references. On the other hand, even a small tendency for more people to mention something favorable to Stevenson than to Eisenhower is noteworthy.

Two attributes of the Eisenhower image stand out in comparison to that of Stevenson. Eisenhower was more often seen as a man with the qualities of leadership, and in particular he was seen as a man able to do something about the foreign situation. One out of seven respondents spoke favorably of Eisenhower as a person of leadership ability, strength, and decisiveness as contrasted to only a handful who spoke of Stevenson in those terms.[3] More than one out of five spoke favorably about Eisenhower's ability to handle the foreign situation (many of them specifically referring to the Korean War), whereas very few spoke of Stevenson in this connection.

The marked accent given to the foreign situation in the positive perceptions of Eisenhower is particularly striking when compared with the emphasis given this area in the reactions to the parties. We have

[2] These distinctions are similar to some that have been made in studies of "authoritarian" reactions to leadership figures. See, for example, Sanford, F. H., "The Follower's Role in Leadership Phenomena," in Swanson, Newcomb and Hartley, *Readings in Social Psychology* (New York: Dryden Press, 1951), 328–39.

[3] The tendency to perceive Eisenhower in "leadership" terms needs to be interpreted with caution. Although we were primarily interested, in this category, in coding out responses to the "charismatic" leader, the "man on horseback," very few of the responses were of that nature. Most of the responses had a strong functional flavor, being rather matter-of-fact references to the fact that Eisenhower had certain demonstrated leadership abilities. In general, the interviews evidenced very little reaction to Eisenhower as a strong authoritarian figure, much less, certainly, than was evidenced in many of the newspaper comments and editorials during the campaign. An analysis of the study data in terms of the charismatic response to Eisenhower is being carried out by Dr. James C. Davies.

already noted that foreign policy, to the extent that it was a party issue, was almost exclusively a pro-Republican issue; but a comparison of Tables 4.3 and 4.12 suggests that foreign policy was much more a pro-

TABLE 4.12

FAVORABLE PERCEPTIONS OF EISENHOWER AND STEVENSON

FAVORABLE REFERENCES	MENTIONED IN CONNECTION WITH:	
	Eisenhower	Stevenson
Experience and abilities:		
Good man; qualified; capable	17%	11%
Governmental or political experience	1	11
Military experience	11	—
Successful record	14	8
Other references to experience or ability	6	4
Leadership	14	2
Personal attractiveness	15	7
Other personal qualities:		
Integrity; principle; honesty	15	6
Intelligence; education; understanding	7	9
Other personal references	14	7
Issues and policies:		
Domestic policies	9	7
Foreign policy; ability to handle foreign situation, Korean War	22	2
General references to policies and issues	2	4
Association with certain groups (working people, farmers, etc.)	3	7
Party representativeness:		
He's a Republican (Democrat)	5	15
Other party references	1	1
Good campaign; good speaker	2	8
"Time for a change"; he'll bring a change	4	—
Made no favorable reference	31	46
Total	**	**
Number of cases	1,614	1,614

** Columns total more than 100 per cent because some people gave more than one reason for liking Eisenhower or Stevenson.

Eisenhower than a pro-Republican party issue. Whereas many more people responded favorably to Eisenhower in terms of the foreign situation than in terms of what he might do on the domestic scene, the reverse was true of the favorable perceptions of the Republican party: many more people mentioned favoring the Republican party because of the domestic situation (clean up corruption, lower taxes, etc.) than because of its ability to do something about the foreign situation and the Korean War (Table 4.3). The favorable perception of Eisenhower in this area, then, was not just a symptom of dissatisfaction with the Korean War, nor a mere echo of the public's reaction to the Republican party. Eisenhower, because of his background and experience, seems to have been perceived as a person peculiarly able to cope with the nation's international problems.

In the face of the greater Eisenhower appeal, there were very few ways in which Stevenson was viewed more favorably than Eisenhower. One asset was his governmental and civil experience, although this was counterbalanced by Eisenhower's military experience. There was also a slight tendency for more people to speak favorably of Stevenson's intelligence and his speeches and campaign. On the whole, however, Stevenson's main advantage over Eisenhower does not appear to have been anything that Stevenson himself brought to the campaign. Rather it lay in his party representativeness. Among the respondents, 15 per cent said they liked Stevenson because he was a Democrat, whereas only 5 per cent spoke of liking Eisenhower because he was a Republican. In part, this difference probably reflects the respondents' inability to think of other reasons for favoring Stevenson. Half of the people who said they liked Stevenson because he was a Democrat gave no other reason for liking him.

Although we have emphasized the differences between the public perceptions of Eisenhower and Stevenson, they were also similar in some ways. In spite of the fact that the number of references to Eisenhower was much larger, many of the same qualities were attributed to both candidates—their capabilities, their commendable records of past service, their attractive, "likeable" personalities, and their positive domestic policies.

When we consider the images of the candidates in relation to the respondents' voting behavior, the similarities are even more striking and overshadow the differences. Comparison of the Democratic and Republican voters' perceptions of Eisenhower is presented in Table 4.13, and the comparison with respect to Stevenson appears in Table 4.14. Although many more Democrats than Republicans gave pro-Stevenson responses, and many more Republicans made favorable references to Eisenhower, Stevenson and Eisenhower voters did not differ greatly in the particular aspects of the candidates that they responded to.

There is little relation between the respondents' presidential vote and the particular characteristics of the candidates that they mention, but a few of the specific findings in Tables 4.13 and 4.14 deserve notice. For example, in Table 4.13 it is interesting that there is only one category in which a larger proportion of Stevenson than Eisenhower voters commented favorably on Eisenhower, and that was his past record. There was some tendency for Stevenson voters to speak favorably of Eisenhower's past record rather than of his present capacities and competencies for the job of president. Looking at

TABLE 4.13

RELATION OF VOTING BEHAVIOR TO FAVORABLE PERCEPTIONS OF EISENHOWER

Favorable References to Eisenhower	Eisenhower Voters	Stevenson Voters
Experience and abilities:		
Good man; qualified; capable	22%	13%
Governmental or political experience	1	*
Military experience	15	6
Successful record	15	17
Other references to experience or ability	10	2
Leadership	25	6
Personal attractiveness	21	13
Other personal qualities:		
Integrity; principle; honesty	23	10
Intelligence; education; understanding	10	5
Other personal references	25	5
Issues and policies:		
Domestic policies	16	3
Foreign policies; ability to handle foreign situation, Korean War	35	10
General references to policies and issues	4	1
Association with certain groups (working people, farmers, etc.)	4	1
Party representativeness:		
He's a Republican	8	*
Other party references	2	*
Good campaign; good speaker	3	1
"Time for a change"; he'll bring a change	8	*
Made no favorable reference	9	47
Total	**	**
Number of cases	687	494

** Columns total more than 100 per cent because some people gave more than one reason for liking Eisenhower.

Table 4.14, the figures on the responses to Stevenson's campaign are also noteworthy. Stevenson's campaign approach, which aroused considerable interest and speculation in the months preceding the election, was reacted to favorably by as large a proportion of Eisenhower as of Stevenson voters. To the extent that this made a positive impression on the voters, the effect seems to have been a bipartisan one. Finally, examination of both Tables 4.13 and 4.14 underscores the observation already noted that being a Democrat was apparently a much stronger basis for support of Stevenson than being a Republican was for Eisenhower. Whereas 29 per cent of the Stevenson voters mentioned the fact that their candidate was a Democrat as a reason for

TABLE 4.14

RELATION OF VOTING BEHAVIOR TO FAVORABLE PERCEPTIONS OF STEVENSON

Favorable References to Stevenson	Eisenhower Voters	Stevenson Voters
Experience and abilities:		
Good man; qualified; capable	8%	18%
Governmental or political experience	7	20
Successful record	7	13
Other references to experience or ability	2	6
Leadership	1	4
Personal attractiveness	6	10
Other personal qualities:		
Integrity; principle; honesty	5	11
Intelligence; education; understanding	9	12
Other personal references	6	13
Issues and policies:		
Domestic policies	2	12
Foreign policy; ability to handle foreign situation, Korean War	*	4
General references to policies and issues	1	9
Association with certain groups (working people, farmers, etc.)	2	14
Party representativeness:		
He's a Democrat	3	29
Other party references	*	2
Good campaign; good speaker	9	9
Made no favorable reference	60	19
Total	**	**
Number of cases	687	494

** Columns total more than 100 per cent because some people gave more than one reason for liking Stevenson.

approving of him, only 8 per cent of the Eisenhower voters mentioned his being a Republican as a reason for supporting him.

The unfavorable reactions to Eisenhower and Stevenson were much less extensive than were the favorable reactions, as is evident in Table 4.15, but certain aspects of these perceptions deserve mention. There appears to have been very little personal rejection of the candidates. The most frequent objection to Eisenhower was that he was a military

man and had no governmental or political experience.   The objection
to Stevenson mentioned most often was his supposed connection with
Truman, the feeling that he was "Truman's man."   It would appear
that there was not much "voting against a candidate" in the 1952
election, not much rejection of the personalities.

TABLE 4.15

Unfavorable Perceptions of Eisenhower and Stevenson

Unfavorable References	Mentioned in Connection with:	
	Eisenhower	Stevenson
Experience and abilities:		
Military man	25%	—%
Lack of governmental or political experience	10	1
Other references to experience or ability	4	5
Lack of leadership	1	2
Personal unattractiveness	1	3
Stevenson's divorce	—	5
Other personal factors or qualities	5	9
Issues and policies:		
Domestic policies	4	4
Foreign policies; likelihood of getting us into war	5	2
General references to policies and issues	2	2
Association with special interest groups (mostly "upper classes," "rich people")	2	1
Party representativeness:		
He's a Republican (Democrat)	8	6
Connection with Taft, "Old Guard"	3	—
Connection with Truman	—	11
Other party references	3	4
Bad campaign; poor speaker	1	3
Made no unfavorable reference	50	61
Total	**	**
Number of cases	1,614	1,614

** Columns total more than 100 per cent because some people gave more than one reason for disliking
Eisenhower or Stevenson.

The comparisons of the unfavorable reactions of the Stevenson and
Eisenhower voters do not add greatly to the picture.   As indicated in
Tables 4.16 and 4.17, there is a high relationship between voting behavior and the number of unfavorable references to the candidates,
with Eisenhower voters giving many more anti-Stevenson responses,
and Stevenson voters making many more unfavorable references to

Eisenhower, but there was no particular tendency for the two groups of voters to stress different aspects of the candidates in their negative perceptions of them.

Before concluding this section, some further comment might be made on one of the items that appears in the unfavorable references to

TABLE 4.16

RELATION OF VOTING BEHAVIOR TO UNFAVORABLE PERCEPTIONS OF EISENHOWER

Unfavorable References to Eisenhower	Eisenhower Voters	Stevenson Voters
Experience and abilities:		
Military man	17%	41%
Lack of governmental or political experience	8	18
Other references to experience or ability	2	8
Lack of leadership	1	2
Personal unattractiveness	—	1
Other personal factors or qualities	3	10
Issues and policies:		
Domestic policies	2	7
Foreign policies; likelihood of getting us into war	3	8
General references to policies and issues	1	4
Association with special interest groups (mostly "upper classes," "rich people")	1	4
Party representativeness:		
He's a Republican	1	14
Connection with Taft, "Old Guard"	2	7
Other party references	2	4
Bad campaign; poor speaker	1	1
Made no unfavorable reference	66	23
Total	**	**
Number of cases	687	494

** Columns total more than 100 per cent because some people gave more than one reason for disliking Eisenhower.

Eisenhower: his lack of governmental or political experience. In an election that was determined to a considerable extent by Democrats who deserted their candidate and voted Republican, we would expect that Eisenhower's lack of political background and consequent ambiguity with relation to the party system may have been an asset as well as a liability. Democrats with some antipathy to the Republican party may have been able to vote for Eisenhower in 1952 because they did not see him as clearly identified with the Republican party.

Although Eisenhower's nonpolitical background was rarely mentioned directly as a reason for favoring him, there is some evidence from one further question in the pre-election interview that it may have been a positive aspect of Eisenhower's appeal. In an attempt to

TABLE 4.17

RELATION OF VOTING BEHAVIOR TO UNFAVORABLE PERCEPTIONS OF
STEVENSON

Unfavorable References to Stevenson	Eisenhower Voters	Stevenson Voters
Experience and abilities	9%	2%
Lack of leadership	3	1
Personal unattractiveness	5	1
Divorce	7	4
Other personal factors or qualities	16	3
Issues and policies:		
Domestic policies	6	4
Foreign policies; likelihood of getting us into war	3	*
General references to policies and issues	4	1
Association with special interest groups	2	1
Party representativeness:		
He's a Democrat	12	*
Connection with Truman	20	3
Other party references	8	1
Bad campaign; poor speaker	7	1
Made no unfavorable reference	35	80
Total	**	**
Number of cases	687	494

** Columns total more than 100 per cent because some people gave more than one reason for disliking Stevenson.

measure the extent to which Eisenhower was differentiated from the Republican party, the following question was asked:

Some people say that Eisenhower is not a real Republican. What do you think about this? Is he the kind of man that *you* think of as being a real Republican? (Why do you say that?)

Responses to this question indicate that a large number of people looked upon Eisenhower as different from their image of the Republican party. If this ambiguity of Eisenhower was a significant factor in enabling former Democrats to switch their votes, one would expect this perception of him to be particularly marked among those people who voted Democratic in 1948 and Republican in 1952. In Table 4.18 these people are contrasted with the regular Democrats and Republicans in their perceptions of Eisenhower as a "real Republican." There we see that the Democratic-Republican switchers did tend to see Eisenhower as less clearly Republican than did the regular Republicans. But contrary to what we might expect, there was no difference between the switchers and the regular Democrats in this perception.

TABLE 4.18

RELATION OF 1948–1952 VOTING PATTERN TO PERCEPTION
OF EISENHOWER AS A REPUBLICAN

PERCEPTION OF EISENHOWER†	1948 AND 1952 VOTE FOR PRESIDENT		
	Dewey, Eisenhower	Truman, Eisenhower	Truman, Stevenson
Eisenhower is a "real" Republican	50%	32%	33%
Eisenhower is not a "real" Republican	31	44	41
Don't know; it depends	15	21	24
Not ascertained	4	3	2
Total	100%	100%	100%
Number of cases	385	165	362

† The question used is shown in the text.

The relationships presented in Table 4.18 are by no means conclusive, but they do suggest that Eisenhower's lack of political background may have had some positive connotations, particularly for the critically important group who switched from the Democrats to the Republicans in 1952.

Comparison of Perceptions of Parties and Candidates in the 1948 and 1952 Elections

We have noted a number of differences in the perceptions of the Democratic and Republican parties and candidates in the 1952 election. It would be interesting to be able to compare these perceptions with those from the 1948 election, particularly in view of the significant shift in the vote that occurred between the two election years. This comparison cannot be made for the data discussed thus far in this chapter, since they were obtained from questions and coding operations unique to the 1952 study. However, there are some limited data from the 1952 study bearing on the popular perceptions of the parties and candidates that are roughly comparable to data gathered in our 1948 survey. In the postelection interviews of both studies, all respondents who voted were asked to give the reasons for their presidential votes. In the 1952 study the question was, "What would you say is the most important reason you voted for him?" In the 1948 study the question was phrased, "What made you decide to vote the way you did?" Although the responses were coded somewhat differently in the two studies, fairly parallel distinctions can be made among responses that referred to party allegiance, candidate personality, domestic issues, foreign policy, and other broad factors of this kind. It is possible, therefore, to obtain

TABLE 4.19

RELATION OF VOTING BEHAVIOR TO REASONS FOR VOTE, 1948 AND 1952

REASONS FOR CHOICE OF CANDIDATE[†]	1948		1952	
	Dewey Voters	Truman Voters	Eisenhower Voters	Stevenson Voters
Party allegiance	25%	27%	8%	32%
Domestic policies and issues[‡]	15	36	36	56
Foreign policy	10	3	32	2
Personal characteristics of candidate	10	6	24	18
Experience of candidate[§]			8	14
Tautological, voted for best man	28	21	15	14
"Time for a change"	26	—	37	—
General satisfaction: no time for a change	—	9	—	3
Total	**	**	**	**
Number of cases	178	212	687	494

** Columns total more than 100 per cent because some people gave more than one reason for their vote.
† The questions used are shown in the text.
‡ In order to make this category comparable to the one used in the 1948 study, it includes the "association with groups" category.
§ This category was not included in the coding of the 1948 responses.

some indication of the changes that occurred in the significance of these different factors for the Democratic and Republican presidential supporters between 1948 and 1952.

These data are presented in Table 4.19. The coding categories of the 1952 study have been combined here to make them comparable to those of the 1948 study, but certain unavoidable differences remain. In general, a somewhat greater attempt was made in the 1952 study to code out the specific reasons for the vote. Because of the greater refinement of the code, general categories such as "general satisfaction: no time for a change" and "tautological, voted for best man" were used less often than they had been in 1948. For example, a number of responses which would have been coded "tautological, voted for best man" in 1948 may have been coded in the "candidate experience" category in 1952. Another difference is that in 1948 only the first two reasons given by an individual respondent were tallied, whereas in 1952 the maximum was set at three. This change helps to explain the larger total number of responses shown for 1952.

Because of these differences, the figures in Table 4.19 should be interpreted cautiously, particularly when comparing the extent to which any particular category is mentioned in the two election years. For example, the fact that "personal characteristics of candidate" was mentioned much more often by both groups of voters in 1952 than in 1948, while probably reflecting the greater salience of the candidates in the 1952 election, is also probably a function of some of the differences in the coding operations employed in the two studies. These qualifications are much less applicable when Table 4.19 is viewed as a comparison of the *relative* prominence of the different factors for Republican and Democratic voters in the two elections. Therefore, in examining the table the reader should look primarily for increases or decreases in one group of voters' responses in a given category that are not paralleled by increases or decreases in the other group.

Looking at Table 4.19 from this point of view, we may observe a number of interesting findings. First of all, "party allegiance," which was a prominent reason given by both Dewey and Truman supporters in 1948, was much more exclusively a Democratic factor in 1952. Relatively few Eisenhower voters gave this as an important reason for their vote. Secondly, foreign policy, which was not particularly salient for either group of voters in 1948 (although even then more often mentioned by Republican voters), was one of the most prominent factors mentioned by the Eisenhower supporters but remained inconsequential among Democratic voters. Thus, two of the main differences we have already noted in our discussion of the perceptions of the parties and candidates in 1952—the greater relevance of party allegiance in the responses of the Stevenson voters and the almost exclusive relevance of foreign policy as a Republican argument—were both very different from the comparable perceptions in 1948.

A third finding, less striking than the two already mentioned, may also be noted in the table. In 1952, domestic issues were again more often mentioned by Democratic than Republican voters as a reason for their votes, but the ratio had changed somewhat. Whereas over twice as many Truman as Dewey voters mentioned domestic issues, the comparable ratio for Stevenson and Eisenhower voters was only about 1.5 to 1. Domestic issues seem to have been relatively more salient for the Republican voters in 1952 than they were in 1948.

Summing up these differences between 1948 and 1952 in another way, we may say that the differences in the rationale of voting given by the Republican presidential supporters in the two elections are much greater than the differences in those of their Democratic counterparts. Both in 1948 and 1952, party allegiance and domestic issues were the two major factors stressed by the people who voted for the Democratic presidential candidate. Among the Republican presidential voters, however, party allegiance was given much less prominence and issues (particularly foreign policy issues) were relatively more frequently mentioned in 1952 than in 1948.

These findings are not surprising when we recall the 1952 election situation and the Republican and Democratic campaigns. The Democrats in 1952 were running on their New Deal–Fair Deal record, on the Democratic party as the party of prosperity, the party of "the people." Even with the substitution of Stevenson for Truman, the Democrats presented a traditional appeal. Their arguments were basically the same in 1952 as they had been in 1948, and this fact was reflected in the similarity of the perceptions of their supporters in the two election years. Much of the Republican campaign, on the other hand, was devoted to issues that had arisen since 1948, particularly "Korea" and "corruption," and one would expect their supporters to have evidenced an increased consciousness of issues. The much lower reference to traditional party allegiance on the part of Eisenhower supporters in 1952 no doubt derived in part from the fact that a large proportion of Eisenhower's support came from people who had previously been Democratic supporters or nonvoters. It may also reflect the more immediate significance of issue and candidate considerations to the Eisenhower voters, who gave higher priority to these specific factors than they did to the more traditional, general factor of party loyalty.

It should be noted that in Table 4.19 there is an interesting discrepancy with respect to other data from the study. The small difference between Eisenhower and Stevenson voters in their references to "candidate personality" does not indicate the greater relevance of the Eisenhower personal appeal that one would expect to find. This apparently results from the fact that a large proportion of the favorable comments given by Republican voters regarding Eisenhower linked him with the international situation. They favored him because a central aspect of his appeal was his presumed ability to do something personally about Korea and the cold war. In answering the question, these people explained their approval of Eisenhower in specific terms, rather than in more general terms that would have been coded in the "personal characteristics" category. This peculiarity of coding makes it difficult to compare the two candidates directly in this table, and the disagreement of these data with the tables presented earlier is probably not real.

Summary

The data presented in this chapter have given us, at least in broad outline, a picture of the two parties and candidates as they were seen by the electorate. Noteworthy differences have been pointed out between the perceptions of the two candidates and also between the images of their respective parties. We have also indicated some of the differences between the perceptions of the parties and candidates in the elections of 1948 and 1952.

In summary, it appears that people in general had more feeling about the Democratic party than about the Republican, and although they were critical of it in the 1952 election their perception of it as the party of the common people and the "prosperity" party persisted. Ability to deal with international problems—which to many in 1952 consisted of the Korean War—was seen almost exclusively as an attribute of the Republican party, but it was associated more with the candidate of that party than with party philosophy. The Democrats were also somewhat handicapped by the public's lack of acquaintance with their candidate, particularly in comparison to the well-known popular figure representing the Republican party.

The reader will recognize that these are broad generalizations from data of considerable complexity. They do not establish a clear causal relation between any of these data and the vote, suggestive though they may be. Along with the information presented in the next chapter, on the demographic characteristics of the voters, the data presented here regarding the public images of the parties and candidates will serve to provide a setting for the analysis of political motivation to be undertaken in Part Two.

V

The Demography of the Vote

The broad sociological differences between the Republican and Democratic followings have long been a matter of common knowledge. Throughout the Roosevelt-Truman period the Democrats drew their support largely from the voters of the big cities, the less advantaged socio-economic groupings, the ethnic and religious minorities. The 1948 election showed this political pattern quite clearly. What happened to the pattern in 1952?

What happened, too, to some of the occupational groups for which the parties were bidding so vigorously during the campaign? Is it true, as some observers believed, that the women's vote was especially attracted to Eisenhower? And how about young people—did their political bias differ from that of voters whose political education began under the New Deal? Many such questions may be asked, and for some of them answers may be found in the tables in this chapter.

1948 and 1952

Table 5.1 presents the relationships between presidential preference in the 1948 and 1952 elections and a number of demographic characteristics. It also enables us to compare the turnout of the various demographic groups. There we may see the party biases of, for example, people of different levels of income (as evidenced by their choice of presidential candidate), how these biases differed as between 1948 and 1952, and what the ratio of voters to nonvoters was at each level in each election.

Study of the table as a whole shows that in the general shift to the Republicans in 1952 the Democrats lost their large majorities in many of the groups formerly associated with them, but that, since most of the other classifications also became more Republican, the usual relationships between demographic characteristics and voting behavior tended to persist.

The most significant conclusion to be drawn from Table 5.1 is that the force or forces which made the 1952 election so different from that of 1948 were felt throughout the entire population. If one examines the two-party division among the groupings, it becomes obvious that

TABLE 5.1

RELATION OF DEMOGRAPHIC CHARACTERISTICS TO PRESIDENTIAL PREFERENCE IN 1948 AND 1952 ELECTIONS

DEMOGRAPHIC CHARACTERISTIC	VOTED FOR:			TOTAL VOTING	DID NOT VOTE, BUT PREFERRED:			TOTAL NOT VOTING	NUMBER OF CASES§
	Republican	Democratic	Other†		Republican	Democratic	Other‡		
SEX									
1952									
Male	44%	34	1	79%	9%	10	2	21%	738
Female	41%	28	*	69%	13%	15	3	31%	876
1948									
Male	28%	36	5	69%	7%	17	7	31%	302
Female	26%	29	4	59%	5%	29	7	41%	357
AGE									
1952									
21–34	37%	31	*	68%	13%	17	2	32%	485
35–44	41%	34	1	76%	11%	11	2	24%	381
45–54	45%	33	1	79%	10%	9	2	21%	284
55 and over	48%	27	2	77%	9%	11	3	23%	442
1948									
21–34	19%	32	5	56%	6%	32	6	44%	199
35–44	24%	38	4	66%	5%	21	8	34%	174
45–54	37%	33	5	75%	3%	16	6	25%	125
55 and over	31%	27	5	63%	8%	21	8	37%	156

TABLE 6.1 (continued)

Demographic Characteristic	Voted for:			Total Voting	Did Not Vote, but Preferred:			Total Not Voting	Number of Cases§
	Republican	Democratic	Other†		Republican	Democratic	Other‡		
RELIGION									
1952									
Protestant	45%	26	1	72%	12%	13	3	28%	1,156
Catholic	41%	43	1	85%	5%	10	*	15%	343
1948									
Protestant	28%	25	5	58%	6%	28	8	42%	461
Catholic	25%	49	5	79%	2%	15	4	21%	140
RACE									
1952									
White	47%	31	1	79%	10%	9	2	21%	1,453
Negro	6%	26	1	33%	15%	42	10	67%	157
1948									
White	29%	33	4	66%	6%	22	6	34%	585
Negro	10%	18	8	36%	3%	46	15	64%	61
TYPE OF COMMUNITY									
1952									
Metropolitan areas	44%	33	2	79%	8%	13	*	21%	438
Towns and cities	42%	31	*	73%	11%	13	3	27%	928
Rural areas	42%	25	1	68%	16%	10	6	32%	248
1948									
Metropolitan areas	32%	46	5	83%	2%	12	3	17%	182
Towns and cities	30%	28	5	63%	6%	25	6	37%	354
Rural areas	12%	25	4	41%	8%	37	14	59%	126

TABLE 5.1 (*continued*)

Demographic Characteristic	Voted for:			Total Voting	Did Not Vote, but Preferred:			Total Not Voting	Number of Cases§
	Republican	Democratic	Other†		Republican	Democratic	Other‡		
EDUCATION									
1952									
Grade school	31%	30	1	62%	15%	18	5	38%	660
High school	46%	34	*	80%	9%	10	1	20%	712
College	65%	24	1	90%	6%	4	—	10%	238
1948									
Grade school	16%	35	4	55%	6%	30	9	45%	292
High school	29%	34	4	67%	6%	21	6	33%	266
College	54%	17	8	79%	4%	13	4	21%	100
OCCUPATION OF HEAD OF FAMILY									
1952									
Professional and managerial	59%	27	2	88%	7%	5	—	12%	333
Other white collar	52%	28	1	81%	9%	9	1	19%	155
Skilled and semi-skilled	34%	39	1	74%	11%	13	2	26%	462
Unskilled	19%	40	1	60%	12%	23	5	40%	174
Farm operators	42%	24	1	67%	17%	11	5	33%	178
1948									
Professional and managerial	58%	14	3	75%	7%	14	4	25%	118
Other white collar	38%	38	5	81%	7%	9	3	19%	78
Skilled and semi-skilled	15%	52	4	71%	5%	21	3	29%	164
Unskilled	12%	33	5	50%	6%	34	10	50%	85
Farm operators	13%	25	4	42%	3%	41	14	58%	105

Demographic Characteristic	Voted for: Republican	Democratic	Other†	Total Voting	Did Not Vote, but Preferred: Republican	Democratic	Other‡	Total Not Voting	Number of Cases§
TRADE UNION AFFILIATION OF HEAD OF FAMILY									
1952									
Member	33%	43	1	77%	8%	13	2	23%	411
Nonmember	46%	26	1	73%	12%	12	3	27%	1,165
1948									
Member	13%	55	5	73%	2%	23	2	27%	150
Nonmember	32%	26	4	62%	6%	24	8	38%	493
INCOME									
1952									
Under $2,000	30%	23	*	53%	17%	22	8	47%	315
$2,000—2,999	36%	31	1	68%	13%	15	4	32%	255
$3,000—3,999	40%	35	1	76%	11%	12	1	24%	364
$4,000—4,999	41%	41	1	83%	8%	8	1	17%	233
$5,000 and over	59%	28	1	88%	6%	6	*	12%	415
1948									
Under $2,000	16%	28	2	46%	8%	35	11	54%	178
$2,000—2,999	17%	38	6	61%	6%	28	5	39%	185
$3,000—3,999	35%	34	5	74%	3%	18	5	26%	142
$4,000—4,999	36%	33	6	75%	5%	14	6	25%	66
$5,000 and over	53%	25	4	82%	4%	7	7	18%	84

† Includes respondents whose vote was not ascertained as well as those who voted for minor-party candidates.
‡ Includes nonvoters who expressed no preference as well as those who preferred minor-party candidates.
§ The 1952 sample consisted of 1,614 cases, the 1948 sample of 662 cases. The number of cases within a set of demographic groups does not always add to the full total, because of the omission of those respondents who did not fall into the categories represented or from whom the relevant information was not obtained.

the same trend persisted in almost all of them : groups strongly Democratic in 1948 were but weakly Democratic in 1952, groups evenly
divided in 1948 were likely to be clearly Republican in 1952, and
groups predominantly Republican in 1948 remained strongly Republican in 1952. Inasmuch as many of the groups of nonvoters in 1948
were heavily Democratic in their sentiments that year, it is not surprising to discover that a slight pro-Democratic margin persists in
many groups of nonvoters in 1952. Despite this pro-Democratic
margin, it seems evident that the nonvoters were affected by the same
pervasive pro-Republican forces which attracted their voting counterparts to the Republican candidate.

The generality of the movement from Democratic to Republican is
highlighted by the fact that in only three of the numerous demographic
groupings represented in Table 5.1 can one observe clear evidence of a
deviation from the general 1948–1952 trend. Negroes, the college
educated, and the professional and managerial groups all showed a
slightly greater proportion voting Democratic than was found in 1948.
None of these shifts was large enough to be very significant, but they
stand out against the general trend. Why these particular groups
should not have moved with the others is a question which requires
closer examination than we can give it here.

The greatest shift in preference between 1948 and 1952 was reported
by people living in rural areas and their occupational subgrouping,
farmers. These rural people moved from a strong majority for Truman
to an almost as strong majority for Eisenhower. We do not know
whether they were merely returning to a traditional Republican position they had temporarily abandoned in 1948, or whether they have
become a politically volatile group capable of swinging from one party
to the other as the political scene changes.

While the 1952 election brought a shift toward the Republican
candidate in most of the demographic classes, the increase in turnout
was somewhat less evenly distributed. If we examine Table 5.1 again,
we see that although many of the groupings increased their turnout,
several did not. The most striking change was again found among
people living in rural areas, of whom some 68 per cent reported casting
a ballot where only 41 per cent had so reported in 1948. It is significant
that most of the groups that fell below the general level of increase in
turnout were nominally Democratic groupings. These were headed
by metropolitan dwellers. Far from increasing their 1948 voting
record, residents of the large cities dropped from 83 per cent voting in
1948 to 79 per cent voting in 1952. Negroes also had a lower record in
1952 than in 1948, although the change was not significant. Three
other pro-Democratic groups showed a disproportionately small increase
in turnout. Union members changed only from 73 per cent voting in

1948 to 77 per cent in 1952, skilled and semi-skilled workers went from 71 to 74 per cent, and Catholics increased their voting record from 79 per cent in 1948 to 85 per cent in 1952.   All of these groups are largely metropolitan, of course, and their performance may reflect some general factor that affected metropolitan and other people differently. These findings are particularly interesting in the light of the rather commonly held belief that a large turnout in national elections should favor the Democratic party.   This belief is based on the fact that the traditionally pro-Republican classes uniformly have a high turnout, even when the vote as a whole is light, so that increases in size of vote might be expected to come mainly from working-class groups.   This expectation was clearly not fulfilled in the 1952 election.

We may summarize these 1948–1952 comparisons by stating that no single demographic class was responsible for the great increase in the Republican vote.   Farmers and rural people generally made the most dramatic shift of votes, but they were not a large enough group to account for the Eisenhower majority.   Women did not contribute any greater proportion of the Republican vote in 1952 than they had in 1948.   Young people gave Eisenhower a small majority, but their contribution to his total vote was proportionately less than that of any of the older groups.   General Eisenhower won because virtually every major demographic group in American society gave him more votes than it had given the preceding Republican nominee.

Regional and Ethnic Differences

The study also undertook to provide information regarding the voting behavior of two other social classifications which have been thought to have political relevance.   They are geographical region and ethnic background.   Since there are no comparable data from the 1948 survey, we cannot relate these 1952 data to any earlier election.

Regional Differences and the 1952 Vote

The South has for many years been politically unique among the regions of the United States.   In 1952, even though the Democrats' grip on this region was severely shaken by the Eisenhower sweep of six of its states, the South, taken as a whole, still gave Stevenson some 52 per cent of its total presidential vote (Table 5.2).   This, of course, was in contrast to the rest of the nation, where the Democrats succeeded in capturing about 40 per cent of the two-party vote.   The high rate of nonvoting among Southerners was also evident in 1952.   Less than half of the sample of this region reported casting a vote for president.

We also see in Table 5.2 that the Northeast and Midwest resembled each other very closely, both in turnout and in party preference.   The

Far West, however, reported half again as many nonvoters as did the other two regions outside of the South, and those nonvoters preferred the Democratic candidate to the Republican candidate by a margin of approximately two to one.

The sample of this study was specifically designed to make possible the separate study of each of the four major geographical regions.

TABLE 5.2

RELATION OF REGION TO PRESIDENTIAL PREFERENCE IN THE 1952 ELECTION

REGION	VOTED FOR:			TOTAL VOT- ING	DID NOT VOTE, BUT PREFERRED:			TOTAL NOT VOT- ING	NUM- BER OF CASES
	Eisen- hower	Steven- son	Other†		Eisen- hower	Steven- son	Other‡		
Northeast	49%	34	1	84%	8%	6	2	16%	390
Midwest	51%	33	1	85%	8%	6	1	15%	580
South	24%	25	*	49%	20%	25	6	51%	440
Far West	47%	29	1	77%	7%	15	1	23%	204

† Includes respondents whose vote was not ascertained as well as those who voted for minor party candidates.
‡ Includes nonvoters who expressed no preference as well as those who preferred minor party candidates.

While the data on the vote presented in Table 5.2 might also have been derived from the election statistics as they were reported by states, it will be apparent to the reader that the other data of the survey make possible an intensive study of each of the major areas. It is expected that subsequent analysis will provide a detailed statement of political differences among the four regions.

Ethnic Background and Presidential Preference

Although there is a substantial folklore regarding the voting proclivities of different ethnic groups in this country, evidence of these relationships is based almost exclusively on the relatively gross data afforded by studies of voting districts, rather than on studies of individual voters. In order to supplement the available data in this interesting area of study, a series of questions on nationality background was included in the pre-election survey. All respondents were asked where they were born. Those born in the United States were asked the birthplace of their parents. When the parents were also native-born Americans, the respondents were asked to identify the birthplace of their grandparents. No attempt was made to identify national origins beyond the grandparents' generation. Only six national groupings were represented by more than a scattering of individuals in the sample: Scandinavian, German, English-Scotch, Irish, Italian, and Polish.

The 1952 voting behavior of these six groupings is presented in Table
5.3. Because of the separate ethnic identity maintained by the Jewish
group in most European countries, these six classifications do not
include Jews. Also, since most speculation about the "Irish" vote
refers to Irish Catholics, Protestants are not included in the Irish
grouping.[1]

Although the figures in Table 5.3 are based on small numbers of
cases, the ethnic differences shown are consistent with those commonly
noted by political observers. Americans of Scandinavian, German, and

TABLE 5.3

RELATION OF ETHNIC BACKGROUND TO VOTING BEHAVIOR IN
THE 1952 PRESIDENTIAL ELECTION

VOTING BEHAVIOR	ETHNIC BACKGROUND†					
	Scandi-navian	German	English-Scotch	Irish-Catholic	Italian	Polish
Voted for:						
Eisenhower	59%	58%	55%	38%	38%	42%
Stevenson	24	20	25	55	49	40
Other, or not ascertained	—	2	1	2	2	5
Did not vote	17	20	19	5	11	13
Total	100%	100%	100%	100%	100%	100%
Number of cases	54	139	76	42	63	38

† The questions on which these classifications are based are described in the text. Ethnic background
was not ascertained for native-born individuals whose parents and grandparents were all native-born,
and such respondents are not included here. Jews are also omitted.

English-Scotch background favored the Republican candidate much
more than did Americans of Irish, Italian, and Polish descent. The
findings with respect to amount of political participation are also of
interest. The "Democratic" ethnic groupings tended to vote in somewhat greater proportion than the "Republican" groupings, a fact
associated with their urban residence.

[1] Although the number of Americans of Irish Protestant background represented in the sample was small (28) and figures based on them consequently
unreliable, it is interesting to note that their voting preference was very different
from that of the Irish Catholics. As we see in Table 5.3, Irish Catholics tended
to support the Democrats, 55 per cent having voted for Stevenson and only
38 per cent for Eisenhower. The Irish Protestants in the sample, on the other
hand, favored the Republicans, 57 per cent having voted for Eisenhower and only
21 per cent for Stevenson.

Because of the history of immigration in America, factors related to ethnic background also tend to be related to the period of arrival in America. Scandinavians, Germans, and English tended to predominate among the earlier immigrants, while Italians, Poles, and to some extent Irish were among the later arrivals. We would expect, therefore, that the relationship between voting preference and ethnicity would be paralleled by a relationship between voting preference and generation-time in America. This is borne out by the findings presented in Table 5.4. Third-generation Americans were more Republican than were foreign-born first-generation American citizens or

TABLE 5.4

RELATION OF GENERATION-TIME IN AMERICA TO VOTING BEHAVIOR
IN 1952 PRESIDENTIAL ELECTION

VOTING BEHAVIOR	GENERATION-TIME IN AMERICA†			
	First Generation	Second Generation	Third Generation	Fourth Generation or More
Voted for:				
Eisenhower	41%	45%	57%	44%
Stevenson	35	40	26	27
Other, or not ascertained	5	1	1	*
Did not vote	19	14	16	29
Total	100%	100%	100%	100%
Number of cases	120	362	328	548

† Negroes, and individuals whose generation-time in America was not ascertained, are omitted from this table. First generation refers to foreign-born American citizens; second generation, native-born Americans one or both of whose parents were foreign-born; third generation, native Americans of native American parents, but with at least one foreign-born grandparent; fourth generation, native Americans with native-born parents and grandparents.

native-born Americans whose parents were foreign born. The relationship is not a completely linear one, since people from families who have been in America for more than three generations were somewhat less Republican than third-generation Americans. This deviation reflects the heavy concentration of Southerners among the old American group.

The relationship between voting preference and generation-time in America raises the question of the extent to which the relation between voting preference and ethnic background would hold up, if length of time in this country were controlled. Are the political inclinations of the "Democratic" ethnic groupings a function of their more recent immigrant status, and do these groups become increasingly Republican as they become "integrated" into American society?

The size of the sample was too small to permit us to compare the political characteristics of the six ethnic groupings within each of the different generations. However, we may estimate what the result of such an analysis would have been from an examination of the relation between voting preference and religious affiliation within the different generations. Since people of Scandinavian, German, and English descent are predominantly Protestant, and people of Irish, Italian, and Polish background predominantly Catholic, relationships involving the "Democratic" and "Republican" ethnic groupings should be very similar to those involving the two major religious groupings. These relationships involving religious background, generation-time in America, and voting preference, are presented in Table 5.5.

TABLE 5.5

RELATION OF RELIGIOUS AFFILIATION TO 1952 VOTE FOR PRESIDENT, WITH GENERATION-TIME IN AMERICA HELD CONSTANT

RELIGIOUS AFFILIATION	GENERATION-TIME IN AMERICA†			
	First Generation	Second Generation	Third Generation	Fourth Generation or More
	Proportion of Two-Party Vote for Eisenhower			
Protestant	71%	70%	71%	64%
Number of cases	31	138	193	354
Catholic	53%	42%	64%	46%
Number of cases	40	137	67	28

† Negroes and individuals whose generation-time in America was not ascertained are not included.

Although some of the figures in Table 5.5 are based on small numbers of cases, it would appear that the greater Republicanism of the Protestant groupings is not merely a reflection of the fact that Protestants are more heavily concentrated among the older American settlers. Protestants of all generations were more likely to vote for Eisenhower than were Catholics of the same generation. By implication, this was probably also generally true of the major ethnic groupings which make up these religious categories (although not, of course, necessarily true for each particular ethnic group).

Summary

We have devoted this chapter to a statement of the demographic characteristics of voters and nonvoters because of the widespread interest in this type of data. There is an undoubted fascination in the concept of great blocs of voters moving from one party to another, or from apathy to action, and much political analysis has sought to explain political behavior in these terms.

We have not attempted to elaborate the implications of the differences we have pointed out between the various social classifications that make up American society. Previous authors have examined the historical origins of these group differences; others have related them to considerations of economic and other types of self-interest. It is possible to analyze them in terms of group effects and group identification. There is clearly much more that might be said about the data presented in this chapter.

Our approach to the study of political behavior is not, however, at the level of groups. We are interested in analyzing the motivation of the individual voter or nonvoter. How does he regard himself politically? Does he feel himself to belong to one or the other party? Is he involved in partisan issues—does he take a partisan position regarding issues? Is he concerned with the candidates? It is from the point of view implicit in such questions that the next section of our analysis proceeds.

Part Two

THE MOTIVATION OF
VOTING BEHAVIOR

VI

Introduction to Part Two

Part One has presented a wide range of information regarding the vote cast for president in November, 1952. We have seen how the vote crystallized from the period prior to the nominations down to Election Day, we have noted the extent and character of individual participation in the campaign, we have examined in detail public perceptions of the parties and the candidates, and we have compared the demographic characteristics of the Eisenhower and Stevenson supporters. Where possible, data from the 1948 presidential election have also been presented so as to provide a comparison between the two elections.

Many interesting facts may be singled out of the tables which have been presented in Part One, and many intriguing interpretations are suggested by them. It is now appropriate to ask, "Have these data told us why the voters turned out in record numbers in 1952 and why they elected General Eisenhower by a sizable majority?" The data we have examined do not in fact answer these questions. They do offer a detailed documentation of the manner in which these events came about, but the forces which impelled the voters can, as yet, only be inferred. How can we come to a closer account of the motivation of the vote? Three methods of approaching this problem come to mind.

The Study of External Events

Any survey of voters will uncover an occasional individual who will explain that his voting decision was in doubt until he heard a particular speech, saw a convincing television program, or read something impressive in his magazine or newspaper. How well can we explain the motivations of the general electorate through the analysis of such individual events during the campaign and pre-campaign period?

The prospects of this procedure of linking events directly to action do not seem encouraging. It would be a hopeless undertaking to attempt to record and assess all of the individual stimuli which enter the individual mind during the period prior to an election, hopeless indeed if we were to think of doing this for any significant group or sample of people. A sheer enumeration of all of the conversations, advertisements, media appeals, exhortations both oral and written of which one becomes aware, would pose a problem of discouraging proportions—and infinitely more so if an attempt were made to assess the relative intensity of all these experiences.

It is, moreover, very questionable whether one can accept without reservation a voter's report of the influence of specific campaign events on his decision. The lifelong Republican who tells us that Eisenhower's promise to visit Korea settled the issue for him may satisfy his own need to sound reasoned and deliberate, but his explanation may not be very convincing if we examine the total range of factors to which he may be reacting. No single campaign experience exists in a vacuum. Every new event is perceived against a background of attitudes and predispositions of which the individual himself may be only dimly aware. Perceiving is a highly selective process, influenced both by past experience and present needs. Few voters could be expected to introspect so accurately as to be able to assess reliably the impact of the specific attributes of a situation as complex as an election campaign.

For these reasons, the present study did not attempt to take a detailed record of the campaign events which the members of the sample could remember and considered important. It sought rather for some more generalized conceptualization of the factors which underlie the vote.

The Study of Sociological Setting

Certainly the most widely current explanation of voting behavior which goes beyond the simple accounting of campaign events is that which depends on the concept of broad group or class interest. Practical politicians have for many years attempted to exploit the pulling power of an Irish, Italian, Jewish, or other name on their tickets. Special appeals to the farm vote, the labor vote, the women's vote, and to numerous other special groups in the population are a dependable feature of political campaigns in this country. All of this group-directed pleading is based on the assumption that people of like national, religious, occupational, or other characteristics will respond similarly to appeals which invoke the special interests of their particular group.

There is, of course, ample evidence that, during the past twenty years at least, some of these social groupings have in fact given a large majority of their votes to one or the other of the major parties in the presidential elections. It is apparent that during the Roosevelt-Truman period knowledge of a voter's religion, occupation, income, and place of residence made it possible to predict his vote with much better than random success. An early demonstration of this fact may be found in Lazarsfeld's 1940 study in Erie County, Ohio, from which the authors concluded that "A person thinks, politically, as he is, socially. Social characteristics determine political preference." This sweeping observation was based on a high relationship found among Erie County voters that year between party preference and an index of political predisposition based on three sociological variables : socio-economic level, place of residence, and religion. According to the authors this "simple combination goes a long way in 'explaining' political preferences."

The experience of the last two presidential elections has shown us, however, that the simple classification of voters into sociological categories does not have the explanatory power that at first appeared. It has been demonstrated[1] that the application of the Lazarsfeld index to the national electorate in 1948 resulted in a prediction of the vote not remarkably better than chance. In 1952, the great shifts in group preferences which we have seen would have been very difficult to predict on the basis of previous voting records. Many a political prognosticator has been led into difficulties by the confident assumption that the major population classes will vote in the next election as they have voted in the recent past, and seldom has this been more true than it was in 1952.

It is sometimes possible to infer the motivations of certain classes of voters by analyzing the changes in their votes rather than the consistencies. This has been done, for example, by Lubell in his study of the vote in counties predominantly German in ethnic background.[2] The behavior of the vote in these counties from 1936 to 1948 led him to conclude that "ethnic and emotional" factors related to the Second World War were motivating large blocs of voters in these areas. Can we find evidence of this kind in our data regarding the 1948 and 1952 votes of the major sociological classes ?

We have seen in Chapter V that the most impressive fact about the 1948–1952 shifts in group voting was their generality; the movement toward Eisenhower occurred in virtually all of the groups represented. The broad character of the shift suggests that some factor or factors which transcended narrow class interests were operating in the 1952 election, and we shall have to look beyond the simple demographic comparisons for evidence as to what these factors were.

The Study of Intervening Variables

Additional information regarding the dynamics of voting behavior can be obtained by an approach at the level of attitudes, expectations, and group loyalties, the psychological variables which intervene

---

[1] Janowitz, M., and Miller, W. E., "The Index of Political Predisposition in the 1948 Election," *Journal of Politics*, 1952, **14**, 710–27.

[2] Lubell, S. *The Future of American Politics* (New York : Harper & Brothers, 1951, vii–285).

between the external events of the voter's world and his ultimate behavior. Successful identification and analysis of these "intervening variables" should provide insights into the problem of voter motivation beyond anything we can hope to achieve through attempting to relate specific campaign events to the vote, or by classifying the votes of the major demographic classes.

What are the major psychological variables that we might think of as relevant to an individual's decision to vote and to his choice of candidate? In the planning of the present study, six factors were proposed as having sufficient importance to warrant specific investigation in the interviews. They were:

1. Personal identification with one of the political parties;
2. Concern with issues of national governmental policy;
3. Personal attraction to the presidential candidates;
4. Conformity to the group standards of one's associates;
5. A sense of personal efficacy in the area of politics;
6. A sense of civic obligation to vote.

Each of these factors may be thought of as having significance in the total motivation of the vote. The first four of the six have the effect of not only stimulating the individual to vote but also of influencing the direction of his vote. The remaining two have relevance only to the act of voting, not to the direction of the vote.

Although data were collected in the interviews regarding each of these six variables, particular attention was given to the first three—those representing concern with parties, issues, and candidates. The other three factors have all been subjected to detailed analysis (portions of which are presented in the Appendices of this volume), but it seemed apparent from the outset that the major factors of parties, issues, and candidates would make the largest contribution to our understanding of voter motivation.

Part Two will deal with three concepts which we have labeled *party identification, issue orientation,* and *candidate orientation.* Although we shall be mainly concerned in this volume with relating these concepts to political behavior in the 1952 election, it may be hoped that they will have interest beyond the confines of this limited objective. Because of this broader interest, each of these concepts will be discussed in some detail in the chapters which follow. The variables used to represent these conceptualized forces are described in each case, and certain expectations regarding the behavior of each of the variables in relation to other data of the study are tested. This discussion is followed by three chapters in which we consider the way in which the three variables interact, how they are related to voting behavior, and how they may be applied in an analysis of the motivation of the 1952 vote.

It must be emphasized that the argument of Part Two is based on the assumption that no single-factor theory will account for voting behavior. In other words, we assume that most citizens are acted upon by more than one of the factors we are considering and probably by others as well. We expect their behavior to be a resultant of the total impact of these forces. That is to say, we expect that the greater the number of positive forces activating an individual in the election situation the more likely he will be to respond. When the forces acting on a person are in conflict, however, we expect that his response will be reduced. These two hypotheses will be tested in the chapters which follow, as they relate both to participation in the election and to choice of candidate.

VII

Party Identification

Political activity during the national election campaigns is centered around the major political parties. These sprawling, loosely knit organizations, relatively quiet during the off-election years, provide the mechanism through which the activities of millions of partisan followers are stimulated and integrated during the campaigns.

The nature of the political parties, their history, their internal organization, their techniques and activities, have interested students of politics for many years. Much detailed information is available regarding these attributes of the parties. Our present objective is to explore a different aspect of the total phenomenon of political parties than has ordinarily been the subject of investigation. We propose to consider the parties as social groups and in this and later chapters, to analyze the perceptions, evaluations, and actions of those who identify with them.

Broadly defined, a group is any aggregation of individuals who share a sense of common characteristics or common goals. Every member of our society relates himself either formally or vicariously to a variety of different kinds of groups, some of a small, face-to-face character, others of a much more diffuse and impersonal nature. The particular groups with which a person may choose to associate himself differ in different strata of society, at different stages of life, and in different areas of experience. Some groups imply actual physical proximity among members. Other important groupings are physically dispersed and have little or no ritual of membership. Group-belonging in this latter sense may consist largely of a person's considering himself a member of the group—of identifying himself with it.

Group membership may be said to have importance psychologically in the degree to which it influences the attitudes and behaviors of those who share it. The same group may have very different degrees of significance to different individual members. To some church members the dogma pronounced by the official hierarchy may have the force of law; to others it may seem merely casual. If the group has high positive significance to the individual, he will tend to conform to what he perceives to be its standards.

The sense of personal attachment which the individual feels toward the group of his choice is referred to in this chapter as identification and, with respect to parties as groups, as *party identification*. Strong identification is equated with high significance of the group as an influential standard.

Political Parties as Groups

The political parties represent a unique kind of social grouping in American society. They are not formal membership groups in the usual definition of the term. Most of their adherents are not elected or invited to membership, they pay no dues, they go to no meetings and they have no contact with any official representative of the party. On the other hand, it is apparent that for many of these silent partisans the fact of "being a Republican or a Democrat" represents much more than a merely nominal association. As V. O. Key observes:

> Despite the informality of acquisition of legal membership in a party the psychological attachment of the great mass of partisans to their party possesses remarkable durability. Even if the party member is an unfaithful attendant at party functions and an infrequent contributor to its finances, he is likely to have a strong attachment to the heroes of the party, to its principles as he interprets them, and to its candidates on election day.

The two major parties in the United States have served as rallying points for political partisans for almost one hundred years. Generations of Americans have sorted themselves into Republicans and Democrats, usually for reasons of a purely pacific variety, but occasionally with implications of more serious conflict. The executive and legislative branches of both federal and state government have been controlled by the two parties as long as contemporary Americans can remember. An elaborate folklore regarding the parties, their history, their great leaders, their policies, has grown up and is widely shared in the population.

One of the important peculiarities of political parties is the fact that for the most part they make no formal requirements of their followers. An individual is free to call himself a Democrat and to consider himself such without getting anyone's approval, paying any fee, or taking any pledge. He is equally free to desert the Democratic party whenever he sees fit and proclaim himself a Republican. While some people have a much more formal connection with their party, for the most part association with a political party in the United States is largely a matter of what one regards himself as being, a Republican or a Democrat.

The fact that people are free to choose their party or shift from one party to the other should not be taken to imply that party identification is typically a frivolous attachment with no serious implications. It is a commonplace experience that some fervid individuals arrange their lives around their partisan obsessions, giving money, doing volunteer work, following the party line in word and deed. Of course most people are a good deal more restrained about their political interests, although as we have seen a good many of them can be stimulated into action during the heat of a presidential campaign. The fact is that individuals differ greatly in the involvement they feel with political events, and it may be taken for granted that great variation exists in the degree of influence party identification exerts.

The present analysis of party identification is based on the assumption that the two parties serve as standard-setting groups for a significant proportion of the people of this country. In other words, it is assumed that many people associate themselves psychologically with one or the other of the parties, and that this identification has predictable relationships with their perceptions, evaluations, and actions. These relationships would be expected to be in areas of experience relevant to the activities of political parties. We would expect high party identification to be associated with conformity to perceived party standards and support of perceived party goals.

We are asking the reader to think of the influence of personal attachment to a political party as one of the important factors that act as psychological forces in determining political behavior. Two other factors, issue orientation and candidate orientation, will be considered in the chapters which follow. An analysis of the interaction of these three motivational factors and of their combined relation to voting and related behavior will be presented in Chapters X and XI.

The Measurement of Party Identification

The first step we can take in attempting to establish an individual's group attachment is to ask him whether or not he associates himself with this or that organization or social grouping. Is he a Baptist, a Californian, a Rotarian, a Rutgers alumnus? If answered honestly, this can serve as a screening question to divide the population into nominal groups, with no implication as to the personal importance of these group associations.

A direct categorical question of this kind was asked in the present study to separate the respondents into party groups. It read as follows: "Generally speaking, do you usually think of yourself as a Republican, a Democrat, an independent, or what?" Of the sample, 22 per cent answered this question by saying they were "independents." They were asked a second question, as follows: "Do you think of yourself as closer to the Republican or Democratic party?" Most of these self-styled independents agreed that they were closer to one party than the other, and they are subsequently referred to as independent

Republicans and independent Democrats. Those independents who insisted they were not closer to either party are henceforth referred to simply as independents.[1]

It may be assumed that some of these people who accepted a party label when it was offered to them in the interview gave a merely superficial answer to the question. The fact that they chose one party label rather than the other may imply very little regarding the actual importance of the preferred party to them. It is clearly necessary to assign those people who placed themselves in one or the other party a value representing the strength of their identification with that group. If we propose to correlate party attachment with various aspects of political behavior, it is essential for our analysis that we at least be able to divide the party identifiers into those for whom party connection is purely nominal and those for whom it has some psychological importance.

Since party identification is regarded in this study as the perception of oneself as attached to one or the other of those vaguely defined agglomerates known as the Democratic party or the Republican party, it was decided to rate the intensity of this identification on the basis of the individual's own perception of himself as being strongly or weakly associated with these party groups. Each respondent who answered the first question on party identification by saying he usually thought of himself as a Republican (or a Democrat) was asked, "Would you call yourself a strong (R) (D) or a not very strong (R) (D)?" In each case the party identifiers divided themselves about equally into strong and weak partisans. Those people who classified themselves as strongly attached to one or the other party often expanded their remarks in terms which left no doubt as to their preference. The following excerpts illustrate the language which they used in speaking of their party:

> "All my ancestors all the way up have always voted Democratic and I felt like it would have made my poor old daddy turn over in his grave if I voted any other way. He fought in the Civil War and went through too much."

[1] The reader will recognize that there are a variety of ways of defining political "independents." Usually some aspect of voting record, such as ticket-splitting or irregular voting, is taken as the basis of classification. Eldersveld ("The Independent Vote: Measurement, Characteristics, and Implications for Party Strategy," *The American Political Science Review*, September, 1952, **46**, No. 3, 732–53) has pointed out that the method of self-designation used in this study does not yield the same results as the more familiar methods of definition. It should be emphasized that in the present context the "independents" were defined as those people who rejected the party labels when asked to identify their political affiliation. Their voting behavior was not considered as a criterion of classification.

"There's no party but the Democratic party as far as I'm concerned. Eisenhower's a good man—he's got a good record, but he's with the wrong party."

"I was just raised to believe in the Democrats and they have been good for the working man—that's good enough for me. The Republicans are a cheap outfit all the way around. I just don't like Republicans, my past experience with them has been all bad."

"I'm a borned Republican, sister. We're Republicans from start to finish, clear back on the family tree. Hot Republicans all along. I'm not so much in favor of Eisenhower as the party he is on. I won't weaken my party by voting for a Democrat."

"I think the differences between the parties are so wide they can't be calculated. It's a matter of personal experience. I've always found the Republicans a finer type of mind and conduct. I think they are on the right side and whatever they do is right."

"It's hard to explain, but I've always been a Republican and I just don't know why or anything about the reasons, issues, or such. I just think they're better than the Democrats in everything, nothing in particular."

As a consequence of this series of questions, it was possible to sort all but a small fraction of the sample into seven categories ranging from strong Democrats to strong Republicans.[2] The distribution of the population into these categories within the four major geographical areas of the nation is presented in Table 7.1.

It is apparent from this table that in October, 1952, about three out of four Americans identified themselves at least nominally with one or the other of the traditional parties, while almost one in four called himself an "independent." It is also clear that at the time of this survey many more people thought of themselves as Democrats (47 per cent) than thought of themselves as Republicans (27 per cent).

If our basic assumption is to be supported—the assumption that party identification is a psychological force with important relationships to political behavior—these self-classifications must imply something more than a capricious choice of proffered labels at the time of the interview. It would have been very desirable if the stability of reported party identification could have been studied by means of panel surveys extending over months or years, with successive reinterviews with the same sample of respondents. Lacking this, a measure of group, rather than individual, reliability can be obtained by comparing the distributions of identification scores obtained from independent samples at different points in time. Evidence of this kind is available from two surveys conducted by the Survey Research Center,

[2] Some four per cent of the respondents, largely Southern Negroes, seemed unable to relate themselves to this type of classification.

one in June, 1952, and the other in September, 1953, in which the same questions[3] on party identification were asked as were asked in the October survey. Table 7.2 demonstrates the way these three independent samples of the national population identified their party association. The distributions are essentially similar, the only difference being a drop in the independent category after June, 1952, with a

TABLE 7.1

DISTRIBUTION OF PARTY IDENTIFICATION WITHIN REGIONS

PARTY IDENTIFICATION[†]	REGION				TOTAL SAMPLE
	North-east	Mid-west	South	Far West	
Strong Democrat	18%	17%	31%	22%	22%
Weak Democrat	18	25	32	24	25
Independent Democrat	13	9	8	10	10
Independent	8	7	2	7	5
Independent Republican	9	8	5	6	7
Weak Republican	18	15	8	13	14
Strong Republican	14	18	6	16	13
None, minor party, or not ascertained	2	1	8	2	4
Total	100%	100%	100%	100%	100%
Number of cases	390	580	440	446‡	1,614

† The questions on which this classification is based are shown in the text.
‡ See pages 3 and 4.

corresponding small rise in both the party categories.[4] In other words, within the limits of the present data, the self-classification of party identification appears to be relatively stable. The difference between the three distributions only slightly exceeds what might have been expected from errors resulting from sampling, even though the period between the first two surveys was one of intense political activity, and a change in the national administration intervened between the second and third.

[3] They differed slightly in the wording of the question on strength of party identification, which in June read, "Would you say you are a strong (R) (D) or a weak (R) (D)?" and in the later surveys read, "Would you call yourself a strong (R) (D) or a not very strong (R) (D)?"
[4] In the June survey those respondents who did not identify themselves in any of the categories offered were classified with the "independents."

A procedure commonly used to establish the validity of a classification, such as the one with which we are here concerned, is to correlate it with other classifications or scales which may be considered on the basis of a priori judgment to be measuring the same trait or variable. In order to accomplish this in the present study, two questions were asked which posed the problem of party loyalty in suppositional terms. The expectation was that people who had classified themselves

TABLE 7.2

DISTRIBUTION OF PARTY IDENTIFICATION IN JUNE, 1952,
OCTOBER, 1952, AND SEPTEMBER, 1953

Party Identification	June, 1952	October, 1952	September, 1953
Strong Democrat	19%	22%	22%
Weak Democrat	20	25	23
Independent Democrat	9	10	8
Independent	14	5	4
Independent Republican	7	7	6
Weak Republican	13	14	15
Strong Republican	15	13	15
None, minor party, or not ascertained	3	4	7
Total	100%	100%	100%
Number of cases	999	1,614	1,023

as strong party adherents would be more likely to express a willingness to follow their party line than would people of weak party attachment, or people independent of parties.

The first of these questions asked the respondents to imagine what they would do if their party ran a candidate they "didn't like or didn't agree with." Only those people who had identified themselves as Democrats or Republicans were asked this question, the answers to which are summarized in Table 7.3.

Although the conjectural character of this question may be thought to have introduced some degree of unreality into the answers, the differences between the party groups are marked. Strong partisans were very much more likely to say they would support their party in spite of a candidate they didn't like than were party identifiers who had been classified as less strong.

The second question read, "Some people think that if a voter votes

TABLE 7.3

RELATION OF PARTY IDENTIFICATION TO EXPECTED REACTION TO UNATTRACTIVE CANDIDATE ON PARTY TICKET

"SUPPOSE THERE WAS AN ELECTION WHERE YOUR PARTY WAS RUNNING A CANDIDATE YOU DIDN'T LIKE OR YOU DIDN'T AGREE WITH. WHICH OF THE FOLLOWING THINGS COMES CLOSEST TO WHAT YOU THINK YOU WOULD DO?"	PARTY IDENTIFICATION				TOTAL IDENTIFIERS
	Strong Demo-crat	Weak Demo-crat	Weak Repub-lican	Strong Repub-lican	
I probably would vote for him anyway because a person should be loyal to his party	40%	11%	9%	28%	22%
I probably would not vote for either candidate in that election	26	25	18	18	23
I would probably vote for the other party's candidate	32	61	71	53	53
Don't know	1	1	*	—	1
Not ascertained	1	2	2	1	1
Total	100%	100%	100%	100%	100%
Number of cases	351	402	222	217	1,192

TABLE 7.4

RELATION OF PARTY IDENTIFICATION TO ATTITUDES TOWARD STRAIGHT PARTY VOTING FOR NATIONAL OFFICES

" . . . A VOTER SHOULD VOTE FOR THE SAME PARTY [FOR CONGRESS AS FOR PRESIDENT]. DO YOU AGREE OR DISAGREE . . . ?"	PARTY IDENTIFICATION							TOTAL SAMPLE†
	Strong Demo-crat	Weak Demo-crat	Inde-pendent Demo-crat	Inde-pendent	Inde-pendent Repub-lican	Weak Repub-lican	Strong Repub-lican	
Agree	57%	33%	24%	26%	24%	41%	58%	40%
Don't know, it depends	5	9	10	5	8	7	6	9
Disagree	37	57	66	68	67	51	36	50
Not ascertained	1	1	—	1	1	1	*	1
Total	100%	100%	100%	100%	100%	100%	100%	100%
Number of cases	351	402	164	87	114	222	217	1,614

†Including 49 people who identified themselves otherwise than as Democratic, Republican, or independent, and eight whose party identification was not ascertained.

for one party for president he should vote for the same party for senator and congressman. Do you agree or disagree with that idea? " It will be noted that this question has a stronger ideological content than the first question and is not framed in terms of specific, personal behavior. The answers to this question are shown in Table 7.4.

Half of the respondents rejected this basic proposition of the party system, most of them on the grounds that the voter should always select "the best man." However, those with strong partisan attachments were more than twice as likely as the independents to agree with this statement.

Two conclusions are apparent from these two tables. In the first place, it is clear that the relationships between the classifications of party identification and the expressions of willingness to conform to party position are in the expected direction and are high. To this extent, we may feel some reassurance regarding the validity of the party identification measure. It is also evident, however, that the two conjectural questions posed more severe tests of party discipline to the respondents than did the simple naming of oneself as a strong Republican or Democrat. One-third of the people classified as strong Democrats and one-half of the strong Republicans declared themselves prepared to vote for the other party's candidate in the event that they didn't approve of the man put up by their own party.[5] A third or

[5] It is of interest that a larger proportion of the Republican party identifiers than of the Democratic identifiers declared themselves ready to vote for the other party's candidate. The explanation of this may lie in the difference in the average educational levels of the followers of the two parties, Republicans having a considerable advantage in years of formal schooling. It is known from the Survey Research Center study of the 1948 election that higher education was clearly associated with ticket-splitting in the election of that year, and this relationship has been found again in the present study. It may be surmised that advanced education may tend to free the individual from the restraints of party voting, make him better informed and more selective regarding the individual candidates, and give him greater confidence in his ability to manipulate a split rather than a straight ticket. In other words, the somewhat greater Republican willingness to cross party lines may be a characteristic of highly educated people primarily and of Republicans only secondarily. It will be noted in Table 7.4 that the followers of the two parties did not differ in their reaction to the somewhat sophisticated concept of party uniformity in presidential and congressional votes. In this case the relationship to education disappears. People of high education are no less likely to accept the desirability of party voting on national officers than are people of low education. It appears that the concept of party responsibility in the executive and legislative branches of the federal government is sufficiently well understood and accepted among more highly educated people to make this otherwise relatively selective group of people as willing as other sections of the public to conform to party nominations at this particular level, or at least to accept the stereotype of party responsibility when they recognized it in the question.

more of both these groups rejected the concept of party uniformity in voting for national officers. These distributions lead us to conclude that while for the most part we are justified in regarding our "strong" identifiers as having greater party attachment than our "weak" identifiers, we must keep in mind that these classifications are relative and that the "strong" categories undoubtedly contain some individuals whose party loyalty is not as great as the term "strong" might imply.[6]

Finally, returning to Table 7.2, it should be remarked that the five-to-three advantage which went to the Democratic party in the self-identifications of the October sample contrasted sharply with a five-to-four advantage which these same people gave to the Republican nominee for president. This discrepancy supports the presumption which is implicit in this analysis that for most people party identification is not the same thing as current intention to vote for one party or the other. This distinction was made very explicitly by some of the respondents who answered the question on whether "they usually thought of themselves" as Democrats, Republicans, or independents in the following kind of language:

"I'm a Democrat. There are times when I split my vote but I've always considered myself a Democrat. I'm going to split my vote for Eisenhower this time."

It is possible, of course, that some people answered the party identification questions entirely in terms of their current voting intentions. In other words, they called themselves strong Republicans or strong Democrats because at that moment they were strongly supporting Eisenhower or Stevenson and not because of any attachment to either party. The ensuing section of this chapter, which presents data on the personal history of party identification, suggests that for most people these party attachments do not change easily as candidates come and go on the national scene.

The Personal History of Party Identification

Virtually nothing is known about the genetic development of personal identification with political parties. Some vague awareness of party politics is probably widespread among American schoolchildren, but there has been no systematic study of how party consciousness develops. The present study has made some preliminary explorations

---

[6] It would have been possible to "refine" the two groups of strong identifiers by taking out those who rejected the party position on either of the two questions regarding support of party candidates. However, this would have reduced the size of the "strong" groups below a desirable level and would not have proved advantageous in the analysis which is presented in this chapter.

into the personal history of party identification. It has had to rely on the respondents' recall of early experiences, a notoriously fallible source of information. The data are presented here with full recognition of their shortcomings and with the expectation that they will subsequently be replaced by new data gathered by more adequate methods.

Most Americans of voting age, when asked if their parents "thought of themselves mostly as Democrats or Republicans," remember their parents as being associated with one or the other party rather than as shifting between parties (Table 7.5). As might have been expected, those people who remember both their parents as preferring one of the two parties tend strongly to prefer that party themselves. When parental partisanship was reported as mixed or unknown, the identification of the offspring was more evenly divided.

These findings are subject to three possible interpretations: (a) Party attachment, like church preference, may tend to be passed from parent to child and to persist into adult life. (b) It may be that most people remain in the same class, ethnic, and religious groups as their parents and are subject to the same group influences as their parents. (c) People may tend consciously or otherwise to make their memory of their parents' partisanship conform to their own current attachments. While there is no way of assessing the relative weight of these mechanisms from the data of the present study, there is no apparent reason to expect that the factor of biased recall should have been pre-eminent among them. In our society, no public opprobrium attaches to a person who votes differently from his parents. The need to conceal intrafamily differences would seem rather slight.

It will be observed from Table 7.5 that more people identified their parents as Democratic (41 per cent) than as Republican (24 per cent). A sizable proportion of this discrepancy was contributed by the South with its traditional adherence to the Democratic party. Of the Southern respondents, 56 per cent remembered both their parents as Democrats; 15 per cent classified their parents as Republicans. When the rest of the country is considered without the South, the division of parental partisanship is more nearly equal, although the Democrats hold an advantage in every region (Table 7.6).

There is also a substantially greater tendency for younger respondents to report their parents as Democratic than for older. Those people reaching voting age prior to the 1928 election reported their parents as dividing about 55 to 45 in favor of the Democratic party, an advantage contributed entirely by the South. Those people coming of age after the 1928 election reported their parents as favoring the Democrats by slightly more than a two-to-one margin.

In considering these data on family partisanship, it must be remembered that they cannot be directly equated with the division of the

TABLE 7.5

Relation of Parents' Party Identification to That of Offspring

"Do you remember when you were growing up whether your parents thought of themselves as mostly Democrats, or Republicans, or did they shift around from one party to another?"

Party Identification	Both Parents Democrats	Both Parents Republicans	One Democrat, One Republican	One Democrat or Republican, Other Uncertain	Both Parents Shifted	Don't Know About Either	Neither Parent Voted
Strong Democrat	36%	7%	12%	14%	11%	15%	15%
Weak Democrat	36	9	32	23	23	21	22
Independent Democrat	10	6	10	13	13	14	14
Independent	3	4	—	10	14	5	15
Independent Republican	3	10	—	10	12	11	7
Weak Republican	6	30	22	12	14	9	9
Strong Republican	6	33	22	15	11	3	3
None, minor party, or not ascertained	*	1	2	3	2	22	15
Total	100%	100%	100%	100%	100%	100%	100%
Number of cases	657	387	41	102	103	140	59
Proportion of total sample†	41%	24%	3%	6%	6%	9%	4%

† Omitted from this table are 125 respondents whose parents belonged to minor parties, whose parents had unusual combinations of party connections, who did not grow up with their parents, or from whom this information was not ascertained.

TABLE 7.6

DISTRIBUTION OF PARENTS' PARTY IDENTIFICATION WITHIN REGIONS

PARENTS' PARTY IDENTIFICATION	REGION			
	North-east	Mid-west	South	Far West
Both parents Democrats	33%	35%	56%	37%
Both parents Republicans	25	31	15	27
One Democrat, one Republican	1	2	3	4
One Democrat or Republican, other uncertain	8	7	4	7
Both parents shifted	7	9	2	5
Don't know about either	6	5	15	8
Neither parent voted	8	2	2	3
Other combinations, including minor parties	10	7	2	8
Not ascertained	2	2	1	1
Total	100%	100%	100%	100%
Number of cases	390	580	440	446

presidential vote during the period when the respondents were "growing up." People over 40 in this country grew up at a time when the Republican party was rather consistently in power in Washington. One would expect that the total number of votes cast during the period when the present electorate was growing up would show a Republican majority. However, there is evidence both from this study and from earlier research that, as a group, people who regard themselves as Democrats are significantly less likely to vote than those who identify themselves as Republicans (see Table 7.7). If this differential in turnout has characterized the two parties for any significant period of time, as Table 7.7 indicates it has, it would be reasonable to expect that reported family partisanship would run more strongly Democratic than the recorded vote.

It would have been very desirable for the study of the development of party identification, if a full record could have been obtained from each respondent of his voting history from the time he reached voting age. This seemed clearly beyond the possibility of achievement, and it was not attempted. However, it was felt that an individual's first vote for president might be a sufficiently salient experience to be reliably recalled many years later. A question regarding first vote was asked in the survey with the results shown in Table 7.8. Three-fourths of the people who report their first vote as going to one or the

TABLE 7.7

RELATION OF PARTY IDENTIFICATION TO REGULARITY OF VOTING IN PRESIDENTIAL ELECTIONS

"IN THE ELECTIONS FOR PRESIDENT SINCE YOU HAVE BEEN OLD ENOUGH TO VOTE, WOULD YOU SAY YOU HAVE VOTED IN ALL OF THEM, MOST OF THEM, SOME OF THEM, OR NONE OF THEM?"	PARTY IDENTIFICATION							TOTAL SAMPLE
	Strong Democrat	Weak Democrat	Independent Democrat	Independent	Independent Republican	Weak Republican	Strong Republican	
All of them	42%	36%	41%	32%	51%	47%	65%	43%
Most	22	17	21	23	9	20	19	18
Some	15	22	15	23	13	15	5	16
None	14	18	15	16	17	12	5	16
Not of age or not a citizen in previous elections	6	7	8	4	9	4	4	6
Don't know	—	—	—	1	—	—	—	*
Not ascertained	1	*	—	1	1	2	2	1
Total	100%	100%	100%	100%	100%	100%	100%	100%

other of the two major parties still associate themselves to some degree with the same party. Only one person in ten has clearly shifted his allegiance from the party of his original choice to the other.

Additional evidence regarding the constancy of party attachment was obtained by asking those people who called themselves Democrats

TABLE 7.8

RELATION OF REPORTED FIRST VOTE TO PARTY IDENTIFICATION

PARTY IDENTIFICATION	FIRST VOTE FOR PRESIDENT		
	Democratic	Republican	Don't Remember or Have Never Voted
Strong Democrat	33%	4%	20%
Weak Democrat	34	6	27
Independent Democrat	12	6	10
Independent	5	6	5
Independent Republican	5	11	7
Weak Republican	7	27	13
Strong Republican	4	39	8
None, minor party, or not ascertained	*	1	10
Total	100%	100%	100%
Number of cases	710	387	498
Proportion of total sample†	44%	24%	31%

† Nineteen people who voted for minor parties or whose first vote was not ascertained are omitted from this table.

or Republicans whether they had ever thought of themselves as identified with the opposite party. As Table 7.9 demonstrates, at the time of the survey 90 per cent of the Democrats said they had never thought of themselves as Republicans, while approximately one-quarter of the Republicans admitted that they had once thought of themselves as Democrats.

The character of the party switching reported by people calling themselves Republicans in 1952 becomes clearer when it is found that most of it occurred in the late 1930s and 1940s, and in large part among people who reported their first vote as pre-Roosevelt Republican, or who came from families with a Republican preference. In other words, the apparent instability in the Republican ranks is largely an expression of a return to the Republican party of those who had strayed into the Roosevelt camp in 1932 and 1936.[7]

First vote, as reported by the respondents, is clearly associated with region. For the South, first votes, like family partisanship, are heavily Democratic (82 per cent, as against 17 per cent Republican).

TABLE 7.9

RELATION OF PARTY IDENTIFICATION TO PARTY SWITCHING

"WAS THERE EVER A TIME WHEN YOU THOUGHT OF YOURSELF AS A REPUBLICAN [DEMOCRAT] RATHER THAN A DEMOCRAT [REPUBLICAN]?"	PARTY IDENTIFICATION			
	Strong Demo-crat	Weak Demo-crat	Weak Repub-lican	Strong Repub-lican
Yes, a Democrat	—%	—%	30%	16%
Yes, a Republican	6	12	—	—
No	92	87	68	83
Don't know	1	—	—	—
Not ascertained	1	1	2	1
Total	100%	100%	100%	100%

In the other three regions, first votes for Democrats outnumbered those for Republicans by about three to two.

The explanation of the heavy Democratic majority among first votes (44 per cent Democratic to 24 per cent Republican) becomes apparent when the first votes are divided by election years. Two types of analysis are possible:

1. We can examine the votes cast by the respondents in the first election after they reached voting age. Considering each election beginning with 1916, we find that these coming-of-age voters followed the national trend in every election down to 1932. In 1932 there was a massive shift of preference to the Democratic party among this group. This heavy Democratic majority continued through the Roosevelt era, although it declined somewhat in the Truman victory of 1948, reaching a low of slightly over five to three. The total coming-of-age vote from 1916 through 1948, as reported in this survey, favored the Democratic party by a two to one majority.

2. It is also possible to look at the character of the "delayed" first votes, votes cast sometime later than the first election for which the

[7] There is also evidence that Republican identifiers are less rigid in other aspects of political behavior, i.e., split-ticket voting, and that this may be associated with their high education level.

person was eligible. This brings to light a significant number of delayed first votes reported for Roosevelt in 1932 and to a lesser extent in his subsequent elections. Virtually no compensatory delayed first votes appear during these years for the Republican nominees. The total number of delayed first votes brought into the Democratic column, from 1932 to 1948 inclusive, outnumbered those captured by the Republicans by a margin of five to one.

Although these data on first votes are consistent with the general trend of election statistics over the last 40 years, there is no sure way of establishing their validity. It is possible to compare the reported coming-of-age vote in recent elections to data on the young voters obtained in earlier surveys. The two kinds of data support each other closely. There is, however, no external criterion against which the survey information on delayed first votes can be checked. In view of these facts, the possibility must be admitted that the high degree of internal consistency which characterizes these data on first votes may result from a conscious or unconscious wish on the part of the respondents to tell a consistent story.

Data on one further aspect of the political history of the respondents are available from the survey. Those people who reported that they had at some time or another voted in a presidential election were asked whether they had always voted for the same party. As Table 7.10 demonstrates, about two-thirds of the people who claimed to have voted said they had always voted for the same party, and among them the Democratic party enjoyed a two-to-one advantage.

The high degree of party regularity indicated by this table needs to be modified by one important consideration. When a person reported that he "always" had voted Republican, this might mean in fact that he had voted only once and then for the Republican candidate. Number of times voted is disregarded in this table. With this provision, it is not surprising that the proportion of party regulars is as high as it is reported. As shown in Table 7.9, the amount of switching of party identification is relatively small, especially among Democrats.

The large majority of Democratic voters among the party regulars is very largely a phenomenon of the Roosevelt era. It must be kept in mind that approximately half of the adult population in 1952 had reached voting age after the 1928 presidential election. An even larger proportion of the 1952 population had cast their first votes after 1928, approximately 60 per cent. Thus, the Roosevelt period, with its great appeal to coming-of-age voters and delayed first voters, contributed a substantial Democratic bloc to the 1952 electorate. It must also be noted that a sizable number of Republicans crossed into the Roosevelt column during the thirties, and even though they later returned to their party they could not be classified here as party

TABLE 7.10

RELATION OF PARTY IDENTIFICATION TO PARTY REGULARITY IN VOTING

PARTY IDENTIFICATION

"HAVE YOU ALWAYS VOTED FOR THE SAME PARTY OR HAVE YOU VOTED FOR DIFFERENT PARTIES FOR PRESIDENT?"	Strong Demo-crat	Weak Demo-crat	Inde-pendent Demo-crat	Inde-pendent	Inde-pendent Repub-lican	Weak Repub-lican	Strong Repub-lican	TOTAL SAMPLE
Always Democratic	71%	56%	30%	9%	8%	6%	2%	34%
Mostly Democratic	2	3	2	1	*	1	1	2
Always Republican	*	*	2	3	24	39	66	16
Mostly Republican	—	—	—	—	—	5	7	2
Different parties	6	15	41	64	40	32	15	22
Don't know	—	*	1	3	—	*	*	1
Not ascertained how voted	1	*	1	—	2	1	*	1
Have not voted, or not ascertained whether voted	20	26	23	20	26	16	9	22
	100%	100%	100%	100%	100%	100%	100%	100%

regulars (see Tables 7.9 and 7.10). Considering these facts and the fact that Democrats were more likely to fail to vote in some of the elections for which they were eligible, it is reasonable to expect that a majority of the people who have never crossed party lines should be Democrats.

Two additional facts of interest emerge from Table 7.10. It will be seen that a small but visible fraction of those people who called themselves Republicans in October, 1952, said they had always voted Democratic in previous years. This switching of allegiance is almost entirely absent in the Democratic columns; virtually none of the self-identified Democrats reported having voted Republican exclusively in earlier elections. This discrepancy is a reflection of the sizable drift of Democrats into the Eisenhower camp which occurred in the 1952 election. Most of these defectors still called themselves Democrats but, as Table 7.10 shows, a small number of them not only supported Eisenhower, but now called themselves Republicans.

The second interesting item from the table is the distribution of people who say they have voted for different parties. Reasonably enough, these people appear in greatest proportion among those who call themselves independent of party affiliation and in decreasing proportions among the groups with increasing party attachment. As noted above, the proportion of bipartisan voters among Republicans is considerably higher than that among Democrats, largely a consequence of the Roosevelt inroads into the Republican ranks during the 1930s.

In summarizing these data on the personal history of party identification, we must observe again that report based on recall of events years in the past is subject to serious question. However, the data presented have a reassuring consistency with such outside information as is available. If we were to assume that within the limits of random memory error the respondents were reporting the facts as they remembered them, we would be justified in stating the following conclusions:

1. As of the time of the survey in October, 1952, about two Americans out of three remembered both their parents as identified with one of the two major parties, more commonly with the Democratic party than with the Republican. They tended very strongly to hold the same party identification they attributed to their parents.

2. Most people who identified themselves with one of the major parties had cast their first vote for that party and had never voted for the presidential candidate of the other party.

3. First votes were more frequently reported as Democratic than as Republican, largely as the result of the appeal of the Roosevelt administration to young voters and to older people who had not voted prior to 1932.

4. People who identified themselves as Democrats were more likely to be nonvoters and occasional voters than people who called themselves Republicans. However, Democrats who had voted were more likely to have stayed with their party in votes for president than were Republicans.

Relation of Party Identification to Participation and Presidential Preference

The evidence presented in the preceding pages documents our assumption that most people in the United States recognize the political parties as significant social entities toward which they feel a continuing sense of personal identification. The high degree of family similarity in party identification, the relatively small percentage of party switching, the small number of people who call themselves independents—all these indicate the importance of the parties as points of psychological anchoring.

It has also been assumed in the preceding discussion that identification with parties has predictable relationships with the way the individual sees the political world around him and how he reacts to it. A full development of the nature of these relationships cannot be undertaken here, but we can examine the degree to which differences in party identification were associated with differences in participation, and preference, in the 1952 election.

Our concept of party identification leads us to assume that a person who associates himself strongly with a party will conform to what he sees to be party standards and will support party goals. Taking the role of party member means, of course, supporting the candidates of the party. This, in a sense, is the ultimate test of party regularity. We might thus expect the strong party identifiers to be most unwavering in their preference for their party's standard bearers and most active in supporting them during the campaign and on Election Day.

If we look first at the extent of participation in the 1952 campaign reported by the different party groups, we discover that they do not differ as much as one might have expected (Table 7.11). The strong Republicans were much the most active of all the groups, both in percentage voting and in the proportion supporting their votes with other activity. Strong Democrats were the most active of the Democratic groups, although their record was not outstanding. However, there is not a high relationship between party identification and extent of participation.

What are we to deduce from Table 7.11 regarding the nature of party identification? It appears that the degree to which a person actively takes part in an election is determined largely by factors which are not reflected in our measure of party identification. At least, this was true in 1952. In that year we could not have made a very much better prediction of whether a person would vote or otherwise support his candidate from knowing which party category he put himself in than if we knew nothing about his party identification—unless he called

TABLE 7.11

RELATION OF PARTY IDENTIFICATION TO POLITICAL PARTICIPATION

POLITICAL PARTICIPATION†	PARTY IDENTIFICATION						
	Strong Demo-crat	Weak Demo-crat	Inde-pendent Demo-crat	Inde-pendent	Inde-pendent Repub-lican	Weak Repub-lican	Strong Repub-lican
High	30%	19%	26%	22%	32%	29%	42%
Medium	46	50	48	52	46	49	50
Low	24	31	26	26	22	22	8
Total	100%	100%	100%	100%	100%	100%	100%
Index of participa-tion‡	+ 6	− 12	0	− 4	+ 10	+ 7	+ 34

† It will be remembered that the three steps of participation ("high," "medium," and "low"), as discussed in Chapter III, refer respectively to voting plus other participation, voting only, and nonvoting.
‡ The index of participation is derived by subtracting the proportion of "low" participators from the proportion of "high" participators. It is included in this and following tables to summarize the data as an aid to the reader.

himself a strong Republican, in which case we could have been almost sure he would vote and reasonably sure he would participate in other ways, too.

We must conclude that, for many people, calling oneself a Democrat or a Republican does not imply a serious obligation to exert oneself on behalf of that party, even to the extent of voting for it. This is especially true of those people who call themselves Democrats. On the other hand, it is clear that many people vote and otherwise support their candidate without any admitted sense of strong attachment to either party. Their behavior must derive from other kinds of motivation.

It may be that for many people party identification does not have the capacity to stimulate overt activity, but does have the power to command support on the psychological level of preferences and attitudes. That is to say, a party-identified person might feel impelled to take his party's position when confronted with a choice between parties, even though his sense of party loyalty was not sufficient to move him into action. This would seem to be implied from the data presented in

Table 7.12, where we see the presidential preferences of the voters and nonvoters. The high relationship between party identification and preference for that party's candidate is apparent.

We saw in Chapter II that there were serious defections in the 1952 election among former Democratic voters. As we would expect, this

TABLE 7.12

RELATION OF PARTY IDENTIFICATION TO PRESIDENTIAL PREFERENCE
OF VOTERS AND NONVOTERS

PRESIDENTIAL PREFERENCE OF VOTERS AND NONVOTERS	PARTY IDENTIFICATION						
	Strong Demo- crat	Weak Demo- crat	Inde- pendent Demo- crat	Inde- pendent	Inde- pendent Repub- lican	Weak Repub- lican	Strong Repub- lican
Voted for:							
Eisenhower	12%	26%	28%	57%	73%	73%	91%
Stevenson	63	42	44	14	5	5	1
Other, or not as- certained	1	1	2	3	—	*	*
Did not vote but pre- ferred:							
Eisenhower	3	12	7	17	16	17	8
Stevenson	20	17	17	6	4	5	—
Other, none, or not ascertained	1	2	2	3	2	*	—
Total	100%	100%	100%	100%	100%	100%	100%

is reflected in the groups of Democratic party identifiers, especially among weak Democrats. In contrast, the strong and weak Republicans were virtually monolithic in their preference for Eisenhower, both those who voted and those who did not.

Two explanations might be put forward to clarify these impressive differences in the support given the candidates of the two parties by those who identify with these parties. It might be proposed, on the one hand, that those people who identify themselves with the Republican party in fact have a stronger group attachment than those people who identify with the Democratic party, and that the questions used in this survey to classify people by party identification were too crude to show this difference. On the other hand, it might be argued that in 1952 those factors other than party identification which influenced the public favored the Republican party, in which case the identifiers of the two parties may have been equally loyal to their parties, but the Democrats were subjected to a greater degree of pressure to break away from their party ticket.

There are three facts which make it appear that the first of these two explanations will not adequately account for the data: (*a*) The preceding tables in this chapter have not shown any consistent evidence that Republicans are more strongly attached to their party than are Democrats. A review of these data will show that in some cases the Republican partisans seem less ready to follow party discipline than are the Democrats. (*b*) As an inspection of Table 7.13 will show, the

TABLE 7.13

RELATION OF PARTY IDENTIFICATION TO VOTE FOR CONGRESSMAN IN 1952

VOTE FOR CONGRESSMAN IN 1952	PARTY IDENTIFICATION							TOTAL SAMPLE
	Strong Demo-crat	Weak Demo-crat	Inde-pendent Demo-crat	Inde-pendent	Inde-pendent Repub-lican	Weak Repub-lican	Strong Repub-lican	
Republican	6%	12%	21%	43%	54%	58%	75%	31%
Democrat	54	42	39	16	13	7	4	30
Other	1	1	—	1	—	—	—	*
Party not ascertained	5	7	7	6	7	6	8	6
Voted but not for Congressman	5	5	5	5	3	5	3	4
Not ascertained whether voted for Congressman	5	2	2	3	1	2	2	3
Did not vote	24	31	26	26	22	22	8	26
Total	100%	100%	100%	100%	100%	100%	100%	100%

difference between the voting regularity of Democrats and Republicans in 1952 was much smaller in the congressional vote than it was in the presidential vote. Although defections among the Democrats were still more common than among the Republicans, the discrepancy between parties was not so large. (*c*) It seems evident that the preponderance of Republican votes, both presidential and congressional, among the independent group must be due to factors other than party loyalty, probably to the same factors which produced the defections among the Democrats.

The present discussion may be concluded by the statement that conformance to party line in preference for candidate for president in the 1952 election was high among strong partisans of both parties, and less high among those less strongly identified with party. Factors conflicting with party loyalty were apparently more important for Democrats than Republicans in 1952.

Summary

The data of this chapter have been organized around the assumption that most Americans identify themselves with one or the other of the two major political parties, and that this sense of attachment and belonging is predictably associated with their political behavior.

The measurement of this experience of party identification presents difficulties. For some people party identification is undoubtedly largely nominal, implying little or no influence on the individual's perception of the political world and his reactions to it. For others, it is obviously a factor of great importance, affecting every aspect of their political lives. The present study has had to content itself with a simple division of those who identified themselves with each party into the strong partisans and the weak partisans, based on their own statements of the strength of their party attachment.

Following this method of classification, it has been found that party identification has both wide distribution and high stability. Three-fourths of the sample usually thought of themselves as either Republicans or Democrats, and there is substantial evidence that for the most part these party attachments are lasting and unchanging. A large majority of these people deny ever having thought of themselves as belonging to the party other than the one of their current choice.

We have conceptualized the personal attachment an individual feels toward his party as a psychological force which, along with other motivating factors, accounts for his voting behavior. Our analysis indicates that the extent of active participation people engaged in during the 1952 election was largely determined by factors other than party identification. The partisan direction of their choice for president, however, was very highly related to their sense of party attachment. We have not demonstrated, of course, that party identification has a direct causal effect on these presidential preferences, but the data follow the pattern we would expect to find if it did.

As we pointed out at the beginning of this chapter, party identification is not the only variable we need to consider in our analysis of the motivation of the vote. The presence of other important factors which influence political attitudes and behavior has been clearly indicated in the tables which have been presented. The succeeding chapters are devoted to their analysis.

VIII

Issue Orientation

If the party identifier is a person for whom parties provide the focus of political thought and action, the issue-oriented citizen is a person for whom questions of governmental policy are of paramount importance. We would expect this individual to perceive parties and candidates as they give promise of coping with major problems of state. Such a person is not, at least in his conscious thought processes, bound by traditional allegiance to the party of his fathers. He will not knowingly accept the warmth and kindliness of one candidate's personality, nor will he reject the retiring or arrogant candidate. For him the party and candidate are but vehicles through which one policy or its alternate will be enacted. He will not "vote for the man" nor will he "vote his party," except as the man or the party represents governmental policies which he himself wishes to see enacted or protected. For him, we assume, the electoral contest is given meaning by the backdrop of congressional voting behavior or administrative action which precedes it.

We propose to treat the concept of *issue orientation* as embracing two major components. These components are—

1. Sensitivity to differences in party positions on issues related to governmental action;
2. Involvement in issues which are perceived as being affected by the outcome of an election.

In the context of the American political system, most issue-oriented behavior will be determined by the perceived choices of action which the two major parties offer the citizen. A vote for party A, or candidate X, will follow from the perception that support of party A, or candidate X, may result in governmental action which will enhance values dear to the heart of the issue-oriented citizen, while support of party B, or candidate Y, might lead to governmental action which would threaten those same values. Inasmuch as the issue-oriented person evaluates his own behavior in terms of its eventual consequences for governmental action, it is postulated that he will be more likely to see policy differences between contesting parties or candidates than will citizens who are more prone to candidate or party orientations. In the midst of an election campaign, the candidate-oriented individual responds primarily to the personal attributes of the candidates for office, the party-oriented individual responds to his party's appeal for his support, and the issue-oriented individual responds to both parties and candidates in terms of what he sees to be the relative differences in their stands on issues.

The second and perhaps more obvious component of issue orientation is the involvement that the individual himself has in controversial questions of governmental policy and action. Personal involvement in issues has in turn two distinct dimensions. One dimension is the quantitative extent of involvement, varying from lack of concern with any issue to intense preoccupation with a multitude of issues. The second dimension is direction of involvement. Where extent of involvement varies in quantity or strength, direction of involvement varies in quality or kind. In the American political system, with its two clearly dominant political parties, the direction of involvement may be said to vary, for the most part, on a single continuum from pro-Democratic on one extreme to pro-Republican on the other.[1]

Although there may be a theoretically infinite variation from pro-Democratic to pro-Republican on a single issue, the data used in this analysis are not so refined as to allow distinctions among more than three different positions on a given issue. Throughout this presentation these positions will be: pro-Democratic (D), neutral (?), and anti-Democratic (R).[2] Consequently, for this discussion any greater complexity in the partisan nature of issue involvement can be expressed only with involvement in more than one issue.[3]

[1] To some degree, the neatness of such a simple conceptualization is achieved at the expense of ignoring the wide range of ideologies exhibited by prominent members within either of the two major parties. Many of the data which will be examined indicate that this is not a fatal flaw in the conceptualization. Nevertheless, the reader should keep this limitation in mind throughout the discussion.

[2] For the purpose of this discussion anti-Democratic attitudes will be equated with pro-Republican attitudes. If the focus of our interest were state and local elections, or the nomination of presidential candidates, this implied congruence would not be acceptable. In partisan strongholds of the North or the South, or in a presidential convention, opposition to the policies espoused by the major party can be expressed (or must be expressed) by support of likeminded candidates *within* the party. However, in the study of a presidential election the two points of view (anti-Democratic and pro-Republican) must, for many purposes including the purposes of this discussion, be interpreted as equivalent points of view. With only two real alternatives available to the voter, anti-Democratic behavior must be the same as pro-Republican behavior. Carrying this one step further, anti-Democratic attitudes must, in determining a presidential vote, have much the same meaning as pro-Republican attitudes.

[3] Once involvement includes two or more issues, direction of issue involvement may include being pro-Democratic on at least one issue while being pro-Republican or ambivalent on one or more additional issues, etc. Involvement in three issues,

In developing measures of issue orientation as a factor influencing political behavior, we shall need to take account of all three of these elements: *sensitivity to partisan differences* on issues, represented by the degree to which the individual sees differences in the parties' stands on major issues; *extent of involvement* in issues, represented by the existence or nonexistence of partisan attitudes toward issues involving governmental action; and *direction of issue involvement*, represented by the extent to which the individual favors the position of one of the two parties in his own attitudes toward issues. Simultaneous handling of all the data pertaining to the three aspects of issue orientation will not be attempted. We propose, instead, to create two measures based on these three variables. One measure is intended to represent the extent or amount dimension of issue orientation, as expressed in sensitivity to party differences and in extent of involvement in issues. This we shall refer to as *extent of issue orientation*. The second measure will focus on the partisan character of issue orientation, again using sensitivity to party differences, but this time in combination with direction of issue involvement. This we shall call *issue partisanship*.[4]

These components of issue orientation are analogous to the single measure of party identification discussed in Chapter VII. We may speak either of strong party identifiers or of people who are highly issue oriented, and we may refer to a nonidentifier as well as to a person who is not issue oriented. In either instance, the strength of the orientation in question can be specified without regard for the partisan nature of the orientation. It is, of course, also appropriate to describe people as

for example, would allow the following variations in direction of involvement: DDD, DDR, DRR, RRR, DD?, DR?, RR?, D??, R??, and ???. At the same time, the amount of involvement might be any one of four degrees, namely, (a) involvement in three issues, DDD, DDR, DRR, or RRR, (b) two issues, DD?, DR?, or RR?, (c) one issue, D?? or R??, or (d) none, ???.

[4] The third possible measure, created by pairing the two dimensions of involvement and ignoring the sensitivity to differences component, will not be used. Although the two dimensions of issue involvement can be combined to form an issue matrix which provides a rather full description of the patterns of issue involvement within a population, their study without a consideration of the sensitivity to differences component is not appropriate to this particular discussion of issue-oriented behavior.

The sensitivity variable will be included in each of the two measures to be used because it is essential both to the theory of the nature of issue-oriented behavior and to the empirical demonstration of its existence. Its existence is crucial to the production of either major dependent variable, i.e., amount of participation and direction of participation. On the other hand, sheer amount of issue involvement is *not* related to direction of political partisanship, and, with one notable exception, direction of issue involvement is not pertinent to amount of political participation.

Republican party identifiers or as Republican issue partisans in instances where the directional or partisan components of the orientation are pertinent.

Although the similarities between the dimensions of issue orientation and party identification are most important, the nature of the two variables differs in at least one important respect. It is reasonable to expect that many people will be strongly issue oriented and yet show no extreme issue partisanship. Questions of governmental policy are of crucial importance for those people, but they may well be pro-Republican on some issues while being equally pro-Democratic on others. This sort of balanced partisanship cannot be experienced by a party identifier. By the very nature of party identification, being a strong Democrat rules out being a Republican identifier, and vice versa.

While the two orientations differ in this fashion, they are again similar in that extreme partisanship within either orientation also implies a high degree of involvement with the orientation. Thus, issue orientation is very important to the person who is an extreme Democrat·on issue partisanship, just as party identification is very important to the person who calls himself a strong Democrat.

The Measurement of Issue Involvement

The relevance of governmental activity to individual goals may take many forms, varying from the enduring and all-embracing relevance experienced by the ideologically persuaded individual to an occasional and probably casual feeling that "Washington" could or should do something to alleviate or eliminate a personal grievance. The relevance may be perceived as strictly personal, as with the concern over taxes, or prices, which affect the individual's pocketbook. It may also be much broader, perceived as affecting not only the individual but his or her business or social associates as well. In the latter case, the issue involvement is possibly reinforced by a sense of group involvement in which the individual feels that his group, and not he alone, has a stake in some governmental action. Issue involvement may also be experienced in relation to governmental action which has no conceivable consequences for the individual's material well-being, or for that of family or friends, but which, rather, enhances or threatens values held by the individual.

Just as the range and depth of involvement in issues may vary, so may the particular content of the issues include all manner of items. The ideology may be focused on the extent of governmental economic activity, or on the amount and kinds of governmental participation in foreign affairs. The more particularized concern with issues may concentrate on specific economic, social, or social welfare activities of the government, even raising questions about the execution of authorized policies rather than about the policies themselves. A proposed change in import duties on pocket watch crystals, a bill to accept 100 additional immigrants from the country of one's nativity, or a Senate resolution condemning all opposition to military conscription—any of these may prompt the issue-oriented citizen to act.

A full exploration of issue involvement would seem to call for at least two areas of study. The first step would be the collection and treatment of data which would allow one to specify, concerning each individual being studied, that there is or is not evidence of issue involvement or commitment. The second step could then entail exploration and specification of the content of each involvement. The following discussion will not give detailed consideration to this second step but will, instead, center on questions of the existence and relative importance of issue involvement.

Data Regarding Issue Involvement

The data on issue involvement were provided by responses to seven specific questions asked in the pre-election interviews. The questions were chosen for inclusion in the interview schedule on the basis of their judged relevance to political behavior in the 1952 election. Although the final selection was quite adequate for providing issue information which was related to the total context of the election study, it did impose severe limitations on the independent analysis of issue involvement.

In the first place, the questions were deliberately constructed to encompass a wide range of issues. No two questions were intended to tap any single dimension of issue involvement. Consequently, the task of constructing meaningful scales or typologies by combining items which have a single dimension in common becomes quite difficult. Second, the additional criteria which were employed in selecting issues for investigation were not, except coincidentally, criteria which were relevant to a study of different types of issue involvement.

The questions were chosen to represent (a) both domestic and foreign policies, (b) differences of partisan opinion which, in point of time, were both of long duration and of very recent origin, and (c) broad, more or less fundamental or ideological controversies, as well as the more particularized "bread and butter" disagreements over specific policy acts. Using the three criteria as guides, issues were chosen to represent a broad range of government activities which were judged to be foci for relatively clear expressions of party differences. The only additional limiting criterion was an insistence that all questions be about issues on which the incumbent Truman administration had accepted responsibility for a particular position. This, of course, eliminated specific inquiry about "corruption" or "communism in government," although these and other such controversial areas are usually included in discussions of campaign issues of 1952. We have seen evidence of the role of some of these latter items in Chapter IV.

Inasmuch as the questions were chosen to explore partisan differences, the categorization of responses which was used highlighted such differences.[5] The responses to each question were grouped under one of three headings, namely, "Support Democratic Administration Policy," "Oppose Democratic Administration Policy," and "Not Partisanly Committed on Democratic Administration Policy."[6] This procedure minimized the extent to which the data could accommodate the factional differences which existed within both parties. It opened the possibility of a certain lack of precision in thinking about partisan differences in that it obscured very real differences which did exist within the parties. It did, however, provide an understandable and communicable basis for specifying a common meaning attached to responses. The seven questions are listed below.

GOVERNMENTAL SOCIAL WELFARE ACTIVITY: "Some people think the national government should do more in trying to deal with such problems as unemployment, education, housing, and so on. Others think that the government is already doing too much. On the whole, would you say that what the government has done has been about right, too much, or not enough?"

FEPC: "There is a lot of talk these days about discrimination, that is, people having trouble getting jobs because of their race. Do you think the government ought to take an interest in whether Negroes have trouble getting jobs or should it stay out of this problem? Do you think we need laws to deal with this problem or are there other ways that will handle it better? Do you think the national government should handle this or do you think it should be left for each state to handle in its own way? Do you think the state governments should do something about this problem or should they stay out of it [also]?"

TAFT-HARTLEY LABOR LAW REVISION: "Have you heard anything about the Taft-Hartley Law? [If yes] How do you feel about it—do you think it's all right as it is, do you think it should be changed in any way, or don't

[5] Although there were many possible dimensions which could be utilized in establishing categories for responses to the questions, the categories actually used in the coding operation were directed only at capturing that substantive content of each response which was directly relevant to the question asked. Dimensions such as specificity-generality of response were not coded.

[6] Detailed description of the responses subsumed under each of the three categories may be found in the *American Political Science Review*, June, 1953, 47, No. 2, 359–85.

you have any feelings about it? [If should be changed] Do you think the law should be changed just a little, changed quite a bit, or do you think it should be *completely* repealed?"

U.S. FOREIGN INVOLVEMENT: "Some people think that since the end of the last world war this country has gone too far in concerning itself with problems in other parts of the world. How do you feel about this?"

U.S. CHINA POLICY: "Some people feel that it was our government's fault that China went communistic—others say there was nothing that we could do to stop it. How do you feel about this?"

U.S. ENTRY IN KOREAN WAR: "Do you think we did the right thing in getting into the fighting in Korea two years ago or should we have stayed out?"

CURRENT U.S. KOREAN POLICY: "Which of the following things do you think it would be best for us to do *now* in Korea? (*a*) Pull out of Korea entirely? (*b*) Keep on trying to get a peaceful settlement? (*c*) Take a stronger stand and bomb Manchuria and China?"

Issue Involvement and Presidential Preference

Each of the seven questions evoked responses which were significantly related to the presidential preference of the respondents. On all issues people taking a pro-Democratic attitudinal position were the

TABLE 8.1

RELATION OF DIRECTION OF INVOLVEMENT IN ISSUES TO
PRESIDENTIAL PREFERENCE

ISSUE†	PRESIDENTIAL PREFERENCE‡	ISSUE INVOLVEMENT		
		Pro-Democratic	Anti-Democratic	Neutral
Governmental social welfare activity	Eisenhower	43%	85%	48%
	Stevenson	52	14	49
	Other	5	1	3
	Total	100%	100%	100%
	Index of presidential preference§	−9	+71	−1
	Number of cases	400	293	921
FEPC	Eisenhower	48%	59%	54%
	Stevenson	48	39	35
	Other	4	2	11
	Total	100%	100%	100%
	Index of presidential preference	0	+20	+19
	Number of cases	732	765	117

TABLE 8.1 (*continued*)

Issue†	Presidential Preference‡	Issue Involvement		
		Pro-Democratic	Anti-Democratic	Neutral
Taft-Hartley Law	Eisenhower	29%	77%	52%
	Stevenson	68	23	43
	Other	3	*	5
	Total	100%	100%	100%
	Index of presidential preference	−39	+54	+9
	Number of cases	275	355	984
U.S. foreign involvement	Eisenhower	45%	62%	39%
	Stevenson	53	36	49
	Other	2	2	12
	Total	100%	100%	100%
	Index of presidential preference	−8	+26	−10
	Number of cases	521	899	194
U.S. China policy	Eisenhower	45%	71%	52%
	Stevenson	52	27	42
	Other	3	2	6
	Total	100%	100%	100%
	Index of presidential preference	−7	+44	+10
	Number of cases	776	406	432
U.S. entry in Korean War	Eisenhower	45%	62%	54%
	Stevenson	54	35	38
	Other	1	3	8
	Total	100%	100%	100%
	Index of presidential preference	−9	+27	+16
	Number of cases	641	664	309
Current U.S. Korean policy	Eisenhower	45%	61%	53%
	Stevenson	51	37	35
	Other	4	2	12
	Total	100%	100%	100%
	Index of presidential preference	−6	+24	+18
	Number of cases	734	772	108

† The questions asked in the interview about each of these issues are shown in the text.
‡ The term "presidential preference" is used to cover the choice of candidate made by voters and also the preference expressed by nonvoters in answer to the question, "Who would you have voted for if you had voted?"
§ The index of presidential preference is derived by subtracting the proportion who preferred **Stevenson** from the proportion who preferred Eisenhower. It is included in this and following tables to summarize the data as an aid to the reader.

most Democratic group on presidential preference, while people expressing anti-Democratic attitudes were the most pro-Republican (Table 8.1).
On most issues, the people in the neutral issue position were, as a group,
clearly less partisan than either of the other groups.   The relationship
between direction of issue involvement and presidential preference
was lowest for the FEPC issue.   This might be expected both because
of the extreme division within the Democratic party on that issue,
and because the issue was not a salient issue for a large part of the
population.   Even this relationship, however, was high enough so that
it clearly could not be attributed to errors of sampling.   The relationships appeared to be somewhat higher for the other two domestic
issues than for any of the foreign affairs issues.[7]

Issue Involvement and Participation

Involvement with issues was, in the case of six issues, unmistakably
related to level of political participation as we have defined it in
Chapter III.   For each of the six issues, people who took either a pro-
Democratic or an anti-Democratic stand on an issue participated
significantly more than did people who were categorized as neutral
on the issue (Table 8.2).   For the seventh issue, U.S. Entry in Korean
War, the over-all relationship is clearly lower than that for all other
issues, but is still significantly high.

[7] The question labelled U.S. Foreign Involvement had been asked in a number
of earlier Survey Research Center studies.   In surveys in 1946, 1947, and 1948
approximately one-third of our national samples answered this question by
saying they thought this country had "gone too far" in its foreign involvements;
this figure stood at 56 per cent in our 1952 pre-election survey.   The implications
of this shift cannot be developed here, but it is undoubtedly related to the
increased significance that the general problem of foreign policy had in the 1952
election as compared to 1948.

TABLE 8.2

RELATION OF INVOLVEMENT IN ISSUES TO POLITICAL PARTICIPATION

ISSUE	POLITICAL PARTICIPATION	ISSUE INVOLVEMENT		
		Pro-Democratic	Anti-Democratic	Neutral
Governmental	High	29%	40%	23%
social welfare	Medium	48	45	46
activity	Low	23	15	31
	Total	100%	100%	100%
	Index of participa-tion	+6	+25	−8
	Number of cases	400	293	921

TABLE 8.2 (*continued*)

| ISSUE | POLITICAL PARTICIPATION | ISSUE INVOLVEMENT | | |
		Pro-Democratic	Anti-Democratic	Neutral
FEPC	High	25%	32%	14%
	Medium	47	47	45
	Low	28	21	41
	Total	100%	100%	100%
	Index of participation	−3	+11	−27
	Number of cases	732	765	117
Taft-Hartley Law	High	42%	39%	19%
	Medium	43	48	47
	Low	15	13	34
	Total	100%	100%	100%
	Index of participation	+27	+26	−15
	Number of cases	275	355	984
U.S. foreign involvement	High	33%	27%	12%
	Medium	46	49	38
	Low	21	24	50
	Total	100%	100%	100%
	Index of participation	+12	+3	−38
	Number of cases	521	899	194
U.S. China policy	High	27%	41%	16%
	Medium	47	47	45
	Low	26	12	39
	Total	100%	100%	100%
	Index of participation	+1	+29	−23
	Number of cases	776	406	432
U.S. entry in Korean War	High	33%	24%	23%
	Medium	45	49	45
	Low	22	27	32
	Total	100%	100%	100%
	Index of participation	+11	−3	−9
	Number of cases	641	664	309

TABLE 8.2 (*continued*)

ISSUE	POLITICAL PARTICIPATION	ISSUE INVOLVEMENT		
		Pro-Democratic	Anti-Democratic	Neutral
Current U.S.	High	24%	31%	20%
Korean policy	Medium	46	48	45
	Low	30	21	35
	Total	100%	100%	100%
	Index of participation	−6	+10	−15
	Number of cases	734	772	108

The data which we have examined suggest the following conclusions with respect to involvement in each of the seven issues:

1. Direction of issue involvement was clearly and positively related to presidential preference.

2. Amount of issue involvement was highly related to political participation.

The Measures of Issue Involvement

The measures of issue involvement which will be used henceforth in this analysis are based on four issues selected out of the seven available. These issues include the four which are most highly related to both participation and voting preference. They are: Governmental Social Welfare Activity, Taft-Hartley Labor Law Revision, U.S. Foreign Involvement, and U.S. China Policy. This selection also results in choosing two general and two specific items, two on foreign policy and two on domestic affairs, two on which a relatively large number of people are not partisanly committed and two on which most of the population have taken sides. It also results in omitting the two foreign policy questions of most recent development, and omitting the one domestic question which is most likely a unique issue insofar as regional differences are likely to occur.

When the four issues are combined, 15 different patterns of involvement result. Amount or extent of issue involvement will be measured on a three-point scale ranging from High to Medium to Low. The 15 different patterns of issue involvement will be distributed among the three categories, as shown in Figure 8.1.

HIGH INVOLVEMENT	MEDIUM INVOLVEMENT	LOW INVOLVEMENT
DDDD	DD??	D???
DDDR	DR??	????
DDRR	RR??	R???
DRRR		
RRRR		
DDD?		
DDR?		
DRR?		
RRR?		

Number of cases

813	497	304

Proportion of total population

(50%)	(31%)	(19%)

FIG. 8.1.—Amount of Issue Involvement

The directional component of issue involvement will be measured on a five-point scale. The scale will include the following categories: pro-Democratic with no conflict, pro-Democratic with conflict, no predominant partisan commitment, pro-Republican with conflict, and pro-Republican with no conflict (Fig. 8.2).

DEMOCRATIC NO CONFLICT	DEMOCRATIC WITH CONFLICT	NO PARTISAN PREDOMINANCE	REPUBLICAN WITH CONFLICT	REPUBLICAN NO CONFLICT
DDDD	DDDR	DDRR	RRRD	RRRR
DDD?	DDR?	DR??	RRD?	RRR?
DD??		????		RR??
D???				R???

Number of cases

357	252	391	268	346

Proportion of total population

(22%)	(16%)	(24%)	(17%)	(21%)

FIG. 8.2.—Direction of Issue Involvement

The Measurement of Sensitivity to Partisan Differences on Issues

The possible importance and meaning which may be attached to the data on perception of difference between party positions falls somewhere between two rather wide extremes. The minimum expectation concerning the role of perception of partisan issue differences is that an individual's perceptions of party positions on a given issue will affect only the single relationship between his involvement in that issue and his presidential preference and participation. At the other extreme lies the possibility that, in the context of the defined nature of issue orientation, the perception of difference in the parties' positions on a major item of policy may be a crude manifestation of the individual's general predisposition to perceive most political phenomena in terms of partisan differences on issues.

An immediately apparent limitation of the perception of difference data is found in the fact that the available data pertain only to perceptions of the political parties and omit perceptions of the candidates. It is, of course, quite possible that many issue-oriented citizens may have perceived the 1952 election as a contest between the major candidates, with parties playing only a secondary role, and with party differences being consequently much less salient. If this were in fact the case, the available data could not be expected to provide a satisfactory reflection of issue orientation. This would follow because many people who did perceive differences in the candidates' positions on issues might, in this analysis, be incorrectly classified as perceiving no partisan differences, because the data relate only to the parties and not to the presidential candidates.

Accepting the fact that the data do not provide full information, it is still possible to explore the adequacy of the interpretation that the questions which were asked about perceptions of party issue positions did provide crude measures of a basic component of issue orientation.

Data Regarding Perception of Partisan Differences on Issues

Information on perception of differences between the parties was obtained in connection with two issues, Governmental Social Welfare Activity and U.S. Foreign Involvement. Immediately following the response to each of these two issue questions, the people being interviewed were asked, "Now, how do you think the two parties feel about this question—do you think there are any differences between the Democratic and Republican parties on this issue, or would you say they feel the same?" The responses to these questions about party differences were categorized in five groups: (a) Democrats will (go further) (do more) than the Republicans; (b) both parties have the same position; (c) Republicans will (go further) (do more) than the Democrats; (d) I don't know the parties' positions on the question; and (e) not ascertained.

As can be seen in Table 8.3, very few responses fit the third or the fifth categories.[8] There are, therefore, three principal distinctions

[8] The last category is somewhat larger for these two questions than for other questions asked in the interview. This probably was a function of two factors—level of difficulty of the question and the relatively narrow framework of the code. The question was undoubtedly difficult both for the well-informed people who were aware of intraparty differences on the two issues and for the poorly informed people who were not accustomed to differentiating party stands on policy matters. Following from this, the code for perceptions of differences did not

among the respondents: (a) people who see the parties as taking different stands (and, specifically, see the Democrats being more active); (b) people who see the parties taking the same position; and (c) people who don't know on which side of the issue either party is to be found.

TABLE 8.3

DISTRIBUTIONS OF VARYING PERCEPTIONS OF DIFFERENCES
IN PARTY POSITIONS ON TWO ISSUES

Perception of Difference†	Governmental Social Welfare Activity	U.S. Foreign Involvement
Democrats will (go further) (do more)	30%	30%
The two parties have the same position	34	33
Republicans will (go further) (do more)	2	2
Don't know the parties' positions	27	26
Not ascertained	7	9
Total	100%	100%
Number of cases	1,614	1,614

† The interview questions on which this table is based are shown in the text.

One factor which lends not inconsiderable weight to the broader of the two interpretations of the meaning of "perception of difference" is the nature of the issues which were the basis for the inquiries. These two issues were the most fundamental of all seven issues. They represented both domestic and foreign policies, and they represented issues which have more or less defined the major Democratic and Republican differences in Congress and elsewhere for two or more decades. It is not hard to imagine that people who had no perceptions of party positions on those issues were people who, by and large, would not likely be aware of other issues either. People specifying "both parties have the same position" on the two issues would, presumably, be generally less aware of issue differences between the parties than would people who saw differences on the test issues.[9]   Finally, people

accommodate the carefully weighed pro-con responses nor the evaluative responses ("I think the Republicans should do more," or "The Democrats have done too much").

[9] There are, however, at least three additional possible interpretations of the meaning of the "Same" response (interpretations which do not assume that "Same" means lack of awareness). People who said the parties did not differ may also have been responding to any of the many observable instances in which the wide range of difference within each of the two parties is more spectacular

who did perceive differences between the parties' policy positions, are more likely to be issue-oriented in their behavior than are people who saw no such crucial difference.

Perceptions of Difference and Presidential Preference

There is nothing in the assumed meaning of the perception of difference variable which would lead to any particular expectation concerning possible relationships between perceptions of difference and presidential preference. Consequently, the only prediction which could be made concerning possible relationships between the variables was that varying perceptions of party differences would be distributed in the same manner among both Democratic and Republican presidential preferrers. This expectation was confirmed by the data.

Perceptions of Difference and Participation

The three major categories of response to the perception of difference questions did, however, demonstrate very different relationships with level of political participation. It can be seen in Tables 8.4 and 8.5 that the differences in relationships persisted for perceptions based on both the foreign and domestic issues. People who, on either issue, perceived differences between the parties' positions participated significantly more than any other group.[10] People who perceived the parties as not differing exhibited a distribution on participation which was no different from that of the total population. At the bottom extreme, people who did not know the parties' positions tended to be low participators. For both issues, the people whose perceptions of party positions were not ascertained showed a distribution which was similar to that of the intermediate, nondifferentiating "both parties have the same position" group.[11]

than the relatively obscure difference between them. They may include those people who perceive differences as existing among candidates but not among parties. They may also include people who wish to minimize the deficiencies which they perceive in their own party, or who are unwilling to grant a possible popular advantage to the opposing party.

[10] People perceiving the Republicans as "doing more" were not significantly different from those seeing no difference between parties, but on the social welfare issue they were most like the people who said "Democrats will do more." The empirical position of the "Republicans will do more" group, relative to the other groups, was quite ambiguous. This ambiguity, combined with the apparent lack of reality orientation of the response, made this a suspect category. It probably contained both poorly informed people and people who were highly involved in politics, but who were experiencing severe enough conflicts to create distorted perceptions. In the absence of further clues concerning this group they were eliminated from the analysis.

[11] In the analysis which follows, the "Not ascertained" categories were combined with the "Same" categories. This can be defended only on the basis that

TABLE 8.4

RELATION OF PERCEPTIONS OF DIFFERENCES BETWEEN PARTY POSITIONS ON
GOVERNMENTAL SOCIAL WELFARE ACTIVITY TO POLITICAL PARTICIPATION

POLITICAL PARTICIPATION	PERCEPTION OF DIFFERENCE				
	Democrats Will Do More	No Difference	Republicans Will Do More	Don't Know	Not Ascertained
High	41%	25%	36%	16%	23%
Medium	43	51	47	46	43
Low	16	24	17	38	34
Total	100%	100%	100%	100%	100%
Index of participation	+25	+1	+19	−22	−11
Number of cases	477	551	36	443	107

TABLE 8.5

RELATION OF PERCEPTIONS OF DIFFERENCES BETWEEN PARTY POSITIONS
ON U.S. FOREIGN INVOLVEMENT TO POLITICAL PARTICIPATION

POLITICAL PARTICIPATION	PERCEPTION OF DIFFERENCE				
	Democrats Will Do More	No Difference	Republicans Will Do More	Don't Know	Not Ascertained
High	41%	26%	24%	12%	30%
Medium	46	49	52	44	45
Low	13	25	24	44	25
Total	100%	100%	100%	100%	100%
Index of participation	+28	+1	0	−32	+5
Number of cases	489	534	33	417	141

empirically they were most like the "Same" group, and the arbitrary lumping
together of the groups thereby preserved some 230 cases which would otherwise
have been eliminated from the analysis. Those respondents who were classified
as "Not ascertained" on *both* questions were, at this point, eliminated from the
analysis.

Measurement of the Perception of Difference Variable

It will be remembered that in Table 8.3, and the tables which
followed, perceptions of party differences on Governmental Social
Welfare Activity and perceptions of party differences on U.S. Foreign
Involvement were observed to be similarly distributed throughout
the population and similarly related to participation. This demonstrated similarity of the two items, and the absence of any theoretically
relevant difference between them, appeared to justify combining them
into a single measure.[12]

The first step in constructing a single measure of the perception of
difference variable involved combining the data to create the six
possible patterns of response to the two trichotomized items. The
three content categories retained from each item were: (a) Democrats
will (do more) (go further); (b) the parties' positions are the same; and
(c) I don't know the parties' positions.[13] The six resulting patterns
included: (a) different-different (D-D), (b) different-same (D-S), (c)
different-don't know (D-DK), (d) same-same (S-S), (e) same-don't
know (S-DK), and (f) don't know-don't know (DK-DK). (In each
instance, "different" refers to "Democrats will (do more) (go further).")
These six categories included over 95 per cent of the total sample, with
the remaining 84 cases combined in a nonmeaningful "other"
category.[14] Table 8.6 shows the relationship between the new measure
of perception of difference and level of participation.

TABLE 8.6

RELATION OF PERCEPTIONS OF DIFFERENCES IN PARTY POSITIONS
TO LEVEL OF PARTICIPATION

POLITICAL PARTICIPATION	PERCEPTIONS OF DIFFERENCES					
	D-D	D-S	D-DK	S-S	S-DK	DK-DK
High	48%	36%	28%	24%	18%	8%
Medium	41	49	47	50	51	41
Low	11	15	25	26	31	51
Total	100%	100%	100%	100%	100%	100%
Index of participation	+37	+21	+3	−2	−13	−43
Number of cases	226	356	132	343	231	242

[12] The two measures were, of course, highly correlated with each other. They
did not, however, combine to form any sort of an ordered scale.

[13] See footnotes 10 and 11, this chapter.

[14] This includes people who responded "Republicans will do more" to either
of the issue questions, and people whose responses were coded "Not ascertained"
on both questions. See footnotes 10 and 11, this chapter.

Sensitivity to partisan differences will be measured by a three-point scale (Fig. 8.3). Adjoining pairs of positions in the above six-point measure of perception of difference will be collapsed (e.g., D-D will be combined with D-S, D-DK with S-S and S-DK with DK-DK), and only the three resultant positions will be retained. Three degrees of sensitivity to differences will be distinguished as High, Medium, and Low. High will therefore include people who saw differences on both

	HIGH SENSITIVITY	MEDIUM SENSITIVITY	LOW SENSITIVITY
Perceptions of Difference	Different-Different	Different-Don't Know	Same-Don't Know
	Different-Same	Same-Same	Don't Know-Don't Know
Number of cases	582	475	473
Proportion of total population	(36%)	(30%)	(29%)

FIG. 8.3.—The Measure of Sensitivity to Differences

issues and people who saw differences on one, but said the parties did not differ on the other. Medium will include people who saw differences on one issue but did not know the parties' positions on the other, and people who saw no difference on either issue. Low sensitivity will include people who saw no difference on one issue and did not know the parties' positions on the other, and people who did not know the parties' positions on either issue.

The Measurement of Issue Orientation

The development of the measure of sensitivity to party differences provides a tool for manipulating the third and last independent variable needed for our study of issue orientation. As suggested earlier, these three variables can be combined to form relatively simple summary measures of two different aspects of issue orientation. We have designated these two summary measures of issue orientation as the measure of extent of issue orientation and the measure of issue partisanship. These measures are produced by a simple combination of the measure of sensitivity to party differences with the measure of one of the issue involvement components, amount or direction.

Extent of issue orientation will be measured by a five-point scale on which greatest extent of issue orientation, position 1, designates high amount of issue involvement and high sensitivity to party differences, position 2 designates either medium involvement and high sensitivity *or* high involvement and medium sensitivity, and position 3 designates low involvement and high sensitivity *or* medium involvement and medium sensitivity *or* high involvement and low sensitivity, etc. (Fig. 8.4).

Issue partisanship is also measured on a five-point scale. The combinations of direction of issue involvement and sensitivity to

SENSITIVITY TO PARTY DIFFERENCES	AMOUNT OF ISSUE INVOLVEMENT		
	High	Medium	Low
High	1	2	3
Medium	2	3	4
Low	3	4	5

FIG. 8.4.—The Measure of Extent of Issue Orientation

party differences which form each scale position are similar to those observed in the measures of extent of issue involvement (Fig. 8.5).

SENSITIVITY TO PARTY DIFFERENCES	DIRECTION OF ISSUE INVOLVEMENT				
	Democrat	Weak Democrat	Non-Partisan	Weak Republican	Republican
High	1	2	3	4	5
Medium	2	2	3	4	4
Low	2	3	3	3	4

FIG. 8.5.—The Measure of Issue Partisanship

With our two measures of issue orientation thus established, we can now examine the relationships which exist between these variables and the extent and character of political participation.

Issue Partisanship

In Table 8.7 the presidential preferences of people differing in issue partisanship are compared. The very strong tendency for people of extreme partisan position on issues to prefer that party's candidate for president is apparent. It may be remarked, however, that this relationship has many individual exceptions—a sixth or so of each extreme group preferred the candidate of the other party.

In the basic planning of this study, attention was given to the hypothesis that conflict among independent variables will tend to reduce the incidence of resultant variables. This may now be translated to the case of conflict within issue partisanship as it is related to political participation. Inasmuch as weak partisanship and non-partisanship (as defined by the mid-positions in the issue partisanship measure) are, in large part, reflections of conflict over issues, it should follow from the hypothesis that political participation will be lower for the middle categories of issue partisanship than for the extreme categories.

The data do, in fact, indicate that some people who were in conflict over their commitments on various issues may have resolved that

TABLE 8.7

RELATION OF ISSUE PARTISANSHIP TO PRESIDENTIAL PREFERENCE

PRESIDENTIAL PREFERENCE	ISSUE PARTISANSHIP SCORE					TOTAL SAMPLE
	(Demo-crat) 1	2	3	4	(Repub-lican) 5	
Eisenhower	17%	36%	52%	69%	86%	54%
Stevenson	81	59	43	29	14	43
Other	2	5	5	2	—	3
Total	100%	100%	100%	100%	100%	100%
Index of presidential preference	−64	−23	+9	+40	+72	+11
Number of cases	118	417	449	406	140	1,614
Proportion of total sample	7%	26%	28%	25%	9%	

conflict by refraining from becoming involved in an election which focused on those issues. For each of the four comparisons which can be made in Table 8.8 between patterns of more or less conflict (comparisons between steps 2 and 1, 3 and 2, 3 and 4, and 4 and 5 of issue partisanship) members of the group with greater conflict participated significantly less than the members of the group with less conflict.

Before we accept these relationships involving issue partisanship,

TABLE 8.8

RELATION OF ISSUE PARTISANSHIP TO POLITICAL PARTICIPATION

POLITICAL PARTICIPATION	ISSUE PARTISANSHIP SCORE					TOTAL SAMPLE
	(Demo-crat) 1	2	3	4	(Repub-lican) 5	
High	37%	26%	20%	29%	43%	27%
Medium	45	45	47	47	51	47
Low	18	29	33	24	6	26
Total	100%	100%	100%	100%	100%	100%
Index of participation	+19	−3	−13	+5	+37	+1

we must check one additional factor. Reference to the description of the way in which the issue partisanship measure was constructed (pages 123 and 130) may suggest that variations in the *amount* of issue involvement for various steps on the issue partisanship scale could have been responsible for the correlation shown in Table 8.8. In other words, it may be that people fall into the middle (neutral) positions on the issue partisanship scale because they are not involved in issues and have no opinion on them. Their low record of participation may depend more on their lack of involvement than their lack of partisanship.

This possibility is easily explored by examining the relationship between issue partisanship and participation found among people involved in different numbers of issues. When this is done (Table 8.9)

TABLE 8.9

RELATION OF ISSUE PARTISANSHIP TO POLITICAL PARTICIPATION
FOR VARYING LEVELS OF ISSUE INVOLVEMENT

AMOUNT OF ISSUE INVOLVEMENT	ISSUE PARTISANSHIP SCORE				
	(Democrat) 1	2	3	4	(Republican) 5
Four issues	+64†	+23	+20	+35	+61
Three issues	+30	+13	− 9	+20	+38
Two issues	0	− 9	−10	+ 2	+31
One issue	−29	−40		−36	+ 5
No involvement			−57		

† Cell entry is index of participation.

it is immediately apparent that the sheer number of issues in which the person is involved is not responsible for any large part of the relationship between issue partisanship and participation. The evidence is quite striking, particularly at the upper two levels of involvement. At the highest level of involvement (groups with the patterns of DDDD, DDDR, DDRR, DRRR and RRRR), three of the four differences are statistically significant. All four differences support the conflict hypothesis. In like manner, all four differences on the next level of involvement (issue patterns DDD?, DDR?, DRR?, and RRR?) are in the correct direction and statistically significant. In the middle level, although the differences are not all statistically significant, they are all in the predicted direction. It seems clear that variations in amount of issue involvement do not affect the conclusion that conflict in issue partisanship is related to lowered political participation.

Extent of Issue Orientation

We see in Table 8.10 that extent of issue orientation is also highly related to the level of political participation. People broadly concerned with issues and party positions on issues are very likely to vote and to take other political action.

TABLE 8.10

RELATION OF EXTENT OF ISSUE ORIENTATION TO LEVEL OF PARTICIPATION

POLITICAL PARTICIPATION	EXTENT OF ISSUE ORIENTATION					TOTAL SAMPLE
	(High) 1	2	3	4	(Low) 5	
High	46%	32%	20%	13%	7%	27%
Medium	43	50	51	53	35	47
Low	11	18	29	34	58	26
Total	100%	100%	100%	100%	100%	100%
Index of participation	+35	+14	−9	−21	−51	+1
Number of cases	405	371	336	228	190	1,614
Proportion of total sample	25%	23%	21%	14%	12%	

The degree of success with which the extent measure separates people with high and low participation scores is apparent in Table 8.10. Only 11 per cent of the people receiving a high score failed to vote (and were therefore rated "low" in participation). Over one-half of the people showing the least evidence of issue orientation did not vote. Conversely, almost one-half of the people who were ranked high on issues both voted and participated in the election in some other manner and only 7 per cent of the low scorers were such active participants. Its ability virtually to eliminate nonvoters from the category of high issue orientation and active participators from the lowest category of issue orientation suggests that the measure of extent of issue orientation may prove a powerful tool for future analysis of issue-oriented behavior.

" Third Factors " and the Measures of Issue Orientation

Statistical analyses of the kind under discussion here are constantly plagued by the possible existence of crucial "third factors." Any simple relationship which is apparently discovered between two variables must remain suspect until the effect of additional factors known to be highly related to them have been explored. For example, in the instance of issue orientation it is possible to establish that extent of issue orientation is positively correlated with education so that strong orientation and college education are very often characteristics of the same people, while the absence of issue orientation and little formal education frequently go hand in hand. It is also true that participation is positively correlated with the same education variable. These facts open the possibility that a correlation between extent of issue orientation and participation is merely a reflection of some common third factor which is associated with years of formal education. Only by demonstrating that the orientation-participation relationship exists within each level of education, or within levels of any other variable that is significantly correlated with both orientation and participation, can we discard the possibility that our supposed relationship is merely a function of a "third factor." It is not appropriate in this particular discussion to engage in a lengthy exploration of all possible third factors. It does seem desirable, however, to examine the one most obvious item—education—which is well known to be related to attitudinal data on issues.

Education is related to both issue partisanship and extent of issue orientation, and to both presidential preference and level of participation. These five variables almost certainly have some degree of common determination. The important fact for our present analysis is that when variations in education are removed by the method we have indicated, the crucial relationships involving our two measures of issue orientation with either presidential preference or participation still remain. It is clear that in using our measures of issue partisanship and extent of issue orientation we are not simply manipulating some underlying factor that might just as well have been represented by years of formal education.

Summary

The argument of this chapter has been sustained by the repeated demonstration that personal involvement with matters of governmental policy is related in a predictable way to political behavior.

The measurement of issue orientation has been accomplished by ignoring and omitting many of the nuances and refinements which would be necessary to a thorough understanding of the phenomenon. In particular, no attempt was made to distinguish various types of issue orientation in order to place domestic and foreign problems in some relationship to each other. The presentation was focused, instead, upon simple measures of the gross tendency toward issue orientation and crude distinctions between the major parties' positions on selected national issues. These measures were sufficient, however, to allow us to discriminate between different degrees of extent of issue orientation and between varying partisan positions with regard to issues.

The extent of issue orientation has been demonstrated to be highly related to the amount of political participation in an election. The partisan nature of issue orientation has been demonstrated to be highly related to the presidential preference of both voters and nonvoters. As with party identification, there has been no crucial proof that issue orientation bears a direct causal relationship to voting behavior, but all hypotheses compatible with such a notion of causality have been firmly supported.

IX

Candidate Orientation

Candidate orientation may be broadly defined as the structuring of political events in terms of a personal attraction to the major personalities involved. Paralleling the argument presented in the discussion of issue orientation, two dimensions of candidate orientation may be distinguished which, following the terminology of the preceding chapter, will be referred to as *extent of candidate orientation* and *candidate partisanship*. Extent of candidate orientation refers to the degree of personal involvement with the candidates, and candidate partisanship refers to the direction of this involvement (varying in the 1952 election from strongly pro-Eisenhower to strongly pro-Stevenson).

In Chapter IV we described in some detail the electorate's perceptions of the presidential candidates in the 1952 election. We examined Eisenhower's and Stevenson's appeal in terms of the complex interaction of many factors—their experience and background, their personal qualities, their party representativeness, their relation to the crucial issues of the day. In evaluating the total impact of a candidate on the electorate and attempting to assess his effect on the vote, all of these factors must be considered. However, candidate orientation, as utilized in this study, is defined in terms of a much more limited aspect of this candidate appeal, and is restricted to the response to the personal attributes of the candidates.

Limitation of the concept of candidate orientation in this manner is consistent with most other general theorizing in this area. Conceptualizations of reactions to public figures evidenced in such terms as "identification," "father figure," "charismatic leader," "authoritarian follower," all imply a personal attraction to these figures, and not a response to such things as their "liberalism," or "governmental experience," or "Republicanism." Restriction of the concept of candidate orientation is also dictated by the demands of the theoretical framework of the study. Since we are concerned, in the analysis, with differentiating "party identification," "issue orientation," and "candidate orientation," it is important to exclude from the concept (and measures) of the candidate variable, reactions to the candidates in "party" or "issue" terms. In making this distinction we do not, of course, imply that people in their reactions to the candidates psychologically separate the "personal" qualities of the candidates from their other characteristics. In defining the concept of candidate orientation, as in our definitions of party identification and issue orientation, we are attempting to differentiate analytic constructs, and are not attempting to isolate psychologically pure "types."

Because of the psychological difficulty of separating one's reactions to the "personal" qualities of a candidate from one's total reaction to him, any attempt to measure candidate orientation by forcing the respondents to make such a separation would probably not be particularly fruitful. As a result, it seemed more meaningful to base the measures of candidate orientation on the spontaneous personal references to the candidates made by the respondents during the course of the interview. In separating out "personal" references to the candidates, certain arbitrary distinctions had to be made, since no response can be coded as purely "personal" or "nonpersonal." Consequently, the selected responses included only the most obvious personal references—statements about personal characteristics (leadership, honesty, sincerity) or statements suggesting the respondents' personal attraction toward a candidate ("I like him," "he's wonderful"). This meant that a number of responses with probable "personal" overtones were excluded. For example, the positive reference to Eisenhower's ability to do something about the Korean situation was coded as an "issue" response and not included in the measures of candidate orientation, even though we have observed that for many people this undoubtedly was a response to "Eisenhower" and not just an expression of concern over the Korean War. However, since the measures of candidate orientation were based on material gathered from most of the pre-election interview, it was assumed in such cases that there would be adequate opportunity for other responses to occur during the course of the interview that could be coded in the "personal" categories.

One serious problem in measuring candidate orientation on the basis of spontaneous references involved the weighting of these responses in combining them into meaningful summary scores. There was no theoretical or empirical basis on which differential weightings for various responses could be systematically assigned. Although "he's a great leader" is obviously indicative of a stronger personal attraction than the cliche "he's a man of integrity," the intensity of most of the responses could not be so clearly differentiated. Since any weighting system would be arbitrary, and any summary score a crude approximation at best, the simplest weighting procedure was adopted. This meant giving equal weights to positive and negative responses, and to different types of personal responses. The measure of extent of candidate orientation was formed from a simple tally of all positive and negative personal references to the candidates. A five-point index was constructed, with a score of 5 indicating that no personal references were made to either candidate and a score of 1 indicating that 4 or more such references were made.   For the measure of candidate partisanship, each pro-Eisenhower and anti-Stevenson personal reference was given a weight of $+1$, each pro-Stevenson and anti-Eisenhower reference was given a weight of -1, and a summary score based on the algebraic sum of these weightings was assigned to each respondent.   Since relatively few scores exceeded $+2$ or -2, those which did were included in the $+2$ and -2 classifications.   This yielded a five-point index of candidate partisanship, with a score of $+2$ representing a "strong" personal preference for Eisenhower, $+1$ a "moderate" pro-Eisenhower attraction, a score of 0 representing a point of balance or indifference with respect to the personal qualities of the two candidates, and -1 and -2 representing a "moderate" and "strong" personal response to Stevenson.

Before relating these measures to voting behavior in the 1952 election, one further comment might be made.   In neither dimension of candidate orientation are we considering the nature of the personal reaction to the candidates.   For example, no distinction is being made between the individual attracted to the strong leadership qualities of a candidate and one attracted to a candidate's broad humanitarian qualities.   This is not meant to imply that such a distinction is not an important one, just as the lack of differentiation among the different issues in the issue orientation measures does not negate the meaningfulness of those differences.   For many interesting and significant investigations in this area, one would want to make such distinctions.   However, for the purposes of the present analysis we have attempted only to delineate a very broad and general concept, parallel to the party and issue concepts discussed in the two preceding chapters.   In our two dimensions of candidate orientation we are attempting to differentiate people who evidence a personal reaction to the candidates from those who don't (the "extent" dimension), and people attracted to Eisenhower from those attracted to Stevenson (the "partisanship" dimension).   The use of these dimensions will thus be restricted to the analysis of those relationships where these broad differentiations are meaningful.

Candidate Orientation and Presidential Voting Behavior

The major analyses involving the use of the two measures of candidate orientation will be presented in the chapters that follow.   We shall confine ourselves, in the remainder of this chapter, to a brief presentation and discussion of the relationships between candidate orientation and the two main dependent variables, political participation and presidential preference in the 1952 presidential election.

Let us first examine the relationship between extent of candidate orientation and level of political participation. As we see in Table 9.1, these two variables are highly related. People showing a high personal attraction to the candidates were very likely to vote and to take other political action in the 1952 election. Political participation was much lower among people who gave no evidence of any personal reactions to the candidates. Their participation, when it occurred, was mostly confined to voting, and almost two out of five did not even do that.

TABLE 9.1

RELATION OF EXTENT OF CANDIDATE ORIENTATION TO
LEVEL OF PARTICIPATION

POLITICAL PARTICIPATION	EXTENT OF CANDIDATE ORIENTATION SCORE					TOTAL SAMPLE
	(High) 1	2	3	4	(Low) 5	
High	46%	44%	32%	25%	18%	27%
Medium	44	45	52	52	43	47
Low	10	11	16	23	39	26
Total	100%	100%	100%	100%	100%	100%
Index of participation	+36	+33	+16	+2	−21	+1
Number of cases	166	161	254	342	691	1,614
Proportion of total sample	10%	10%	16%	21%	43%	100%

In the discussion of the parallel relationship in the previous chapter (i.e., the relation of extent of issue orientation to political participation) we discussed the problem of the relationship being merely the reflection of possible "third factors," and showed that this was not true for the most obvious possible one, education. Controlling for education is even more relevant in the case of the candidate measure because of the means by which the measure was derived. Since extent of candidate orientation is a function of the number of remarks made by a respondent during the course of an interview, it is in part a reflection of verbal facility, and is thus highly related to education. It should be noted, therefore, that when variations in education are removed by the method of control, a high relationship between extent of candidate orientation and political participation still remains.

One other possible contaminating factor should be noted. Although theoretically the extent dimension has no directional component, in the 1952 election it was actually significantly related to voting choice. Because of the greater personal appeal of Eisenhower, people who indicated a high personal reaction to the candidates tended to be Eisenhower supporters, and those evidencing minimal personal attraction to the candidates were more often Stevenson voters. However, this does not seriously affect the relationship shown in Table 9.1; when

TABLE 9.2

RELATION OF CANDIDATE PARTISANSHIP TO PRESIDENTIAL PREFERENCE

PRESIDENTIAL PREFERENCE	CANDIDATE PARTISANSHIP SCORE					TOTAL SAMPLE
	(Stevenson)			(Eisenhower)		
	−2	−1	0	+1	+2	
Eisenhower	21%	31%	42%	67%	90%	54%
Stevenson	78	67	52	32	10	43
Other	1	2	6	1	*	3
Total	100%	100%	100%	100%	100%	100%
Index of presidential preference	−57	−36	−10	+35	+80	+11
Number of cases	83	160	778	276	317	1,614
Proportion of total sample	5%	10%	48%	17%	20%	100%

Eisenhower and Stevenson voters are examined separately, the strong relationship between extent of candidate orientation and political participation persists.

Turning to the partisanship dimension of candidate orientation, Table 9.2 shows the relationship between this dimension and presidential preference. As expected, this relationship is very high. One may also note in this table the much stronger personal predilection for Eisenhower recorded in the survey. Of our sample, 37 per cent were scored as Eisenhower partisans as contrasted to only 15 per cent scored as Stevenson partisans.

Candidate partisanship is also clearly related to level of political participation, as Table 9.3 demonstrates. Candidate partisans (particularly those favoring the Republican candidate) both voted and took other political action more often than the nonpartisan group.

A problem arises in interpreting the relationship demonstrated in Table 9.3. Since the group with a candidate partisanship score of 0 consists mainly of people who made no personal references to the candidates at all, the different score positions on the candidate partisanship dimension vary not only with relation to the partisan nature of the personal references, but also differ with relation to the total number of personal references made. Consequently, the relation obtained between candidate partisanship and political participation may be a function of the *number* of personal references made (i.e., the extent of

TABLE 9.3

RELATION OF CANDIDATE PARTISANSHIP TO POLITICAL PARTICIPATION

POLITICAL PARTICIPATION	CANDIDATE PARTISANSHIP SCORE					TOTAL SAMPLE
	(Stevenson)			(Eisenhower)		
	−2	−1	0	+1	+2	
High	36%	28%	20%	30%	41%	27%
Medium	45	51	44	49	50	47
Low	19	21	36	21	9	26
Total	100%	100%	100%	100%	100%	100%
Index of participation	+17	+7	−16	+9	+32	+1

candidate orientation) and not of the degree of partisanship of the references. Does the relationship between candidate partisanship and political participation add anything to the relationship between extent of candidate orientation and political participation already observed in Table 9.1 ? We can answer this question by presenting the relationship between candidate partisanship and political participation, and controlling for the extent of candidate orientation. This is done in Table 9.4. (Because of the small number of cases in the two highest "extent" categories, they are combined in this table.)

Because of the large number of empty cells, and the small number of cases (23) in one of the most crucial cells, Table 9.4 should be interpreted cautiously. However, it is clear that political participation is much more related to the number of personal candidate references made than it is to the homogeneity in partisan direction of these references. For people who indicate some reaction to the candidates in personal terms, the lack of a clear choice between the candidates does not appear greatly to inhibit their political participation. This presents an interesting contrast with the issue partisanship dimension, where a "middle" position was strikingly associated with lower political participation (see Table 8.9). This difference may possibly be explained in terms of the different meaning of a "middle" position with respect to the candidates and issues in the 1952 election. To take one party's position on the issues investigated in this study necessarily involved opposition to the other party's position. Therefore, to have a Democratic position on some issues and a Republican

TABLE 9.4

RELATION OF CANDIDATE PARTISANSHIP TO POLITICAL PARTICIPATION
FOR VARYING LEVELS OF EXTENT OF CANDIDATE ORIENTATION

NUMBER OF PERSONAL CANDIDATE REFERENCES	CANDIDATE PARTISANSHIP SCORE				
	(Stevenson)			(Eisenhower)	
	−2	−1	0	+1	+2
Three or more	+34†	+24	(+22)‡	+38	+39
Two	−3		+8		+24
One			0	+2	
None			−21		

† Cell entry is index of participation.
‡ Figure is based on only 23 cases.

position on others meant that whatever voting choice was made involved the support of some things that one was opposed to. We would expect that in some cases this would create a conflict situation and would lead to nonparticipation. In contrast to this situation, the positive perception of one candidate does not necessarily involve the negative perception of the other. Since data presented earlier (Chapter IV) indicate that there was very little negative personal reaction to either candidate, a "middle" position on candidate partisanship probably represents, in most cases, a favorable perception of both candidates. Voting either way, in such a case, would not involve supporting anything one was opposed to, and represents a situation of much less potential conflict than that existing for the person with conflicting partisan positions on issues. We would not expect that this type of situation would exert any inhibiting effect on political participation.

In conclusion, then, we have indicated two relationships between candidate orientation and political behavior in the 1952 election. High relationships have been demonstrated between the extent of candidate orientation and political participation, and between the partisan nature of this orientation and presidential preference. The usual caution that the existence of a correlation between two variables does not necessarily imply any particular causal relationship should be particularly stressed in the interpretation of these two relationships. We do not know to what extent people with certain voting predilections tend to stress the good points of their candidate and the bad points of the opposing candidate, or to what extent personal attraction to a candidate tends to influence people's voting preferences. The meaningfulness of our conceptualization of candidate orientation as a force influencing voting behavior, and the adequacy of the indices developed to measure it cannot be judged on the basis of the analysis presented thus far. Such a judgment can more properly be made after the discussion of the following chapters.

X

Differences Among the Motivating Factors

The preceding three chapters have presented and discussed three concepts which we have felt to be important to the understanding of the motivation of voting behavior. Each of the concepts—party identification, issue orientation, and candidate orientation—has been considered independently of the other two. In the remaining chapters we shall compare and integrate our measures of these three forces. The present chapter will be devoted to an examination of the relationships of each of the three measures to the others and to certain attitudinal, behavioral, and demographic characteristics. Chapter XI will demonstrate how combinations of the three measures relate to various facets of voting behavior. Finally, Chapter XII will present a motivational analysis of the different patterns of voting change that occurred between the 1948 and 1952 elections. The reader will recall that we have identified two dimensions for each of these three variables. However, in order to simplify the presentation and avoid repetition, most of the discussion in these concluding chapters will refer to the partisanship measures.

We have seen that, with the exception of party identification, the three factors with which we have been concerned are closely related to our measure of participation, and that they are without exception highly related to presidential preference. This raises the natural question as to whether our three measures are not in fact merely reflecting some common underlying factor which we have not identified. If we cannot demonstrate that the three variables we have developed have a significant degree of independence of one another, the preceding chapters will lose most of their force.

There are three methods by which degree of independence may be shown. First, and most obvious, we shall want to see how closely the three variables correlate with one another; second, we shall find out whether the capacity of one variable to order our participation and preference data is eliminated if one or both of the other variables is controlled; and finally, we shall determine whether the three variables behave in different ways in their relationships with some of the other variables we have considered.

The simple intercorrelations of the three measures are shown in Table 10.1. Considering only the partisanship dimension in each case,

TABLE 10.1

INTERRELATIONS OF THREE MEASURES OF POLITICAL MOTIVATION

ISSUE PARTISANSHIP	PARTY IDENTIFICATION				
	Strong Demo-crat	Weak Demo-crat	Inde-pendent	Weak Repub-lican	Strong Repub-lican
Strongly Democratic	18%	8%	5%	3%	1%
Moderately Democratic	37	30	26	21	13
Nonpartisan	23	38	30	33	21
Moderately Republican	18	19	27	33	42
Strongly Republican	4	5	12	10	23
Total	100%	100%	100%	100%	100%

CANDIDATE PARTISANSHIP	PARTY IDENTIFICATION				
	Strong Demo-crat	Weak Demo-crat	Inde-pendent	Weak Repub-lican	Strong Repub-lican
Strongly Democratic	9%	5%	6%	2%	1%
Moderately Democratic	18	9	9	8	6
Nonpartisan	56	54	45	37	33
Moderately Republican	11	18	18	23	19
Strongly Republican	6	14	22	30	41
Total	100%	100%	100%	100%	100%

CANDIDATE PARTISANSHIP	ISSUE PARTISANSHIP				
	Strongly Demo-cratic	Moderately Demo-cratic	Nonpar-tisan	Moderately Repub-lican	Strongly Repub-lican
Strongly Democratic	17%	5%	4%	3%	2%
Moderately Democratic	21	12	9	7	4
Nonpartisan	42	54	55	44	31
Moderately Republican	14	18	15	19	21
Strongly Republican	6	11	17	27	42
Total	100%	100%	100%	100%	100%

we find that each variable correlates significantly with each of the other two. In general, people who identify themselves as Democrats are more likely to take a Democratic position on issues and to regard the Democratic candidate more favorably than are the Republicans. Republican identifiers similarly tend to have Republican attitudes and preferences. It would be remarkable if this were not true. A close inspection of Table 10.1 will reveal, however, that there are many exceptions to these general trends. There is clearly sufficient independence between the three variables to justify the separate consideration they have been given.

The technique of partialling out the influence of one or two variables in order to reveal the independent relationship of the third variable to the participation and preference scores requires a more elaborate presentation than is appropriate here. It is essentially a procedure of observing the correlation of the third variable with the dependent variables within segregated brackets of the other two variables. This analysis results in very small numbers of cases in some of the final cells, but the fact can be clearly shown that each of the variables correlates independently, both with extent of political participation and with the direction of presidential preference.

The third type of analysis proposed has particular significance, since it permits us not only to extend our demonstration of the relative independence of the three variables, but also to reveal to some extent the ways in which they are different. In comparing the relationships of party identification, issue orientation, and candidate orientation to other variables, two types of findings may be anticipated. Since all three variables are intended to represent positive motivational influences on political attitudes and actions, we would expect to find some types of data with which they would show similar relationships. However, since we have conceptualized these motivational forces as qualitatively different, we would also expect to find other variables to which they would relate differently.

Although we shall present both similar and differential relationships in the present chapter, our primary interest lies in demonstrating the latter. It is important to show that our three variables do in fact relate to meaningfully distinct constructs, and are not merely different measures of the same thing. The major usefulness of these variables as analytic constructs depends not on their ability to predict the same dependent variables, but on their ability to make differential predictions, derived from their differentiating characteristics.

Let us look first at variables that we would expect to be similarly related to party identification, issue orientation, and candidate orientation. Since all three of these concepts carry the inherent implication of personal awareness and sensitivity to political affairs, we would expect all three to be positively related to the various non-behavioral measures of interest and involvement in the election that were investigated in the study. As we noted in Chapter III, three direct questions were asked in the pre-election interviews concerning different aspects of interest in the 1952 election. The respondents were asked about their interest in "following the political campaigns," about how much they "personally cared" which party won the election, and whether or not they felt that the outcome of the election would make a "good deal of difference to the country." Without presenting the tables here, it can be said that party identification, issue partisanship and candidate partisanship are, as anticipated, all highly related to these three attitudinal measures of political interest and involvement. Although some minor variations occur in these relationships, one is struck by their high degree of similarity.

Considering now the differential relationships, we have already seen in the preceding chapters that party identification is much less closely related to level of participation than are the other two motivational variables. A further distinction among these three variables is revealed when we examine their relationships to the characteristics of the voting decision. The relationships of party identification, issue partisanship, and candidate partisanship to straight ticket voting, time of voting decision, and consideration of voting for the opposing candidate are presented in Tables 10.2, 10.3, and 10.4. It will be recalled from Chapter II that these measures of voting behavior were designed to tap the extent of conflict and ambivalence over the voting decision.

In our discussion of the concept of party identification, we emphasized the group conformance character of this postulated force on the voter. It was our assumption that a party-identified person would feel himself impelled, either from his own sense of loyalty or from outside pressures, to comply with the standards which his party sets. Early decision, lack of vacillation in decision, and straight-ticket voting may all be thought of as behavioral manifestations of conformance to party standards. We would therefore expect them to be highly related to party identification, with strong party identifiers who voted for their party showing a minimum of conflict and equivocation, and strong party identifiers who voted against their party showing a maximum of such conflict. We would also expect some evidence of conflict among people who voted in a direction inconsistent with their candidate or issue partisanship. However, because of the somewhat different nature of the issue and candidate variables, we would not expect the relationships to be as marked as those found for party identification.

The clearest test of this hypothesis which our data present is in the analysis of ticket splitting. The straight ticket is the traditional mark of party loyalty. The voter who resolutely follows his ticket down the

TABLE 10.2

RELATION OF PARTY IDENTIFICATION, ISSUE PARTISANSHIP, AND CANDIDATE PARTISANSHIP TO SPLIT-TICKET VOTING

ALLOCATION OF VOTES FOR ALL CANDIDATES IN 1952	PARTY IDENTIFICATION					ISSUE PARTISANSHIP					CANDIDATE PARTISANSHIP				
	Strong Democrat	Weak Democrat	Independent	Weak Republican	Strong Republican	Strongly Democratic	Moderately Democratic	Nonpartisan	Moderately Republican	Strongly Republican	Strongly Democratic	Moderately Democratic	Nonpartisan	Moderately Republican	Strongly Republican
A. Among Eisenhower Voters															
Voted straight Republican ticket	30%	30%	49%	71%	81%		58%	61%	59%	57%		59%	55%	62%	62%
Split away from their presidential votes:															
At national level only	5	5	4	—	3		2	3	2	6		—	2	3	4
At state or local level only	23	23	33	22	12		21	21	26	25		15	27	20	21
At both levels	42	42	14	7	4		19	15	13	12		26	16	15	13
Total	100%	100%	100%	100%	100%	†	100%	100%	100%	100%	†	100%	100%	100%	100%
Number of cases	43	104	178	160	197	17	108	175	230	116	15	39	225	147	261
B. Among Stevenson Voters															
Voted straight Democratic ticket	86%	70%	57%			77%	77%	71%	80%		71%	80%	76%	71%	
Split away from their presidential votes:															
At national level only	3	4	8			7	3	3	5		6	2	4	7	
At state or local level only	7	19	27			6	17	17	10		19	13	13	13	
At both levels	4	7	8			10	3	9	5		4	5	7	9	
Total	100%	100%	100%	†	†	100%	100%	100%	100%	†	100%	100%	100%	100%	†
Number of cases	220	170	90	11	2	81	183	129	66	15	51	84	263	68	28

† Too few cases to permit computation of percentages.

ballot or pulls the party lever on his voting machine demonstrates thereby his unreserved support of his party.   We see in Table 10.2 not only that strong party identifiers were heavily inclined to vote their party's ticket straight, but it is also evident that the less strongly attached a voter was to a party the less likely he was to vote a straight ticket.   We also see that, in the case of Democrats at least, when a voter crossed party lines to support the opposing party's presidential candidate he usually stayed with his own party for part or all of the rest of the ticket.   In marked contrast to this are the data showing the votes of issue- and candidate-oriented people.   Although their presidential votes also followed the direction of their issue and candidate interests, voters strongly motivated by these factors were no more likely to vote a straight ticket than those weakly motivated or indifferent to issue or candidate considerations.

Differences of a similar kind, but less pronounced, are found when we compare the time at which people of different motivations reached their decision to vote (Table 10.3).   Here again, strong party identifiers who supported their own party's candidate made this decision very early in the campaign.   People of weaker party attachment were more deliberate, and people (Democrats) who voted against their own party's candidate were very late in reaching this decision.   The same pattern between strength of motive and time of decision is seen in the case of the issue and candidate factors, but the relationship is not nearly as close. Attachment to a party seems to have a significance for early or late decision regarding voting that partisanship with respect to issues or candidates has only in much less degree.

The difference between party identification and the other two variables is much less apparent in the relationships with vacillation over voting decision, as measured by the extent to which the respondents reported considering voting for the candidate opposite to their final voting choices.   As shown in Table 10.4, among Eisenhower voters party identification, issue partisanship, and candidate partisanship are all highly related to this particular measure of voting indecision. However, there is some evidence among the Stevenson voters that the relation of vacillation in voting decision to party identification is greater than its relation to the other two variables, although the incomplete data on party identification make such a comparison difficult.

To summarize these three tables, we may say that party identification as a motivating force has shown itself to have a somewhat different character than the issue or candidate factors.   This is particularly apparent in its relation to straight- and split-ticket voting.   This further supports our assumption that the three factors differ significantly in quality, and it reveals an important attribute of the phenomenon of party identification.

TABLE 10.3

RELATION OF PARTY IDENTIFICATION, ISSUE PARTISANSHIP, AND CANDIDATE PARTISANSHIP TO TIME OF VOTE DECISION

A. Among Eisenhower Voters

Time of Decision	Party Identification					Issue Partisanship					Candidate Partisanship				
	Strong Democrat	Weak Democrat	Independent	Weak Republican	Strong Republican	Strongly Democratic	Moderately Democratic	Nonpartisan	Moderately Republican	Strongly Republican	Strongly Democratic	Moderately Democratic	Nonpartisan	Moderately Republican	Strongly Republican
Before the conventions	9%	12%	22%	27%	43%	†	17%	22%	34%	33%	†	20%	25%	29%	28%
At the time of conventions	30	35	38	44	44		37	39	40	42		38	34	40	48
During campaign	26	27	21	17	10		21	22	15	17		18	19	23	15
Within two weeks of election	28	18	12	7	2		22	9	7	7		15	15	6	5
On Election Day	5	2	2	1	—		1	2	*	—		3	2	—	1
Do not remember	2	1	1	—	—		—	2	*	—		3	1	—	*
Not ascertained	—	5	4	4	1		2	4	4	1		3	4	2	3
Total	100%	100%	100%	100%	100%	†	100%	100%	100%	100%	†	100%	100%	100%	100%

B. Among Stevenson Voters

Time of Decision	Party Identification					Issue Partisanship					Candidate Partisanship				
	Strong Democrat	Weak Democrat	Independent	Weak Republican	Strong Republican	Strongly Democratic	Moderately Democratic	Nonpartisan	Moderately Republican	Strongly Republican	Strongly Democratic	Moderately Democratic	Nonpartisan	Moderately Republican	Strongly Republican
Before the conventions	45%	31%	18%			31%	34%	39%	35%		26%	36%	41%	31%	
At the time of conventions	30	26	22			26	32	21	27		29	24	25	34	
During campaign	18	23	38			35	21	24	15		35	27	20	22	
Within two weeks of election	3	10	12			6	6	6	11		6	8	6	6	
On Election Day	1	5	8			2	4	4	6		2	4	4	4	
Do not remember	—	—	—			—	—	—	—		—	—	—	—	
Not ascertained	3	5	2			—	3	6	6		2	1	4	3	
Total	100%	100%	100%	†	†	100%	100%	100%	100%	†	100%	100%	100%	100%	†

† Too few cases to permit computation of percentages.

TABLE 10.4

RELATION OF PARTY IDENTIFICATION, ISSUE PARTISANSHIP, AND CANDIDATE PARTISANSHIP TO CONSIDERATION OF VOTING FOR THE OPPOSING CANDIDATE

Consideration of Other Candidate	Party Identification					Issue Partisanship					Candidate Partisanship				
	Strong Democrat	Weak Democrat	Independent	Weak Republican	Strong Republican	Strongly Democratic	Moderately Democratic	Nonpartisan	Moderately Republican	Strongly Republican	Strongly Democratic	Moderately Democratic	Nonpartisan	Moderately Republican	Strongly Republican
A. Among Eisenhower Voters															
Considered Stevenson	47%	32%	23%	14%	6%		31%	19%	17%	12%		38%	21%	16%	13%
Did not consider Stevenson	51	67	77	86	94		69	80	83	87		59	78	84	87
Other	—	1	*	—	—		—	1	*	1		—	1	*	—
Not ascertained	2	—	—	*	—		—	—	—	—		3	*	—	—
Total	100%	100%	100%	100%	100%	†	100%	100%	100%	100%	†	100%	100%	100%	100%
B. Among Stevenson Voters															
Considered Eisenhower	12%	28%	52%			25%	26%	22%	32%		22%	17%	23%	34%	
Did not consider Eisenhower	87	71	48			72	74	78	67		76	82	77	65	
Other	1	1	—			3	—	—	1		2	1	*	1	
Not ascertained	—	*	—			—	—	—	—		—	—	*	1	
Total	100%	100%	100%	†	†	100%	100%	100%	100%	†	100%	100%	100%	100%	†

† Too few cases to permit computation of percentages.

There is an additional way in which we can study the degree of independence and the qualitative differences of our three variables—through an exploration of their incidence in various demographic subgroups within the population. In other words, we can find out whether people in a particular occupational, economic, educational, or other classification have a common level of involvement in party, issue, and candidate considerations, or whether particular groups are characterized by particularly high concern with one or two of these factors with little apparent motivation from the third.

It is clearly impossible to present an analysis of the motivational characteristics of the great number of demographic groups which this study isolated. We may summarize these diffuse data by saying that evidence of differences among the variables is to be found within almost every demographic grouping studied.

The following illustrations may be sufficient to demonstrate the point:

1. Table 10.5 presents the motivational characteristics of people of college education. The figures in this table represent the proportion of college educated people in each category of the different motivational variables. For example, the first figure means that 11 per cent of the strong Democratic party identifiers are people of college education.

If all three partisanship dimensions were only measuring the same underlying factor of political motivation, we would expect them to relate similarly to college education in Table 10.5. Since college educated people voted heavily Republican, we would expect them to be much more heavily represented on the Republican end of the three partisan dimensions than on the Democratic end. This turned out to be true for both party identification and issue partisanship. College educated people contributed almost twice as heavily to the extreme Republican groups on these variables as they did to the comparably extreme Democratic groups. On candidate partisanship, however, an unmistakable difference in relationship occurred. The college educated group which was so markedly Republican in its vote did not contribute a larger proportion of the people attracted to Eisenhower than it did of those attracted to Stevenson.

The same rationale may be applied to the examination of the extent dimensions in Table 10.5. If the three extent dimensions had no significant degree of independence of each other, we would expect them to relate similarly to college education in the table. However, it is apparent from the table that such is not the case. Party identification shows a pattern that is very different from that of the other two variables. On both the issue and candidate variables, college educated people are over-represented in the "high" orientation groups, and under-represented in the "low" groups. Although the college educated people made up 15 per cent of the total population studied, they made up 34 per cent of the high candidate orientation group and 27 per cent of the group most involved with issues. On the other end of these indices, they constituted only 1 per cent of all the people who were lowest on issue orientation, and only 7 per cent of the people who were least concerned about candidates. These findings are consistent with

TABLE 10.5

MOTIVATIONAL CHARACTERISTICS OF PEOPLE OF COLLEGE EDUCATION†

MOTIVATIONAL VARIABLES	PARTISANSHIP				
	Strongly Democratic	Moderately Democratic	Non-partisan	Moderately Republican	Strongly Republican
Party identification	11‡	10	19	19	23
Issue partisanship	14	13	11	19	25
Candidate partisan-ship	20	18	9	20	21
	EXTENT OF ORIENTATION				
	(High) 1	2	(Medium) 3	4	(Low) 5
Party identification	15		13		19
Issue orientation	27	19	10	7	1
Candidate orienta-tion	34	27	17	13	7

† College educated people comprised 15 per cent of the sample, voted 72–28 for Eisenhower, with a participation index of +35.
‡ Figure is the percentage of the category which is made up of college educated people.

the fact that college educated people constituted one of the highest participation groups in the 1952 election. However, this disproportionate representation is not found among the strong party identifiers. Some 19 per cent of the group who were low in extent of party identification were college educated, whereas the college educated contributed no more than their share, 15 per cent, to the strong party identifiers. (This distinction between party identification and the other two variables parallels the finding already noted that party identification is less clearly related to political participation than are the other two variables.)

2. Although members of labor union families were much less pro-Democratic in 1952 than in 1948, they were the largest demographic grouping to give the Democrats a clear majority of their 1952 votes. The rather "average" participation rate of union people, as contrasted

to the college educated group, is consistent with their less intense concern about two of the three major orientations. While union people did not differ from the rest of the population in the extent of their concern with parties or candidates, they were clearly more likely to be concerned with issues (Table 10.6). Union people (who made up 27 per cent of the total population) contributed 31 per cent of the people

TABLE 10.6

MOTIVATIONAL CHARACTERISTICS OF MEMBERS OF UNION FAMILIES†

MOTIVATIONAL VARIABLES	PARTISANSHIP				
	Strongly Democratic	Moderately Democratic	Non-partisan	Moderately Republican	Strongly Republican
Party identification	32	31	27	25	21
Issue partisanship	43	31	26	22	17
Candidate partisanship	37	36	25	27	23

	EXTENT OF ORIENTATION				
	(High) 1	2	(Medium) 3	4	(Low) 5
Party identification	28		29		27
Issue orientation	31	29	28	22	17
Candidate orientation	28	25	25	33	26

† Members of union families comprised 27 per cent of the sample, voted 58–42 for Stevenson, with a participation index of +5.

who were in the strong issue-oriented category and only 17 per cent of those weakest on issue orientation.

Union membership was associated with a pro-Democratic predisposition on all three of the partisan measures, and union people showed most partisanship on the variable with which they were most involved, issue orientation. The association with issue partisanship was clearly higher than with either of the other two measures, with union people constituting 43 per cent of the extreme Democratic issue partisans and only 17 per cent of the extreme Republican partisans.

3. The vote division among women in 1952 was not significantly different from that among men, and their participation, although somewhat on the restrained side, was not greatly different from that of men. The relationship between sex differences and partisanship conforms, by and large, to the lack of a sex difference in the vote

(Table 10.7).   On the measures of partisanship their pattern is one of balance.   The interesting differentials between variables occur in relation to the measures of extent or amount of the orientations.   Of particular interest is the sex difference concerning issues and candidates.   Women were disproportionately low in their concern with issues, contributing only 39 per cent of the highly issue-involved people

TABLE 10.7

MOTIVATIONAL CHARACTERISTICS OF WOMEN†

MOTIVATIONAL VARIABLES	PARTISANSHIP				
	Strongly Democratic	Moderately Democratic	Non-partisan	Moderately Republican	Strongly Republican
Party identification	52	58	48	58	53
Issue partisanship	50	52	61	52	51
Candidate partisan-ship	55	50	53	57	58
	EXTENT OF ORIENTATION				
	(High) 1	2	(Medium) 3	4	(Low) 5
Party identification	52		58		48
Issue orientation	39	47	61	65	75
Candidate orienta-tion	61	58	56	53	51

† Women comprised 53 per cent of the sample, voted 56–44 for Eisenhower, with a participation index of −8.

and 75 per cent of the uninvolved.   On the other hand, they showed a somewhat greater than average concern with candidates.   While 61 per cent of the people in the group much concerned with candidates were women, only 51 per cent of the people in the group least concerned with candidates were women.

In each of these three cases, we have seen clear evidence of differences among the three motivational variables.   Moreover, it should be stressed that the differences seem to be meaningful ones, and not merely capricious variations within a set of generally consistent relationships. College educated people's self-identification as "independents," the particular relevance of issues for the union vote, and women's concern with candidates, are all findings which, although not necessarily predicted, are consistent both with our conceptualization of the motivational variables and our expectations about the political attitudes of these demographic groupings.

One final point should be noted : In the above discussion we have deliberately emphasized the differences among the three variables, and have utilized the demographic groupings to demonstrate these differences.   However, the same data serve not only to differentiate the variables, but also to demonstrate differences among the demographic groupings.   By focusing our attention on the differences among these groupings, it would be possible to utilize the three variables as the basis for an analysis of the groupings' different political motivational patterns. Such an analysis could add to our understanding of the meaning of relationships   between   demographic   characteristics   and   political behavior.

Summary

The analysis presented in this chapter has been necessary to establish the independent identity of the three factors with which Part Two has been concerned.   We have accomplished this by intercorrelating our three measures, by looking for their independent effects when two of the three are held constant, and by comparing the relationships of each of them to certain other variables.   The evidence seems to demonstrate that while these measures of party identification, issue orientation, and candidate orientation share an appreciable degree of common element, they nevertheless reflect factors which are qualitatively different.

Indications of the character of the qualitative differences between the motivational forces have been suggested by some of the different ways in which the various measures correlate with other variables. We have not, however, been able to develop this analysis as fully as would be desirable.   Additional information is available from the study which could be used in this manner to illuminate further the content of our major variables, but this extension of the analysis cannot be undertaken here.

XI

The Interaction of the Motivating Factors

The evidence presented in Chapter X supports our original assumption that the three motivational forces we have conceptualized do in fact have a significant degree of independence of each other. It now becomes meaningful to ask, How do combinations of these forces relate to the vote? The reader will remember that in the Introduction to Part Two two basic hypotheses were proposed regarding the relations of these variables to the vote. It was proposed first that the greater the number of congruent forces activating a person in the election situation the more likely he will be to respond to them. Second, we expect that when the forces motivating a person are in conflict his response will be reduced. These hypotheses are tested in Table 11.1 as they apply to extent of participation in the 1952 election, and in Table 11.2 as they apply to the choice of candidate in that election.

In Table 11.1 people represented by different combinations of the three motivational factors we have been discussing have been combined and their participation records are presented.[1] Thus, we find the people who were Democratic in all three factors (DDD), party identification, issue orientation, and candidate orientation, had a relatively high participation record with 29 per cent in the most active category and only 17 per cent not voting. Their Republican counterparts (RRR) were even more active, having the highest record of participation of any of the pattern groups. If the reader will follow down the sides of the triangular matrix of Table 11.1, going either from DDD through DD? and D?? to ??? or from RRR through RR? and R?? to ??? he will find a decreasing amount of participation recorded. Since each of these steps represents a decrease in the number of effective motivational forces (from three to none) these findings may be seen to support our expectation that people would be found to be politically active in direct relation to the number of factors which motivated them.

[1] As described in the previous chapters, the three variables are measured on a five-point scale, which includes strong and moderate categories of pro-Democratic and pro-Republican response, and one nonpartisan category. To facilitate the handling of data for this discussion, the strong and moderate categories have been combined to form scales containing the following three categories: pro-Democratic (D), pro-Republican (R) and nonpartisan (?).

The hypothesis that conflict of forces would reduce political participation can be tested by reading across the top two rows of pattern groups in Table 11.1. In the top row the relevant comparisons are between the DDD and DDR groups and between the RRR and DRR groups, since these patterns are similar in the number of active forces (three)

TABLE 11.1

RELATION OF POLITICAL PARTICIPATION TO MOTIVATIONAL PATTERNS

Political Participation	Motivational Patterns			
	DDD (90)†	DDR (99)	DRR (105)	RRR (138)
High	29%	29%	35%	46%
Medium	54	52	50	50
Low	17	19	15	4
	DD? (233)	D?R (248)	RR? (217)	
High	32%	20%	40%	
Medium	41	49	47	
Low	27	31	13	
	D?? (242)	R?? (160)		
High	16%	19%		
Medium	44	49		
Low	40	32		
	??? (82)			
High	10%			
Medium	38			
Low	52			

† Figures in parentheses are number of cases.

but differ in the consistency of these forces. In the first of these cases, the conflicted pattern does not have a lower participation record than does the nonconflicted group. In the second case, RRR as compared to DRR, the expected difference is found. In the second row the DD? and RR? patterns should be compared to the D?R pattern. In this case all three patterns have two active forces, but in D?R they are in conflict. Here again the conflicted pattern has a lower participation record. We may conclude that our data incline toward support of our expectation that conflict in motivation would be associated with reduction in extent of political participation.

Two additional facts should be noted from Table 11.1. The reader will observe that the participation records on the Republican side of the triangular matrix are all higher than the corresponding values on the Democratic side. Our two hypotheses give us no clue as to why this should be the case. It may be conjectured that in the 1952 situation the factors we have been considering were not equally strong for Republicans and Democrats. It is possible, for example, that Republican candidate orientation may have been a stronger motivating force than Democratic candidate orientation. They have been regarded as equal in this presentation, and we have no way of assigning differential values to them.

On the other hand, the greater participation of the Republican pattern groups may result from other factors which are not taken account of in the three variables which we have been considering. Considering the demographic and regional differences which we have seen to exist between Republicans and Democrats, it would not be surprising to find that there are additional psychological factors which differentiate the party groups and are themselves correlated with readiness to participate in politics. Some of the factors which were measured in this study but not included in the present analysis, such as sense of political efficacy or sense of civic obligation, may be found in subsequent investigation to explain part of the difference we have seen between the participation records of people with Republican and Democratic motivational patterns.

One further aspect of Table 11.1 supports this suggestion that additional factors must be brought into the analysis before we can consider variations in political participation to be fully accounted for. The pattern at the bottom of the matrix shown in the table represents the participation record of those people who were given neutral or indifferent scores on all three of the major variables of this study. Half of these people reported having voted. Although this is a small group, comprising approximately 5 per cent of the total sample, we must assume that some other forces than the ones we have dealt with impelled them to go to the polls. It may be hoped that the analysis of additional data gathered in this study will tell us something of what these forces were.

Table 11.2 presents the preference between Eisenhower and Stevenson expressed by people in the various pattern groups. If the reader will examine this table in the same manner as he did Table 11.1, he will find that the same general trends appear. Clear-cut choice of one candidate over the other diminishes as one proceeds down the sides of the matrix, until the bottom pattern is found to show no preference between the two candidates.   Conflict between forces is reflected in ambiguity in preference for candidates, as may be seen by reading across the top two rows of pattern groups.   And, just as in the previous table, the Republican-oriented patterns are in every case more consistent in their preference for the Republican candidate than are the corresponding

TABLE 11.2

RELATION OF PRESIDENTIAL PREFERENCE TO MOTIVATIONAL PATTERNS

Presidential Preference	Motivational Patterns			
	DDD (90)†	DDR (99)	DRR (105)	RRR (138)
Eisenhower	7%	29%	81%	98%
Stevenson	93	69	17	1
Other, or none	—	2	2	1
	DD? (233)	D?R (248)	RR? (217)	
Eisenhower	18%	50%	94%	
Stevenson	78	48	6	
Other, or none	4	2	—	
	D?? (242)	R?? (160)		
Eisenhower	28%	81%		
Stevenson	64	15		
Other, or none	8	4		
	??? (82)			
Eisenhower	39%			
Stevenson	40			
Other, or none	21			

† Figures in parentheses are number of cases.

Democratic-oriented patterns in their preference for the Democratic candidate.

The conclusions to be drawn from Table 11.2 are essentially similar to those we have drawn from Table 11.1.   Preference for a candidate is strongest among people reporting the largest number of factors impelling them toward that candidate.   This preference is weakened if conflict exists among these motivating factors.   From a comparison of the two tables, we may conclude that our motivational analysis has been somewhat more successful in accounting for presidential preference than it has for extent of political participation. In the "pure" positive patterns (DDD and RRR), the number of people properly classified as to presidential preference approaches 100 per cent; in the "pure" nonpartisan pattern (???), the difference in the proportions choosing each candidate falls to zero. Considering the fact that actual participation in an election is undoubtedly influenced by many factors that do not affect the simple statement of a preference between candidates, i.e., weather, illness, change of address, inconvenience, conflicting obligations and the like, it is not surprising that it should be relatively more difficult to predict.

Consistency and conflict in motivational forces relate not only to political participation and preference, but also to the other measures of voting behavior examined in the study. We would expect to find the character of the motivational pattern related to time of voting decision, presence or absence of vacillation between candidates, and straight- and split-ticket voting. The greater the summation of forces activating the voter, the earlier and less ambiguous we would expect his

TABLE 11.3

RELATION OF MOTIVATIONAL PATTERNS TO STRAIGHT-TICKET VOTING

A. AMONG EISENHOWER VOTERS

	Motivational Patterns			
	RRR	RR ?	RRD	R ?D
Voted straight Republican ticket	75%	69%	44%	52%
Voted split ticket	25	31	56	48
Total	100%	100%	100%	100%
Number of cases	131	181	75	91

B. AMONG STEVENSON VOTERS

	Motivational Patterns			
	DDD	DD ?	DDR	D ?R
Voted straight Democratic ticket	84%	78%	75%	72%
Voted split ticket	16	22	25	28
Total	100%	100%	100%	100%
Number of cases	70	137	56	78

decision to be. Where conflict in motivation is present, we would expect evidences of indecision in the choice of candidate.

Table 11.3 presents the record of the different motivational patterns in regard to straight-ticket voting. Only those patterns in which at least two of the motivational forces were active are considered. We see by reading across the table—comparing RRR and RR?, RRD and R?D, DDD and DD?, and DDR and D?R—that the summation hypothesis is generally supported, although there is one reversal among the Republican groups. In Table 11.4 we find similar results for the presence of vacillation over the choice of candidate. Table 11.5 shows the record of the different groups in time of decision. Here, strength of motivation is seen to be associated with early decision. One exception to this pattern appears among the DDDs, who were somewhat later in reaching their decisions than we would have expected.

In order to show the influence of conflict among the motivational forces, the number of forces should be held constant. Therefore, in testing the conflict hypothesis in these three tables, the relevant comparisons for the Eisenhower voters are the RRRs compared to the RRDs and the RR?s compared to the R?Ds. For the Stevenson voters

TABLE 11.4

RELATION OF MOTIVATIONAL PATTERNS TO CONSIDERATION OF
VOTING FOR OPPOSING CANDIDATE

A. AMONG EISENHOWER VOTERS

	Motivational Patterns			
	RRR	RR ?	RRD	R ?D
Considered voting for Stevenson	5%	12%	25%	23%
Did not consider voting for Stevenson	95	87	75	75
Other, or not ascertained	—	1	—	2
Total	100%	100%	100%	100%

B. AMONG STEVENSON VOTERS

	Motivational Patterns			
	DDD	DD ?	DDR	D ?R
Considered voting for Eisenhower	16%	16%	29%	35%
Did not consider voting for Eisenhower	81	84	69	64
Other, or not ascertained	3	—	2	1
Total	100%	100%	100%	100%

the relevant comparisons are between the DDDs and the DDRs and between the DD?s and the D?Rs.

We see in Table 11.3 that people whose presidential vote was supported by a consistent pattern of motivational forces were more likely to vote a straight ticket than were those with a conflicting motivational pattern. Table 11.4 shows a similar relationship between conflict in the three motivational variables and the presence of vacillation in the voting decision and consideration of the opposing candidate. Finally, we see in Table 11.5 that a conflicting motivational pattern tended to be associated with a late decision regarding one's vote and a consistent pattern with an early decision, although, as we saw in the preceding paragraph, Stevenson voters who were Democratic on all three of the motivational measures were somewhat slower in coming to a decision than we would have predicted.

TABLE 11.5

RELATION OF MOTIVATIONAL PATTERNS TO TIME OF VOTING DECISION

A. AMONG EISENHOWER VOTERS

	Motivational Patterns			
	RRR	RR?	RRD	R?D
Before the conventions	40%	35%	20%	23%
At the time of conventions	47	42	47	35
During campaign	9	15	24	22
Within two weeks of election	3	4	7	16
On Election Day	—	—	—	2
Don't know, or not ascertained	1	4	2	2
Total	100%	100%	100%	100%

B. AMONG STEVENSON VOTERS

	Motivational Patterns			
	DDD	DD?	DDR	D?R
Before the conventions	33%	42%	34%	24%
At the time of conventions	23	26	39	31
During campaign	33	22	14	23
Within two weeks of election	11	3	9	12
On Election Day	—	4	—	6
Don't know, or not ascertained	—	3	4	4
Total	100%	100%	100%	100%

Summary

The reader will recognize that the data presented in this chapter provide a critical test of the argument on which Part Two is based. We have talked about voting behavior in terms of individual citizens reacting to a complex of motivating forces. We have limited our analysis of these forces to three broad factors on the assumption that they, acting together, would represent a large part of the total motivation which underlies the vote. We have stated certain expectations, based on general motivational theory, as to how these three factors would interact. As we have seen, the data conform in a satisfactory way to these expectations.

It is important to add that while the conclusions reached in this chapter are based on data from 1952 we would expect the rationale of our analysis to apply equally well to any other presidential election in this country. The motivating factors we have conceptualized do not depend on any specific candidates, issues, or parties. The changes in candidates and issues that occur from year to year give each election a quality of its own, but as contributors to the total motivation of the voters, candidates, issues, and parties are present every year. The relative importance of each of the three factors may well vary from one election to the next, but we would assume that in any election they will account for a major share of the total motivational force affecting the public. We would also expect them to facilitate and inhibit each other in much the same way as we have observed in this report.

Chapter XI has described the interaction of the forces which the preceding chapters of Part Two have discussed individually. It remains now to apply this technique of analyzing motivational patterns to the particular circumstances of the 1952 election. Is it possible to go beyond the over-all generalities with which this chapter has dealt and come to specific conclusions regarding the forces which motivated the voters in 1952? We shall attempt to accomplish this by studying the motivational patterns of each of the major voting groups which made up the 1952 electorate.

XII

A Motivational Analysis of the 1952 Vote

Elections are won and lost by the ability of each of the contesting parties to hold and activate the support of their accustomed followers, to attract new voters entering the electorate, to capture the uncommitted voters with no party loyalties, and to win away, at least temporarily, the supporters of the opposition. It is apparent from analyses of the 1948 election that the Democratic success of that year resulted from the considerable advantage enjoyed by the Democratic party in the number of people who had, during the previous sixteen years, been supporting it rather than the Republican party, and from the inability of the Republican party to attract any substantial number of these Democratic voters to their side.[1] The closeness of the Truman victory resulted not so much from Republican strength as from the failure of large numbers of 1944 supporters of Roosevelt to go to the polls in Mr. Truman's behalf in 1948.

Chapter II of this volume has presented comparable data from the 1952 election. We have seen that one of the decisive factors in the Republican victory of that year was the switching of a large number of former Democratic supporters to Eisenhower. With the Republican party having only a narrow margin over the Democrats in the total number of their party faithful that they were able to muster out to the polls, and with no major advantage gained by the Republican party in its ability to attract the new voters, it was the shift of almost one out of every four of the 1948 Truman Democrats to the Republican ranks which gave General Eisenhower his clear margin over Governor Stevenson.

These conclusions regarding the nature of the Democratic successes and failures in 1948 and 1952 lead directly to the further question, What caused these crucial changes in voting behavior? We propose now to apply to the data of the 1952 election the method of motivational analysis which we have developed in the preceding chapters of Part Two.

There are two ways in which such an analysis may be undertaken. In one approach, we can focus our attention on the motivational

[1] From unpublished data in the Survey Research Center study of the 1948 election.

variables themselves, and attempt to estimate the changes that occurred in them between 1948 and 1952. This will be treated briefly in the concluding section of this chapter. In a somewhat more refined approach, we can consider the groups of people whose voting behavior changed between the two election years, and attempt to understand the factors influencing this change by comparing their motivational patterns with those of the people whose voting behavior remained unchanged from 1948 to 1952. This latter type of analysis, which provides us with much more detailed information regarding the motivational bases of the 1948–1952 change, will be our major concern in this chapter.

A Motivational Analysis of 1948–1952 Voting Groups

Inasmuch as all gains and losses in voting strength are of more or less importance in the outcome of an election, we need to consider each of the major categories of voters and nonvoters who contributed to the final balance of Republican and Democratic votes. The ensuing discussion will, consequently, focus on four segments of the population: (*a*) party regulars, people who voted Democratic both in 1948 and 1952 (DDs) or who voted Republican in both elections (RRs); (*b*) new voters, people who did not vote in 1948 but did vote in 1952 (NDs and NRs); (*c*) switchers, who voted Democratic in 1948, but Republican in 1952 (DRs);[2] and, (*d*) nonvoters, people who may or may not have voted in 1948, but did not vote in 1952 (NNs, DNs, and RNs). Because of the particular significance of the defection of a large segment of the normally "solid South" to the Republican fold in 1952, a further subdivision will be made within each of these groups to allow a comparison of voter change between Southern and non-Southern parts of the population.[3] The term "North" will be used to refer to all of the country outside the 15 border and Southern states. Each group of voters will be described in terms of the three major variables which make up our motivational pattern—party identification, issue orientation, and candidate orientation.[4]

---

[2] The number of 1948 Republicans who shifted to Stevenson in 1952 was too small to consider in this analysis.

[3] Only minor differences exist among the other three regions, Northeast, Midwest, and Far West. Although the question of regional differences demands further study, it seems clear that South–non-South differences constitute the most significant regional differences with regard to the motivational items considered here.

[4] Again Chapter XII deals mainly with the directional measures although references are also made to the strength of the three factors. In order to simplify the presentation only the directional measures are given in the tables which accompany the text.

An examination of the data for South and North immediately reveals a number of significant differences between the motivational patterns predominating in the two parts of the nation. It is evident from Table 12.1 that Southerners were much more often identified with the Democratic party than were people in the rest of the nation; moreover, Southerners were more likely to describe themselves as strong identifiers and less likely to accept the "independent" label than were residents of the other sections of the country. However, they were somewhat less clearly favorable to Eisenhower in their attitudes toward the candidates, and a smaller proportion of them showed an

TABLE 12.1

REGIONAL DIFFERENCES IN MOTIVATIONAL PATTERNS

	PARTY IDENTIFICATION		ISSUE PARTISANSHIP		CANDIDATE PARTISANSHIP	
	North	South	North	South	North	South
Strongly Democratic	18%	31%	8%	5%	6%	3%
Moderately Democratic	22	32	26	26	11	7
Nonpartisan	26	15	27	33	42	66
Moderately Republican	16	8	24	26	18	13
Strongly Republican	16	6	10	5	23	11
Other	2	8	5	5	—	—
Total	100%	100%	100%	100%	100%	100%
Number of cases	1,174	440	1,174	440	1,174	440

interest in the candidates as individuals than was true of people of the North. Interestingly enough, neither of these two all-inclusive segments of the American electorate showed any over-all partisan bias in its attitudes on the major issues which were presented in the survey; pro-Democratic and pro-Republican sentiment on these issues was evenly balanced in both sections. Insofar as extent of involvement with governmental policy was concerned, however, people of the North were clearly more involved than were Southern residents.

Within each of the major regions, North and South, we find substantial differences in the motivational patterns reported by the four main classes of people ve propose to consider, party regulars, new voters, switchers, and nonvoters. Consider first the characteristics of these four groups in the North.

Among people living outside of the South, new Democrats of 1952 were quite similar to regular Democrats insofar as the three motivational factors are concerned. Only two differences between these groups merit comment. In the first place, while new Democrats were no less likely than regular Democrats to express an identification with the Democratic party, they were less inclined to call themselves "strong" party identifiers (Table 12.2). Second, the new Democrats did show somewhat less enthusiasm for Stevenson than did the Demo-

TABLE 12.2

RELATION OF 1948–1952 VOTE PATTERN TO PARTY IDENTIFICATION

PARTY IDENTIFICATION	1948–1952 VOTE PATTERN							
	ND	DD	DN	NN	RN	DR	RR	NR
A. In the North								
Strong Democrat	28%	44%	42%	13%	—%	16%	1%	4%
Weak Democrat	46	34	37	29	9	32	3	18
Independent	26	19	12	36	22	36	22	32
Weak Republican	—	2	6	15	35	11	29	27
Strong Republican	—	1	—	*	30	5	44	16
Other	—	—	3	7	4	—	1	3
Total	100%	100%	100%	100%	100%	100%	100%	100%
Number of cases	65	295	35	136	23	122	357	96
B. In the South								
Strong Democrat	51%	65%	48%	21%		30%	—%	7%
Weak Democrat	38	25	40	32		47	11	41
Independent	11	6	4	15		14	28	14
Weak Republican	—	2	4	9		9	11	21
Strong Republican	—	—	—	4		—	50	17
Other	—	2	4	19		—	—	—
Total	100%	100%	100%	100%	†	100%	100%	100%
Number of cases	39	67	23	194	3	43	28	29

† Too few cases to permit computation of percentages.

cratic regulars (Table 12.4). However, in their views on issues the new Democrats were no less involved or partisan than the regular Democrats (Table 12.3).

It may be said, then, that as a group the new Democrats reacted positively to the influence of party and issues and, while not overly impressed with Stevenson, they were not sufficiently diverted by Eisenhower to throw their votes to him.

The new Republicans of 1952 were quite distinctly different from the regular Republicans. Although nearly half of the new Republicans called themselves "Republican" in their party identification, the group included far fewer "strong" Republican identifiers, and many more independents and Democratic identifiers, than did the group of Republican regulars. Even more striking was the failure of the new Republicans to take a Republican position on issue partisanship. While regular Republicans clustered heavily at the Republican end of the issue distribution, new Republicans were about as likely to take a

TABLE 12.3

RELATION OF 1948–1952 VOTE PATTERN TO ISSUE PARTISANSHIP

ISSUE PARTISANSHIP	1948–1952 VOTE PATTERN							
	ND	DD	DN	NN	RN	DR	RR	NR
A. In the North								
Strongly Democratic	18%	19%	14%	4%	—%	5%	1%	5%
Moderately Democratic	31	39	34	33	22	28	9	25
Nonpartisan	32	23	40	39	22	30	23	24
Moderately Republican	14	12	9	17	34	25	38	27
Strongly Republican	2	2	—	1	9	10	23	9
Other	3	5	3	6	13	2	6	10
Total	100%	100%	100%	100%	100%	100%	100%	100%
B. In the South								
Strongly Democratic	13%	7%	13%	4%		—%	—%	—%
Moderately Democratic	28	45	22	26		14	25	10
Nonpartisan	31	26	26	37		40	18	31
Moderately Republican	20	16	35	26		28	39	45
Strongly Republican	3	4	4	1		9	18	10
Other	5	2	—	6		9	—	4
Total	100%	100%	100%	100%	†	100%	100%	100%

† Too few cases to permit computation of percentages.

Democratic as a Republican position on this scale. Only in the direction of their attitudes toward the candidates did the new Republicans disclose a clear-cut explanation of their support of the Republican cause; they were almost as unreserved in their admiration of Eisenhower as were the party regulars.

Virtually the same pattern of motives was demonstrated by the DR switchers as by the new Republicans, with the major (and not unexpected) exception of the direction of their predominant party identification. Half of the switching group still called themselves Democrats, albeit "weak" Democrats for the most part. Relatively few of them (16 per cent) were prepared to identify themselves as

Republicans. As with the new Republicans, an even split among the switchers in the direction of their issue commitments removed issue partisanship as an effective motivational factor for them as a group, and only a strong positive orientation toward Eisenhower is left as clearly related to the switch.

The Northern nonvoters of 1952 may be divided into three groups: those people who voted neither in 1948 nor 1952 (NNs), those who voted Democratic in 1948 and did not vote in 1952 (DNs), and those

TABLE 12.4

RELATION OF 1948–1952 VOTE PATTERN TO CANDIDATE PARTISANSHIP

CANDIDATE PARTISANSHIP	1948–1952 VOTE PATTERN							
	ND	DD	DN	NN	RN	DR	RR	NR
A. In the North								
Strongly Democratic	8%	12%	3%	7%	4%	2%	3%	1%
Moderately Democratic	15	21	23	8	4	5	6	3
Nonpartisan	49	49	60	63	26	35	26	40
Moderately Republican	22	13	11	15	40	24	21	25
Strongly Republican	6	5	3	7	26	34	44	31
Total	100%	100%	100%	100%	100%	100%	100%	100%
B. In the South								
Strongly Democratic	3%	6%	4%	1%		2%	—%	—%
Moderately Democratic	13	6	4	7		9	—	3
Nonpartisan	61	70	66	76		42	43	55
Moderately Republican	13	14	26	10		14	32	11
Strongly Republican	10	4	—	6		33	25	31
Total	100%	100%	100%	100%	†	100%	100%	100%

† Too few cases to permit computation of percentages.

who voted Republican in 1948 but did not vote in 1952 (RNs). The contribution which these people make to the outcome of an election is negative, but it is not unimportant. Their failure to vote provides an interesting opportunity for a further test of the hypotheses discussed in the preceding chapter.

The two-time nonvoters (NNs) are clearly the least highly motivated of any of the voting pattern groups in the North. They have the smallest proportion strongly identified with a party, they have the largest number indifferent to both candidates, and they are least involved in partisan issues. As a group they do not seem highly motivated by any one of the three factors we have considered. Their failure to participate in the election conforms, of course, to our expectations.

The 1948 Democrats who failed to vote in 1952 (DNs) are like the NNs in the weakness of their issue partisanship and candidate orientation, but differ sharply in the strength of their identification with the Democratic party. In the absence of support from the other two motivational factors, party identification alone was apparently not sufficient to activate these people to vote.

Unlike the NNs and DNs, the motivational pattern of the 1948 Dewey voters who failed to vote in 1952 (RNs) is not one of over-all weakness. This is a very small group in the sample (23 cases) and does not merit detailed discussion. Since they appear to contradict one of the basic hypotheses of this study, however, it is of interest to search for an explanation of this fact. For all three of the variables considered, the strength of motivation recorded for the RNs approaches (but does not equal) that of the regular Republicans. Taken as a whole, the pattern of the three factors would indicate considerably stronger motivation for this group than for either of the other two nonvoting groups. Why then did they not go to the polls? The reasons must lie beyond the components of our motivational pattern.

A variety of explanations will occur to the reader as to why a person who is highly motivated by political factors will fail to vote in a particular election. Several have been suggested in the preceding chapter. If we now look at the individual interviews of the 23 people who make up the RN group, we discover that in almost all of these cases some obvious impediment to their voting was present. Nine of these people reported being ill on election day, and three others had been called out of town on short notice. Four of this group were women in their seventies who felt too infirm to go to the polls. In five cases there had been a recent change of residence which prevented registration. In only two cases was there no apparent obstruction of this kind.[5]

This analysis of the RN group documents the observation made in the preceding chapter that, because of the kinds of extraneous obstacles to political participation we have just enumerated, it is impossible to account fully for differences in participation solely on the basis of psychological factors. It also explains why a group which, on

[5] In 19 of the 21 cases, the reason for not voting was either confirmed by the interviewer or was given credence by other evidence given in the interview. Two of the reports of illness, however, were not confirmed and may have been suggested by the wording of the question. The high proportion of apparently valid explanations of nonvoting in this highly motivated group contrasts sharply with the relatively low incidence of such explanations in the weakly motivated DN group in the North. Less than 1 out of every 3 members of this group reported being unable to vote because of residence requirements, illness, and the like. Twenty of the 35 persons in the DN group gave explanations such as "I just didn't feel like it; I had a cold," "I didn't want to walk that far," or "I was too tired after work."

the basis of their motivational pattern, we would have expected to be voters were in fact nonvoters.

Turning now to the South, we must note first that the sample from this area was much smaller than that from the North and conclusions regarding Southern voting groups must be drawn with this in mind.

We have seen that new Democrats in the North were very similar to Democratic regulars in that region. This is also true in the South where new Democrats even more closely resembled the Southern Democratic regulars. The greater tendency of DDs over NDs to be "strong" rather than "weak" party identifiers seen in the North persisted as a difference between DDs and NDs in the South. Otherwise, in concern and partisanship regarding issues and in candidate partisanship, new Democrats and regular Democrats in the South did not differ significantly.

Party identification and issue orientation apparently combined to form the basis for the new Democratic vote in the South as well as for the new Democratic vote of the North. Again, candidate orientation did not seem to exert any strongly partisan influence.

New Republicans and Republican regulars are both relatively small groups in the South. Keeping in mind the relative unreliability of our samples from these groups, we may observe that the similarity in positive attitudes toward Eisenhower found between Northern NRs and RRs was also found between Southern NRs and RRs, and was supplemented by a strong resemblance in attitudes on issues. Both groups showed a strong bias toward the Republican end of the issue scale. Only a relatively weak attachment to the Democratic party, held by a large minority of the new Republicans, stood as a barrier separating them from the Republican regulars of the South.

The Southern switchers constitute one of the most interesting of the voting groups. They comprised 43 per cent of the total 1952 Republican vote in the South (while the Northern switchers made up only 21 per cent of the Northern Republican vote).[6] These new-found supporters of the Republican presidential candidate still carried the marks of their earlier allegiance to the Democrats. In overwhelming numbers they maintained their identity as Democrats, with only a small minority willing to call themselves even "weak" Republicans. In the matter of partisanship regarding issues and candidates, on the other hand, Southern switchers were almost as Republican as regular Republicans in the South. Both groups were above the Southern average in their degree of involvement in issues. Although the DRs were not as solidly

[6] A number of these Southern Eisenhower voters who say they voted for Truman in 1948 are undoubtedly people who actually voted for Dewey. As we noted in Chapter I, there was an over-report of the Truman vote and under-report of the Dewey vote among our Southern respondents.

Republican in the direction of their attitudes on these issues, they were not likely to be found on the Democratic side of this scale. Both groups were decidedly Republican in their attitudes toward the presidential candidates.

Making allowance again for the restricted size of these samples, the similarity between Southern switchers and Southern Republican regulars is unmistakable on all these measures except direction of party identification.

Only one of the nonvoting groups in the South is large enough to warrant detailed analysis—those people who failed to vote both in 1948 and 1952, the NNs. Like their counterparts in the North, they are characterized by a very weak motivational pattern. Their concern with issues was lower than that of any of the other groups, North or South; their attitudes regarding these issues were weak and not predominantly biased toward either party position. Their indifference to candidates was virtually complete. Like all other of the Southern groups except the regular Republicans, they maintained a degree of attachment to the Democratic party, but even this was relatively weak. Their failure to vote is not difficult to understand.

A word may be added regarding the 1948 Democratic voters in the South who did not vote in 1952, the DNs. They are a small group (23 cases) and like the RNs in the North their three-factor pattern shows greater evidence of positive motivation than one would expect among nonvoters. Extraneous obstacles of the kind described earlier account for about half of these cases, but there still remains a much larger proportion unaccounted for than was the case with the Northern RNs. There is an interesting suggestion of conflict in the motives of this group with a high identification with the Democratic party and an inclination toward the Republican position on issues and candidates, but the data are too fragmentary to warrant drawing any conclusion regarding this.

If we now review the motivational patterns of the several groups of voters and nonvoters we have discussed, we shall find interesting differences in the components of the total Democratic and Republican votes.

The Democratic vote in 1952 totalled over 27 million, the highest vote for a Democratic presidential nominee since the Roosevelt sweep in 1936. In terms of the voting groups described in this chapter, this near-record turnout was made up almost entirely of two groups, a large group of party regulars (DDs) and a much smaller group of new voters (NDs), who were just reaching voting age or who had failed to vote in 1948. The contribution made by 1948 Republicans now voting Democratic was of no practical consequence in 1952.

The significant fact about these two Democratic components is their similarity. Both appeared to be motivated both by feelings of party loyalty and by adherence to the Democratic position on partisan issues. Neither group took a strongly partisan position on the two candidates. North and South were alike in these respects. In spite of certain adverse issue factors, and in the face of the unusual personal appeal of the Republican candidate, these people stood firm for the Democratic standard-bearer.

The Republican vote in 1952 was composed of three groups—the party regulars (RRs) contributing the largest proportion, the new voters (NRs), and the erstwhile Democrats now supporting Eisenhower (DRs). These groups differed substantially in their commitment to parties and issues. They had only one strong resemblance—a positive attitude toward the Republican rather than the Democratic candidate. In the North only the party regulars were clearly Republican in all three of these respects. Both the new Republicans and those switching to the Republicans fell between the Democratic and Republican positions on issues. The situation of the switchers was further compromised by the fact that their party identification was still much more clearly Democratic than Republican. In the South there was more resemblance in the three components of the Republican vote in their issue position than there was in the North, all three groups inclining to the Republican end of the issue scale. While the Republican regulars in the South were strong in their identification with their party, the other two groups supporting Eisenhower maintained the traditional Southern identification with the Democratic party, especially those who were switching from a Democratic vote in 1948.

The tremendous importance of General Eisenhower to the Republican vote in 1952 cannot be doubted. This is not the only conclusion to be drawn from these data, however. Of possibly great long-term significance is the fact that General Eisenhower attracted the votes of several million people from the ranks of the Democrats and the young and previously inactive voters without thereby effecting any substantial reorientation in their attitudes regarding parties, and with only partial agreement from them with the Republican position on issues. Only in the South were the new adherents to his party people who, as a group, shared the Republican point of view regarding partisan issues. Even they maintained at least a nominal association with the Democratic party.

A Comparison of Motivational Forces in 1948 and 1952

In the preceding section, we sought to gain some understanding of the changes represented in the 1952 election by a motivational analysis of the different groups of 1948–1952 voters and nonvoters. We may also approach this problem by attempting a direct comparison of the motivational forces operating in the two election years.

Let us first consider the phenomenon of the great increase in turnout in 1952. If we extend the logic of our first major hypothesis, which related the likelihood of individual voting to the summation of motivating forces, we have the basis of an explanation of the substantial differences which occur from year to year in the total participation of the electorate in the current campaigns and elections. Thus it would follow that in those elections in which relatively large numbers of people were moved by a variety of reasons for voting, the voting turnout and general political activity would be relatively large. Conversely, when fewer factors were exerting widespread influence, the level of activity would be expected to be low.

The presidential elections of 1948 and 1952 present an interesting test of this hypothesis. Although we do not have information regarding voter motivations in 1948 comparable to that available for 1952, it is clear that in 1948 the total number of people voting was low, and the general level of public activation was comparatively modest. In 1952 the total vote was approximately 20 per cent higher and evidences of public excitement and involvement were manifest. What differences existed in public motivation in the two campaigns? If we consider only the three factors reviewed in this study, we would probably assume that so far as party identification was concerned no significant differences existed in the two years, either in the number of people who identified with one or the other party or in the intensity of their identifications. It seems evident, however, that the factors of issues and candidates both differed greatly in the two years.

There were clear party differences in 1948 in attitudes regarding domestic issues, and these differences were in some ways magnified in 1952. There were also marked differences in 1952 between followers of the two parties in reference to issues of foreign policy. The Korean War, the loss of China to the Communists, the Soviet threat in Europe, and the general frustrations of the period of cold war moved the American electorate to a degree quite unknown in 1948. Foreign policy became a dynamic component of total public motivation in 1952 in a manner which contrasted sharply with the "bipartisan" era of 1948.

The other great difference in the two elections was the candidates. Neither Truman nor Dewey could have been described as a popular hero in 1948. Truman was favorably seen by some people as a friend of the "little man," but it seems unlikely that either candidate influenced the election greatly through direct personal appeal. Our study in 1948 concluded that "neither of the candidates was seen as an inspiring leader by the voting population." The presence of General Eisenhower as a candidate in 1952 provided a personal element in the campaign which was largely missing in 1948. We have seen the very widespread and favorable reputation he enjoyed among the public, even among people who voted against him. It is difficult to assess exactly the influence he personally exerted on the election, but it can hardly be doubted that, largely because of his candidacy, the total positive impact of the candidates on the 1952 electorate was greater than that created by Truman and Dewey in 1948.

Note one further interesting fact regarding these two factors. Not only was there a highly charged foreign policy issue and a candidate of great appeal but, perhaps most significantly, for many of his supporters the Eisenhower appeal was very largely in terms of his presumed ability to handle this very problem of foreign policy, specifically the Korean War. As we have seen, the voters found it much easier to associate him favorably with their concern over the international crisis than they did Governor Stevenson. For a great many voters, it was a happy combination of the man and the hour.

Following our hypothesis in this broad application, the increase in the vote in 1952 can be seen as the result of the increased pressure exerted by issues and candidates during the campaign of that year. Other factors, extraneous to the analysis presented here, doubtless had their effects on the voters as well. However, the high salience of both domestic and international issues, and the personal character of the Eisenhower candidacy, undoubtedly contributed heavily to the high turnout in 1952. Whether our reasoning regarding the relation of turnout to plurality of motivational forces can be usefully applied to other election situations is a question which remains to be investigated.

Although we have concentrated in this discussion on the increased turnout in 1952, the method of analysis also has obvious application to the change in the proportions of the total vote that went to each party. It appears that the increased pressures exerted by issues and candidates in 1952 were predominantly Republican in direction. They served, consequently, not only to increase participation in the 1952 election, but to incline it in favor of the Republicans.

It is not the function of this book to speculate as to the ultimate implications of these findings for party politics in the United States. It will suffice at this point to offer certain limited observations regarding the relative stability of the three factors with which we have been primarily concerned. It seems clear that the sense of political group attachment which we have been calling party identification does not change easily. There are numerous evidences, both in this chapter and in Chapter VII, of the tenacity with which most people hold to their party label, even when they are crossing party lines to support the opposition. We do not know how long it takes to convert any appreciable segment of the electorate from one party to the other, or under what conditions. Apparently such a phenomenon occurred during the

Roosevelt era. It has not occurred thus far during the Eisenhower period.

Issues undoubtedly fluctuate in the significance they have in succeeding national elections. There is survey evidence from as early as 1932[7] that the followers of the two parties differ in their views on domestic economic and social issues. We observed this difference in 1948 and we have seen it again in the present report. It would be pretentious to speak of a "party ideology" on these domestic policies, but it is clear that Republican and Democratic voters as groups have persistently held contrasting points of view on these matters, at least since the beginnings of the New Deal. As we have seen, foreign policy, on the other hand, assumed a much greater significance in 1952 than it had in 1948. Reflecting the impact of world events, international issues took on a party relevance which was much less apparent during the days of the "bipartisan" foreign policy.

The relative importance of domestic and foreign issues in future elections cannot be predicted without knowledge of future events. It is clear, however, that the prevailing public images of the two parties render them both vulnerable to public disapproval which might be activated by new developments on the national or international scene.

Of the three factors we have considered, candidate appeal would appear to be the most susceptible to the vagaries of public sentiment. Although there are many examples of office holders who have maintained their popularity in one election after another, there are at least as many others whose hour of public acclaim was fleeting. It seems likely that the success of a public figure in maintaining his popular appeal will be determined not only by the personal attributes of the man, but also by the extent to which he is associated favorably or unfavorably with the partisan issues which become salient in the public mind during his term of office.

[7] Hayes, S. P., Jr., "The interrelations of political attitudes: I. Attitudes toward candidates and specific policies," *Journal of Social Psychology*, 1937, 8, 459–82.

Part Three

SUMMARY

XIII

Summary

The study of political behavior encompasses a much broader range of phenomena than we have dealt with in the research described in this report. We have been concerned exclusively with voting in a national election and the perceptions, attitudes, and activities related thereto.

Voting behavior has obvious attractions as an object of research. The vote has the great advantage of being a discrete act which can be isolated and measured with a high degree of validity. It is, moreover, an act of considerable intrinsic significance. Other things being equal, most researchers would prefer to analyze data which hold some promise of more than trivial consequence. Finally, it is possible to use the vote as a vehicle for the investigation of a rich array of closely associated facts, as the present study has attempted to do.

This research was intended as a study of voters rather than of votes. This meant that we gathered our data from individual citizens rather than from election statistics or other aggregative data. Our objectives specified that our data have national and regional significance, and this required the use of a national cross-sectional sample. We wanted to measure both intentions to vote and actual voting behavior, and this meant that we interviewed our sample respondents both before and after the election.

Part One of this report has presented a detailed description of the 1952 election. It is possible to describe an election in a variety of different terms. We can assess the amount of interest and involvement people felt in the election and show the ways in which they expressed their interest. We can follow the course of the voting decision, tracing the gradual resolution of conflict into the final vote. We can compare the present vote with previous voting experience in order to reveal changes in voting behavior. We can describe the images of the parties and candidates as they existed in the minds of the public. We can compare the demographic characteristics of the voters and nonvoters, Republicans and Democrats. All of these kinds of data were anticipated in the planning of this study, and all have been presented in this report.

Descriptive information of this kind has both immediate and more lasting value. Simply as documentation of an important political event, it has undoubted interest. The study of political behavior is not so advanced that descriptive facts are no longer useful. The general significance of such data is greatly enhanced, however, if they can be integrated with comparable data from preceding and succeeding elections. The study of political change holds much greater promise for the effective testing of theory regarding political behavior than does the analysis of any particular event. Repeated measurements of the kind reported here are necessary for a fully developed program of research in this area.

Part Two has undertaken a dynamic analysis of voting behavior. It has not concerned itself primarily with attempting either to relate specific campaign events to the vote or to classify the votes of the major demographic classes, although data of both these kinds have been presented. Our approach has been at a different level, that of the intervening variables of attitudes, perceptions, and group loyalties. The basic assumption of the study has been that a major portion of the total motivation of the individual citizen in the election situation can be reduced to a manageable number of variables, and that these variables can be adequately measured. Three concepts of personal orientation toward political behavior have been developed, emphasizing parties, issues, and candidates, respectively. These orientations have been treated as motivational factors, and measurements of each have been devised.

The analysis has been organized around two related hypotheses: first, that the motivation of political behavior is effective in direct relation to the number of congruent forces that motivate a person, and second, that the effectiveness of these motivating forces is reduced if there is conflict among them. We have applied these two hypotheses both to extent of participation and choice of candidate.

Participation in the 1952 presidential election has been found to relate with various degrees of significance to each of the three variables which have been the main concern of this study. Those people who were motivated by all three of these factors, with no partisan conflict among them, nearly all participated in the election, at least to the extent of voting. The fewer of these factors present for an individual, the less likely he was to vote or to engage otherwise in the election process. In other words, we have shown a direct relationship between the number of political factors motivating a person and the likelihood of his taking political action.

Similarly, we expected that a combination of congruent forces favoring a candidate would be more likely to result in preference for that candidate than would a smaller number of such forces. We have found that those people who felt themselves strongly identified with one of the major parties, held strongly partisan views on issues which were consistent with those of their party, and were strongly attracted by the personal attributes of their party's candidate expressed preference in nearly every case for the candidate their party put forward. In contrast, among those people for whom none of these factors was active, equal numbers preferred each of the two candidates.

Our hypotheses have proposed that voting behavior depends not only on the cumulative effects of self-consistent factors but also on the inhibiting effect of conflicting factors. In contrast to the highly predictable behavior we observed among people with consistent motivational patterns, we found that when the three motivating factors were not congruent people were less clear in their choice of candidate, they were not so likely to vote, and those who did vote showed the conflict in their motivations by a greater incidence of vacillation, postponement, and divided votes.

These findings regarding the influence of conflict on voting behavior may be recognized as basically similar to the earlier data published by Lazarsfeld, and developed by him under the concept of "cross-pressures." For the most part the "pressures" measured by Lazarsfeld were not the same as those considered in this study. However, the results of both studies may be said to conform to the basic psychological principle that when strong and opposing forces act on an individual the resultant behavior will demonstrate the characteristics of conflict. In the present case, this took the form of, (*a*) negative reaction to the total situation, as expressed through failure to vote or postponement of the decision to vote, (*b*) alternate reaction to one force and then the other, as shown in vacillation between the two candidates, and (*c*) an attempt to satisfy both conflicting forces by reacting positively to both, expressed by dividing the ballot between the two parties.

The three motivational forces with which we have dealt do not, of course, represent the full range of motivations which may influence an individual in his voting decision. Although taken together they do account for a substantial part of the total variance of the vote, there are undoubtedly other factors of both a psychological and nonpsychological character which play a part. Subsequent analysis of data not presented in this report should make possible a more complete accounting of the variations we have seen in voting behavior.

No attempt has been made in this presentation to compare the relative influence exerted on the vote by each of the three variables studied. It seems probable that the respective weights each of these factors has would vary from election to election. The importance of party identification appears to have bulked large in both 1948 and 1952 and, given a continuation of the present party division, this factor may be expected to contribute a substantial portion of the total motivation in any presidential election in this country. In any particular year, the more variable factors of issues and candidates may have unusual importance; 1952 appears to have been such a year. In contrast, 1948 appears to have been largely a party year.

It is apparent that our three basic concepts can be employed as analytical tools in the investigation of types of research problems other than those that have been the concern of this volume. The study of factors related to the three different orientations, the application of these variables to a motivational analysis of the political inclinations of demographic groupings, and other such investigations should add to our understanding of political phenomena above and beyond the limits of any given election.

The present volume has not presumed to interpret the political implications of the data which have been discussed. We have analyzed the characteristics of the major groups which make up the electorate, and we have found that the Republican victory in 1952 was made possible by the successful activation of their party regulars and the recruiting of substantial support from previous nonvoters and former Democrats. Neither of these latter groups had a strongly Republican motivational pattern, however, and it is problematic how long and under what conditions the Republican party can depend on their support. The Republicans profited in 1952 both from the attractiveness of their candidate and from the public temper regarding partisan issues. This profit was sufficient to overcome their persistent deficit in the number of people who identify themselves with their party. While party identification seems to change slowly, both issues and candidates are more variable factors. Whether the balance of forces which we have observed in 1952 will endure or not depends in large part on the extent to which domestic and foreign events force a reëvaluation of these factors in the minds of the voters.

Appendices

A. Sense of Political Efficacy

The preceding chapters have been concerned, in large part, with a discussion of the relationship of political participation and direction of vote to three variables, which have been identified as party identification, issue orientation, and candidate orientation. This section will be devoted to a discussion of one of two other variables, which it was hypothesized in the planning of this study would also be related to political activity, namely, *sense of political efficacy*. The other variable, discussed in Appendix B, is called *sense of citizen duty*. These variables were explored on an experimental basis in the present study, and the data presented in these appendices are intended primarily to stimulate interest in the concepts they represent.

Although the level of citizen interest and participation in any one election may be explained largely in terms of such factors as the attractiveness of one or both candidates and the perceived importance of the campaign issues, an understanding of long-range trends in level of electoral participation requires, in addition, the consideration of broader and more enduring political values and attitudes. For that matter, individual differences in involvement in any particular election are also better understood if we have some notion as to the basic attitudes held by these individuals with regard to political activity. Sense of political efficacy, as defined and used in this study, represents an attempt to investigate one of these broader political attitudes.

Sense of political efficacy may be defined as the feeling that individual political action does have, or can have, an impact upon the political process, i.e., that it is worth while to perform one's civic duties. It is the feeling that political and social change is possible, and that the individual citizen can play a part in bringing about this change. To the extent that this feeling of political efficacy is measurable, we would predict that it would be positively related to political participation.

In an attempt to measure some of the components of political efficacy, five items (calling for a simple "agree" or "disagree" response) were included in the pre-election questionnaire. These items were :

1. I don't think public officials care much what people like me think.

2. The way people vote is the main thing that decides how things are run in this country.

3. Voting is the only way that people like me can have any say about how the government runs things.

4. People like me don't have any say about what the government does.

5. Sometimes politics and government seem so complicated that a person like me can't really understand what's going on.

"Disagree" responses to items 1, 3, 4, and 5, and an "agree" response to item 2 were coded as "efficacious." To respond in contrary fashion (i.e., to think that public officials are not responsive to the will of the electorate, to feel that most major policy decisions are the work of "wire-pullers" and pressure groups and the product of "backroom deals," to be unaware that means of expressing one's political wishes other than voting are available to the average citizen, and to be of the opinion that the modern complexities of government have made citizen participation either impossible or unavailing) indicates a high degree of political futility.

There are a number of different ways to combine a set of items into a single measure. Because it represents one of the more psychologically meaningful methods, it was decided, if possible, to construct a Guttman-type scale from the political efficacy items.[1] Several procedures have been developed for applying the scale analysis technique. The one that seemed best suited to our purposes was Ford's method for scoring six (or fewer) attitude questions with an IBM counter-sorter.[2] It is the procedure used in the following analysis.

One of the main problems in constructing a scale involves the establishment of criteria for judging the adequacy of the scale and of the individual items in it. Several different (and, it must be admitted, largely arbitrary) criteria have been used. Guttman demands 90 per

[1] A scale, psychologically speaking, is an instrument for placing the members of a given population in their proper positions relative to one another with regard to a particular characteristic, attitude, or behavior. One of the criteria of a good attitude scale is that it be unidimensional, by which is meant that it must measure but one attitude or set of closely interrelated attitudes or, in other words, that it must measure just one continuum, or dimension. The Guttman scale analysis methods were perfected to eliminate from scales items that proved to be unreliable or off the continuum being measured. Behind the technique is the notion that a perfect scale would be one by which it would be possible to reproduce the exact pattern of the respondent's answers to each item in the scale from the score he obtained. This scale would have 100 per cent reproducibility. Actual scales cannot be expected to produce these perfect results, but something approaching this should be demanded of every usable scale. Guttman settled on 90 per cent as the minimum "coefficient of reproducibility" necessary for an acceptable scale. For a full discussion of this particular concept of "scalability" and the techniques involved see S. A. Stouffer, *et al.*, *Measurement and Prediction*, Vol. IV of *Studies in Social Psychology in World War II* (Princeton, N.J.: Princeton University Press, 1950).

[2] For a detailed description of this method see Robert N. Ford, "A Rapid Scoring Procedure for Scaling Attitude Questions," *Public Opinion Quarterly*, Fall, 1950, **14**, 507–32.

cent reproducibility for the total scale, i.e., a total error of greater than 10 per cent means that the scale is unsatisfactory. Jackson, on the other hand, has devised what he calls a "plus percentage ratio" (PPR) for measuring scalability. By this criterion, a PPR of .70 is required for the data to be considered scalable.[3] For individual items, different researchers have established criteria of not more than either 10 or 15 per cent error for acceptability. An item with greater than 15 per cent error in it should be dropped from the scale.

When a scale analysis was carried out using the aforementioned five political efficacy items, an over-all coefficient of reproducibility of 92.3 resulted; or, stated another way, there was 7.7 per cent error for the five-item scale. The range of error was 6 to 8 per cent for four of the individual items, but for the second item ("the way people vote is the main thing that decides how things are run in this country") it was 10.8 per cent. Since this was a somewhat ambiguous question with a relatively large per cent error, it was dropped from the scale, and the percentages of error were recomputed on the remaining four questions. The coefficient of reproducibility for the four-item scale is 93.5, and none of the individual items yields more than 7.3 per cent error. This scale also meets Jackson's criterion for scalability with a PPR of .75.

The next task was to convert the response patterns into scale types. For those patterns that were not perfect scale types two methods were used: (a) "Minimum error assignment," wherever possible, and (b) Henry's "distribution of perfect types" for the "ambiguous" response patterns.[4] The end product was a five-point scale, the frequencies for which are to be found in Table A.1.[5]

[3] The formula for a plus percentage ratio is

$$PPR = \frac{C.R. - \text{minimum C.R.}}{1 - \text{minimum C.R.}}$$

where C.R. is Guttman's "coefficient of reproducibility," and the minimum C.R. for each item equals the frequency of responses to the category with the greatest frequency, divided by the total number of responses to that item. This PPR is computed for each item in the scale, and the PPR for the whole scale is simply the arithmetic mean of the item PPRs. See Jay M. Jackson, "A Simple and More Rigorous Technique for Scale Analysis," Part II of *A Manual of Scale Analysis* (unpublished manual, McGill University, Montreal, Canada).

[4] See Andrew F. Henry, "A Method of Classifying Non-Scale Response Patterns in a Guttman Scale," *Public Opinion Quarterly*, Spring, 1952, 16, 94–106.

[5] For approximately 3 per cent of the cases in the total sample there were one or more "Not ascertained" responses. Half of these had two or more such responses and were therefore coded "Not ascertained" for the entire scale. The remaining cases, however, each had only one such response, and it was possible to assign them to one of the five scale types. In addition a few cases, in which the two "easiest" items (items 1 and 4) had been negatively responded to and the two "hardest" items (items 3 and 5) had been positively responded to, were considered to be nonscalar and were also classified as "Not ascertained."

To test the hypothesis that political participation is positively related to the sense of political efficacy, the political efficacy scale was related to the index of political participation. The relationship between these two variables is presented in Table A.1. This table clearly indicates that the higher one's sense of political efficacy, the higher the level of his participation in the 1952 election. The index scores range from +29 for the highest political efficacy category to −35 for the lowest, and the relationship is consistent throughout.

TABLE A.1

RELATION OF POLITICAL EFFICACY SCALE SCORES TO POLITICAL
PARTICIPATION

POLITICAL PARTICIPATION	POLITICAL EFFICACY SCALE SCORES				
	(High) 4	3	2	1	(Low) 0
High	42%	43%	27%	20%	12%
Medium	45	42	50	54	41
Low	13	15	23	26	47
Total	100%	100%	100%	100%	100%
Index of participation	+29	+28	+4	−6	−35
Number of cases	106	326	629	202	331

Although Table A.1 dramatically demonstrates the size and consistency of the positive relationship between political efficacy and political participation, there are some obvious considerations which suggest that the relationship might be largely derivative. One would predict, for example, that political efficacy (as well as political participation) is also positively related to education—the higher one's education, the more likely he is to rate high on political efficacy. Perhaps, then, the political efficacy differences shown in Table A.1 are merely a reflection of educational differences. Or, in similar fashion, one might suspect that the demonstrated differences are merely artifacts of race, or region, or sex, or age differentials in political activity. We would predict, however, that they are not, and that the positive relationship between political efficacy and political participation will not disappear even when the crucial demographic variables are held constant.

Table A.2 presents some of the demographic correlates of political efficacy. As was expected, education is highly related to the efficacy scale; one-half of those respondents who attended college rank high on this scale, as compared with only 15 per cent of those who have completed no more than grade school. The other two socio-economic status variables, income and occupation, are also highly related to political efficacy. In addition, men are somewhat more inclined than women to feel that the average citizen can make his influence felt upon governmental policy, Negroes feel more politically impotent than the

TABLE A.2

SOME DEMOGRAPHIC CORRELATES OF SENSE OF POLITICAL EFFICACY

DEMOGRAPHIC VARIABLES	DEGREE OF POLITICAL EFFICACY†					NUMBER OF CASES
	High	Medium	Low	Not Ascertained	Total	
Sex						
Male	35%	47	17	1	100%	738
Female	20%	55	23	2	100%	876
Race						
White	28%	53	18	1	100%	1,453
Negro	14%	36	48	2	100%	157
Age						
21–34 years	27%	55	17	1	100%	485
35–44 years	31%	52	17	*	100%	381
45–54 years	30%	52	17	1	100%	284
55 years and over	22%	48	28	2	100%	442
Education						
Grade school	15%	49	34	2	100%	660
High school	30%	56	13	1	100%	712
College	50%	44	6	*	100%	238
Income						
Under $2,000	11%	49	38	2	100%	315
$2,000–2,999	19%	54	25	2	100%	255
$3,000–3,999	25%	57	17	1	100%	364
$4,000–4,999	33%	51	16	*	100%	233
$5,000 and over	43%	46	10	1	100%	415
Occupation of head						
Professional and managerial	41%	50	8	1	100%	333
Other white collar	39%	46	14	1	100%	155
Skilled and semi-skilled	25%	57	17	1	100%	462
Unskilled	15%	47	37	1	100%	174
Farm operators	13%	55	31	1	100%	178

TABLE A.2 (*continued*)

DEMOGRAPHIC VARIABLES	DEGREE OF POLITICAL EFFICACY†					NUMBER OF CASES
	High	Medium	Low	Not Ascertained	Total	
Region						
Northeast	30%	53	15	2	100%	390
Midwest	30%	50	19	1	100%	580
South	18%	49	32	1	100%	440
Far West	30%	56	12	2	100%	204
Type of community						
Metropolitan areas	33%	50	15	2	100%	438
Cities and towns	27%	51	21	1	100%	928
Open country	16%	55	28	1	100%	248

† For the purposes of this table and of Table A.3, political efficacy scale scores 1 and 2 were combined to form a "medium" political efficacy category, and scale scores 3 and 4 were grouped together to produce a "high" political efficacy category; scale score 0 thereby became the "low" political efficacy category. Some such combination was necessary in order to avoid ending up with cells with too few cases. The relationship of these five scale scores to political participation (Table A.1) dictated the particular grouping effected.

rest of the population, the South ranks significantly lower than the other three regions of the country in political efficacy, and sense of political potency increases directly with population density.

Having demonstrated the relationship of these demographic variables to political efficacy, and having previously demonstrated their relationship to level of political participation (Chapter V), we are now in a position to discover what happens to the political efficacy–political participation relationship when these demographic factors are held constant. This is done in Table A.3.

Inspection of Table A.3 reveals that the relationship between political efficacy and political participation holds for every one of the categories of the eight demographic variables used as controls. High participation index scores are obtained by the college-educated, middle-aged and high-income respondents who also score high on political efficacy. The lowest participation index score (– 82) is obtained by Negroes who are "lows" on political efficacy. People of low efficacy scores in the South and in the "under \$2,000" income bracket are not far behind, with participation index scores of – 66 and – 62.

As has already been suggested, education is a particularly crucial control variable; but even among the college educated the strength of the respondent's sense of political efficacy seems to make some difference in the extent of his political activity. The same also holds true in the "highest" categories of the other two socio-economic status variables, income and occupation. It should be noted, however, that there is

TABLE A.3

RELATION OF SENSE OF POLITICAL EFFICACY TO POLITICAL PARTICIPATION,
WITH RELEVANT DEMOGRAPHIC VARIABLES HELD CONSTANT

DEMOGRAPHIC VARIABLES	DEGREE OF POLITICAL EFFICACY		
	High	Medium	Low
Sex			
Male	+34†	+11	−27
Female	+22	− 6	−39
Race			
White	+32	+ 6	−21
Negro	(−50)‡	−41	−82
Age			
21–34 years	+12	− 6	−38
35–44 years	+31	+ 1	−44
45–54 years	+41	+ 8	−27
55 years and over	+35	+ 6	−29
Education			
Grade school	+17	−16	−48
High school	+26	+ 8	− 8
College	+43	+31	§
Income			
Under $2,000	+ 8	−15	−62
$2,000–2,999	+14	−15	−33
$3,000–3,999	+16	+ 1	−18
$4,000–4,999	+30	+19	−13
$5,000 and over	+43	+19	+ 2
Occupation of head			
Professional and managerial	+40	+26	(+10)‡
Other white collar	+37	+ 5	(−33)‡
Skilled and semi-skilled	+20	− 4	−19
Unskilled	(− 8)‡	−17	−50
Farm operators	(+22)‡	+ 1	−51
Region			
Northeast	+47	+ 8	−12
Midwest	+26	+12	−11
South	+ 6	−26	−66
Far West	+28	+14	(−12)‡
Type of community			
Metropolitan areas	+35	0	− 9
Cities and towns	+25	+ 4	−39
Open country	+25	− 8	−43

† Cell entries are indices of participation.
‡ Indices based on between 20 and 30 cases.
§ Too few cases to permit computation of a reliable index.

less spread between the political efficacy "highs" and "lows" among those respondents with a college education, with incomes of $5,000 or over, and in families where the head of the household pursues a professional or managerial occupation, than there is among those of poorer education and lower income. These data suggest that factors other than sense of political efficacy may have somewhat greater relevance for the political participation of people of upper socio-economic status than they do for those of lower status.

In summary, it is reasonable to conclude that citizens who feel that public officials are responsive and responsible to the electorate, who think that individual political activity is worth while and capable of influencing public policy, and who see that the private citizen's channels of access to governmental decision-makers are not confined to the ballot box, are much more likely to be politically active than those citizens who feel largely overwhelmed by the political process. It is also possible to state that this relationship is not merely a function of education or any other likely demographic factor. It does appear, however, that the effect of differing levels of political efficacy is not as great for the more socially advantaged citizenry as it is for the less socially advantaged.

B. Sense of Citizen Duty

The second general political attitude included in this study is what has been termed *sense of citizen duty*. Alternative labels for this concept might be "sense of political responsibility" or "sense of civic obligation." It is the feeling that oneself and others ought to participate in the political process, regardless of whether such political activity is seen as worth while or efficacious. It was predicted that the strength of this sense of citizen duty would be positively related to the level of political participation.

Citizen duty, like political efficacy, was to be measured by a scale composed of several different items, which were intended to tap the more important components of this political value. The following four statements (requiring a simple "Agree" or "Disagree" response) were included in the pre-election interview:

1. It isn't so important to vote when you know your party doesn't have a chance to win.
2. A good many local elections aren't important enough to bother with.
3. So many other people vote in the national elections that it doesn't matter much to me whether I vote or not.
4. If a person doesn't care how an election comes out he shouldn't vote in it.

Obviously, the respondent must disagree with these statements if he is to express feelings of political obligation. He must feel that all elections (national, state, and local) deserve his participation, that neither overwhelming electoral odds nor the apparent insignificance of the single vote should stand as barriers to voting, and indifference to the outcome of a particular election should be no deterrent.

The first fact to be noted concerning these four items is the high degree of disagreement that they evoked. Nearly seven out of every eight respondents took exception to the first and third statements, and four out of five expressed disagreement with the second item. A little less than half, however, could not accept the fourth statement. The obvious discrepancy between the average citizen's professed sense of citizen duty and his political performance should occasion no great surprise when two facts are borne in mind: First, in an area involving socially valued attitudes or activities, there is bound to be a certain amount of deliberate distortion on the part of respondents who wish to cast themselves in a more favorable light; and, second, there is both much honest inconsistency between people's thoughts and actions and also much honest failure to live up to perfectly good intentions.

The same type of scale analysis as was applied to the political efficacy items was also used with the citizen duty statements. The coefficient of reproducibility for the four-item scale was 96.0, with the amount of error ranging from 3 to 5 per cent for the individual items.[1] The "plus percentage ratio" for this scale is a satisfactory .77. The response patterns were then assigned to scale types in accordance with the methods described in the preceding section.[2]

Table B.1, constructed in the same fashion as Table A.1, shows the nature of the relationship between citizen duty and political participation. Again, we have a five-point scale related to three categories of political participation. The citizen duty scale is, as would be expected, highly skewed, with approximately four out of every five respondents falling in the highest two scale types. The data, however, give considerable support for our hypothesis that political participation is positively related to citizen duty. The range of participation index

[1] It must be admitted, of course, that with three of the items yielding 80 to 90 per cent disagreement, the opportunity for error was relatively small, as the amount of error in a dichotomous item cannot exceed the percentage given by the response with the smaller frequency. Jackson's PPR, however, takes this fact into account and attempts to correct for it.

[2] The cases for which there were one or more "Not ascertained" responses were also handled as were the similar cases in the political efficacy scale. The cases having two or more such responses were coded "Not ascertained" for the citizen duty scale, the remaining being assigned to one of the scale types. Two response patterns were considered to be nonscalar and were also classified as "Not ascertained."

scores is from $+17$ for those respondents possessing the greatest sense of political responsibility to -69 for those possessing the least, and there are no reversals among the intervening scale types; and looking at the "high" and "low" political participation rows, we discover an orderly and predicted progression throughout.

TABLE B.1

RELATION OF CITIZEN DUTY SCALE SCORES TO POLITICAL PARTICIPATION

POLITICAL PARTICIPATION	CITIZEN DUTY SCALE SCORES				
	(High) 4	3	2	1	(Low) 0
High	32%	29%	24%	6%	4%
Medium	53	46	46	23	23
Low	15	25	30	71	73
Total	100%	100%	100%	100%	100%
Index of participation	+17	+4	−6	−65	−69
Number of cases	698	631	106	52	103

It will be noted that the five citizen duty scale types divide themselves into three rather distinct groups so far as extent of political activity is concerned: Scale types 0 and 1 seem to go together to form a category of respondents (approximately 10 per cent of the sample) who rank very low in political participation. Scale types 2 and 3 may be combined to make a grouping whose index of participation conforms very closely to that of the total sample ($+2$ as compared with $+1$). And scale type 4 stands by itself as a category which rates fairly high ($+17$) on the index, although, it should be noted, not nearly as high as the top political efficacy category. The combinations just described are the ones that will be used in the remaining analysis of citizen duty.

As in the case of political efficacy, the question arises as to whether the relationship between citizen duty and political participation is primarily the reflection of the influence of education or some other demographic variable. This is a problem, because of the relationship between citizen duty and a number of demographic factors. A summary of some of these demographic correlates of citizen duty is presented in Table B.2. Generally speaking, this table shows the same types of relationships as were found with respect to political efficacy. Education, income, occupation, and race are highly related to sense of civic obligation; the regional and type of community relationships are

TABLE B.2

SOME DEMOGRAPHIC CORRELATES OF SENSE OF CITIZEN DUTY

DEMOGRAPHIC VARIABLES	DEGREE OF CITIZEN DUTY†					NUMBER OF CASES
	High	Medium	Low	Not Ascertained	Total	
Sex						
Male	44%	48	7	1	100%	738
Female	42%	44	12	2	100%	876
Race						
White	45%	46	7	2	100%	1,453
Negro	24%	39	36	1	100%	157
Age						
21–34 years	42%	50	7	1	100%	485
35–44 years	43%	48	8	1	100%	381
45–54 years	44%	45	10	1	100%	284
55 years and over	46%	39	13	2	100%	442
Education						
Grade school	32%	46	19	3	100%	660
High school	49%	46	4	1	100%	712
College	57%	43	*	—	100%	238
Income						
Under $2,000	31%	41	25	3	100%	315
$2,000–2,999	41%	47	11	1	100%	255
$3,000–3,999	39%	53	7	1	100%	364
$4,000–4,999	43%	52	3	2	100%	233
$5,000 and over	58%	40	1	1	100%	415
Occupation of head						
Professional and managerial	54%	43	2	1	100%	333
Other white collar	55%	41	2	2	100%	155
Skilled and semi-skilled	39%	52	8	1	100%	462
Unskilled	32%	48	20	—	100%	174
Farm operators	34%	47	17	2	100%	178
Region						
Northeast	50%	41	7	2	100%	390
Midwest	49%	43	6	2	100%	580
South	28%	51	20	1	100%	440
Far West	45%	51	2	2	100%	204
Type of community						
Metropolitan areas	52%	41	5	2	100%	438
Cities and towns	42%	47	10	1	100%	928
Open country	35%	48	16	1	100%	248

† The combination of sense of citizen duty scale scores into high, medium, and low categories is described on page 196.

TABLE B.3

RELATION OF SENSE OF CITIZEN DUTY TO POLITICAL PARTICIPATION
WITH RELEVANT DEMOGRAPHIC VARIABLES HELD CONSTANT

DEMOGRAPHIC VARIABLES	DEGREE OF CITIZEN DUTY		
	High	Medium	Low
Sex			
Male	+24†	+13	−58
Female	+11	− 8	−72
Race			
White	+20	+ 6	−53
Negro	−30	−52	−93
Age			
21–34 years	+ 6	− 7	−73
35–44 years	+25	− 5	−66
45–54 years	+29	+16	(−77)‡
55 years and over	+17	+ 8	−61
Education			
Grade school	− 5	−11	−73
High school	+23	+ 6	(−44)‡
College	+39	+32	§
Income			
Under $2,000	− 9	−17	−77
$2,000–2,999	+ 1	−16	(−57)‡
$3,000–3,999	+10	+ 1	(−48)‡
$4,000–4,999	+31	+12	§
$5,000 and over	+34	+25	§
Occupation of head			
Professional and managerial	+32	+35	§
Other white collar	+23	+ 3	§
Skilled and semi-skilled	+13	+ 1	−70
Unskilled	− 1	−25	−82
Farm operators	+15	−11	(−72)‡
Region			
Northeast	+28	+14	(−41)‡
Midwest	+19	+13	−32
South	−12	−22	−91
Far West	+28	+ 9	§
Type of community			
Metropolitan	+23	+ 3	(−43)‡
Cities and towns	+15	+ 4	−73
Open country	+11	− 7	−70

† Cell entries are indices of participation.
‡ Index number based on between 20 and 30 cases.
§ Too few cases to permit computation of a reliable index.

substantially the same as those for political efficacy.   Only in the case of the sex and age variables do differences largely disappear.

In spite of these demographic relationships, the relationship between citizen duty and political participation holds up very well, even when each of these eight demographic factors is held constant.   This is clearly demonstrated in Table B.3.   Unfortunately, in several categories (and several of the more crucial ones) there were too few cases to permit the computation of a reliable participation index.   These consist of the "low" citizen duty respondents in the highest education, income, and occupational groupings and in the Far West category.   It might be noted, however, that the indices constructed from each of these groupings do yield the expected *negative* scores.   This being the case, there is only one minor reversal in Table B.3—between the "high" and "medium" citizen duty categories for the professional and managerial class.   There are no reversals between the "high" and "low" citizen duty groups.

We are able to state with a fair degree of certainty, therefore, that the more strongly a person feels a sense of obligation to discharge his civic duties, the more likely he is to be politically active.   And this relationship is not peculiar to any particular demographic status.   At all levels of age, education, income, and occupational status, in different sections of the country, and regardless of race or sex, a higher sense of citizen duty accompanies a greater likelihood of active political participation.

C.   Primary Group Influences and Political Behavior

Students of political behavior have long been aware of the vital role that interpersonal forces play in shaping an individual's political attitudes.   Studies on populations varying from the national electorate to college sophomores have demonstrated the striking congruence between an individual's political attitudes and voting choice and those of his primary group associates—his family, his work group, his circle of friends, and neighbors.   This has led many investigators to single out these primary group influences as the major determinants of political attitudes and behavior.

In an attempt to determine the extent of primary group homogeneity in the 1952 election, the postelection interviews included a series of questions about the voting behavior of three significant primary groups. All respondents were asked how their "friends" had voted.   Married people were asked how their spouses voted, and unmarried people were asked about their families.   Finally, all people who worked in a situation involving other people were asked about the voting behavior

of "the people where you work."[1]   The questions about spouses and
families were phrased in terms of whether they voted Democratic or
Republican.   In the questions about friends and work associates, the
respondents were also offered a neutral alternative ("Did they vote
mostly Republican, mostly Democratic, or were they pretty evenly
split?") in order not to force a Democratic or Republican choice in
those cases where the group was divided.

On the basis of the data obtained from the responses to these questions, we can conclude that the 1952 election again demonstrated the
political homogeneity of the face-to-face group.[2]   This is clearly
illustrated in Table C.1, which presents the relationships between the
respondents' presidential preferences and their primary group members'
votes.   In those cases where the primary group was seen as voting in
predominantly one direction, there was a strong tendency for the
respondent's presidential preference to agree with the group choice.
This agreement was greater for husbands and wives than it was among
friends and work associates, but in all cases it was very clear.   Even in
the case of lowest agreement, three-quarters of the respondents who
perceived their work associates as going predominantly for one of the
parties also took the dominant group position.[3]

[1] Respondents were also asked, in the pre-election interviews, about the vote
intentions of their "five best friends" and (in the case of married people) of their
husbands or wives.   Relationships between respondents' voting behavior and the
pre-election perceptions of the voting intentions of friends and spouses were very
similar to the relationships between respondents' voting behavior and the
postelection perceptions presented in Table C.1.

[2] In making this statement, we are assuming that the respondents' perceptions of their primary group associates' voting choices represents an accurate
reflection of reality.   We have no reason to suspect that conscious, purposeful
misrepresentation of their associates' votes would be any greater than the
respondents' misrepresentation of their own votes, which, as we noted in
Chapter I, we have reason to believe was small.   However, in cases where the
group referent was somewhat vague and political discussion among group
members minimal, so that accurate information about the group was not readily
available, we might expect some tendency for respondents to "project" their own
preferences on to the group.   This would occur more often in the perception of
the voting behavior of friends and "people where you work" than it would in the
case of husbands and wives.   In general, however, we would expect that there
would be more information available on which to base a realistic perception of
how one's primary group associates voted (and hence less "projection") than
there would be in the case of the broad demographic groupings discussed in
Appendix D.

[3] It should be noted that this statement does not mean that three-quarters
of the respondents who expressed a presidential preference saw themselves in
agreement with their work associates.   Since well over one-quarter of the
respondents did not see their work associates as taking a predominant position,
it would not be possible for three-quarters of them to see themselves in agreement with these work associates.

Also of interest in Table C.1 are the presidential preferences of the respondents in those cases where the primary group was not seen as taking a clear party position. Those people whose primary group associates did not vote indicated a decided preference for Stevenson, which is consistent with the frequently documented finding that people of Democratic inclination tend to predominate among the nonvoting groups. On the other hand, those people who did not know how their

TABLE C.1

RELATION OF PRIMARY GROUP MEMBERS' VOTES TO
RESPONDENTS' PRESIDENTIAL PREFERENCES

PRIMARY GROUP VOTE	RESPONDENTS' PRESIDENTIAL PREFERENCES				INDEX OF PRESIDENTIAL PREFERENCE	NUMBER OF CASES	PROPORTION OF SUBSAMPLE†
	Eisenhower	Stevenson	Other	Total			
Spouse's vote							
Democrat	11%	88	1	100%	−77	337	(27%)
Republican	93%	7	*	100%	+86	496	(40%)
Don't know	52%	39	9	100%	+13	77	(6%)
Didn't vote	40%	54	6	100%	−14	311	(25%)
Family's votes‡							
Democrat	20%	79	1	100%	−59	75	(22%)
Republican	91%	8	1	100%	+83	108	(32%)
Split	41%	54	5	100%	−13	22	(6%)
Don't know	45%	43	12	100%	+ 2	51	(15%)
Didn't vote	39%	50	11	100%	−11	38	(11%)
Friends' votes							
Democrat	17%	83	*	100%	−66	355	(22%)
Republican	84%	15	1	100%	+69	574	(36%)
Evenly split	47%	50	3	100%	− 3	373	(23%)
Don't know	49%	39	12	100%	+10	236	(15%)
Didn't vote	34%	54	12	100%	−20	41	(3%)
Work associates' votes§							
Democrat	20%	78	2	100%	−58	271	(30%)
Republican	76%	24	*	100%	+52	290	(32%)
Evenly split	55%	43	2	100%	+12	195	(21%)
Don't know	47%	43	10	100%	+ 4	114	(13%)
Didn't vote	‖	‖	‖		‖	8	(1%)

† Proportions were computed on the basis of the subsamples asked about each primary group; for example, the subsample for "Family's vote" includes only unmarried respondents. These figures do not total to 100 per cent because they do not include people whose primary group associates voted for a third party candidate or whose vote was not ascertained.
‡ Asked only of unmarried people.
§ Asked only of people who work with other people.
‖ Number of cases too small for computation of percentages.

primary groups voted took neither an unusually Democratic nor Republican position, but showed an Eisenhower preference similar to that evidenced by the total sample population. The findings with reference to those cases in which the primary groups were seen as split in their allegiance are not too clear, but there does appear to be some tendency for people whose friends or family were politically divided to indicate a higher preference for Stevenson than that obtaining in the total sample population. This may be due to the fact that, in a year of marked shift to the Republican party, a number of the evenly split groups were probably groups of normally Democratic allegiance.

In studying the relationship between an individual's political behavior and that of his primary groups, the focus is usually on the *direction* that political activity takes. There is also a relationship between the *extent* of an individual's political activity and that of the other people in his primary group. The relationships between primary group voting behavior and amount of individual political participation in the 1952 election are presented in Table C.2. It is apparent from this table that nonvoting, as well as direction of voting, tends to be a shared behavior. Over half of the married people whose spouses did not vote, 74 per cent of the unmarried people whose families did not vote, and 90 per cent of the people whose friends did not vote were themselves nonvoters.

A number of other items may be noted in Table C.2. As would be expected, individuals in Republican groups tend to participate more than individuals in groups of Democratic inclination, a reflection of the fact that Republicans generally tend to participate more than Democrats. Also of interest is the difference between those individuals whose primary groups were seen as split and those who said they did not know how their groups voted. Not knowing how one's primary group associates voted seems to be a reflection of lack of interest and involvement. Except in the case of one's husband or wife (where a "don't know" response may have special meaning), people who don't know how their primary groups voted tend to be low participators.[4] Those who saw their groups as divided in allegiance behaved quite differently. Their participation tended to fall between the participation of those from the Democratic and Republican groups, being lower than that of people whose group members were predominantly Republican, but higher than that of the respondents who associated with

[4] A "don't know" response may not only indicate low interest and participation on the respondent's part, but may also reflect low participation of his primary group associates. It will be noted in Table C.2 that relatively few people indicated that their families, friends, or work associates did not vote. It is possible that many people who gave a "don't know" response when asked about their groups' voting behavior were members of groups where most of the members actually did not vote.

people of Democratic persuasion.   Being in a group of divided political loyalty does not appear to produce any inhibitory effect on the individual's political participation.   If being in such a situation creates conflict in the individual, this conflict does not evidence itself in reduced participation.

TABLE C.2

RELATION OF POLITICAL PARTICIPATION TO PRIMARY GROUP MEMBERS' VOTES

PRIMARY GROUP VOTE	POLITICAL PARTICIPATION				INDEX OF PARTICIPATION	NUMBER OF CASES†
	High	Medium	Low	Total		
Spouse's vote						
Democrat	31%	53	16	100%	+15	337
Republican	39%	54	7	100%	+32	496
Don't know	30%	56	14	100%	+16	77
Didn't vote	10%	31	59	100%	−49	311
Family's votes‡						
Democrat	27%	42	31	100%	− 4	75
Republican	31%	56	13	100%	+18	108
Split	32%	41	27	100%	+ 5	22
Don't know	20%	37	43	100%	−23	51
Didn't vote	5%	21	74	100%	−69	38
Friends' votes						
Democrat	22%	49	29	100%	− 7	355
Republican	39%	46	15	100%	+24	574
Evenly split	29%	49	22	100%	+ 7	373
Don't know	11%	49	40	100%	−29	236
Didn't vote	2%	8	90	100%	−88	41
Work associates' votes§						
Democrat	32%	43	25	100%	+ 7	271
Republican	41%	41	18	100%	+23	290
Evenly split	31%	48	21	100%	+10	195
Don't know	9%	54	37	100%	−28	114
Didn't vote	‖	‖	‖		‖	8

† Does not include people whose primary group associates voted for a third party candidate, or whose vote was not ascertained.
‡ Asked only of unmarried people.
§ Asked only of people who work with other people.
‖ Number of cases too small for computation of percentages.

As we have already noted at the beginning of this discussion, the tendency for the political behavior of the individual to conform to the patterns set by his primary group associations has long been part of our basic knowledge in this area.   However, the explanations and interpretations of these groups' political homogeneity are by no means obvious. The mechanisms by which the group influences the individual are exceedingly complex. They vary from the subtle, unconscious mechanisms by which a group structures the political perceptions of its members, even when political events are of little concern to the group, to the extreme cases where political attitudes are tied to the basic values of the group members, and any attempt at individual deviation leads to interpersonal conflict and guilt reactions. Moreover, although it is customary to explain the homogeneity of the group's political attitudes in terms of the influence of the group on the individual, this is by no means the only factor operating. To mention only two other factors, group homogeneity is probably to some extent a function of the similarity of the socio-economic conditions and politically relevant life experiences of the primary group members, and also to some extent a function of the selective factor by which people tend to seek out individuals of like attitudes in forming their close relationships.

Intensive investigation of the nature of the mechanisms underlying the relationships between individual and group political behavior lies beyond the scope of this study. A national sample survey is not the method of choice for a study of group influence processes. However, an attempt was made to obtain some information in this area. In the coding of the reasons people gave for their voting choices, and in the codes which summarized the respondents' positive and negative perceptions of the parties and candidates, separate note was made of all responses which indicated that attitudes or behavior had been influenced by family, friends, work associates, etc. However, only a handful of people made such references—too few to permit any systematic analysis.

In addition to this coding of the responses to open-ended questions, a direct attempt was made to get information on primary group influence. All respondents who voted were asked the following question about the four primary groups whose vote had previously been ascertained: "Do you think any of [his] [her] [their] opinions about the election had anything to do with the way you decided to vote?"

This question has obvious limitations. Depending as it does on the respondent's perception of whether or not he was influenced, it does not measure the multitude of interactive processes affecting the individual that he does not recognize as influence. Moreover, admitting that one's voting decision has been affected by the opinions of others runs counter to an important American value and stereotype which stresses the independent thinker, the man who examines the relevant political facts and makes up his own mind.

Because of these and other limitations, responses to the question on perceived primary group influence cannot be interpreted as an accurate measure of the actual political influence exerted by these groups. As one would expect, very few people admitted being influenced.   Despite these limitations, however, an investigation of some of the correlates of the responses to this question may be of some interest.   Although we cannot pursue this analysis here, we may cite one example for illustrative purposes.   It is a common observation that concern with

TABLE C.3

RELATION OF SEX TO PERCEPTION OF PRIMARY GROUP INFLUENCE

PRIMARY GROUP INFLUENCE†	SEX	
	Male	Female
Spouse		
Influenced	6%	27%
Not influenced	87	70
Not ascertained	7	3
Total	100%	100%
Number of cases	502	449
Family‡		
Influenced	7%	10%
Not influenced	82	73
Not ascertained	11	17
Total	100%	100%
Number of cases	75	134
Friends		
Influenced	5%	6%
Not influenced	91	88
Not ascertained	4	6
Total	100%	100%
Number of cases	585	603
Work associates§		
Influenced	4%	5%
Not influenced	90	88
Not ascertained	6	7
Total	100%	100%
Number of cases	454	195

† Asked only of people who voted.
‡ Asked only of unmarried people.
§ Asked only of people who work with other people.

politics, in American life, is much more relevant to the man's role than it is to the woman's, and that women are less involved and informed in political events. We would expect, therefore, that there would be a relationship between sex and the importance of interpersonal influences on one's vote, with women both depending more on the opinions of others in arriving at their own decision, and being more willing than men to admit this dependence. The comparative perceptions of primary group influence for men and women are presented in Table C.3.

Two interesting findings appear in the table. First of all, political influence in the marriage relationship seems to go predominantly in one direction. Of the married women who voted, 27 per cent said that their husbands' opinions helped them decide on their voting choices, as contrasted with only 6 per cent of the married men voters admitting influence by their wives. This tends to support the widely held assumption that political agreement between husband and wife is more a function of wives voting the way their husbands vote than it is a function of husbands voting as their wives vote. (However, this difference is probably also partly a function of the fact that it is more socially acceptable for women to admit being influenced by their husbands than for men to admit influence by their wives.)

Perhaps of even greater interest than this difference between husbands and wives is the lack of any significant differences between men and women in the perception of political influence of family, friends, and work associates. Several interpretations for this finding are possible. It may indicate that, except in the marriage relationship, women are no more subject to interpersonal influence in forming their political attitudes than are men. Or, since we would expect that women's friendship and work groups would consist largely of other women, the fact that they did not feel they were influenced by these groups might indicate that women, though looking to men for help in making their election decisions, do not put other women in such a role. A third possible explanation must also be considered: in terms of the limitations discussed above, the lack of consistent differences noted in Table C.3 may be a function of the inadequacy of our measure of influence. Judgment on this point may better be made after the use of this measure in further analyses.

D. The Perceived Political Relevance of Demographic Groups

Chapter V presented a detailed discussion of the relationships between demographic characteristics and voting behavior in the 1952 election. To a considerable extent, these relationships conformed to patterns that have long been observed by students of American elections. However, the fact that these relationships are well known does not necessarily mean that they can be explained in simple terms.

In certain ways, the analysis of the effects of demographic group membership on political attitudes and behavior involves complexities even greater than those encountered in the study of primary group influences (see Appendix C). This is particularly true when one examines these relationships in terms of their meaningfulness as psychological group phenomena. The main focus in the study of primary group influences is on the mechanisms and processes by which the group influences the individual. There is no need to argue the fact that primary groups do influence their members' attitudes and behavior. In the case of attitudinal homogeneity within demographic categories, however, one is first faced with the problem of attempting to determine whether in fact this is a psychologically meaningful group phenomenon. The first question one must answer is the extent to which the members in the demographic category are behaving as members of a psychological group. To what extent is a Catholic's vote an expression of identification with the Catholic group? To what extent are farmers psychologically voting as farmers? Or, can the relationship between demographic characteristics and political behavior be explained in terms of the similar life experiences of people of similar demographic background, or in terms of other factors which do not require the conceptualization of these broader social categories as psychological groups?[1]

We were interested, therefore, in measuring the extent to which people in different demographic classifications saw their membership in these classifications as relevant for their voting decision. For this purpose, two questions were included in the pre-election interview. Since the respondents could obviously not be asked about all relevant demographic classifications, the two questions referred only to the following nine categories: farmers, working-class people, Negroes, middle-class people, big-businessmen, labor union members, Protestants, Catholics, and Jews.

[1] It is interesting to observe in this connection that even Lazarsfeld's Erie County study, which placed such a primary emphasis on the influence of demographic characteristics, did not conceptualize this influence in terms of the individual's psychological relationship to the demographic grouping as such. Although the concept of social group conformity pressures plays an important role in Lazarsfeld's explanation of the influence of the demographic characteristics, these are primary group influences rather than forces induced by identification with the broader social grouping. The influences of the broad social categories are reduced to primary group influences; they are seen as important primarily because they define a person's primary group relationships. In such an explanation, Catholics vote alike because a Catholic's primary group relationships are mostly with other Catholics; psychologically they are voting as their "friends" and "family" vote, not as "Catholics" vote.

The respondents were first asked how they thought people in the nine different demographic categories would vote—whether they would be "mostly Republican," "mostly Democratic," or "evenly split."[2] This type of question has become fairly standard in group studies. It is based on the assumption that when an individual's group membership is psychologically relevant in influencing his attitude in a given area, he will tend to see the group as taking a particular position on that issue. For example, we would assume that a person whose sense of community with other Catholics was a significant determinant of his voting behavior would tend to be aware of Catholics' voting position, i.e., he would not say that he didn't know how Catholics would vote, and would also tend to see them as taking a predominant position rather than as politically divided, i.e., he would tend to see them acting as a group with a common set of political attitudes.

In those cases where the respondents saw a demographic grouping as voting either Democratic or Republican, they were asked the additional question of why they thought that the group would vote that way. Examination of these reasons gives further information on the extent to which the group is seen as relevant politically. We would assume that a reason which singles out the particular group's interest, and ties this interest to the fortunes of one of the parties, indicates a greater sense of the political relevance of this group than a general reason which has applicability to the total population. For example, we would assume that being a farmer was a more important influence on the vote of a man who saw farmers voting for a given party because that party "has always tried to help the farmer" than it was on the vote of a farmer who saw other farmers as voting for a given party because there would be a "better chance for peace" if that party won. The former reason ties the farmer's interest specifically to one of the parties; the latter reason could have been used equally well for any other grouping.

The reasons were coded with this distinction in mind. Reasons such as "party of the working man," "a lot of candidates in the party are Catholics," and "Negroes will vote Democratic because of FEPC" were all coded as "group-relevant" reasons. Reasons such as "better for peace," "time for a change," and "corruption," which clearly have no special group relevance, were coded as "other" reasons. In addition, a third major category was used so as to single out those responses

[2] The question was worded as follows: "Now, I'd like to ask you some questions about how you think *other* people will vote in this election. For instance, take *farmers*—do you think farmers around the country will vote mostly Republican, mostly Democratic, or do you think they will be about evenly split?" This question was then repeated for the eight other demographic groupings.

which were not clear as to their group relevance. These were mainly responses which referred to good economic conditions, prosperity, etc., where, particularly in the case of the economic groupings, it was not clear whether the respondent was referring to conditions that affected the whole country or conditions that had special relevance for the particular group. These responses were categorized as "general economic interest reasons."

The question on the perception of how a group would vote can be combined with the question on the perception of the reasons why the group would vote that way to form a measure of "political group relevance." A group is then most relevant politically when it is seen as voting a given way for "group-relevant" reasons, next most relevant when seen as voting a given way for "general economic interest reasons," next when seen as voting a given way for "other" reasons, next when seen as "split" in vote intention, and least relevant politically when the respondent doesn't know how the group will vote.

Other data in the pre-election interviews enabled us to obtain some check on the adequacy of this measure of group relevance. In the coding of the pre-election interviews, all responses which referred favorably or unfavorably to one of the parties because of its helping or hurting a particular group were recorded and tabulated in a summary code (see Chapter IV). Since a respondent's spontaneous reference to a particular group, when commenting on the two parties, is in all probability a more valid indication that the group is psychologically relevant for him than his responses to a question which presents him with the group stimulus, these spontaneous references, when they occur to any great extent, may be used as an internal validity check of the group-relevance measure. This could not be done in the case of five of the demographic groupings—Negroes, middle-class people, and the three religious groupings—because only a very few respondents made spontaneous references to them. However, the internal validity analysis was made with reference to working-class people, farmers, and big-businessmen,[3] where considerable numbers of respondents had made spontaneous references. Of the total sample, 33 per cent spoke favorably of the Democratic party as having helped the working people, common people, poor people, etc.; 14 per cent spoke negatively of the Republican party as being the party of big business, rich people, etc.; 8 per cent spoke favorably of the Democrats in connection with farmers.

Table D.1 presents the relationship between the respondents' spontaneous statements that the Democratic party was good for working

---

[3] The analysis was not made with reference to labor union members, since it was felt that it would have duplicated the findings with reference to working-class people.

people, and their responses to the specific questions on how they thought working-class people would vote and the reasons for their perception. A very clear relationship is evident. Two-thirds of the respondents who felt that working-class people would vote Democratic, and gave group-relevant reasons for this belief, had previously spontaneously associated working people's welfare with the Democratic party. This figure decreases regularly down to 12 per cent for those who felt that working-class people would vote Republican and 9 per cent for those

TABLE D.1

RELATION OF PERCEPTION OF WORKING-CLASS PEOPLE'S PARTY PREFERENCES TO SPONTANEOUS ASSOCIATION OF DEMOCRATIC PARTY WITH WELFARE OF WORKING PEOPLE

	PERCEPTION OF WORKING-CLASS PEOPLE'S PARTY PREFERENCES					
	Democratic for Group Relevant Reasons	Democratic for General Economic Interest Reasons	Democratic for Other Reasons or Reasons Not Given	Split	Republican†	Don't Know
Spontaneous association of Democratic party with working people's welfare	66%	48%	34%	24%	12%	9%
No spontaneous association of Democratic party with working people's welfare	34	52	66	76	88	91
Total	100%	100%	100%	100%	100%	100%
Number of cases	259	328	226	392	129	278

† The perception of working-class people as voting Republican is not divided according to reasons, because very few respondents who had this perception gave group-relevant reasons.

who didn't know how working-class people would vote. Thus, the spontaneous identification of working people's interest with the Democratic party was related both to the perception that working-class people would vote Democratic and to the group-relevant nature of the reasons for this perception. Similar relationships were obtained in relating the perception of the vote and reasons for the vote of "farmers" and "big-businessmen" to the spontaneous references to those groups (although these relationships were much less sharp than that presented in Table D.1).[4] There is some evidence, then, supporting the validity of the group relevance measure.

[4] Since many fewer people made spontaneous references to big-businessmen and farmers than to working people, we would not expect the relationships to be as large.

In examining the perceived political relevance of different demographic groupings, we are mainly interested in the members' perceptions of their own demographic groupings.   However, the attitudes and behavior of one's nonmembership groups can also be psychologically relevant, as findings from many group studies have demonstrated. Tables D.2 and D.3, therefore, present the total sample's perceptions of the voting behavior of the nine demographic groupings. The perceptions of the members of each group are presented in Table D.4.

Table D.2 presents the respondents' pre-election perceptions of how the nine demographic groupings would vote.   Although there are a number of interesting items in this table, two generalizations might be

TABLE D.2

PERCEPTION OF PARTY PREFERENCES OF DIFFERENT
DEMOGRAPHIC CLASSES

DEMOGRAPHIC CLASSES	PERCEPTION OF PARTY PREFERENCES						NO. OF CASES
	Demo-cratic	Repub-lican	Split	Don't Know	Not Ascer-tained	Total	
Farmers	35%	14	27	24	*	100%	1,614
Labor union members	61%	5	12	22	*	100%	1,614
Working-class people	51%	7	25	17	*	100%	1,614
Middle-class people	19%	24	31	26	*	100%	1,614
Big-businessmen	12%	55	9	24	*	100%	1,614
Negroes	34%	10	15	41	*	100%	1,614
Protestants	4%	11	40	44	1	100%	1,614
Catholics	17%	8	25	49	1	100%	1,614
Jews	11%	8	19	61	1	100%	1,614

noted.   First, taking a "split" or "don't know" response as an indication that the group is seen as less politically relevant, a sharp difference appears between the economic and the religious groupings, with the economic groupings being seen as much more relevant.   This is particularly true with respect to big-businessmen, who were seen as taking a predominant party position by 67 per cent of the respondents, and labor union members, whom 66 per cent of the respondents saw as going Democratic or Republican.   In contrast to this, all the religious groupings were seen as of low political relevance by at least three-quarters of the population.   Although this was to be expected in the case of Protestants and Jews, it is interesting that it was also true for Catholics—at least in the 1952 election.

It is also interesting to observe, in Table D.2, that the perception of group voting tends strongly to favor the Democrats. "Big-business-men" is the only group which is seen as heavily favoring the Republicans. Labor union members (and working-class people), Negroes, and farmers are put solidly in the Democratic camp. Although the perception of the first three groups as Democratic was anticipated, the

TABLE D.3

RELATION OF PERCEPTION OF PARTY PREFERENCES OF DIFFERENT DEMOGRAPHIC CLASSES TO PERCEPTION OF REASONS FOR PREFERENCES

PERCEPTION OF PARTY PREFERENCES OF DEMOGRAPHIC CLASSES	PERCEPTION OF REASONS FOR PARTY PREFERENCES					No. OF CASES
	Group Relevant Reasons	General Economic Interest Reasons	Other Reasons	Reasons Not Ascertained	Total	
Farmers						
Democratic	46%	35	10	9	100%	549
Republican	18%	14	57	11	100%	228
Labor union members						
Democratic	41%	19	29	11	100%	982
Republican	13%	16	52	19	100%	69
Working-class people						
Democratic	32%	40	19	9	100%	813
Republican	3%	29	53	15	100%	129
Middle-class people						
Democratic	12%	47	29	12	100%	308
Republican	20%	13	52	15	100%	378
Big-businessmen						
Democratic	21%	47	17	15	100%	193
Republican	44%	4	41	11	100%	893
Negroes						
Democratic	53%	15	21	11	100%	546
Republican	26%	5	53	16	100%	151
Protestants						
Democratic	8%	14	58	20	100%	71
Republican	9%	2	72	17	100%	176
Catholics						
Democratic	16%	13	58	13	100%	269
Republican†	42%	11	38	9	100%	126
Jews						
Democratic	44%	20	27	9	100%	182
Republican	55%	6	25	14	100%	126

† The high proportion of group-relevant reasons among people who saw the Catholics as going Republican is almost completely a function of the Stevenson divorce issue.

perception of farmers is somewhat surprising. Although it conforms to the farmers' 1948 vote, it diverges sharply from their 1952 vote and runs counter to the stereotype, held in some quarters, of the farmer as an individualistic, conservative Republican.

This tendency to identify the Democratic party with the interests of the broad population groupings is even more clearly demonstrated when the reasons for the perceptions of group voting are examined. This is done in Table D.3.   Farmers, working-class people, labor union members, and Negroes are not only more often seen as voting Democratic than Republican, but are also much more often seen as voting that way for group-relevant reasons.   For example, 46 per cent of the people who felt that farmers would vote Democratic gave group-relevant reasons for their perceptions, whereas only 18 per cent of the respondents who thought that the farmers would vote Republican gave group-relevant reasons for that perception.   When these groups were seen as voting Republican, the group vote was much more often cast in a general context and not given a specific group meaning.[5]

Turning now to a consideration of the way that membership in a demographic grouping influences one's perception of its political relevance, Table D.4 compares group members and nonmembers in their perceptions of the vote of the nine demographic categories.[6]   A number of differences appear.   We would expect a grouping to be more relevant for members of the grouping than it is for the general population. This is supported by the data presented in Table D.4, if we consider only the "don't know" response category.   For example, 61 per cent of the non-Jews said that they didn't know how Jews would vote, whereas only 32 per cent of the Jews in the sample didn't know how their group would vote; 53 per cent of the non-Catholics in the sample said they didn't know how Catholics would vote as compared to only 32 per cent of the Catholics.   However, much of this difference between members and nonmembers disappears if "split" voting as well as a "don't know" response is taken to represent minimal psychological relevance of the group.   Only one-third of the Catholics and Jews in the sample saw their groups as making a predominant party choice. Even among their members, there was not very much perception of religious groupings as politically relevant.[7]

[5] This tendency to identify the Democratic party with group interest, particularly with economic group interest, is consistent with other data from the study.   As was noted in Chapter IV, some of the major arguments offered by respondents in favor of the Democratic party were that it was the party of the common people, the working man, and that it meant good times and prosperity. The Republican party was rarely spoken of favorably as a party that would bring better economic conditions, or as a party that would help particular groups.

[6] Group members and nonmembers differed in their perceptions of how their groups would vote, but did not differ systematically in their perceptions of the reasons for their groups' votes.   Contrary to expectations, there was no relation between membership in a group and the tendency to see that group as voting a given way for group-relevant reasons.   For this reason, we have not included the table showing the relation between group membership and the perception of the reasons for the group's vote.

[7] This may be partly a function of a reluctance of people to identify religion with politics, at least publicly.

TABLE D.4

RELATIONSHIP BETWEEN MEMBERSHIP AND NONMEMBERSHIP IN DIFFERENT
DEMOGRAPHIC CLASSES AND PERCEPTION OF PARTY PREFERENCES
OF THESE CLASSES

MEMBERSHIP IN DEMOGRAPHIC CLASSES†	PERCEPTION OF PARTY PREFERENCE						No. OF CASES
	Demo-cratic	Repub-lican	Split	Don't Know	Not Ascer-tained	Total	
Farmers							
Members‡	26%	18	37	18	1	100%	183
Nonmembers	34%	14	27	25	—	100%	1,431
Labor union members							
Members§	72%	3	14	11	—	100%	440
Nonmembers	57%	5	11	27	*	100%	1,174
Working-class people							
Members‖	54%	8	22	16	*	100%	504
Nonmembers	48%	8	26	18	*	100%	1,110
Middle-class people							
Members#	15%	47	29	9	—	100%	200
Nonmembers	19%	21	32	28	*	100%	1,414
Negroes							
Members	45%	6	13	35	1	100%	157
Nonmembers	32%	11	15	42	—	100%	1,457
Protestants							
Members	5%	11	39	44	1	100%	1,156
Nonmembers	2%	12	42	42	2	100%	458
Catholics							
Members	22%	6	38	32	2	100%	343
Nonmembers	15%	9	22	53	1	100%	1,271
Jews							
Members	31%	2	31	32	4	100%	52
Nonmembers	11%	8	19	61	1	100%	1,562

† Does not include "big-businessmen" because very few respondents could be objectively placed in that class.

‡ Includes people who were themselves farmers or whose family heads were farmers.

§ Includes people who were themselves union members or whose family heads were union members.

‖ Working-class members consist of people who subjectively identified themselves as "working-class" and whose occupational status or that of the family head was that of a skilled, semi-skilled, or unskilled worker.

Middle-class members consist of people who subjectively identified themselves as "middle class" and whose occupational status or that of the family head was professional, managerial, or self-employed businessmen.

We would also expect that group members would have a truer perception of how their groups' votes actually would go. This tends to be supported by the data. It is interesting to learn, however, that even among farmers the perception of the farmers' vote, though slightly more Republican than the perception among the general population, was still more Democratic than Republican.

We would expect the perceived political relevance of a group to be related to a number of other factors, in addition to membership in the group. Following some of the findings derived from recent social-psychological experiments on factors influencing perception, we would expect the perception of the political relevance of a group to be related to such dimensions as the ambiguity of the group's political position, the strength of the individual's identification with the group, and the positive or negative attitude toward the group. We would also expect such factors to affect the relation between the perceived group vote and the individual's own vote. Investigation of these hypotheses and relationships lies beyond the scope of the present discussion.

E. The Questionnaires

Pre-Election Questionnaire

I'm mainly interested in talking to you about the election this fall and how you feel about it.

1. Who do you think will be elected president in November?
    1a. [If R makes choice] Do you think it will be a close race or will [answer to 1] win by quite a bit?
2. How about here in [your state]? Will the vote for president be pretty evenly split or not?
    2a. [If necessary] Who do you think will win for president here in [your state]?
3. Do you think there are any important differences between what the Democratic and Republican parties stand for, or do you think they are about the same?
4. I'd like to ask you what you think are the good and bad points about the two parties. Is there anything in particular that you like about the Democratic party? (What is that?)
5. Is there anything in particular that you don't like about the Democratic party? (What is that?)
6. Is there anything in particular that you like about the Republican party? (What is that?)
7. Is there anything in particular that you don't like about the Republican party? (What is that?)
8. Do you think it will make a good deal of difference to the country

whether the Democrats or the Republicans win the elections this November, or that it won't make much difference which side wins?

8a. [If yes] Why is that?

8b. [If no] Why do you feel it won't make much difference?

9. Do you think it will make any difference in how you and your family get along financially whether the Democrats or Republicans win? (How is that?)

   9a. [If makes a difference and not answered in 9] Well, do you think you'll be better off or worse off financially if the Republicans win the election?

10. Now I'd like to ask you about the good and bad points of the two candidates for president. Is there anything in particular about Stevenson that might make you want to vote for him? (What is it?)

11. Is there anything in particular about Stevenson that might make you want to vote against him? (What is it?)

12. Is there anything in particular about Eisenhower that might make you want to vote for him? (What is it?)

13. Is there anything in particular about Eisenhower that might make you want to vote against him? (What is it?)

14. Now, adding up the good points and the bad points about the two candidates, and forgetting for a minute the parties they belong to, which one do you think would make the best president?

15. Some people say that Eisenhower is not a real Republican. What do you think about this? Is he the kind of man that *you* think of as being a real Republican? (Why do you say that?)

16. [If not answered in 15] What about Eisenhower's ideas and the things he stands for? Do you think that he is pretty much the same as most other Republicans, or is he different from them? (Why do you say that?)

17. How about the candidates for vice-president? Aside from their parties, do you have any strong opinions about either of them? (How is that?)

18. Generally speaking, would you say that you personally care a good deal which party wins the presidential election this fall, or that you don't care very much which party wins?

19. How about state and local elections? When you have state and local elections around here would you say that you care a good deal who wins, or that you don't care very much who wins those elections?

20. Some people don't pay much attention to the political campaigns. How about you? Would you say that you have been very much interested, somewhat interested, or not much interested in following the political campaigns so far this year?

Now, I want to ask you how you feel about some of the issues that people are talking about these days. For example—

21. Some people think the national government should do more in trying to deal with such problems as unemployment, education, housing, and so on. Others think that the government is already doing too much. On the whole, would you say that what the government has done has been about right, too much, or not enough?

21*a*. Now, how do you think the two parties feel about this question—Do you think there are any differences between the Democratic and Republican parties on this issue, or would you say they feel the same? (How is that?)

22. There is a lot of talk these days about discrimination, that is, people having trouble getting jobs because of their race. Do you think the government ought to take an interest in whether Negroes have trouble getting jobs or should it stay out of this problem?

22*a*. [If government should take an interest] Do you think we need laws to deal with this problem or are there other ways that will handle it better?

22*a*(1) [If "other ways" to 22*a*] What do you have in mind?

22*a*(2) [If "laws" to 22*a*] Do you think the national government should handle this or do you think it should be left for each state to handle in its own way?

22*b*. [If government should stay out] Do you think the state governments should do something about this problem, or should they stay out of it also?

23. Have you heard anything about the Taft-Hartley Law?

23*a*. [If has heard] How do you feel about it? Do you think it's all right as it is, do you think it should be changed in any way, or don't you have any feelings about it?

23*a*(1) [If should be changed] Do you think the law should be changed just a little, changed quite a bit, or do you think it should be *completely* repealed? (How is that?)

24. Some people think that since the end of the last world war this country has gone too far in concerning itself with problems in other parts of the world. How do you feel about this?

24*a*. Now, how do you think the two parties feel about this question—Do you think there are any differences between the Democratic and Republican parties on this issue, or would you say they feel the same? (How is that?)

25. Some people feel that it was our government's fault that China went Communist, others say there was nothing that we could do to stop it. How do you feel about this?

26. Do you think we did the right thing in getting into the fighting in Korea two years ago, or should we have stayed out?

27. Which of the following things do you think it would be best for us to do *now* in Korea? Should we—

☐ (*a*) Pull out of Korea entirely?

☐ (*b*) Keep on trying to get a peaceful settlement?

☐ (*c*) Take a stronger stand and bomb Manchuria and China?

[Qualifying comments]_____

Now I would like to ask you a little more about the political parties.

28. Generally speaking, do you usually think of yourself as a Republican, a Democrat, an independent, or what?

If Republican or Democrat to Question 28 : (*if independent or other skip to Question* 28d.)

28a. Would you call yourself a strong (R) (D) or a not very strong (R) (D)?

28b. Was there ever a time when you thought of yourself as a (R) (D) rather than a (D) (R)?

28b(1). [If yes to 28b] When did you change?

28c. Suppose there was an election where your party was running a candidate that you didn't like or you didn't agree with. Which of the following things comes closest to what you think you would do?

☐ (1) I probably would vote for him anyway because a person should be loyal to his party.

☐ (2) I probably would not vote for either candidate in that election.

☐ (3) I probably would vote for the other party's candidate.

28c(1). [If 3 is chosen to 28c] How would you feel about voting for the other party—would it bother you in any way?

If independent or other to Question 28 :

28d. Do you think of yourself as closer to the Republican or Democratic party?

28e. Was there ever a time when you thought of yourself as a Democrat or a Republican?

28e(1). [If yes to 28e] Which party was that?

28e(2). [If yes to 28e] When did you change?

Ask of everyone

29. Do you remember when you were growing up whether your parents thought of themselves mostly as Democrats or Republicans, or did they shift around from one party to another?

30. In the elections for president since you have been old enough to vote, would you say that you have voted in all of them, most of them, some of them, or none of them?

If R has ever voted for president to Question 30, *ask Questions* 31–33; *if R has never voted for president, skip to Question* 34.

31. Have you always voted for the same party, or have you voted for different parties for president?

31a. [If same] Which party was that?

32. Do you remember who you voted for the first time you voted for president?

32a. [If yes] Who was it? What party was it?

32b. [If yes] Do you remember what year that was? [If yes] When?

33. In 1948, you remember that Truman ran against Dewey. Do you remember for sure whether or not you voted in that election?

33a. [If yes, does remember voting] Which one did you vote for?

Ask of everyone

34. Now how about the election this November? Do you know if you are (registered) (eligible to vote) so that you could vote in the November election if you wanted to?

    34a. [If necessary] Are you (registered) (eligible to vote)?

35. So far as you know now, do you expect to vote in November or not?

If yes to Question 35, ask Questions 36–39; if no to Question 35, skip to Question 40.

36. How do you think you will vote for president in this election?

    36a. [If mentions candidate or party] What would you say is the *most important reason* why you are going to vote for [answer to 36]?

37. Who do you plan to vote for as United States senator?

38. How about congressman? Who do you plan to vote for there?

39. Who do you think you will vote for as governor here in [your state]?

If no to Question 35:

40. If you *were* going to vote, how do you think you would vote for president in this election?

    40a. [If mentions candidate or party] What would you say is the most important reason why you would vote for [answer to 40]?

Ask of everyone

41. Some people think that if a voter votes for one party for president he should vote for the same party for senator and congressman. Do you agree or disagree with that idea?

    41a. Why do you feel that way?

42. Was there some other candidate whom you would rather have seen nominated at Chicago last July? [If necessary] Who?

    42a. [If yes to 42] Why would you like to have seen him nominated?

43. Do you think the party conventions like they had in Chicago are a good way to nominate candidates for president, or do you think there is a better way?

    43a. [If a better way] What would you suggest?

44. Now I'd like to ask you some questions about how you think *other* people will vote in this election.

    For instance, take *farmers*—do you think farmers around the country will vote mostly Republican, mostly Democratic, or do you think they will be about evenly split?

    ☐ D   ☐ R   ☐ Split   ☐ DK

    Now, how about *working-class people*—do you think they will vote mostly Republican, mostly Democratic, or do you think they will be about evenly split?

    ☐ D   ☐ R   ☐ Split   ☐ DK

    Now, how about:

Negroes	☐ D	☐ R	☐ Split ☐ DK
Middle-class people	☐ D	☐ R	☐ Split ☐ DK
Big-businessmen	☐ D	☐ R	☐ Split ☐ DK
Labor union members	☐ D	☐ R	☐ Split ☐ DK

Now, how about people in different religious groups, like Protestants, Catholics, and Jews? For instance, how about Protestants —do you think Protestants around the country will vote mostly Republican, mostly Democratic, or do you think they will be about evenly split?

	□ D	□ R	□ Split	□ DK
Now, how about Catholics?	□ D	□ R	□ Split	□ DK
How about Jews?	□ D	□ R	□ Split	□ DK

44a. [Ask only for groups seen as mostly supporting one or the other party to question 44.] Now let me check back and ask you why you feel that _____ are more likely to vote (R) (D), etc.

45. Are you married?

45a. [If yes] How do you think your husband (wife) will vote?

46. Now how about your five best friends? How do you think they're most likely to vote?

47. Now I'd like to read some of the kinds of things people tell me when I interview them and ask you whether you agree or disagree with them. I'll read them one at a time and you just tell me whether you agree or disagree.

47a. It isn't so important to vote when you know your party doesn't have a chance to win.   □ Agree   □ Disagree

47b. I don't think public officials care much what people like me think.   □ Agree   □ Disagree

47c. The way people vote is the main thing that decides how things are run in this country.   □ Agree   □ Disagree

47d. Voting is the only way that people like me can have any say about how the government runs things.   □ Agree   □ Disagree

47e. A good many local elections aren't important enough to bother with.   □ Agree   □ Disagree

47f. So many other people vote in the national elections that it doesn't matter much to me whether I vote or not.   □ Agree   □ Disagree

47g. People like me don't have any say about what the government does.   □ Agree   □ Disagree

47h. If a person doesn't care how an election comes out he shouldn't vote in it.   □ Agree   □ Disagree

47i. Sometimes politics and government seem so complicated that a person like me can't really understand what's going on.   □ Agree   □ Disagree

And now I'd like to ask you just two more questions.

48. There's quite a bit of talk these days about different social classes. If you were asked to use one of these four names for *your* social class, which would you say you belonged in—the middle class, lower class, working class or upper class?

49. Some people say there's not much opportunity in America today—that the average man doesn't have much chance to really get ahead. Others say there's plenty of opportunity, and anyone who works hard can go as far as he wants. How do you feel about this?

Postelection Questionnaire

We're calling on all the people we interviewed before the election and asking them how they feel about the way the election came out.

1. Do you think it will make a good deal of difference to the country that Eisenhower won instead of Stevenson, or don't you think it will make much difference?
   1a. [If yes] Why is that?

2. We're mainly interested in this interview in finding out whether people paid much attention to the election campaign this year.
   Take newspapers for instance—did you read about the campaign in any newspaper?
   2a. [If yes] Would you say you read quite a lot ☐ or not very much ☐ ?

3. How about radio—did you listen to any speeches or discussions about the campaign on the radio?
   3a. [If yes] Would you say you listened quite a lot ☐ or not very much ☐ ?

4. How about television—did you watch any programs about the campaign on television?
   4a. [If yes] Would you say you watched quite a lot ☐ or not very much ☐ ?

5. How about magazines—did you read about the campaign in any magazines?
   5a. [If yes] Would you say you read quite a lot ☐ or not very much ☐ ?

6. [If yes to two or more] Of all these ways of following the campaign which one would you say you got the most information from—newspapers, radio, television, or magazines?

7. In talking to people about the election, we find that a lot of people weren't able to vote because they weren't registered, or they were sick, or they just didn't have time. How about you, did you vote this time?

If R voted: (If R did not vote, skip to Question 23)

8. Who did you vote for for president?

9. What would you say is the most important reason you voted for him?

10. How long before the election did you decide that you were going to vote the way you did?

11. Did you ever think during the campaign that you might vote for [opposite candidate]?
    11a. [If yes] What made you decide not to vote for him?

12. How about the election for United States senator? Did you vote for a candidate for senator?
    12a. [If yes] Who did you vote for?

13. How about the vote for congressman? Did you vote for a candidate
    for Congress?
    13a. [If yes] Who did you vote for?

14. How about the vote for governor here in [your state]? Did you vote
    for one of the candidates for governor?
    14a. [If yes] Who did you vote for?

15. How about the elections for other state and local offices—did you vote
    a straight ticket or did you vote for candidates from different parties?
    15a. [If voted a straight ticket] Which party did you vote for?

16. You know that the parties try to talk to as many people as they can to
    get them to vote for their candidate. Did anybody from either one of
    the parties call you up or come around and talk to you during the
    campaign?
    [If yes]
    16a. Which party were they from?
         ☐ D   ☐ R   ☐ Both D and R   ☐ Don't know   ☐ Other
    16b. Do you remember what they talked to you about?
         [If Democrat]   ———
         [If Republican]   ———
    16c. Do you think that anything they said had anything to do with
         the way you decided to vote?

Now I'd like to ask you some questions about how you think some people
you know voted in the election.

17. Could you tell me how your friends voted in the election? Did they
    vote mostly Republican, mostly Democratic, or were they pretty evenly
    split?
    17a. Do you think any of their opinions about the election had anything
         to do with the way you decided to vote?

18. How about the people where you work? Did they vote mostly Republi-
    can, mostly Democratic, or were they pretty evenly split?
    18a. Do you think any of their opinions about the election had anything
         to do with the way you decided to vote?

19. [If married] How about your (husband) (wife)? Did (he) (she) vote
    Democratic or Republican?
    19a. Do you think any of (his) (her) opinions about the election had any-
         thing to do with the way you decided to vote?

20. [If not married] How about your family? Did they vote Democratic
    or Republican?
    20a. Do you think any of their opinions about the election had anything
         to do with the way you decided to vote?

21. Is there anything in particular that happened during the campaign,
    something you saw, read, or heard about, that helped you decide how
    you were going to vote?

22. I have a list of some of the things that people do that help a party or a
    candidate win an election. I wonder if you could tell me whether you
    did any of these things during the last election campaign.

22*a*. Did you talk to any people and try to show them why they should vote for one of the parties or candidates? ☐ Yes ☐ No

22*b*. Did you give any money or buy tickets or anything to help the campaign for one of the parties or candidates? ☐ Yes ☐ No

22*c*. Did you go to any political meetings, rallies, dinners, or things like that? ☐ Yes ☐ No

22*d*. Did you do any other work for one of the parties or candidates? ☐ Yes ☐ No

22*e*. Do you belong to any political club or organizations? ☐ Yes ☐ No

Skip to Question 32 if R voted

If R did not vote:

23. Who would you have voted for if you had voted?
24. What was the main reason you didn't vote?
25. Were you registered to vote?
26. You know the parties try to talk to as many people as they can to get them to vote for their candidate. Did anybody from either one of the parties call you up or come around and talk to you during the campaign?
26*a*. [If yes] Which party were they from?
    ☐ D ☐ R ☐ Both D and R ☐ Don't know ☐ Other

Now I'd like to ask you some questions about how you think some people you know voted in the election.

27. Could you tell me how your friends voted in the election? Did they vote mostly Republican, mostly Democratic, or were they pretty evenly split?
28. How about the people where you work? Did they vote mostly Republican, mostly Democratic, or were they pretty evenly split?
29. [If married] How about your (husband) (wife)? Did (he) (she) vote Democratic or Republican?
30. [If not married] How about your family? Did they vote Democratic or Republican?
31. I have a list of some of the things that people do that help a party or a candidate win an election. I wonder if you could tell me whether you did any of these things during the last election campaign.

31*a*. Did you talk to any people and try to show them why they should vote for one of the parties or candidates? ☐ Yes ☐ No

31*b*. Did you give any money or buy tickets or anything to help the campaign for one of the parties or candidates? ☐ Yes ☐ No

31*c*. Did you go to any political meetings, rallies, dinners, or things like that? ☐ Yes ☐ No

31*d*. Did you do any other work for one of the parties or candidates? ☐ Yes ☐ No

31*e*. Do you belong to any political club or organizations? ☐ Yes ☐ No

Ask of everyone: [Questions 32–40 were asked only of 585 people selected at random from the postelection sample.]

32. I have a list here of different kinds of clubs and organizations that people can belong to. I would like you to go over this list with me and tell me if you belong to any organizations like a labor union, a lodge, a veterans' organization and so on.
[List names of all organizations to which R belongs at bottom of page.]

LABOR UNIONS: A local of some union.

CHURCH CONNECTED GROUPS: Like a club connected with a church, such as men's clubs, ladies' aid societies, Holy Name societies, Missionary societies.

FRATERNAL ORGANIZATIONS OR LODGES: Like the Masons, Knights of Columbus, Elks, Eastern Star.

VETERANS ORGANIZATIONS: Like the American Legion, Veterans of Foreign Wars, Am. Vets.

BUSINESS OR CIVIC GROUPS: Like Rotary, Kiwanis, Lions.

PARENT-TEACHER ASSOCIATION.

NEIGHBORHOOD CLUBS OR COMMUNITY CENTERS.

ORGANIZATIONS OF PEOPLE OF THE SAME NATIONALITY BACKGROUND: Like the Polish National Alliance, the Italian American Society, etc.

SPORT TEAMS: Like bowling or baseball teams.

PROFESSIONAL GROUPS: Like the American Medical Association, or a builders' association.

NEIGHBORHOOD IMPROVEMENT ASSOCIATIONS.

WOMEN'S CLUBS.

CHARITABLE AND WELFARE ORGANIZATIONS.

INFORMAL CLUBS OR GROUPS: Like sewing circles, bridge clubs, poker clubs.

33. We want to be sure we have all of the organizations you belong to. Are there any others that are not on the list? [Add any mentioned to list below].

34. [For each group mentioned which is not a well-known national organiza tion] Just what does this organization do? I mean what is its main activity? [Write in answers below]

35. [For all groups] Now I would like to ask you how active you are in this (these) organization(s).
First, let's take the _____ group. Would you say you are an active member of this group or not very active?
   Active ☐ Not very active ☐ [repeat for each group]

36. Now I'd like to read some of the kinds of things people tell me when I interview them, and ask you whether you agree or disagree with them. I'll read them one at a time, and you just tell me whether you agree or disagree with them, and whether you agree or disagree a little or quite a bit.

36a. Human nature being what it is, there must always be war and conflict.
Agree: A little ☐   Quite a bit ☐
Disagree: A little ☐   Quite a bit ☐

36b. What young people need most of all is strict discipline by their parents.
Agree: A little ☐   Quite a bit ☐
Disagree: A little ☐   Quite a bit ☐

36c. A few strong leaders could make this country better than all the laws and talk.
Agree: A little ☐   Quite a bit ☐
Disagree: A little ☐   Quite a bit ☐

36d. Most people who don't get ahead just don't have enough will power.
Agree: A little ☐   Quite a bit ☐
Disagree: A little ☐   Quite a bit ☐

36e. Women should stay out of politics.
Agree: A little ☐   Quite a bit ☐
Disagree: A little ☐   Quite a bit ☐

36f. People sometimes say that an insult to your honor should not be forgotten. Do you agree or disagree with that?
Agree: A little ☐   Quite a bit ☐
Disagree: A little ☐   Quite a bit ☐

36g. People can be trusted.
Agree: A little ☐   Quite a bit ☐
Disagree: A little ☐   Quite a bit ☐

36h. One main trouble today is that people talk too much and work too little.
Agree: A little ☐   Quite a bit ☐
Disagree: A little ☐   Quite a bit ☐

36i. Sex criminals deserve more than prison; they should be whipped publicly or worse.
Agree: A little ☐   Quite a bit ☐
Disagree: A little ☐   Quite a bit ☐

36j. It is only natural and right that women should have less freedom than men.
Agree: A little ☐   Quite a bit ☐
Disagree: A little ☐   Quite a bit ☐

37. What was your occupation four years ago? I mean, what kind of work were you doing around the time of the 1948 election?
37a. [If R was employed] Were you working for yourself then, or were you working for someone else?

38. [Ask only if R is not head of the household] What kind of work was the head of your household doing four years ago, around the time of the 1948 election?
38a. [If head was employed] Was he working for himself then, or was he working for someone else?

39. When you were going to grade school or high school, did you go to a parochial school, a private school, or a regular public school?

40. Were you or the head of your household ever in the armed services of the United States?

[If yes]

40a. Which one of you was that?

40b. What years did that cover?

Personal Data

1. Sex: ☐ Male ☐ Female.
2. Race: ☐ White ☐ Negro ☐ Other _____
3. What year were you born?
4. How many grades of school did you finish? 1, 2, 3, 4, 5, 6, 7, 8, 9, 10, 11, 12.

    4a. [If high school] Have you had any schooling other than high school?
        ☐ Yes ☐ No

        4a(1). [If yes to 4a] What other schooling have you had?

    4b. [If attended college] Do you have a college degree? ☐ Yes ☐ No.

5. What is your occupation? I mean, what kind of work do you do?

    5a. [If R is employed] Do you work for yourself or for someone else?

    5b. [If R is unemployed] What kind of work do you usually do?

    5c. [If R is retired] What kind of work did you do before you retired?

6. [Ask only if R is not head of the household] What kind of work does the head of your household do?

    6a. [If head is employed] Does he work for himself or for someone else?

    6b. [If head is unemployed] What kind of work does he usually do?

    6c. [If head is retired] What kind of work did he do before he retired?

    6d. Age of head: | 21–24 | | 25–34 | | 35–44 | | 45–54 |
        | 55–64 | | 65 and over |

7. Do either you or the head of your household belong to a labor union?

    7a. [If necessary] Who is it that belongs?

8. What kind of work did your father do for a living while you were growing up?

9. Where were you born? [If United States, which state?]

10. What part of the United States did you grow up in? (Which state or states?)

11. Were you brought up mostly on a farm, in a small town, or in a large city?

12. Were both your parents born in this country? ☐ Yes ☐ No.

    [If yes to Question 12:]

    12a. Which country did your father's parents come from?

    12b. Which country did your mother's parents come from?

    [If no to Question 12:]

    12c. Which country was your father born in?

    12d. Which country was your mother born in?

13. How long have you lived in this county [Note: *county*, not country.]

14. How long have you lived in (state)?

15. Do you feel that you have settled down to stay here in [face sheet designation] or do you feel that you may not stay here very long?
16. Do you folks own your home here, or rent, or what?
    ☐ Own   ☐ Rent   ☐ Other _____
17. Do you have any children in school here in _____ ?
    ☐ Yes   ☐ No.
18. Is your church preference Protestant, Catholic, or Jewish?
    ☐ Protestant   ☐ Catholic   ☐ Jewish   ☐ Other   ☐ None.
19. Would you say you go to church ☐ regularly ☐ often ☐ seldom or ☐ never?
20. About what do you think your total income will be this year for yourself and your immediate family?
    ☐ Under $1,000   ☐ $3,000–3,999   ☐ $7,500–9,999
    ☐ $1,000–1,999   ☐ $4,000–4,999   ☐ $10,000 and over
    ☐ $2,000–2,999   ☐ $5,000–7,499

F. Sample Design

General Method for Selection of Sample

The individuals interviewed in this survey are a representative cross-section of citizens of voting age living in private households in the United States.   Since the survey was restricted to private households, those people residing in military establishments, hospitals, religious and educational institutions, logging and lumber camps, penal institutions, hotels, and larger rooming houses were excluded from the sample. These excluded groups, which comprise very roughly about five per cent of the adult population of the United States, were omitted from the defined population because the usual sampling procedures would cause serious practical difficulties when applied to these groups, and because a large proportion of these people are legally or otherwise disfranchised.

The sample was selected by a probability method with procedures known as area sampling.   By this method every member of the population sampled had a known chance of being selected.   The basic procedure is first to select randomly a sample of primary sampling areas (each of which contains one or more counties).   This was done by dividing the entire country into 66 strata, and selecting one primary sampling area from each stratum.   Each of the twelve largest metropolitan areas in the country formed a stratum by itself and was selected with certainty, so as to represent itself.   In each of the remaining 54 strata, one primary sampling area was selected to represent the entire stratum.

Within each sample point (selected primary sampling area), a sample of places (cities, towns, rural congested areas) was selected. Open country areas were selected in 40 of the sample points.

Within each sample city or town, or rural congested area, scattered blocks were selected at random. For cities with populations of 50,000 or more, census statistics showing average rental value and number of dwelling units are available for each block, and this information was used as a basis for stratification of the blocks and for measures of size used in the selection procedure.

A sampling rate was applied such as to yield an average of two expected dwellings in each block, on the basis of census figures. In the larger cities each block was chosen with a probability directly proportional to its expected number of dwelling units, and the dwellings within the blocks were selected with probability inversely proportional to the same number; therefore, all dwellings had the same chance of being included in the sample (except when they were deliberately oversampled). It should be noted that if there were any major changes in population since the census figures were obtained, these changes would be reflected by area sampling in an increased or decreased yield of interviews from the affected areas. Census figures were not used to establish a quota of interviews, but only a sampling rate. This procedure of sampling, with probability proportionate to measure of size, was used similarly at each stage of the sample selection.

In smaller cities, towns, and rural congested areas, the map was divided into blocks and numbered in such a way as to yield a rough geographical stratification when sampled systematically. The dwelling units found on the selected blocks were listed and subsampled systematically.

Open country areas were divided into small segments containing one to six dwelling units, and a random selection was made from these segments. All the dwellings in the selected segments were included in the sample.

Each sample block or segment was marked on a detailed map or aerial photograph of the area. These materials and detailed instructions guided the interviewers in carrying through the sampling procedure.

Within each dwelling unit which fell into the sample, only one adult was interviewed. The respondent was designated by an objective procedure of selection,[1] and no substitutions were allowed. If an individual to be interviewed was not at home on the first call, from three to ten call-backs were made in an attempt to reach him. However, even after repeated calls a small proportion of the designated individuals were not found at home, and some refused to be interviewed.

[1] Kish, Leslie, "A Procedure for Objective Respondent Selection within the Household," *Journal of the American Statistical Association*, 1949, **44**, 380–87.

The selection of only one adult within each sample dwelling unit means, of course, that if each dwelling unit had an equal chance of being included in the sample, then people who live in households where there are a large number of adults have a smaller chance of being interviewed than people in households where only one or two adults live. This can be adjusted for through a system of weights. The data presented in this report have not been adjusted in this way. However, from the analysis of data from this survey and many previous surveys, it was found that the weighting produces only minute changes in the data.[2]

The Sample for the Pre-Election Survey

In order to obtain a large enough sample to permit regional estimates and comparisons, the West was sampled with a probability twice as large as was used for the rest of the country. The double sampling in the West was handled as follows: For three sample places (each of which were large cities) three extra large cities were selected, and the interviews were taken from them. In the remaining sample places the number of interviews was doubled. This made it possible to make more precise estimates for the West. Altogether 2,021 interviews were taken on the pre-election survey.

The Sample for the Postelection Survey

For this survey, the West was "unloaded," i.e., only half of the dwellings in the West which had been selected for the pre-election survey were retained for the postelection survey. This subselection was made randomly, stratifying on sex, income, and party preference of the respondent. All selected dwellings in the other three geographic areas (Northeast, Midwest, and South) were retained.

This left a sample of dwellings in the United States, all of which had been selected with equal probability. This sample was randomly divided into two parts, one consisting of one-third of the sample, the other consisting of the other two-thirds of the sample. This was done because two different forms of questionnaires were used. All respondents were asked certain basic political questions. The additional

[2] By comparing properly weighted data with unweighted data on a selection of items, it was found that for most items the differences ranged around 0.3 per cent. The largest differences were found on age, sex of respondent, and income. The unweighted results underestimate the proportion of people under forty years old by 1.3 per cent, underestimate the proportion of males by 0.9 per cent, and overestimate the proportion with incomes under $2,000 per year by 2.8 per cent. The unweighted results for 1952 voting behavior underestimated the Democratic vote by 0.1 per cent.

questions were political in nature for the one-third sample, and economic in nature for the two-thirds sample.

The same respondents that were interviewed on the pre-election survey were reinterviewed on the postelection survey. If the family occupying the selected dwelling had moved, the interviewers were instructed to go to the new address and interview the designated respondent there. No substitutions were allowed.

TABLE F.1

THE DISPOSITION OF INTERVIEWS ON THE PRE-ELECTION
AND POSTELECTION SURVEYS

Number of respondents who gave:		
Both pre-election and postelection interviews		1,614
Pre-election interviews only		407
Postelection interviews not obtained because:		
(a) West overload	222	
(b) Other reasons	185	
Postelection interviews only		100
Total		2,121

No reinterview was attempted with those respondents who had refused to be interviewed in the pre-election survey. It was assumed that they would refuse a postelection interview, so they were merely counted as refusals on the reinterview, and incorporated into the "nonresponses."

Altogether 1,714 postelection interviews were taken, and of these 1,614 respondents had also given pre-election interviews. The 100 respondents giving only postelection interviews were not interviewed in the pre-election survey for reasons such as: not at home, respondent absent, house vacant during the time of the pre-election survey, etc.

Sampling Errors

Survey results are subject to two major kinds of error. First, there are whatever inaccuracies occur in the respondents' answers and in the way they are recorded by the interviewers—the so-called "reporting" errors. In most cases the magnitude of these errors can only be surmised. Another type of error is called sampling error. It results from the fact that the survey is based upon a sample rather than upon interviews with the entire population. There is always the possibility that by chance the sample will contain too many or too few Republicans, too many or too few people who believe foreign involvement is undesirable, etc. The extent to which sample findings may overestimate or underestimate the true figures is largely dependent on the number of interviews, but there are other factors involved as well. With a sample of a given size, the smallest sampling error would be achieved if the cases in the sample were widely scattered through the area sampled, with no two interviews taken in the same place. This kind of sample is prohibitive from the standpoint of time and expense, however, and in practice the interviews are "clustered" within sample points and within blocks or segments. Clustering increases the sampling error. To some extent, however, certain reductions in sampling error are achieved through the use of stratification.

The sampling error measures the limits on either side of the obtained figures within which the true population value has a given probability of falling. It is customary to give, as "the sampling error," a figure representing two standard errors; this represents the limits within which the true value will lie 95 out of 100 times.

The sampling error varies somewhat for the different findings of the survey. Despite these differences, tables representing the approximate magnitudes of the sampling errors of various estimated percentages will give a general picture of the degree of variability that should be attached to the estimates. Tables F.2, F.3, F.4, and F.5 represent a generalized compromise result. However, the sampling error for any particular item may in fact be one percentage point lower or higher than that given in the tables.

Table F.2 may be used to determine the sampling error for the difference of two proportions when comparing two subgroups, both of which are based on all sample points. The ns of the two subgroups and the average size of the two proportions being compared are necessary for entering the table.[3] If, for example, the two groups being compared were based on ns of 200 and 500 respectively, the proper "box" in the table is found in the row marked $n = 200$ and the column marked $n = 500$. Where the proportions being compared are about 50 per cent, the sampling error is about 9 per cent; where the proportions being compared are about 20 per cent, the sampling error is about 7 per cent; etc. Thus, the proper "box" is determined by the ns of the two subgroups, and the line within the "box" is determined by the size of the proportions being compared.

[3] The average of the two proportions being compared would be obtained by the following formula:

$$\frac{n_1 p_1 + n_2 p_2}{n_1 + n_2} = \text{average proportion},$$

where n_1 and n_2 refer to the sizes of the two groups being compared, and p_1 and p_2 refer to the two proportions being compared.

TABLE F.2

DIFFERENCES REQUIRED FOR STATISTICAL SIGNIFICANCE (Probability=95%) IN COMPARING TWO SUBGROUPS, BOTH OF WHICH ARE BASED ON ALL SAMPLE POINTS

n \ n	40	70	100	200	300	500	1,000	1,500	p
40	23	20	19	18	17	17	17	17	50%
	18	16	15	14	14	14	13	13	20%
	18	16	15	14	14	14	13	13	10%
	18	16	15	14	14	14	13	13	5%
70		17	16	14	14	13	13	13	50%
		14	13	12	11	11	10	10	20%
		14	13	12	11	11	10	10	10%
		14	13	12	11	11	10	10	5%
100			15	13	12	12	11	11	50%
			12	10	10	9	9	9	20%
			9	8	7	7	7	7	10%
			9	8	7	7	7	7	5%
200				11	10	9	9	8	50%
				9	8	7	7	7	20%
				7	6	6	5	5	10%
				5	5	4	4	4	5%
300					9	8	8	7	50%
					7	7	6	6	20%
					6	5	5	5	10%
					4	4	4	3	5%
500						7	7	7	50%
						6	5	5	20%
						5	4	4	10%
						3	3	3	5%
1,000							6	6	50%
							5	5	20%
							4	4	10%
							3	3	5%

Table F.3 may be used to determine the sampling error for estimated proportions of groups based on all sample points. The size of the group and the size of the proportion being estimated are needed for entering the table. If, for example, the size of the group is 300, then the proper "box" is found in the row marked $n=300$. Proportions around 50 per cent have a sampling error of about 6 per cent;

TABLE F.3

SAMPLING ERRORS (Probability = 95%) FOR ESTIMATED PROPORTIONS
FOR GROUPS BASED ON ALL SAMPLE POINTS

n		p
40	16	50%
	13	20%
	13	10%
	13	5%
70	12	50%
	10	20%
	10	10%
	10	5%
100	10	50%
	8	20%
	6	10%
	5	5%
200	8	50%
	6	20%
	5	10%
	4	5%
300	6	50%
	5	20%
	4	10%
	3	5%
500	5	50%
	4	20%
	3	10%
	3	5%
1,000	4	50%
	3	20%
	3	10%
	2	5%
1,500	3.6	50%
	2.9	20%
	2.2	10%
	1.6	5%
1,800	3.4	50%
	2.7	20%
	2.0	10%
	1.4	5%

proportions around 20 per cent have a sampling error of about 5 per cent; etc. Thus, if a proportion based on an $n = 300$ were estimated to be 45 per cent, then the true population value has a 95 per cent probability of falling within the range $45-6$ per cent and $45+6$ per cent —thus, between 39 and 51 per cent.

TABLE F.4

DIFFERENCES REQUIRED FOR STATISTICAL SIGNIFICANCE (Probability $=95\%$) IN COMPARING TWO SUBGROUPS FORMED ALONG REGIONAL LINES

n \\ n	40	70	100	200	300	500	1,000	1,500	p
40	25	22	21	20	19	19	19	19	50%
	20	18	17	16	16	16	15	15	20%
	20	18	17	16	16	16	15	15	10%
	20	18	17	16	16	16	15	15	5%
70		19	18	16	16	15	15	15	50%
		16	15	14	13	13	12	12	20%
		16	15	14	13	13	12	12	10%
		16	15	14	13	13	12	12	5%
100			17	15	14	14	13	13	50%
			14	12	12	11	11	11	20%
			11	10	8	8	8	8	10%
			11	10	8	8	8	8	5%
200				13	12	11	11	10	50%
				11	10	8	8	8	20%
				8	7	7	6	6	10%
				6	6	5	5	5	5%
300					11	10	10	8	50%
					8	8	7	7	20%
					7	6	6	6	10%
					5	5	5	4	5%
500						8	8	8	50%
						7	6	6	20%
						6	5	5	10%
						4	4	4	5%
1,000							7	7	50%
							6	6	20%
							5	5	10%
							4	4	5%

Table F.4 and Table F.5 may be used when the groups are formed along regional lines, since in this case, only part of the sample points are involved. The procedures for using Tables F.4 and F.5 are the same as noted above, for Tables F.2 and F.3 respectively.

TABLE F.5

SAMPLING ERRORS (Probability=95%) FOR ESTIMATED PROPORTIONS
FOR GROUPS FORMED ALONG REGIONAL LINES

n		p
40	17	50%
	14	20%
	14	10%
	14	5%
70	13	50%
	11	20%
	11	10%
	11	5%
100	11	50%
	9	20%
	7	10%
	6	5%
200	9	50%
	7	20%
	6	10%
	4	5%
300	7	50%
	6	20%
	4	10%
	3	5%
500	6	50%
	4	20%
	3	10%
	3	5%
1,000	4	50%
	3	20%
	3	10%
	2	5%

Index